The Death of SHAKESPEARE

The Death of SHAKESPEARE

As It Was Accomplisht in 1616
& The Causes Thereof

A Novel by Jon Benson

PART TWO

Copyright © 2022 Nedward, LLC

ISBN-13: 978-0-9970899-2-9

Library of Congress Control Number: NRC110174

Published by Nedward, LLC, Annapolis, Maryland
Typeset in Garamond 11

Cover Design by Gerard A. Valerio, with Sherri Ferritto
Maps drawn and hand-lettered by Joan B. Machinchick

The 🜲 at the end of each chapter
is the crown in the Earl of Oxford's signature.

The story of how The Earl of Oxford
wrote the poetry and plays attributed to
William Shakespeare
begins in *The Death of Shakespeare – Part One*

Readers interested in further information can purchase
The Reader's Companion to the Death of Shakespeare for comments keyed to
each chapter.

The Death of Shakespeare, Part One and *Part Two* and *The Reader's
Companion* are also available as E-Books. Both print and E-Book
versions can be purchased at amazon.com. For more information, visit
www.doshakespeare.com.

*To Elizabeth Regina, who took many
secrets with her to the grave.*

Degree being vizarded,
The unworthiest shows as fairly in the mask.

       Troilus and Cressida, Act I, Scene 3

Why write I still all one, ever the same,
And keep invention in a noted weed,
That every word doth almost tell my name,
Showing their birth and where they did proceed?

       Sonnet LXXVI

Far fly thy fame,
Most, most of me beloved, whose silent name
One letter bounds.
Thy unvalu'd worth
Shall mount fair place when Apes are turned forth.

       Scourge of Villainy, John Marston (1598)

To the Gentle Reader

This Booke, that thou here seest put,
It was for gentle Oxford cut;
Wherein the Author had a strife
With History to show Lord Oxford's life.

O, if only those who knew his wit
Had said the plays by him were writ,
There'd be no need to here reclaim
The name purloined by Shakespeare's fame.

Grave Spenser need not shift more nigh
Our Chaucer, nor Beaumont nearer Spenser lye;
Let them sleep, Westminster lords,
The world now knows the plays are Oxenford's.
Their every word sings he wrote the plays,
And in his Moniment Shakespeare slays.

Elizabeth knew of noble lords
Who wrote well but suppressed their words,
Or let them publish in another's name,
Thereby losing deservèd fame.

The author here his name must also feign,
Lest he, too, in academia, be slain.
Therefore, Gentle Reader, looke
Not on his name but on his Booke.—J.B.

The Authorship Question

William Shakespeare is believed by many to have written the greatest plays the world has even seen. There is no record of his education, if he had any. His parents, wife, and children may have been illiterate. He left no books. No one reported in any diary or letter that they had met him or talked about him or even talked *about* him.

He left six signatures, all different. Three were on his last will and testament, which makes no mention of any plays, poems, or books; two were on deeds to real property; the last was found on an affidavit he gave in a court case.

The records show a businessman who acquired considerable property during his lifetime, hoarded grain during a famine, and engaged in a number of lawsuits, one over as little as five pounds. He was connected with the theater, but there is nothing that *independently* proves he was the author of the plays attributed to him.

These missing facts, plus the nature of the plays themselves – thirty-seven of the thirty-eight plays he supposedly wrote were about royalty and nobility with only *The Merry Wives of Windsor* being about commoners – have created the Authorship Question. Many students of the plays have concluded Shakespeare was a front for someone else. The list is long. It includes Walt Whitman, Mark Twain, Sigmund Freud, Sir Derek Jacobi, Hugh Trevor-Roper and many others. Visit https://doubtaboutwill.org/declaration to learn more.

But if Shakespeare did not write the plays, who did? And if someone else was the greatest writer who ever lived, why was Shakespeare give the credit? *The Death of Shakespeare* explains how this happened, and why the Bard of Avon paid with his life for his part in, to use the words of Henry James, "the biggest and most successful fraud ever practiced on a patient world."

The story of how the Earl of Oxford wrote the poetry and plays attributed to William Shakespeare begins in Part One of *The Death of Shakespeare*. Readers interested in further information can purchase *The Reader's Companion to the Death of Shakespeare* for comments keyed to each chapter. *The Death of Shakespeare*, Parts One and Two, and *The Reader's Companion* are available in print and E-Book versions at amazon.com. For more information, visit *www.doshakespeare.com*.

Table Of Contents

Maps of England and London

Floor Plan of Oxford Court, London

Floor Plan of King's Place, Hackney

Lineage Tables
(*At end of text*)

The Earls of Oxford
William Cecil, Baron Burghley
The Earls of Southampton
The Earls of Derby
Peregrine Bertie, Lord Willoughby de Eresby
The Earls of Pembroke
The Lords Hunsdon
The Sidney Family
Margaret Douglas, Countess of Lennox

Glossary

Afterword

Questions for a Stratfordian

More Information

N
Grimsthorpe
Stamford
Stratford-upon-Avon
Billesley
R. Avon
Cambridge
Castle Hedingham
Ditchley
Earls Colne
R. Colne
Oxford
Colchester
Theobalds
Wivenhoe
R. Thames
Hackney
Bristol
Windsor
LONDON
Richmond
Greenwich
Bath
Gads Hill
Wilton
Canterbury
Southampton
Dover
Titchfield Abbey
English Channel
England

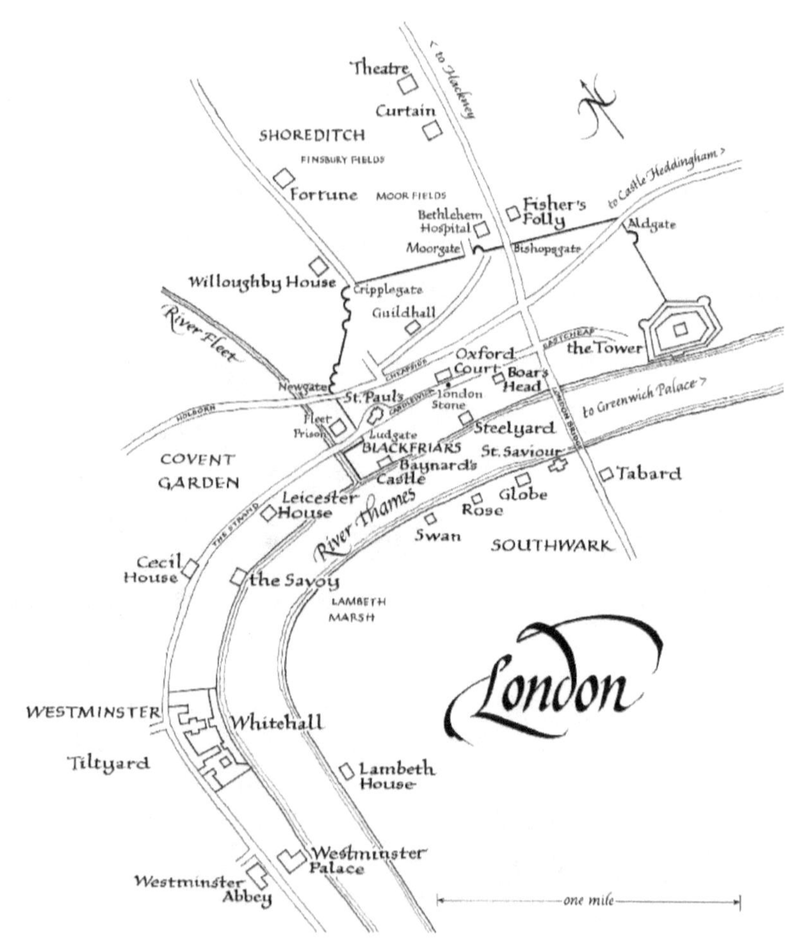

Theatre
< to Hackney
Curtain
SHOREDITCH
to Castle Heddingham >
FINSBURY FIELDS
Fortune
MOOR FIELDS
Fisher's Folly
Bethlehem Hospital
Aldgate
Moorgate
Bishopsgate
Willoughby House
Cripplegate
River Fleet
Guildhall
CHEAPSIDE
Oxford Court
EASTCHEAP
the Tower
Newgate
St. Paul's
London Stone
Boar's Head
HOLBORN
CANDLEWICK
Fleet Prison
Ludgate
Steelyard
LONDON BRIDGE
to Greenwich Palace >
COVENT GARDEN
BLACKFRIARS
Baynard's Castle
St. Saviour
Tabard
Leicester House
River Thames
Rose
Globe
Swan
SOUTHWARK
Cecil House
the Savoy
LAMBETH MARSH
London
WESTMINSTER
THE STRAND
Whitehall
Lambeth House
Tiltyard
Westminster Palace
Westminster Abbey
one mile

Oxford Court

First Floor

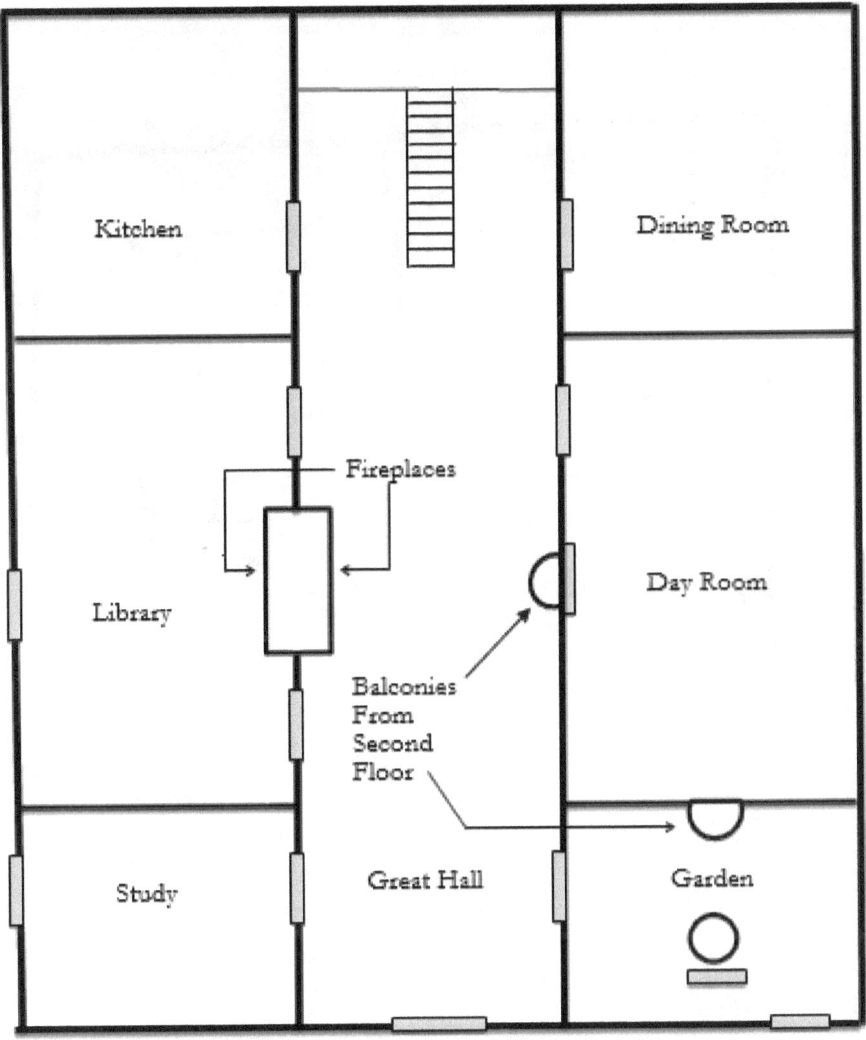

Candlewick Street

King's Place, Hackney

First Floor

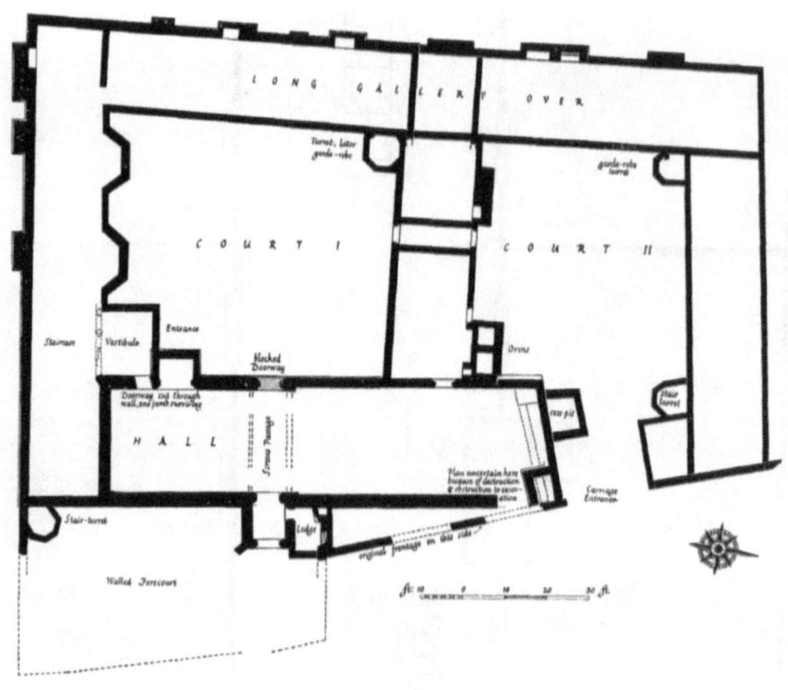

Dramatis Personae

(Names of historical figures are boldfaced)

Edward de Vere, 17th Earl of Oxford (Oxford)

> **Anne Cecil** (Nan), Oxford's first wife, mother of his daughters **Elizabeth (Lisbeth), Bridget,** and **Susan**

> **Elizabeth Trentham** (Elspeth), Oxford's second wife, mother of his son and heir, **Henry de Vere**, 18th Earl of Oxford.

> **Anne Vavasour** (Anne), lady-in-waiting to Queen Elizabeth, mother of Oxford's bastard son, Edward Vere

William Shakespeare (William Shackspear, Willum)

> **Anne Hathaway,** Shakespeare's wife, mother of his children, **Susanna, Hamnet,** and **Judith**

Elizabeth Tudor, Queen Elizabeth I of England

Henry Wriothesley, 3rd Earl of Southampton, putative son of Oxford and Queen Elizabeth

William Cecil, Baron Burghley, Oxford's guardian and father-in-law, and the Queen's most trusted minister

Sir Robert Cecil, Burghley's second son and successor to his father's offices

William Stanley, 6th Earl of Derby, married Lisbeth Vere

Francis Norris, Baron of Rycote, married Bridget Vere

Philip Herbert, Earl of Montgomery, married Susan Vere and was one of the "incomparable pair of brethren" to whom the First Folio was dedicated

Peregrine Bertie, Lord Willoughby de Eresby, twice ambassador to Denmark, who married **Mary Vere**, Oxford's sister

Aemilia Bassano, first published English female poet, the Dark Lady of the sonnets, mistress to **Henry Carey**, 1st Lord Hunsdon

Arthur Golding, Oxford's uncle and translator of Ovid's *Metamorphosis*; brother of **Marjory Golding**, wife of **Earl John**, 16th Earl of Oxford, Oxford's father

Lettice Knollys, dowager Countess of Essex and Leicester, widow of the 1st Earl of Essex and mother of **Robert Dudley**, 2nd Earl of Essex, beheaded in 1601

William Brooke, 10th Baron Cobham, Lord Chamberlain from August 1596 until his death on 6 March 1597; father of **Elizabeth Brooke**, wife of Sir Robert Cecil

Anthony Munday, John Lyly, Christopher Marlowe, Ben Jonson, John Marston, playwrights

Philip Henslowe, manager/impresario of the Rose Theater

James Burbage, manager/impresario of the Theater

Richard Burbage, actor, member of the Lord Chamberlain's Men

Dr. Rodrigo López, physician to the queen, executed for allegedly trying to poison her

Michael Lok, to whom Oxford owed £3,000, induces Oxford to write a play about Jews that becomes *The Merchant of Venice*

Rowland Yorke, servant to Earl John and father of **Rowland Yorke**. Oxford knew the father as Yorick. The son falsely told Oxford that Nan had cheated on him while he was in Italy and, therefore, Lisbeth was not his daughter

Thomas Brincknell, undercook in Cecil House. Oxford, while a ward at Cecil House, stabbed him in the thigh, killing him; Lilah Stanhope, his fiancé/maidservant to Oxford's daughter, Susan

Joan Jockey, love interest of Earl John, whose retainers cut off her face so he would put her away

Marcus Gheeraerts, Dutch artist, who painted the Ditchley Portrait and the Pregnancy Portrait

Sir John Falstaff, knight; Tupp, his page

Peaches Bottomsup, barmaid in the Boar's Head

Robin, Oxford's page

Finley, former classmate of Oxford's at Cambridge, failed playwright, seeking to have plays considered worthy of study

Malfis, Oxford's lawyer

Nigel, Oxford's steward

Timson, Oxford's manservant

Thomas Digby, Oxford's steward at Hedingham Castle

Tobias, Oxford's whiffler

The Death of SHAKESPEARE

Author's Note to Part Two

At the conclusion of Part One, the Earl of Oxford is talking with the dowager Countess of Southampton who has just married Sir Thomas Heneage. They are watching her guests move through a complicated dance when her son, Henry Wriothesley, now 3rd Earl of Southampton, whirls past them. Oxford remarks that it is a pity Henry's father had not lived to see how handsome his son had turned out to be.

"But he *is* here," the Countess says to Oxford.

"Who?"

"His father." She looked out over the dancers.

"His father is dead, my lady. You buried him."

"I buried the 2nd Earl of Southampton, my lord, not Henry's father."

"My lady, you do yourself ill by slandering your former husband on the occasion of your second marriage."

"But truth is truth, is it not, my lord?"

Oxford was beginning to think the Countess may have had too much to drink but then realized she was implying *he* was Henry's father. "My lady, you suggest an honor I must decline."

"Because you and I have never …?" she said mischievously, letting her voice trail off.

"Yes."

"Your mistake, my lord, is assuming I am Henry's mother."

"Of course, you are."

"I would know, wouldn't I?" The woman Oxford had thought drunk or mad now sounded completely sober. She turned to look at him. "He has your eyes and her hair, your mouth and her nose. His arrogance he gets from both of you."

Oxford looked out at Southampton dancing gracefully across the floor. She waited.

"Then, if you are not his mother, who is?" Oxford asked.

The Countess leaned in and gave his arm a squeeze: "She who just left in the royal barge."

Oxford and the Queen

Oxford's mouth fell open. The Countess was beaming. She waited for Oxford's reaction. Instead, he strode away across the room and ran out onto the pier. The royal barge was barely perceptible in the distance.

"God's blood!" he called out. He ran back down the pier and out into the courtyard on the Strand. He grabbed the reins of a big red being held by a hostler and vaulted into the saddle.

"Hey!" the hostler cried out. He let go when he saw the Earl of Oxford astride the horse. Oxford twisted his head around to glare down at him. The hostler stepped back. Oxford pulled the horse's head around and gave him the same look, startling the beast as much as he had frightened the hostler. He dug his heels in and the stallion bolted through the gates onto the Strand and flew off toward Ludgate.

The Londoners filling the road ahead peeled away like water before a ship under full sail. They were used to being run down by a nobleman in hot pursuit of a lady or a play. The big red flew past Paul's, past London Stone to Bishopsgate where it turned downhill to cross London Bridge at full gallop.

Oxford and the horse sped off the bridge into Southwark, turning left to follow the Thames past Deptford. At Greenwich Palace, Oxford carried on through the gate, scattering the few guards on duty. He brought the horse to a halt in the rear courtyard, leaped off, and ran into the palace. The big red wandered off. A servant ran after him.

No one challenged him. They were all somewhere else the queen was later told when she demanded to know how Oxford had gotten all the way to her private apartments. Elizabeth had just slipped off the gown she had worn to the Countess of Southampton's wedding when Oxford burst into her bedchamber.

"My lord!" Elizabeth cried out. One of the ladies-in-waiting threw a robe over the queen's shoulders.

"Get out!" Oxford said, waving an arm at the other women in the room. Elizabeth could sense something awful had happened but knew Oxford intended her no harm. She gestured and the ladies-in-waiting backed out of the room. Oxford closed the door behind them.

"How dare you!" Elizabeth said, recovering some of her composure. "How dare you come into our presence without permission."

Oxford came back to the bed and stopped in front of her, hands on hips. "You have lied to me."

"About what?" she shot back, her own anger at his violation of her private space beginning to match the choler she saw in his face.

"*Our son!*"

"*Our son?*" Elizabeth repeated. She listened to herself. She laughed. "My lord, you have been too long in the playhouse."

Oxford stood in front of her, breathing heavily.

"I have been accused of motherhood before," Elizabeth said, her smile tightening. "Lord Seymour when I was fourteen. Some have claimed I gave birth to *his* son, but a week's examination failed to prove that claim. Then there was Leicester, and d'Alençon, as well as his minister, Monsieur Simier, my little monkey, and Leicester, of course. And you in there somewhere. *All with access to the royal apartments like I was a hackney in a house of pleasure!*" She was not referring to the horse or the hamlet north of the City.

Oxford was not persuaded. But was she toying with him because she was *not* Southampton's mother? Or because she *was*. Elizabeth was as fine an actor as any on the London stage. There was more than one reason she and Lord Burghley got along so well, and why the examination into her relationship with Lord Seymour failed to reveal what had actually happened when she was fourteen.

"And who, my lord, is *our son?*"

"Henry Wriothesley."

She started. "The Earl of Southampton?" She answered her own question. "No. I would know, wouldn't I?"

Oxford drew in his breath. The Countess had said the same thing to convince Oxford *she* was not Southampton's mother!

"Piffle. He's a sweet boy. Long fingers."

"Like yours, Your Majesty." She hardened. She was proud of her long fingers and forever showing them to foreign guests. "And his red hair?" Oxford added.

Her amusement disappeared. Her hair had hints of red in it. She had always thought it a sign. She was superstitious about many things, including the gold medallion she always wore around her neck for good luck. She reached up to touch it. The old woman who had given it to her had said she would reign as long as she wore it around her neck.

"Enough!" she cried out. "Who told you this?"

"Lady Mary."

Elizabeth's anger grew. "My lord, you are a bigger fool than I thought you were. She knew you would come running to me. I hate it when that she-wolf finds a way to reach *into my very bedroom and ruin my evening!*"

She turned away. "It was bad enough I had to attend Lady Mary's wedding and wish her well but my reward is for you to bring me this *canard!*" She looked toward the river, distant in the gathering dusk. "She is laughing at us, my lord. *Both* of us."

Oxford was studying her, the way a seamstress looks at a dress for an errant thread. Elizabeth saw what he was doing.

"Stop it. I am *not* the mother of the Earl of Southampton. And why, my lord, would you want more sons? You have two already: an heir and a bastard."

"The bastard gotten here, Your Majesty. And no one knew Anne was pregnant. Not even you, *who knows all.*"

Elizabeth leaned toward him. She did not like being reminded of Anne Vavasour's pregnancy. Her own lady-in-waiting, gotten with child by the man standing in front of her, the babe delivered in these very rooms, and, yes, *without her knowing anything about it!* She had sent mother, father, and child to the Tower. Elizabeth had been humiliated: how could she be queen if a baby could be conceived and birthed in her own chambers *without her knowing it!* Oxford heard her teeth grind, something he had not heard since they had slept together as lovers.

He dropped another thought into the conversation: "Both sons named Henry, Your Majesty." She was confused for a moment, then realized he was referring to Henry, his son and heir, the future 18th Earl of Oxford, and Henry Wriothesley.

Elizabeth's eyes widened. They looked at each other, each imagining the same image: long fingers, red hair, and the word "Henry" floating over both children. Elizabeth was momentarily speechless. The Earl of Oxford was always shocking and surprising her. Most times, it was a healthy tonic to the bureaucratic babbling she had to put up with. Not this time, though.

"You recall the *Book of Prophecies*, don't you, the one Charles Arundel said I had in my desk?" This startled her. "The one with paintings in it he said were 'after the manner of a prophecy and by interpretation resembled a *crowned son to the queen?*"

Elizabeth remembered it well. Oxford was quoting from a written statement Arundel had given while in the Tower. Oxford had named Arundel as part of a plot to replace Elizabeth on the throne. Arundel denied the charges and penned a laundry list of accusations against Oxford, one of which was that Oxford had a *Book of Prophecies* "in his deske." In it was a painting of a child Oxford claimed was Elizabeth's son! With a crown on his head!

Arundel told the queen Oxford was lying – he still had the book. The other conspirators agreed. Elizabeth tended to believe them and not Oxford. They were gullible, for sure. They had believed Oxford when he told them he had slept with a mare and seen the ghost of his mother's second husband coming at him with a whip.

She released them eventually. Arundel fled to France where he died, poisoned by the Spanish. He, at least, was indeed a spy, as Oxford had said he was. But she remained convinced the *Book* existed. Arundel and the others had seen it. Oxford didn't deny he had such a book in his possession at one point. He said he had given to it to Dee who had taken it with him to the continent where he remained.

Not having it vexed her. What did it contain? Genealogical charts and other such nonsense? Something about Southampton? Over the years, she listened to every word Oxford wrote, knowing hidden messages filled his plays. When Pericles said at the Hampton Court performance of *Pericles, Prince of Tyre*, "*Who has a book of all that monarchs do, / He's more secure to keep it shut than shown*," she knew Oxford was teasing her about *The Book of Prophecies*.

"Did you name him?" Oxford asked, taking her away from thoughts about *The Book*. He was trying to sound blasé.

Elizabeth bristled. "I did not name him. What do you *not* understand? I am *not* his mother. He is *not* my son!"

Oxford nodded, a complacent *we-both-know-you-have-to-say-you're-not-his-mother* look on his face. She had more to tell him.

"This claim goes no further, Edward." Her use of his given name underscored the seriousness of her command. "If you tell anyone about this, if you put this in one of your plays or in a poem, I shall have you immediately committed to the Tower again. This time, you won't be there long. I will forthrightly sign the warrant for your execution, after which your head will appear on London Bridge to show my people what happens when one of my subjects disobeys me, even one who stands as high in my court as the Earl of Oxford."

Oxford did not feel threatened. She hadn't sent him to the Tower for *Venus & Adonis*. If she sent him now, it would only confirm Southampton was their son.

But he was beginning to understand why she couldn't acknowledge Southampton. She was the virgin queen, wasn't she? How could she admit she had given birth to a son? Oxford thought he had the answer. He walked back to her.

"You have no heir, Your Majesty. The succession is fraught with danger. England cries out for a proper heir. Our son is royal by virtue of being your son. He can succeed you."

She glared at him. Oxford went on before she could interrupt him.

"Your own father has shown you the way. He had an illegitimate son, Henry Fitzroy. He could not marry the boy's mother because he was still married to Catherine. What did he do? He acknowledged the boy as his own and made him the 1st Duke of Richmond *and* Somerset at age six. Had he lived, he would have succeeded your father."

"And I would never have been born," she snapped.

"But the step your father took to acknowledge Henry Fitzroy set a precedent that allows you to acknowledge Southampton as your successor. The Act of Succession supports this. Up to 1571, the Act of Succession required that a successor had to be the 'issue of the queen's body lawfully begotten.' In 1571, '*lawfully begotten*' was struck out by Parliament. The Act now reads: 'except the same be *the natural issue of her Majesty's body*.' Henry Wriothesley can succeed you."

She refused to look at him.

He leaned in. "I asked Camden about the change but he refused to tell me what he knew." Oxford dropped his voice to imitate the gravelly tones of the noted historian and Clarenceux King of Arms: "*Oh, my. It were incredible the jests made by lewd catchers of words on the occasion of this clause, forasmuch as the lawyers term those children natural which are gotten out of wedlock.*"

Oxford thought his imitation good but Elizabeth's stony face told him she was not impressed. He decided to tack in another direction.

"Your subjects do not want another War of the Roses after you're gone. Telling them you have hidden away an heir would bring joy to the land. *The constant virgin who planned for their well-being once she was gone.*"

"But I am the Virgin Queen, and virgins, except for our Lord's blessed mother, do not have children!"

"They will know it was a clever ruse to protect Henry before he becomes king! Your people will love you for it."

Elizabeth glared at him. "I am *not* the mother of *any* son, much less the Earl of Southampton." She leaned toward him. "The moment I acknowledge him, I become Richard II and my reign is over."

Oxford thought she was protesting too much. Elizabeth read his thoughts.

"You may believe the English people will embrace Henry if they think he is my son but others will surely want him dead. Think of Edward's sons, murdered in the Tower so that Gloucester could become Richard III. You have shown us the man: '*Now is the winter of <u>our</u> discontent,*' you have him say. You don't have him say '<u>*my*</u> *discontent.*' He says '<u>*our*</u> *discontent,*' showing he already thinks himself king. In real life, someone is *always* having a *winter of discontent.* Words matter, my lord, much more in my world than yours. If you speak of what Lady Mary told you today, you will be signing Henry's death warrant. It will come when he least expects it, in a dark corner on his way home or in a tavern, upstairs, like Marlowe." She looked at him closely. "Is that what you want?"

Oxford didn't say anything.

She continued. "I do this out of love for the Earl of Southampton, my lord, not because I think he is my son. You should do the same. Otherwise, you will be sacrificing the boy on the altar of your pride."

This brought Oxford up short. But was she putting on a wonderful performance? He couldn't tell. He nodded and rose. "With your permission." She waved a hand.

He retraced his steps through the palace. The big red was nowhere to be seen. A warm breeze from the southwest washed over him. He went back through the palace to the side that faced the Thames. As he recrossed the empty hallways, he felt a sense of exhilaration rise within him. He was probably fooling himself but hopeless quests had always excited him. After all, he was the last of the medieval knights. Who better to be the father of the next king? With every step toward the water, he became more convinced Elizabeth was Southampton's mother *and he was the boy's father!*

The tide was coming in. A good sign, he thought. He hailed a wherry and stepped aboard. He felt as light as a feather. "Where to I go?" he asked himself. "The Boar's Head; Fat Jack will love this."

~ 99 ~
The Boar's Head

Sir John Falstaff was asleep in his customary booth.

"Best leave him be, my lord," Peaches said, as she crossed paths with Oxford in the middle of the inn. "Asleep, he can do no harm. Awake …" Her voice trailed off.

"He is of use to me," Oxford replied, continuing past her. He sat down opposite Falstaff.

"Jack," he said. To Oxford's surprise, Falstaff immediately sat up.

"My lord," he said. His basso profundo sounded like it was coming from beneath the inn's thick oak floor. "And we are to …?"

"Nowhere," Oxford said. Falstaff's face fell. "I have just come from the queen," Oxford continued, "but what I learned at the Countess of Southampton's wedding today is of great interest."

Falstaff assumed a look of concern to match his lordship's. He folded his enormous hands over each other.

Oxford leaned forward and lowered his voice. "The Earl of Southampton is my son."

Falstaff blinked. "Your son? Who told you that?"

"The Countess of Southampton."

"The Countess of Southampton? She who married old Heneage today?"

"Yes."

A sly smile spread across Falstaff's face. "Ye dog, ye."

Oxford shook his head. "You give me credit where none is due. The Countess told me she is not the boy's mother."

This further confused Falstaff. "She isn't?"

"No."

"Now, let me get this aright. You go to a wedding and the bride tells you she is *not* the mother of the boy everyone thinks is her son. And, she says *you* are the boy's father."

Oxford nodded.

"And why now, my lord, after all these years? *And at her wedding to her second husband?*" He looked away, not in disgust but to savor the moment. His lordship was always presenting him with outrageous stories, characters, and events. It was the reason he had taken the young earl under his wing when Oxford had arrived at Cecil House, a twelve-year old royal ward by way of his father's untimely death. The queen had given his wardship to her most senior minister, then known as Sir William Cecil. He would not be made Baron Burghley until much later.

Oxford had presented himself at Cecil House at the head of 80 men on horseback and 100 yeomen dressed in reading tawney with a blue boar on their left shoulder. Gold chains hung around their necks.

Falstaff had been one of Burghley's 'men,' former soldiers and drifters who gravitated to men of power in return for food, lodging, and occasional assignments. Falstaff had sought entrance to Cecil House to be closer to the London taverns but he had begun to tire of Burghley's oily ways when Oxford arrived, fresh, young, and arrogant. Watching the pup earl dismount in the inner courtyard and bid his retainers a fair journey back to Hedingham, Falstaff put off his decision to leave. He could see at a glance that the young earl would be a handful. Burghley might have to throw him out, thereby losing the fees and honors the queen's appointment had brought him. Falstaff decided to stay to see what happened.

Oxford made it clear that he expected Elizabeth to be calling on him and was soon ordering everyone around, including Burghley. Falstaff took delight in this and subtly encouraged Oxford to rub Burghley the wrong way in the hope that Burghley would eventually throw Oxford out.

But Burghley never did. 'Pondus,' as he was called because of his long speeches, knew how to fawn and dissemble to get what he wanted. He had sought the guardianship of Oxford's personal property whilst telling the queen he had no interest in Oxford's property. This allowed the queen to give the guardianship of the lands Oxford inherited to the Earl of Leicester, the queen's newest favorite. This helped elevate Leicester to the power and influence he had lost when his father had been executed for putting Jane Gray on the throne. The queen could have given Leicester back his father's lands, which had been forfeited to the crown at his father's conviction, but she made Leicester guardian of Oxford's lands to avoid this. How much Leicester pillaged from Oxford is unknown. There were rumors he sold off the lead downspouts at Castle Hedingham. Oxford, forever ignorant of how he was financed or robbed, never knew how much he lost and Leicester gained. The queen had no reason to protect the Earl of Oxford. Their affair and love child would not come for a decade.

An outsider might have thought Burghley had made a mistake seeking guardianship of Oxford's personal property instead of his lands but the old fox wanted to control who Oxford married. Being Oxford's guardian, he could – and did - force Oxford to marry his daughter, Nan. This move allowed him to talk the queen into elevating him to the peerage by making him Baron Burghley so that his grandchildren could inherit Oxford's titles. Burghley was gambling that the queen would remain childless and one of Oxford's children – one of *his* grandchildren – would inherit the throne if the queen died without a successor. In moments of warm reflection, he imagined his offspring marching off into the future as kings, all descended from William Cecil, commoner, who first became Sir William Cecil and was then made Baron Burghley by a grateful queen.

While Burghley bided his time, Oxford grew into a fair poet, a better athlete, and such a good dancer that the queen was soon asking him to court. He took to practicing sword-fighting, of course, and thus, it came about one day that he was dueling with his tailor's assistant in a side yard at Cecil House when he saw a man spying on him through a hedge. Oxford knew Burghley used all his servants as spies. Enraged, Oxford ran over to the hedge and thrust his sword into it, stabbing the man in the upper thigh. The poor fellow, an undercook in the house kitchen, fell through the hedge at Oxford's feet and died in twenty minutes.

A coroner's jury was convened the next day. Oxford and the tailor's assistant made themselves ready to testify. Oxford, seventeen years of age and imbued with honor and duty, steeled himself to tell the truth. His family motto, after all, was *vero nihil verius – nothing truer than truth.*

Burghley had other plans. He intended to tell the jury that Oxford was defending himself when the undercook attacked him, but Falstaff had a better idea. Before Burghley came downstairs, he ambled past Oxford into the room where the jurors waited and shut the door behind him. He told the men in the room that the undercook had run onto the end of Oxford's sword and committed suicide.

The jurors were overjoyed to hear this. They had been dreading what Burghley would do if they returned a verdict against Lord Oxford. They immediately declared that the undercook had committed *felo de se* and ran out the door, winking and nodding at Oxford as they went by.

Oxford had no idea what had happened. He plucked the sleeve of a clerk who came out of the room. "What happened?" he asked. The clerk smiled. "Ye're free. Falstaff told them the cook ran onto the end of your sword and killed himself."

Oxford was stunned. This was a lie. Oxford had stabbed the poor man through the hedge! *And Falstaff hadn't even been there!*

Falstaff came out. He saw the look on Oxford's face. "Come with me," he said, putting his massive arm around Oxford's shoulders. He took him down to the Thames where they sat under a willow tree and watched the boats scurrying back and forth across the Thames. "It's a shame about the undercook, my lord, but hanging you won't bring him back. The wheel of fortune has taken the poor man away but I decided to put my thumb on it to prevent you from joining him. This way, ye get the life ye deserve. Let it go."

Oxford sat next to Falstaff looking out over the water. He was in shock. He had been given his life back because of a lie? All his ideas about truth, beauty, and goodness disappeared.

The two of them never spoke about the undercook again but the poor man's death and Falstaff's lie bonded the fat knight and the young earl in ways they did not understand. Falstaff could see that Oxford was gifted. Everyone did. At seventeen, the young earl had mastered several languages. Some thought he was destined for greatness.

Sir John stayed on at Cecil House. He left when Oxford married Burghley's daughter, Nan. He took lodgings down an alley off Eastcheap. He and Oxford would see each other periodically, sometimes at a play or a prize fight behind an inn, but mostly at the Boar's Head. He drifted back and forth between being a distant uncle and a boon companion to Oxford. They came together and went away from each other like comets passing through the heavens on long elliptical orbits. Oxford's sudden arrival in the Boar's Head with news he might be the father of the Earl of Southampton did not surprise Falstaff. He always felt like they were simply picking up where they had last left off, the in-betweens not worth talking about.

Falstaff sighed. "Okay, you're the boy's father, and she's not his mother. Did she say who is his mother?"

"She did."

"And her name is?"

"Elizabeth Tudor."

Falstaff's mouth dropped open. "Nooo!" he said in disbelief. "Holy Mary, God a mercy! *St. Agnes on a broomstick!*"

Oxford put up a hand. He looked around.

Falstaff calmed down. "It's times like this that make a man wish he hadn't wasted his stock of bad words on trivial events." He looked at Oxford with admiration. "If you are the earl's father and the queen is his mother, you will be prince consort, without doubt, and I" - here tears appeared in the corners of his eyes - "*I will be lord treasurer at least!*"

"I think not."

"Why not?"

"Elizabeth says the boy is not hers."

"You've been to her?" Oxford nodded. "Of course, you would. And, of course, she'd deny she was his mum."

"And if I say a word, I'm to the Tower, and then my head …"

"Aye. I get it. My lips are sealed. But let's see. You and the queen were close for a time. How many years ago was that?" Falstaff grimaced as he tried to do the math.

"Just about when the Southampton boy was born."

"Aye. The time the two of you went to the Bishop of Croydon."

"Yes. We exchanged rings and bound ourselves in marriage, but she changed her mind almost immediately. She ordered me to never speak of it."

Falstaff gave Oxford a sly look. "Ye needed more than the exchange of rings to make Southampton," he said. "Sex with the queen," he mused, but changed course when he saw the look on Oxford's face. "And didn't she go to Bath about the same time? When you ran off to the continent?"

Oxford nodded again. "She told me she had delivered a boy but that he had died immediately. 'He was one hour mine,' I remember her saying."

"Well, it appears that he *didn't* die," Falstaff announced. "It sounds like he was farmed out to the 2nd Earl of Southampton."

"Who was in the Tower when 'his' son was conceived."

"Even more proof Southampton's your boy!" Falstaff ran a hand over the stubble on his face. "And the Countess would surely know if she were Southampton's mother." Then he shook his head. "But her word means nothing if the queen says no." He looked at Oxford. "So, what do you say? Is Southampton yours?"

"I don't know. I want to believe the Countess and not the queen, but is that because I *want* Southampton to be my son? Is Elizabeth lying to me? Is she mistaken? She may not have been told the boy lived."

"Someone knows." Falstaff held a fat finger up next to his nose. "Someone *always* knows. Finding out who is the trick."

"The witnesses are probably all dead."

"Not if Jack Falstaff puts his ear to the ground."

"But this is about something that happened twenty years ago."

Falstaff looked up, indignant. "Didn't I find Joan Jockey and Yorick when Sir Robert tried to take away yer titles, eh? I had to go back *forty* years." His mind raced on to another thought. "But list, list. We don't *have* to be positive here, do we? It's not what *really* happened, it's what people *think* happened." Oxford's jaw dropped open. Falstaff made like he didn't notice it. "Her Majesty needs an heir, doesn't she? We can give her one. Or one the people will accept."

"No, Jack. No, no, no. No more Yoricks, their heads filled with lies."

"Oh, yes. I forgot. The truth. Always the truth."

"Yes. This isn't about who owns a piece of property, or even whether I am the lawful issue of my father, the 16th Earl of Oxford. *This is about whether Southampton is Elizabeth's son and rightful heir.* A lawful sovereign can only be succeeded by a lawful successor. If Henry is not my son by Elizabeth, he has no right to be king. Don't blur this question out of existence with your frabbles and quibbles."

Falstaff disagreed. "What about Henry Tudor? Didn't he push Richard III, a lawful sovereign, aside so he could become Henry VII, *our queen's grandfather?* Was he lawfully descended? And wasn't Elizabeth twice declared a bastard, *first by her own father,* so he could lie with Ann Boleyn?"

"*God works in mysterious ways.*"

"*He also helps those who help themselves,*" Falstaff replied. He glanced at Oxford, pleased he could throw something Biblical back at his lordship. "Do ye want me to help or not?"

The glint in Oxford's eyes told him he did.

Falstaff nodded magisterially, as if he were Theseus agreeing to rid Attica of the Bull of Marathon. "Then I will. This is wonderful news, my lord. My hams are tingling, which is always a good sign. We need to celebrate. Ye might be the father of the next king of England. That calls for beer. *Peaches!*" he called out.

Before Peaches could come out of the kitchen, Robin came in.

"Robin!" Falstaff called out.

Oxford put a hand on Sir John's arm. "Not a word, Jack."

Falstaff nodded. "Pint-man! Come over here. Have a beer with us."

Robin stopped in the middle of the inn. "Pint-man?" He folded his arms.

Oxford interceded. "No, Jack. You know how he gets."

"All right. *Big* Robin, it is, then."

Robin unfolded his arms and walked over to them. "I'm bigger than ye think," he said defiantly. He slid into the booth next to Oxford. "My lord," he said, tipping his head. "If the fat knight," he gestured toward Falstaff, leaning forward and lowering his voice, "that bolting-hutch of beastliness, that huge bombard of sack, that …" here he drew in his breath, "that swollen parcel of dropsies, and, my all-time favorite, that roasted Manningtree ox with pudding in his belly, to wit, Sir John Falstaff, pushes at ye, *ye push him back!*"

"Bravo," Oxford said.

Even Falstaff was impressed. "Ye've been reading Thomas Nashe. And drinking with him."

Robin nodded and hiccupped at the same time. Peaches came up.

Oxford glanced up at her. "Sir John and I will be having a brace of Fleet River Double Bock," Oxford said. "Our friend here has already had his share."

Robin did not deny he had. He sat there staring straight ahead, a look of forced seriousness on his face.

"Have you seen him like this before?" Oxford asked.

Falstaff shook his head. He leaned over the table. "Ye need to have something to pour the beer into, little friend. Unlike me, ye've been shortchanged by He who made ye. It's got nowhere to go."

Robin nodded, then raised his head to look at them. "And what's the play?" he asked, hiccupping again.

Oxford and Sir John laughed.

"And what makes you think a play's in the offing?" Oxford asked.

"Because ye've been to the queen."

This surprised Oxford. "How do you know?"

"Because ye rode through London on a horse ye stole from the Earl of Warrington, knockin' people over on the way." He looked at Oxford with admiration. "Including a woman carrying smelts. Ye knocked her into the Thames!"

"I did?"

Robin nodded. "Fortunately for you, a wherryman pulled her out of the river, saving her from drowning, he did, as she couldn't swim."

Falstaff chuckled. "Someone's already working on a ballad, I'm sure," he said, appreciating the image of Oxford's headlong flight through London's crowded streets.

"Mr. Lyly's on it," Robin said, nodding vigorously. "Ye'll be famous my lord. Mr. Lyly says he'll get William Byrd to put it to music. *The Earl of Oxford's Dash,* he says he'll call it."

Oxford groaned. "Remembered for a ride through London."

"All the more reason to write," Robin said, his face aglow, more from the prospect of working on a new play than from the beer. He leaned further forward, a sly look on his face: "And the play is …?"

Oxford tried to look away. Robin leaned toward him. After a long pause, Oxford said: "Two plays."

"Oh, boy!" Robin said.

"A love tragedy, so the queen will stop telling me she saw a play once that so well-limned love that no one could best it."

"Spurring you on, of course, as she always does," Falstaff said.

"And the second?" Robin asked, eyes bright.

"Something for Lisbeth's wedding, I think."

"If she marries him," Robin said.

Falstaff looked at him. "Why wouldn't she?"

"Because the widow of the Earl's older brother says she's expecting. If she births a boy, he will 'un-earl' Lisbeth's betrothed." Robin grinned. "Lisbeth says she's not marrying someone who's an earl today and common tomorrow."

Oxford nodded. "She said as much. She can be a willow made of steel to get what she wants. She got that from Burghley, not me."

"Or maybe she got it from someone else," Robin suggested, an impish look on his face.

A cloud swept over Oxford's face. Robin cringed. He knew Oxford could not abide jokes about who Lisbeth's father was.

Falstaff chortled. "He meant nothing, my lord. It's the beer."

"You cheeky little upstart," Oxford growled. Robin shrank further down. "You dare to imply Lisbeth is not my daughter?" His voice rose as the enormity of what the little page had implied swept over him.

"I'm so sorry, my lord. It is, indeed, the beer talking. I lack the wit of Sir John or your lordship. You both can slide words and thoughts together and make people laugh. I thought connecting Lisbeth's pushiness with a different father would let you avoid having to explain how she got her personality from you, but … but…." He realized he was digging himself in deeper. "You know how much I love you," he finally said in desperation.

Falstaff shook his head. "He's a squirrel in a forest, your lordship. He doesn't know which way to run. A tree is about to fall on him."

"I like the image."

Robin cowered. Oxford had been told when he returned from Italy that Lisbeth was not his daughter. The queen thought she had disabused him of this by showing him a bowl she gave Nan on Lisbeth's birth. But the queen was unaware that Oxford had refused to sleep with Nan before he left so he could annul his marriage to Nan if the queen changed her mind and asked him to become her consort.

Burghley knew Oxford had declined to sleep with Nan, though. Nan had told him. She had to; he kept pestering her about it. Burghley was not pleased but, being a patient man interested in the long game, he was content to wait out his feckless son-in-law until the queen made it clear she was never going to marry. But then out of the blue she granted Oxford permission to go abroad. This raised the specter of Oxford dying somewhere in Europe and frustrating Burghley's goal of spawning a line of noble descendants through his grandchildren.

Burghley realized he had to get his son-in-law into Nan's bed before Oxford left for Italy but Oxford deflected attempts to bring this about. Burghley vexed over this until he realized the solution to his problem was getting Nan into *Oxford's* bed! But how? By smuggling Nan into Oxford's farewell party as a going-away present.

Nan readily agreed. Burghley arranged for Oxford's "friends" to host a going-away party for him in the Savoy. The wine and beer flowed. Musicians played. Nan, appropriately hidden in swathes of rich cloth, was presented to Oxford for his enjoyment and her husband climbed into bed with his own wife, not knowing who she was. Lisbeth was apparently the result.

When Oxford returned, a then-trusted retainer told him Lisbeth was *not* his daughter because she had been born more than nine months after he had left. This was a lie, of course, but Oxford didn't think Lisbeth was his daughter anyway because he hadn't slept with Nan before he left. In either case, he was a cuckold. Then he was told Lisbeth *was* his daughter because he had been tricked into sleeping with her before he left! *And didn't know it!* Cuckolded and tricked! Humiliated! He imagined people belittling him for not keeping his wife on a tether and then laughing at him when he accepted Burghley's preposterous story that he had slept with his wife *and didn't know it!*

For all these reasons, Robin's attempt at being a wit brought back bitter memories for Oxford. Falstaff said nothing. Robin waited.

Oxford's face finally began to relax. "All right, Robin. We all know what happened. Or maybe we don't."

"You saw yerself in her face," Robin immediately said, referring to when Oxford visited Cecil House and met with his daughters. Lisbeth was twelve then. "You said you saw yerself in her eyes, the way she held her head back, her nether lip."

"Aye," Oxford admitted. It was true that he had seen himself in her. It was part of the reason he had come to accept Lisbeth as his daughter. "Still…," his voice trailed off.

"Still…?" Robin asked hopefully. He wanted out of jail.

Oxford thought for a moment. "It's amazing how the blood rushes through me when Lisbeth's birth brings back my fear of being cuckolded. It is a fierce current. I will use it someday."

"How?" Robin asked.

"Why, to write a play, of course!"

Robin burst out laughing. "Oh, my lord," he began, but Oxford cut him off.

"Enough of that. And of what you think of as your 'wit.'"

"Yes, my lord." Robin became serious. "I am your pen. Fill me with your words."

"Mary, mother of God," Falstaff said. "Ye certainly had plenty of your own to describe me, you little worm!"

~ 100 ~
A Play About Young Love

R omeus?" Robin said over his shoulder as he walked into the library at Oxford Court.

"You know it?" Oxford asked.

Robin nodded. He opened the cupboard and began taking out quills and ink. "Inartful, wordy, dull, plodding, and full of advice that would warm a Puritan's heart if they bought books, which they do not."

Oxford liked his little page's summation. "But what I will write will be a far cry from Mr. Brooke's ham-handed poem with its happy ending. I will tell a different tale, one I heard many times in Italy. It was known as *La Giuletta*."

"No happy ending? I thought you said this was going to be about young people in love."

"Yes, it will be about young people in love. The bride and groom will marry but die shortly thereafter."

"A tragedy, then."

"A tragedy *and* a love story."

"A love story," Robin repeated, sounding unconvinced.

Oxford frowned. "Pen. Ink." He pointed at the table. Robin bent over the page in front of him. "I first began to work on this in 1581 while I was in the Tower. Elizabeth had sent me there for making Anne Vavasour with child."

"Your first son, Edward," Robin said brightly, looking up.

Oxford scowled. Robin put his head back down.

"My son," Oxford added. He glared at the back of Robin's head, who sat there as still as a marble statue. Robin had eagerly cross-examined Oxford about Edward, Oxford's bastard son. They were working on *Much Ado About Nothing*. Robin, realizing he must have been the same age as Edward, wondered how the boy felt about being Oxford's son, albeit a bastard. After all, Robin had no idea who his parents were. Oxford had cut him off. Robin remembered how Oxford had reacted and decided to keep silent.

Oxford returned to how he felt about being in the Tower.

"I was taken to the Tower in a boat filled with Yeomen of the Guard. You would have thought I was full of fear as the boat passed under the portcullis at Traitor's Gate which had looked down on Anne Boleyn, the Earl of Surrey, and so many others who had met their end in Tower Yard. But I knew Elizabeth was not going to send me to the block for getting a lady-in-waiting pregnant. I was full of stories and poetry. The queen thought she was punishing me but I am never less idle, lo! than when I am alone. *My mind to me a kingdom is*," Oxford said.

"The cell she put me in looked out over the city. I poured out the poetry in my head, uninterrupted by servants, lawyers, bill-collectors, and nagging queens. It was a wonderful time. I enjoyed it so much the old boot let me out early. Someone told her I was as happy as a seal pup who'd found his cave."

He walked around the table to the window that looked out into the garden. "There are moments, Robin, when the fire that poetry stokes pours out molten verses that cool and stiffen into phrases that require no revision, no fine filing. Such was the case with the poetry I had been carrying around in my head since I, too, had seen *Palamon & Arcite*. She didn't remember I had been with her when she saw it. I agreed it was the best display of love I had ever seen. Unlike her, however, I did not think it the last word on the subject. After all, I was only twelve at the time."

"Of course. But she obviously thinks you can write a story that will outdo *Palamon & Arcite*."

"Yes. But in poetry?" He shook his head. "Poetry is dead the moment the pen is lifted from the page, Robin. The same is true for sculpture and painting. But a play comes alive every time it is staged. It is nothing on the page, but when players speak its lines?" Oxford gazed off across the room, having taken himself to an imaginary theater somewhere far away.

"And *La Guiletta*?" Robin asked, eager to get into the play.

"All here," Oxford said, tapping the side of his head. "Ready to be unlocked."

"God be praised," Robin could not keep himself from saying.

"A prologue will lay out the course of the play:

> *Two households, both alike in dignity,*
> *In fair Verona, where we lay our scene,*
> *From ancient grudge break to new mutiny,*
> *Where civil blood makes civil hands unclean.*

From forth the fatal loins of these two foes
A pair of star-cross'd lovers take their life;
Whole misadventured piteous overthrows
Do with their death bury their parents' strife.

Robin scrambled to get this down. He looked up when he was finished. "You're going to tell the audience the whole story at the start?"

"The story is well-known. The prologue merely gives an outline of how this version is going to be told. Brooke's mistake was to drag it out and turn it into a morality lesson. The tale I will tell will proceed at breakneck speed to the death of the lovers. Are they fated to die because they are from different families who hate each other? Because a letter went astray? Because a poison that was not a poison was suspected of being so?"

"Star-crossed lovers. Doomed from the start."

"Doomed no matter what they do. Life, in other words." He thought for a moment. "Be aware that the Romeo in this play is not in love with Juliet; he's in love with love. They are not the same."

"But when the play begins, he's in love with Rosaline, isn't he?"

"He is indeed. His love for her will show how fickle Romeo is. Rosaline will never appear on stage. The mention of her name will be enough."

"And who is Rosaline?"

"The queen, of course."

"The queen?" Robin looked up, worried. "And she never appears on stage?" He looked down at the paper in front of them. "Oh, boy," was all he said.

Oxford frowned. "I was in the Tower, wasn't I?" He walked back from the window to loom over Robin. "She rejected me and then locked me up! She will not like being a character who never appears onstage. This is how I get my revenge."

Robin was not enthused. "I would think *Venus & Adonis* had accomplished that."

"She needs reminding. Small annoyances will do for now, such as being named in one of my plays and then not getting a line to speak. And how the love interest – Romeo – falls in love with someone else!"

"And who are *you* in this play?"

"How many of me were there in *Two Gentlemen of Verona?*"

"Two. Proteus and Valentine."

"We are back in Verona, are we not? What if there are three of me in *Romeo & Juliet?*"

"Three?" Robin thought for a moment. "Why not? Let me guess. One must be Romeo because you are always the lead character."

Oxford nodded. "But how will the audience know that?" Robin shrugged. Oxford went on. "Because one of Romeo's friends will say, *"Here comes Romeo, here comes Romeo,"* to which another will reply: *"Without his roe."*

"*Without his roe?*" Robin screwed up his face. "Oh, this is going to be difficult." He wanted Oxford to help him.

Oxford's silence showed that he would not help him.

"Okay," Robin went on. "If Romeo is you without 'your roe,' I take away "Ro." This leaves 'me-o.'" He paused. "Good grief: *'I am Oxford.'*" He shook his head. "I thought you were getting tired of puns. *Two Gentlemen* was packed with them."

"You forget that this is an early play."

Robin sighed. "And who are the other characters in the play who are you?"

"Mercutio and Benvolio."

"Signor Mercurial and his cousin, Benevolent." Robin stopped. "Signor Benvolio: *'Good-Will-To E.O.'*"

"Well-done. Me as the madcap; me as the kindly one. Add Romeo and you have three."

"Yes," Robin said, "but will the audience enjoy a play where they are watching the same man appear three times in front of them?"

"Well, if I can be two characters in *Two Gentlemen*, why can't I be three in this one?

Robin had no answer to this. "And the two households of ancient grudge? I have heard of the broils in the streets of

London when you and your men went at it over Anne Vavasour. Is this where you got the brawl in this play?"

"Yes. Romeo will try to separate the Capulets and the Montagues, as I did on more than one occasion."

"Is that why Thomas Knyvet, Anne's cousin, stabbed you that night in Pudding Lane?"

"That was later. Much later. But it was still part of the Vavasour brawls."

"Ye still limp from it."

"For which he will be Tybalt in *Romeo & Juliet*."

Robin nodded. "And Mercutio?"

"Based on a man I met in Italy. A bargeman on the Adige River who steered the raft that carried me from Bolsano to Verona. He was big, rough, and full of life. Always twisting a word into a pun."

"And why is he needed in this play?"

"To set off Juliet's pure love."

"I like Benvolio better."

"You have not yet met Mercutio.

"Yes, but I think I know Mercutio." He meant his master. It was Oxford's turn to frown. Robin decided to move away from Mercutio. "And Romeo? Will I like Romeo?"

"Oh, yes. Romeo will appear as a young man besotted with Rosaline when the play begins. He will praise her to Benvolio, expressing his love:

> *She'll not be hit*
> *With Cupid's arrow; she hath Dian's wit;*
> *And, in strong proof of chastity well arm'd,*
> *From love's weak childish bow she lives unharm'd.*
> *She will not stay the siege of loving terms,*
> *Nor bide the encounter of assailing eyes,*
> *Nor ope her lap to saint-seducing gold:*
> *O, she is rich in beauty, only poor,*
> *That when she dies with beauty dies her store.*

"Elizabeth," Robin said, as his pen sped across the page. "She'll like this."

Oxford shrugged. "Benvolio will urge Romeo to come to a ball where he'll see faces that "*will make thee think thy swan a crow.*"

"*Thy swan a crow?*" Robin asked, looking up. "His Rosaline?" Oxford nodded. "Uh, oh."

"Romeo will defend Rosaline: *One fairer than my love! the all-seeing sun / Ne'er saw her match since first the world begun.*"

"Good. This will take you back onto safer ground."

"Until Romeo sees Juliet at the ball:

> *O, she doth teach the torches to burn bright!*
> *It seems she hangs upon the cheek of night*
> *Like a rich jewel in an Ethiope's ear;*
> *Beauty too rich for use, for earth too dear!*
> *So shows a snowy dove trooping with crows,*
> *As yonder lady o'er her fellows shows.*
> *The measure done, I'll watch her place of stand,*
> *And, touching hers, make blessed my rude hand.*
> *Did my heart love till now? forswear it, sight!*
> *For I ne'er saw true beauty till this night.*

"Lovely," Robin said, writing all this down. "*She doth teach the torches to burn bright*, and *hangs upon the cheek of night like a rich jewel in an Ethiope's ear.* Aren't these the words you spoke aloud on the way back from meeting Aemilia Bassano?"

This stopped Oxford. He drifted away. Robin knew his master loved nothing more than to call up an earlier moment of poetic creativity and, like a cow munching contentedly in a field, bring it up to enjoy it again.

Robin continued. "And the poetry evoked by the sight of Aemilia Bassano at Lord Willoughby's has been sitting in your head all this time, only to come out when you decide to revisit *Romeo & Juliet?*"

"Of course, dear Robin. I'm *always* writing something in my head. *Hamlet* you know of. The trunk of plays may be upstairs but a copy of everything sits in here. *My mind to me a library is.*" He reassumed the contented look Robin had seen when the subject of Aemilia Bassano had come up. "I rummage through rhymes whilst Burghley goes on and on at court, sifting soil from what he, or the queen, is droning on about to make my garden grow. Sometimes I'll work on a sonnet or a poem or stretch a line out in my head as they fill the room with colorless, efficient bureaucratic words. I call what they say 'dry-speak.'"

Robin looked at his notes. "So much for Rosaline. Romeo has seen Juliet. Can he marry her?"

"No. Her family tells her she will marry Paris."

"Paris? Oh, you mean like Paris in the Trojan War. He will be a sneaky, underhanded noble of no more than second rank for, if I remember rightly, you would not otherwise name him after the coward who shot Achilles dead with an arrow instead of facing him sword to sword, like a man."

This outburst surprised Oxford. He didn't know Robin knew anything about the Trojan War, much less that his page would think Paris a coward for using a bow and arrow to kill Achilles. "Yes. But let us return to Romeo. He sees Juliet at a party and falls instantly in love with her. He comes back at night, vaults over the wall into the garden behind her home and spies a light in a room above him:

> *But, soft! what light through yonder window breaks?*
> *It is the east, and Juliet is the sun.*
> *Arise, fair sun, and kill the envious moon,*
> *Who is already sick and pale with grief,*
> *That thou her maid art far more fair than she.*

"The envious moon?" Robin asked. "You make the queen *envious? Sick and pale with grief* because *her maid*—Juliet—is *far more fair than she is?*

"You don't think she'll like this?"

"Well, it's better than describing her as a *panting, sweating, overweight, aging love goddess, with a taste for choir boys.*"

Oxford smiled. Robin was describing how his master had painted Elizabeth in *Venus & Adonis*. He forced himself to concentrate. "As he gazes up at Juliet, Romeo realizes she doesn't know he is in the garden below her."

"Spying on her," Robin muttered. He looked up at Oxford. "He's spying on her. Not gazing."

Oxford, about to launch into poetry, stopped. "Gazing. Spying. What's the difference? Particularly if you are a nobody clerk writing down what I say. *What I say*," he repeated.

Robin put his head down.

Oxford began again. "Juliet still doesn't know Romeo is looking up at her. Audiences love knowing something characters on the stage don't know."

"*Henry VI*. The father holding the body of a man he has killed not knowing it's his son, book-ended by a son who has done the same to his father."

"Yes. With the king looking on. At your suggestion, I must acknowledge."

"Without the two men being aware the king was there," Robin added, a happy grin on his face as he remembered Oxford accepting his idea.

But Oxford was not thinking of *Henry VI*. "Romeo is wondering if he should emerge from the shadows or stay hidden. Realizing Juliet is speaking to the heavens, he speaks to himself *sotto voce*:

> *I am too bold, 'tis not to me she speaks:*
> *Two of the fairest stars in all the heaven,*
> *Having some business, do entreat her eyes*
> *To twinkle in their spheres till they return.*
> *The brightness of her cheek would shame those stars,*
> *As daylight doth a lamp; her eyes in heaven*
> *Would through the airy region stream so bright*
> *That birds would sing and think it were not night.*

"Oh, this I like," Robin said.

"I'm so very glad you do, but *basta!*" Oxford erupted, shattering Robin's enthusiasm. "*Enough* with what you think. You are my pen. Pens do not speak!"

Oxford drew himself erect and walked toward the window at the end of the library. "Juliet leans her cheek upon her hand." He raised his hand and put his cheek upon it. "Romeo sees it: '*O, that I were a glove upon that hand, that I might touch that cheek!*' Juliet still doesn't know he's below her. She asks the sky why he has to be Romeo:

> *'Tis but thy name that is my enemy; it is nor hand, nor foot,*
> *Nor arm, nor face, nor any other part*
> *Belonging to a man. O, be some other name!*
>
> *Romeo, doff thy name,*
> *And for that name which is no part of thee*
> *Take all myself.*"

"Romeo hears this. He reveals himself:

> *I take thee at thy word:*
> *Call me but love, and I'll be new baptized;*
> *Henceforth I never will be Romeo.*

"This will surprise Juliet, who will step out into the light." Oxford opened the window and leaned into the garden, becoming Juliet:

What man art thou that thus bescreen'd in night
So stumblest on my counsel?"

"*Stumblest*, my lord?" Robin asked. "He didn't stumble. He climbed over the wall. He's a spy. A bit of Paris here."

Oxford turned from the window. "It's what *she* says that's important. Not him. Or you. She can't call him 'spy' or say 'you're just like Paris.' She's in love with him. Just like he is with her. When you're in love, Robin, you don't see the other person. That's why Cupid is blind. It's not the person one sees; it's the state of being, in which case, anyone will do."

"Cock-a-doodle-do," Robin cried "Any-cock'll-do!"

Oxford stopped, shocked. So was Robin. Oxford asked. "Where did you learn *that?*"

Robin grimaced. "Sir John."

"So, he's corrupting you too," Oxford said, recalling Elspeth's complaint that Falstaff was corrupting Lil Henry. Maybe she was right. "I'm not talking about 'any cock'll do!' That's lust. Lust is despised as soon as it is enjoyed; hunted past reason, and no sooner had, than past reason hated. Witness Romeo, aflutter over Rosaline a few hours ago, who is now, *instamente*, in love with Juliet. She will not object to his intrusion because she's *in love* with him! 'Stumble' will do."

Robin wanted to ask Oxford whether he had spied on Nan. 'All the things I don't ask,' he thought to himself, 'and don't get credit for not asking.'

Oxford resumed walking around the table.

"Now, where was I? Ah, Romeo is worried he has offended her. He will make up to her by saying he will get rid of his name:

My name, dear saint, is hateful to myself,
Because it is an enemy to thee;
Had I it written, I would tear the word."

"*Had I it written, I would tear the word,*" Robin said approvingly, "Marvelous."

"Romeo, of course, is too dense to realize Juliet doesn't care what his name is. She acknowledges her love for him but starts to have second thoughts about his love for her:"

Dost thou love me? I know thou wilt say 'Ay,'
And I will take thy word: yet if thou swear'st,
Thou mayst prove false; at lovers' perjuries

> *They say, Jove laughs. O gentle Romeo,*
> *If thou dost love, pronounce it faithfully.*

"But she pauses," Oxford continued, "realizing she may be moving too fast for the young man below her window:

> *Or if thou think'st I am too quickly won,*
> *I'll frown and be perverse and say thee nay*
> *So thou wilt woo.*

Oxford waited for Robin to catch up before he went on. "Romeo immediately thinks he has to swear that he truly loves her: *Lady, by yonder blessed moon I swear / That tips with silver all these fruit-tree tops*—but she interrupts him, taking over the conversation:

> *O, swear not by the moon, the inconstant moon,*
> *That monthly changes in her circled orb,*
> *Lest that thy love prove likewise variable.*

"Oooh," Robin said. "The moon is now 'inconstant.' Another dig?"

"Well, isn't she?" Robin said nothing. "Romeo," Oxford continued, "not being as swift as the young girl he is wooing, is at a loss as to what to do."

"Were you?" Robin asked.

"Of course, I was. I was a boy, with no experience in wooing a woman."

"Nan," Robin guessed, not looking up. 'So, Juliet is Nan,' he said to himself.

Oxford ignored him. "Romeo is still trying to figure out what to say. He will ask: *What shall I swear by?* and Juliet will answer:

> *Do not swear at all;*
> *Or, if thou wilt, swear by thy gracious self,*
> *Which is the god of my idolatry,*
> *And I'll believe thee.*

"Ah. He has his instructions."

"But fails to follow them. *If my heart's dear love*--he will begin, but she will interrupt him again: *Well, do not swear: although I joy in thee.*

"She is moving toward the door."

"Or pulling herself out of the window and back into her room."

"My lord, why do you make her this way when Romeo only wants her to love him?"

"She *already* loves him. That's what he doesn't get. And Juliet is starting to have second thoughts about the man she has decided to fall in love with. She tells him:

> *I have no joy of this contract to-night:*
> *It is too rash, too unadvised, too sudden;*
> *Too like the lightning, which doth cease to be*
> *Ere one can say 'It lightens.' Sweet, good night!*

Robin shook his head. "Romeo won't accept this. He'll want to stay in the garden longer, with a climb up the vines into the lady's bedroom, eh, my lord?" Robin glanced up at Oxford with a sly look.

"Yes, *as I was*, before you ask." He glared at Robin and went on. "Romeo wonders: *O, wilt thou leave me so unsatisfied?*

"Well, that is to the point."

"She asks: *What satisfaction canst thou have to-night?* To which Romeo responds *The exchange of thy love's faithful vow for mine.*"

"She's already told him that, hasn't she?"

"She has. She will take him to school:

> *I gave thee mine before thou didst request it:*
> *And yet I would it were to give again.*

Romeo:

> *Wouldst thou withdraw it? for what purpose, love?*

"Truly, my lord. He misses her again? This is you?"

Oxford waved a hand. "Juliet goes on to describe her love:

> *To give my love to thee again.*
> *My bounty is as boundless as the sea,*
> *My love as deep; the more I give to thee,*
> *The more I have, for both are infinite.*

"*The more I give to thee, the more I have, for both are infinite,*" Robin said. His voice told Oxford he liked what he was hearing. "And so, they part?"

"Not quite yet. She goes in but comes back out almost immediately. They can't leave each other. They're in love." Oxford smiled. Robin could see that his master was reliving a tender moment when he was young and innocent and courting Nan. "Juliet says to Romeo:

> *'Tis almost morning; I would have thee gone:*
> *And yet no further than a wanton's bird;*
> *Who lets it hop a little from her hand,*

Like a poor prisoner in his twisted gyves,
And with a silk thread plucks it back again,
So loving-jealous of his liberty.

Romeo says: *I would I were thy bird,* to which Juliet responds: *Sweet, so would I: / Yet I should kill thee with much cherishing. / Good night, good night! parting is such sweet sorrow, / That I shall say good night till it be morrow.*

"To which I say, young Robin, good night as well. More on the morrow."

~ 101 ~
Two Lovers, Still in Love

Oxford and Robin were back in the library before the sun rose the next morning. Despite being as English as two people can be, neither thought of breakfast. They were both eager to get back into the play.

"And where do we find the young lovers this morning, my lord?"

"Romeo is up early, of course:

> *The grey-eyed morn smiles on the frowning night,*
> *Chequering the eastern clouds with streaks of light,*
> *And flecked darkness like a drunkard reels*
> *From forth day's path and Titan's fiery wheels:*

"Who speaks these lines?"

"Friar Laurence, who is happily working his heap of compost when Romeo bursts in and asks the good friar to marry him to Juliet."

"But the friar doesn't know about her yet, does he?"

"No. He thought Romeo was in love with Rosaline:

> *Is Rosaline, whom thou didst love so dear,*
> *So soon forsaken? young men's love then lies*
> *Not truly in their hearts, but in their eyes.*

Robin liked this. "A good and *wise* man."

"Yes. But Romeo has grown tired of listening to the friar: *Thou chid'st me oft for loving Rosaline,* he says, to which Friar Laurence tells him *for doting, not for loving, pupil mine.* Romeo says he thinks the friar told him to *bury love.* The friar protests. *Not in a grave, / To lay one in, another out to have.*

"*Not in a grave,*" Robin repeated to himself, the quill in his hand racing across the page, "*to lay one in, another out to have.* I 'spect the word 'grave' will appear often in this play."

"It's a tragedy, isn't it?" Oxford looked at the ceiling. "How many times will 'grave' appear, you ask? Ten times? No, twenty, at least. Let me see." Robin almost expected Oxford's hand come up, index finger extended, but Oxford's hands remained by his sides. "It's in a line where Juliet, when she first sees Romeo, wonders if he is married, in which case, she says, *my grave is like to be my wedding bed.*"

Robin shook his head. "Nice, but I'm guessing the friar will not marry Romeo and Juliet."

"Oh, but he will. He thinks marrying Romeo and Juliet will unite the Capulet and Montague houses and *turn rancor into love*. Juliet comes in and the friar marries them at once."

"Well, that's moving right along. Things are looking up."

"Not for long. Romeo finds Mercutio and Tybalt spoiling for a fight. He tries to separate them. Tybalt hides behind Romeo and stabs Mercutio, who falls wounded. Romeo stabs Tybalt, killing him."

"Oh, my goodness: the family feud is on again!"

"It is. The Prince banishes Romeo, who visits Juliet for one night before he runs to Mantua where he will hide until Friar Laurence figures out a way for him to come back."

"Ah. There will be a happy ending."

Oxford frowned. "Romeus might have gotten one, but Romeo will not. Juliet's parents have pledged her to Paris, who goes to Friar Laurence to marry him to Juliet."

"Paris goes to Friar Laurence? But the friar can't marry him to Juliet; he's already married her to Romeo!"

"Yes. And if he marries her to Paris, she will be guilty of bigamy."

"And he will be guilty of helping her!"

Oxford nodded. "The friar can't tell Paris what he has done because he is obligated to keep silent about her marriage to Romeo. He puts Paris off. Paris leaves and Juliet comes in. She is desperate. She doesn't want to marry Paris. She wants to kill herself. Friar Laurence tells her he has a plan. He says she will tell everyone she will marry Paris but he will give her a drug that will put her to sleep and make her look like she has died:

> *Take thou this vial, being then in bed,*
> *And this distilled liquor drink thou off;*
> *When presently through all thy veins shall run*
> *A cold and drowsy humour, for no pulse*
> *Shall keep his native progress, but surcease:*
> *Thou shalt continue two and forty hours,*
> *And then awake as from a pleasant sleep.*

"He says her family will think she is dead. They will bury her in the family tomb. While she sleeps, Friar Laurence will send a letter to Romeo to come back and rescue her."

"I like this, but wouldn't Juliet worry the friar has given her *real* poison?"

Oxford hadn't thought of this. "Why would she think that?"

"The friar married her to Romeo without her parents' permission. Might not Juliet think the friar would be happy if she never wakes from her sleep? Everyone *thinks* she's dead. If she stays dead, the friar would not have to explain why he married her to Romeo."

"And what about Romeo?" Oxford asked. "Are you going to poison him next?" Robin hadn't thought of this. "You leave the plotting to me, young man, and forget the conspiracies your little fervid mind dreams up. Besides, the friar would never give her real poison. He's a good man."

"Oh. Friar Laurence is one of your tutors."

Oxford looked like he'd been caught. Both decided not to talk about who that might be.

Robin leaned toward him. "But I still think Juliet is going to worry that the sleeping potion is poison and she is not going to wake up. After all, she's what, thirteen?"

"Two months short of fourteen," Oxford couldn't stop himself from saying, Nan's age when he courted her.

"A young girl, then. Who knows what they think?" Robin asked, glancing at Oxford out of the corner of his eye. "There is ore here to mine, my lord. She might ask herself:

> *What if it be a poison, which the friar*
> *Subtly hath minister'd to have me dead,*
> *Lest in this marriage he should be dishonour'd,*
> *Because he married me before to Romeo?*

"I like this," Oxford conceded. "She will have other worries too, like what happens once she's lying in the coffin:

> *How if, when I am laid into the tomb,*
> *I wake before the time that Romeo*
> *Come to redeem me? There's a fearful point!*

"Yes," Robin chimed in. "She is going to be frightened. Ghosts. Devils. And worried there might not be enough air in the tomb."

> *Shall I not, then, be stifled in the vault,*
> *To whose foul mouth no healthsome air breathes in,*
> *And there die strangled ere my Romeo comes?*

Oxford thought this good. "And where is Tybalt lying?" he asked.

Robin grinned. "Right next to where they're going to place her! It's the family tomb!"

"Indeed. And so, this is what she will say:

> *I will be in a vault, an ancient receptacle,*
> *Where bloody Tybalt, yet but green in earth,*
> *Lies festering in his shroud;*
> *If I wake, shall I not be distraught,*
> *And pluck the mangled Tybalt from his shroud?*

Robin looked up. "Maybe she'll decide not to drink the poison Friar Laurence has given her."

"No. Really, Robin, you forget we are in the theater. She needs to take the drug. I will expand her fears, as you suggest - after all, she is only a girl - but she will abruptly down the poison and collapse onto her bed."

Robin shrugged. "Well, as you say, she is only a girl."

"But you miss something else, Robin. *The audience also won't know whether the drug is true poison or not!*"

"But they know she's going to die."

"Yes, but not *when*. Juliet will be discovered in her bed when Friar Laurence arrives to marry her to Paris. Paris, thinking he has been cheated of Juliet, will cry out:

> *Beguiled, divorced, wronged, spited, slain!*
> *Most detestable death, by thee beguil'd,*
> *By cruel cruel thee quite overthrown!*
> *O love! O life! not life, but love in death!*

"*Cruel cruel?*" Robin asked. "*O love! O life! not life, but love in death!*" He was suddenly mystified. "Thou didst never pen such lines since I have come into your service, my lord."

"Shh, Robin. It is not I who is speaking."

"Oh, Paris is …" He strained to figure out who Oxford intended him to be. "Sidney," he finally said.

"Well done."

"But Sidney is dead, my lord. You beat him up as Claudio in *Much Ado About Nothing* and put him in *Love's Labour's Lost* as Boyet. Wasn't that enough?"

"No. Never."

"Oh. Then Juliet is Nan, you are Romeo, and Paris is Sidney." He looked up at Oxford, a grin on his face. Oxford was having trouble keeping one off his face for he always loved it when someone started to see other characters staring at them through the shrubbery of the play, as Oxford liked to put it. "But you didn't have to kill her. Juliet, I mean. Uh, Nan."

"She lives at this point in the play, doesn't she? And in real life, she married Romeo, didn't she?" Robin nodded. "You forget I wrote this play whilst I was in the Tower. Sidney was alive then, and fresher in my mind."

"So, why did you wait so long to finish it?"

"Because I did not know the ending then. I was too young when I put the story down in the Tower. It's the same thing with *Hamlet*. Too soon. It's *still* too soon for *Hamlet*."

"And what is the ending you came up with for *Romeo & Juliet*?"

"I will have the letter from Friar Laurence go astray so that Romeo never learns of Friar Laurence's plan, only that Juliet is dead. In despair, he will buy poison from an apothecary in Mantua. *Real* poison this time. He will rush back to Verona to see Juliet's tomb but find it locked. He will break in. Paris, coming to put flowers on Juliet's grave, will find Romeo in the vault. They will fight. Romeo will kill Paris and then drink the apothecary's poison:

> *O true apothecary!*
> *Thy drugs are quick.*

"I'm starting to feel sorry for Paris," Robin said as he took this down.

"Don't. Juliet will wake and find Romeo lying next to her:

> *What's here? a cup, closed in my true love's hand?*
> *Poison, I see, hath been his timeless end:*
> *O churl! drunk all, and left no friendly drop*
> *To help me after? I will kiss thy lips;*

She sees his dagger:

> *O happy dagger! This is thy sheath;*

She stabs herself and falls on Romeo's body."

"And where is Paris while this is going on?" Robin asked, as he took this down. "He was in the tomb when Romeo killed him. Is he still lying there?"

Oxford was at first irritated at the question but realized Robin had a point: Where had Paris fallen? There was a body lying on the stage somewhere.

"If I may suggest, my lord, you may want to add lines for Romeo to speak to Paris before he dies. You have an opportunity here to end the hatred between them."

"And why should I do that?" Oxford asked, sounding irritated.

"To bring the two households together and end their 'ancient grudge.'"

"And you suggest?"

"Give Paris a dying speech. Not too long. Just long enough for him to ask Romeo to lay his body beside Juliet's."

Oxford didn't understand. "Romeo hates Paris."

"*You* hate Paris because he's Philip Sidney, but Paris should have married Juliet, except that Romeo kills him! My lord, let Romeo be gallant in his victory! The audience will love him for doing so."

Oxford was still frowning. "All right:

> *In faith, let me peruse this face.*
> *Mercutio's kinsman, noble Paris!*
> *I'll bury thee in a triumphant grave;*
> *For here lies Juliet, and her beauty makes*
> *This vault a feasting presence full of light.*

"Very gallantly done," Robin said, writing down Oxford's lines.

"But there's much to fill in. We will come back to this, once it is no longer fresh, for it is then that the mason and the playwright can see the cracks and imperfections in their work and putty them over."

Midsummer Madness

I have tired of Romeo," Oxford said the next morning. "And Juliet as well, his too-smart young love. I see too much of Nan when I write Juliet. I will come back to her and her silly boyfriend later. I have need of some foolery now for Lisbeth's wedding."

"Foolery," Robin said aloud. "A new word." He rolled it around in his mind as he sat down at the library table. "But we can't abandon *Romeo,* can we? It's to be presented at Christmas. Shouldn't we finish it first?"

"Of course. But I won't."

"Oh. A deadline to make the juices flow." He was grinning from ear to ear. Oxford knew the little page was excited because they had a *second* play to work on. And then they would have to come back to *Romeo.* Robin's cup was overflowing. Without looking up, he said: "And if you're tired of Romeo, you're tired of you."

"Yes. I'm tired of me. Particularly the young me, who gushed poetry and sonnets all the time. Whoever was not embarrassed by the excesses of youth?" He sighed.

"But the poetry in *Romeo,* is good, my lord. The sonnets too, when Romeo and Juliet are devouring each other with their eyes and their imaginations ..."

"And their words," Oxford interjected. "Never forget the words."

"Yes. Who would have thought to do it in perfect sonnets?"

Oxford liked Robin's praise. "Yes. I was young, when the forges of love burned hotter. I can still retrieve what I wrote then. I can still bring Nan to life with the purity she had before it was besmudged by what was to come." Robin was poised, pen in hand, but Oxford could tell Robin's ears had gone up when he heard the word 'besmudge.' "I said we're not going back to *Romeo.*"

"Just give me a touch, my lord. Some of Nan's 'purity' before she was 'besmudged by whatever was to come.'" He looked up, his face glowing.

Robin's question made Oxford realize that his description of Nan as pure "before she was besmudged" was an unconscious admission he was the cause of her fall from perfection. He frowned, angry with himself. He scanned Robin's face to see if his page had heard the same thing but saw only adoration. He couldn't resist. "Juliet is standing in the garden, eager for night to come so that she can see her Romeo again:

> *Come, gentle night, come, loving, black-brow'd night,*
> *Give me my Romeo; and, when he shall die,*
> *Take him and cut him out in little stars,*
> *And he will make the face of heaven so fine*
> *That all the world will be in love with night*
> *And pay no worship to the garish sun.*

"Ooo," Robin said as he wrote this down. "And these little stars, your words, will make the world love *you* when they read them."

"If they *know* I wrote them," Oxford said, a touch of anger slipping into his voice. He looked up at the ceiling. Robin could tell his master was running Juliet's lines through his mind, finding no changes were needed, as if they were chiseled in granite. The gods were nodding approval.

Robin was gazing in admiration at Oxford. "You were really good when you were young, my lord," he said.

"Not now?"

Robin sat up. "No, no, my lord. I meant you were *so* good *so* young. Most poets have to wait years before they can pen *take him and cut him out in little stars. You're even better today!*"

Robin's outburst brought Oxford up short. Had he peaked when he was young? Was he empty now of the inspiration that had given him lines such as *But, soft! what light through yonder window breaks?* He didn't like to think so. "For now, we shall turn to *Midsummer Madness.*"

"A working title, I hope."

Oxford shrugged. "Who cares what a play is called? What's in a name? It's the words that make it sing."

Nigel appeared in the doorway. "Mr. William *Shake-spare,*" he announced, his nose pointed at the ceiling.

"Yes. Mr. Shacksmear," Oxford said, unconsciously calling up the Countess of Southampton's mispronunciation of the name of the man now striding into the library.

"My lord," Shackspear said, sweeping a wide-brimmed hat off his head. "We are back from the provinces." Oxford and Robin looked at each other. "The theaters have been closed for a year, my lord," Shackspear added, to jog Oxford's memory. "We had to go on tour to make enough money to stay alive."

"Ah. Your investments were insufficient?"

"The plague closed more than the theaters, my lord. The houses of pleasure as well. Who wants to spend money on a play if they can't have sport with a lady after they see it, eh? Or," he went on, his face assuming the low-browed look of a pederast eyeing a young boy at a fair, "while the play is going on?"

"Indeed," Oxford said. Robin turned away.

Shackspear looked pleased, thinking Oxford finally understood him. "And what is the play?" he asked, leaning on a new walking stick he rotated so that Oxford could see the ivory inlay that ran down one side.

"Two plays, actually."

Shackspear's face lit up. "Two? Wonderful! And when can I take them to Burbage."

"What happened to Henslowe?"

"We fell out in Coventry. I'm not going to give him any more plays. Burbage is the man." He pulled out a chair on the other side of the table and gestured that he would like to sit down. "My leg is not what it used to be, my lord, what with walking up and down England all these months. When I become a made-man, I will buy a house and travel no more."

Oxford didn't want Shackspear to join them at the table but the mention of a bad leg, something Oxford was feeling that very morning, stopped him for a moment. Shackspear took advantage of the silence and sat down. "Of course, as co-author of the plays we have written together, it is only natural that I join you." He put what he thought was a kind smile on his face and leaned his cane against the edge of the table.

Oxford glared at him. "What cheek, sir! You are *not* co-author!" His anger at being tricked into letting Shackspear sit down at the table rose in his throat.

Shackspear protested. "I gave the world Launce and his dog, Crab, in *Two Gentlemen*, did I not?"

"No, you did not."

"What about the 'grandam who, having no eyes, wept herself blind?' Ye liked that one."

Oxford had to admit the scene with Launce and his dog was good. "But that doesn't make you co-author."

"Well, it may not have been much but I think I should get *some* credit for my contributions. I am, you must admit, the soodness author of the plays, even though my name is not hyphenated."

Oxford had no idea what Shackspear was talking about. Robin did. "My lord, when Mr. Shackspear and I took *Venus & Adonis* to Mr. Field, Mr. Field suggested he print Mr. Shackspear's name as *Shakespeare*."

"Without the hyphen, of course," Shackspear went on, "because that would mean I was soodness - not the author - which I am not."

Oxford had a dazed look on his face. He still didn't know what Shackspear was talking about.

"I write my name *Shakespeare* now and speak it thus: *Shake-spare*."

Oxford finally understood. "Congratulations," was all he could manage to say.

Shackspear shrugged. "What's in a name anyway? Is there anything I can take to Burbage?"

"No."

"At least tell me what they're about, Burbage will want to know."

"A tragedy about two young lovers, and a comedy that ends with three marriages."

"Lovely. And when can I expect them, or either one?"

"Christmas."

"Christmas? But that is so far off, my lord. I need money now."

Oxford shrugged. "Get Langley to open the whorehouses."

"He's already done that, but while the theaters were closed because of the plague, we had to go to the money lenders, you know, the Spinozas, the Baptistas. They want their money now that the theaters and the happy houses are open again."

Oxford was surprised to hear that he and Shackspear might have something *else* in common: being in debt to moneylenders. Oxford knew the Spinozas and the Baptistas, but he was not going to tell Shackspear that. Realizing he and Shackspear had another connection made Oxford even angrier. "And did you find time to see your son, *Hamnet*," he asked, "whilst you were walking around England?"

At this moment, Lady Elspeth came into the library towing Henry, saving Shackspear from having to answer Oxford's question. He heaved himself up. "My lady," he said, bowing to her. He grabbed his cane and headed for the door.

Lady Elspeth nodded to him as he went by. Once Shackspear had left, Lady Elspeth walked Henry over to his father. "And here is your son, my lord, handsomely dressed to go out for his morning walk." It was at this point that she spotted Falstaff stretched out in a chair behind the door. The big man looked like he was fast asleep. "Oh," was all Lady Elspeth said.

Oxford followed her eye. "I didn't know he was here."

Elspeth looked like she didn't believe him. "Bona Fortuna is going to take Henry to St. Paul's and back. It's a fine day outside."

Henry finally saw Falstaff. "Sir John!" he cried out. He started toward him but Lady Elspeth held him back. "Not now, my dear," she said. "Some other time." She towed Henry out of the room.

Falstaff, eyes still shut, made a sound like an earthquake far away. "I'm not bad for 'im," he said, opening an eye. "He loves it when I call him 'Lil Henry' and let him ride my good leg." He pulled himself up in the chair and opened his other eye. "And you," he said, casting a disapproving look at Oxford. "Asking 'His Soodness' if he visited his son, *Hamnet*. Really. He may be a worthless Warwickshire hack but you need him. He's your highway to the public stage. And under all that bluster, he's a man, like you and me."

"Like you and me?" Oxford was dumbfounded by this.

"He wants fame and fortune, doesn't he? Isn't that what everyone wants? *Isn't that what Achilles wanted?*"

Oxford glanced at Robin, who looked away. He turned back to Falstaff, still angry, with Shackspear for interrupting his morning and with Falstaff for objecting to how Oxford had treated the man who had just left. "So, what have you been up to? Sharing a pint with Willum?"

"Of course not. But you saw Hamnet in Stratford. You said something was missing. Even the boy's grandfather said he was 'a fire made with little twigs.' I think His Soodness stays away from Stratford because he doesn't want to see his boy. He sees Lil Henries everywhere, including here, and he doesn't know what to do with his son. 'Willum' may be a bit slow and lack what it takes to succeed as a playwright or a player but I bet his heart aches when he sees the boy.'"

Oxford gaped at Falstaff. But then he remembered how Shackspear had sworn on his son's life to keep secret Oxford's help while they were writing *Titus Andronicus*: "*On the life of my son, whom I revere and adore*," he had said.

Robin was watching all this. He knew his master was thinking how little he had thought of Hamnet, or even his own son, for that matter. He jumped in. "Shackspear didn't get the sarcasm, my lord. I passed him as he went out the door. Your words went right over his head."

"Liar," Oxford said. Robin looked away. "You have never been good at lying," Oxford went on, sounding like he was going to make the little page a lightning rod for his frustrations, but then Nigel came in again: "Lady Lisbeth Vere and the Earl of Derby" he announced, as if his words would wash the sound of Shake-spare's name out of his mouth.

Oxford's eldest daughter and her betrothed came into the library. Oxford stood up. Lisbeth curtsied. "Father," she said. Derby extended his hand which Oxford shook vigorously. "We came to see how it goes with the play," Derby said, a broad smile on his face.

"What play?" Oxford asked, his face all innocence.

"For the wedding, of course," Lisbeth said, looking at him with alarm.

"Lisbeth, my dear, you told me I was forbidden from writing plays because of how embarrassing it would be if the grandfather of the next king of England - your son by his lordship here - was discovered to be a playwright."

"I said *after* our wedding; not *before*."

Oxford looked away for a moment. "Parts have been written, parts have not."

"Will you have it ready in time?" Lisbeth demanded.

"Yes. It will be ready." Oxford glanced at Robin, seated in his accustomed chair at the table. Lisbeth and Derby followed Oxford's eyes. Robin nodded.

"Well," Lisbeth said, "there it is. If anyone knows, *he* knows," she said, referring to Robin. "We will leave you to your ink and things." She swept out of the room.

Derby lingered. "I have always wanted to be a player, my lord. Is there any way I could appear in this new play you're writing? Not as myself, of course. A small role, if that were possible."

"Indeed, it is. In fact, I was wondering if you would play Theseus, the Duke of Athens."

"What an honor, my lord." Derby's hand came up to his chest. "I will go home and brush up on my Greek."

"No need to. You will not find the Duke I am writing in Plutarch or Xenophon. The role will require a player who possesses gravitas, someone who can announce decisions in a way that brooks no cavil."

"I am your man, my lord. I will practice before the glass." He bowed and turned to leave. "Oh," he said, turning back. "You should know that I was in France when Catherine de Medici and her daughter, Marguerite, traveled to Navarre to settle Marguerite's marriage negotiations with Henri IV. Unfortunately, I was forced to stay behind in Paris."

"*Quel dommage!*" Oxford said. "Robin, here, actually went with them."

"You did?" Derby exclaimed. "Oh, what I would have done to have been on that voyage to Navarre!" Derby reached out to take Robin's hand. "I want to kiss the hand of the man who kissed the hands of the members of the l'escadron volant. Oh!"

Robin snatched his hand away before Derby could press his lips against it.

Derby sighed. He was imagining himself with the French ladies, not kissing Robin's hand. "We are brothers," he said to Robin, "bonded at the heart."

Robin was worried what Derby meant by 'heart.' *Certainly not there!* he thought to himself. He glanced at Oxford.

Derby continued. "According to my sources in Paris, my lord, *Love's Labour's Lost* conveyed exactly what happened during the visit of the ladies to Navarre. The play has been translated into French. The French think it *merveilleuse,* a reflection of a scintillating episode in their history."

Derby bowed and continued out the door.

"You are fortunate, Robin," Oxford said, "to have spent only a few months in France; he spent three years there and look how affected he has become." Oxford looked like he was reconsidering whether the Earl of Derby should marry his daughter when he recalled how 'Italianate' he had been upon his return from Italy.

"He is madly penning plays, my lord," Robin said. "He spends every day going to plays. He is of the theater."

Oxford considered this. "Well," was all he said.

"But back to *Midsummer Madness,* my lord. Does it already exist in your head and you only have to speak it to me to get it down on paper or does it need work?"

"Both. Unlike *Romeo*, which is entirely in my head, some of *Midsummer* has been written down. Those pages lie upstairs in the trunk of plays."

This was thrilling news to Robin. On their first visit, Oxford had pulled a sheaf of papers out of the trunk and handed them to Robin with a flourish. "*The Famous Victories of Henry the Fifth*," Oxford had announced, "a fledgling barely hatched out if its egg. The queen wants history; you shall write it. Add feathers and see if the heir of your first invention has wings."

Thus, *Famous Victories* became Robin's first play. Shackspear, of course, claimed it was his. The queen didn't like it. "You have buried three plays in this coffin," she told Shackspear. She ordered him to write three new plays from the bones he had presented.

On their second visit to the trunk of plays, Oxford pulled out an early play the two of them turned into *A Double Maske* for the Countess of Southampton's wedding. They subsequently learned it had been staged at the Rose as *Love's Labour's Lost*.

On this third visit, Oxford pulled out a sheaf of papers and announced "*Phyllida & Choryn*." He closed the lid and headed back downstairs, a disappointed Robin in tow. "Too much classical knowledge can crush a story," he said over his shoulder, waving the papers in his hand. "Like decoration on a building, or the finish on the top of a cake. This early attempt spent too much time trying to impress the listener with allusions to ancient Greece and obscured the story. I had forgotten the first rule of writing: *Toujours l'histoire, toujours l'histoire.*"

They arrived in the library. Oxford put the papers on the table and began to shuffle them like they were giant playing cards, sliding them back and forth and over and under each other. Robin went around to the other side and watched. He thought his master might be reabsorbing what he had written years earlier by simply passing his eye over the pages as they flew by. After a few minutes, Oxford looked up.

"*A Pastorall of Phillyda & Choryn*, I called it. Two wooden characters sighing and calling out to each other in the middle of a field. Too much Sidney; too much Spenser. Grandiose words but not a human being in sight. I shall replace Phillyda and Choryn with not one but two pairs of lovers." Oxford tore off the top of one of the papers on the table and threw it on the floor.

Robin, aghast, looked at the paper on the floor. "Are we going to pick these up again, my lord, like the scraps you threw on the floor while we worked on *Henry VI*?"

"No. What's on the floor will stay there." Oxford tore off part of another page and threw it after the first. "*Midsummer Madness* will open with an angry father whose daughter is refusing to marry the man he has chosen to be her husband."

"Ah, old Capulet choosing Paris as Juliet's betrothed."

"If this were *Romeo & Juliet*, but it's not."

"Will lovers die in this play, my lord?"

"No. It's a comedy. The angry father will go to the Duke of Athens to demand justice against the young man his daughter wants to marry. The Duke, at the time, will be in the middle of planning his wedding to Hippolyta."

"Did you go to Athens, my lord?"

"No. I didn't have to. There is a small town called Sabbioneta. The Italians call it '*La Picola Atena*', or 'Little Athens.' Like the sycamores in Verona, there will be a scene where the men who act a play for the Duke will meet at the Duke's Oak to rehearse, and any knowledgeable traveler will instantly know that our scene is set in Sabbioneta."

"The opening, then?" Robin asked. His hand hovered over the pot of ink.

"The Duke's palace. Theseus, the Duke, is talking to his bride: *Now, fair Hippolyta, our nuptial hour draws on apace.* He is interrupted by Egeus who is complaining about his daughter, Hermia. Egeus has given his consent for Hermia to marry Demetrius but she wants to marry Lysander. The only reason this could be possible, the father thinks, is that Lysander has bewitched his daughter. Theseus orders them all to appear in front of him. The father tells Demetrius to step forward:

> *Stand forth, Demetrius. My noble lord,*
> *This man hath my consent to marry Hermia.*
> *Stand forth, Lysander: and my gracious duke,*
> *This man hath bewitch'd the bosom of my child;*
> *Thou, thou, Lysander, thou hast given her rhymes,*
> *And interchanged love-tokens with my child:*
> *Thou hast by moonlight at her window sung,*
> *With feigning voice verses of feigning love,*
> *And stolen the impression of her fantasy.*

"*Stolen the impression of her fantasy*," Robin said aloud as he wrote down Oxford's words, "*by moonlight at her window*, no less." He looked up. "Romeo did not die in Verona, my lord: he is alive and well in *Midsummer Madness*. Is he Lysander?"

Oxford ignored him. "The Duke will tell Hermia that Demetrius is a worthy choice and she must marry him because her father says so, but Hermia refuses. She presses her case:

> *I do entreat your grace to pardon me.*
> *I know not by what power I am made bold,*
> *Nor how it may concern my modesty,*
> *In such a presence here to plead my thoughts;*
> *But I beseech your grace that I may know*
> *The worst that may befall me in this case,*
> *If I refuse to wed Demetrius.*

Theseus is blunt:

> *Either to die the death or to abjure*
> *Forever the society of men.*

Robin looked up. "Death or the convent? Isn't that a little severe, my lord?"

"Hush, sweet Robin. Isn't any daughter her father's property?" Robin couldn't tell if Oxford truly believed Hermia was owned by Egeus or if his master was mocking him. And then Robin remembered Petruchio in *The Taming of the Shrew* describing the woman who was about to become his wife. Robin said:

> *I will be master of what is mine own.*
> *She is my goods, my chattels; she is my house,*
> *My household stuff, my field, my barn,*
> *My horse, my ox, my ass, my any thing.*

"Very good," Oxford cut in, "but this is a comedy. Theseus stands for order. He *has* to say she dies or goes to the convent. It tightens up the fear that Hermia will be killed or locked away."

"Will she find true love?" Robin asked. He looked worried.

"Of course, she will. But if I have caused my little page to fret, Theseus and Egeus have done their jobs."

"Who will she marry?"

"Lysander, but only after falling in love with Demetrius for a while."

"How can that be?"

"Because you will fetch a magic flower from far away that contains a juice that, when squeezed into someone's eye, makes them fall in love with the next person they see."

"Me?" Robin asked. He looked at Oxford. He was confused. Then he realized Oxford was imagining him onstage actually getting the flower. "Oh, no, my lord."

"You will love being Puck."

"Puck?! Robin repeated, uttering the word in a weak voice.

"A woodland fairy, who I will command to:

> *Fetch me that flower; the herb I shew'd thee once:*
> *The juice of it on sleeping eye-lids laid*
> *Will make or man or woman madly dote*
> *Upon the next live creature that it sees.*

"*You* will command?" Robin asked. His eyes opened wider.

"I will be Oberon, the king of the fairies."

"Since when did you cast ourselves in a play?"

"Since we began work on a comedy to celebrate the wedding of my oldest daughter. Her husband-to-be, as you heard me promise him, will play Theseus. Lisbeth will play Hippolyta, although she doesn't know it yet."

Robin looked away. Words he had happily taken down for others to speak were now words *he* would have to utter. The curtain he had hid behind was being pulled aside. He was both thrilled and frightened.

Oxford brought Robin back to the task at hand. "Oberon will have a queen who has disobeyed him. Her name will be Titania."

"Ovid's name for Diana," Robin said quickly. "Which is the name the poets use to refer to Elizabeth." His face paled. "Her Majesty will be watching a play in which there will be a fairy queen she will recognize as … her?" Oxford nodded. "And who will play Titania, my lord?" Robin was worried his master would ask him to 'double' the roles of Puck and Titania. He didn't want to play Titania. Not in front of Elizabeth.

"Lettice Knollys."

Robin's jaw dropped. "The Dowager Countess of Leicester? She who Elizabeth banned from court for marrying her Robin?"

"One and the same."

Robin immediately recalled the trial where his master had almost been unearled. The Countess had been ejected from the court for yelling at the jury, all noblemen. She told them she knew what they were doing. She said the queen was a bitch. 'Make sure you spell it with a capital B' she had cried out, as palace guards manhandled her out of the courtroom.

"But, my lord, the queen, will not take kindly to Lettice Knollys returning to court without her permission *and* playing a queen whose name is the same as the one the poets use to refer to Elizabeth!"

"Yes. Don't you love it?"

Robin drew in his breath. "Falstaff says every decision has two parts, my lord: *now* and *later*. He rarely takes his own advice, but don't you think you are enjoying the moment too much when the queen figures out what is going on and not paying enough attention to what she might do afterwards?

"Oh, Robin, you are so practical."

Robin was dismayed. He made a note to be far away from the queen when Lettice Knollys walked onto the stage. "And Oberon and Titania will argue in this play."

"Of course."

"Over what?"

"A little changeling boy."

"A *what?*"

Nigel appeared in the doorway. "Forgive me, my lord, but would you care for some supper?"

Oxford looked around. It was dark out. "Where is my lady?" he asked.

"She has gone out, my lord, but did not inform me as to where she was going. Bona Fortuna went with her."

"And Henry?"

"The wet-nurse is with him."

"She didn't take him with her? She hasn't done that before."

Nigel did not comment. He returned to the question of whether his lordship wanted anything to eat. "We have some ox tongue Frangellica can provide, smoked by Digby at Hedingham, with some manchet bread she made this morning."

Oxford nodded. "That would be very nice. Thank you, Nigel. I shall have it here and continue working."

Nigel glanced at Robin before he turned to leave. He gave Robin a glance to let him know he would take care of him as well.

103

The Little Changeling Boy

I think I may like squeezing love-juice into the eyes of sleeping lovers," Robin said the next morning as he and Oxford walked into the library. He looked mischievous. The sun was not yet over St. Swithin's next door. "Tell me about the little changeling boy," he asked. Then his face darkened. "Titania," he said, listening to how her name sounded. "Will I have to put love-juice in *her* eyes?"

"No, pages do not squeeze love-juice into the eye of a queen."

"Most certainly not." Robin felt better.

"I will do it, as Oberon, King of the Fairies."

"You? Oh, of course. And where will I – Puck - get the flower to put love-juice in the eyes of the lovers?"

"Off-stage. Oberon will describe how Cupid once fired an arrow toward the heart of the 'imperial votaress' but the arrow missed so that she was able to *pass on, in maiden meditation, fancy-free.*"

Robin's brow furrowed. "Cupid doesn't miss, does he?"

"No, but when the target is the queen's heart, Cupid's arrow has to miss because it is *quenched in the chaste beams of the watery moon.*"

"Oh, she'll like that. But you already had Romeo use the same words to describe how *Rosaline* could not be hit by Cupid's arrow:

> *she hath Dian's wit;*
> *And, in strong proof of chastity well arm'd,*
> *From love's weak childish bow she lives unharm'd.*

Robin stopped. "Oh. I forgot. Rosaline is the queen in *Romeo.*"

"She is. She was safe from Cupid in *Romeo* because she was chaste. In *Midsummer, because she is heartless!*"

"Oh. She is not going to like that."

"I certainly hope not. She has kept my name from appearing on the plays I write, and I will make her pay for it." He started to anger. "Still, Cupid's arrow will miss her again. She cannot love." This brought him to a halt.

Robin waited. After a moment, Oxford returned to *Midsummer.* "The arrow that misses her will fall *upon a little western flower, before milk-white, now purple with love's wound, which maidens call love-in-idleness.*"

"'*Purple with love's wound*,'" Robin said, writing down Oxford's words. "Lovely. And the love-juice from this flower will change the way people see things."

"Yes. It will make them fall in love with the first person they see after it is squeezed into their eyes. I thought of using it in *Romeo* but decided it would work better in *Midsummer*. Didn't Romeo have love-juice in his eyes when he saw Juliet?"

> *Did my heart love till now? forswear it, sight!*
> *For I ne'er saw true beauty till this night.*

"I hear Marlowe: *Who ever loved that loved not at first sight?*'"

Robin's comment stopped Oxford for a moment. To Robin's surprise, his master was not displeased by the comparison. Oxford went on. "Remember how Romeo tells Juliet he found her garden: *By love, who first did prompt me to inquire; / He lent me counsel and I lent him eyes.*"

"Eyes." Robin looked up. "I'll wager *eyes* fill *Romeo & Juliet*."

"Fifty times, at least. In *Midsummer*, even more!"

Robin laughed. "I love the love-juice, my lord, but what is going on between the fairy king and Titania over the little changeling boy."

"You, as Puck, will be the first to mention the boy. You will meet a fairy and tell her:

> *Oberon is passing fell and wrath,*
> *Because that she as her attendant hath*
> *A lovely boy, stolen from an Indian king;*
> *She never had so sweet a changeling;*
> *And jealous Oberon would have the child*

"*A changeling boy, stolen from an Indian king*. Why mention India? Isn't *Midsummer* supposed to be taking place in Athens?"

"Yes. But Captain James Lancaster is just back from India, having completed the first voyage to that ancient continent in a British ship. I supped with him to find out what he learned there. Among other things, he saw a boy in the court of an inland rajah who looked English."

"Was he?"

"He didn't find out. The changeling-boy will be the son of an Indian king. This will throw a garland over Captain Lancaster, recently knighted by the queen for his exploit."

Robin liked this. "And those who come to the theater and treat the lines they hear like chicken bones to suck on after the play is over will wax eloquent over hidden meanings they will claim to see in the reference to the Indian boy." He returned to looking at the papers in front of him. "So, Titania stole the boy from an Indian king."

"That's what *you* will say. Titania's account will be different:

> *His mother was a votaress of my order:*
> *And, in the spiced Indian air, by night,*
> *And sat with me on Neptune's yellow sands,*
> *Marking the embarked traders on the flood,*
> *When we have laugh'd to see the sails conceive*
> *And grow big-bellied with the wanton wind;*
> *But she, being mortal, of that boy did die;*
> *And for her sake do I rear up her boy,*
> *And for her sake I will not part with him.*

Robin wrote this down. "Okay, so the boy's mother was a *votaress* of Titania, the Fairy Queen. But if she was, she violated her duties to Titania by sleeping with a man and giving birth to a child, right?" He looked down at his notes. "*We laugh'd to see the sails conceive and grow big-bellied with the wanton wind.*" Robin looked up. "Titania should be furious with her, but you describe them as bosom friends."

"Yes. Puzzling, isn't it?"

The two of them looked at each other. Robin was still adrift as to what was going on with the little changeling boy.

"Maybe the votaress is not the boy's mother," Oxford suggested.

"But Titania says she is: *For her sake do I rear up her boy, / And for her sake I will not part with him.*"

"That's what *Titania* says, Robin, but what if she's not telling the truth? What if *she* slept with the king, and not her votaress?"

"That would make her the mother of the boy, but if she is, why lie about it and say the votaress is the mother?" He frowned, trying to understand what was going on. Suddenly, he looked at Oxford. "Because she *can't* admit she is the mother, so she invents a mother who died."

Oxford nodded. "Bravo."

"But if Titania is Elizabeth, then Elizabeth is the boy's mother. And if *you* are Oberon, you are the father ..." His eyes got bigger. "*The boy is your son by Elizabeth?*" His voice rose. "And the boy is a changeling? *What is this all about?*"

"It's a mystery," Oxford said. "The queen will understand."

"Understand or no, this is not good, my lord," but Oxford cut him off.

"We have a play to write."

"But does Oberon - do you - get the boy? In the play, I mean." He was floundering.

"In the play, yes. In our world ...?"

Robin waited.

"I am now tired of Oberon. I don't like him much anyway. He is too commanding. Too demanding. It is to Bottom we must go. I like Bottom. Bully Bottom. He loves everyone. He loves words. And whatever is new."

"Will someone put love-juice in his eyes?"

"No. He will go offstage as a man and come back with the head of an ass! He will be transformed, not blinded."

Robin gulped. "My lord. You – Bottom – will come back as an ass?" He was already imagining Oxford with the head of an ass.

"I, as Oberon," Oxford continued, "will squeeze love juice into Titania's sleeping eyes while Bottom is being transformed offstage. Bottom will come back on stage and be the first thing Titania sees when she awakes. She will fall instantly in love with him and ask," and here Robin took up his pen again, "*What angel wakes me from my flowery bed?*" I/Bottom will sing a song about birds to her. In Siena, a monk read me Aristophanes' play *The Birds*, a comedy about birds being philosophers who dislike men. It was full of songs and laugh-out-loud scenes. Bottom will sing:

> *The finch, the sparrow and the lark,*
> *The plain-song cuckoo gray,*
> *Whose note full many a man doth mark,*
> *And dares not answer nay;--*

Titania, having awakened and fallen madly in love with Bottom/me/the ass will respond:

> *I pray thee, gentle mortal, sing again:*
> *Mine ear is much enamour'd of thy note;*
> *So is mine eye enthralled to thy shape;*
> *And thy fair virtue's force perforce doth move me*
> *On the first view to say, to swear, I love thee.*

Robin joined in Oxford's laughter. "She will reach up and stroke your furry ears!"

"She will, indeed. She will purr and say, *I will purge thy mortal grossness so / That thou shalt like an airy spirit go,* which," Oxford continued, his voice dropping to his normal speaking voice now full of anger: "she promised to do by making me her consort—*a promise she gave before an archbishop, for God's sake!*" His fist slammed down on the table, causing the cups and papers to jump. Socrates, sleeping on one of the chairs out of sight, bounded out of the room.

"My lord," Robin said quietly.

"Yes. The play. The queen - Elizabeth - will well-like a scene where her most noble lord is an ass, even as it implies that *she* was an ass for falling in love with him."

"Particularly when the ass is being played by you," Robin added.

"Yes, a detail that will drive the point home."

Robin tensed, thinking Oxford was going to pound the table again. "But why show yourself a motley to the world, my lord? Let someone else play Bottom."

"Because she still loves me, Robin. I know it. If someone else plays Bottom, she will tell herself that Bottom is not me, just another character in an endless cycle of plays performed for her amusement. With me leering at her through the eyeholes of the head, she will not be able to wiggle away and claim that it is not I who is talking to her. *Midsummer Madness* will be presented at Greenwich after the wedding. A low stage will be added to the left side of the hall for her to sit on. She will be close at hand. When she sees me parade across her, there will be no doubt that the ass in the mask is me."

Oxford started to walk around the table. "People who love *Romeo & Juliet* will love the transformation I give them in *Midsummer Madness*. We accept that Romeo switched his love from Rosaline to Juliet because he thought he had found his true love. The love juice was in both their eyes, you might say. But what if the love-juice is squeezed into the wrong eye?"

Robin suddenly looked worried. "Because of me?"

"Yes. Recall that Hermia and Lysander love each other and want to marry, but Hermia's father has ordered her to marry Demetrius. Demetrius was in love with Helena before the play begins but has abandoned her to marry Hermia. Helena still loves him, though. When she learns that Hermia and Lysander are going to run away to a nearby forest, Helena tells Demetrius of their plans. Demetrius runs after them with Helena tagging along because she wants Demetrius to love her again."

"So, I will put the love-juice into Demetrius's eyes to make him fall in love with Hermia."

"No. You will put the love-juice in Lysander's eyes by mistake. Helena will come by and, when Lysander awakes, he will instantly fall in love with Helena who will think he's playing a joke on her."

"Oh, my goodness. I should have put it in Demetrius's eyes."

"Yes."

"Will you berate me?"

"Most roundly. You are my servant, are you not?"

Robin nodded glumly. "In life and in this play."

Oxford liked this. He continued. "Oberon will take you to task:

> *What hast thou done? thou hast mistaken quite*
> *And laid the love-juice on some true-love's sight:*
> *Of thy misprision must perforce ensue*
> *Some true love turn'd and not a false turn'd true.*

"*Some true love turn'd and not a false turn'd true,*" Robin said, as he wrote down Oxford's words. "So, my mistake will make Lysander switch his love from Hermia to Helena."

"Yes, creating conflict between Demetrius and Lysander because they both now love the same girl - Helena."

"And showing us what happens when the *wrong* person becomes the desire of our love."

"Which is doubled when Titania falls in love with me as an ass."

Robin shook his head in wonderment. "Wonderful. I think."

"Titania will summon the fairies to wait on me, Bottom."

"Their names?" Robin asked, his pen raised.

"Is that important?" Oxford was irritated at being interrupted. "Oh, all right. They shall be called Peaseblossom, Cobweb, Moth,' and 'Mustardseed!' This pleased Robin. "Titania will instruct them to take care of me:

> *Be kind and courteous to this gentleman;*
> *Hop in his walks and gambol in his eyes;*
> *And pluck the wings from Painted butterflies*
> *To fan the moonbeams from his sleeping eyes.*

"And what conversation will Bottom – you - have with them?"

"With the fairies?" Oxford asked.

"Won't they speak?"

Oxford frowned. "What do you suggest?"

Robin sat up, all business. "There are four of them: First, ask them their names. Speak to Cobweb first. Say you will come to him if you cut your finger."

"Lines," Oxford said curtly. "What are my lines? Don't give me descriptions. Give me words."

Robin nodded. His master didn't care much about the fairies and was going to make him pay for making him put them in the play. "*I shall desire you of more acquaintance, good Master Cobweb: if I cut my finger, I shall make bold with you.*"

"Good. And what will I say to Peaseblossom?"

"*I pray you, commend me to Mistress Squash, your mother, and to Master Peascod, your father.*"

Oxford laughed. "Master Peascod."

Robin continued. "To Mustardseed, you will say: *Good Master Mustardseed, I know your patience well: that same cowardly, giant-like ox-beef hath devoured many a gentleman of your house: I promise you your kindred had made my eyes water ere now.*"

Oxford laughed again. "Mustardseed a victim of ox-beef? And each seed a gentleman?" Robin paused to hear whether Oxford approved. "Write it down," Oxford said. Robin did so with vigor, enjoying being the author instead of the scribe for the moment. But Oxford put up a hand: "We need hear nothing from Moth."

"Oh," Robin said, disappointed. "And what does Titania tell the fairies to do with you?"

"Listen:

> *Come, wait upon him; lead him to my bower.*
> *The moon methinks looks with a watery eye;*
> *And when she weeps, weeps every little flower,*
> *Lamenting some enforced chastity.*
> *Tie up my love's tongue bring him silently.*

Robin took this down. "The moon *looks with a watery eye*. This is the moon in the sky, not the moon who sometimes is Elizabeth our queen."

"Oh, no, no, no. The moon *is* Elizabeth. The *enforced chastity* the moon is lamenting is her own."

"Oh," Robin said. He sighed. "This is all very complicated."

"No, it's not."

"Well, certainly not when Titania orders the fairies to *tie up* your tongue so they can bring you *silently* to her bower."

"Hasn't she tied up my tongue?" Oxford held his head back, looking at Robin as if the little page was never going to get it.

"Okay. But I thought Titania had fallen in love with your singing." He looked down at his notes. "*Mine ear is much enamour'd of thy note; / So is mine eye enthralled to thy shape,*"

"My note is my poetry. She is *much enamor'd of my poetry.*"

Robin shrugged. "What about Theseus? I haven't heard much about him. Or Hippolyta."

"Theseus and Hippolyta will frame the play; they will take no part in the action."

"Like Christopher Sly in *The Taming of the Shrew.*" Robin liked Christopher Sly, a character who sat on the stage believing he had somehow become a lord and was married to the woman sitting next to him. A play within a play, with the tension of when he was going to reach over and exercise his marital duties."

"You almost played his wife."

"You suggested the role; I rejected the idea."

"But you *will* play Puck."

"Yes. No one is going to grab Puck."

Oxford laughed. "Methinks you look forward to being a player."

Robin dipped his head. "Does Oberon get the changeling boy?"

"He does. He comes upon Titania after the love juice has taken its effects and begins to pity her for *seeking favors from this hateful fool.*

"You," Robin said simply.

"Yes. Me. As Bottom. But now I'm speaking as Oberon, who will first taunt Titania until she begs my patience and gives me the boy."

Robin's pen sped across the page. "That's a quick turnaround. *Not for thy fairy kingdom!*" she said the first time you asked her.

Oxford shrugged. "Maybe the drug I put in her eye was stronger than I thought."

"She does sound a little wobbly here."

Oxford liked that. "She will wake from her trance and say: *Methought I was enamour'd of an ass,*" to which I will point to the still-sleeping Bottom and say: *There lies your love.* She will cry out in fright. I will take her hand and we will compass the earth *swifter than the wandering moon* while she wonders:

> *Tell me how it came this night*
> *That I sleeping here was found*
> *With these mortals on the ground.*

"But how can both Bottom *and* Oberon be in this scene at the same time, my lord? Even you can't double yourself."

"Because it will be Bottom's head that Titania will be nestling in her lap. I will be Oberon. When I take Titania and leave, the audience will think Bottom is still asleep."

Robin shuffled through the papers in front of him. "And there will be a scene with the other players that follows so that you have time to slip back into Bottom's costume."

"Yes. One must keep track of who's coming in and who's going out. After I leave, Theseus and Hippolyta will discover the four lovers sleeping naked on the ground."

"I hope they bring Hermia's father with them too," Robin suggested, looking excited about writing the scene.

"Yes. We will come back to that."

"After which you-Bottom will come out on stage sans ass-head."

"Yes. He will be confused at first, like Titania.

> *When my cue comes, call me, and I will answer: Heigh-ho!*
> *Peter Quince! Flute, the bellows-mender! Snout, the tinker!*
> *Starveling!*

"I love the names," Robin said, as he took this down.

"I'm so glad," Oxford commented dryly. "Me/Bottom will stand in the middle of the stage and try to figure out what has happened:

> *I have had a most rare vision. I have had a dream, past the wit*
> *of man to say what dream it was: man is but an ass, if he go*
> *about to expound this dream. Methought I was — there is no*
> *man can tell what. Methought I was,--and methought I had,--*
> *but man is but a patched fool, if he will offer to say what*
> *methought I had.*

Robin's pen flew across the page. "The poor man can't get away from being an ass, can he?" Robin asked, chuckling to himself.

Oxford eyed him. Oxford continued. Robin wrote faster.

The eye of man hath not heard,
The ear of man hath not seen,
Man's hand is not able to taste,
His tongue to conceive,
Nor his heart to report, what my dream was.

Robin finished capturing Bottom's speech. "*The eye of man hath not heard?*" He looked up. "*The ear has not seen?*"

"Isn't this how a man who transformed into an ass might speak?"

"But does he have to mock St. Paul," Robin asked, a look of worry on his face.

"You know who Bottom is misquoting?" Oxford asked. "First Book of Corinthians 2.9: *But as it is written, the things which eye hath not seen, neither ear hath heard, neither came into man's heart, which God hath prepared for them that love Him.?*"

From the uncomfortable look on Robin's face, there was no doubt Robin knew what Paul had written to the Corinthians. "As you have told me many times, my lord, I will not go to Hell for writing down what you speak, even if you go so far as to twist the words of St. Paul into something he did not say. But will the audience know whose words you are twisting?"

"Oh, yes. They know their Bible." He looked at Robin. "As you do, apparently." Robin looked away. "But, Robin, this is a play about transformation. Can I not transform the words of Paul as well as myself?" He looked pleased.

"I am forced to admit you can, since it seems you can do *anything*."

Oxford could tell Robin was not being sarcastic. "Yes." He took Robin's praise at full value. "The theater is all about transformation. I write to make the audience feel like they are gods looking down on mortals. They think they know more about what is going on than the actors, and they are right. Theseus will limn the tenor of the play:

The forms of things unknown, the poet's pen
Turns them to shapes and gives to airy nothing
A local habitation and a name.
How easy is a bush supposed a bear!

Oxford walked back to look over Robin's shoulder as his page wrote this down. Socrates, sitting on the pages Robin pushed away to write on a new one, moved down the table toward the window where he flopped himself down in a pool of sunlight like he was the Queen of Sheba arriving in a golden barge to see Solomon.

Oxford put his hand on Robin's shoulder. "This is why you crave admission to the world of playwriting, Robin. You want to give an 'airy nothing a local habitation and a name.'"

"Don't we have an 'airy nothing' here to capture, my lord?" reminding Oxford they still had a play to finish.

"Yes," Oxford said, walking off down the table toward Socrates, who eyed him warily. Oxford went around the table and stopped on the other side. "In fact, we have *another* play to write."

"You mean *Romeo*."

"No. It is *Pyramus & Thisbe* that calls to me now."

"What does *Pyramus & Thisbe* have to do with *Midsummer*?"

"It will be a play within the play. It will crown the evening, the three couples now together as they should be: Demetrius with Helena; Lysander with Hermia; and Pericles with Hippolyta."

"But Bottom has lost his head."

"Oh, no, my good Robin. Bottom has only lost his 'ass-head.'"

"Of course. Forgive me, my lord. I had forgotten you will play Bottom."

Oxford looked at him out of the corner of his eye but Robin, pen in hand, had his eyes focused on the paper in front of him. Oxford went on. "Bottom's associates, rude mechanicals - a carpenter, a joiner, a bellows-mender, a tinker, a tailor, a weaver, Bully Bottom - *me! …*"

Robin broke in: "Who have been left worried sick because their prime fellow has been transformed into an ass and disappeared!"

"Yes." Robin had seen something he hadn't. "How do *you* think *hard-handed men who never labour'd in their minds before* would react?" Oxford asked.

"They would be greatly frightened to see Bottom with the head of an ass."

"I think they would indeed. Go on."

"They would lament his transformation and disappearance and say there was no one to replace him."

"Of course. Particularly with me playing the part. Very good. Go on. Lines now; not words."

"Flute will say: *If he come not, then the play is marred: it goes not forward, doth it?* Another will say: *you have not a man in all Athens able to discharge Pyramus but he.*"

"Good. Good. Write it down."

Robin was happy his suggestions were being accepted, but he felt pressure because he had to scribble them down before they floated away like gossamer threads. "One of the mechanicals will tell the others that the Duke would have paid them six pence a day for the rest of their lives if they had put on the play: *we had all been made men,*" he will wail.

"I will rescue them," Oxford said. "Bottom will come charging back: 'Where are these lads? where are these hearts?' The others will crowd around him, begging him to tell them where he'd been. He will refuse to answer.

> *Not a word of me. All that I will tell you is, that the duke hath dined.*
> *We shall meet presently at the palace; our play is preferred.*
> *every man look o'er his part. No more words: away! go, away!*

"And this play they will put on, what will it be about?"

"*Romeo & Juliet,* as imagined by the mechanicals."

"Two lovers, separated by family names."

"And a wall. The lovers will speak to each other through a crack in the wall, which one of the mechanicals will represent by holding up his thumb and index finger like this and saying:

> *This loam, this rough-cast and this stone doth show*
> *That I am that same wall; the truth is so:*
> *And this the cranny is, right and sinister,*
> *Through which the fearful lovers are to whisper.*

"A wall that speaks." Robin's head wagged back and forth. "Theseus and his bride will love a talking wall."

"They will. I/Bottom/Pyramus now, will peer through the hole in the wall to see Thisbe, but she will not be there. Pyramus will curse the wall:

> *O wicked wall, through whom I see no bliss!*
> *Cursed be thy stones for thus deceiving me!*

"*Cursed be thy stones?*" Robin asked, looking up.

"Aren't walls made of stones?" Oxford asked, all innocence. He went on. "Theseus will wonder aloud if Pyramus should curse again and I/Bottom/Pyramus will tell him *no!*"

Robin looked up in surprise. "You, a player in a play being staged before an audience, will speak to a member of the audience? Players don't address the audience, my lord."

Oxford laughed. "Doesn't every play have a know-it-all in the audience who has to interrupt the play to add his tuppence?"

"More than one, usually, but the players ignore hecklers."

"But Bottom will not be talking to someone in the audience watching *Midsummer Madness*. He will be talking to the players on stage who are watching *Pyramus & Thisbe*."

Robin shook his head. "This is dizzying."

"So many layers, eh? Oxford said, smiling. "Don't you love it?" Robin nodded, although somewhat reluctantly. Oxford continued. "A lion will appear and scare Thisbe into running away, but she will leave a bloody scarf behind. Pyramus will find it and think she has been killed:

> *Eyes, do you see?*
> *How can it be?*
> *O dainty duck! O dear!*
> *Thy mantle good,*
> *What, stain'd with blood!*

Robin, scribbling away, wagged his head.

Oxford went on. "Bottom will lament that Nature made lions:

> *O wherefore, Nature, didst thou lions frame?*
> *Since lion vile hath here deflower'd my dear:*
> *Which is--no, no--which was the fairest dame*
> *That lived, that loved, that liked, that look'd.*

"*Deflowered*, my lord?" Robin looked at him. "And Thisbe *was the fairest dame that lived, that loved, that liked, that look'd.* He burst out laughing. "Spenser!"

"Sidney," Oxford corrected him. "The queen still loves him. His poetry too. I can't stop myself. He gobbled like a turkey: *But God wot, wot not what they mean.* I told Her Majesty English poetry was better off without him, God having called him home for that reason."

Robin did not follow Oxford's trip into his reasons for loathing Sidney. He was looking at the pages in front of him. "And what will Bottom do when he finds the bloody mantel? Kill himself, right?"

"Yes. Just like Romeo, who also thought - wrongly - that Juliet was dead. Pyramus will pull out his sword and fall on it. Thisbe will come back and find Pyramus/Bottom/me/the ass dead and kill herself with the sword Pyramus fell on."

"A fun retelling of *Romeo & Juliet*. Will *Midsummer* end with everyone married?"

"Yes. And the house blessed by fairies flying through it."

"But you haven't told me what happens with the two couples after I mistakenly place the love-juice in the eye of Lysander instead of Demetrius."

"Your mistake will drive this part of the plot. I will order you to put love-juice in Lysander's eyes to make him fall in love with Hermia."

Robin took this in. "You realize I only put the love-juice into the men's eyes, not the women's."

"Because women are steadfast' men are variable. For example, you remember Lady Mary, the Countess of Southampton coming by to ask me to write a comedy for her wedding to Sir Thomas Heneage."

"Yes."

"I asked her how Sir Thomas came to propose. I didn't think he had it in him. She agreed. I suggested she had proposed to him, something not impossible, knowing her. She denied it and protested: 'What do ye take me for? Men propose, not women. But what makes a man do it? They never know. Neither did he.'" Oxford looked at Robin. "What do you think? Would love-juice work in Lady Mary's eye?"

"Not even if it were real."

104

Shackspear and Mumblecrust

Oxford and Robin returned to the library to finish *Midsummer Madness*. They were sliding different sheets of paper around the table to figure out how to show Hermia, Helena, Demetrius, and Lysander arguing with each other when Nigel came in. "Master Shakes-spare," he announced. Shackspear swept by him.

"No!" Oxford said, putting up a hand.

"My lord, I can help. I need to. *I need the money.*" He sounded like he had slammed the door behind him in the face of a pack of poursuivants chasing him down Candlewick Street.

"Which play?"

"Either one, my lord. I'm good for more than one."

Robin intervened. "How about two couples in love."

Shackspear cocked his head. "Each Jack in love with his Jill?"

"It depends on where they are in the play," Oxford said.

"So, the ladies change their minds."

"The men, not the ladies," Robin said. Shackspear looked puzzled. "Whether they change their minds turns on where they are in the play," Oxford said again.

Shackspear assumed what he thought was a dignified air. "Meaning, if the men change their minds, the ladies will be affected."

Oxford was surprised by this. "In what way?"

"Well, if a man abandons a lady for another, the lady who's been abandoned will blame the other lady. She won't blame her man. She'll blame her rival. If they get within arms' reach, they'll fight."

"Actually fight?" Robin asked.

"With blows?" Oxford added. He looked at Robin. Shackspear could see they thought his claim ridiculous.

"Without doubt, my lord." Shackspear drew himself up. "I have some experience in this. With ladies who want the same man. It weren't pretty, I can tell you that."

"Tell us."

Shakespeare grinned. Having been given the floor, he began. "One was older than I, the other younger. One was fair, the other dark."

"An Ethiope," Oxford suggested.

"She was."

Oxford gestured for Robin to start taking notes. "How old was the older?"

"Twenty-six, my lord. Anne Hathaway of Stratford was twenty-six."

"And the other?"

"Fourteen."

"A good age for this play. And you were?"

"Eighteen."

"So, Anne Hathaway was a fine catch for you, being that you were only eighteen at the time."

"Not when everyone else had passed on her."

"As you did, then?"

Shackspear grimaced. "It was more complicated than that."

"How so?"

Shackspear sighed. "Six months earlier, I had spent a warm spring afternoon in a hayfield with her. Unfortunately, I left a present behind I didn't know about."

"And then you began courting the Ethiope."

Shackspear nodded. "Anna Whatley. I saw her every day in town and watched her blossom into a lovely young girl. I had no reason to remember Anne, who lived six miles away down Alcester Road in Temple Grafton. I had forgotten her. One and done, ye know."

"So, you never went back to Temple Grafton?"

"No."

"And Anna?"

"I asked her to marry me. She accepted. I got the license, but Anne found out the same day. She's an Arden, you know. One of them must have been working in the courthouse and told her."

"What did she do?"

"She came to my house. Er, my father's house. I was still living there. Anna and I were in the garden in the back when Anne suddenly appeared. She had two burly uncles with her. Her father having passed, they had decided she needed a guardian."

"To talk to you about your new fatherly duties."

"Aye."

"And?" Robin couldn't keep himself from asking.

Shackspear sighed. "Anne was six months gone and showing. I saw the three of them appear at the top of the garden. Anna didn't know who they were, but I did." He looked put upon. "Anna didn't know what was going on but put two and two together fast. She could tell the woman charging down the hill was pregnant and that I must be the father of her child."

Robin made a clucking sound. "The women tore into you."

Shackspear was puzzled by this. "No. Anne came barreling down the path and headed for Anna. Anne was spittin' mad. She started pulling her hair. She said Anna had stolen me from her."

Robin was surprised by this. He glanced at Oxford. "Yes," Oxford said, "but what of the two uncles?"

"They made sure I married Anne and not Anna."

Oxford took this in. "On reflection, Willum, I've changed my mind. You may be able to help us." He motioned for Shackspear to sit down at the table. Shackspear, trying not to look too pleased, pulled out a chair and sat down opposite Robin. "Let me tell you, Willum, where we are. We have a young man named Lysander who is in love with Hermia."

"Is Hermia the little one?" Shackspear asked.

"She is. And she's dark."

"She's Anna, then." He looked relieved. Being little and dark would help him remember who Hermia was.

"Which means the other woman is taller," Oxford continued.

"Yes. But not by much." He was getting this, he thought. So did Oxford.

"Hermia, the little one, will be the daughter of a rich man who will order her to marry a man named Demetrius."

"This will work, my lord. Anna Whatley was the daughter of a rich man in Shottery. He never told me to marry her, but ..." His voice wandered off as he tried to pack this into his now crowded mind.

"Demetrius wants to marry Hermia, but she wants to marry Lysander."

Shackspear nodded. "My Anna wanted to marry me; Anne stood in the way. Two women who both wanted me." He liked the idea. "But there is only one of me, my lord. I can't be both Demetrius and Lysander."

"Of course, you can."

"How can that be?"

"Because there will be fairies in this play, Willum. If there be fairies, is there be any doubt that there can be more than one of you?"

"Will they get along with each other, the two me's?"

"Being both of you, how could they not?" Oxford did not glance at Robin for fear his little page would put them both to laughing. Oxford went on. "Sometime before the play begins, you, as Demetrius, will be in love with Helena, while you as Lysander will be in love with Hermia. Each Jack, as you put it, would have his Jill. But before the curtain goes up, Demetrius will have switched his love to Hermia. We won't spend time on the reason." Oxford checked to see if Shackspear was still with him. A blank face and a partially-opened mouth encouraged Oxford to go on. "This means that Hermia is now loved by both men and Helena is loved by neither."

Shackspear thought about this. "I wish there had been two of me in Stratford." The wistful look on his face disappeared as quickly as it had appeared. "No. No. That would have been worse."

"Well, there will be two of you on the stage in London. That's not bad, is it?"

Shackspear nodded. He was still trying to figure out how he could be two when he was only one. "But in your play, you have me, my two me's, fighting over Hermia. I didn't fight over Anna in Stratford, my lord. I wanted to marry her. It was Anne - Helena - who blocked me." He thought about this. "How do you resolve this?"

Oxford and Robin were surprised that Shackspear was picking up something of the plot of *Midsummer Madness*. "By having the men switch back and forth," Oxford explained.

"And why would they – me - do that?"

"Magic love potions," Oxford said. "A potion made from a flower that, when squeezed into a lover's eyes, makes the lover fall in love with the first person they see when they wake up."

"Oh," Shackspear said. "I once fell asleep in a field and, when I woke up, a pig was pushing its nose into my face! Imagine if someone had put love juice in my eye!" He burst out laughing. His eyes widened. "Maybe that's what happened with Mumblecrust!"

Oxford and Robin looked at him. "Who?"

"Mumblecrust. My name for Anne. Course, I don't call her that to her face. She mumbles all the time, drooling and spitting bubbles that form a crust around her mouth." He shook his head. "I must have been under a spell when I lay down with her. That would explain it." He looked like he had finally solved a puzzle that had been bothering him for a long time. He looked at Oxford. "Why do ye think I live in London?"

Oxford nodded. Stratford must be worse than he thought.

"But what about me in your play?" Shackspear asked. "Or me's?"

"Yes. The Fairy King will have one of his minions put love-juice in Demetrius' eyes so that Demetrius – you – will go back to loving Helena. Unfortunately, the minion will put the love-juice into Lysander's eyes by mistake. Lysander will wake up and see Helena …"

"And fall instantly in love with her," Shackspear cut in. Shackspear *was* getting it. "But Demetrius is not going to be happy that Lysander still loves Helena. The two of me will start fighting over Helena." He suddenly looked disappointed. "I thought I'd like myself."

"Do not despair. You will not be able to play both Demetrius and Lysander because they will be on stage at the same time. I'll get you another part. In the meantime, tell us what happened between Anne and Anna?"

"Oh, my lord, it was awful. Anne went after Anna with her nails." Here, Shackspear switched into a falsetto voice, a sneer on his face: "Mumblecrust screamed: '*You juggler! you canker-blossom! You thief of love! what, have you come by night and stolen his heart from him? You puppet, you!*'"

Oxford glanced at Robin to make sure he was getting this down. "Can you remember what Anna said in response?"

"Oh, yes, my lord. Every word. Every word:

> *Puppet? Ah, so that's how the game goes.*
> *Now I perceive that she hath made compare*
> *Between our statures; she hath urged her height;*
> *And with her personage, her tall personage,*
> *Her height, forsooth, she hath prevail'd with him.*
> *And are you grown so high in his esteem;*
> *Because I am so dwarfish and so low?*
> *How low am I, thou painted maypole? speak;*
> *How low am I? I am not yet so low*
> *But that my nails can reach unto thine eyes.*

Oxford and Robin looked at each other in amazement. Shackspear was repeating verbatim what he had heard years ago in Stratford. The hack from Stratford, without depth or education, could apparently remember things. On reflection, Oxford thought, this shouldn't have been a surprise. Shackspear couldn't have become an actor without being able to memorize his lines.

"How did Mumblecrust react to being called a 'painted maypole'?" Oxford asked.

"Not well. I was holding Anna back, who really wanted to tear out Anne's eyeballs. Anne, suddenly afraid, stepped behind her uncles who had come up. She asked them for help:

> *I pray you, gentlemen, let her not hurt me;*
> *Let her not strike me. You perhaps may think,*
> *Because she is something lower than myself,*
> *That I can match her.*

"Anna, trying to get free of me, called out: '*Lower! hark, again.*' Anne, made brave by standing behind her uncles, replied: '*You dwarf,*' she screamed. '*You minimus of hindering knot-grass made; you bead, you acorn. She was a vixen when she went to school; And though she be but little, she is fierce.*'

Oxford and Robin wanted to ask about '*you minimus of hindering knot-grass made,*' but Oxford had a better question. "They went to school together?"

"Aye. A school for girls in Wilmcote. I didn't know they knew each other. But Anna was a fierce one: '*Little' again!*' she cried from behind me. '*Nothing but 'low' and little! Let me come to her.*'"

He rearranged himself in his chair, obviously enjoying his retelling of how Anne met Anna. "Anna finally got around me and started for Anne, who was afraid of her. My father, hearing the row going on in the garden, came out to see what was going on. The uncles decided it was time to leave. They must have been worried my father would charge them with trespass. They took Anne with them and headed for the gate past the barn but not before telling me they'd see me in church."

"What did your father do when he saw what was going on?"

"Nothing. He looked around, hawked his nose with his thumb, and went back in the house."

"And Anna?

"She stood there, breathing in and out. 'That witch put a spell on you, didn't she?' She stamped her foot. 'She's not going to win. I will marry you; not her!'"

"But you didn't."

"No. My father told me the town was scandalized and our family shamed. Marrying Anne would restore the honor of the family. Knowing him better now, I think he rather liked having me stuck in Stratford. He never got out."

"I thank thee for your help with *Midsummer,* ..." Oxford said, surprising himself as well as Shackspear and Robin. An earl did not refer to a commoner as 'thee.' Robin was shocked; Shackspear was shocked and surprised. What they didn't know was that Oxford had come very close to calling Shackspear 'William,' something he and Falstaff had taken away from Shackspear one beery night in the Boar's Head.

These thoughts brought Oxford to a halt. Robin and Shackspear were used to Oxford "disappearing." They waited for him to return. He finally looked at Shackspear.

"I have no doubt that we will have further need of your services, *Willum*. In fact, there will be a play within the play we are writing. I think you might be interested in playing one of the parts in that play."

Shackspear beamed. "I'm sure I would, my lord."

"When I get it further along, we will talk."

"Thank you, my lord. And when should I come back?"

"Next week. Wednesday will do."

"I will be here."

Shackspear nodded to Oxford and Robin, picked up his walking stick and left.

Robin looked at Oxford. "A part in *Pyramus & Thisbe? Come back next Wednesday?* My lord, what is going on?"

"He has shown us he has a memory. He can learn a part. And we're going to need more players than normal. The cast is getting very large: Theseus, Hippolyta, Demetrius, Lysander, Hermia, Helena, Egeus, the butler who will bring the entertainment list to Theseus, the mechanicals who will perform *Pyramus*—Quince, Snug, Flute, Snout, Starveling, Bottom, and *me!*, not to mention Oberon, Titania and the fairies—Peas-Blossom, Cobweb, Moth, and Mustardseed!" He was out of breath.

"Puck?" Robin asked, trying to sound unconcerned.

"Yes, Puck. How could I forget Puck?"

"Quite easily, it seems."

"Only because there are so many characters in this play!"

"Or the character you want me to play is a *minimus of hindering knot-grass, a bead, an acorn*, compared to the characters you will play."

"Not at all," Oxford insisted. He was stopped by what Robin had just said. "A *minimus of hindering knot-grass*. Who would have thought our friend from Warwickshire could harbor such treasures. It's another reason I invited him back. What other precious ore lies within that minimus of meandering mediocrity?"

Robin laughed.

"And *Midsummer Madness* will need more players than have been required for any play I have done before."

"I'll get John Lyly to help. He'll gather up Paul's Boys to play the fairies and the girls."

"We will need help from the Admiral's Men, the Lord Chamberlain's, Worcester's, mine. There will be grudges among them. Some will refuse to help."

"Shackspear knows them all. Give him the task."

"An excellent idea."

Robin shook his head. "But who will he play in *Pyramus?*"

"Peter Quince, one of the rude mechanicals who have never before labored in their minds. Quince will write the script and rehearse the players. That will limit the damage Willum can cause."

Robin was still worried that bringing Shackspear on board might turn out to be a mistake. "You remember how he got blood all over himself when he played York in *Henry VI*. Edward Alleyn said he'd never work with him again."

"Yes, but when Alleyn finds out he will play Demetrius and Burbage will play Lysander, neither one will be able to turn me down."

A Letter from Anne Vavasour

Oxford and Robin had been working on *Midsummer Madness* which Shakespeare had suggested would be better named *A Night's Dream*. 'Dream' better conveyed what the play was about, he said. Having the word 'madness' in the title might turn people away.

At first, Oxford had been indignant at Shackspear's cheek and was about to reject the idea when Robin wondered if adding 'midsummer' might lighten the mood of the play. Oxford reminded them that the play would be presented in January. 'All the more reason, my lord," Robin said; "Who won't want to see a play about midsummer in January?'

Oxford reluctantly agreed and *Midsummer Madness* became *A Midsummer Night's Dream*. They were about to resume work when Lady Elspeth came into the library. She told him she had received a letter from Anne Vavasour that contained a second letter addressed to him.

Oxford was suddenly apprehensive. He glanced at Elspeth, expecting to see arched-eyebrow cynicism on her face but saw none. She explained.

"Anne and I became friends when you and I went to Ditchley. I thought at the time she might be wanting to rekindle her relationship with you but quickly realized she had no such intentions. She had found comfort, if not love, she said, with Sir Henry. She could not marry him – he was already married, his wife living elsewhere on his estates – but he loved her and was a good father to Edward."

"And what does she want to speak to me about?"

"I don't know." Elspeth handed him the envelope.

Oxford opened it and read the letter aloud. "Edward will be going to university in January and will not be able to attend Lisbeth's wedding to the Earl of Derby. It would be meet if you would let him visit you before he leaves for the continent."

This surprised Oxford. Was Edward already old enough to go to university? What was he, fourteen, fifteen?

"She says he's a fine young man now," Elspeth said, as if reading Oxford's mind. "In truth, I think she has arranged for Edward to be somewhere else because he might be embarrassed to be at Lisbeth's wedding, being her bastard half-brother."

Oxford didn't know what to say. Did one invite a bastard half-brother to a sister's wedding? When had he seen Edward last? A feeling of guilt washed over him. "I should see the boy," he said,

"I will let Anne know," Elspeth said. She left him in the library.

"Blast!" he shouted after she'd gone. That he had quite forgot he had a son named Edward, named after him, for goodness sake, made it clear that he might be a great playwright and poet but he was a failure as a father. Elspeth's comment that Anne found Sir Henry a 'good father' cut him. His realization of how disappointed he was with himself, and others with him as well, boiled over into anger.

"Why can't I just write plays?" he said aloud to the empty room. "That's all I want to do. I write plays and offend no one, and for that the women in my life - *the women!* - make me think poorly of myself."

Robin had reappeared in the doorway holding a tray of pasties from Frangellica. "Maybe it's because they care about you."

"*Care about me?*" Oxford exploded.

Robin put the tray on the table. "You have a son whose mother wants him to reconnect with his father. Think of what a benefit that would be to him." Oxford was not interested in hearing he might be good for something, or anyone. Robin pushed on. "Or what he might bring to *your* life."

Oxford remembered Robin peppering him with questions about Edward the first time the boy came up. Oxford reminded himself that the little page had been left at a monastery as a baby and had no family. He would love to know who *his* father was.

And what do fathers do? Oxford asked himself. He thought of how little he knew about Henry, his son by Elspeth. He didn't know much about his son, Edward, either. Had Sir Henry displaced Oxford as the boy's father? Had Sir Henry taught him Latin? If so, Oxford could show him *Il Cortegiano* and discuss what it takes to have *sprezzatura* – 'studied carelessness' - a nonchalance that conceals art and makes whatever one does or says appear to be without effort or thought. Except how to be a father, that is.

Robin realized his master had retreated inward. He took one of the pasties and quietly slipped out of the room, leaving Oxford alone with his thoughts.

~ 106 ~
Romeo & Juliet

Billy Ostler carried the audience away as Juliet, his velvet tenor voice and uncanny hand movements - *Too elegant for a young man playing a woman. How does he do it?* - the theatergoers in the audience asked each other as they applauded the exquisitely painful death Billy had just given them.

Above the groundlings, hidden from view in a special box the elder Burbage had built into the north wall of the Curtain, the queen applauded as well. She thought the younger Burbage had played Romeo well, despite being a tad old for the role. Her pleasure at seeing the play only increased her sense of freedom the box brought her.

Elizabeth Regina did not attend plays, of course, just as everyone 'knew' she was a virgin. Certain pretenses had to be maintained. Within her screened box, she could attend plays without having to give up her claim that she did not. She loved secrets. When the play ended, she lingered, listening to the happy theatergoers digesting the love story they had just seen. '*Very properly done,*' one said.

She sent a messenger down to Oxford to let him know she wanted to speak with him. He pushed his way through the crowd and climbed a hidden set of stairs to her box.

"You have finally brought us something, my lord, that surpasses *Palamon & Arcite*," she told him. Her voice showed how difficult it was for her to admit this. "Had I not been urging you all these years to do so, well, we might still be waiting."

Oxford said nothing. He didn't need Gloriana's opinion to know *Romeo & Juliet* was like nothing anyone had seen before. They both knew it would bring luster to her court all over Europe, something she craved. Her brow furrowed. Oxford waited to hear what she *really* wanted to talk about.

"You continue to lard your plays, my lord, with allusions you don't think anyone will ferret out, a private game you play, laughing at the rest of us as you bury hidden meaning in what you write. Rosaline, for example. Everyone knows who she is supposed to be, and yet you give her not one line to speak." She sounded more hurt than angry.

"And who Romeo abandons at his first glimpse of Juliet," Oxford added, unable to keep himself from rubbing it in.

"Why have her in the play at all?"

"Romeo has to be somewhere before the play begins. And characters who never appear need not be paid, increasing profits."

She didn't believe him. "You were afraid she might o'er balance the play, being such a *powerful* figure."

"Like Mercutio."

"I thought it was Juliet's play."

"Hers too."

She harrumphed. "At least Rosaline had many fine lines in *Love's Labour's Lost*," she said, almost to herself.

"Your Majesty thinks Rosaline, was you?" he asked.

"Oh, please, I was as fine an opponent to Berowne – *you* – as there ever was."

Oxford was touched. "A passing fancy."

The queen didn't know whether he was referring to the play or himself. She brought him up short with the following:

Berowne:	*Did not I dance with you in Brabant once?*
Rosaline	*Did not I dance with you in Brabant once?*
Berowne:	*I know you did.*
Rosaline	*How needless was it then to ask the question!*

Oxford laughed. "Well-remembered."

"Also, I loved hearing my character say, when 'you' – Berowne – are first mentioned: '*He hath been five thousand years a boy*.'"

"Little of the boy left, I'm afraid."

"We'll have none of that. When will I see your next play?"

"In January, Your Majesty. To celebrate the marriage of my daughter to the Earl of Derby."

"Oh, yes. And who will I be in *that* play?"

"I haven't written it yet. It's all still nothing more than vapors, up here." He waved a hand over his head.

His refusal to tell her who she would be turned her sour again. "And you. Making sure everyone knows who Romeo is."

"And who *is* Romeo?" Oxford asked, all innocence.

"You, of course. You have Mercutio saying, '*here comes Romeo, without his roe*'. A disgusting image, to be sure, but not unexpected."

"Well-spotted, Your Majesty."

"From a well-spotted man," Elizabeth replied.

"*A spotted man*," Oxford said. "A goodly phrase. I think I shall use it, if Your Majesty permits."

"Are you going to do this in every play?"

"Robin has asked the same question."

She looked over at Shackspear accepting accolades. "Yes," they could hear him saying. "Thank you. I most enjoyed crafting the swordsmen going at each other."

A cloud passed over Oxford's face. Elizabeth saw it. "You may not believe me when I say I regret the loss of your name, my lord, but I want you to know I wish it were otherwise."

'Yes,' Oxford thought, 'but not enough to allow me to put my name on my plays.'

"What most surprises me, Edward," she said in a voice that showed how much she was in awe of him by using his Christian name, "is how you took the bare framework of the story, much like a dress-maker's shape, and covered it with words that turned it into something altogether new. Juliet, lamenting Romeo's going:

> *'Tis almost morning; I would have thee gone:*
> *And yet no further than a wanton's bird;*
> *Who lets it hop a little from her hand,*
> *Like a poor prisoner in his twisted gyves,*
> *And with a silk thread plucks it back again,*
> *So loving-jealous of his liberty.*

"The story you stole from Arthur Brooke has Juliet simply asking Romeo to stay. Every person who has been in love hates the moment when they must part from their lover. *Parting is such sweet sorrow*, you write, and even that far surpasses Brooke, but you take this moment, a bare wire in the framework of Mr. Brooke's poem and turn it into a *wanton's bird that* can only *hop a little from her hand* before it is pulled back by a *silk thread*. Who can resist a little bird kept captive by a *silk thread?* A *wanton's bird* at that, for, after all, aren't all lovers wanton?"

Oxford realized his words were washing away the dull, dark, words of business and statesmanship that daily clogged her mind. "*Is there no pity sitting in the clouds*," Elizabeth asked, "*that sees into the bottom of my grief?*" She looked at Oxford. "How can a fourteen-year-old girl express better than I can the grief I have borne?"

Oxford was surprised. Juliet was real to her. He had rarely seen Elizabeth so open, even when, years earlier, they had been lovers.

She looked out over the people still in the Curtain. "The words Juliet uses to express her love for Romeo is more than anyone has ever said about love before:

> *My bounty is as boundless as the sea,*
> *My love as deep; the more I give to thee,*
> *The more I have, for both are infinite.*

"I spoke these very words to you when we were closer," Oxford said quietly. "You don't recognize them?"

She hadn't. Elizabeth's euphoria disappeared. Was she embarrassed for having forgotten, Oxford wondered, or had what he'd written brought her pain?

"You have our permission to retire." She waved a hand at him. She didn't wait for him to leave. She rose and turned away.

Oxford watched her go. How could he bring her so much joy and then be dismissed as if she didn't know him? He remembered her promise to marry him and then, only a few days later, abruptly changing her mind. Perhaps today, Oxford thought, he had failed to meet the expectations of her memory as much as she did of his. Or perhaps words whispered to her many years ago, spoken by Juliet to Romeo, did more than take her back to an earlier time when they were lovers. Perhaps it took her back to a time when she thought she would marry him and give birth to his child.

Oxford watched her striding away from him, trying to look ageless, and doing a good job, he thought. Robin came up to him.

"She wanted to know what the next play would be," he said to Robin, "and who she would be."

"Did you tell her?"

"Of course not. Wait till she sees the little Indian boy," Oxford said, grinning like a little boy himself. The grin disappeared as his leg reminded him of how Thomas Knyvet had lamed him in Pudding Lane one snowy Christmas.

The Bastard

Master Edward Vere," Nigel announced from the doorway of the library. Oxford's bastard son marched into the room, head high. He wore a ruffed shirt and an oversized codpiece someone thought would make him look like a man.

"My lord," he said, bowing low.

Oxford rose from the table where he had been working. Robin slipped out the door. As he did so, Oxford noted that Edward was not much bigger than his page.

"Edward," Oxford gestured to a chair on the other side of the table. "Please sit down."

Edward did as instructed. He sat stiffly erect and said nothing. He had, after all, completed the task his mother and Sir Henry Lee had given him – take himself to Oxford Court and meet his father.

Oxford retook his seat. He didn't know what to say. "Your mother thought we should meet before you went to university. I had no idea you were old enough to go. Which school will you be attending?

"Leiden."

"A fine university." Edward nodded. "And because of this, you will be unable to attend your sister's wedding to the Earl of Derby next month."

"I wasn't invited."

"Oh, I'm sure you were."

Edward's face showed that he had not received an invitation.

Oxford looked away. "I apologize. I am not in charge of such things. I thought you would have been invited as a matter of course. When it comes to Lisbeth's wedding, I am told what to do and when to appear."

"As you are now," Edward said matter-of-factly.

Oxford didn't know how to take this. "Sir Horatio has spoken highly of you. He said he has encouraged you to study Polybius."

Edward nodded again. "I have made Polybius my companion."

Oxford smiled. "An excellent choice. Has my cousin set you to translating any of his work?"

"He has urged me to do so. Caesar is easiest for me."

"Indeed," Oxford said. He was glad to hear that his son was becoming comfortable with Latin. "Did you bring any examples?"

"I did." Edward reached behind him and brought out a sheaf of papers. "Sir Horatio said you might want to see them." He pushed the papers across the table.

Oxford looked though them. "You study Polybius to seek preferment or to write history?" he asked.

"I study Polybius as a pastime, my lord. I intend to train as a soldier. Sir Henry's position as Master of the Armouries has allowed me to learn a great deal about arms."

"As well as Latin," Oxford said, glancing at Edward's translations. He perused a few pages. "I see you are making a good beginning."

Oxford was impressed but Edward took his father's comment as dismissive. He leaned forward. "I'm sure you had great sport in my making," the boy said, sarcastically, "for *my* mother must have provided you with more joy than whatever that Puritan you married gave you in the making of Henry, your *legitimate* son! He may have been gotten between better sheets than I but he and I are separated only by words spoken at your wedding to Henry's mother which, not being spoken to my mother, made me a bastard! My dimensions are as favorable as his, my mind e'en more so being older than he." He reached across the table and snatched the papers he had handed to his father.

"Edward," Oxford said, but Edward was not finished.

"I will not tarry, my lord. I have much to do, for the bastard son has a longer row to hoe than does his legitimate brother. I worship no god but nature since it is but by the vagaries of nature that my brother will engorge himself on your titles and property when you are gone whilst I will receive nothing."

He strode out the door, leaving a thoroughly perplexed and confused Oxford behind him.

A Midsummer Night's Dream

Shackspear took to his new duties with alacrity. He arranged for John Lyly and his boys to play the fairies in *Midsummer*. Richard Burbage from the Lord Chamberlain's Men and Ned Alleyn from the Admiral's Men put down their real cudgels to pick up verbal ones and go at each other as Lysander and Demetrius. Billy Ostler and Layton Pennycuick signed on to play Helena and Hermia. He rounded up players from the Chamberlain's Men to fill out the remaining roles. Tilney agreed to loan costumes and stage paraphernalia because the queen would be in attendance.

The wedding was scheduled to take place in the early afternoon with a splendid feast in the Great Hall to follow. *Midsummer* would be performed after the feast had ended and the tables cleared. The royal carpenters built a stage at one end of the hall with an extension to the left for the queen.

"And the ass's head?" Oxford asked Robin a week before the performance.

"Shackspear knows a tyrer in Silver Street whose wife makes headpieces and trimmings for the ladies at court. She made a helmet for Lisbeth so she could be Athena in a performance before Lord Burghley at Theobalds. Did you attend, my lord?"

"No. Not that they would have invited me," he said, but immediately heard Edward saying *he* had not been invited to Lisbeth's wedding. He pushed these thoughts away to think how ironic it was that his headpiece would be fashioned by the same hand that had turned Lisbeth into Athena. In his case, she would turn him into an ass!

Robin was watching. "My lord?"

"Nothing." Oxford waved a hand. "I am sure the ass's head will serve me well. Lisbeth would never wear anything that was not well-made."

Robin agreed. "I am told, my lord, that it will be covered in fine fur."

"And, thereby, look even more like the head of an ass."

Robin didn't know how to take this.

Oxford sensed Robin's worry. "Do not worry, my little choux. The sillier I look, the more the queen will love it."

Robin was not so sure. His prior experience had not prepared him for *Midsummer*. In the past, he had merely taken down Oxford's words and made ready the script. Here, he would have to move from the page to the stage. He would be Puck, a good role for him if there ever was one. He had already learned his lines. No need to scan the cue roll that would be hung in the tiring house. But would there be a tiring house? he asked himself. The play would be at Greenwich, not in one of the theaters. Did the carpenters build a tiring house at the rear of the stage? 'My goodness,' Robin thought. 'Where will the cue roll be if there was no tiring house? What if I can't remember my lines?'

He ran off looking for his master. "Oh dear, oh dear," he kept repeating as he checked the rooms looking for Oxford.

1595

The Dream at Greenwich Palace

The queen was a master-mistress of many faces. The smile she presented to foreign emissaries that promised them money and alliances was completely different from the glance she flicked past fawning favorites to keep them on their knees. Those who failed her saw a face filled with anger.

The face she brought to *A Midsummer Night's Dream* was one of indifference, more flint than royal sternness, Oxford thought. He knew she had been trying to find out what she would see in *Midsummer*. She, along with everyone else of note, worried they might miss an allusion and be laughed at after the play was over. Worse, they might be the butt of a hidden joke, for everyone thought they were important enough to merit being lashed by Oxford's wit, even if they were not. Because Oxford's allusions were faintly limned, connections were missed, and targets imagined that Oxford had not been aiming at.

Their attempts, reported back to him, were a source of amusement. Gabriel Harvey had set the table years earlier at Audley End by warning people they should avoid antagonizing Oxford *"for feare he be moved, and make a Play of you, and then is your credit un-undone for ever and ever."* He was no doubt punning on Oxford's name when he wrote 'ever and ever', an obvious attempt to imitate Oxford's love of doing the same thing. Harvey had spoken these words in the hope Oxford would hire him as secretary. Instead, Oxford hired John Lily, making Harvey a lifelong enemy.

The upshot of all this was that everyone, from the queen on down, tried to find out who the subject of ridicule might be in a play *before* it opened. But no one had been able to find out what awaited them in *A Midsummer Night's Dream*. Spies who tried to sneak into the rehearsals at the Swan were turned away. They did manage to find out that Burbage and Alleyn were going at each other, hoping their chance to perform in front of the queen would send fortune their way.

Thus, Elizabeth knew nothing about what she was going to see when she took her seat. The hall was packed: courtiers mingled with joiners and churchmen with ladies of pleasure. Everyone had heard that the play would be filled with magic and fairies, something in short supply on a cold, blustery day in January.

The opening scene - an angry father refusing to let his daughter marry the man she loved - set a few heads nodding in agreement. This they liked better than Romeo stealing Juliet out from under Paris and her father. "Fit for the stage," a man said loudly to the man seated next to him, indicating his approval. He had obviously seen *The Taming of the Shrew*. "'She is my goods,' in't she?" another proclaimed loudly. "Didn't Petruchio say his bride was 'my chattels, my house, my household stuff, my horse, my ox, *my anything?*'"

The queen heard the reference to Petruchio. She smiled in the man's direction, a not unexpected reaction given that she had proclaimed there were few things as difficult as stopping a woman's mouth. "*Petruchio has shown us how it can be done,*" she had announced. "*All hail Shackspear, whose wife, no doubt, cowers on the back stairs when she hears his boots returning home to Stratford. Hah, hah, hah!*" she had laughed.

Oxford had written *The Shrew* to laugh at his sister, Mary. He thought the audience would laugh at Shackspear too. Instead, they adopted Petruchio as their role-model and pounded up the steps when they came home. Lettice Knollys told Oxford that *The Shrew* had done more damage to her and other women than anything since Eve handed the apple to Adam.

The Earl of Derby took the stage and, as Theseus, glowered down at the speaker. He remembered Oxford's instructions to speak in a commanding voice and ignore the rabble standing in front of him but he had never been on stage before. He felt his dignity, as the 6th Earl of Derby, had been impugned. He quite forgot he was not the 6th Earl of Derby but a character in a play. "*Theseus!*" Lyly called from the edge of the stage, having recognized what was going on.

Derby took his eyes off the man in the audience he was glowering at and put one foot forward. "*Now, fair Hippolyta, our nuptial hour draws on apace*" he thundered into the now-silent hall, and the evening of magic was underway.

Derby magisterially dealt with Hermia and her father and ceded the stage to Richard Burbage as Demetrius and Edward Alleyn as Lysander. The two grappled with each other at a pitch that some in the audience thought more than acting, but both claimed afterward they had only played their assigned parts. A torn ear and a bloody cuff, however, suggested their mutual dislike may have increased the intensity of their performances. Shackspear was later forced to deny he had written the parts to send them to fisticuffs. He had more difficulty explaining why he had parodied *Romeo & Juliet* with *Pyramus & Thisbe* so soon after the ill-fated lovers from Verona had taken London by storm.

All this mattered little to the queen or the audience. They were enthralled by the fairies and love-juice. Robin, as Puck, charmed everyone. When he mistakenly placed the love-juice into Lysander's eyes, everyone laughed. But it was the candles the children of Paul's brought with them to play the fairies in Titania's train that made the performance memorable. No one cared that Oberon and Titania were fighting over a 'little changeling boy.' Titania's refusal to give the boy to Oberon was merely a dramatic excuse to have her fall in love with an ass!

Oxford, strutting across the stage as Bottom, found that the headpiece was even better than he had expected. No one had any idea who was inside, including the queen. They loved hearing the ass describe what it was to be loved by a queen: *I have had a dream,"* he said, coming out to the front of the stage: *"A dream past the wit of man to say what dream it was."* He wagged his ears back and forth. *"But man is but an ass, if he go about to expound this dream."* At which point he bent over and picked up a glove Elizabeth had unknowingly dropped:

Although engag'd on this high embassy,
Yet stoop we to pick up our cousin's glove.

He handed the glove back to a thoroughly startled queen who realized for the first time her most senior lord was playing an ass *who had just made love to a queen! Her!* And what was a queen who fell in love with an ass? *An ass herself!*

Her anger knew no bounds. And then she realized why the little Indian boy was in the play. *The little Indian boy was Southampton!* Her rage grew. She gripped and ungripped the arms of the chair she was sitting in. She wanted to jump up and storm out of the room but Oxford held her captive, smiling down at her through the eyeholes in the head he was wearing. How could she run? Everyone would spend the next two weeks trying to figure out why she had bolted. And it wouldn't take a week for someone to figure out the answer.

She forced herself to stay seated, her anger hidden behind a face that showed only boredom. She, of all people, of course, knew how to wear a mask, even when one hadn't been given to her.

Oxford, as Bottom, drifted away. Elizabeth chided herself: she should have seen this coming. After all, hadn't he once debarked at Dover claiming he was the Turkish ambassador? Swaths of cloth had gotten him all the way to Greenwich before she saw him winking at her from beneath a turban no Turk ever wore, like he had just winked at her from inside the ass head. Back then, she had turned away to hide her laughter and prevent a scandal when the real ambassador arrived. But not this time. This time she could hardly contain herself.

She watched *Pyramus* and *Thisbe* unfold and *The Dream* end with fairies blessing the newlyweds. The players came out, crowding the stage, and bows were taken, but Oxford did not appear. Elizabeth leaned over to one of her ladies-in-waiting: "*Get him,*" she hissed. The woman had no doubt who she was to fetch. She turned away and Elizabeth waved an arm over the crowd, dismissing them. The hall emptied.

Oxford appeared. He bowed.

"*Not without the ass-head,*" Elizabeth said in a low voice. A servant ran behind a partition and came back with the head. "*Put it on.*"

Oxford slipped the head over his shoulders and leered out at her through the eye holes, the way he had looked at her when he picked up her glove.

Elizabeth waved the remaining servants away. She leaned toward him. "Would that I could tie up *your* tongue!" she said into the empty room. Oxford started to take off the head. "Oh, no, you don't. I may not be a fairy queen, but as Elizabeth I, Queen of England, Wales, and Ireland, I can command you to remain an ass, *for that is what you are.*"

Elizabeth thought this would humiliate Oxford, but she couldn't see his eyes. He tipped his head. *He was smiling!* "*Off!*" she cried.

Oxford slid the headpiece off his head and offered it to her.

"Oh," she said, disgusted. Oxford could see her jaw working. He thought she was going to explode. The listeners outside the hall waited for the queen to say something. Silence in her case, they knew, was more dangerous than words.

Elizabeth finally calmed down. "To make me Rosaline in *Romeo and Juliet* and deny me time on the stage was bad enough," she growled. "To make me Titania and show me onstage besotted with an ass is quite another."

"A joke only you and I …," Oxford began, but she cut him off.

"No, they get it," she snapped. "Everyone knows Titania was Ovid's name for Diana. Am I not Diana?" Her voice rose another octave. "Haven't there been others who have called me Titania?" She tried to remember. "Spenser, wasn't it, in one of his interminable poems?" She stopped, her eyes opening wider. "But, wait! Who played Titania? She had a deeper voice than I expected."

Oxford didn't answer.

"*Who was it?*"

"Well," Oxford shrugged, "Lettice Knollys turned down the role."

Elizabeth looked at him wide-eyed. "*You offered the role of Titania to Lettice Knollys?* She who I banned from court for marrying my Robin?" Bringing up 'her Robin' was intended to goad Oxford who, she knew, couldn't stand it that the Earl of Leicester had become her lover after she had grown tired of Oxford. "She who called me a 'bitch' with a capital 'B' at your trial?"

Oxford nodded. Her Majesty *did* have long ears.

"And why would she turn down the chance to so egregiously annoy me?" Elizabeth asked.

"She thought you would immediately leave the play when you recognized her."

"*Which I most certainly would have done!*" Elizabeth shouted.

"Which is to say that the Countess knows Your Majesty exceedingly well," Oxford pointed out.

Elizabeth didn't like to hear that.

"So, who *did* play Titania?" Elizabeth asked again, realizing that Oxford had not answered her question.

"Dorothy Soer," Oxford answered.

"Dorothy who?"

"Dorothy Soer, the wife of John Soer, who runs the Swan theater in Paris Garden."

"A woman?" Elizabeth repeated in amazement. "*A woman on the stage?*"

"Not the first time."

"*Not the first time?*" Elizabeth didn't want to know who had played a woman on the stage before but couldn't keep herself from asking.

Oxford read her mind. "Dorothy also played Margaret in *Henry VI*, for one."

Elizabeth's jaw dropped. "She who gave a handkerchief to York dipped in the blood of his son?" Oxford nodded. "She who York described as a 'tiger's heart wrapped in a woman's hide.'" Oxford nodded again. "How could this woman play such an awful person?"

"Dorothy runs the pleasure house behind the Swan, Your Majesty. If you ever met her in an alley, you would go the other way."

Elizabeth could no more imagine what it was like to be walking in an alley than to accept the notion that a common woman could play Titania. "Titania did seem less fairy than I would have imagined," she said, almost to herself. "But you went too far with the little changeling boy." She glared at him. "'*In the spiced Indian air?* my lord? '*Indian heir?*'" I get it." She stuck out her chin. "You didn't." She watched to see if she had hurt him, but he was as much a master of putting a mask on as she was. He was still smiling, almost gloating. She pressed on. "I know why you wrote a little changeling boy into your play. We will have no more of that. You are to write nothing about me and your," here, her voice dropped, "wild claims about someone we both know, someone who is *not* my issue."

"So, you say," Oxford said calmly. "But Heaven guards our kingdom, does it not? Only a true heir can succeed a king. Or a queen."

His use of "our" kingdom dismayed her. Was he using the royal "we" to imply he was royal? Or was he talking as a citizen, proud to be an Englishman? He was exasperating here now; somewhere else an instant later. His face, she could tell, showed that he was even more convinced than ever that Southampton was their son.

She was tiring. "I thought my noblest lord scribbling plays was bad enough, but seeing you on the stage … with an ass head on your shoulders …" Her voice trailed off. She wanted to deny she had ever been in love with him, but that would be a lie. They had been besotted with each other at one point. Part of what drew her to him, Falstaff as well, was Oxford was never the same, always brilliantly different.

Oxford knew what she was thinking. "Yes, a short time, but long enough for me to get you with child."

This was said loud enough for the eavesdroppers outside to hear. Elizabeth suddenly realized he might be using their conversation to spread rumors about his claims about Southampton. She stood. A servant immediately appeared. "My lord claims much on the strength of a few words."

"Art can be efficient, Your Majesty, just as we were many years ago when you had love juice in your eyes and made love to an ass."

She turned away, acting as if she had not heard him, but they both knew she had.

"Your Majesty," Oxford said to her retreating back.

A Visit From A Lady-in-Waiting

Nigel appeared in the doorway, his shoulders squared, his back straighter than usual. "Lady Elizabeth Howard, my lord, who has just dined with the Countess, craves a word." Oxford had no idea who Lady Elizabeth was. "She is the Admiral's youngest daughter and the queen's newest lady-in-waiting," Nigel added.

There was only one "Admiral" in England; Lord Charles Howard, 1st Earl of Nottingham, the man who had defeated the Spanish Armada. He was also the sponsor of the Admiral's Men, Philip Henslowe's favorite company at the Rose. Perhaps Lady Elizabeth craved a part in a play?

He got up and followed Nigel across the Hall to where he found his wife dining with a slip of a girl who looked up at him from beneath an explosion of feathers and furs that covered her head.

"My lord," she said, a look of condescending benevolence spreading across her face.

"Lady Elizabeth," Oxford said, bowing. "Please accept my congratulations on your appointment as lady-in-waiting to Gloriana."

"My lord," she said, the collection of objects on her head nodding gravely in thanks. "My father sends his greetings."

"Please give him my best wishes in return." He was amused. The young lady had immediately established her patrimony lest he be unaware of who she was.

Elspeth, seated at the far end of the table, thought they sounded like two birds in a forest establishing their territories. Ever the observer, she loved watching people interact. She sat back to watch.

"Her Majesty was disappointed by *A Midsummer Night's Dream*," Lady Elizabeth said, wasting no time getting to the reason for her visit. "Something about the little changeling boy, I think."

Oxford nodded. "Yes. She seemed to have been put off by that."

The young lady was disappointed Oxford was unconcerned to hear Her Majesty was displeased. He was amused, in fact. She had expected apologies, or possibly the prospect of seeing Oxford grovel, given the power she thought her new position gave her. "She expects to hear no more about the boy." The smile on Oxford's grew wider. She looked away. "And a play, my lord. Her Majesty suggests something spring-like. When Lent is over. She will be at Richmond."

"But why ask me, my lady. I am not a writer of plays."

"That may be what the world believes, my lord, but, for those of us in the know, Her Majesty speaks with my Lord of Oxford after a play has ended, not Mr. Shakespeare. Spring-like, she said."

Lady Elizabeth considered her message delivered. She smiled down the table at Elspeth.

Oxford was no longer amused. He left the room without bidding his guest farewell.

"*In my own house,*" he cried aloud as he crossed the Great Hall and strode into the library. "*A child!*"

Robin was seated on the right side of the table in his customary position. Oxford picked up a book and slammed it on the table. Socrates flew out the door. Robin sat completely still.

Oxford finally pulled out a chair and sat down. He glared at Robin across from him. "*Dismissed in my own house! By a child!* All bodged up with hoops and silks, a jungle of feathers and dead animals on her head, dressed with a little authority and most ignorant of what she's most assured!"

"Who, my lord?"

"Lady Elizabeth Howard, the queen's newest lady-in-waiting." He got up and walked around the table. "A play about *springtime*, she said." Robin sat up. "Yes, a new play. You can smile, Robin. Her wish is my command." Oxford was irritated but Robin could tell he was also intrigued. He paused. "Springtime. I have just what she wants. To the trunk of plays," he announced.

The two of them headed for the second floor and the trunk of plays. Oxford slid the trunk away from the wall and opened it. He reached in and pulled out a sheaf of musty papers. He held them up for Robin to see. "She wants springtime? I'll give her springtime." They went back down to the library where he spread the pages on the table. He took his customary seat; Robin sat down opposite him.

"Many years ago, the queen decided to engage in a chess match with France and Spain. Spain had sent troops to the Netherlands. Everyone thought they would soon invade England. Elizabeth decided to use France to keep Spain at bay. She started marriage negotiations with the king's brother, the Duke d'Alençon. He didn't know it but she had no intention of marrying him."

"The back and forth went on for some time. Those Englishmen who thought Elizabeth was serious begged her to stay our virgin queen. Some of us – me included – thought it might be a good idea. Alençon, the third son, loved the attention; his older brother, the king, did not."

"After a long period, Alençon realized Elizabeth was not going to marry him and the negotiations came to a halt. The ending to this farce occurred about the time the queen allowed me to return to court. I wrote a play to thank her for allowing me to come back. The play recycled the events surrounding her negotiations with 'her frog,' as she called him."

"What did you call the play?"

"It was never given a name. When the negotiations came to an end, it became old news. *En fin*, into the trunk of plays it went."

"And what needs to be done to present it at Richmond at the end of Lent?"

It was at this point that Nigel announced, in grand fashion, "*William Shake-spare*, my lord" and the Bard from Stratford-upon-Avon strode into the room. "My lord," he said, sweeping off his head a new hat crowned with a brown turkey feather from the new world. Oxford groaned. "I am ready for our next venture," Shackspear announced. He did not try to sit down. "*Midsummer* went over very well. Our public eagerly awaits our next invention."

"'Our' public? 'Our' next invention?" Oxford said, his voice rising. A slight nod from Shackspear' acknowledged he may have gone too far. "God's blood! Man," Oxford went on. "I write for the queen and the queen only! *There is no public!*" he shouted. "And when I want your help, *I will ask for it!*"

Shackspear nodded again, this time more affirmatively.

"And no," Oxford went on, "there is no play, before you ask. I will advise you when I have something. In the meantime, visit Stratford and see your wife and family."

Shackspear straightened up. "My investments do not allow me time to visit Stratford, much as I would like to. If there is nothing to work on at the moment, I will leave off seeking everlasting fame to further secure my financial future." He stroked the feather that rose out of his hat. "My lord," he said, giving Oxford a slight bow. "Master Robin," he said to Robin across the table. He put his hat on his head and walked out of the room.

"God, God," Oxford muttered to himself. He forced himself to think about the play. "Alençon's older brother, Henri, became king when their father died whilst tilting with a Scotsman, of all people."

"I know the story. Nostradamus predicted the king would die in a gilded cage. Nobody believed him but the king was wearing a golden helmet when the Scotsman's lance came in through the visor."*

"Indeed. And so, the King's son, Henri, came to the throne. Henri didn't trust his brother, Alençon, who he thought was scheming to take his place, so he kept him poor. In the play we're going to work on, an older brother inherits his father's estate but keeps his younger brother uneducated and poor. I want you to help me bring it up to today because I owe a play to the Jew who sits outside our door every Monday morning and I don't have time to write both."

"Of course," Robin said. He was thrilled to work on another play. "And what needs to be done to get this play ready for Holy Saturday?"

"A few scenes and characters. Touchstone, for one. He will be the court fool, named after the stone used to test gold or silver."

"Ah, you."

"Yes. I will sketch Touchstone for you. There will be another me - Jacques - a melancholic fellow. He will shed tears for the deer whose tender hides are gored to provide meat for the table. You stay there," he said, pointing to where Robin was sitting. "I will shift to the end of the table and start working on my suggestions."

He picked up some scrap papers on the table, leftovers from the wrappings that had carried chickens and pork to Oxford Court, and began to write, muttering to himself as he did so. He sounded like carpenter bees boring through the table. Socrates appeared to see if the storm that had driven him from the room had passed. Whatever he saw, it wasn't enough. He went back into the Great Hall.

Oxford kept writing through dinner. So did Robin. Robin left him there when he finally pushed himself up from the table and went to bed.

~ 111 ~
Call Me Rosalind

Robin was at the table when Oxford came in the next morning. "This reads like Thomas Lodge's *Rosalynde*," Robin said, turning over the pages Oxford had given him.

"It does."

"But *Rosalynde* was only recently published, wasn't it?"

"It was."

"But you told me you wrote this back in 1583 or thereabouts."

"I did."

"So how … Oh. Lodge saw it in manuscript and copied you."

"He did."

"But he didn't write a play. He wrote the story in prose."

"Yes."

"Do you think he's not capable of writing it as a play?"

"It's easy to write prose."

"And difficult to write a play."

"Even if someone has given you the plot."

Robin nodded. This was certainly the case with him.

"A play," Oxford said, "is a story told through words and action. The early plays had characters named Vice or Gluttony. Ideas, not people. Ideas don't have feelings, fear of failure, lust, or overwhelming ambition."

"Richard, Duke of Gloucester," Robin said. He thought Oxford was testing him. "Jack Cade; Juliet; Arthur!" he added, recalling the boy Hubert was sent to blind with hot pokers in *King John*.

Oxford liked Robin's enthusiasm. "Yes, Lodge buries Rosalynde in a flood of words, a technique adopted by many would-be writers in the hope that one word will hit the mark. A play does not have this luxury."

"And your play. The one I will finish. Is there a love interest?"

89

"Yes. When our story opens, Duke Senior, the rightful ruler of a French Duchy, has been dispossessed by his younger brother and banished to the Forest of Ardennes."

"The Ardennes?"

"It's a forest in France."

"Shackspear will want to rename it the Forest of Arden, my lord. It's near Stratford. He'll use it to claim he's the author, like he did with the fat alewife of Wilmcote."

Oxford groaned. He decided to ignore where Shackspear might put the Forest of Ardennes.

"Rosalind is the daughter of the banished Duke. She has been allowed to stay in the Duchy because she is the best friend of Celia, the daughter of the usurping brother. They lament the banishment of Rosalind's father."

Oxford paused for a moment. "There is a young man in the Duchy named Orlando whose older brother has been denying Orlando the money and education he deserves."

"Ah. The French prince surfaces. And the queen will like the reappearance of Rosalind in this play."

"She will. This Rosalind will have more lines to speak than any other female character I have created."

"And make up for muzzling her in *Romeo & Juliet*."

Oxford shrugged. "Orlando will fall in love with Rosalind and she with him but before they can get together, Orlando realizes his brother intends to kill him to avoid having to share their father's estate. Orlando, with an ancient servant named Adam, flees to the forest. Then Rosalind is banished by her father and she and Rosalind flee to the forest as well."

"How can they make the trip?" Robin asked. "Ladies don't go off alone to a forest. It would be too dangerous."

Robin had a point. "May I suggest," Robin said, "that they disguise themselves as young men? Dressed as boys, a world of mistaken identities opens up. You had fun in *A Comedy of Errors* with the Antipholus twins, but they weren't disguised. Julia disguised herself as a page to get near Proteus in *Two Gentlemen*. And you had Helena in *All's Well* sneaking into Diana's bedroom …"

"Yes, yes," Oxford said, putting up a hand. *All's Well* had been Oxford's attempt to purge himself of the humiliation he had suffered when he returned from Italy and heard Nan had cuckolded him.

Robin realized he shouldn't have mentioned *All's Well*. He waited. Oxford finally sat down opposite him. "All right, the young women put on men's clothes before they leave. And what if I suggest something is going on between them *as women?*"

"Oooh. More forbidden fruit." Robin smiled slyly at Oxford. "If I may take your suggestion a little further, my lord, we can accomplish this by having our heroine call herself Ganymede when she is dressed as a boy."

Oxford laughed. "Oh, you devil. The Trojan boy swept up to Heaven to be Jupiter's love-toy."

"Marlowe painted him as a mincing cherub in *Dido, Queen of Carthage.*

"'*Come, gentle Ganymede, and play with me,*'" Oxford said. "God, how I miss him."

Robin knew Oxford meant Marlowe, not Ganymede. "Remember, my lord, how the courtiers copied Ganymede's walk as they strutted around London? Hunsdon loved him."

"Yes," Oxford's face suddenly darkened. "Hunsdon. Aemilia Bassano."

'Uh oh,' Robin muttered to himself. He had drifted into another forbidden area. Hunsdon's mistress, Aemilia Bassano, had swept Oxford off his feet when they first met. He had become besotted with her. He sent her sonnets which she, to his dismay, found 'antique.' She had fallen in love with the poems of another poet: *William Shackspear!* Oxford could only grind his teeth as Aemilia praised the 'rustic genius from Stratford' as she swooned over words *Oxford* had written!

But her adoration of Shackspear didn't last long. It ended when he couldn't recite Sylvia's lines from *Two Gentlemen* one night. The scales fell off her eyes. Recalling something Oxford had said, she realized who the true author was. When Oxford had no trouble reciting Sylvia's lines, the heat she had felt for Shackspear was redirected toward Oxford. She and Oxford began to plot how to sneak him into the lodgings she shared with Hunsdon but they never pulled it off *before she became infatuated with another poet!* She refused to tell Oxford who his new rival was and, when he demanded to know who had taken his place in her heart, she slammed the door on him.

Oxford thought at first that Marlowe had seduced her but Marlowe laughed and told Oxford he preferred boys. He pointed to *Dido* and asked Oxford if his plays showed any appreciation of women. Oxford had to accept that Marlowe had not bedded Aemilia Bassano.

Any hope of enjoying the favors of the dark-eyed beauty ended when she became pregnant. Hunsdon, fifty years older than she was, claimed the child was his and promptly married her off to a ship captain. Thus, wittingly or unwittingly, he repeated what Hunsdon's real father, Henry VIII, had done when he got Mary Boleyn pregnant. Great Harry married Hunsdon's mother to a nobody who was immediately knighted and became Hunsdon's official father. Hunsdon, when he was old enough to understand what might have happened, was happy to wink and let people think he was Henry VIII's son.

Marlowe told Oxford Hunsdon was almost certainly *not* the father of Aemilia's child because he *also* liked boys. In fact, it was this love that drove Hunsdon to seek the office of Lord Chamberlain so that he could be around sweet-voiced boys. He had only taken Aemilia on as his mistress to make people believe he liked women, when he didn't.

Marlowe said he had used Hunsdon's love of boys to get *Edward II* past the Office of the Revels by telling Hunsdon that if he had liked *Dido,* he would love *Edward II.* Hunsdon spoke to Tilney and the Office of the Revels approved *Edward II* for performance.

Whatever Hunsdon's preferences, Aemilia Bassano's pregnancy and quick marriage took her away from court and out of Oxford's life, thus ending Oxford's pursuit of her. He resented not having bedded her and became haunted by the thought that Shackspear was the 'poet' who had beat him to her.

Oxford pushed thoughts of the dark lady aside and returned to the play he and Robin were working on. "Her name alone – *Ganymede -* will have the audience leaning forward to hear what she says to her friend, also dressed as a boy."

Robin was pleased Oxford liked his idea "There is more here, I think. We can have Rosalind, who Orlando will think is a young man, teach him how to wean himself off his love for her."

Oxford guffawed. "Oh, excellent. Rosalind as a young man, convincing Orlando how to stop loving her as a woman. Marvelous. But can we make the audience believe Orlando does not know he's standing in front of the woman he is in love with?" He looked askance at Robin.

"He will sense he has seen her somewhere else and drift close to discovering who she is, but I will make him so in love that he won't be able to see what is in front of him."

"Love juice?" Oxford asked.

Robin nodded. "As you well know, my lord, young men have very little wit when they are in love."

Oxford looked closely at his little page and wondered if he was being cheeky. Was he referring to Oxford's pursuit of Aemilia Bassano? Nan? The queen? "True enough," Oxford acknowledged.

"I, of course, am not yet man enough to know how such a young man feels when he is in love." Robin said this as he coughed behind his hand. "But I think an audience would never accept a blind *female* character. A man?" He looked off.

Robin *was* being cheeky. But about what?

"And," Robin continued, "if Orlando is blind, he should be a terrible poet. Have him compose love poems to Rosalind that he carves into the trees in the forest. The queen will know these are the letters her little frog sent her from France."

"Ah," Oxford said. His little page was on a roll.

"And may I ask why you want to name this character Rosalind?" Robin asked. "A different name here *would* make a difference, particularly when Rosalind very quickly becomes Ganymede and changes into a boy. She won't like that."

"Yes, she will."

"We can't call her something else?"

"I am calling her Rosalind. *Capiche?*" Robin didn't know what *capiche* meant but understood it was time to shut up.

"What shall I write down?" he asked, Oxford's spaniel once again.

"This is your effort, Robin. What you have in your hands is the version I wrote many years ago. I will say, however, that you should have the two girls bring Touchstone with them to the Forest of Ardennes."

"Arden."

"Arden. And what will Celia call herself when she transforms herself into a young man?"

"Aliena," Robin immediately said. He looked up. "She will be 'alien' to her sex, won't she?"

Oxford smiled. He rose from the table. "You keep working on this. We will resume tomorrow morning."

"And what will you be working on?"

"You have, no doubt, noticed a man in gabardine outside our door each Monday morning."

Robin nodded. "He sits next to London Stone. Tobias says you said to let him be."

"I did. He is there to remind me of a promise I made."

"And what was that, my lord?"

"You remember Rodrigo López, physician to the queen?"

Robin's face became grim. "I was there when he was executed."

"But you didn't stay to the end. You ran away as the executioner carved him up and splattered everyone with blood."

Robin's hand started to shake. "I didn't leave *soon* enough. I too was sprayed with his blood. It was hot and sticky! I ran to the conduit but couldn't wash it off. Sometimes I swear I can still see it! Look!" He held up his arm. Oxford couldn't see anything. "Do you remember his last words?" Robin went on. He assumed a voice Oxford had never heard before, as if the boy had been transformed into a town crier addressing a crowd: "*Be it known that I have always loved the Queen as well as I love Jesus Christ!*" He looked at Oxford. "He was a good Christian, my lord. No man lies in the face of death."

Oxford didn't say anything.

"I remember a man kneeling next to you as the executioner cut into Dr. López. Is he the man outside?"

"Yes. His name is Michael Lok. He is a Jew. He asked me to promise I would write a play to show how Jews love their children and grieve when they suffer loss. 'If you cut us, do we not bleed?' he asked me, pointing to López. I promised I would. His presence outside the door is to make sure I don't forget. His appearance every Monday is enough. He knows that whenever I go out– Tuesday, Wednesday, or any other day of the week – he is there in my mind, silently asking me to fulfill my promise."

"But Marlowe has already done a play about a Jew, my lord."

"*The Jew of Malta* gave us what Christians think a Jew is, not *who* he is. I promised Michael I would write a play about a man like you and I are, who is not different from us simply because he believes in a different path to God. It is time for me to honor my promise."

~ 112 ~
Ipse is not William

"Good morrow, my lord," Robin said, looking up as Oxford entered the library.

Oxford had a sheaf of papers under his arm. He sat down at the table opposite Robin. "You mentioned Touchstone yesterday. I'm looking forward to hearing more about him, but, if I may be so bold, you need to add more characters to Thomas Lodge's pathetic story."

"You think so?"

"Yes. Who shall I add?"

"A man who irritates Touchstone greatly."

"Wherefore?"

"Because he wants to marry the same rustic Touchstone wants to marry."

"His name?"

"William."

"*William*? As in *William* Shackspear?"

"We will call him by his first name only. We will leave off his surname to be consistent with the way the other characters are named in the play. And to allow us to deny, with great dismay, if asked, any intent to connect *this* William with the William we so unfortunately know. The windy side of the law, and all that."

"*William*?" Robin asked again.

"Yes. Am I stopped from having a character named William in a play because the first name of the man we know is William?"

Robin could tell the answer to this question was 'no.' Oxford was done with any further discussion of William's name. "And what does William say?" Robin asked.

"William will appear in only one scene. He will be joined by Touchstone and Audrey, a rustic who is the object of Touchstone's affection."

"The rustic," Robin said, writing down what Oxford said. "Will Touchstone marry Audrey at the end of the play?"

95

"He will. Their marriage will be one of four, which will be a record for all those who count these types of things. Rosalind will marry Orlando; Celia will marry Orlando's older brother, who I will make a good man by the end of the play; a shepherd will marry his shepherdess, who, up until then, has been in love with Ganymede, thinking she was a man; and Touchstone will marry Audrey."

"That's a lot of change to bring about."

"All will end happily"

"What will Touchstone say to William when they are together with Audrey?"

"He will first ask William if he is learned, to which William will answer 'no, sir.'"

"Telling the truth, for once," Robin said.

"Touchstone will then say to William:

> *Then learn this of me: to have, is to have; for it is a figure in*
> *rhetoric that drink, being poured out of a cup into a glass, by*
> *filling the one doth empty the other; for all your writers do*
> *consent that ipse is he: now, you are not ipse, for I am he.*

Robin took this down. "Who is ipse?" he asked.

"I am ipse."

"But Touchstone said he was ipse."

"He is, but I am Touchstone."

Robin blinked. "Ipse means 'he himself,' right?"

Oxford nodded. "Do not fret, my little cabbage. William will be as confused as you are. He will say *Which he, sir?* to which Touchstone will reply:

> *He, sir, that must marry this woman.*
> *Therefore, you clown, abandon, - which is in the vulgar leave, -*
> *The society, - which in the boorish is company, - of this female, -*
> *Which in the common is woman; which together is,*
> *Abandon the society of this female, or, clown, thou perishest;*
> *Or, to thy better understanding, diest; or, to wit I kill thee,*
> *Make thee away, translate thy life into death, thy liberty into bondage:*
> *I will deal in poison with thee, or in bastinado, or in steel;*
> *I will bandy with thee in faction; I will o'errun thee with policy;*
> *I will kill thee a hundred and fifty ways: therefore tremble and depart.*

"This is rather strong, my lord. What has William done to deserve such execration?"

"Execration?" Oxford asked.

"Touchstone is denouncing him. He paints William with words that make him sound despicable."

"He is, but I didn't think I would ever hear the word 'execration' come out of your mouth."

Robin looked smug. "I am a lover of words, aren't I? A wordsmith?"

"Aye."

"But William hasn't done anything *in the play*."

"He wants to marry Audrey."

"That's a crime?"

"You don't know who Audrey is."

Robin could tell Oxford was presenting him with a puzzle and expected him to solve it. "Okay, I don't know who Audrey is. Does Audrey say anything after Touchstone tells William to depart?"

"She does. She says: *Do, good William.*"

"Well, that's to the point. What does William do?"

"He leaves."

"And never comes back?"

"No."

"What is going on here?"

"It's a mystery."

Robin sighed. He was about to give up when he said: "Wait! If you are Touchstone, and William is William, *Audrey must be the plays!*" He looked up, his mouth hanging open.

"I said it was a mystery."

Robin didn't know whether Oxford meant he had solved the puzzle of who Audrey was in the play or the mystery of who actually wrote the plays. "Audrey as the plays," he mused. "Is there else I should know?"

"Yes. We will add a character named Jaques."

"Jay-quews?" Robin asked, repeating the way Oxford pronounced the name of this new character."

"Yes. If Touchstone be the clown, Jaques will be a deep soul to offset him. The Duke will want to converse with him."

"Oh. another you."

"Of course. The Duke will hear that Jaques wept into a brook over the death of a deer the hunters killed for supper."

"He weeps over a deer?"

Oxford looked at Robin. "You wouldn't?"

Robin didn't know where this was going but his master was bristly, which usually signaled a bad end. "I guess."

"You guess? You, who eat meat carved in the kitchen from a carcass someone else shot and thus miss the tears that fell down the poor beast's nose as it collapsed to the ground, wouldn't have any feelings for the poor beast."

Robin blinked.

"Who do you think killed the stag whose antlers hang over the mantel at Hedingham? I was ten when I did that. He was a magnificent beast. He died while I held his head, his tears running down his face, my tears running down mine. His eyes accused me of murdering him."

"Oh. So, Jay-ques will express grief over the deer."

"Most assuredly:

> *The wretched animal heaved forth such groans*
> *That their discharge did stretch his leathern coat*
> *Almost to bursting, and the big round tears*
> *Coursed one another down his innocent nose*
> *In piteous chase; and thus the hairy fool*
> *Much marked of the melancholy Jaques,*
> *Stood on the extremest verge of the swift brook,*
> *Augmenting it with tears.*

Oxford continued. "The Duke is told that Jaques memorialized what he saw 'into a thousand similes' and railed against the dying deer's friends, who ignored him as they ran away: '*Sweep on, you fat and greasy citizens,*' Jacques will cry."

"Interesting. A thousand similes."

He noticed Oxford had suddenly become very sad. Was it the memory of the stag he had shot? The '*fat and greasy citizens?*' "I will play you a tune at supper, my lord, to cheer you up."

"Nay, nay. I am for melancholy. Give me a melancholy song. I can suck melancholy out of a song as a weasel sucks eggs."

"Oooh," Robin said, picking up his pen. "Something Jaques might say."

"Yes. Sad, he will be, as I am now. He will tell the Duke:

All the world's a stage,
And all the men and women merely players:
They have their exits and their entrances;
And one man in his time plays many parts,
His acts being seven ages. At first the infant,

"Wait!" Robin cried, as he tried to keep up. "Seven stages?"

"Yes. *At first the infant, mewling and puking,* the whining school-boy, *creeping like snail to school,* ending as an old man going into *mere oblivion sans teeth, sans eyes, sans taste, sans everything!*"

"Oh, my goodness," Robin muttered. "Where did this come from?"

"The floor of a church in Siena. I will fill in the blanks."

"And Rosalind? Can you help me a bit with Rosalind?"

"She will spend most of the play as Ganymede, pulling Orlando this way and that, abusing him about his love for her, reeling him in and out like a big, stupid fish."

"Oh. A big, stupid fish."

"How else describe Orlando after reading one of the poems he carves into trees in the forest:

From the east to western Ind,
No jewel is like Rosalind.
Her worth, being mounted on the wind,
Through all the world bears Rosalind.
All the pictures fairest lined
Are but black to Rosalind.
Let no fair be kept in mind
But the fair of Rosalind.

"Well, he's no poet."

"No, indeed. While Rosalind has fun with stupid Orlando, she will be pursued by the shepherdess who thinks she is a man. All of this will be resolved when Rosalind reappears as Rosalind."

"If the audience likes it," Robin said, showing his anxiety about whether he was up to the task of crafting a play the audience would like. "As much as you like it."

Oxford shrugged. "That's as good a name as any: *As You Like It,*" he announced. "There. You have the name for your play."

Robin preferred *Rosalind* but could tell his master had decided otherwise. "Does Rosalind cross paths with Jaques?"

"Of course. The two foremost wits in the play will combat with each other. When they meet for the first time, Rosalind will tell Jaques she has heard that he is *a melancholy fellow*. Jacques will agree: *I love it better than laughing*. This will cause Rosalind to laugh. Jacques will say: *Why, 'tis good to be sad and say nothing*. Rosalind's response will be: *Why then, 'tis good to be a post.*"

Robin laughed.

"Jacques will go off into a long aside about a scholar's melancholy – you fill in the different types – and confess that he is sad because of his travels, whereupon Rosalind will say:

> *A traveller! By my faith, you have great reason to be sad: I fear*
> *you have sold your own lands to see other men's; then, to have seen much*
> *and to have nothing, is to have rich eyes and poor hands.*

Robin sniggered. "Footprints. And to make sure we know who the true author is, Rosalind will bid Jaques goodbye thus:

> *Farewell, Monsieur Traveller: look you lisp, wear strange suits,*
> *disable all the benefits of your own country, be out of love with your*
> *nativity, or I will scarce think <u>you have swam in a gondola</u>!*

Robin laughed out loud. Oxford was caught between admiring his page's cleverness and resenting his cheek. But he did lisp on occasion, wear strange weeds, and disparage England. "Swam in a gondola?" he asked, reaching for something with which he could abuse his little page.

Robin looked up. "Past tense. Oh, you mean it should be 'swam *with* a gondola.'"

"One rides *in* a gondola."

"Oh, I'll change it."

"No. No. It's perfect. It's just what Shackspear would say, not having been to Venice."

Smiling, he got up and left Robin alone to continue working.

~ 113 ~
As You Like It

Lent came to an end and everyone was eager to forget the prayer, penance, repentance, almsgiving, and self-denial they had endured the past forty days, not to mention the dried fish and steamed lentils. The queen's kitchen was ordered to prepare a better than normal bouche of court - beer, wine, and bread - and roast three bucks in the great fireplace Henry VIII had built in the basement. The pastry chefs battled the sauce-makers. The end result was a banquet to remember in the great hammer-beam hall where *As You Like It* was performed before the queen. Edward Alleyn played Jaques; Robert Armin, Touchstone. The queen liked it.

"Good fun," she announced. "A fitting ending to a cold winter. Words to sweep our heads clean as the days warm." She looked around for Oxford, glancing furtively down at a small piece of paper in her hands where she had scribbled some lines from the play:

"Hath not old custom made this life more sweet than that of painted pomp?" she asked the audience, still in the room. She thought to dazzle them by making them think she could recall what she had heard only once. *"Are not these woods more free from peril than the envious court?"* She looked up. "That cannot be true, can it?"

The loyal subjects in front of her murmured 'no, no,' and 'hear, hear.'

"And where is Master Shakespeare? Didn't he play the old man Adam?"

"No, Your Majesty," someone said. "He is not here."

"A pity." She saw Oxford. Her hand came up. Oxford was soon at her side. "Me as Ganymede?" she asked him.

He couldn't tell whether she was intrigued by the idea or angry about it.

"As woman *and* man, Your Majesty."

She leaned forward. "Lisp, for me."

Oxford was shocked. "Your Majesty! Here?"

Elizabeth looked away, disgusted. "Do you have to twist everything?"

"I am a poet."

"At least I didn't have to worry this time I would find you leering up at me through a mask, or Lettice Knollys might be … by the way: who played Rosalind?"

"Nathan Field."

"Oh, thank God. I dreaded it might be that woman who played Titania."

"She did a good job, though, didn't she?"

"Why did she not return?"

"She liked not the theater. She said faking it was not good for her business."

Elizabeth rolled her eyes. "How did Shackspear react to William?" she asked, changing the subject.

"He has been away on a trip with Francis Langley, Your Majesty. Business called him. I would be surprised if he's read the script."

"He'll not like it."

"*Tant pis*," Oxford replied. "His price for fame."

She realized he was going to ask her to let his name appear on the plays. "No, no. We'll have none of that," she said. "You agreed."

She got up and left.

Falstaff

Falstaff looked up as the Earl of Oxford sat down on the other side of the table.

"Think ye can sneak up on old Jack, eh?" Falstaff said, cracking an eye open as he looked across the table at Oxford.

Oxford put up a hand. He didn't want to hear a long story about avoiding death or capture while in service to the Duke of Norfolk by lying down in battle and acting dead. Oxford had heard it all before. More than once.

Disappointed, Falstaff rearranged himself on the bench he'd been sleeping on.

"Get up, Jack. Why do ye lie there?"

"If one lies on the ground, one can fall no farther."

Oxford growled.

"She didn't like the little changeling boy," Falstaff said, meaning the queen.

"No, she didn't. But I didn't come in here to find out something I already know. What have you found out about Southampton? Is he my son?" He looked around the Boar's Head. "You won't find answers here."

"Oh, ye of little faith," Falstaff demurred. "Shackspear likes to tell the ladies he learned all he needed about Verona from listening to an Italian seaman in the Mermaid."

Oxford didn't want to talk about Shackspear. "And?"

Falstaff pouted. "Ye want me to find information from a long time ago. Twenty years!"

"You found Yorick and Joan Jockey, didn't you? They'd been missing for *forty years*." The big knight took this as a compliment. He smiled and leaned back to reflect on his cleverness.

"So?" Oxford asked.

Falstaff got down to business. "Blanche Parry," he began, but Oxford interrupted him.

"Blanche Parry died in 1590, Jack. Unless you have powers I am unaware of, you cannot ask her what she knows *about anything* because she is dead."

Falstaff straightened himself. "Blanche Parry," he began again, ignoring Oxford's interruption, "was lady-in-waiting to the queen from the time of the queen's accession in 1558. In 1565, she became Chief Gentlewoman of the Privy Chamber after Kat Ashley died. She held that position until she died in 1590."

"And is *still* dead."

"She was Burghley's cousin."

This Oxford didn't know. "Well, Jack, Pondus is still alive, though not by much. If you're planning on asking him what he knows about Southampton, you'd better hurry up."

Falstaff cast a baleful eye at Oxford. "He wouldn't say if he knew. Ye know that."

"Finally, something we can agree on. So, if Blanche *can't* talk, and Burghley *won't* ..."

"I'm to Bacton, my lord. I am told Blanche has a tomb there. She's not in it, of course, having been buried at the queen's expense in Westminster Abbey, but relatives maintain a tomb there for her."

"What's to maintain?" Oxford said exasperatedly. "No one's going in or out." He was reaching his limits.

Falstaff was unruffled. He loved it when he had his lordship on a short chain and made him jump about like a bear led by a gypsy child. He drew himself up. "I would think your lordship would be interested in what goes on at a tomb, my lord, with all the comings and goings ye had in *Romeo & Juliet*. Now, there was a busy tomb. Hard for a dead person to get any rest." He paused. "Not that yer descendants will have to worry about *that* ..."

He looked out of the corner of his eye and saw Oxford was seething. It had nothing to do with Falstaff's refusal to answer Oxford's questions, or even the remark about Oxford not needing a tomb. It was because Falstaff was winning what had turned into a 'goad' contest, a subcategory of wit contests Oxford usually won. Not this time, though. Falstaff grinned. Oxford forced himself to calm down.

"All right. Bacton is closer than Scotland," Oxford admitted, referring to how far Falstaff had to go to find Yorick and Joan Jockey.

"Aye. Thank goodness for that," Falstaff said, basking in Oxford's silent acknowledgement that the big man was winning. "Blanche Parry was descended from a relative of William Herbert, 1st Earl of Pembroke. When she went up to London, she took a girl with her as maid who stayed till Blanche died in 1590. The girl is now an old lady living in a cottage behind the Bacton church. I'm hoping she might know something. I'll bring her some sweets and gossip from London." He smiled to himself. "Jack'll see what he can pry out of her. Old ladies love to give up secrets to a handsome knight paying them court." He began to imagine her as a young lady, himself as a young man, too.

Oxford interrupted his revery. "And when do you leave?" His tone made clear Falstaff should be going out the door.

"Oh," Falstaff said, lying over on his side like an old barnacled whale rolling over to dive beneath the sea. "Any day now. It took me quite a while to find out who worked in the palace back then. It's not something that's published in a listing, you know. Tiring it was." He sighed and disappeared below the table.

"And if the young-girl-now-old-lady doesn't remember?"

"On to Wilton, my lord," Falstaff said unseen. "Some of the people who followed Blanche to court found work at Wilton when their services were no longer needed. Wilton needs hundreds to keep it up. If no luck, there, then on to Titchfield, where Southampton lives. I'm told he was one of two sons."

"Two?" Oxford asked. "His father only had one son."

"There are rumors there were two. One may have gotten lost. Or died. Or switched. They all look alike, don't they? Little children?"

Oxford had to agree: they *did* all look alike. His son looked like every other child he saw in London. If Southampton was Elizabeth's child, he could have been swapped for another at Titchfield, what with wet nurses and all. Children were so rarely seen or heard in the vast mansions nobles lived in, who would have noticed a child swapped out for another one?

He sat up. Could someone switch Lil Henry, he wondered, and no one notice? No: Elspeth was with him all the time. She would never let that happen. But this made Oxford realize he hadn't seen his son in weeks. Where was he? What does Elspeth do with him? It can't be much, he thought, because she's either in the garden digging up the ground or upstairs moaning in front of her Bible. So, who was raising Lil Henry, he wondered?

"I have high hopes, my lord," Falstaff rumbled from beneath the other side of the table, startling Oxford. "It's only been twenty years. I'll rest up a bit and be on my way. And you?"

"I owe a Jew a play."

"Better than owing him money."

William

William Shackspear brushed his way past Tobias and strode into the library. Oxford and Robin were seated at the table. They looked up.

"My lord," he said in a tense voice. "I have it on good authority that *your* play - *As You Like It* - contains an exchange between a character named Touchstone and one named 'William,' in which Touchstone tells 'William' to depart immediately or suffer death a thousand different ways."

"A hundred and fifty," Oxford said. Shackspear didn't understand. "Different ways for 'William' to die," Oxford explained.

It was obvious that Shackspear had not read the play, *which he had supposedly written,* Oxford angrily reminded himself.

"Oh," Shackspear said. But Oxford had not answered his question: "Is this 'William' me?" he asked.

"William?"

"Yes?" Shackspear said, thinking Oxford had asked him a question, then realizing Oxford was, as usual, trying to confuse him. "I am asking about the character 'William' in *your* play. Is he me?"

"Ipse?"

"Ipse?"

"He himself."

"Me myself?"

Oxford smiled. He was having a good time. "Of course not. The character named 'William' in *your* play is a country bumpkin. Unlearned. Unlettered. Uneducated. Dull. How could such a character be you, the 'western comet blazing across the English stage,' the 'rustic genius from Warwickshire?'"

Shackspear liked hearing he was a 'comet' and a 'rustic genius,' except that he had learned he shouldn't trust anything Oxford said. He felt at sea when he was with his lordship,

despite the fact he had never been to sea. These thoughts —
'feeling he was at sea' whilst never having been to sea —
unnerved him. The concept kept coming back to him in a
loop, like a burglar running around a house at night, a thought
that further unnerved him.

And Oxford's supposed compliments took him in
another direction. He had come up to London to dazzle the
theater with his plays but his first venture had emptied the
Rose before the third act. Oxford collaborated with him on
Titus Andronicus, which became a smash. It played at the Rose
thirty-seven times. Shackspear might claim a word or two, but
the play was otherwise entirely Oxford's.

After *Titus,* Shackspear assumed he would take a larger
role in writing the plays that followed but found himself
letting Oxford write everything instead. *The man was so damn
good!* he told himself. There was also the fame that came from
being hailed as author, which seduced him into letting Oxford
continue to write the plays that he then carried to the
playhouses as his.

The way Oxford had treated him in *As You Like It,*
however, pushed him to finally say enough was enough. He
thought he could now pick up his pen and write plays without
Oxford's help. After all, hadn't he added key scenes to *Two
Gentlemen* and *Romeo and Juliet?* Hermia and Helena in
Midsummer?

"Everyone is *laughing* at me, my lord. They pull me aside,
drop their voices, and ask how I could write a play with a
character in it named 'William' *who is driven from the stage with
threats of being killed a thousand different ways!*"

"A good question," Oxford said, ignoring Shackspear's
continued failure to get the number right. "And how have you
responded?"

"I could only think to say I had written other lines for
'William' to speak but that they must have been cut from the
cue roll."

"An excellent answer."

Shackspear was still exasperated. "And I am told, on good
report, my lord, that when the players arrived at Hampton
Court, not one of them would take the part of 'William.' A
footman, of all people, was found standing next to a carriage
and talked into acting the part."

"Oh, perfectly cast." Shackspear didn't understand. "And a compliment to you, don't you think?"

Shackspear hadn't thought of this. He wasn't quite sure he understood what Oxford was saying. "I guess."

"But Willum, it was a court play for the queen; that's all. It will never be brought to the public stage. The audience has to work too hard to understand what is going on. It will soon be forgotten. Don't bother your handsome featherhead about it."

This reminded Shackspear that he had forgotten to take off his hat, the one with the turkey feather on it. He snatched it off his head. Despite what Oxford had said, he didn't believe him. *As You Like It* would be staged again, he thought, but William would not be in it. He would make sure of that.

This decision emboldened him. He jammed his hat back on his head. "I can tell you one thing, my lord. I will never carry paper to the theater for you again … *without reading every word of it!*" He had wanted to say he was done with Oxford but couldn't bring himself to say it.

"An excellent idea."

He left. Oxford chuckled to himself as he watched him go. "A footman."

Robin did not share his master's joy. "He knows you're laughing at him, my lord."

"Of course, he does. It is *his* price for the fame he gets by claiming he is me." His dark face made it clear that he would brook no ex-*pressions of sympathy for the hack from Stratford.

"The Jew was not outside this morning," Robin said.

"He wasn't?"

"He apparently thinks he has accomplished his mission."

Oxford nodded.

"And the play you work on for him is set where?"

"Venice. A beautiful woman is courted by several men. One is a young man named Bassanio who wants to marry her. Unfortunately, he does not have the money to buy the clothes and jewelry he needs to convince her to marry him. He goes to a rich merchant named Antonio to borrow what he needs. They are good friends. *Very good friends*, I should add. Antonio is willing to help him but he has no cash because his ships are at sea. Antonio decides to borrow what Bassanio needs from a Jewish moneylender. The Jew agrees to loan Antonio the money if Antonio gives his bond to pay it back. Antonio's ships sink and the Jew will demand his bond."

"And the bond is?"

"A pound of flesh."

Robin's jaw dropped open. "A pound of flesh?"

"To be cut off and taken from what part of your body pleaseth me."

"The Jew says this?"

"It's what he and Antonio agree to."

"My lord! Antonio will die if the Jew cuts a pound of flesh from him."

"Probably."

"Will this be done on stage?"

"Possibly."

Robin's eyes grew bigger.

"There will be a trial, of course. A wonderful trial! The Jew will demand justice." A glow appeared in Oxford's eyes. He moved to the end of the table. "Is he entitled to justice? The terms are clear, as is the penalty on default."

"My lord! How can you resolve this?"

"I will blend Bassanio's love story with justice for the Jew. It will be difficult." He sat down and pulled papers in front of him. He began to hum.

"May I help?"

"No."

Robin, disappointed, left the library.

~ 116 ~
Justice

For a Jew?" Robin asked. "A Jew can't get justice even when he converts!"

"My little page is full of indignation this morning."

"I am thinking of Dr. López."

"Who died because he was going to poison the queen."

"No, he wasn't! You don't believe that!" Oxford's face showed he didn't. "He was a *Christian!*" Robin went on. "He said he loved Jesus and the queen. He spoke these words as he was about to die! Nobody lies when they are about to die!"

Oxford knew the law agreed with Robin, but what if López had fooled them all, his last words given as his 'bond,' to save his family? Michael Lok had said as much.

The vision of the executioner holding up the poor man's heart flooded into him. 'López's heart' he said to himself. 'López's heart' will be the 'pound of flesh. And the Jew's name will be Shylock, for Michael Lok, the man to whom Oxford still owed £3,000 for funding Frobisher's voyages to the new world. Michael Lok had agreed to void the bond if Oxford wrote a play that showed Jews as human beings: "*If you prick us, do we not bleed? if you tickle us, do we not laugh? if you poison us, do we not die?*" Oxford said aloud.

"My lord?" Robin asked, bringing Oxford back to the library.

"The name of the Jew shall be Shylock; *The Jew of Venice* the play." He leapt up and went out into the street.

The Jew of Venice

T*he Jew of Venice,* I call it," Shackspear announced proudly, bearing the manuscript Oxford had given him into the Curtain. Richard Burbage was by his side. They went into a small office. Shackspear laid the manuscript on a table and stepped aside. "I daresay, Richard, you will once again star across the heavens. Only *you* can play the Jew."

Burbage grunted. He opened the manuscript and began to read. He knew Shackspear's praise meant he would give the manuscript to Alleyn if he turned it down. Or the script had already been offered to him and rejected. "Has Alleyn seen this?"

"Not yet." Shackspear reached over to roll up the script. He started to put it under his arm. "I'm sure he'd be interested in playing the Jew. It's just a hop, skip, and a short boat ride across the Thames to Bankside ..."

"No need," Burbage said, pulling the script out of Shackspear's hands. "He may be a Jew," Burbage was, referring now to Alleyn, who was *not* a Jew, "but that does not mean he can *act* the part of a Jew. Only a great *Christian* actor can bring the Jew to life for a Christian audience, and that actor is me. I can already sense how I will move, how I will lean into those who stand near me. I will dye my hair red." He spread out the script and began to read.

Shackspear relaxed his grip but didn't leave. He watched Burbage read through the script, grunting as he turned pages. "Well, this Jew is no Barabbas," he said, referring to Christopher Marlowe's Jew.

"No, indeed." Shackspear had read the script this time. No 'William' in this one.

"Yes," Burbage said, reading further. "Oh, choice. Shylock will loan money to Antonio but the bond will be a pound of flesh." Burbage looked up at Shackspear. "A pound of flesh! And the Jew will carve it from the merchant!" He raised his arm like he had a knife in his hand. He was, in his mind, already carving into Antonio.

Shackspear shook his head. "Not exactly. The Jew gets close, but he never cuts him."

Burbage dropped his arm. "Why not?

"He demands his bond when the merchant fails to repay the loan, of course. He says to the judge," Shackspear continued:

> *The pound of flesh which I demand of him,*
> *Is dearly bought; 'tis mine and I will have it.*
> *I stand for judgment: answer; shall I have it?*

"But the judge tries to get Shylock to forgo the bond. He asks him to be merciful:"

> *The quality of mercy is not strain'd,*
> *It droppeth as the gentle rain from heaven*
> *Upon the place beneath: it is twice bless'd;*
> *It blesseth him that gives and him that takes.*

Burbage was not impressed. "That may get some nods from the Sisters of We-Love-Every-One, William, but the groundlings hear this in St. Paul's."

"Oh, have no fear. Shylock will have none of mercy: *I crave the law, the penalty and forfeit of my bond.*"

"Good. Good," Burbage said. He turned back to the script. "The judge says Shylock is right! He tells Shylock to sharpen his knife! But he doesn't get to use it, you say?"

"No."

"What stops him?"

"The judge will give Shylock judgment and tell him he can *cut off the pound of flesh, but no more nor less.* If he doesn't cut off exactly one pound, or the merchant dies, all of Shylock's goods will be confiscated. Faced with this, the Jew decides to forgo his bond."

"What?" Burbage exclaimed. "He has to carve up the merchant, doesn't he?" His arm came up again. "Imagine how this will look on the stage."

"No. The merchant will give Shylock back his loan, having borrowed it from another, and go home. What's wrong with that?"

"Who do ye think will be in the audience: a bunch of Jews?"

Shackspear didn't know what to say to this. He hadn't thought about the audience. He remembered Oxford telling him the pound of flesh story was in all the sources. "The story is extent, Richard. It's in all the sources."

"I don't care if it's 'in the sources.' We have to make it better." He flipped the script over and grabbed a pen. "The Jew is an alien, is he not?" Shackspear nodded. "And he has threatened the life of a Venetian citizen, has he not?" Shackspear nodded again. "He was going to cut a pound of flesh from him, wasn't he?" Burbage continued. How was Antonio going to survive that?"

Shackspear finally understood. But he had never changed one of Oxford's scripts. He had always treated Oxford's plays as if they were the Ten Commandments. Oxford was God; Shackspear was Moses. Moses only delivered; he didn't edit.

But the thought of *adding* to a play made Shackspear giddy. If he did, he would finally be striking out on his own.

"You're right," Shackspear said forcefully. "Shylock has threatened the life of a Venetian. The judge will tell the Jew he's in trouble:

> *He that seeks the life of any citizen,*
> *The party 'gainst the which he doth contrive*
> *Shall seize one half his goods; the other half*
> *Comes to the privy coffer of the state.*

Here Shackspear gestured for Burbage to take down his words. If he were to be his own man, he thought, he would dictate like Oxford did. He pointed to the blank paper on the table. "You are better at this than I am," he said to Burbage, doing what he always did, which was to get other people to do his work. Burbage pulled a stool over and began to write. Shackspear continued.

> *And the offender's life lies in the mercy*
> *Of the Duke only, 'gainst all other voice.*

Shackspear was feeling good. "And, since I am of a benevolent nature at the moment, the Duke shall show the Jew what Christian mercy is like:

> *That thou shalt see the difference of our spirit,*
> *I pardon thee thy life before thou ask it.*
> *For half thy wealth, it is Antonio's;*
> *The other half comes to the general state.*

"Oh, excellent. The Jew loses everything."

This made Shackspear suddenly feel apprehensive. What would Oxford do when he saw the changes in the script?

"Maybe this is going too far?" he asked. Burbage looked at him. "Not that I have any concern for the Jew, of course, or the Jews," Shackspear quickly added, laughing nervously, "but maybe we shouldn't strip Shylock quite so bare? After all, Antonio is supposed to be the Christian here. Maybe we should make him more … merciful. What if Antonio takes only the *use* of Shylock's money during his lifetime?"

"And then where would it go?"

Shackspear thought for a moment. "To the Jew's daughter and the Christian she has run off with!"

"Excellent," Burbage said. He was looking at Shackspear in a different way. "You have experience in these matters. You are clever." Shackspear liked this. He fluffed up a bit. There weren't many times he felt clever, but if Burbage thought he was, he'd take it.

He said nothing. Isn't that what Her Majesty had told him to do when she coupled him to Oxford? He never answered questions, particularly after a play, but no one ever noticed. Silence apparently made people think more highly of him. He was acquiring gravitas, the way birds acquire feathers or bears fur.

"So, what should we add?"

"I would have Antonio say the following:

> *So it please my lord the Duke*
> *I will quit the fine for one half of the Jew's goods*
> *As long as he will let me have*
> *The other half in use, to render it*
> *Upon his death unto the gentleman*
> *That lately stole his daughter.*

Burbage chuckled. "'Stole' his daughter. A lovely reminder of the Jew's humiliation."

Shackspear agreed. "But Antonio isn't finished:

> *Two things provided more: that for this favor*
> *He presently become a Christian;*
> *The other, that he do record a gift,*
> *Here in the court, of all he dies possessed*
> *Unto his son Lorenzo and his daughter.*

"Oh," Burbage crowed, "how merciful! Instead of half his estate going to Venice and the other half to Antonio, Antonio will let the Jew have the use of his estate for life with the balance at his death going to the Jew's daughter and his new 'son,' the Christian boy who has stolen his daughter! And Shylock becomes a Christian! What could be more merciful than that?"

Shackspear wasn't sure. Forcing a Jew to convert to Christianity might be good for Christianity but was it good for the Jew? Besides, how does one ever know whether a Jew has really converted? He's still a Jew, isn't he? Did López lie when he cried out that he was a Christian as the executioner cut into him? Shackspear felt a vague feeling of wonder and admiration well up in his bosom.

But would God forgive López for lying because he did it out of love for his family? A Christian God might not, but would a Jewish God forgive him? Shackspear's brain rattled on, causing more confusion. He felt a headache coming.

"Richard, would ye turn Turk if ye were captured by a Muslim? Or Jew if ye were sold to a Jewish merchant?"

"Not something to worry about this week."

Shackspear wished he had answered his question. Maybe his headache was caused by what Oxford would do to him if he found out *The Jew* had been altered.

Burbage was still looking through the script. "I say, William, some of this makes the Jew out to be very human."

"These are lines spoken early in the play, Richard. By the end, he is stripped of his property and forced to become a Christian. Leave it at that."

Shackspear gathered up the script and turned toward the door. "I'll come by tomorrow morning to work out the sheets for the players. The rest is a romance between a young man and a rich woman pursued by many suitors. There will be caskets for them to choose which one marries the bride."

He left. 'Things are going to change,' Shackspear said to himself as he left. Revenues from tenements and fees from the stews he and Langley controlled were growing. His share from the Lord Chamberlain's Men was also on the rise. Very satisfying, he thought. Soon he would be both famous *and* rich. He expected *The Jew of Venice* would be well-received and further cement his reputation.

Whistling to himself, he headed off toward Bishopsgate. He felt entitled to a pint. Not at the Boar's Head. Falstaff might be there. Nothing ever good came from running into him. The fat knight was obviously jealous of Shackspear's growing relationship with the earl. 'No,' he said almost aloud, as he rounded into Bishopsgate and headed downhill. 'I'll to the Mermaid. Ben Jonson might be there. He thinks he's an actor. Maybe I can talk him into playing Bassanio. Yes. That would be interesting. I shall offer him the role of Bassanio.'

~ 118 ~
The Jew of Venice at the Curtain

Richard Burbage, as the Jew of Venice, his hair dyed red, his body wrapped in a heavy gabardine cloak that fell to the top of his shoes, staggered across the stage. His shambling, interminable walk back to the tiring room after uttering his last line – *I pray you give me leave to go from hence: I am not well* – was cheered by some in the audience and jeered by others. He was hit by fruit and knuckle bones from the floor of the pit, some thudding into his back with an audible thwack. Burbage's performance would be remembered by all. Everything that preceded his slow disappearance off stage was mere window dressing, an excuse for Portia and Nerissa to give their male partners awkward moments before everyone went off to supper.

"How different from Marlowe's Barabas," Elizabeth remarked. "He was all darkness and evil. Shylock here is presented almost … almost human." She glanced around, looking for Oxford, who she saw moving rapidly toward the door to the street. "My lord," she said. It was low enough that Oxford could have claimed he hadn't heard it but he had. He turned around. She leaned out into the empty theater.

"Your Majesty." He bowed slightly.

"I liked being Portia more than Titania or Rosalind."

"If you say so." She could tell he was angry.

"Well, I do" she said, wondering what was causing him to be out of sorts. "And the suitors. Are they not *my* suitors?"

"Some might say they were the suitors who sought Mary Queen of Scot's hand, Your Majesty."

She bristled. "Wasn't my choice of suitors governed by the will of a father? As Portia so excellently put it, '*my will curbed by the will of a dead father*'? Didn't Henry hem me in with *his* will?"

Oxford was forced to agree.

"And who else," Elizabeth continued, shifting from being confidant to sovereign, "could dispense mercy that '*becomes the throned monarch better than his crown?*'"

Oxford nodded again.

"So why doth thou sway and fret in front of me now? You've written a work of art, my lord, a love story, a trial about justice, and, oh yes, £3,000, of course. But I must say I think you were a bit hard on the Jew at the end. I guess you thought too much Christianity in a Jew would not go over well in the theater, eh?"

Oxford was having trouble keeping a forced smile on his face.

"Ah. Someone *else* may have had that thought."

Oxford's eyes pleaded with her to let him go.

She waved him away.

Oxford found Shackspear in the Mermaid. Ben Jonson had his arm around Shackspear's shoulders. He was calling himself 'Bassanio.'

"Willum," Oxford said in a low voice. He gestured for Jonson to go away. Jonson saw a man who looked like he wanted to kill someone a thousand different ways. He took his arm off Shackspear's shoulder and walked away. "Come with me," Oxford said.

He went over to the front door and out into the street. Shackspear followed him, feeling like he was back in Stratford grammar school and the headmaster was going to give him a licking. Shackspear had a good idea why Oxford was angry. He straightened his back. If his lordship overreacted, he would end his 'servitude' to him. It was time to go out on his own.

Oxford went around the corner into Bread Street. He found an empty alley. He turned around and put his face up against Shackspear's. "How dare you make changes to *The Jew*. Don't you *ever* do that again! You will go back to the Curtain and get the script from Burbage. You will bring it to me. I will correct it, after which you will take it back to Burbage and make him understand *in no uncertain terms* that Richard Topcliffe will visit him in the name of the queen if he makes any further changes to it. This will be the same for any other play I give you in the future. You have forgotten your place."

"And you, yours, my lord."

"What?"

"The world knows your plays as mine, my lord. They know nothing of the Earl of Oxford. The queen ordered *you* to stop writing plays but she didn't tell *me* to stop. I do not need you anymore. Goodbye, my lord. My audience and immortal fame await me."

He marched out into Bread Street and headed back to the Mermaid, leaving an astonished Earl of Oxford behind him.

1596

~ 119 ~
Hedingham

Hedingham," Robin said happily. "We're going to Hedingham." He marveled at the sound of the word.

"Yes," Oxford said, sorting through some papers.

"Will Lil Henry be coming with us?"

"No. His mother is off to Staffordshire to show him off to her relatives. The roads have finally dried out."

Robin thought he saw something flick across Oxford's face. His master and her ladyship had seen little of each other lately. Robin initially thought Oxford might have been pleased to be left behind, but her leaving had somehow put him out of sorts.

"Will Falstaff be coming with us?" Robin asked.

"I have no idea where he is. Off to Wales, was the last thing I heard."

"I miss him."

"Then visit him when he comes back," Oxford said acerbically as he continued to look through the papers.

"Will Shackspear visit?"

"Certainly not." Oxford turned to look at Robin. "Shacksmear rewrote *The Jew* and destroyed it. I am through with him."

Robin's jaw dropped. "Does that mean no more plays, my lord?"

"I don't know." Oxford pushed some papers to his right in an irritated gesture. "I thought I had brought *Timon of Athens* down from the trunk of plays upstairs, but I can't find it."

"The play you pulled out and threw on the floor? The play you told me was 'an effort distilled from anger?' A play about a man who gives everything to his friends who then abandon him when he has nothing left?"

Oxford nodded again, surprised Robin remembered so much from only a glance at the play. They had not talked about it for years.

Robin remembered more. "No female characters. No romance. You told me at the time: 'Never write from anger, Robin. Your effort will be as cold as Damascus steel on a winter morning.'"

Oxford was still looking through papers in front of him. "True."

121

"We are still to Hedingham, are we not?"

Oxford nodded.

"And maybe Cambridge?"

"Perhaps."

"I'll pack."

"Do."

--------⊛⟨⊛⟩⊛--------

Hedingham was a long ride from Oxford Court. Oxford and Robin were tired when they clattered through Hedingham village. The houses and buildings were rundown or abandoned. Robin had been told the people who staffed the castle lived there, or at least until Oxford's father died and Oxford went off to London to become Burghley's ward. With Oxford gone, staff and servants melted away, leaving many homes in the village abandoned and boarded-up.

Castle Lane was a narrow way that curved left around a copse of trees to the top of a hill that overlooked the village. A 100-foot-high Norman Keep rose into the sky at the top. It was surrounded by a great hall, chapel, kitchens, apartments, stables, granaries, butts, a tennis court, and an open area for tournaments. Many of the buildings showed the decades of neglect and the efforts of the Earl of Leicester to steal as much as he could while he was guardian of Oxford's lands, even down to the lead gutters.

Digby, Hedingham's steward, was waiting for them at the top of the hill.

"My lord," he said warmly. He took the reins to Oxford's horse.

"Thomas," Oxford replied. He climbed down. He gestured to Robin. "Robin, my page."

Digby nodded to Robin and took the reins to his horse as well. "A venison stew awaits you in the dining hall, if you would be so kind as to follow me." He took Oxford and Robin across the drawbridge that separated the Keep from the stables and outbuildings. Oxford, tired and hungry, only wanted to eat something and go to bed. Robin lagged behind, staring up at the tower that loomed over them. He thought it high enough to reach the heavens. The individual stones were the size of giant hay bales.

"Watch yerself, young sir," Digby said, as he began to climb the steps into the first floor of the Keep. "The doorstep'll get ye."

Robin looked down. Digby was right. The steps were bigger than any he had seen in London. Giants again!

He and his master were soon well-fed. Oxford headed up to sleep in a room high above them while Robin happily slipped into a niche in the stone walls that was just wide enough for him. He slept like a baby.

Oxford went hunting the next day with Digby. Robin was not asked to come along, which suited him fine. He climbed to the top of the Keep and spent most of the day gazing out over the Essex countryside, a quilt work of fields and streams. He dreamed he was Robert de Vere, 3rd Earl of Oxford, one of the barons who forced King John to sign Magna Carta but who later lost the Keep to John in a bloody siege. Robin leaned over the side and swore he could hear soldiers fighting below him.

Oxford and Digby returned with a fat doe at the end of the day. Digby butchered it on a table near the drawbridge. Throwing the offal to the dogs, two assistants carried the meat off to be aged. "I'll hang it for ten days," Digby said, "but look at this." He held up two miniature fawns, one in each hand. "She would have birthed 'em in a few days." Oxford could see faint spots on the flanks of the carcasses. "Nothing better," Digby said with relish, eyeing Oxford. "A quick toss in a pan with a little cream, some saffron to color and flavor them. Nutmeg - six or seven, I think - ginger, raisins 'o the sun, and prunes, onions, all baked in a pie."

"It should be extraordinary," Oxford said.

Robin came up. He had been exploring a dovecote on the edge of the hill that had housed a thousand doves before it was abandoned and stripped. Oxford greeted him. "Well, my young page; are we to Cambridge tomorrow?"

Robin could see that the outing had been good for his master. "We are," Robin forced his eyes to look away from Digby and what he was doing.

"Freshwater prawns are what I crave. The Cam is full of them at this time of the year. We will partake and return."

Cambridge

Oxford and Robin rode down to the village the next morning and out the other side. They headed north through the villages that dotted the gentle Essex countryside - Horseheath and Steeple Bumpstead, Haverhill and Little Abington - before descending into Cambridge.

Oxford was still feeling good. His spirits picked up even more when Cambridge came into view. He waved Robin up next to him. "Oxford University claims it is older than Cambridge," he said. "Those who went to school there say Oxford scholars founded Cambridge here when they were forced to flee when Oxford town hung three students for causing the death of a woman. The university felt the students should have been tried by ecclesiastical authorities. If they had, they would have been acquitted."

"And the woman?"

"What about the woman?"

"What had the students done to her?"

"Who knows? She is lost in the history of time."

Robin's face fell. Oxford did not see it.

"I was eight when I came here," Oxford continued. "I was admitted to Queens' College as an impubes."

"That sounds disgusting."

"It was. Queen Mary died a week after I arrived. She had devoted her reign to making England Catholic again. Elizabeth, our right royal sovereign, succeeded her and reversed course. While Mary lived, many claimed they were Catholics, Lord Burghley among them. When she died, many claimed they had never left the Anglican church, Lord Burghley among them again. The university colleges, run by religious orders, suffered. Those who claimed they had always been Anglicans attacked those who had remained Catholic. As a result, the beginning of my formal education was turbulent."

"Did you have any idea what was going on?"

"Very little. Thomas Fowle of St. John's was my first tutor, but the university thought him too Catholic and dismissed him. Sir Thomas

Smith took his place. He remained my tutor, even after I became a royal ward and moved to Cecil House on the Strand."

"Was he the old man you talked to at Runnymede when we were on our way to Windsor?"

"Yes. Although I'm not sure he knew who I was."

"Did you stay here long?"

"No. I left before the end of the first term. The president and most of the tutors had already fled, afraid they would also be labeled Catholic. Sir Thomas was building a new home in Theydon Mount near Epping and I went there. When my father died, I went to Cecil House. Lady Mildred took over my education. Sir Thomas visited to make sure it was up to what he thought it should be."

They rode across the bridge into Cambridge. A short distance further, they turned off Silver Street and dismounted in front of the Gatehouse to Queens' College. Porters took their horses.

"We'll look for Finley," Oxford said. "I sent a message ahead. He was here when I came to Queens. He stayed here, teaching from time to time and hoping to convince the college to allow plays to be studied alongside poetry and rhetoric."

"I thought the universities considered plays the work of the devil."

"They do. Finley, always on a hopeless quest, thinks he can convince them otherwise."

A tall, lanky man came out. "My lord," he said enthusiastically.

"Finley," Oxford replied. "My page, Robin." He gestured toward Robin.

"Pleased," Finley replied. "You look well, my lord. Greetings from Cambridge." Without pause, he raced on, obviously enthused to have Oxford as his guest. "We've had three plays put on this year, my lord. The students loved them — entertainment and no work for them — but a don or two attended. I am winning."

His long hair flapped over his shoulders like waves at a Norfolk beach. His clothes hung off him, hand-me-downs from someone even bigger than he was. He looked, as always, Oxford thought, like an unmade bed. He probably hadn't eaten a decent meal in months, yet Oxford had never heard him complain of hunger. Perhaps he lived on morning dew, as some starving poets claimed they did.

"And, pray tell," Finley continued, "what I can do for my Earl of Oxenford this day?"

"Prawns," Oxford replied.

"Of course. They still hide beneath the Cam's velvet banks."

"Is Double-Blind Billy still doling them out from his pushcart?" Oxford turned to Robin. "The man is blind in both eyes and wears eyeglasses made of black glass."

"Was," Finley said. "The Billy you knew died years ago. However, his son carries on his father's trade. Under the same name, in fact."

"The same name?" Finley nodded. "And is he blind in both eyes, like his father?" Oxford asked.

"Of course."

This surprised both Oxford and Robin. "How can a blind man roast prawns?" Robin wondered. "How can he know where they are on the grill?"

Finley agreed. "I wonder myself, Robin, but he always seems to know where they are and when to pull them off. Blind people have extraordinary senses, you know."

Something in the way Finley said this made Oxford realize Double-Blind Billy was not blind. Oxford laughed. "Oh, who is the blind man now?"

"As I was blind, my lord, thinking Shackspear wrote *Titus, The Comedy of Errors, Venus & Adonis,* and all the rest. Oh, and *Love's Labour's Lost,* although it is beyond me why someone would give a name to a play that invites so many misspellings." He looked exasperated.

Oxford smiled. "Someone in love with apostrophes," he said.

"And alliteration," Robin chimed in.

Finley shook his head. "It causes us so much trouble when we try to catalogue and index them."

Oxford commiserated with him. But he was surprised to hear Finley hadn't known Oxford had written the plays. "How did your 'sight' return?" he asked.

"I last saw you in London, my lord, at the Countess of Southampton's wedding to Sir Thomas Heneage. I had been told *A Double Maske* – I know it's now being staged as *Love's Labour's Lost* – was to be performed after the ceremony and slipped in to see it. Shackspear was touted as being the author. He was not there, of course, but I had come up to London for more than seeing a play. I was looking for scripts. I need them to bring the study of the theater into academia but they are very difficult to get a look at. The companies buy them and lock them away in a strongbox. The biggest man in the house guards it. They don't publish them because, if they did, they couldn't put them on again. Ergo, scripts are difficult for me to come by."

"But, then, where do the quartos come from?" Robin asked.

"Aye. Good question. The publishers have no more access to proper scripts than I do. To get around this, they pay actors and theatergoers to write down what they hear during a performance. They rush these notes into print whilst always claiming them 'newly corrected' and 'as played before Her Majesty, the Queen,' when they are nowhere near what the public heard in the theater."

He was disgusted. "How can I prepare a course of study for a field of art that is not yet twenty years old," he complained, looking at Robin to make sure he was listening, "when the written record is so incomplete and what little exists is inaccurate!"

"And?" Oxford asked. Finley had not answered his question: "How *did* you find out Shackspear was not the author?"

"The same way I found out Double-Blind Billy wasn't blind. Watch and observe, my mother always said. I ran Shackspear down in the Mermaid. It was not difficult to engage him in conversation since he was full of himself and the beer he had been drinking. It took no time to realize the man in front of me could not have written the plays I love. A few more questions, a few more blank looks, a shrug, followed by a smug – *who's-going-to-out-me?* – and the dark glasses fell off my face!"

"Indeed."

"Yes. With him cleared out of the way, you immediately appeared. *Voila!* And that is how I recovered my sight!"

They all laughed.

"On that note, it is time for prawns, is it not?"

"It is indeed."

Finley, with his long legs, strode off toward the river, Oxford and Robin in tow. They went over the wooden bridge that crossed the Cam to where they could see smoke curling up from a cart parked under a willow tree.

"Billy," Finley called out. "Three freshwater prawns in Diablo sauce, if you please."

A small man turned in their direction. The afternoon sun reflected off his round black eyeglasses. Finley held up three fingers. "Aye, Dr. Finley. Three prawns." He turned to the grill behind him.

"Diablo sauce?" Robin asked.

"Billy's prawns are steeped in malt-vinegar and brushed with a sauce Billy says he got from a Spanish sailor shipwrecked off Boddam Head when the Spanish Armada was fleeing home around Scotland."

"'*Dr. Finley*'," Oxford said appreciatively. Finley looked at him, puzzled. "Billy just called you Dr. Finley," Oxford cocked an eye at Finley.

Finley shrugged. "I have more degrees than published plays," he said. "I don't know which is worse."

Oxford laughed. "But, if Shackspear did not write the plays, how did you conclude I did?"

Finley became serious. "These degrees I have acquired have been to expand my register, as they say about singers and composers, so I can analyze and understand plays. I have assembled a library of documents, which I will donate to Queens when appropriate. What I have learned, however, tells me that the man who wrote the plays so many have come to love – *Titus Andronicus*; *The Comedy of Errors*; *Two Gentlemen of Verona*; *Henry VI* …"

"*King John*," Oxford couldn't keep himself from adding.

"Yes," Finley agreed. "The man who wrote them is standing in front of me as we speak. Once you know who the author is, the plays open up like bottomless trunks, like the clowns that keep coming out of a trunk at a fair. They are bottomless because they contain so much more than one would think possible to put into a play." He glanced at Oxford to see what his guest thought of his leap into extravagant similes. "And once you know who the author is, you realize he likes to put himself into the plays as one of the characters. Benedict, for example. Sometimes twice! *Two Gentlemen*, where he is Proteus *and* Valentine!"

"Mercutio and Benvolio!" Robin blurted out.

Finley was surprised, both because the little page had jumped into the conversation and because he had identified something Finley had missed. "I didn't realize that, little Robin. Thank you. And *Romeo* makes three, of course. Oberon and Bottom in *Midsummer*," he added, as more thoughts came tumbling out."

"Wait till you see him in *Hamlet*," Oxford said.

"Oh!" Finley exclaimed. He put a hand to his chest. "And when will that be?"

"When Pondus no longer walks the earth. He must be gone before I put on *Hamlet*. Even a double-blind spectator will know who

Polonius is. The Earl of Surrey will visit me twixt the departure of His Verbalness and his burial. It will be an interesting time."

This puzzled Finley and Robin, who knew nothing about the Earl of Surrey or 'His Verbalness.'

Double-Blind Billy handed them the prawns, each seared on a willow stick. Before they could peel off the shells, a queen's messenger thundered over the bridge and came to a halt in front of them. The messenger vaulted from his horse and dropped to one knee before Oxford.

"My lord," he said, holding out a rolled-up scroll tied with a dark red ribbon.

Oxford sighed and handed his prawn to Robin. He took the scroll, untied the ribbon, and opened it. "A play. For Accession Day."

"Congratulations," Finley said.

A broad smile spread across Robin's face.

"Thank you, but no thank you. I am done with plays," he announced." This was said to both Finley and Robin, as well as the messenger still kneeling before him.

"What?" Finley and Robin exclaimed.

"Or, rather, I am done with His Highness from Stratford, the son of a glover! Done with him, and thereby done with writing plays."

The messenger was still on one knee. Finley waved him up. The man rose. He had more. "Her Majesty instructed me to tell you that your lordship owes her three plays about King Henry IV and his son, Prince Hal."

"Oh, my God," Oxford said. He turned away in disgust. He dropped the scroll the messenger had given him. Robin retrieved it.

The messenger continued, sounding like he was quoting the queen's actual words, his voice shifting into a more nasally register: "'*Famous Victories* was a failed, juvenile attempt. It must be disinterred and brought to life. This much you owe your art.'"

"'*You have buried three plays in this coffin,*'" Robin said in a voice that mimicked the queen's.

The messenger, having heard the same voice the day before, almost guffawed. He forced a wooden smile onto his face.

Oxford glared at Robin, who found something to look at across the river. Finley, never having heard the queen speak, missed what the messenger and Oxford heard in Robin's voice.

Finley was at a loss. He could tell that Oxford was upset but not why. The messenger thought it an opportune time to inform them that Lord Hunsdon had died. "My lord, it is with great regret that I must also inform you that Lord Hunsdon died on July 22."

Oxford's jaw dropped. "Old Hunnie?" This shocked Finley and Robin, who had never heard Lord Hunsdon referred to this way, but not as much as the messenger, who was familiar with Hunsdon's nickname. "Great Harry's most successful blowby," Oxford said, shaking his head.

This the messenger had also heard, which made him even more uncomfortable. Everyone, including Hunsdon, thought he was the son of Henry VIII and Mary Boleyn, the *other* Boleyn girl. Elizabeth had ennobled Hunsdon for his loyal service, possibly because she knew he was her cousin at least, if not her half-brother.

The messenger had gained control of himself and thought he should complete his message, at least as it related to Lord Hunsdon. "The queen visited Lord Hunsdon on his deathbed. She wanted to make him Earl of Wiltshire, which he declined, telling her that if she did not count him worthy of the honor whilst he lived, he did not account himself worthy of it in death."

"Vintage Hunnie," Oxford acknowledged.

"The players thought well of him," Robin said. "He loved the theater."

Oxford agreed. *He also loved boys,* according to Christopher Marlowe, *which was the real reason he wanted to be Lord Chamberlain.* Oxford turned to the messenger. "Who has replaced him as Lord Chamberlain?"

"William Brooke, Tenth Baron Cobham."

Oxford groaned.

"Wherefore?" Finley asked. He didn't know who Cobham was.

"Cobham's oldest daughter is married to Sir Robert Cecil."

"Oh."

The messenger now worried the earl and his companions would start to wax eloquent about Sir Robert. This was a subject the messenger had *no* interest in hearing. No one worried about Hunsdon: he was dead; Sir Robert, on the other hand, was very much alive and running England now that his father, Lord Burghley, had taken to his sick bed.

"Baron Brooke has stepped fully into his new duties," the messenger announced. "He has ordered the theaters closed."

Oxford, Finley, and Robin looked at the messenger in disbelief. The messenger, in turn, was surprised. He had no idea why they would be upset to hear this. "Of course, the theaters are already closed because of the plague, and the City is always petitioning the Council to close the theaters, so the immediate effect of the Baron's order is unclear."

"And the odds?" Finley asked. Londoners bet on everything, from when someone would be executed to wild swings in law enforcement. He knew the bookmakers would have set odds on when the theaters would be closed if such an order had been made.

"Ten to one against, but the odds may have changed since I left."

Finley nodded. He turned to Oxford. "No worry. Brooke can bay at the moon. The people will never allow the theaters to be closed."

Robin was relieved to hear this but suddenly remembered Oxford had announced he was done with plays. "No more plays, my lord?" His lower lip quivered. Oxford waved a hand at the messenger, who leapt onto his horse and galloped over the bridge, happy to get away.

Robin moved himself around in front of Oxford. "No more plays, my lord?" He assumed a fierce countenance. "You don't need Shackspear, my lord." He sounded like a sergeant ordering a young recruit to buck up. "You can pick a new name for them. Or you can put *his* name on them. The queen won't care, even if she finds out. I'll take the scripts to Henslowe or Burbage. They won't care either." He looked pleased with himself, like a street urchin who had found a coin.

"They know, by the way" Finley said quietly.

"Who knows?" Oxford asked.

"Burbage and Henslowe."

"That I am the author?"

Finley nodded.

"Who else knows?"

"Can anyone keep a secret in the theater?" Finley asked.

"So why is it not common knowledge?"

"Because everyone loves a con, my lord. Particularly when everyone thinks they're the only ones who know it." He gestured toward Billy behind him. "Take Billy here. He's not blind, but when we figure out he's having us on, we smile and let him con the next customer. We don't share his secret; we keep it."

"A bit of theater," Robin chimed in.

Finley agreed. "The same for those who realize you wrote the plays. It's more fun to keep it a secret than tell the world. T'wouldn't be a secret, then, would it?"

"Ye can do it," Robin said firmly.

Oxford studied him. "Ye think?" He did not appear convinced.

Robin's head went up and down. "What can Shackspear do? He can't admit he *didn't* write the plays. He won't be famous anymore."

Finley joined in. "There are lots of plays by 'anonymous'. Make your next play by 'anonymous,' my lord. No one will care!"

Robin liked this. He could tell Oxford was wavering. "So, what shall it be" he asked.

"*Timon*," Oxford said. "It will keep the bitch away from me."

This startled Finley. He glanced around to see whether anyone had heard what Oxford had called the queen. He had cause to worry. Some 'protectors of the realm,' as they billed themselves, delighted in telling officers in her majesty's government what they heard in the streets. Finley knew of colleagues who had been taken away to be questioned, even tortured, about intemperate remarks they had made in the street or at a college meeting. To his relief, no one was in earshot.

"*Timon*, is old, my lord. Nothing newer?" he asked.

Oxford demurred. "No need. Robin will make it new."

Robin smiled. Finley did not. "Good for you, my lord, and good for Robin here, but not for those of us who wait for the streams of nectar and honey you can give us. New plays, my lord," Finley said sternly. He now sounded like a sergeant berating a new recruit. Maybe Robin had given him the courage to speak out. "New plays."

Oxford hesitated.

Robin, a mischievous look on his face, made like he would tap the side of Oxford's head. "We know they're up there. *Lots of them!*"

Oxford laughed. "Have I told you so?"

"You have indeed."

Robin and Finley waited.

Oxford gave in. "I am halfway through a tale I heard in Palermo."

"Sicily!" Finley said. "*Much Ado* is set in Messina. Tell me what Palermo is like, my lord. I fear I may never get there myself."

"A warm city spread out around a bay. Everyone spends their time outdoors, drinking, talking, and eating."

"And what did you do there?"

"I drank, I talked, I ate." They all laughed.

"But what happened while you were there?"

"I issued a challenge to fight anyone for the honor of the queen, but no one accepted. I met a Spaniard who had lost an arm at Lepanto who told me he was working on a story about a madman who tilts at windmills because he thinks they are dragons." Oxford chuckled at the memory. "His knight had a manservant who was wiser than he was."

"They always are." Finley said. He looked at Robin to see what Oxford's little page thought of this.

"I wasn't there," Robin said quickly. He didn't want to talk about servants smarter than their masters. "And what will this story be?"

"Jealousy."

Finley and Robin groaned.

"Is there anything else?" Oxford asked. He finished his prawn and threw his willow stick into the river. "I've had my prawn. Time to go."

He headed for the bridge. Finley came up next to him. "We are planning plays for the winter season, my lord. The students are excited. Original material. It should be fun. I think you would be proud to see the seeds I have planted. They are producing new works. Why, you could write one yourself," he added brightly.

"I've enough dealing with the queen," Oxford replied. "She will be hounding me for plays." Finley's disappointment was plain to see. Oxford saw it. He felt bad for so brusquely pushing away Finley's offer. "But let me know what you plan to put on and I will see if I can come back. For now, it is back to Hedingham. Robin will go on to London and give Henslowe *Timon*. After reworking it, I hope."

Robin nodded. "My second play," he said to Finley proudly.

"My condolences," Finley deadpanned. "An awful place to end up, in love with plays."

Oxford agreed.

"Isn't it?" Robin asked. He was beaming.

~ 121 ~
Filet of Unborn Fawn

Oxford and Robin returned to Hedingham where it became clear that Oxford was bored. Digby tried to get Oxford out of his doldrums by rising early each morning and taking him out to view the grounds. He thought it might recreate memories of his years spent growing up at Hedingham. Robin tagged along as they traversed the many paths that went past the dovecotes, the stables, the outbuildings in which the servants lived, the exercise yards, and the gardens for vegetables bordered by geraniums to keep out the pests. They set snares for hares the second morning and fished the pond the other side of Castle Lane in the afternoon.

But Oxford never stopped looking distracted. Digby and Nell, his wife, worked hard in the kitchens putting familiar dishes in front of him, but Digby knew it was only a matter of time before Oxford left for London. He decided to grace Oxford's final supper with venison from the deer they shot the first day.

The long table in the dining hall was covered with a white tapestry woven by weavers in Normandy. Digby said the Veres had brought it over when they crossed the Channel with William the Conqueror. A parade of dishes began to emerge from the corner stairwell. Sorrel soup was followed by baked pheasants hung to perfection before being put over the fire. The fawns appeared in a pie, its crisp top capping a bubbling broth made from ox tongue, shallots, and truffles, with spices the identity of which Nell would not divulge. Digby placed the pies in front of Oxford and Robin and sat down with one himself.

"Food you will never experience in London, my little Robin," he said, cutting into the pie in front of him.

Robin peeled back the crust on his pie and looked in at the medley of meat and vegetables. He inhaled the saffron, the nutmeg, the ginger and fresh cream. He cut himself a slice of the venison in the pie and swept it to his mouth. "Ah," he exclaimed, acknowledging that Digby had outdone himself.

"You like?" Digby asked. Robin nodded. "Filets of unborn fawns."

Robin stopped chewing. His jaw froze. He couldn't swallow. A rainbow of emotions ran across his face, a potpourri of surprise, awe, shock, and disgust. He looked like a sheep that had just been told he was going to the butchers instead of the barbers. "Yes" was all he managed to get out, his voice so high that he sounded like he had turned into a bird and was trying to fly out of the top of the Keep high above them. Oxford and Digby, eyes shut as they enjoyed Nell's masterpiece, did not realize how Robin had reacted to Digby's creation.

Robin thought he saw spots in the pie in front of him. The piece of meat at the back of his throat hung there, growing larger and more revolting. He imagined it growing legs. Hairy legs. He started to gag. "Sorry," was all he could say before bolting from the table and running outside.

Oxford and Digby watched him go. "He loved it till he found out what it was, eh? You?"

"Delicious," Oxford said. He dug into the pie for another piece.

"Such a strange reaction. It *is* delicious. Venison from a full-grown buck? Marvelous. From an unborn fawn? Repulsive." He shook his head. "Nothing is either good or bad but thinking makes it so, eh, my lord?"

"Hmm," Oxford said.

Digby reached over and pulled Robin's plate toward him. "I should have told him what it was *after* he had eaten it."

———◆◆◆◆———

The sun was not yet pushing its golden fingers through the treetops when Oxford and Robin left for London the next morning. They cantered down the hill and through the village. There would be no stops. Oxford was impatient to get back; so was Robin. They were both eager to return to the world of playwriting.

~ 122 ~
Two Plays; Two Failures

Oxford came around a corner into Bread Street and ran into Shackspear. "My lord!" Shackspear said, jumping back.

Oxford was startled as well. He started to go around Shackspear.

"My lord," Shackspear said again, putting up a hand but making sure he did not actually touch Oxford. "Much has happened."

"As it does every day," Oxford said, starting to go around Shackspear again.

"My son has died," Shackspear blurted out, shifting into Oxford's path again. He stood in front of Oxford, his eyes filled with grief. "You have also lost a son, have you not, my lord?"

"Yes," Oxford said, and was immediately angry with himself for sharing anything with the man in front of him. He had no wish to dredge up the loss of his first son, dead only two days after Nan had given birth to him. He pushed Shackspear aside.

"My lord," Shackspear said, still blocking Oxford's path, his hand now resting firmly against Oxford's shoulder. He leaned into Oxford. "I never went back to Stratford to be with him, always finding excuses for not going. I knew he lacked something. I was ashamed to see him; to be *with* him. He died alone, in Stratford, *never having known me!*"

Shackspear began to sob. "Now I am bereft, at my own cause, worse than if I had been told he had died *when he hadn't!*"

This startled Oxford. Up to now, Shackspear's outburst had only made Oxford think of the boy Nan had given him, but Shackspear's cry had thrust Oxford up against the loss of *another* son, his son by Elizabeth! 'He was but one hour mine,' he had exclaimed when told the child had died. *But he hadn't died!* His son had been smuggled out of the palace and raised as the Earl of Southampton!

Shackspear thought Oxford didn't understand Shackspear's loss.

"My lord, I would give anything to spend an afternoon fishing with my boy or watching him ride a pony I bought him."

Oxford, filled with anger at the queen, was surprised at this. "You bought him a pony?"

"No, but I would if I could." Shackspear began to sob again. *"But I can't,"* he wailed, collapsing into Oxford again.

Oxford pushed him away.

Shackspear tried to get control of himself. "How did *you* manage?" he asked.

"Stiff upper lip and all that," Oxford said sarcastically. Shackspear may have lost his Hamnet, but he had a son for a few years. *I have been denied mine!*

Shackspear heard the sarcasm in Oxford's voice. "Easy for you," he said, a sneer slipping into his voice. "Silver spoon. Land rents comin' in every month. Ye've had other sons. *I had one. I ignored him. And now he is gone!"*

Shackspear's despair was folding into contempt for Oxford, who was surprised by this turn. The two men stood in the street, Shackspear still leaning into Oxford, swaying back and forth like trees being pushed around by swirling winds.

"How did yer Anne take the loss of her son?" Shackspear went on, trying to rub some salt in Oxford's wound. But this comment only reminded Oxford that he and Shackspear were both married to Annes, which increased Oxford's anger toward the man in front of him and brought back the grief he felt at the loss of his first son. He could see Nan's face holding the little baby. She was wailing the way Shackspear was now.

Nan had turned to poetry to cope with her loss, her quiet scratchings fulfilling some ritualistic need. Oxford had kept her poems, mediocre and repetitive though they were. He knew them by heart.

> *Had with the morning the Gods left their wills undone*
> *They had not so soon herited such a soul:*
> *Or if the mouth, time, did not glotton up all*
> *Nor I, nor the world were depriv'd of my son.*

But Nan had mourned her loss; Oxford had not. He never talked to anyone about their son's death, even with Nan. Instead, he suppressed any memory of it. Perhaps the grief he had so successfully contained was now being released by Shackspear's loss. He could see Nan standing next to a tiny grave as their son was lowered into the ground. At the same time, he imagined his son by Elizabeth being carried through a door into a dark night, wrapped in a blanket stripped from one of the royal beds. He felt overwhelmed.

Shackspear realized Oxford was struggling with his own memories. Shackspear thought the loss of their sons had somehow bonded them. He put his arm around Oxford's shoulders. Oxford flinched, but a part of him welcomed the contact.

"Into the Mermaid, my lord," Shackspear said, turning Oxford around and walking him back toward the tavern. Oxford felt like he was being captured by pirates again. Shackspear carried the two of them into the Mermaid where they sat down in a booth. Shackspear ordered two pints, his voice sounding to Oxford as if it were coming from far away. The anger Oxford felt toward him and the queen was beginning to seep away.

Shackspear and Oxford remained lost in their separate thoughts as they waited for the beer. They were both startled when the tapster banged the mugs down on the table. They picked up the mugs and took a sip. Shackspear spoke first.

"He was dead by the time I got there, of course" Shackspear said, as if he had been speaking to Oxford all along. "News takes two days to travel from Stratford to London. It only took me a day to get back there. They hadn't put him in the ground yet so I was able to say good-bye to my boy before the earth took him forever."

Shackspear seemed comforted by this. "My thoughts about Hamnet changed as I made the trip, my lord. A journey can be a good time spent if ye let memories well up, sifting through them at a pace uninterrupted by the busy-ness that swirls around us every day."

He took another sip of his beer. "Hamnet had been conceived during a short visit to Stratford, repeating the mistake that forced me to marry Anne. A two-fer this time: Hamnet and his talkative sister, Judith. As different as two children can be."

He paused for a moment. "But Hamnet was different from other children, not just Judith." He glowered. "I hadn't noticed it the first time I returned to Stratford, but the second time I could tell something was missing. He had been short-shrifted. My father blamed the Ardens, but I started to wonder if Hamnet was mine. After all, how could I have had such a child? Judith seemed normal. Anne claimed I was father of both, but who knows what she does when I'm not there ..." His voice trailed off.

"You thought Hamnet might be by a different father?"

"Anything's possible, in 'it?"

Oxford didn't know. He'd never wondered if twins had to be by the same father. If it were true, was it possible Anne had cuckolded Shackspear twice? Double cuckolded him? Was there a play in here somewhere?'

"But," Shackspear went on, unaware that Oxford had wandered off, "there's no use running down that road, eh? Ye can never know, right?" He took a long pull on his beer. "All I knew was that he would hobble into a room and look around with his dull, vacant eyes and I couldn't deal with it. I basically shifted myself to London to get away from the sight of him."

He thought about this. "Funny thing is, when I got news he had died, I bolted out the door. Whatever doubt I had felt in London was gone by the time I got to Stratford."

Oxford marveled at how easily Shackspear had been able to talk himself into believing he was Hamnet's father. A simple mind may miss the deeper satisfactions in life, he thought, but it obviously had its advantages.

A simple mind could also believe in God and an afterlife, something Oxford could not do. He had learned there were many paths to Heaven. The rabbi at the Scola Levantina in Venice who taught him law and history took him to a Jew who had converted from Islam. This man told Oxford there were Hindus and Buddhists in India. There was Giordano Bruno, who waxed eloquent one night at the top of the Keep about the stars and galaxies above them, each point of light, he said, a separate universe that had never heard of Jesus or Buddha. All of this knowledge ended up being a curse, for Oxford ended up forever barred from the Garden of Eden others enjoyed, including, apparently, Shackspear.

Elspeth too. He had watched her recede into a faith that excluded others. She erected walls that kept people out rather than inviting them in. Cyclops-eyed, she was happy to believe in a Protestant God as given to her in Tyndale's Bible. Jesus had told her all she needed to know.

These thoughts caused Oxford to go silent. Shackspear, deep in his own grief, didn't notice. The two of them sat there, heads bent, eyes on the surface of the table.

Shackspear was the first to speak. "Once I buried Hamnet, I went back to London. I couldn't stay in Stratford, even with Hamnet gone. Anne seemed relieved she would never have to look up again and see him lurking in a doorway. I gave her money to keep her in Stratford. That's all she wants from me. She wants to buy tithes and land. She wants to buy the big house on Church Street, the one Hugh Clopton built. You know about him, don't you?" Oxford didn't know who Clopton was. "Mayor of London, he was," Shackspear said, hoping Clopton's birth in Stratford would improve his standing with Oxford.

"Before my time," Oxford said.

Shackspear went back to Hamnet. "His two sisters ignored him when he was alive and didn't care that he had died. They hated each other *and* their mother. They all hated each other, like pine trees oozing sap."

Oxford was beginning to understand Shackspear's grief. Stratford sounded like a horrible place for him.

"One night, Judith told me Susanna was the cause of her mother's pregnancy."

Oxford didn't understand. "*Judith said Susanna caused her own pregnancy?*" Shackspear nodded. He had that look true believers get when they are imparting something of great importance to someone who has not yet seen the light.

"Susanna wasn't in existence when you got Anne pregnant with her."

"Not even a gleam in my eye," Shackspear said, "or, as father likes to say, a carrot in the ground."

"That's incredible. Where did Judith get such an idea?"

"A woman in Snitterfield, Judith said."

Shackspear nodded gravely as he said this. Oxford thought Judith's explanation far outstripped claims by the father of a newborn child that he had been seduced into sleeping with the child's mother by potions, a leg, or a wink.

Shackspear was still thinking. "She - meaning Susanna - could be another Arden throw-off." He said this with a you-know-what-I-mean look. "She huddles next to the fireplace, reading her books. She never looks up or acknowledges anyone. It's like her body is seated in the chair but she's somewhere else. She despises her mother, who returns the favor. 'I was doing good until *she* showed up,' Anne declared once."

"In Susanna's presence?"

Shackspear nodded. "She resented her mother for that. She resented Hamnet because he was a boy. She resented Judith because Judith got all the spunk in the family. And she reads silently." Shackspear imparted this in a tone of wonder, as if this confirmed everything odd about his oldest daughter. "Whoever heard of such a thing?"

'St. Augustine,' Oxford almost said aloud. But if Susanna seemed odd, Judith sounded interesting. "Have you thought about spending time with her?" Oxford asked. "Judith," he added, to make sure Shackspear knew which daughter he was referring to.

Shackspear frowned. "She's a girl," he said, as if this was all that mattered. "Besides," he went on, "she might have had something to do with Hamnet's taking off."

This Oxford hadn't expected: "Judith might have had a hand in Hamnet's death? Why would you say that?"

"The day we buried Hamnet, Anne muttered to me that Judith had vowed to 'fix things, and now we all know what she meant.'"

"'Fix things?' You mean, poison him?"

Shackspear shrugged. "Who knows?" The vicar said Hamnet died of the plague, but a neighbor told me my boy had sores on him that didn't look like he got them from the plague. He didn't explain." Shackspear shrugged again, as if to say, who knows?

"Another road without end."

Shackspear nodded. "Maybe Judith poisoned him. Maybe she didn't. Fact is, he's dead, and there's an end to it."

Oxford was impressed: Shackspear was accepting things he couldn't change. Like Hecuba in *The Trojan Women*, sitting on the ground with the other women at the end of the Trojan War, Troy burning behind her. They were waiting to be told which Greek warrior they would be awarded to as slaves. Hecuba had lost her husband, her sons, and her grandchildren. Euripides has her saying: 'Up foot. Leg on. The next step.' Short. Concise. Mighty writing.

Shackspear took another pull on his beer. He leaned back and looked around. "Did ye know *Famous Victories* was put on here?"

Oxford hadn't known.

"Aye. The tables were pulled out from the back and a stage built on top of 'em. Four nights it ran the first time, three weeks when it was brought back." He sighed as a contented man. He obviously measured happiness in money. "I made enough to buy land on Alcester Road."

Oxford only knew how to sell land. Shackspear's comment about *Famous Victories* being played in the Mermaid made Oxford recall the queen's comment when she saw it. "She didn't like *Famous Victories*," Oxford said. "She said I had buried three plays in it. She has commanded me to 'dig them out' and 'give her three new ones.'"

Shackspear started to think this was good news but remembered he and Oxford no longer worked together. This, in turn, reminded him that he had written a play after he and Oxford split. "I wrote a play after we last talked, my lord."

"You did?"

Shackspear missed the surprise in Oxford's voice. "I wanted to put it on at Kenilworth, but they wouldn't let me."

"Kenilworth?"

"Yes. It's walking distance from Stratford, my lord. The queen was there in '72. I was eight. My father took me. The fireworks were amazing! They went over the castle walls and set fire to a farmer's house outside!"

Oxford knew all about Kenilworth and the queen's visit in '72: he had been there himself. A farmer's house had indeed been set on fire during the visit. Oxford and George Gascoyne had to jump into the water to rescue the farmer and his wife. The queen was very pleased, thinking it part of the show and not a fireworks display gone awry.

Shackspear could see this had piqued Oxford's interest. He thought Oxford hadn't been there and wanted to know more. "She came back three years later, my lord, when I was eleven. I snuck my way onto a bridge and watched a huge mermaid swim by. There was a Triton on top what sang to her!" He glowed at the memory. "The Mermaid," he announced, waving an arm to indicate the tavern they were sitting in. "Named, I am told, after the mermaid that swam past the queen at Kenilworth that year."

Oxford scowled. The Mermaid was more than a hundred years old. It had not been named after a float the queen saw in '75. He said nothing.

Shackspear returned to his play. "*Arthur*, I called it, but no one would let me stage it. 'No' was all I heard. I finally put it on in Bath. The Admiral's Men were there, the plague having closed the theaters in London. They were happy to have it."

Oxford was surprised to hear this. He realized he was hoping it had failed. "And how was it received?"

"Not well. After two performances, the Master of the Revels shut it down."

"Tilney's reach extends to Bath?"

Shackspear nodded. "I had apparently wandered into forbidden territory. I didn't know that Great Harry had an older brother named Arthur. Tilney thought *Arthur* was a parody about Harry's brother. It wasn't; how can I parody someone I didn't know existed?"

"Yes," Oxford agreed. "Guilt by an association that doesn't exist."

Shackspear looked like he appreciated Oxford's sympathy, even though he wasn't sure what Oxford meant.

"Your mistake, then," Oxford said, "was picking the name of a man no one wanted to hear about."

"Yes. But why is that? Who was this Arthur?"

"Arthur was Henry VII's eldest son. Henry had arranged for him to marry Catherine of Aragon. She came to England and they married. Unfortunately, he died almost immediately. Henry was unfazed by this. He wrote to Catherine's parents and told them he had a second son - Great Harry - who would take up Arthur's burden. Catherine's parents agreed and, even though Catherine was six years older than Harry, they married."

"As Anne was eight years older than I was when we married," Shackspear exclaimed, happy to hear of a parallel between himself and Henry VIII.

This inane comment made Oxford wonder what he was doing wasting his time in the Mermaid with – what did Falstaff call him? – *the son of a glover?* He started to get up but realized Shackspear had not told him what happened with *Arthur.*

"Your play. Was it good?"

Shackspear shrugged. "I thought it was. I *always* think what I write is good, but I could tell the Admiral's Men were glad to see it go. So, no."

Oxford was happy to hear this. Shackspear saw it out of the corner of his eye.

"And you? You wrote *Timon* after I left. Gone in two nights, I heard, and not because the Master of the Revels called it in." He smirked.

This was news to Oxford. He hadn't heard anything about *Timon* after he told Robin to dust it off and send it over as Shackspear's.

"And ye put my name on it," Shackspear continued. "As if I wouldn't know."

"No one cares whose name is on a play, Willum. It doesn't matter if it's your name or my name or someone called *anonymous!*"

"Unless ye want the fame," he said with a satisfied look on his face. But then he realized pushing Oxford away was not what he wanted to do. He needed the Poet Earl. *Arthur* had taught him that much.

"My lord, we have much in common," he announced.

This was the last thing Oxford expected to hear. He started to put his hand up to stop him but Shackspear went on. "The loss of our sons; women who drag us down; Tilney; our love of plays; cobbling works together that will live down the ages."

Exasperated, Oxford pulled his hand down.

"We have done well together."

This brought Oxford to his feet.

Shackspear was finished. "*Arthur* taught me, my lord, that I am no playwright. My dream of being a playwright is ended. You, on the other hand, *are* a playwright. But, as *Timon* proves, ye need help in writing a story people want to hear. Words ye write are beautiful, no doubt, in poetry, but sleep-inducing in the playhouse."

Oxford bristled.

Shackspear ignored him. "Who wants to listen to Timon, my lord? Everyone knows he is you, angry at being abandoned by his 'friends' after he's given away all his money. I went to the playhouse to see it. I thought I might learn something. I did. Listen to what Timon says as he leaves Athens:

> *Matrons, turn incontinent!*
> *Obedience fail in children! slaves and fools,*
> *Pluck the grave wrinkled senate from the bench,*
> *And minister in their steads!*
> *Maid, to thy master's bed;*
> *Thy mistress is o' the brothel!*

"This goes on for pages! Curses are good in small doses, my lord, but too much will ruin the soup! The audience ran for the exits!"

Oxford was not used to being harangued about a play *he* had written but the hack from Stratford was right about one thing: *Timon* had failed.

Shackspear could tell he was winning. "By yerself, you will be a playwright, but an *unsuccessful* one. Word will get out that no one wants to come to yer plays. Burbage and Henslowe will start telling you they have younger playwrights who are writing what the public wants. Your work will disappear into the trunk of plays, never to be seen again."

The trunk of plays? How did Shackspear know about the trunk of plays? Oxford was beginning to feel like he'd been burglarized. Worse, Shackspear was telling Oxford his plays would end up being dissected by dead minds at Cambridge, like the butterflies encased in glass cabinets there, dimly lit and never visited.

Shackspear leaned closer. "Plays are not poems, your lordship. Plays are about life. The actors need lines the audience can understand, plots that make sense. You give them Timon, who ends up living in a cave by himself."

Oxford was trying to regain control of himself. How could a provincial slow-wit help him, the 17th Earl of Oxford? But was Shackspear right? Was Shackspear smarter than he appeared and Oxford the slow-wit?

The tapster swept in over the table, bringing new beer. Oxford pushed his away. How many had he had? He wasn't sure. He got up. He felt dizzy. Shackspear asked him where he was going. Oxford didn't answer.

~ 123 ~
Pursued by a Bear

Oxford came into the library the next morning and found Shackspear seated at the far end of the table.

"What are *you* doing here?"

Nigel followed Oxford into the room. "My lord, Mr. Shakes-pare appeared this morning and demanded entrance. Tobias was in the kitchen at the time and, therefore, did not have an opportunity to prevent Mr. Shakes-pare from proceeding into the library. I ran off to find you, but you were not in your room. I did not think to look in my lady's room ..."

Oxford waved an arm, cutting Nigel off. Robin drifted in.

Shackspear spoke from the end of the table. "Ye told me last night we would work together on your new play this morning." He pointed to a script on the table. "Ye said not to keep ye waiting." He put on a face of innocence. "Have I done wrong?"

Oxford did not recall the conversation. Was Shackspear making this up? But then, how would he have known there about a new manuscript on the library table?

"Truly, my lord, we discussed many things in the Mermaid last night. *Timon*, your play, and how it failed. *Arthur*, my play, and how *it* failed. We agreed we needed each other. Ye said to come early and look through it." He pointed toward the script.

Oxford remembered leaving the script at the near end of the table. Shackspear had moved it to the end where he was now sitting. Was this out of respect for Oxford, who normally sat near the door, or was Shackspear staking out territory for himself at the far end of the table?

Shackspear had initially thought Oxford's blank face meant his lordship had forgotten their agreement but he began to worry Oxford had changed his mind. Shackspear couldn't quote passages from Plutarch but he could read faces. Oxford was fast receding from him.

"Ye said last night ye were halfway through another *Timon*," Shackspear said. "No joy, no happiness. White-hot anger from a king in Sicily who thinks his wife has cheated on him with his best friend."

Shackspear couldn't have known this unless Oxford had told him.

147

"Not only that," Shackspear went on, "but the king disowns his own child, thinking she's not his!"

Oxford's face showed he was beginning to remember their conversation, including talk about the rejected child.

"Aye. Cuckoldry. A subject ye keep bringing up again and again. Claudio in *Much Ado*. The Bastard in *King John*. Hints of it in *All's Well*. It's a wonder you kept it out of *The Merchant of Venice*. I half expected Antonio to seek Portia's hand, until I realized he was in love with Bassanio." He shook his head. "A bit of Marlowe there, I think. And now this." He pointed at the pages on the table in front of him.

Shackspear may have been enjoying his review of Oxford's plays, but Oxford was not.

"*Basta!*" Oxford shouted down the table. Nigel and Robin jumped. They both immediately left the room. "How dare you speak of my plays like you were at a county fair judging melons or Melton Mowbray pies!"

Shackspear was unaffected by this outburst. He smiled in an understanding way, as if Oxford's anger was directed at someone else. "But cuckoldry works, my lord. 'Tis the fear in every man's heart. Or," he continued blithely, "in the hearts of those who care what their wives are up to." It was clear that this had never bothered him.

Not so for Oxford. Part of his anger at Shackspear was being reminded of how many times he had written about cuckolded husbands in his plays. But Shackspear was right: cuckoldry works.

"Who goes to plays, my lord?" Shackspear asked. "Men, not women. And it is men who worry about what their wives are up to." A smile that would have sent a priest to the confessional spread across his face. "It would be interesting to know how many children have been spawned whilst their supposed fathers were watching a play about cuckoldry! They love to watch someone else being cuckolded but hate it when they're the victim!"

Shackspear leaned back, thinking himself full of wise counsel. He was as fluffed up as a bird sitting on a fence rail in cold weather. "Cuckoldry works, my lord," Shackspear repeated, spreading out the pages of Oxford's play. "In this new play, the king – Leontes – suspects his queen is unfaithful. Is she?"

"No."

"The good wife, then, unjustly accused. Odysseus, wondering about Penelope all those years he was away."

This surprised Oxford. He would never have thought Shackspear knew anything about Odysseus or Penelope. Maybe, Oxford thought, Shackspear had received a better education in Stratford than he had been given credit for.

"Then why does Leontes suspect her?" Shackspear asked.

"Jealousy."

"But *what* makes him suspect her?"

"She laughs when she's with his best friend, Polixenes, who is the King of Bohemia."

"That's all?" Oxford nodded. "No lies whispered in the king's ear by a servant who feels he has been passed over?"

"No. The king's rage will burst forth fully-formed, like Athena from the head of Zeus."

Oxford realized he had thrown Athena into the conversation to see if Shackspear had heard of her, but this only made Oxford angry with himself for letting himself get dragged into a duel at Shackspear's level of 'how much do you know about Greek mythology?'

"Ye might want to add a whisperer, my lord," Shackspear suggested. "The audience will wonder what drove the king to cast out his wife. Shouldn't there be something to suggest she's at fault?"

"No. She will be pure. She will do nothing with her husband's friend but be kind and courteous to him. The husband will go mad, thinking they're hiding their love from him. The audience will despise him."

Shackspear wasn't convinced. "I've read through what's been written so far. Leontes, upon no cause, locks up his wife and orders their child abandoned. He thinks she cheated on him with Polixenes and the child is not his. The babe is taken away and left on a wild shore. The wife – Hermione - dies of grief. The king's young son soon dies from a wasting sickness brought on by his mother's death. Finally, Leontes wakes up and realizes how mistaken he has been."

Shackspear looked at Oxford, shaking his head. "The child is not the only thing abandoned here, my lord. The play itself is hard aground, mired in gloom."

Oxford nodded. "Yes. And it will be years before the child is old enough to come back and be reunited with her father. I can't wait that long."

"Sure you can. Just skip over the years in between! We'll add Father Time to the play. He will come out and tell the audience the tale has jumped ahead a few years. Ta-da! Problem solved."

Oxford looked at him in disbelief. "You must be mad. That will never work. Sidney was right when he railed against plays where two hours' time on the stage is expanded into years. He laughed at battlefields where soldiers fought first on one continent and then on another, depending on which side of the stage they were standing on!"

"Who cares about Sidney? What he knew about plays wouldn't fill a gnat's codpiece. Poetry? Maybe. Plays? No. The audience wants a story, your lordship, so let's give 'em one."

He picked up a pen. "Father Time will get us to where we want to go, but before we go roaring off into the rest of the play, there is one scene Henslowe or Burbage will probably want to cut."

"Which scene is that?" Oxford asked sarcastically.

This pleased Shackspear no end. He had 'reeled in' his lordship, he thought. They were partners again. He tried to look humble and obeisant but looked more like he was auditioning to play the title role in *Tamburlaine*. He sat up. "Before the king orders the babe abandoned, a lady servant wants to lay the child before the king to make him realize it is his:

> *Behold, my lords,*
> *Although the print be little, the whole matter*
> *And copy of the father — eye, nose, lip,*
> *The trick of 's frown, his forehead, nay, the valley,*
> *The pretty dimples of his chin and cheek, his smiles,*
> *The very mold and frame of hand, nail, finger.*

"Now, I agree the king can't recognize the child yet because we are only in Act II and, if he says 'she's mine,' the play is over." He looked down the table. "And ye stretch it out to good effect, but where did ye get this from?"

Oxford didn't answer.

"It reads like something from real life."

Oxford still didn't answer. He was not going to admit Lady Suffolk had laid his own daughter in front of him one day *hoping Oxford would recognize Lisbeth as his own child!* According to Lisbeth, Oxford went by her *without so much as a glance.*

Shackspear sensed he had drifted into something that was off-limits. "Okay, then let's talk about what happens when Father Time jumps the play forward. How old do you think the babe will be when she comes back?"

"Old enough to marry."

"Fourteen years?"

"She's no Juliet. Make her sixteen."

"And who will she marry?"

Oxford shrugged. He didn't know. Shackspear thought for a moment and then said: "What if she marries the son of Polixenes, the man Leontes thought had cuckolded him."

Oxford blinked. "Now, that *would* be a coincidence."

"Audiences love coincidences."

Oxford had to agree. "This would mean that the babe would have to be abandoned on a shore that was part of the friend's kingdom."

"Easily done. Ye can blow her boat anywhere you want."

Oxford nodded.

Shackspear went on. "Abandoning the child on a barren shore is too poignant not to show on stage. It'll make a great scene." His eyes narrowed. "I see a bear."

"A bear?"

A smug look appeared on Shackspear's face. "Where have the lads been before they come to watch a play? Where are they going after it ends?" He paused dramatically. "The Bear Garden, my lord."

Oxford was lost. "And what does a bear have to do with this play I am trying to write?"

"The bear will eat the man who carries the babe ashore."

"*Eat him?*"

"Not on the stage, of course. The bear will come in from the left and chase the man off to the right. 'Exit – pursued by a bear!' After which, the bear will eat him."

Oxford was now looking at Shackspear in amazement. "And, if the only thing on the stage is a babe, how will the audience find out what happened to the man who brought her to the beach if the bear eats the man *offstage?*"

Shackspear hadn't thought of this. "Well, how about we add a shepherd who comes in from the tiring house and finds the babe. In the middle of a ripping storm," Shackspear added, starting to warm to his tale, "that will flap-dragon and sink the ship that brought the babe to the beach! Ye need a great storm, my lord. Always begin a play with a storm."

"We're in the middle of the play, Willum."

"Oh. Right. Well, a storm works in the middle too." He could see he was starting to lose Oxford. He hurried on. "The shepherd will see the babe lying on the beach and cry out!" Here, Shackspear switched into a Scottish brogue: *Mercy on's, a bairn! A very pretty bairn. A boy or a child, I wonder? A pretty one, a very pretty one.*

Oxford thought he should not interrupt Shackspear at this moment by reminding him that the play is taking place in Sicily and Scotland would be a fairly long voyage to go on to abandon a child on a beach.

Robin slipped into the library. Oxford motioned for him to sit down. Robin looked from Oxford to Shackspear and grabbed a pen.

Shackspear continued, enjoying his role as the shepherd. "The shepherd is followed by a son, who tells him the bear has eaten the man who ran off stage. *I'll go see if the bear be gone from the gentleman and how much he hath eaten. If there be any of him left, I'll bury it.* That takes care of that piece of information. Then, they'll find a box full of gold."

Oxford was looking at Shackspear in dumbfounded amazement.

Robin, wide-eyed, had no idea what Shackspear was talking about. He kept his head down as he captured what he could understand.

Shackspear thought an explanation might help Robin. "When I came in, the wife was dead, the son was dead, and the baby girl had been abandoned on a foreign shore. I've added a bear to lighten things up."

"Does it really eat the man?" Robin asked in a worried voice.

"Of course. Why de ye think the knuckleheads pay good money to see dogs torn to pieces in the bear pits?" He declared this with such enthusiasm that there was little doubt he was a 'knucklehead' himself. "When they hear there's a scene with a bear in it - what're ye calling this play, yer lordship?'

Robin intervened: "*The Knucklehead Husband,*" he said, without looking at Oxford.

""Oh," Shackspear said. "*The Knucklehead Husband,* as good a working title as any. When the knuckleheads who go to the bear pits find out there's a scene in a play where a bear *eats* someone, well, trust me, my lord, they will want to come see it. They will tell all their friends about it! And they'll come back to see it again!" He sat back pleased. "Asses in the seats, my lord, asses in the seats."

The theater was not about 'asses in the seats' to Oxford. He was about to jump up and remind Shackspear he only wrote for the queen but Shackspear was not done. "A 'signature' scene helps a play be remembered. The handkerchief dipped in the blood of a son in *Henry VI*. Titus Andronicus asking his daughter, Lavinia, to carry her brother's head in her teeth. Bottom leering at Titania from inside the head of an ass."

He looked back and forth between Oxford and Robin. "The bear I'm proposing will be the hinge in the play where the audience senses the story swing away from death and darkness toward comedy and light."

If Shackspear had expected applause, he was disappointed. Oxford was looking at Shackspear with his mouth open. But Oxford had to admit that having a bear charge across the stage might work.

"Yes," Oxford finally said, an admission Robin knew was not easy for his master to make. "Yes. I will accept your 'bear' for now."

"And Father Time?"

Robin had not been in the room when Shackspear suggested that Father Time be added to the play. "Father Time?" Robin asked.

Shackspear extended an arm. "See me as Father Time," he announced. Oxford thought Shackspear was giving them the scene and auditioning for the part at the same time. *The man!* Oxford thought.

"Father Time," Shackspear intoned:

> *Impute it not a crime*
> *To me or my swift passage that I slide*
> *O'er sixteen years, and leave the growth untried*
> *Of that wide gap, since it is in my power*
> *To o'erthrow law and in one self-born hour*
> *To plant and o'erwhelm custom.*

Shackspear looked down the table. "Problem solved," he announced. "And to Hell with Sidney. In a play, we can do wherever we want!"

He settled back in his chair. Oxford was still not convinced. He glanced at Robin to hear what he had to say.

Robin had ideas himself. "I think the babe will grow up to be beautiful and modest because she is the daughter of a king. No briars in her hair; no slippery young men staining her honor." Oxford and Shackspear looked at Robin, intrigued, but Robin took their glances as disbelief. "It's a fairytale now, isn't it?" There was a bit of defiance in his voice.

"Yes. She will be modest and beautiful," Oxford said.

"And, being royal," Robin continued, "she will fall in love with the son of the man who the king thinks seduced the queen."

"The son of the man who wrecked the king's marriage?" Oxford asked.

"She's washed ashore in his kingdom, hasn't she?" Shackspear asked.

Robin took this as support.

Oxford gave up. "What's the boy's name?"

"Florizell," Robin said.

Oxford and Shackspear looked at each other. "Awful name," they agreed. Robin stuck his chin out. "What's the babe's name?" Oxford asked.

"Perdita," Robin suggested.

"Good name," Shackspear said. "*The little lost one.*"

"Who will *not* know she is royal," Oxford said.

"No," Shackspear agreed. "The bear took care of that when he ate the man who brought her to the beach!"

The image of the bear eating the unfortunate man, even offstage, momentarily stopped them. Shackspear was the first to speak.

"But she will think herself unworthy of Florizell," Robin said:

> *That I should love a bright particular star*
> *And think to wed it, he is so above me.*

"Helena," Oxford said. "From *All's Well That Ends Well.*"

"Act I, Scene 1," Robin said, but did not add that Helena was Nan in Oxford's mind and Bertram was Oxford.

Oxford looked at Robin to see if his page was being cheeky. All this went by Shackspear, of course.

"So, Helena got Bertram. Will Perdita get Florizell?" He grimaced. He really didn't like the name.

"Yes, because *Florizell,*" Robin said, stressing the pronunciation of Florizell's name to irritate Shackspear, "will see her true nature and disregard her disavowals."

"Okay," Shackspear said. "Not Bertram."

"Can we stay with *this* play?" Oxford asked. He was now the one irritated. "I think the father will object to the match because he will think her common and not good enough to marry his son."

"But the son will see her true nature," Robin enthused, "and disregard her disavowals."

"But not his father," Oxford added. "He will think her common and not good enough to marry his son."

"A knucklehead himself," Robin added.

Shackspear liked this. "Excellent! We will make the king of Bohemia as blind to Perdita's nobility as Leontes is to his wife's faithfulness. *Knuckleheads all!*"

Robin smiled. He was almost beginning to like Shackspear, who looked down the table at Oxford. "This is good, my lord. Very good."

Oxford scowled. He had not been caught up in Shackspear's enthusiasm. "We have work to do. We may, by way of Father Time, make Perdita grow up quickly, but she is still in Bohemia. How do we get her back to Sicily?"

"Easy. Her future father-in-law will put the hammer down on Perdita marrying his son. We all know what happens when young men are denied what they want: they run away!"

"God," Oxford said. He put his head in his hands. "Where?"

"To Sicily, of course."

"Oh," Oxford said. For the first time, he thought Shackspear's idea might work. "Pursued by the father who created this mess in the first place."

Shakespeare nodded. "This will bring them all together for the grand finale. The First Knucklehead will recognize Perdita as his daughter, clearing up the first mess. The Second knucklehead, learning that his son wants to marry the daughter of his good friend, the king, will say, oh, okay, since she's of royal blood, you can marry her!"

Shackspear announced this with a touch of sarcasm. As a commoner, he knew what it was like to have decisions made on descent rather than merit. Oxford, on his part, had no problem with this.

"But the queen is dead," Robin pointed out.

"Unless," Shackspear said, looking slyly at Oxford and Robin, "she isn't."

Oxford frowned. "Paulina said she was dead."

"She *said* she was dead. There was no inquisition, no postmortem. We can bring her back."

"After so many years?" Robin asked. "Where's she been?"

"Who cares?" Oxford said, unconsciously repeating Shackspear's comment about Sidney. "We'll leave it to the theatergoers to guess where she's been. Did she run away? Is she back from the dead?"

"What if she's a statue?" Shackspear suggested. "Ovid had a sculptor, didn't he, who fell in love with a statue he was carving? The gods brought the statue to life so he could marry her, didn't they?"

"Just so," Oxford said. "The queen, then, will come back as a statue, carved by Julio Romano."

No one asked Oxford why Julio Romano was now in the play. Nobody cared who carved it. They were trying to figure out how the statue could help them. They were stuck.

"Why a statue, my lord?" Robin asked. "Where's it been? In a closet, ready to be taken out and dusted off at the end of the play?"

The room went silent. After a while, Oxford said: "Paulina will explain that she commissioned the statue as a keepsake of her mistress. When everyone recognizes Perdita as the queen's daughter, they will go to see if she looks like her mother. The statue will come to life and everyone will realize the queen has returned."

"Or never left," Robin said sarcastically. He thought everything his master and Shackspear had concocted was ridiculous. "This will be hooted off the stage, my lord."

"No," Shackspear said. "They will love it." His face glowed. He became the statue, arm extended. "She will cast her eye o'er the audience, turning to look at each directly, bringing a shiver to their hearts." He rotated slowly, the way a dignified queen would turn when called.

Oxford laughed. "I think Robin is worried I will ask him to play the queen."

"I'm too small," Robin said defiantly.

Shackspear agreed. "He may be little, but he knows his limitations."

"At least as to height."

Oxford and Shackspear laughed. Robin did not. "I'm working on it," he declared.

"To work," Oxford announced. "I'll divide up the scenes and you will fill in the parts. Agreed?"

"Aye," Shackspear and Robin replied.

"And William," Oxford said.

Shackspear and Robin stopped in their tracks.

"William?" Robin asked.

Shackspear, for once, said nothing.

"I owe you something for what you have brought to this play. It is time I returned your name to you. I shall call you William from now on. You've earned it."

Shackspear was surprised. "Thank you, my lord."

"It may have been wrong of me to take the 'i' from your name."

Shackspear shook his head. "T'was Falstaff who did that, my lord." He glanced at Robin, who was looking at his master in amazement.

"That's very kind of you, William, to offer me an out by blaming Jack, but I did it."

"Yer lordship," was the only thing Shackspear could say.

"And, truth be told, Jack has of late been abusing me for my treatment of you. He will be happy to call you William too."

"He will?" Shackspear was now amazed even more. He turned to Robin. "Who would've thought? Who can ever say what life'll bring ye, eh? It's a mystery!"

~ 124 ~
A Visit from Baron Cobham

Nigel swept into the library. "My lord: Sir William Brooke, 10th Baron Cobham, Lord Warden of the Cinque Ports, Lord of the Manor of Cobham, Kent, et cetera, et cetera, *as well as* Her Majesty's new Lord Chamberlain."

Robin slipped in behind Nigel and quietly padded down the table to a chair at the far end.

A large man strode through the open door. He was dressed in a black jerkin embellished by a thick white pleated ruff so tight against his neck that he could not turn his head without turning his body. The whiteness of the ruff was repeated at the cuffs. A compact round black cap —the latest court fashion — covered his head. In his right hand he carried the staff of the office of the Lord Warden of the Cinque Ports, a thin nondescript stick like one a young boy might pluck from a riverbank. An extravagant curling mustache masked tight lips pinched together in a combination of indignation and apprehension caused by having to enter the residence of the 17th Earl of Oxford.

Oxford rose. Brooke bent from the waist, acknowledging Oxford's greater lineage. He was only a baron, and only the 10th one at that. Oxford's bow, slightly shy of Cobham's, showed his acceptance of Brooke's deference. The formalities over, Oxford gestured toward a chair at the end of the table.

"Thank you, my lord," Brooke said as he sat down.

Oxford took the chair opposite him. "My congratulations on being named Lord Chamberlain," Oxford said. Brooke was pleased to hear this. "But you must find the office a burden, with all the obligations you have to your family, your liegemen, and the queen."

Brooke was tanned and leathered and looked fit despite being three score and ten. "*Pas de tout,*" he said, slipping in some French to show he was a man of parts. "I welcome the opportunity. I have always been a lover of the theater, my lord. Being Lord Chamberlain lets me put my hand on the tiller, so to speak. There is a particular enjoyment in watching a new production on the stage and taking modest credit for having *cleaned it up,* as it were, before it was presented to the public."

159

He preened. Oxford thought he looked like a duck spreading his feathers out to dry in a rare moment of English sunshine.

Brooke went on. "*The Winter's Tale*," he announced. Oxford reacted like he didn't recognize the play, which was true: he didn't. "A capital piece of work," Brooke said. "I had seen *Pandosto*, of course, and knew from whence Mister Shackspear derived the plot, but the falsely maligned queen dies at the end of Mr. Greene's play whilst Mr. Shackspear had the genius to unite all the characters at the end and bring a statue to life!"

Oxford finally realized that *The Knucklehead Husband* had become *The Winter's Tale* on its way to the playhouse.

Brooke was reliving the statue coming to life. "This man Shackspear knows how to stage a play, my lord, those *incidents*" – here he effected a French accent, '*ahn-see-dents*, but pronounced both the 't' and the 's' which showed the true extent of his education – "that will become the mark by which this play will be remembered. No one will forget the statute turning slowly round to look out at the audience! A dead man rising from his coffin could not have had equal effect!"

He looked around the library, clearly disappointed no one else was in the room to hear his review of the play. Robin did not count, of course. He would have been invisible to Brooke anyway. Unbeknownst to all of them, however, Falstaff lay stretched out in his favorite chair behind the open library door, which, Oxford and Robin would soon discover, was wide enough to hide all of the fat knight.

Oxford was irritated to hear that Shackspear's idea of having the queen return as a statue had worked. Robin had thought the idea would be hooted off the stage. They were both wrong. Oxford looked down the table to see what his page thought of the statue now, but Robin avoided his glance.

Brooke was not finished. "There has been too much laxness in the theater of late," he continued, running his eyes over the books that lined the room. He would not have approved of them had he been able to read the titles on their spines. Like many earls and barons, his education had been limited. Why waste time on sums and Latin when you are an earl-in-waiting? A title, like a football, is only temporarily 'held' by the father until, by dying, he passes it on to his son. If the father's death took too long, some earls-in-waiting didn't wait. Arsenic, 'inheritance powder' to some, was often used, like Father Time to advance the clock. Learning how to survive politics at court and fend off people trying to borrow money was what the 10th Baron Cobham had devoted himself to while he waited for his father to die. One trick to keep people at bay was called 'distancing,' where a person of higher station constantly shifted his gaze to avoid eye contact with a person of lower rank and avoid having to say 'no.'

It could be used to avoid a person of higher station as well, Oxford realized, as he watched Brooke's head flicking back and forth as if he suffered from some kind of fit. Oxford could tell Brooke had no interest in books; glancing at the bookshelf was part of his 'distancing' ploy.

"The City, you know," he said, bringing his gaze back to Oxford, "has called for the theaters to be closed. Now, whilst I enjoy a good play once in a while, *vide* my appreciation of *The Winter's Tale,* the theater is inimical to the moral and civic requirements of our society. Therefore, I will be working with the City to close the theaters. After all, they've only been operating, what, twenty years or so? A weed is more easily pulled out, my lord, when ye pluck it early rather than waiting until it has put down deep roots."

"Indeed," Oxford forced himself to say.

"I am pleased to find you consanguant," Brooke said.

This was a word Oxford had never heard. *'Consanguant'? 'Related by blood? To such a degree that marriage would be prohibited?* His guest had made a linguistic reach that exceeded his grasp. "And what does your lordship think I can do to assist?" Oxford asked, hoping his guest would complete his business and leave.

"Shackspear has a new play he is working on."

"Oh?"

Brooke nodded sagely. "I have spies everywhere. It's in rehearsal at the Curtain. An expanded version of *The Famous Victories of Henry the Fifth.*"

"Really." Oxford tried not to look at Robin, who was listening with eyes as big as Shrove Tuesday pancakes.

"The queen didn't like that play."

"No, she didn't."

"She thought there were *three coffins in there!*" he said, bursting out into a toothy grin that lifted the ends of his mustache. From his description of the queen's comment, Brooke had heard Her Majesty's verdict personally. Probably when she appointed him Lord Chamberlain.

It sounded like Brooke didn't know Oxford had written *Famous Victories* or the other plays Shackspear claimed were his. As a newcomer to the theater world, Brooke might not know who the real author was, but this meant the queen hadn't told him. Of course not, Oxford realized. She had intentionally withheld this important piece of information and sent Brooke to Oxford to complain about *Famous Victories*, without telling him Oxford had written it! He could hear her laughing. She knew it would be a good jest for her, and *for E. Ver*. 'She's a sly one,' he thought. He could already hear her jarring laughter when they next met, hers more genuine than his.

"I didn't like it either, but the queen's objections were general; mine are personal and specific."

Oxford cocked his head.

"There was an Oldcastle in *Famous Victories*," Brooke continued. He drew himself up. "I am descended from him."

"Ah," Oxford said. "And you did not like the way he was treated in *Famous Victories*. That must have been humiliating."

"It was. It was. Sir John Oldcastle was a martyr. It says so in *Foxe's Book of Martyrs*. He was burned at the stake in St. Giles Fields. *Famous Victories* has him committing robbery on the highway in Kent County!"

"With Prince Hal," Oxford added, "the future Henry V, England's greatest king!"

"*All the worse!*" Brooke cried. "My ancestor is shown consorting with Hal *before* he shakes off his ill behavior, not *after* he ascends the throne and everyone sees that his vile behavior was but bright metal on a sullen ground to show his worth the brighter when he became king." Robin saw his master's eyebrows flicker. Brooke, in full stride, was still venting. "In *Famous Victories*, Sir John is a reprobate. He was a martyr, my lord. I will not have it." He assumed what he thought was a fierce countenance.

"So, you shall say to Shackspear," Oxford said.

"Nay, my lord. *You* shall say this to him. Speaking directly with him would be beneath me, given the difference in rank between him and me, me, a lord of the realm, him, a ... a."

"But such distance does not extend to me?" Oxford asked, his voice rising. Brooke had gone too far. And, to boot, he was acting as if he were the senior lord in the room.

Brooke realized his error. "My lord, I ask this boon of you because of the love the players have for you, not because I am too proud to deal with the man directly. Shackspear won't listen to me. I am only newly minted as Lord Chancellor."

"But if he doesn't agree to make changes, you could bar his new play from making it onto the stage."

"I didn't say that," Brooke protested, looking at the bookcases again. "I only said Sir John should not be presented to the public as a highway robber and besotted fool. He was a martyr."

"I will speak with Shackspear," Oxford said, his dislike of Brooke growing by leaps and bounds. Silently, he nicknamed him the 10th Earl of Gossip.

"Thank you, my lord." Brooke said. He looked relieved. "Although it escapes me why he would paint Oldcastle as such."

"He?"

"Shackspear.

"You think Shackspear wrote *Famous Victories?*" The scowl on Oxford's face showed how affronted he was by the suggestion. Yet he couldn't admit he had written *Famous Victories.* Brooke was looking at him closely. Oxford had to backtrack. "The play, my good man, was performed over twenty years ago. Shackspear is what, thirty or so? Do you think he wrote it at the age of ten?"

Brooke stuck out his jaw. He didn't like being told he was wrong. "So, who wrote it?" he demanded.

Oxford shrugged. "Anonymous. You've heard of anonymous?"

"Well, anonymous was an obvious Catholic," Brooke said, looking at the bookcases. Oxford's face showed his surprise. Brooke saw it too. "Who else, my lord, would take a Protestant martyr who had been burned at the stake and present him on stage as a fat lecherous knight!"

Brooke didn't know what he had stumbled onto, proving, Oxford thought, that even a blind squirrel can find a nut. Burghley had thought Oxford a budding Catholic at the time a very young Oxford wrote *Famous Victories.* So did the Spanish; they counted him an English lord sympathetic to replacing Elizabeth with Mary, Queen of Scots. Mary was still alive in 1574, a prisoner at Tutbury Castle in Staffordshire.

But *Famous Victories* had nothing to do with the Catholics or Mary. Oxford had written Oldcastle into *Famous Victories* to poke his finger in the eye of all those who believed the lies they read in *Foxe's Book of Martyrs.* Was *Famous Victories* a juvenile effort? Indeed, it was, a screed by an adolescent full-of-himself Catholic-leaning English lord.

"Well, whoever wrote *Famous Victories* was clearly aiming at my father and me," he continued, looking offended.

This surprised Oxford. "Why would you think that?"

"I have no doubt of this because the robbery in *Famous Victories* takes place on Gad's Hill, which is less than a mile from Cobham Hall, where I live." He glowered at Oxford. "The anonymous playwright who wrote *Famous Victories* says that the robbery took place on 'the 20th day of May *in the fourteenth year of the reign of Henry the Fourth.*'" He rearranged himself in his chair. "Except that Henry didn't live till the 20th of May in the fourteenth year of his reign."

"Maybe the robbery took place in a different reign?" Oxford asked.

Brooke exploded. "Ye take me for a fool? I know where Anonymous got the robbery! *He got it from you!*"

Oxford put a hand to his chest. "Me?"

"You, my lord, robbed Lord Burghley's servants on Gad's Hill *on the 20th of May in the fourteenth year of Elizabeth's reign?*" He turned away, his deference to Oxford boiling away in his anger over the Gad's Hill robbery. "Everyone in Kent County knew it. The court buzzed with it. *An earl committing robbery on the highway! And someone putting it in Famous Victories.*"

"But the queen did nothing," Oxford pointed out.

"Of course, she didn't. How could she? Burghley was trying to save his daughter's marriage to you. *And she was in love with you!*" Brooke meant the queen. His face showed the shock he felt, listening to himself recount events that were beyond anything he could imagine, being the strapped-down Puritan that he was.

"And you think I was there?" Oxford said calmly, letting Brooke know he had overstepped his bounds again. No one had proven that Oxford was present when Burghley's servants were attacked. In suggesting Oxford had been there, Brooke opened himself up to an accusation of defamation.

"Of course not, my lord," Brooke said quickly. "The investigation only produced evidence that Lord Burghley's men were set upon by your servants."

"Who may have been acting outside their commissioned duties."

"Of course."

The truth was more complicated. The robbery had nothing to do with Brooke or his family. The robbery had taken place on Cobb's Hill because it was where Burghley's servants would be the most vulnerable as they made their way back to London from Canterbury.

The reason for the robbery? Oxford's annoyance at Burghley's interference in his life, not to mention the young lord's infatuation with Prince Hal and his tavern near-do-wells. Oxford had written *Famous Victories* to encourage the queen to forgive him for his dash to the continent earlier that year. No one came or went from England without Her Majesty's permission. He thought she would laugh at his recreation of Prince Hal's robbery of his father's receivers on Gad's Hill, as reported by Titius Livius and other historians. It would also embarrass Lord Burghley. Brooke and Cobham Hall had nothing to do with it.

Oxford had been there, of course. He chuckled as he remembered the shots fired over the head of the two servants, one, fat William Faunt, falling to the ground when the girth on his saddle broke. Frightened nearly to death, Faunt remounted quickly and rode off to Gravesend where he wrote a frantic letter to Lord Burghley claiming Oxford was behind the attack. Burghley confronted Oxford who refused to reveal what he knew about the incident. Oxford gave his father-in-law a frosty look and said William Faunt would not have lived to write the letter Burghley held in his hand had harm been intended. Clearly, the shots had missed.

Brooke, calming down, began to worry his hot temper had destroyed his chance of getting Shackspear to leave Oldcastle out of the next play. "My lord. We cannot go back and correct *Famous Victories*, but we can, with your assistance, keep my ancestor from returning in the play Shackspear is working on."

Oxford made a vague movement that Brook took as Oxford's agreement to speak with Shackspear. "I thank you for your support, my lord. Now, if you would be so kind as to oblige me, I would like to bring up something of more concern to the court as opposed to my personal interests."

"Such as?"

"The Earl of Essex, my lord. We all live in fear of what he will do next. He acts the petulant schoolboy to get whatever he wants from Her Majesty. He turned his back on her in the Presence Room recently. She smacked him on the head, and he almost drew on her."

Oxford had heard. No one puts a hand on their sword in the queen's presence. Everyone thought Elizabeth would throw Essex into the Tower, but she did nothing. Essex stormed off, angry that she had cuffed him and retired to his country estate where he was pouting.

"What hold does he have over her?" Oxford asked.

"No one knows. Earlier paramours - you, for example - were lovers. No one thinks that is what is going on with Essex."

Oxford's face showed he was not pleased to hear himself referred to as an 'earlier paramour.' Brooke immediately backtracked. "*Via rumore*," he said, thinking he was using Italian correctly, which he was not, and that his shift into Italian would deflect the anger he could see on Oxford's face. He failed on that point as well.

"*Diciere, signor*, is hearsay in Italian," Oxford said with some asperity. "*Rumore* is 'sound.'"

"Ah. Just so. Grazie. Let me return to the Earl of Essex."

"Do."

"There are some who think the earl capable of deciding our great kingdom should be governed by a man."

Oxford didn't think Essex that reckless. "He would try to overthrow Elizabeth?"

"No. It is thought he would try to assume power obliquely, as a guardian, for example, in Her Majesty's declining years."

"Her declining years?" Oxford knew Elizabeth may look older, with her ridiculous cosmetics and walking around bare-breasted to impress a visiting dignitary, but losing her powers.

"You may recall the Duke of Northumberland stealing power from Edward in an attempt to install Jane Grey as his successor. The Earl of Essex may have similar plans."

"I will speak with her."

"A good idea, but you must be roundabout in the way you come to her."

"I know 'roundabout.'"

"In the meantime, it might be worth suggesting to Master Shackspear that he turn his considerable talents away from waking statues and dogs named Crab to pen a story that would show Her Majesty the danger she is in."

"Richard II."

"Yes. He who gave his crown away."

Oxford was beginning to realize he may have underestimated Brooke. The man was uneducated and shallow, but were his pronouncements his conclusions or those of others? He must be spending time with Sir Robert Cecil, his son-in-law. "What sayeth Sir Robert about these *rumores*," Oxford asked, using the Italian word incorrectly to see if Sir William had learned anything. He hadn't. The word, like an errant duck, went right over his head.

Sir William may not have been paying full attention because he was pleased to be asked about his son-in-law, whose marriage to his daughter had polished his escutcheon. In fact, Oxford realized, his visit had almost certainly been coordinated by Sir Robert.

"Sir Robert is all too aware that the Earl of Essex is, shall we say, a loose cannon in the hold of the ship of state." This was a metaphor that almost worked, Oxford thought. "A play about Richard II would be timely," Brooke suggested.

"I will speak to Master Shackspear."

"*Bon*," Brooke said. He rose, taking the cane he had leaned against the table. He paused at the door. "I assume you are aware of the difficulties Mr. Shackspear finds himself in with Justice Gardiner?"

"I am not."

"Francis Langley runs the Swan, my lord. He has filed a writ for sureties of the peace against Justice Gardiner's son, William, as well as a man named Wayte, who is married to Gardiner's daughter. Wayte, in response, has filed for an order of protection himself, claiming he is in danger from Langley as well as Shackspear and two women – Dorothy Soer and Anna Lee."

Oxford sat up. Dorothy Soer? She who had played Queen Margaret in *Henry VI* and done such a splendid job as Titania in *Midsummer?*"

"I have no idea why Wayte added Shackspear to the suit, my lord, but Justice Gardiner is not a man to cross. He and Langley are involved in three other suits between them for slander. Gardiner is known for fleecing widows and taking land away from gullible owners. He sends every defendant who appears in front of him to the Clink where he extracts money from them while they are there. Of more interest to you, he is Justice of the Quorum for Surrey. The Privy Council has issued a letter to all the justices, including him, that orders them to pluck down the theaters."

"Including the Swan, I imagine, seeing that Langley owns it."

"Yes. The Rose as well."

"Thus, the theaters get dragged into their petty disputes."

Brooke nodded.

"Blackfriars as well?" Oxford asked. "Burbage bought space in Blackfriars for a new theater there. The lease on the Theater has expired and the owner won't renew it."

Brooke shook his head. "Burbage will not get approval for a theater in Blackfriars, my lord. Too many important people live there."

"Such as yourself."

"Indeed. My little *pied à terre* while in town." He didn't care whether Oxford might disapprove of his opposition to Burbage's plans. He was the new Lord Chamberlain. "Theaters in Southwark, my lord? That may be one thing. Next door to where I live?" He shook his head.

Oxford knew Brooke would block Burbage as long as he was Lord Chamberlain, but his interest in Justice Gardiner had been piqued. "This Gardiner appears to be a scoundrel. Describe him to me." He glanced down the table to make sure Robin was ready.

Lord Brooke pursed his lips. "Tall and thin, like he never had a groat to his hand, when, in fact, his chests overflow with gold. Stripped, he'd look like a forked radish. Ye could stuff him into an eel-skin. The case for a treble hautboy would be a mansion for him."

"I see him as you speak."

"My pleasure, my lord."

Oxford stood up. Brooke rose also. Oxford followed him into the hall. Tobias opened the front door. Waiting in the street was Michael Lok. Brooke came to a halt, Oxford next to him.

Lok scowled at Oxford, then turned away without a word.

"Most curious," Brooke said.

"Yes," Oxford agreed.

"Someone you owe money to?" the 10th Earl of Gossip asked.

"Something like that."

Exit Oldcastle

Oxford went back into the library. He went around the table to the far end and looked out the window. Robin quietly resumed his place at the table. They had both seen Michael Lok outside the front door, a look of deep sadness on his face. He had obviously seen *The Merchant of Venice*. Robin could tell his master thought he had failed. Instead of making sure *The Merchant of Venice* made it to the theater unchanged, he had naively given it to Shackspear, who had altered it into another rant against Jews, joining Marlowe's *The Jew of Malta* as a nasty description of people banned from England by Edward I in 1290. Lok's face made it clear he wouldn't forgive Oxford for failing him.

Oxford was still at the window when the library door, open against the wall, swung past Robin and slammed shut with a thump. Oxford and Robin jumped. Sir John Falstaff lay slumped in his accustomed chair behind the door. Falstaff had kicked it shut.

"Sir John?" they both said.

"None other," Falstaff said, pulling himself up to a seated position.

When had he entered the room? While Oxford was seeing off Baron Brooke? Had he been in the library the whole time?

Falstaff gazed at Oxford and Robin. "It takes quite a man," he rumbled, "to listen to the Lord of Flatulence drone on without jumping out the window and running away." He tossed his head in exasperation. "I wish you'd taken me with you to Gad's Hill, my lord, when you fired on William Faunt and his assistant. *I wouldn't have missed!* Faunt's days of letter writing would have been over."

"Which may be the reason you weren't invited."

"If ye *had* taken me along," he continued, "I would have taken the time to ride over to Cobham Hall and eliminate your latest guest myself." He waved a fat thumb at the library door. "It would have saved us all a lot of trouble."

He looked at Oxford. "Yer denial about the robbery was pathetic! *Of course*, the baron heard about it. *Everyone* heard about it. People even asked me what it was like, thinking I'd been there."

"Which you, being a modest knight, declined the honor."

"Depended on who was asking. A lord? Ah wasn't there. One who might buy me a pint? A long fight with men in buckram."

Oxford glanced at Robin, whose face showed he had no doubt Falstaff would have done away with Sir William had he been given the chance, even though neither knew where fact ended and fantasy began with the big man.

"Sir William is a scourge to us all!" he thundered. "The pox on him! Closing the theaters! Loving them when they're open - *as long as they're somewhere else* - but not if they're nearby! Poor Burbage. His theater in Blackfriars is worthless now that Sir William will be living there when he is in town!"

"A scourge to us all?" Oxford asked.

"Been part of the supporting cast, haven't I?"

"How so?"

"Lezsee. I think I saved the life of the author once, didn't I? He who writes the plays Shackspear claims are his?"

Oxford glanced down the table at Robin, who was enjoying the show.

"I may not have been in the tiring room, your lordship, but I have rendered assistance - *essential assistance* - to the process by which your thoughts became words the players speak."

"And now?"

Falstaff's chin rose. "The man who just left is thrilled he is Lord Chancellor and can do his worst. He's in league with Gardiner, my lord. Gardiner wants the theaters closed because he thinks Langley is holding out on him on the takings from the Swan - *that's* what Langley and Gardiner are fighting over! Gardiner thinks a threat to tear down the theaters will make Langley pay up; Brooke is willing to go along because he hears Oldcastle may return and humiliate him again. *I am descended from him,*" Falstaff said, mimicking Brooke. "He wants the theaters closed to block any further humiliation."

Oxford wasn't convinced. "He doesn't need to tear down the theaters, Jack. As Lord Chamberlain, he can block any play he wants."

"Aye, but if he only blocks the return of *Famous Victories,*" Falstaff said, "he worries it will look like someone's paid him to shut it down. He is happy to close them all to hide what he's really up to. That's why you need a new name for Oldcastle."

Oxford was surprised by this.

"You were tired of him anyway," Robin said.

Oxford thought for a moment. "Who needs an ancestor of the Earl of Gossip in the next play anyway?" He pursed his lips. "But what can I name him? Knowing me, I'll sail too close to the wind to get a laugh and luff myself into irons, as in prison irons."

"Vex no more," Falstaff announced: "I have the answer." He paused dramatically. "In fact, I *am* the answer." Oxford and Robin frowned. Before they could stop him, he went on. "The character you want to call Oldcastle in your new play - *Prince Hal and the Boar's Head* - should be called *Sir John Falstaff!*" He hooked his thumbs into his waistcoat and looked at Oxford and Robin, who were staring at him with mouths agape. "Why not?" he asked, defensively. "Ye need a name. I'm giving ye one. And I won't sue ye for using it!"

Robin was grinning; Oxford was not.

"On one condition," Falstaff quickly added. "I play the part."

"You?" Oxford and Robin said in unison.

"And who better? Who knows *me* better?" He said this as if that clinched all.

Oxford and Robin were trying not to laugh. "Ye're not a player, Jack," Oxford said, as if *that* clinched all.

"So? Neither is any man before he becomes a player."

"But they train, Jack. They gain experience. They learn many parts before they get to the Rose or the Curtain. It isn't easy to get up on a stage and become someone else."

"But I'll be playing meself."

Oxford, exasperated, looked away. Robin, for his part, was loving it.

"Besides, I've been acting my whole life," Falstaff went on. "I know how to bombast out a line as well as anyone." He winked to let them know, yes, he was parroting Robert Greene. "Who's put on a better performance than my testimony to the coroner's jury when you stabbed one of Burghley's undercooks in the thigh? You were to the gallows if I hadn't stepped in and told them the cook had run onto the end of your sword!"

Falstaff saw immediately he had gone too far. "Okay, I shouldn't have brought up *that* part of my service to you, but I've performed other services to help you write the plays you love. Life can unroll in ways we would prefer to avoid. The undercook, for example. The new Lord Chamberlain, for another. A lie made the gallows disappear in the first case; a new name for Oldcastle – also a lie, I admit - will give the Lord Chamberlain room to let *you* put your beloved Prince Hal on the stage."

Oxford was taking all this in. "I will borrow your name but you can't play the part."

Falstaff folded his arms. "Ye can't have my name unless I get the part."

"I'll use another name."

"No, ye won't."

"Why not?"

"Because ye'll write a man who will sing down the ages with my name in front of ye. Pick another and …"

Oxford glanced at Robin. "It would be a jest *for-ever,*" Robin said softly, a sly look on his face.

Oxford tried not to smile. "You devil."

Falstaff nodded, thinking Oxford was talking about him.

"But you have never been on a stage, Jack, where you'll have to follow a script and memorize a thousand lines." He thought this would force Falstaff to give up.

"Not a problem." He stood up, reaching over Robin to pick up a sheet of paper on the table. "Listen to what the Lord of Flatulence just said:"

> *Being Lord Chamberlain lets me put my hand on the tiller, so to speak. There is a particular enjoyment in watching a new production on the stage and taking modest credit for having cleaned it up, as it were, before it is presented to the public."*

Falstaff dropped the page back on the table.

"You can read?" Oxford asked.

"Can't everyone?" Falstaff replied Falstaff replied nonchalantly. "Not silently, like I'm hiding something, but out loud, where people can hear me."

"And when did this happen?"

"When I realized it was not fitting for me to be in service to a lord and not know his craft. As wood is to a carpenter or flowers to a bee, my lord, words are your nectar, for you are a wordsmith." He paused. "When her ladyship came aboard, she offered to teach me how to read. We would sit in the garden and work our way through Lily's Grammar and the Bible. Not the Geneva one, which you love, with commentary in the margin. She prefers Tyndale. 'From God's mouth to my ear,' she likes to say, 'without the glosses of squeaky men.'"

Oxford and Robin were looking at Falstaff, trying to understand he could read. Oxford began to say something but Falstaff spoke first.

"No 'buts'. Ye want my name, ye take the man."

Oxford sighed. He and Robin looked at each other.

"How bad could it be?" Robin asked.

Oxford thought it could be very bad. He turned to Sir John. "You'll have to get past Burbage."

"Ye leave him to me." He jerked a thumb in the direction of the library door. "What happened to the garden?" he asked.

"What do you mean?"

"It hain't there."

"It isn't?" Oxford looked at Robin, who tried to look like he didn't know what Falstaff was talking about. Oxford turned back to Falstaff. "What do you mean *it hain't there?*"

"I always come in through the garden gate, your lordship. Still have the key." He patted a pouch strapped to his waist that was made of multi-colored cloth. It was large enough to contain bedding to sleep in and a bottle of sack, both of which - and more - Robin had found inside it. "It has been my custom to sit for a moment before entering the Court and enjoy her ladyship's flowers along with the scent from Frangellica's herbs, *but not anymore!* The plants are gone! Plowed under. Nothing left but barren ground." The tilt of his head implied he thought Oxford had something to do with it.

"I know nothing about this." Oxford said. He looked at Robin, who decided to tell his master what he knew.

"My lord, Lady Elspeth has been attending Bible classes at the home of Sir Robert's wife, Elizabeth." By this, they all knew he meant the daughter of the man who had just left.

Oxford blinked. "Bible lessons? At Sir Robert's?"

Robin nodded. "Bona Ventura discovered this when she saw her ladyship leave one morning without telling anyone where she was going. Bona Ventura followed her ladyship but Lady Elspeth waited around a corner and confronted her, wanting to know why she was being followed. Bona Ventura explained she was worried about her ladyship being abroad without servants. Her ladyship decided to take Bona Ventura with her to Sir Robert's house where she saw many strange things. Some at Sir Robert's house attempted to convert her but Bona Ventura is a true Catholic and resisted them."

"How do you know all this?"

"Frangellica and Bona Ventura are both from Venice, my lord. Bona Ventura confided in Frangellica and Frangellica …"

"Confided in you," Falstaff snorted, "whilst, no doubt, you were sampling her lemon biscotti in the kitchen." He was disappointed to have missed the occasion.

"Interesting that they would confide in you," Oxford said to Robin.

"My lord, I am but a boy. Ladies confide in me all the time. My beard has not yet come in."

"Yes," Oxford said. "I can see that. What happened at Sir Robert's?"

"Bona Ventura said there were many prominent ladies there, including Aemilia Bassano."

"Aemilia Bassano?"

"Now Mrs. Aemilia Bassano Lanier," Robin added.

"Aye," Oxford said. "With Lord Hunsdon's offspring in tow."

"That … Bona Ventura did not report."

"What were these women doing at Sir Robert's house?"

"Your ladyship has apparently become a foot-washing Baptist."

Falstaff guffawed. Oxford and Robin looked at him. Falstaff explained. "A foot-washing Baptist believes *any* pleasure is sin. Her ladyship has obviously been told that her love of flowers will send her to hell because they give her pleasure. She will also have been told they take her away from reading the Bible."

Oxford was trying to understand this. "So, she tore out the garden because it gave her pleasure?" Falstaff and Robin nodded. "And Aemilia Bassano is part of this group?"

Falstaff wagged his head. "Yer wife has been drinking witches' brew, my lord." He started to hum and move his arms back and forth as if he were stirring a cauldron. "Double bubble, and so on. But you, hearing how far out to sea yer wife has drifted, don't ask about her: *you ask about Aemilia Bassano, the lady you chased around Lord Hunsdon's bed?*" Robin was shocked by this. "Not literally, little fella. Ye can't but be metaphorical if ye spend time around the likes of him." He looked at Oxford. "Ye never made it into *any* bed with her. She bewitched ye!

Still does! Ye said ye were done with her. Non plus! Fini! Nienté! Terminó! *Bih-TUH!*"

Oxford was surprised Falstaff could recall the words he had brayed out to convince the fat knight that he was done with Aemilia Bassano. She had abandoned him for another poet who Oxford had never been able to identify. Was it Essex, Oxford suddenly wondered? He wrote poetry. He was a hero for climbing the walls of Lisbon and capturing the city. And he was handsome.

Falstaff and Robin were watching. They knew how much his failure to bed her had added to her allure. "Aemilia, a hymn-singer," Oxford said, unable to accept that she had gone over to the Puritans. Essex, maybe, but not the Puritans.

"And writing poetry as well," Robin added.

"Really?" Oxford said. This, he could accept. She loved poetry. Hadn't she loved his?

"In the meantime," Falstaff chimed in, "I now have no garden in which to refresh myself before I make my entrance. *N'est pas?*" he added.

This brought a smile to Robin's face. "Monsieur Le Gros will now claim he can act in French as well as English."

"*Porquoi pas?*" Falstaff went on. Oxford looked away. He was growing tired of Jack, but His Corpulence wasn't finished. "Why not pen a scene entirely in French, my lord? It will scare the merde out of the parvenus at court. They will be frightened to death someone will ask them a question in French they can't answer and show how stupid they are for not knowing the language of William the Conqueror."

"Ignorant," Oxford said.

"Ignorant *and* stupid," Falstaff said.

Oxford was not paying attention. He had drifted off. Aemilia Bassano was in town. He was done with her, of course. *Wasn't he?* But she would never flash her eyes at him again and tell him to meet her somewhere the following night. She was a Foot-Washing Baptist now. She'd been a woman who, with a glance, would have pulled Odysseus' men off his ship if she'd been one of the sirens calling out to them.

"When do we start?" Falstaff asked, his eyes bright.

"Start what?"

"*Prince Hal and the Boar's Head.* I want to write it!"

Oxford shook his head. "I'm borrowing your name, Jack. That will do for now. As to whether you play Falstaff? We'll see. *But write the play as well?* God's blood, man. How much more do you want? I've enough trouble with the 'bard' from Stratford! I don't need another writer!"

To their surprise, Falstaff did not protest. In truth, he knew Oxford would never let him write scenes in a play. He didn't want to. He gave Oxford a toothy grin. By reaching too far, he had gotten what he wanted: *the chance to play himself on stage.* Unbeknownst to anyone, Fat Jack admired Ned Alleyn and Richard Burbage. He had always wanted to imitate them on stage. In fact, it might have been one of the reasons he had stuck with his lordship these many years. Even he didn't know the answer to that question. He got up.

"Stay a moment, Jack," Oxford said. He glanced at Robin who gathered up his things and left. Once he was gone, Oxford turned to Falstaff. "What have you found out?"

"It hain't much, my lord, but I'm making progress, what with all the people I need to talk to lying buried in the ground."

Oxford's face showed he was in no mood for a long introduction.

"We start with nothing. Red hair. Long fingers. *A mother who says she's not his mother.*"

"Go on."

"I've got leads. Not many, but … more like signs, road signs, pointing the way."

Oxford was not pleased to hear this. "Why are you still here?" he demanded.

"I'm going. I'm going." Falstaff headed out the door.

Oxford sighed. No use following him, he thought, even though there was little doubt the big man was heading for the Boar's Head. If Oxford accosted him there, he'd obviously claim he was researching something in the bottom of a tankard of ale. He was, as always, slippier than a freshwater eel. Would he ever bring Oxford resolution and peace?

126

Not Without Mustard

Shakespeare came into the library. His head seemed to be cocked back at an even greater angle than usual. He had a rolled-up parchment under his left arm. With his right hand, he swept his hat, still with turkey feather, off his head.

"You can write me gentleman now, your lordship," he said, bowing low and washing the air in front of hm with the hat.

"And the reason ..." Oxford asked.

"I have arms." Shackspear unrolled the parchment and held it up. "£30 it cost me, by this breath."

Oxford didn't know what to say. Shackspear glanced at Robin, whose mouth was agape. Shackspear took the boy's surprise as disbelief. "I have so toiled among the harrots, you will not believe! They speak the strangest language and give a man the hardest terms for his money that ever you knew."

He handed Oxford the parchment. Oxford ran his eye over it. "Gold, on a bend sable, a spear of the first, the point steeled argent, a falcon as a crest, wings displayed, argent, the falcon standing on a wreath of colors supporting a spear gold, steeled argent."

Shackspear nodded as Oxford put into herald-speak what he was looking at. He looked at Robin. "Didn't I tell ye they spoke a strange language?"

"A very fair coat," Oxford said as he handed the parchment back to Shackspear. "Well charged, and full of armory,"

"Nay," Shackspear protested. "It was checked and approved by all the harrots," he protested. He thought Oxford had said it was 'full of errors.'

Oxford declined to explain. He looked at Robin, who knew nothing about coats of arms. "With a spear. Shouldn't it have been a pen?"

"A pen?"

"You are the author, are you not?"

"Yes."

"I have never seen you with a spear. I get the connection with your name but I still think it should have been a pen, *you being the author!*" Oxford said, his voice rising. "Shackspear started to protest but Oxford had more to say. "And your motto. Very rare: *Non Sanz Droit.*"

Shackspear looked more closely at the parchment. "I hadn't noticed that. It means?" He looked at Oxford.

"*Not without right.*"

"Exactly. That's what they found. I have every right to my coat." Then he frowned. "Although the marking on the one my father filed in 1596 was different."

"In what way?"

"There was a comma after the '*Non.*'"

"Ah. The comma! The little curving line, often mistaken for an eyelash on the page. It changes so much. Look what can happen when you forget it, or put it in the wrong place! Suppose you want to call Falstaff to dinner." Shackspear quickly looked around to see if the big man was in the room. "You call out '*Let's eat,* comma, *Falstaff!* But if you forget the comma, it becomes '*Let's eat Falstaff!*'"

Robin burst out laughing. "That'd be a meal to feed the street!"

"In your case, Master Shackspear, the original motto, with the comma, was '*No, Without Right,* which means someone thought you shouldn't get arms. Apparently, the comma disappeared between 1596 and now. Probably one of the copyists, unwittingly leaving it out. Or," Oxford said with a sly look, "you or your father know someone. Hmm." Shackspear didn't know what Oxford meant by this. "In any case, without the comma, your motto became *Not Without Right,* meaning yes, you do have a right to arms."

Oxford looked at Robin. "I've always loved the comma. Now I positively adore it! *Non Sanz Droit!*" he repeated. "A fine motto."

Shackspear did not understand what Oxford was talking about. He also had no time for commas. He held up the scroll. "What think you of how I am styled, my lord? *Master William Shakespeare, Gent.*"

Oxford smiled, a genuine smile this time. "We will let you gild your lily, William, but how came this about? How did you get the heralds to, how shall we say this, take out the comma and grant you arms?" He avoided looking at Robin.

Shackspear had been standing since he came into the Court. He made a gesture indicating he'd like to sit down. Oxford pointed to a chair. He sat down. "Ben Jonson," he said.

The name didn't register. Robin spoke up. "The bricklayer who writes plays, my lord. You met him coming out of The Sign of the Ship." Oxford still didn't know who Jonson was. "Marlowe was with you at the time."

"Ah. The young man whose hands were in mortar at sunup and cradling a mug of beer as the sun went past the meridian." He looked at Shackspear. "And how is it that this Jonson helped you get arms? Ah. He loaned you the £30."

"No, my lord. I didn't need help with the fee. My investments are paying well, thank you very much. I expect to send Anne the rest of the money she needs to buy the house in Stratford soon. Five sets of windows across the second-floor front." This apparently puzzled him. "Who needs five windows? You can only look out one at a time, can't ye?"

"Yes. And Mr. Jonson? How did he help you?"

"Jonson – Ben - was a student at Westminster when Camden was running it. Camden became Garter King and Ben stayed in touch with him. Ben is writing plays, my lord. He asked me to help him get Burbage and Henslowe to look at one. I agreed if he would talk to Camden about my father's application for arms. He spoke to Camden and, well, there it is."

Oxford had no real interest in how Shackspear got his arms but the mention of Jonson being a budding playwright intrigued him. "What plays has Mr. Jonson written?"

"*The Case is Altered*, my lord."

"I thought Munday wrote that?"

"No. Jonson did. There's a character in *The Case is Altered* named Antonio Balladino. Munday is threatening a reply because he thinks Jonson was aiming at him when he created Balladino."

Robin coughed behind his hand. Oxford and Shackspear looked at him. "Aren't we supposed to be working on *Famous Victories*?" he asked. "Or rather, the three plays you buried in it?"

"Yes," Oxford said. "And one more."

Robin and Shackspear cocked their heads.

"Prince Hal first, in two plays, and then, after he becomes king, a third play to show him before he goes over to France to gain fame."

"And the fourth?" Robin asked.

"Hal got his crown from his father, Henry IV, but where did Henry get the crown he passed on to Hal? From Richard II. Was

Henry Richard's heir? No. Henry took the crown from Richard. Or, rather, Richard gave it up."

"Oooh," Shackspear cut in. "I remember hearing about him when I was at Stratford Grammar School. A scholar was sore vexed for Richard *for giving up his crown!*"

"Aye," Oxford said. "Whether Henry came to the throne legitimately is a vexing question for many. Richard had banished Henry and taken his lands. Henry came back claiming he only wanted his honor and property. But did he come back to take the crown? No one can tell, but Richard gave it away anyway. The question of whether Henry was the rightful heir to Richard has bothered more people than your scholar. In fact, it vexed Henry himself."

"Very interesting," Robin said, his voice showing he wanted to work on the play. "Where do I start?" he asked. He held aloft his pen.

Oxford laughed. "I will keep Richard, my little minion. You and William go through *Famous Victories* and work on the three new plays about Hal. Leave what you write on the table; I will review it each night until all are finished. I'm going upstairs."

He went out into the Great Hall, leaving a very unhappy Robin behind him. He did not want to work with Shackspear. Shackspear, on the other hand, was thrilled to be working with Robin. The wheel of fortune had rolled out a new relationship for him - writing a play with little Robin, who had obviously acquired some talent while hanging on his lordship's every word. Writing them down, in fact. There would be the added benefit of having the genius who had just left the room bring gold to what he and Robin would produce.

Humming to himself, Shackspear sat down at the table and pulled some papers toward him. "Let's work on the robbery first," he said. "In *Famous Victories,* the robbery takes place offstage. This time, let's show the audience what happened."

Robin was forced to agree. "Show, not tell," he muttered to himself.

"Aye," Shackspear said, picking up one of the pages in front of him.

⁂

127

The Earl of Derby

The Earl of Derby," Nigel announced, holding open the library door to let William Stanley, 6th Earl of Derby, pass him.

Oxford got up. "Your lordship," Derby said, extending his hand. Oxford took it. "William. How goeth thou?"

"Well, my lord."

"Let us repair to the Day Room. This room is filled with musty papers."

"No problem with me, my lord. You know how much I love plays."

"Yes. And you were excellent as Pericles, but let's go across the hall." Oxford and Derby crossed to the Day Room.

"I did so love being involved as a player," Derby said, as he sat down in a chair next to a table. Oxford went around to a chair on the other side. Nigel followed them in and placed a decanter of sherry on the table.

"Now what brings you here?" Oxford asked as Nigel left.

"Blast, my lord, I am embarrassed to say it is about your daughter, my wife!" Derby looked at Oxford. "You haven't heard?"

"No."

"Lisbeth has been seen with Essex. More than seen, I am forced to say. I had to issue a challenge, of course."

"He accepted?"

"No, of course not. He's very good at storming castles and what not but he denies he has seen anywhere with 'the lady in question' except in public places. She has also denied it." It was obvious that Derby didn't believe either of them. "I knew I was getting an unruly wife when I married her but I am having more difficulty than I expected in trying to make her understand her rightful place by my side."

"You have reproached her, have you not?"

"Of course, I have."

"How has she responded?"

"By becoming incensed at even being asked about it, combined with a snide 'so-what're-ye-going-to-do-about-it-anyway look? I am at my wit's end."

"How far have the rumors spread?"

"As far as Lady Bacon, who has written to the queen that Essex has been involved in a 'carnal dalliance' with 'a nobleman's wife, and so near Her Majesty.' She cited Thessalonians and Hebrews that 'God will judge fornicators and adulterers!'

Oxford smiled. "This will pass. No one listens to Lady Bacon anymore."

"*You* may not listen to her, my lord, but other people do. Lady Bacon is not only Lisbeth's grandmother but she is cousin to Sir Francis Bacon. To the court, rumors are facts! You must have heard what happened to Richard Fletcher, Bishop of London, when he married a lady from Kent who was so much younger than he was everyone thought he must have bought and paid for her. Their marriage didn't last very long; he died very soon thereafter, a happy man, perchance. The wits in town were soon churning out epigrams about them:

> *We will divide the name of Fletcher:*
> *He, my Lord F; and she, my Lady Letcher.*

Oxford hadn't heard this. He almost laughed but caught himself in time. This was serious business, he reminded himself, although he knew aught how he could bring Lisbeth into line. She was hot out of the marriage oven and not only cuckolding her husband but laughing in his face! At least Nan had not done that to him.

Derby was at a loss as to how to rein her in, but he was fixated even more on Essex. "He didn't win the tilt," he said disdainfully, a fact unrelated to his marital troubles but enough for Derby to dismiss his rival as without merit. Derby meant the Accession Day Tilt held at Whitehall. "No, t'was Southampton who took home the prize. He broke twenty-two staves."

Oxford had been there and proud to see his 'son' take home the prize. "A good man," Oxford said.

Derby was obviously expecting Oxford to help him. "Do you think you can talk to Lisbeth, my lord? She thinks rules are for others and tosses them aside, the way a horse with too many oats in it overturns a fence and runs off."

"I will." He had no idea how he could change his daughter's headstrong behavior. She was too much like him, he realized, which made him wonder how much difficulty he had caused everyone when he was her age.

"She respects you, my lord," Derby went on. Oxford looked at him. "She does. She's told me in the past she would like to make up for the time you two have been apart."

Nigel interrupted them. "My lord, forgive me, but there are two men at the door who have seized Tobias. They are trying to carry him off."

Oxford jumped up and ran to the front door where he found Tobias grappling with two men who were almost as large as he was. He was apparently holding his own and waiting for Oxford to tell him what to do.

"*Let him go!*" Oxford shouted. Tobias took this as permission to slam one of them against the stone wall next to the front door. He was about to do the same to the second man when Oxford put up his hand. "What goes here?"

The second man extricated himself from Tobias. "We have a warrant here, your lordship." He held out a piece of paper.

"For him?"

"For all the blackamoors in London." The man read from the warrant:

An open warrant to the Lord Mayor of London and to all Vice-Admirals, Mayors and other public officers whatsoever to whom it may appertain. Whereas Casper van Senden, a merchant of Lubeck, did procure 89 of her Majesty's subjects that were detained prisoners in Spain and Portugal to be released, and brought them hither into this realm at his own cost and charges, for the which he only desireth to have licence to take up so much blackamoors here in this realm and to transport them into Spain and Portugal, Her Majesty doth think it a very good exchange, and therefore, all are required to aid and assist him.

"Where is Casper van Senden?" Oxford called out.

"In front of ye." The man rolled up the warrant. "Will ye yield to yer sovereign's will, my lord?"

"No!"

"Look ye, sir, ..." but Oxford interrupted him.

"I am no *sir!*" he announced. "*Get thee hence!*"

"But yer lordship, I have been given license to seize and sell the likes of him," he said, pointing toward Tobias, "for a pretty profit in Seville whilst ridding England of the blackamoors that are here."

Oxford was outraged. "Ye'll not be selling anyone."

"But the warrant says: 'with the consent of their masters,' which the queen expects they will yield them up."

"*Have ye asked him?*" Oxford demanded. He gestured toward Tobias, who had a bemused look on his face. "Ye think *he* wants to be a slave in Seville? *Would you?*"

"He's a blackamoor," the man said. "Ye don't ask a table whether it wants to be upstairs or down."

Tobias' face darkened.

Oxford reached over and pulled Tobias away from the two men. "*Get out!*"

Frangellica appeared. She had a great wooden spoon in her hands. "And yoor being disrespectful to two most serenissima lords in all of England," she declared, advancing on the men with the spoon. She began smacking them about the head. They ducked and turned. It was obvious this was not the first time she had laid someone's head open with a spoon.

Oxford glanced at Tobias who quickly stepped in between Frangellica and the two men. Pushing her aside, he grabbed the men and threw them into the street.

"The queen will hear of this, my lord," the second man said, picking himself up.

"*From me,*" Oxford shouted back.

He and Derby went back into Oxford Court. Tobias slammed the door behind them.

"Well," Derby expostulated. "Tobias, you were magnificent."

"He was," Oxford agreed.

Tobias beamed. He went back into his room. Frangellica nodded and gave Oxford a furious look as she went back into the kitchen.

"Meat for a play, my lord?" Derby asked.

"Tobias?"

Derby nodded.

"Already in one. And not as harbinger or doorman. I will talk to the queen about Casper van Senden. And to Lisbeth."

"Thank you, my lord."

Derby shook Oxford's hand and left.

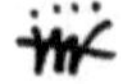

Richard II

Robin was sitting at the far end of the table. It was early in the morning. Daylight was seeping into the room. Oxford came in and stopped. Robin could tell his master was angry and that it had something to do with him. With the manuscript lying on the table in front of him?

"I was up early, my lord," Robin said, "and found your papers here. I thought I could look at them."

Oxford said nothing. He panned away from Robin to survey the room. "What you have done is wrong," he said, in a voice Robin had rarely heard. "I did not give you permission to read this. When you read something I have *not* given you permission to read, you invade my privacy, as if I had found you rummaging in my wardrobe fingering my gowns and sashes."

Robin began to protest, but Oxford put up a hand. "I do *not* share manuscripts with anyone. They are my most prized possessions. You will say that you have only perused them and they still lie on the page where I wrote them."

Robin thought this an excellent response and wished he'd thought of it but realized something else was going on. He lowered his head.

"Yes, the pages can be picked up and read again," Oxford continued, as if he were lecturing a new student at Cambridge, "but you have nevertheless stolen what was on those pages. You now have what I created."

Robin didn't understand. How could he have stolen anything if the pages were still there? "My lord," he cried. "You know I worship the ground you walk on. You know I find it a great privilege to listen to you speak, your words coming out as if you were reading volumes written by scholars who had polished their words before setting them down. You know how fortunate I think I am to help you write your plays. I know how fleeting my good fortune can be. I awake each day in my cubby under the stairs and worry that some boy who's been to university has acquired your livery and will sleep that night where I have just awakened - *while I will sleep in the street!*"

Oxford was taken aback by this. He shook his head. "Where *do* you get these ideas, Robin. There is no 'boy,' university bred or not, about to come into Oxford Court and displace you." Robin was so relieved he almost burst into tears. "The new boy'll sleep upstairs."

Robin's face showed how shocked he was to hear this. Oxford laughed, his anger gone. "Relax, my little Robin. There is no one coming to replace you." Oxford's eyes narrowed. "Nevertheless, you have taken my secrets."

Robin now realized his master had been creating a new scene when he came into the library and found Robin seated at the table. His anger had nothing to do with the manuscript Robin had been looking at.

"What I write is wholly mine," Oxford went on, Robin his audience now and not his victim, "until someone steals it. If you steal my money, it is mine for but a short time. It has been slave to thousands and will be someone else's tomorrow. But what I write is different. It is the jewel of my soul."

"Should I take this down?" Robin asked. Oxford nodded. Robin picked up his pen. Oxford continued:

> *Who steals my purse steals trash; 'tis something, nothing;*
> *'Twas mine, 'tis his, and has been slave to thousands:*
> *But he that filches from me my good name*
> *Robs me of that which not enriches him*
> *And makes me poor indeed.*

Robin's pen raced across the page. Glancing at Oxford's manuscript might not be stealing his good name, but it was enough to propel him into a new scene. Robin looked up when he had captured Oxford's words. "Is this for *Richard?*" he asked.

"No. Another play."

"*Another* play you're working on?"

Oxford nodded. "Still in its shell. Not ready to hatch yet." His anger had passed.

Robin pointed to the manuscript on the table in front of him. "May I ask a few questions about this?" he asked. He tried to sound as deferential as possible. Oxford cocked an eyebrow. Robin went on. "John of Gaunt's description of England in Act II, Scene 1:

> *This royal throne of kings, this scepter'd isle,*
> *This earth of majesty, this seat of Mars,*
> *This other Eden, demi-paradise,*
> *This fortress built by Nature for herself*
> *Against infection and the hand of war,*
> *This happy breed of men, this little world,*

This precious stone set in the silver sea,
Which serves it in the office of a wall,
Or as a moat defensive to a house,
Against the envy of less happier lands,
This blessed plot, this earth, this realm, this England,
This nurse, this teeming womb of royal kings,
Fear'd by their breed and famous by their birth,
Renowned for their deeds as far from home,

"'A precious stone set in a silver sea.'" Robin said. "This is a description of something, a vase, or a painting."

"A footprint?"

"If it's something Shackspear could never see."

"It is. Gloucester is describing a diptych from Richard's time. The right-hand panel has eleven angels in blue on it, all with badges of the white hind, Richard's emblem. The angels float in the air around the Virgin and Child who are gesturing toward Richard, depicted on the left panel. One of the angels is holding the banner of St. George. A globe at the top has a picture of England swimming 'in a shining sea.'"

"Ah," Robin said.

Oxford was enjoying his description of the diptych. He didn't notice he had captured Robin's imagination. "Richard used the diptych as an altarpiece in his private chapel. Elizabeth inherited it when she became queen. She has it in her private chapel. Being the leader of the Anglican Church, she keeps it out of the public eye lest someone ask why she has a painting of Jesus and Mary, given that the Puritans are everywhere now. She loves it for the art, she says, and likes to think the angels will protect her."

"Did they protect Richard?" Robin asked.

"No. He was swept off the throne while still alive, something she worries about. That's why the play I am writing is about Richard. She thinks he gazes down on her as she prays. She thinks of him every time she enters her private chapel and sees the diptych."

"You have been in the queen's private chapel?" Robin asked.

"That's where she keeps it."

Robin smiled. Then he became serious. "This is all in verse, my lord. You've never done that before."

"The characters are noble, apart from a gardener and a groom. It's about ritual, Robin, about who succeeds a king. Elizabeth has no heir and refuses to name a successor. She needs to listen to Richard. Therefore, they must speak in verse."

"But she hates anything that touches on the succession."

"Yes. She thinks she will be in danger if she names her successor."

"And why Richard?"

"If the queen is Richard, who is Bolingbroke?"

"Essex."

"Aye. The upstart she coddles and forgives, promotes to keep him happy, and treats in a way she never treated Leicester. Even Cobham is afeared of where the queen is going. He urged me to write a play that might persuade her to view Essex in a different light."

Robin nodded. "Your picture of Richard is not very flattering. He can't make up his mind about what to do when Bolingbroke comes back to England and ends up giving the crown to him. Is that true?"

"Close enough. How would you describe Richard?"

"A vacillator."

"And what is the queen doing with Essex, her Bolingbroke?"

"Vacillating."

"Indeed. And what is Essex doing?"

"We don't know."

"Yes, as perhaps Bolingbroke didn't know. I present him as conflicted in the play. He says he's come back to claim his rightful heritage but, as the play unfolds, he sounds more and more like he's come back to take the crown."

"But Richard doesn't take advantage of Bolingbroke's indecision."

"No. Richard is like a fish flopping around in the bottom of a boat. He puts a brave face on when he hears that Bolingbroke has come back from France." Oxford searched through the manuscript and pulled up a page:

> *So when this thief, this traitor, Bolingbroke,*
> *Shall see us rising in our throne, the east,*
> *His treasons will sit blushing in his face.*
>
> *God for his Richard hath in heavenly pay*
> *A glorious angel: then, if angels fight,*
> *Weak men must fall, for heaven still guards the right.*

"Ah. The angels on the diptych," Robin said. "He sounds strong here, but starts talking *of graves, of worms, and epitaphs* and *let us sit upon the ground / and tell sad stories of the death of kings.*" He looked up, bewildered.

Oxford was pleased. He liked nothing more than watching a theatergoer flinch as if he were watching something real, for that was what Robin was at the moment.

Robin went on. "It starts to turn so sad. He imagines himself exchanging his royal goods for beads and wooden bowls:

> *And my large kingdom for a little grave,*
> *A little little grave, an obscure grave;*
> *Or I'll be buried in the king's highway,*
> *Some way of common trade, where subjects' feet*
> *May hourly trample on their sovereign's head;*

Robin looked up, a grin on his face. "Oh, *A little grave, a little little grave.* I hear you here, my lord: *Were I a king I might command content,* ending with:

> *A doubtful choice of these things which to crave,*
> *A kingdom or a cottage or a grave*

"to which Sidney replied:

> *An easy choice of these things which to crave,*
> *No kingdom nor a cottage but a grave.*

He was still grinning. He was like a kid pulling toys out of a trunk. "Sidney thought you deserved a grave instead of a kingdom; Richard talks of exchanging his kingdom for *a little little grave.*" He chuckled. "Too bad Sidney isn't alive to hear it."

Robin then became serious. "It may be fun sending up Sidney, my lord, but the scene in which Richard surrenders his kingship to Bolingbroke is even sadder. Richard asks Northumberland if *King Bolingbroke* will give Richard leave to live? *King Bolingbroke?* Bolingbroke has done nothing to challenge Richard up to this point, not even so much as to put his hand on the hilt of his sword!"

Oxford didn't interrupt. He wanted to hear Robin's reaction to what he'd written.

Robin continued. "You have Richard being told that Bolingbroke waits for him in the 'base court.' Richard can't stop himself from waxing lyrical about his imminent fall:

> *Down, down I come, like glistering Phaethon,*
> *Wanting the manage of unruly jades.*
> *In the base court? Base court, where kings grow base,*
> *To come at traitors' calls and do them grace.*
> *In the base court? Come down? Down, court! down, king!*
> *For night-owls shriek where mounting larks should sing.*

"Why does Richard surrender so easily, my lord? He has Heaven on his side."

"Because it's a tragedy, Robin. He can't stop his fall. That's why it is *The Tragedy of Richard the Second*, not simply *Richard the Second*."

"Ah. It's not about him as a king; it's about him as a man."

"No, it's about both. Every king is also a man. Some wear their kingship so close that you cannot separate them without destroying both. Richard slips his kingship off easily, like a light garment, leaving only the man who, without it, is lost."

"And killed."

"Of course. There can't be two kings. Can there be two popes? No. Richard is a threat to Bolingbroke as long as he lives. Richard has to die."

"Will the queen see herself in Richard's fall?"

"Hopefully, she will see Essex as Bolingbroke and rein him in."

"Aye. But, my lord, I have to ask one more question. You begin *Richard II* where *Thomas of Woodstock* left off. Did you write *Woodstock*, my lord?"

"Why would you think that?"

"They both sound like something you wrote, somewhere between the roughness of *Famous Victories* and this." He patted the manuscript on the table. "And how else explain that Earl Robert, 9th Earl of Oxford, is not mentioned in *either* play?"

"Strange, isn't it?"

"According to Camden, Earl Robert was one of Richard's closest companions."

"Closer. They were lovers."

"My lord," Robin said. He was shocked. "Why ever would you say that?"

"Because it is true. Robert was only nine years old when he became the 9th Earl of Oxford. Richard was only ten when he became king. My ancestor, Robert, as Lord Great Chamberlain, washed Richard's hands at Richard's coronation. Two children bonded by an ancient ritual. Is it surprising that Richard made Robert Duke of Ireland? The other nobles hated Robert for this. Robert was eventually forced into exile in France where he was killed by a boar!"

"My lord!" Robin cried out.

"I was told about Earl Robert early in my life. He, earl at nine, me at twelve. Both of us bound over to guardians. He, exiled from court; me exiled in other ways. Could the ending of *Venus & Adonis*, with Adonis being gored to death by a boar, have been any different?"

Robin hadn't thought of this. "Not even if you weren't Adonis," he said, trying not to sound cheeky.

Oxford didn't notice. He was reliving Earl Robert's life. "Richard so loved Robert that he had Robert's coffin brought back to England for burial here. He opened it at Westminster and leaned in to kiss his friend one last time before sending it on to Earl's Colne."

"I guess the close relationship between the two would have besmudged the play with their love," Robin said. Oxford nodded. "And leaving Robert out of *Woodstock* and *Richard II* is another footprint." He eyed his master.

Oxford smiled. His little page still thought his name would become known.

"*Someone, somewhere, someday will say: / The Earl of Oxford wrote this play'*" Robin sang softly.

These thoughts reminded Oxford that the plays still belonged to Shackspear. He looked away, his face clouding over.

"Now, tell me about the horse," Robin asked.

"What horse?"

"Woodstock takes the reins to a visitor's horse when the visitor mistakes him for a groom. The visitor proceeds into Woodstock's house, leaving Woodstock in the courtyard with the horse. Woodstock talks to the horse."

"He does?"

"Yes:

> *Why I say you're a very indifferent beast, you'll follow any man*
> *that will lead you. You look lean. You feed not in Westminster*
> *Hall adays, where so many sheep and oxen are devour'd. I'm*
> *afraid they'll eat you shortly if you tarry amongst them. You*
> *know not your master. And yet I think you have as much wit*
> *as he: Faith, say a man should steal ye and feed ye fatter, could*
> *ye run away with him? Ah, your silence argues a consent, I see.*

Robin glanced at Oxford. "I'm assuming Woodstock is you. Who else would write a scene where the main character has a chat with a horse?"

"Another reason I did not write *Woodstock*."

Robin made a sound like a horse would make as it pulled its head away from a hand it doesn't like.

Oxford laughed. "Go over *Richard* one more time and bring it to me. I've the other play to work on."

"Ah. The *other* play."

Richard II Before the Queen

On Boxing Day, 1596, the queen gave her cousin, Sir George Carey, 2nd Baron Hunsdon, an Indian rock crystal bracelet studded with rubies and diamonds. In the afternoon, she watched Lord Hunsdon's men present William Shakespeare's newest play, *Richard II*. She was not pleased. The royal visage had assumed a permanent scowl by the end of the play. Her hands had worked the arms of the stately chair she sat in whilst Edward Alleyn showed her a pathetic King Richard giving away his crown. The play ended with Richard dying in his prison cell. Elizabeth rose, a look of anger on her face as she surveyed the people in front of her.

"*Get him,*" she said in a low voice. The room emptied. Oxford came around a corner and approached. He bowed, planting his good knee on the floor.

"How dare you," she hissed, leaning over the top of his head. She held a fan made of peacock feathers in her hand. The fireplaces and the people who had come to see the play had overheated the room. She had asked for the fan to cool herself. She snapped it shut and lowered the edge to the back of Oxford's neck. She let it lie there before starting to slide it back and forth across his neck, as if she were looking for the 'sweet spot' where the axe would remove a head in one stroke. She whispered in his ear: "I issue an order forbidding any discussion of my succession and you have the gall to write an entire play about it and *present it in front of me!* You disobey and humiliate me at the same time!"

Oxford remained on his knee. "T'was not about you, Your Majesty; t'was about Richard."

"*Know ye not that I am Richard?*" she almost shouted.

Oxford, still on his knee, head bent, was beginning to think she might order someone to bring her a sword. He pushed the fan aside and rose, even though she had not given him permission to do so.

"And if you are Richard, who is Bolingbroke?" he asked, returning her choler.

She didn't answer. "I have no need of your counsel on who should succeed me, my lord." She got up and stalked off, throwing the fan over her shoulder at him.

Edward Alleyn appeared, still covered in blood. "She didn't like the play," he said, a worried look on his face.

"She loves your art, Edward. That's all that matters. Besides, she never kills the messenger who brings bad news." He opened the fan and began to wave it in front of him. "And, if she only wants to kill me with a fan made of peacock feathers, I am doing well."

"What did she whisper when she bent over you, my lord?"

"If I told you, I'd have to kill you." He snapped the fan shut and made like he would saw Alleyn's neck, who jumped back. "She got the message. *Ça suffit.*"

"She'll like *Prince Hal.*"

"You think so?"

Alleyn nodded. "*Je suis prêt.*"

Oxford frowned. "You're turning French on me? Hal was English."

"I have a very good ack-scent, my lord. Write me a scene in French. The ladies will love it."

Oxford was surprised. Falstaff had urged him to do the same thing. "But you are married, are you not?"

Alleyn made like he was shocked. "I am. I didn't say I'd accept any offers, my lord. But it's good to have them. A scene in French will attract the ladies, who will bring their husbands and lovers, …"

Oxford eyed him. "And who am I speaking with? Edward Alleyn, the player? Or Edward Alleyn, husband and father?"

"Richard II," Alleyn said immediately. A quizzical look passed over his face. "Richard the man? He was so …"

"Human?" Oxford asked. "Ah, you listened to what I wrote. But take the blood off and go home, Edward. Leave Richard here."

Alleyn smiled. "*This happy breed of men, this little world, / This precious stone set in the silver sea,* …

"Yes, yes," Oxford said, waving him toward the door.

"And *merci bien* for those lines."

"You're welcome."

Prince Hal and the Boar's Head

The next day, the day after Boxing Day, the queen was presented with the first of the three history plays she had ordered Oxford to write from the remnants of *The Famous Victories of Henry V*. It arrived with the title of *Prince Hal and the Boar's Head*. Alleyn had preened in front of his fellow players during rehearsals, relishing the chance to shine as Prince Hal. He hoped to push Richard Burbage, playing Hotspur, into the shadows. Burbage thought the opposite, expecting to triumph in front of the queen, but no one had seen Falstaff on stage.

The big knight gained the friendship of the other players by having buttered beer brought in to soothe their throats during rehearsals but he gave no hint that his performance would contain little of what Oxford had written for him. He dropped lines and added others, forcing the other players to scramble to keep up with him. Oxford was appalled but, with sniggers and snide remarks that were not in the script, Big Jack Falstaff walked away with the play.

The audience loved him, probably because they sensed he was ignoring the script like no one had ever done before, not even Tarlton. Everyone in London, from the lowest scullery maid to the queen herself, loved a display of wit, and Falstaff showed himself a master of the form, particularly when the audience knew he was making it up on the fly.

It all began in Act Two when Falstaff decided to expand the number of men who robbed him of the money he had taken on Gad's Hill:

Falstaff: *Four rogues in buckram let drive at me.*

Prince Hal   *What, four? Thou said'st but two even now.*

Falstaff: *Four, Hal, I told thee four.*

Poins: *Ay, ay, he said four.*

Falstaff: *These four came all afront, and mainly thrust at me but took all their seven points in my target, thus.*

Prince Hal: *Seven? Why there were but four even now.*
In buckram?

Falstaff: *Ay, four in buckram suits. Seven by these hilts,*

> *or I am a villain else.*

Not a word of this was in the script Oxford had written. Alleyn, playing Hal, had to make up lines to Falstaff's outlandish claims as they came flying past him. The number of men attacking Falstaff grew and grew until there were eleven men assaulting him, all in buckram suits. And then Falstaff returned to the script, describing how "*three misbegotten knaves in Kendal green came at my back, and let drive at me, for it was so dark, Hal, that thou couldst not see thy hand!*"

This part the actors knew, and Alleyn was ready: *Why, how couldst thou know these men were wearing Kendal green when thou couldst not see thy hand?* Alleyn stood there, looking as regal as Hal, hand on hip. *Come, tell us your reason. What sayest thou to this? Come, your reason, Jack, your reason.*

Alleyn's challenge was the verbal equivalent of a wrestler throwing his opponent to the ground. Or was it? Falstaff snorted:

> *What, upon compulsion? Zounds, an I were at the strappado*
> *or all the racks in the world, I would not tell you on*
> *compulsion. Give you a reason on compulsion? If reasons were*
> *as plentiful as blackberries, I would give no man a reason upon*
> *compulsion, I. I'll be no longer guilty of this sin.*

The audience thought Falstaff was escaping but Alleyn, as the prince, kept him pinned: *This sanguine coward, this bed-presser, this horse-backbreaker, this huge hill of flesh —*

To which Falstaff interrupted with a string of insults of his own: *'Sblood, you starveling, you elfskin, you dried neat's tongue, you bull's pizzle, you stockfish!*

The audience shrieked: the prince described as a *bull's pizzle? A stockfish?* They could hardly contain themselves. Alleyn had so carried off playing Prince Hal that the audience believed he was indeed the heir apparent, and the fat knight showering His Highness with insults was an outrageous sight to behold. The audience howled; the queen did not.

Alleyn decided to tell the audience how he, as Prince Hal, tricked Falstaff into giving up the money he had stolen:

> *We two set on you four and, with a sword, outfaced you from*
> *your prize, and have it, yea, and can show it to you here in the*
> *house. And, Falstaff, you carried your guts away nimbly, and*
> *roared for mercy, and still run and roared, as ever I heard bull-*
> *calf.*

It was the audience roaring now. Alleyn waited for calm and then demanded:

> *What trick, what device, what starting-hole canst thou now*
> *find out to hide thee from this open and apparent shame?*
> *Come, let's hear, Jack. What trick hast thou now?*

"Oooh," went the audience. "He's got 'em now!" someone called out.

Falstaff drew himself up:

> *By the Lord, I knew you, Hal, as well as he that made you.*
> *Was it for me to kill the heir apparent? Should I turn upon*
> *the true prince? Why, thou knowest I am as valiant as*
> *Hercules, but I knew it was thee. The lion will not touch the*
> *true prince.*

The audience gasped, and then burst out laughing. Even the queen was forced to smile.

The play rolled on, with Hal urging Falstaff to play Henry IV so he could practice what to say to his father the next day. *Do thou stand for my father,* Alleyn said, *and examine me upon the particulars of my life.* Falstaff enthusiastically pulled over a stool and sat down. He put a cushion on his head for a crown and called for canary wine to make his eyes red because he intended to be passionate. Mistress Quickly, the hostess of the tavern, exclaimed *O Jesu, he doth it as like one of these harlotry players as ever I see!* which got more laughs.

Falstaff, assuming a regal air, turned to Hal:

> *Harry, that thou art my son, I have partly thy mother's word,*
> *partly my own opinion, but chiefly a villanous trick of thine eye*
> *and a foolish hanging of thy nether lip.*

He leaned toward Hal:

> *The company thou keepest doth defile you: and yet there is a*
> *virtuous man whom I have often noted in thy company, but I*
> *know not his name. He is a goodly portly man, i' faith, and a*
> *corpulent; of a cheerful look, a pleasing eye and a most noble*
> *carriage; and, as I think, his age some fifty, and now I*
> *remember me, his name is Falstaff: there is virtue in that*
> *Falstaff: him keep, the rest banish.*

Alleyn, as Hal, having had enough of this, pulled Falstaff off the stool. *Do thou stand for me, and I'll play my father.*

Falstaff resisted for a moment – *Depose me?* he asked wonderingly – but ceded the stool. The audience was silent for a moment. Hal would now play his father whilst Falstaff would be the prince. Hal – as king now – wasted no time wading into Falstaff:

Thou, ungracious boy. There is a devil haunts thee in the likeness of an old fat man; a tun of man is thy companion. Why dost thou converse with that trunk of humours, that bolting-hutch of beastliness, that swollen parcel of dropsies, that huge bombard of sack, that stuffed cloak-bag of guts, that roasted Manningtree ox with the pudding in his belly, that reverend vice, that grey iniquity, that father ruffian, that vanity in years? Wherein is he good, but to taste sack and drink it? wherein neat and cleanly, but to carve a capon and eat it? wherein cunning, but in craft? wherein crafty, but in villany? wherein villanous, but in all things? wherein worthy, but in nothing?

Falstaff blinked. He put on an innocent face. *I would your grace would take me with you: whom means your grace?*

Hal replied: *thou knowest the man; he is a misleader of youth, an old white-bearded Satan.*

Falstaff nodded:

My lord, the man I know. But if sack and sugar be a fault: if to be fat be to be hated, then Pharaoh's lean kine are to be loved. No, my good lord; banish Peto, banish Bardolph, banish Poins: but for sweet Jack Falstaff, kind Jack Falstaff, true Jack Falstaff, valiant Jack Falstaff, and therefore more valiant, being, as he is, old Jack Falstaff, banish not him thy Harry's company, banish not him thy Harry's company: banish plump Jack, and banish all the world.

To everyone's surprise, Hal said: *I do, I will.*

A hush fell over the audience, as if someone had opened a window and let in a gust of cold air. The queen's smile disappeared. They all felt the play had shifted, like when the bear appeared in *The Winter's Tale*. But no one wanted to hear rumblings that Hal and Falstaff would fall out.

Falstaff was surprised as well. Then the sheriff arrived looking for him and the Gad's Hill robbers. The audience, still absorbing how Hal had turned on Fallstaff, expected Hal to turn the fat knight over to the sheriff, but he didn't. Hal redeemed himself, with the audience, at least, if not the queen, by slipping Falstaff behind an arras and telling the sheriff Falstaff was not there!

This occasioned some gasps: the prince would lie to a sheriff? It got worse: Hal embellished the story and convinced the sheriff to leave, saving the fat knight from being arrested.

After the sheriff had left, Hal looked behind the arras and found Falstaff asleep. He picked Falstaff's pocket in imitation of the Gad's Hill robbery, setting up Falstaff's claim later that someone stole his purse.

The play quickly returned to the serious business of showing Hal becoming his father's right-hand man. He defeated Hotspur and the other rebels. The battle was much appreciated as the players charged back and forth across the stage waving swords at each other.

During rehearsals, Burbage had objected to being killed so early in the play, an event he had not been expecting. In a fit of pique, he refused to lie on the stage while Alleyn, as Hal, triumphed over him. When he found out he would have to lie there while the battle raged around him, he threatened to leave the production. A compromise was reached; a dummy was substituted for him as he lay on the stage, allowing him to stalk out of the theater and retire to the Mermaid where he could try to drink away his humiliation. The switch was accomplished while Hal took the battle to the other side of the stage.

While this was going on, Falstaff suddenly collapsed. This was not in the script. The audience craned forward, thinking he was dead. Oxford and the other players wondered what was going on.

Hal didn't notice Falstaff was down at first. When he did, he couldn't resist turning playwright:

> *What, old acquaintance! could not all this flesh*
> *Keep in a little life? Poor Jack, farewell!*
> *I could have better spared a better man:*
> *Embowell'd will I see thee by and by:*
> *Till then in blood by noble Percy lie.*

Hal ran off to another part of the battle, leaving Falstaff lying not far from the dummy that now represented the dead Hotspur. After a dramatic pause, with the audience and the players wondering what would happen next, Falstaff suddenly got up. "From the grave," a person in the audience whispered loudly. Falstaff brushed himself off. His face showed for an instance that he liked the man's comment but it was what Hal had said that set him to scowling. He thought Hal's description of him insulting.

> *Embowelled! if thou embowel me to-day,*
> *I'll give you leave to powder me and eat me too.*

He looked around, glowering at the audience:

> *'Sblood,'twas time to counterfeit, or*
> *that hot termagant Scot had paid me scot and lot too.*
> *Counterfeit? I lie, I am no counterfeit: to die,*
> *is to be a counterfeit; for he is but the*
> *counterfeit of a man who hath not the life of a man:*
> *but to counterfeit dying, when a man thereby*
> *liveth, is to be no counterfeit, but the true and*
> *perfect image of life indeed.*

He walked to the front of the stage and stopped, hands on hips:

> *The better part of valour is discretion;*
> *in the which better part I have saved my life.*

The audience murmured in appreciation. The cowards among them liked Falstaff's excuse for lying down to save himself. They thought they could use it the next time someone urged them to be brave when they didn't want to.

Falstaff, glancing over his shoulder, saw Hotspur, lying where Hal had killed him:

> *'Zounds, I am afraid of this gunpowder Percy, though he be*
> *dead: how, if he should counterfeit too and rise?*

He eyed the audience to see what they thought. Oxford and the players were dismayed. Where was he going with this?

Why may not he rise as well as I?" he asked.

"Aye!" someone called out. *"Kill him!"* another said.

He surveyed their upturned faces, paused an inordinate amount of time, and then strode back to where Hotspur's body lay. Or, at least his dummy.

> *By my faith, I am afraid he would prove the better counterfeit.*
> *Therefore I'll make him sure; yea, and I'll swear I killed him.*

He drew his sword in dramatic fashion and stabbed Hotspur in the leg.

> *Therefore, sirrah, with a new wound in your thigh,*
> *come you along with me.*

Falstaff hefted Hotspur onto his shoulder and walked out the back of the stage. Hal and his brother, John, came in from the other side of the tiring house, followed immediately by Falstaff returning behind them, still carrying Hotspur. They were astonished to see him. Falstaff had died on the battlefield, hadn't he?

Falstaff threw Hotspur's body down and addressed them:

If your father will do me any honour, so; if not, let
him kill the next Percy himself. I look to be either
earl or duke, I can assure you.

Hal's surprise at finding Falstaff alive was genuine. The scene he now found himself in was not in the script. He could only think to say:

Why, Percy I killed myself and saw thee dead.

Falstaff scoffed:

Didst thou? Lord, how this world is given to lying!

He rearranged his jerkin and shifted his sword in his belt.

I grant you I was down and out of breath; and so was he: but
we rose both at an instant and fought a long hour by
Shrewsbury clock. If I may be believed, so; if not, let them that
should reward valour bear the sin upon their own heads. I'll
take it upon my death, I gave him this wound in the thigh: if
the man were alive and would deny it, 'zounds, I would make
him eat a piece of my sword.

Hal shook his head and said:

Come, bring your luggage nobly on your back:
For my part, if a lie may do thee grace,
I'll gild it with the happiest terms I have.

The play ended. The audience crowded up to the stage. The queen remained seated, watching the nobles and commoners reach up to touch Falstaff who gave his hand to everyone as if he were a king curing them of scrofula. *How much of what she had just heard was Falstaff,* Elizabeth wondered; *How much was Oxford?*

"There will be another play, Your Majesty," an excited lady-in-waiting whispered in Elizabeth's ear. "With Falstaff and Mistress Quickly, the hostess of the tavern. Shrove Tuesday, only five weeks away."

The queen rose. She said nothing as she walked away from the throng still pressed against the stage where Falstaff was holding court. *His court!* Elizabeth noted as she went around the corner. She wanted to talk to Oxford, but he was nowhere to be seen. Strange, she thought, except that he may not have wanted to reappear after what she had said to him after *Richard II*. She frowned. Falstaff being *deposed* by Hal when the prince pulls Falstaff off the joint stool:

> *Depose me? if thou dost it half so gravely, so*
> *majestically, both in word and matter, hang me up by*
> *the heels for a rabbit-sucker or a poulter's hare.*

She began to mutter to herself. What did Hotspur say as he stirred up his rebel lords?

> *In short time after, he deposed the king;*
> *Soon after that, deprived him of his life;*

Aye, she thought. First show me Richard being deposed, coming down, down, down to Bolingbroke, and then bring back the same issue in the next play. "*Enough!*" she cried out, startling the maids and foot servants accompanying her. She hated the way Oxford managed to worm his way into her brain. And he would be back with his questions about Southampton, she knew. Oh, yes, he would be back barking at her about Southampton.

1597

~ 131 ~
The Funeral of Lady Elizabeth Cecil

It was a cold, wet, windy day in February when Sir Robert Cecil laid his wife, Lady Elizabeth, to rest in Westminster Abbey in a free-standing tomb of alabaster and black marble placed alongside the tomb Lord Burghley had built for Lady Mildred, his wife, and Nan Cecil, his daughter.

Lady Elizabeth's three children were too young to attend. The funeral procession was led by two conductors with staves; the number of notables and worthies who followed were more than two hundred. They included Sir Robert Cecil and Sir William Brooke, 10th Baron Cobham, the father of his deceased wife. Diverse gentlemen and doctors of physics and divinity followed. The four corners of the pall were supported by Sir Walter Ralegh, Sir Thomas Gorges, Sir Edward Dyer, and Sir George Carew.

The north side of Lady Elizabeth's tomb displayed an inscription in gold leaf written by Sir Robert. In it, he praised his wife's wisdom and loyalty and memorialized the fact that she had been *blest with two babes, the third having brought her to this* in her thirty-fourth year. A psalm was sung; the preacher held the mourners an hour before they returned to Mr. Dean's house (from whence they had come) for supper.

The queen, along with the sun, did not appear that day. Others could not avoid the ceremony because funerals were one of the visible ways those seeking favors could show themselves to the powerful or hinder themselves by not appearing. Those in the swell of people who trooped through the cold rain into the Abbey and back to Mr. Dean's house came not for the poor woman but her husband, who was now running England. Oxford and many other knights and nobles, including Essex, felt obliged to be seen among the mourners lest their absence be taken as a mark of disrespect to the man had just been widowed.

Mr. Dean's house was on the Strand to the northeast of Cecil House. The walking mourners and the carriages that carried the lords and ladies converged on a large mansion surrounded by a garden. The guests crossed the garden to reach a hall built to entertain guests. The funeral meats were arranged on trestle tables along one wall. No benches or chairs were provided. Mourners were expected to partake and leave. Some, however, stayed. They gathered in knots around Sir Robert trying to put their hands on the levers of power.

Oxford and Essex were both in attendance, although neither was seeking favors from Sir Robert. Essex came up to Oxford and greeted him enthusiastically. "My thanks, my lord, for the good word you put in for me with Bess. She is so difficult to keep happy."

"My pleasure, Robert," Oxford said, not knowing what Essex was talking about. He also didn't think 'Bess' was a word that should be spoken by an upstart such as Essex.

"I fancied *Richard II*," Essex said. "A man racked by conflicts. A man who saw too many possibilities. A man who could not choose which path to take."

"A man who was indecisive."

"Yes."

Oxford was disappointed. Essex had apparently not understood *Richard II*. Oxford had hoped Essex would have taken Richard's fall as a cautionary tale.

"While you are decisive," Oxford suggested.

"Yes, my lord. Action!"

"Including dallying with my daughter."

Essex frowned. "That is nothing but rumor, my lord."

"Her husband does not agree."

Essex scoffed.

"Should I ask Lisbeth?"

This brought Essex to a stop. He knew Lisbeth wouldn't lie to protect him or her marriage.

"I didn't think so," Oxford said. "Robert: be aware. She enjoys chaos. She shows you a shadowed eye and you jump. She shows a different eye to her husband and he runs around in circles. You have enough troubles with the failure of the Islands Voyage." Oxford was referring to the disastrous voyage Essex had commanded that was supposed to destroy the Spanish fleet. You should take off some canvas lest you run aground."

This annoyed Essex even more than being accused of cuckolding the Earl of Derby by sleeping with the daughter of the man standing in front of him. "T'was not my fault," he protested.

"Yes, it was. You disobeyed the queen's order and let the Spanish fleet slip through your hands."

Essex was fuming. He was not used to being criticized. It was only Oxford's titles that kept him from walking away.

Oxford continued. "There are people at court who are disenchanted with you. They will use something you think is inconsequential to get you gone, such as bedding my daughter. Let Lisbeth be wife to the Earl of Derby. And distance yourself from the Earl of Southampton," Oxford added.

This last comment surprised Essex. "Henry?"

"He is still green and susceptible to undue influence."

Essex took umbrage at this. "Any influence I have over Henry benefits him. I am grown to great state with the people. I am the standard around which he and many others rally."

"But in seeking your own destiny, people wonder whether you seek something else. You are being compared to those who have risen against their monarch: Hotspur, Richard, Duke of Gloucester …"

Essex interrupted: "*I seek no throne!*" he practically shouted.

Oxford put up a hand to calm him down. "Did not Bolingbroke make the same claim when he came ashore? Who believes that today?"

Essex began to say something but suddenly stopped. Oxford could tell exactly what he was thinking – *why am I putting up with this agèd relic?* More than one person had said Essex 'carries his love and hatred on his forehead and can conceal nothing,'

Essex huffed off. Over his shoulder, Oxford could see Sir Robert looking across the room at him. Cecil was comforting Baron Cobham, who had aged considerably since Oxford had last seen him. Cecil, on the other hand, looked unchanged despite his loss. He seemed unmoved by Cobham's grief. He resembled Sir Horatio Vere, Oxford's celebrated cousin whose even disposition was compared to the Caspian Sea which neither ebbed nor flowed. But Horatio's steadiness was based on being a principled man; Cecil's was based on being devious.

Cecil disengaged himself from Cobham and came over.

"My lord," Cecil said, bowing slightly. Hunch-backed and lame on one side, the short distance had taxed him.

"Robert," Oxford said. "My condolences."

"Thank you. I appreciate your effort to show the queen how dangerous the Earl of Essex is."

"You've seen *Richard II?*"

"Yes. And so has the queen."

"Has it made her more resolute?"

He shrugged. "She sees the danger one day; the next she does not. She tells me she will rein him in; then she rewards him with a title, like making him Grand Marshall because he was irritated she had given the Admiral a new title. She acts like she's his mother and he the son who can do no wrong."

Was Cecil implying that Elizabeth *was* Essex's mother? She did have a long affair with Leicester. Oxford wondered how much Cecil knew about her affairs and any children she might have had. He decided to fish in Cecil's pond. "I heard there is a young man in Spain claiming he is Leicester's son by Her Majesty."

Cecil knew about Arthur Dudley. He also knew Oxford was claiming that Southampton was his son by the queen. "You reach too far, my lord. Your fancies find no home with me. "But your outrageous claim that Her Majesty and you are the parents of the 3rd Earl of Southampton impugns the queen's honor and endangers the succession."

Oxford looked at Cecil. "I see she shares her most private matters with you."

"And for good reason, my lord. You, unlike that powder keg over there," he gestured toward Essex now talking with Southampton, "have had your fuse watered down by age. Essex, on the other hand, is hot and combustible. He deserves watching. He will o'erstep his bounds soon, and, when he does, Her Majesty will uncouple him from power."

Cecil had been looking at Essex as he said this. He turned to Oxford. "His followers will forget him once he is neutered. Your claim is worse because it may taint the succession, even if you are no longer around, much as a rumor spills through a family long after the source of the lie has left. The damage created by the claim of a false heir - think Perkin Warbeck, for example - can have long-term effects. Her Majesty's successor will be James, not Southampton. You should abandon any hopes for him. It will only harm him."

"But what if he *is* her son?" Oxford said quietly.

"A fact that can never be proven, even if she decided to endorse your outrageous claim, which she will never do. Whatever the case, she has decided that, when she dies, she will ascend to a heavenly kingdom and James will come down from Scotland and take her place. Allow Southampton to live a long and happy life."

"And let you, of course, run England as Secretary."

Cecil nodded. "She has decreed it. James has agreed. The policies my father and I have developed will give James what he wants: a seamless transition."

Oxford had no doubt Cecil was maneuvering Elizabeth into accepting James as her successor to keep himself in power. Pushing Southampton aside must only add a taste of revenge if Cecil thought Southampton was Oxford's son.

Oxford was watching Essex and Southampton over Cecil's shoulder. "I think we can agree that Henry is in danger as long as he associates himself with Essex."

Cecil turned and looked at the two men. "Yes. I will do what I can to pry them apart."

"I would appreciate that. And your father?" Oxford asked. "I hear he is not well. I would like to have a few words with him."

"I'm afraid that will be impossible. A visit from you would do nothing but accelerate his decline. He has never forgiven you for Nan."

"I would apologize for that, my lord, even though I was not at fault."

"You are never at fault."

"I am at times, and not afraid to say so. But not for Nan, or for the kitchen maid you could not marry, Robert. You think I blocked you, Robert, but that was your father's doing."

Cecil glared at Oxford. "You lie. I couldn't marry her because you wouldn't let Sanderson out of a marriage contract that bound her to him. He was one of your retainers. You could have freed her to marry me but you refused."

"Sanderson was not one of my retainers. He was one of the many aspiring poets and musicians who clogged Fisher's Folly when I held it open to starving artists. I knew nothing about Sanderson and his marriage. Your father told me on Accession Day that he had arranged for Sanderson to marry the girl to keep her away from you. 'Bad for the family,' he told me then, 'a decision Robert will regret once his passion for her burns itself out.'"

"I say again - you lie."

"Find Sanderson. He will tell you the truth."

Cecil gave Oxford a withering look and hobbled off into the crowd. Oxford knew Robert would never seek out Sanderson. The truth would end Robert's love affair with his father, which would be even more painful than being denied the love of his life.

A hand touched Oxford's arm. It was Lady Elspeth. Aemilia Bassano was standing next to her, radiant in a black belted doublet with black feathers fanning out behind her over her left shoulder. There was nothing of the exploding colors that had enveloped her when Oxford encountered her at Lord Willoughby's the first time they met. She had been veiled then in translucent silk, gracing the arm of Lord Hunsdon. Her clothing may have changed but her dark mysterious eyes had not.

"My lord," Lady Elspeth said, "I believe you are acquainted with Miss Bassano?"

Aemilia Bassano smiled, a warm glowing smile that Lady Elspeth took as friendship whilst Oxford squeezed it for every bit of unrequited love he could imagine. "My lord," she murmured, holding her hand out. Oxford brushed his lips over it.

"I am sure you two have much to discuss," Elspeth said. "Aemilia has found God, my lord. And poetry. I would think the latter, at least, would interest you." She turned away to speak with a woman who had approached her.

"Poetry," Oxford said to the radiant woman in front of him. He thought his voice sounded more pleasant for being uttered in her presence. "How has that come about?"

"I live now with Lady Margaret Clifford and her daughter, Anne, at Cooke-ham on the Thames. Her estate is a haven for women who pursue the arts."

"I thought you favored a ship captain."

"He was a musician, my lord, who aspired to military success, thinking it would make him rich. He turned out to be a poor musician, a worse soldier, and a terrible businessman. Lord Hunsdon loved me better as his mistress than Alfonso ever did as my husband. He consumed my goods and left me and my son without means. Lady Margaret has been gracious to take me in and nurse my muse."

"Tell me about your muse."

She thought he was genuinely interested. "In my sleep, I am visited by Pilate's wife, who speaks for Our Savior. She asks Pilate why women must endure so much pain when Eve did nothing more than hand Adam an apple."

"A good question."

"I am working on a piece I have named *Hail, God, King of the Jews.* In it, Pilate's wife pleads to save the life of Jesus. She says:

Let us have our Libertie againe:
You came not in this world without our paine.
If one weake woman did simply offend,
This sin of yours hath no excuse, nor end.

Oxford may have thought Aemilia's poetry weak, but her lips were perfect. They reached out to him. The thrill of being so close rendered him momentarily mute. Aemilia took his silence as approval.

"My lord, *my lord of poetry,*" she said: "What think you?"

"You have crafted poetry as lovely as you are," he said warmly.

"Jesus hath saved me, my lord," she said, letting him know she would not let him go any further. She curtsied slightly, as if Jesus were standing nearby. "I was a girl when we crossed paths. My beauty made men grovel at my feet. A silly power based on how I looked, not on who I am. I expect to be judged on better values and use my poetry to bring people to Jesus."

"Yes. But your message may drive wives from their husbands."

"As your *Taming of the Shrew* drove husbands from their wives. Pilate's wife will show women what they can do."

Aemilia yearned to talk about heavenly rewards. He wanted to talk about more earthly things. "I have always imagined us differently. "I have always imagined us differently."

She knew what he meant. She laughed and put a hand on his shoulder, the touch of her hand sending waves of emotion through him. "I see you have not changed, my lord." She said without rancor or judgment.

"You do not blame me?"

"How can I? You are a man." She rotated slightly, making him imagine what was hidden under the swaths of black cloth that wrapped her. "As a man, you are fated to seek admittance to women's charms, no matter what the cost. We women, on the other hand, are fated to resist you so that we are not distracted from pursuing higher goals. In my case, Jesus and poetry. Yours?"

Oxford found himself unable to answer her question. She laughed again, a warm laugh. To his surprise, he blurted out the one question he couldn't stop himself from asking. "Was it Shackspear?"

She knew what he was referring to. He was still obsessed with knowing who had bedded her and given her a son. "You must not look at me like that, my lord. Your ladyship is nearby."

Oxford did not care what Elspeth thought. "Was it Shackspear?"

She laughed. "He had a mustache," she said mischievously.

"A mustache?" Did Shackspear have a mustache, Oxford asked himself. He couldn't remember. Something inside him screamed: *how can I not remember whether Shackspear had a mustache?*

Aemilia felt pity for him. At the same time, she realized she had slipped back into being the woman she had promised Jesus she had put away. "Shackspear has never had a mustache, my lord."

Oxford was instantly relieved.

She could see the pain he had suffered. She decided to give him one more gift. "Do you remember the night when you were to visit me in Lord Hunsdon's chambers and found me otherwise engaged?"

Oxford nodded. "*William I came before Edward VII,*" he said, repeating what the porter had told him.

"William, as in William Shackspear, did not gain access to my bed that night, my lord, although I was content to let you think so."

He looked at her. "He didn't?"

"No. My Lord Hunsdon returned home unexpectedly. Before Shackspear could return, I discovered you were the poet I had fallen in love with. Shackspear has never slept with me, my lord. I tell you this to apologize to you for my behavior and cleanse my soul before God."

Oxford was speechless.

"But you have not answered my question," she said. "You should be seeking Jesus." She smiled but could see he was not ready yet to love Jesus. She bowed and moved off.

She was right about Oxford. But her question made him wonder what he *was* doing. He was about to turn fifty. Marlowe's voice floated into this head: 'Tragedy over comedy, my lord. The audience laughs at comedy and forgets what they heard. No one forgets *Tamburlaine.*'

No one will forget Falstaff, Oxford thought. And plays about kings and queens retold history, which anyone could read in Camden and Holinshed. But *Hamlet* was tragedy. It was time to finish *Hamlet.* And look into old age. Loss. Oblivion. Death is not far away, he reminded himself, the journey on which each of us goes alone.

132

The King Knows Him Not

Shrove Tuesday found England gripped in an ice storm yet no one stayed indoors: they didn't want to miss the return of Sir John Falstaff, who had stolen the theater world from Edward Alleyn in *Prince Hal and the Boar's Head*. The audience loved Alleyn's Prince Hal, but they came back to see the fat knight.

"Must he meet his end here, my lord?" Robin anxiously asked one more time as they settled onto a cold, hard bench in the third tier at The Curtain. Oxford was trying to see if the queen had made her way into the special box Burbage had constructed for her. An ostrich feather had stuck up over the partition that walled her off from the audience during the earlier play. Some thought it was her way of letting everyone know she was there, like the t'gallants on a warship coming up over the horizon, but no feather was visible this time.

"He has to go," Oxford said. "He is a leviathan who has swallowed the play. It was to be about Hal and his progress from wastrel prince to noble king. But no one cares about that now. Not after Falstaff buried the script in snorts and asides, his speeches about valor and conscripts being," here Oxford dropped his voice, 'food for powder, food for powder.' *Gun powder*," Oxford said angrily. "I can now understand the horror Pasiphaë felt as she watched the Minotaur dismount!"

Robin sniggered at the image but Oxford was in no mood for humor. "Truly, Jack has done me a great disservice. When he asked to play the part, I wanted to say 'no' but could not find the words to explain why. That was because no one has ever seen what that bed presser can do to a play. He has broken the mold. He must go."

"The queen loves him."

"Apparently." Oxford scanned the queen's box again. "She has let it be known she wants a 'word' with him after he finishes today."

"Oh, my lord."

"She underestimates the danger she will find herself in."

Falstaff had balked when he read the script to *Henry IV, Part Two*. "I have read the script," he announced, eyeing Shackspear as they sat across the library table from each other. Oxford was sitting in the chair at the end, in front of the window. "Hal becomes king and I race back from Yorkshire to greet him. I get there as he comes out of Westminster Abbey *and you have Hal act like he doesn't know me."* He reached for the script:

> *I know thee not, old man: fall to thy prayers;*
> *How ill white hairs become a fool and jester!*

"He knows me not!" Falstaff exclaimed, waving the script in the air.

"He has changed, Jack, and remember, he is speaking just outside the cathedral, surrounded by the public:

> *Presume not that I am the thing I was;*
> *For God doth know I have turn'd away my former self.*

Oxford continued. "He is speaking o'er the top of you, to reassure everyone that the madcap Hal has become King Henry V!"

Falstaff made a face. He looked down at the script. "Must he banish me ten miles?"

"But he promises to give you means to live and will take you back when you reform yourself. I gave you lines to speak to Justice Shallow to make this clear:

> *Do not you grieve at this,* you say to Shallow: *I shall be sent for in private; he must seem thus to the world.*

"And will that happen?" Falstaff asked. He was suspicious. "I know you are working on the next play, Hal's glory in France. The real Prince Hal made John Falstoff, my ancestor, keeper of Calais. I see myself there, and at Agincourt." He put on a fierce countenance. Neither Oxford nor Robin knew whether the big man was giving them a preview of what he would be like fighting at Agincourt or showing how angry he was at the turn his character had taken in the script. Both, probably.

"Oh, yes. Yes," Oxford said, a little too quickly Robin thought.

The audience sensed a change. Shackspear and Burbage, watching as the play unfolded, realized their patrons understood Hal had to change to become king - what every young boy goes through to become a man - but Falstaff was changing as well. The audience was not happy with this. They sensed the man they had taken to their bosom had been changed into a character they didn't recognize.

At the end, Shackspear came out front to add an epilogue Oxford hadn't written:

One word more, I beseech you.
Our humble author will continue the story with Sir John in it,
And make you merry with fair Katharine of France:
Where, for any thing I know, Falstaff shall die of a sweat,
Unless already he be killed by your hard opinions;
I bid you good night: and so kneel down before you,
but, indeed, to pray for the queen.

The queen liked Shackspear urging the audience to pray for her but she was disappointed with how Falstaff had changed. She summoned Oxford. "Falstaff was a wonderful jewel in Part One, my lord, but the character I have just seen has been sanded down and dulled out. We are not pleased."

Oxford said nothing.

"Go forth and bring him to me. I will have private conference with him."

She had never before asked to talk with any of the players. Oxford went looking for Falstaff, who soon poked his head into the queen's booth. "Yer Majesty?"

She waved him in. "Take a seat," she said. She pointed to one of the chairs in the booth.

Falstaff worked his immense bulk into the booth. He bowed to Elizabeth before gingerly lowering himself onto one of the stools, for he was too wide to sit in any of the chairs.

Elizabeth eyed him. "I thought his lordship had *created* a character we had never seen before, but after watching you in these two plays, I am beginning to wonder if he has only *appropriated* you. Which are you, Sir John? Someone Lord Oxford has created, like Athena from the head of Zeus? Or a man borrowed to dress in fancy clothes and bombast out a line?"

Falstaff smiled. "A good question."

She frowned. She leaned toward him. "I have no time for *bullshit*, Jack!" she said, shocking Falstaff with her language as well as by addressing him as 'Jack.' "I get *bullshit* all the time." Her words came out like punches. "You have no idea how difficult it is to get the truth from someone if you are queen and surrounded by toadies and caterpillars who keep giving you *bullshit!* Answer my question."

Falstaff had entered the booth thinking he'd be in and out with a few pleasantries, but Her Majesty clearly wanted more. "Truth is, yer majesty, I've been with his lordship for so many years, listening to all the words that come out of him, watching him smooth-talk everyone -

not Your Majesty, of course - that I'm not sure where he ends and I begin."

She didn't like his answer. She glowered at him, even lowering her head slightly, reminding Falstaff of a bull he'd escaped when he was a boy. He had climbed a fence to cut through a field when a bull appeared from behind a tree. He managed to get over the fence before the bull got to him but there was no fence for him to leap over and escape from the queen, whose eyes were boring into him.

"I am what I am," he said after a moment.

This was more answer than he knew. Falstaff was quoting Oxford, of course, who had used the same expression in a letter to Burghley in which he had complained about his father-in-law's efforts to control him. Falstaff didn't know Oxford had been quoting Paul.

The queen did, though. But she didn't think Falstaff understood what he'd just said. Was he using Paul's words in the same way Paul had used them? Her cocked head told Falstaff he had not wriggled off the hook yet.

Falstaff drew in a breath. ""His lordship may say I am the cause of wit in others, Your Majesty, but, with all due respect, he misses the mark. I am not the cause of *wit* in others; I am the cause of *happiness* in others. Like the way your grace is the cause of happiness in your subjects."

Elizabeth blinked. Was he now comparing himself to her? Or was he trying to flatter her and had overrun his mark. Her eyebrows rose.

Falstaff realized that his best hope of escaping the 'bull' now eyeing him was to act as if nothing had happened. He told himself to relax. He had to be himself.

He rearranged himself on the stool. "The idea that life is a tragedy is an idea I refuse to accept, Your Majesty. To other people, life is a list of do-nots: do not covet thy neighbor's wife; do not steal; do not lie; do not eat meat on Fridays; do not accept this man because he goes to a different church. I refuse to live that way; I refuse to die each day, like scales falling off a fish. I live only to live."

"And how do you do that?"

"By reminding myself it is not how many days I have but how I live the only day I ever have - today. I refuse to sacrifice today on the ashes of yesterday or on the altar of tomorrow."

The queen nodded. "So, you …?"

"Refuse to take life seriously." He paused for a moment. "Gravity, Your Majesty, is always going to be inferior to gravy." He winked at her. "I bring a bottle of wine to a battle instead of a gun; I lie down to live."

She was looking at him. He couldn't tell whether he was losing her.

"I refuse to age," Your Majesty. "Time means nothing to me. It's a grate of iron that numbers drop over ye, becoming heavier and heavier until it crushes you into old age. I know the year, much less my years. They are false gods other men worship or dread. Give me sack or a wench. Tomorrow always comes, tip-toeing in with the dawn whether I be here or not, whether I worry or not, bringing me a clean fresh day with joys and woes, all different than the day before and yet always the same. The number hung on that day, or hung on me as my age, is but a label, a made-up thing as in a play and could be any number."

The queen was taken aback by this outpouring. "Like the change in the calendar the Pope ordered," she said, in wonderment. "Italy and the rest of the world are ten days ahead of us!"

Falstaff didn't know this. "Another reason the true faith rests here," he said solemnly, nodding his head.

The queen almost took this as sarcasm; how could the corpulent knight in front of her be religious? But then he might be, in his way. Best not to ask him, she thought. Some matters are best left alone.

"And then there were the three women who came upon a naked man sleeping in a field," he said blithely, like they were sharing village gossip over a fence.

She blinked. He was going to tell her a joke?

He didn't wait. "The first woman said, 'he's not my husband.'"

Elizabeth was now startled. He *was* telling her a joke. How *dare* the man! But she couldn't interrupt him. She wanted to hear the rest.

Falstaff saw her reaction and knew he had her. "The second woman said, 'no, he's not.'"

The queen stifled herself.

"The third one," Falstaff went on, "said, 'no, it's not anyone from the village!'"

The queen burst out laughing. Falstaff joined her. The listeners just out of sight looked at each other. The queen carrying on with Sir John!

They stopped laughing. "People laugh, Your Majesty, because I show them how they can get through another day no matter how bad things may seem. In this way, I defeat death. His lordship understands this of me."

Elizabeth watched him settle back on his stool, content with having carried out his 'dooty' to speak truth to her.

"If all that is true, Sir John, why are you changing? The man I see in *Part Two* is not the man I saw in *Part One*. The lusty trencherman of *Part One* is a pitiful remnant at the end of *Part Two*. And, mark you, I know his lordship sees himself as Hal. If he understands you as you say, why has he transformed you into something that is not you?"

Falstaff sighed. "I frighten him." The queen was surprised to hear this. "He understands me, Your Majesty, but he cannot follow me. Neither can you. You both live in a world of obligations; I do not. I can spend days in the Boar's Head doing nothing but he can't. Neither can you. *You* must govern; *he* must write. You govern because you love your subjects who, in return, love you back. He writes for an audience who wants to love him back even though they do not *know* his name. That's the tragedy he should be writing. To be the greatest writer who ever lived and die nameless is a terrible burden."

Elizabeth could tell that Falstaff was not saying this to talk her into letting Oxford's name appear on the plays. That would be beneath him. No, he was still telling her the truth.

"I think you represent the impossible," she concluded.

"But isn't there always hope that the impossible might happen? Isn't that why the churches are full on Palm Sunday?"

Elizabeth smiled wryly. "Tell his lordship to come back in. Thank you, Sir John."

"Yer Majesty." He got up and left the booth.

Oxford came in. "Your Majesty."

"I want you to write a play about Falstaff in love, my lord."

Oxford blinked. "That would be impossible, Your Majesty. He only loves himself."

"Nothing is impossible. For the garter ceremony."

"But that's only a few weeks away!"

She rose. "As I said: nothing is impossible."

133

Falstaff In Love

Oxford came out into the Great Hall. "No," he called out angrily. "No. I will *not* do it."

He bounded up the stairs. He turned left at the top and disappeared into the room that no one was allowed to enter. Not even Bona Ventura. Not even the Countess.

Shackspear and Robin came out of the library.

"He doesn't mean it," Shackspear said, looking up at the stairs.

"He may stand fast this time," Robin said. "He is outraged the queen has ordered another play. He does not take well to commands from anyone, least of all from her. And to tell him to write a play about Falstaff in love? That might be impossible even for him. And, if he doesn't, what can she do?"

"Deny him his pension," Shackspear said. "And me a play. He may not need the money, or even *understand* money, but I do. Anne's going to buy New Place next month. It's going to cost me £60."

"You only get £5 a play. How's that going to help."

"It won't, but, as a sharer, I get more. We made an oxcart of money off *Prince Hal.* But I can't make *any* money without a play!"

"An oxcart?"

"Well, a dogcart. A lot. Every bit helps. Anne hid grain away to sell when the prices went up but someone told the sheriff. They thought she hid 80 bushels of corn! Pshaw! She hid twice that, I warrant."

Robin was shocked to hear this. "Ye'd let people starve when ye had grain they could eat?"

"Why not?" Shackspear replied. "Are bees bound to keep life in drones and idle moths? I don't care a fig about those who don't store enough away to get through the lean times. God's 'winnowing' them out, in't he? But idle tongues about how much she hid away have the town digging up the garden and stripping the barn."

"But if Anne did the buying and the hiding, why are the justices coming after you?"

Shackspear looked at Robin in amazement. "You know women count for nothin', don't ya? You're a man, or almost a man, aren't ye? You helped write *The Shrew*, didn't ye? Sometimes we men pay the price for being on top. The justices figure I must have come up with the idea and hid the grain 'cause Anne's a woman. But I'm in London, ain't I? I mean, I can't be buying corn and burying it in Stratford if I'm here, can I?"

"So, tell them that."

Shackspear thought this even stupider. "I'm the man of the house. I can't say Anne came up with the idea. I would look ridiculous. 'Big man in London run by his wife in Stratford a*nd admits it!'*

For once, Robin thought, Shackspear made sense.

"If she hadn't gotten caught, she'd have the £60 but, no, she treats people like she's pissing on their shoes and never gets it that they're going to come back and piss on hers1 The justices took the grain she hid to sell at below-market prices.. This means she won't have the money to buy the big house she wants in May. I need a play before then to get the cash we need and get her off my back!"

"But I don't think his lordship is going to write you a new play, based on what I know of him."

"Yeah." Shackspear admitted grimly. He thought for a moment. "I'm going to get Ben Jonson to help. He's a playwright as well as a player. I'll get him to do it for nothing. His lordship will be happy to give it to Jonson because it will save him from getting into a fight with the queen."

He headed out the door. Robin watched him go. 'He's right,' Robin thought. 'For a second time. Who would have thought?'

———◆◆◆◆◆———

Shackspear was back within the hour. He pushed his way into Oxford Court, towing Ben Jonson. Jonson was a big, raw-boned man almost the size of Tobias. The African huffed himself up to let Jonson know who was boss.

Jonson was wearing a coach-man's coat with slits under the armpits. He had never been to Oxford Court before although he had heard what went on behind the oak door Tobias closed behind him.

He put a serious look on an ugly face that was full of pocky holes and pimples punched full of oylet holes like the cover of a warming pan. He was trying to frown away the beer he'd been drinking. Shackspear had found him in the Mermaid, bent over a table telling those within reach how he had single-handedly won a battle in the

Low Countries by killing a Spanish soldier in single combat. According to Ben, he was awarded the Spaniard's arms and furniture and was feted by his companions in a nearby town, the name of which he could no longer remember.

Shackspear led Jonson into the library. "Robin," Shackspear said to Robin. "Fetch us your master, if you please."

Before Robin could get up, Oxford appeared in the doorway. He surveyed the room. "Who are you?" he asked Jonson.

"This is Ben Jonson, your lordship," Shackspear said. "He was Bassanio in *The Merchant*. I've asked him to help us write the play the queen wants about *Falstaff in Love*."

Oxford had never imagined that Shackspear would be so brazen as to bring someone in to help write a play. He was about to order Tobias to throw them both into the street when he realized using Jonson might allow him to avoid having to write the play himself. "Oh?"

"You be the conceiver, my lord," Shackspear said, dipping his head deferentially, "whilst Robin and I, with Ben's help, bring *Falstaff in Love* to the stage."

Oxford was trying to tamp down his outrage at Shackspear bringing in someone to help write a new play to consider Shackspear's idea. Maybe they could write a play good enough to satisfy the queen. He stood in the doorway, as motionless as a statue made of marble. A plot began to unfold in his mind.

Shackspear and Robin knew Oxford had gone 'inside.' Jonson, on the other hand, had no idea what was going on. Everyone around him seemed frozen. After an interminable wait, Oxford suddenly turned to Jonson.

"Mr. Jonson; if I give you the bones of a plot, can you put flesh on them?"

"Aye, my lord. It's all I've ever wanted to do. Langley staged my first effort at the Swan. I know how to put a story together that people will want to see."

"And pay good *money* to see," Shackspear added.

Oxford was still looking at Jonson who, Oxford noted, had one eye lower than t'other. He was disheveled and unkempt. He looked like a basket of laundry on its way to the river to be scrubbed hard over rocks. "When do you write?" he asked.

Jonson had expected to be asked *what* he wrote. He hesitated. "Uh, all the time, your lordship. In the morning when I get up. In the middle of the night. *In the middle of having sex!*"

This sounded outrageous but Oxford knew of what he spoke. He had faulted himself more than once for doing the same thing. All he could do was mutter, "poor man."

Shackspear thought Oxford was feeling sorry for Jonson being interrupted by his muse while having sex; Robin thought his master was feeling sorry for Jonson because for being so addicted to playwrighting that it interfered with sex. They were both wrong.

Oxford disliked Jonson, but realized they had one thing in common: playwrighting. "And when you write, *what* do you write?" Oxford asked.

"Comedies. Tragedies. Back-stabbing stories from Plautus. The death of Caesar. The conquest of Mexico!"

"The conquest of Mexico?"

"If not Mexico and the conquistadores, tales from *The Iliad, The Aeneid*, Ovid's *Metamorphoses*, …"

Oxford put up a hand. "No one wants stories like that, least of all Burbage or Henslowe. Or even Langley."

Jonson had to agree. "Indeed, my lord. Those of us who have been to university want to hear stories that uplift us, but the thickheads in the audience want to hear stories about them."

Oxford frowned. "You think plays are written to uplift theatergoers?" He managed to ask this without sarcasm, but Robin knew Oxford only wrote for the queen. And posterity.

"I do, your lordship."

"Pity on you, then, Ben Jonson."

Jonson's face fell. "*The Case Is Altered* did well, my lord."

"Did it?"

Jonson nodded his head up and down, then back and forth as a hundred different emotions flashed across his face.

"No, then. And why is it that you two - three," he said, adding Robin to the two men in front of him, "think you can write something that will allow me to avoid the queen. Let me start with William here," he said, pointing to Shackspear, "whose every effort has failed, and you, Mr. Jonson, whose only effort was not good enough for even Langley - *Langley* - to call you back."

"Because," Robin jumped in, surprising them all, "you will give us the story."

"And shave off our mistakes," Shackspear said.

"And buff up what we do to make it better," Jonson added.

The three of them were clearly desperate: Shackspear needed money; Jonson wanted fame; and Robin, well, Robin wanted to work on a play.

The three looked at him with so much earnestness that Oxford thought they might barricade the door if he refused to help them.

"Very well, then. But Falstaff in love? I'm afraid my muse has abandoned me."

Robin spoke up. "The Falstaff in this play does not have to be the Falstaff everyone saw in *Henry IV*." Oxford and the others were surprised by this. They looked at him. Robin hurried on. "He was Oldcastle in *Famous Victories*, but Baron Cobham objected to using his name so he became Falstaff, right? What's in a name?" he said flippantly. "If the queen wants 'Falstaff in love,' we'll give her 'Falstaff in love.' The name will be the same but Falstaff can be different!"

"Bravo, Robin." Jonson's face broke into a grin. He didn't know how to recreate Falstaff anyway. This way, he could exercise his own 'creativity.' "She won't know he's different until the end," Jonson said. Shackspear didn't quite understand, but it sounded like he might get a play.

"She wants it for the Garter ceremony, gentlemen, which is soon. Can you do it?"

"Aye," all three said together.

"The play will be presented at Whitehall but set in Windsor. I know the castle well; some scenes will be in *The Garter Inn*, below the castle walls."

"And the plot?" Robin asked.

Oxford thought. "The new Falstaff will be older, fatter, and in need of money."

"No change there," Jonson said.

"To get the money he needs, Falstaff will hatch a plan to seduce two married women."

They all murmured approval. "Someone should give away his plans," Shackspear suggested.

"Bardolph and Nym will do it, my lord," Robin said. "If we include them, it will connect it to *Henry IV*. Bardolph and Nym will tell the husbands what Falstaff is up too."

"Excellent," Oxford said. "It will need a love story to run parallel to the comedy. Robin, I charge you with coming up with that. These two know nothing about love." He said this as he waved an arm at Shackspear and Jonson. They did not disagree.

Jonson spoke. "I see Falstaff cornered by the angry husbands. He climbs into a basket filled with laundry to escape them."

"Which will be thrown out the window into the Thames!" Shackspear said.

"With Falstaff in it!" Robin added.

"Yes," Oxford agreed. None of them gave the slightest thought to how Falstaff and the basket could be thrown out a window. This would be left to Henslowe and Burbage to figure out. "But Mr. Jonson, your contribution will be unknown." Oxford pointed to Shackspear. "He will get the billing. Your name will be invisible. Your effort will add nothing to your fame."

"My fame will come, my lord, helped by what I learn helping write *Falstaff in Love*. The queen has not barred *me* from writing plays."

"How fortunate," Oxford said sarcastically. Shackspear and Robin looked away. Oxford left the room.

134

Johnson is Jonson; Shackspear is Shakespeare

Oxford was seated at the end of the table when Robin came in. Oxford had spent the night going through the drafts Robin, Shackspear, and Jonson had written about Falstaff in love. Robin could see a fading mark on the paper where Oxford's head had touched the table when he fell asleep and a corresponding blush on his right cheek. Oxford, just awakened, looked up brightly. Robin took his seat at the table.

"It will do," Oxford said.

This excited Robin. "Let us hope Falstaff will agree to play the part."

"Not if he's the man I think he is."

They heard the front door open. Shackspear and Jonson came in. They tried to come in the library door but bounced against each other like cattle being herded into a narrow loading pen. Whether this was because of growing competition between them or the breakfast of beer porridge they had just finished was not clear.

"Let's settle this outside," Shackspear growled. He turned to leave. Jonson started to go with him.

"Gentlemen!" Oxford called out. They turned around. "Rule 1: pints after work, not before. Understood?" They both nodded.

"Rule 2?" Jonson asked.

"Rule 2: I have no interest in what you two were going to 'settle outside.' If you choose to continue in that direction, I will find someone else to finish *Falstaff in Love*."

Shackspear and Jonson came in and sat down at the table.

"Good," Oxford said. "Now, who is this Justice Shallow?"

"He was in *Henry IV, Part Two*, my lord," Robin said. Shackspear murmured his agreement.

"Yes, but he was only a butt for Falstaff's wit. In this script, something more is going on."

"My lord," Shackspear said, "you may recall that Mr. Langley and I were involved in a proceeding to obtain sureties of the peace from a William Wayte and his father-in-law, Justice Gardiner."

"Oh, him. I've heard of Justice Gardiner."

"Yes. People in Southwark pay Gardiner money when he's not stealing it from them."

"He thinks everyone's garden is his to hoe," Robin said, hoping for a laugh. No one did.

"Langley had to pay Gardiner to keep the Swan open," Shackspear continued. "Otherwise, Gardiner would shut it down. Gardiner started to think the Swan was doing better than Langley let on and demanded more money. Langley refused to pay the increase. Gardiner threatened to close the Swan. Langley wanted to get a restraining order but was blocked because Gardiner is the only justice in Surrey."

"You came to me about this," Oxford said, speaking to Shackspear, "and I sent you to Malfis."

"You did. Malfis told us there were three ways to solve a legal problem: legally, by going to court; illegally, by force or some other method; or non-legally, by finding a way to get what you want that's not either of the others."

"Was it resolved?"

"It was. Mr. Malfis has connections, from the court to the urchins who live in the street drains. Information, he calls it. Worth more than money, he says. Malfis knew that Gardiner liked to sell land he didn't own. Malfis had someone research the land records and came up with proof that Gardiner had taken part in a number of fraudulent transactions."

"Instead of going to the courts, Malfis went to Gardiner and showed him what he had uncovered. He told Gardiner he was doing this as a favor. He said that some of Gardiner's victims were related to members of the Privy Council and one of them had invested heavily in the Swan. Malfis told Gardiner he did not represent the investor and, therefore, had no obligation to tell the investor what he had discovered but thought Gardiner might want to know."

"What did Gardiner do?"

"He panicked. He thought Malfis was going to blackmail him but Malfis denied he wanted anything in return. He suggested Gardiner had time to dismiss the lawsuits and avoid waking up sleeping dogs. He also suggested it might help if Gardiner allowed the Swan to stay open."

"We want to put Gardiner in *Falstaff in Love* as Justice Shallow," Shackspear said, "for all the trouble he has caused us. Malfis has been rewarded for helping us by being given a free pass to any show in town."

"A safe offer to make, for Malfis will never set foot in a theater."

Shackspear shrugged. "His loss."

"Not yers, Mr. Shaaakespeare," Jonson said, dragging out the 'a' in Shackspear's name.

"Nor you, Mr. Jooonson," Shackspear replied, dragging out the 'o' in Jonson's name.

Oxford glanced at Robin whose face revealed nothing. Jonson was on to other matters. "Yer first play about us, your lordship," he said, addressing Oxford. Oxford did not understand. "Ye write about kings and queens, earls and knights, my lord. *Falstaff in Love* is the first play ye've written about Englishmen. This is good because Englishmen buy tickets. They want plays about them, not about Bohemia or Greece. They want to see themselves being tricked, cuckolded, and robbed."

He was beaming. Oxford was not. He could tell Jonson's beer breakfast had not yet been completely absorbed.

Shackspear thought Jonson's comment opened the door for another thought. "How about a play about Stratford?" he asked.

Oxford was fuming. "Never been there."

"Yes, ye have. Ye stayed two times at Billesley, just down the road. I came to visit but ye sent me back to London. Do ye remember me bowing before you, my knee in the snow?" Oxford had forgotten. "My father said ye rode over to Stratford later and talked to him."

This Oxford remembered, but he was beginning to lose his patience. "There will be no play about Stratford, William, or any other provincial backwater that you may have lived in or visited."

"Well, that's definite," Shackspear said matter-of-factly.

"Yer losing him," Jonson said.

"Thank you for your advice, Mr. Jooonson."

"Yer welcome, Mr. Shaaakespeare," Jonson replied. "You ought to consider changing yer name again. Ye should call yourself *Mr. Shakesford*, or *Mr. Oxspeare*. Yeah. *Mr. Oxspeare*."

"*Out!*" Robin suddenly cried out, surprising them all. He jumped up, his left arm pointing toward the door. "*Out!*" he cried again, "you low-life scum-sucking caterpillars." Everyone looked at Robin in astonishment. His other arm came up, pointing toward Oxford. "There sits the right honorable Edward de Vere, 17th Earl of Oxford,

Lord Great Chamberlain of England, Viscount Bolbec, Baron Scales and Badlesmere." He dropped his arms and took another breath. "And you two theater-droppings are what?" He looked at Shackspear. "A provincial tat-swat who's bought a coat of arms for £30?" He turned to Jonson. "And you - a bricklayer who drops an 'aitch' from your name to buy respectability? Ye think ye moved any closer to *him* by doing *that?*" He snorted.

Shackspear glanced at Oxford. He could tell it was time to go. He glared at Robin. "You smidgen of a mushroom smear," he announced. He drew himself up. "Thrown out of his lordship's house by a page." Oxford lowered his head. "And you, Mr. Jooonson?"

Jonson also sensed Oxford wanted them gone. "Ye'll no doubt need help finding yer way home, *Mr. Oxspeare,*" Jonson replied.

The two of them headed for the door, grousing at each other.

Robin turned to Oxford to apologize for his outburst. "Cow flops," he said. "I couldn't put up with how they were treating you."

Oxford smiled. "My little guard dog, my Cerberus. But what is going on with them?"

"Shackspear, ye know, has added an 'e' to his name so he can say it should be pronounced 'Shake-spear.'"

"At the suggestion of Richard Fielding."

"Aye. Jonson, born 'Johnson,' has decided to drop the 'h' from his name to separate him from all the other 'Johnsons' out there, although he can't say who they might be."

"And so, they've been in the Mermaid calling each other names?"

"Yes. But they're mad because of a poem everyone is singing when they come into a pub. They think Tom Nashe wrote it."

"Good old Tom. He likes to stay up all night polishing something he claims the next day he made up whilst standing on a table."

"Aye."

"Ye took it down, I warrant." Oxford said. He meant the poem.

"I did." He gave Oxford a sly look as he pulled out a fistful of papers from a pocket. "I'm good at this, ye know." He laid the papers on the table and straightened them.

> *Ben Johnson, Ben Johnson, of bricklaying fame,*
> *Has laid down his trowel to seek playwriting fame,*
> *He's discovered his name's not good enough now;*
> *It's got too many 'aitches', a name he must now disavow.*

Oxford guffawed. Robin went on:

> *Ben's in a rush to get rid of his shame;*
> *He's heard Shackspear has changed his last name,*
> *For without 'e', it's pronounced 'Shack-spear', or worse,*
> *So Will's adding 'e' to make it Shakespeare and not worse.*
>
> *This means Johnson's now Jonson, though the 'aitch' ye cannot hear,*
> *And Shackspear is Shakespeare with an 'e' ye cannot hear:*
> *Ben's name is now shorter; Shakespeare's an 'e' more;*
> *Which is now better and which has been made poor?*
>
> *No matter - Johnson's now Jonson, and Shackspear's Shakespeare;*
> *They both think they're playwrights, but no one need fear;*
> *One takes plays from another as one of his tricks;*
> *T'other says he writes thunder but he's still laying bricks.*

Oxford laughed. "Work like this is going to get that boy in trouble," he said, referring to Nashe. "Back to the play, Robin. Tell me; is this enough to get the queen off my back?"

"It is. The attempt to woo two wives at once, the scheming by the husbands, Falstaff dumped into the Thames; she'll love it." He looked closer at Oxford. "And I've figured out who you are in this play."

Oxford cocked his head. "Who?"

"Fenton."

"Wherefore?"

"Because he's described by Mistress Quickly as '*he capers, he dances, he has eyes of youth, he writes verses, he speaks holiday, he smells April and May.*'"

"That could be anyone."

"Not after you hear that the woman he's pursing, by name of Anne, comes with £700 a year from her grandfather."

Oxford tried to look puzzled.

"You told me that Anne Cecil, your Nan, came with £700 from Lord Burghley's father. And the father in the play objects to Fenton because he 'kept company with the wild prince and Poins' and was 'of too high a region.' Who else could Fenton be?"

"Does Fenton win Miss Page?" Oxford asked, trying to act like he had no idea what Robin was talking about.

"Fenton's competitors - a Welsh schoolmaster and a character named Slender - are so inept the audience knows from the start who is going to win. Fenton is you. But who is Slender?"

Oxford hesitated. Robin leaned toward him, letting him know he expected an answer. "Sidney," Oxford finally said.

"Sidney?" Robin exclaimed. "Again? What is it with you and him? He's dead years now."

"Burghley wanted Nan to marry him until Burghley found out the little puppy was not going to inherit Leicester's estate. Burghley sent Sidney packing and ordered me to marry Nan."

"That was good, wasn't it?" Robin wasn't sure.

"Marrying Nan meant victory over my nemesis in poetry; the winnings, however, were not what I thought they'd be. It'd been better if Sidney had been forced to marry Nan. In that case, he would've had to put up with her father and not me."

"Well, then, let's make him worse."

"How so?"

"A bit about bear baiting should do it."

"Bear baiting?"

"The queen loves bear baiting more than the theater, my lord. She'd knight Sackerson if she could. Parliament banned bear baiting on Sundays and she overruled them!"

"Oh," Oxford said. He had no idea who Sackerson was.

"Here's what I would have Slender/Sidney say when he hears dogs in the distance and wonders why they bark. He will ask Nan:

> *Why do your dogs bark so? be there bears i' the town?*
>
> *I think there are, sir; I heard them talked of.*
>
> *I love the sport well but I shall as soon quarrel at it as any man in England. You are afraid, if you see the bear loose, are you not?*
>
> *Ay, indeed, sir.*
>
> *I have seen Sackerson loose twenty times, and have taken him by the chain; but, I warrant you, the women have so cried and shrieked at it.*

"He's taken a bear 'by the chain?" Oxford asked. "Not if you know what Sidney looked like. I like what you've done so far. I have a play to work on." He left Robin humming at the library table.

135

Falstaff in Love at Whitehall

Falstaff in Love was presented as part of the Garter ceremony at Whitehall Palace on Sunday, April 23, 1597. Four knights were inducted: Lord Thomas Howard; George Carey, 2nd Lord Hunsdon, who had also just been appointed Lord Chamberlain; Charles Blount, 8th Lord Mountjoy; and Sir Henry Lee, with whom Anne Vavasour had been living for years. The four were invested on May 24.

A fifth new member of the Order of the Garter was supposed to be there: the Duke of Wurttemberg. He was the head of the Duchy of Wurttemberg near Stuttgart. He had visited England in 1592 and lobbied the queen to make him a knight of the Garter. Her Majesty had put off nominating him because she had to pay the cost of his visit. Her Majesty. She put off nominating him. The more he pestered her, the more she resisted nominating him. With five years having passed, she finally gave in but didn't send word that he had finally be selected as a new knight of the Garter in time for him to attend. This was Elizabeth at her best, honoring his request and swatting him away at the same time.

Oxford remembered the Duke's visit and how he had borrowed horses and money he never returned. To give a gift to Her Majesty, he added the Duke to *Falstaff in Love* by including "three cozen-germans who had conned all the hosts of Reading, Maidenhead, and Colebrook of horses and money." Oxford thought the queen would enjoy hearing the Duke held up to ridicule.

The day opened with a morning service in the Chapel, complete with solemn music. All the lords of the Order were present. The queen watched from her royal seat. The lords came and retired, making three congés to her, after which there was a short service conducted by the clergy in their rich copes accompanied by the voices, organs, cornets and sackbuts.

The queen proceeded everyone into the audience hall which had been modified for the play that would celebrate the investiture. The Countess of Warwick, the Countess of Northumberland, and the Countess of Shrewsbury carried her train. The Earl of Bedford carried the Sword of State before her. Six pensioners carried a rich canopy over Her Majesty's head. Trumpets, drums, and fifes opened the play put on before a packed hall. Everyone looked forward to the return of Falstaff, this time in love, and the feast promised afterwards in Lord Howard's chambers.

Falstaff had, as Oxford predicted, refused to play himself. He was insulted by how he had been denied his 'greatness' in *Part Two* of *Henry IV*. He did not appear. Shackspear, and Jonson were glad he refused the part. "Putting Falstaff on stage," some wag had said, "was like putting a match to a powder keg."

The audience was not disappointed, even though they realized early on they would not be seeing the Falstaff they'd come to love. Oxford was surprised. He thought they would feel betrayed. Instead, they were happy to see another Falstaff thrown into the Thames and wear horns to play Herne's ghost. Everyone left feeling good.

Oxford had stayed out of sight during the performance to work with the boys who played the fairies in the final scene. When the play ended, he waited for the royal invitation to speak with Her Majesty. It came. He approached. He put a knee down and waited for the hangers-on to fade away.

Elizbeth used the time to study him. "I thought you were killing Falstaff off in Part Two and now I see I am proven right. This is not the man I ordered you to show in love."

"Shackspear has promised he will be back in *Henry V*."

"No, he won't. He's dead. He died somewhere between Henry's coronation and this farce." She looked away. "Unless he was too heavy to be picked up and thrown into the river. Now, that was a stage direction that must have given the players trepidation."

"We were fortunate to arrange for Dick Tarlton to take his place."

She eyed him. "I know enough about the man Falstaff to know being stuffed into a laundry basket and thrown into the Thames was something he would never have accepted. Good for him."

Oxford did not disagree.

"And by treating him so poorly, you created a Falstaff who was not in love, proving I was wrong to insist you could."

"It is more complicated than that, Your Majesty. In penning *Henry IV*, I wanted to show Prince Hal become Henry V. For contrast, I created a court jester, a fool. I called him Oldcastle to addle Baron Cobham and the Puritans but you made Cobham Lord Chamberlain and, with the power he then had, demanded his ancestor Oldcastle not appear again. I had to change Oldcastle's name. Falstaff said I could use his name but demanded he play the part. I foolishly agreed. I thought he would ruin the play. *Instead, he stole it!* I had to kill him off to write *Henry V*. You were the one who demanded I bring him back."

"Which you gave over to others."

Oxford shrugged.

She sat back. "I looked for your hands on the play and wondered what had changed. The plot wouldn't hold the interest of a grammar schoolboy. The characters are paper cutouts. The unfolding of the scenes is masque-like, something you've not done before. And the poetry? Where's the poetry the great Earl of Oxford is noted for? To think that Falstaff would sign off on a letter like this?"

> *Thine own true knight,*
> *By day or night,*
> *Or any kind of light,*
> *With all his might*
> *For thee to fight, John Falstaff*

I thought you were trying to show Falstaff was a poor poet but this barely exceeded the foreigners who make 'fritters of English' in this play. She was exasperated. "This is not caviar for the general, my lord: this is fish eggs."

She wasn't through.

"You shall return to writing about people you know; earls and dukes, knights and generals. This play is about commerce and trade – *money, for God's sake.* You have no understanding of money, my lord. If you did, we would not have to gift you £1,000 a year, eh?" She eyed him. "You have been bred to hunt big game, my lord, and a fat man in a laundry basket is not it."

She waved a hand, dismissing him. "Oh, and I specifically order you not to bring Falstaff back in *Henry V*. The poor man has suffered enough."

Oxford was happy to stand Falstaff down, but he was surprised to hear that she thought him a failure. But was there anything left in him still worth presenting? He wondered.

136

The Isle of Dogs

*T*he *Isle of Dogs* opened and closed the same day, and not because the audience didn't like it. The audience loved it. The Privy Council did not. By late that evening, they ordered the Swan to be shut down. Carried away by the outrageous insult they thought it was, they ordered all the theaters torn down.

No one saw this coming. Baron Cobham died in March; Justice Gardiner the following month. The loss of these two 'defenders of the faith' gave the theater world the impression they had been unshackled. Their hopes were confirmed when the queen appointed Sir George Carey to replace Cobham as Lord Chamberlain.

Sir George's father had been Lord Chamberlain before Cobham and fielded the Lord Chamberlain's Men while he lived. They became Lord Hunsdon's Men after his death. With Sir George's appointment, they became the Lord Chamberlain's Men again.

In this heady atmosphere, plays that would have been censored burst forth unfettered. *The Isle of Dogs* was one. It presented a kingdom where all the characters were dogs. Instead of putting this fictitious kingdom on a faraway island, the authors put it on a marshy spit of land across the Thames from Greenwich Palace which was known as … the Isle of Dogs. Langley was ecstatic to be rid of Baron Cobham *and* Justice Gardiner. He booked *The Isle of Dogs* into the Swan. The Admiral's Men agreed to play it. Later, when they were dragged before the Privy Council, they claimed they'd had no idea it was such an affront to morals and good order.

The costume maker who provided the head Oxford wore as Bottom in *Midsummer Night's Dream* outfitted each of the players in *The Isle of Dogs*. Each head mimicked a different breed. This caused an uproar that began a quarter hour into the play when everyone realized each dog was intended to represent someone of importance. They quickly concluded that a spaniel was Sir Robert Cecil. It kept bringing a pair of slippers to a great waffling sheepdog seated magisterially in the middle of the stage. This dog was no doubt Lord Burghley, Cecil's father. The spaniel would dangle the slippers in front of the sheepdog and run offstage to give them to someone else. The someone else must be the queen, everyone thought, since none of the dogs appeared to represent Her Majesty.

The plot involved a terrier, thought to be the Earl of Essex, who kept dog biscuits from the other dogs, including a great mastiff who was Richard Topcliffe. A fox hound was Baron Hunsdon, the new Lord Chamberlain. It ran around and around the other dogs - border collies, setters, bloodhounds, and mutts - who crowded the stage. The audience had a lot of fun. Had it not been suppressed, Gardiner ruefully reflected later, it would have run for weeks. "A bit with a dog," he lamented, a sure-fire trick that didn't work this time.

The play had been written by Thomas Nashe and Ben Jonson. Some in the audience thought the play an outrage and reported their dismay to the Privy Council. The order to shut down the Swan and burn the script went out shortly after midnight of the night the play opened. Jonson and the actors were rounded up and thrown into the Marshalsea. Nashe escaped to Great Yarmouth. The order to tear down all the theaters went out the next day.

The Puritans were thrilled but their enthusiasm was not echoed by the general population and some members of court. The order to tear down the theaters was not carried out. The theaters were soon back in business, except for the Swan which remained closed.

Jonson was visited in the Marshalsea by Richard Topcliffe, the queen's personal torturer. Topcliffe told Jonson that certain persons he was not at liberty to identify would like Jonson to became friends with the Earl of Oxford and report back whatever he learned. Jonson was shocked. He held himself in high esteem. He was known in the pubs in London for having volunteered to fight a Spaniard to the death and had been living in the shade of this exploit ever since. He was not such a man, he thought, who would spy on his companions. He refused.

Topcliffe accepted Jonson's refusal and left. Jonson did not. As time went by, he watched other prisoners come in and be released. He listened to accounts of the theaters reopening and the plays being put on and chafed at having to sit in the Marshalsea. He finally sent word he was ready to cooperate but Topcliffe ignored him. When Topcliffe finally sat down with him, Jonson was more than ready to turn informant. He was finally let out in October, only to learn that Oxford had moved to Hackney.

137

She's Not Comin' With Us

The Countess of Oxford had been urging her husband to move out of London for years. "There's nothing but noise and filth here," she would complain, "nothing like where I grew up, a countryside full of forests and rivers, birds and animals. I want our son to have what I had."

She would say this with her hands on her hips and a scowl on her face. "And Falstaff is turning Henry into a sword-swinging foul-mouthed little boy," she would continue. "The other day he asked Henry what he'd do if he found himself in front of a bear! Run! Henry had cried. Falstaff thought this a good answer."

These protests became a constant refrain. She constantly worried about Henry. Of course, he's going to fall down, Oxford would say. Children fall down all the time! Falstaff didn't help when he said children rarely hurt themselves *because they didn't have far to fall!*

It also didn't help that Falstaff began taking Henry sleigh riding on Tower Hill. Elspeth didn't approve; Henry might get hurt. While she was gone one day, Falstaff took Henry over to Tower Hill where he made himself into a giant sled by lying down on his back and holding up his arms. Henry climbed on and, using Falstaff's upraised arms as levers, steered the two of them down the Hill, to the horror of Henry's mother who came upon them as they slid to a stop.

This only added to Lady Elspeth's campaign to move. Oxford continued to ignore her. She finally took matters into her own hands.

She had money; Oxford did not. The only reason he was not in debtor's prison was because nobles could not be imprisoned for debt. She decided to purchase a manor house in Hackney a few miles north of the City. It was still countryside then. She paid £3,300 for it but said nothing to her husband until the conveyancing documents had been signed.

The manor house was known as King's Place because Henry VIII had owned it once. He had used it to meet his daughter, Mary, there in 1536 to persuade her to sign articles that invalidated her mother's marriage to Henry. At the same time, the articles would make her illegitimate. It took quite a few gifts and an unknown amount of money before Mary signed them. She never forgot the humiliation. She never came back to King's Place. Neither did Henry.

Henry sold King's Place to Lord Hunsdon who added his arms and emblems to the ceiling over the long gallery before he sold it on to Sir Rowland Hayward who sold it to Lady Elspeth in 1597.

King's Place was even more famous for having been the home of Lady Margaret Douglas, Countess of Lennox, while it was in Hunsdon's ownership. The Countess was granddaughter to Henry VII, founder of the Tudor dynasty, which made her of royal blood and the center of political intrigue throughout her life. Her part, imaginary or not, in arranging the marriage of her eldest son, Henry, Lord Darnley, to Mary, Queen of Scots, sent her to the Tower. She was sent back much later when her second son, Charles, married Elizabeth Cavendish. This marriage resulted in the birth of Arabella Stuart who became the object of plots to replace Elizabeth after Mary was executed. The Countess died in 1578 at King's Place shortly after entertaining the Earl of Leicester. There were rumors, of course, that he had poisoned her.

King's Place was a large parcel of land with many improvements. It encompassed fifty acres of open land, fifty of meadow, one hundred of pasture, and twenty of wood. The main house was only one of four on the property. It was described as 'fayre' and made 'all of bricke.' It contained a hall, a parlor, a 'faire' kitchen, a pastory, a dry larder with butter pantry, a chapel, a great chamber, and a 'proper lybrarye to laye bokes in.' Gardens, stables, and barns surrounded it.

September 2 was moving day. Everyone had been asked to assemble in the Great Hall at Oxford Court to hear an announcement. Lady Elspeth came down the stairs, stopping midway to command the room. Oxford came out of the library. Robin appeared from where he slept under the staircase. Frangellica came out of the kitchen. Bona Fortuna came out onto the landing with Lil Henry, now five, in her arms. Falstaff leaned in from the garden. Nigel stood at attention next to Tobias at the front door.

Lady Elspeth spoke. "His lordship and I are moving to King's Place in Hackney," she said. "Henry and Bona Fortuna will accompany us, as will Tobias. Frangellica will not; she has decided to return to Italy."

She looked toward Falstaff, leaning against the doorpost to the garden. "Sir John will also not be coming." She turned to Robin standing to the side of the stairs. "Nor will *she*."

Robin didn't realize for a moment that Elspeth was talking about him. Before he could protest, Oxford spoke.

"My lady, Robin is my right-hand. I cannot move to Hackney and leave him behind."

"Her," Lady Elspeth said again. "*Her!*"

Oxford and the others didn't understand. Falstaff guffawed.

"He is not a *he*, my lord," Lady Elspeth said, still looking at Robin. "He is a *she*; and if *she* comes to Hackney, you will be doing *her* under the backstairs before Christmas."

Everyone was dumbstruck.

"Don't give me that look," Elspeth said to Oxford. "She's been banding her boobies for months now. She had a mustache when she came back from France. When it disappeared, she said it wasn't 'thick enough to keep.' You can fool a man every day of the week, but not a woman. *He's a she*, my lord, and she's not comin' with us to Hackney!"

Robin turned and bolted for the front door. Tobias deftly turned her into his room. He slipped in behind her, folding the little page into his greatcoat before closing the door behind him.

Lady Elspeth turned to Falstaff. "You, Sir John, have been corrupting my son. You've been teaching him sword fighting, how to lie, how to laugh at authority. If you come with us, you will ruin him."

Everyone expected Falstaff to issue a stinging retort. Instead, he pivoted into the garden without comment. It was a warm day. They could hear the latch click as he let himself out into Candlewick Street.

Oxford was still trying to absorb the fact that Robin and Falstaff had been banished from his life. Anger rose within him: the prayers at Sir Robert's house, the sessions with Dr. Forman, the growing obsession with their son. Then he realized Aemilia Bassano must have polluted her mind with how women have been unfairly treated by men!

Lady Elspeth was still standing on the staircase. Everyone was looking at Oxford. "What does 'moving' mean?" Henry asked.

Oxford came to life. He strode out the front door. He found Falstaff leaning on London Stone. Tobias came out. He opened his coat, spilling Robin into the street. Robin had been crying. She looked from Oxford to Falstaff and back again.

Falstaff pushed himself off the Stone and headed down the street. "Sometimes," Falstaff said over his shoulder, "words don't work."

They had gotten no more than a few doors when Lil Henry burst out of the Court. He ran after them. "Sir John, Sir John," he cried as he came up to them. "I won't see you anymore?"

Falstaff smiled. "Ye'll be seeing me, my lil musket eyas. We've lots of adventures left in my magic sack." He pulled open the giant purse he always carried and held it open. A puppy stuck its head out!

"Well, can you imagine that? Now, how did he get in there?"

Henry reached in and pulled the puppy out by his ears. He held it up for all to see. "Is he mine?" he asked excitedly.

Robin was horrified to see the dog dangling by its ears. Falstaff saw her fright. "That's the way it's done," he said. "I taught him right. I took him to my apartments to meet Armado and Long Tom and the dogs and cats I live with." He turned to Henry: "He is yours."

Henry squealed. He folded the puppy into his arms and hugged him. "What's his name?"

"He doesn't have a name yet."

"How about Isle?" Henry said.

"I'll?" Oxford asked.

"Aisle?" Falstaff asked.

"*Isle of Dogs!*" Henry shouted. He put his head back and laughed.

Oxford and Falstaff laughed with him. "He deserves a better name than that," Oxford said.

"Bark," Falstaff suggested, trying to look serious. "That way, when you call him, *people will think you're the dog!*" He burst out laughing.

"Don't call him Bark, Henry," Oxford said, shaking his head. "He's going to be your friend for a long time. He deserves a better name than that. But Jack! How can he keep your gift? Elspeth will surely take it from him. Particularly if she finds out it was you who gave it to him."

"No worry. Bona Fortuna will help us. She is a friend and confidant." This was news to Oxford. A sly look slid across Falstaff's face. "How do ye think Lil Henry gets to go sleigh riding with me, or visits the dogs in my apartments?" Then he got serious. He turned to

Henry. "Mark me now, son. You go back to Oxford Court and show your new puppy to Tobias. He'll make sure it gets to Hackney."

"But then what?" Oxford asked. "Elspeth will only send it back."

"Not when she hears it's from a breed Henry VIII started at King's Place." He gave Oxford a knowing wink. "A puppy fit for a king is certainly fit for the 18th Earl of Oxford."

Oxford sighed. "I should have known."

"Ye should've." Falstaff helped Henry slip the puppy into his coat. "Off ye go."

They watched him scamper up the street. Tobias leaned out and gave them a nod before he closed the door.

Oxford and Falstaff, with Robin alongside, continued on to the Boar's Head, stepping down under the battered sign hanging over the street. They went inside and headed toward what had been Oxford's booth. Or was it Falstaff's? The two had argued over it once. They slid into the booth, Oxford and Robin on one side, Falstaff on the other.

Peaches put three mugs on the table. The two men and the young boy who was now a 'girl' picked them up. They took a long pull while Peaches waited. She was looking at Falstaff. "Ye didn't tell them?"

Oxford and Robin expected Falstaff to start waffling and wiggling but he cocked his head and looked across the table at them. "Your lordship," he said, raising his mug and addressing Oxford, then Robin: "I have asked Miss Peaches Bottomsup, this lovely woman here, to marry me." He paused for effect: "and she has said yes."

Peaches was beaming. She looked at Oxford. "A test, yer lordship. There be many a man who will promise marriage in the dark but forget what he said when the sun comes up." She looked at Falstaff. "Well, Sir John Falstaff, ye have confirmed the contract ye made **per verba day pry-sentee.**" She pulled out a fourth mug she had been holding behind her. "A toast!" she announced. "And before the lawyers in the room start pointing out that the contract must be 'consoomated' before it be legal and binding, I can promise you that Sir John will fulfill that requirement this very day!" A sly look came over her face. "Although, we will have to mist the curtains. Can't set them on fire again, can we, chuck?" She reached over and tweaked his cheek. The old knight was beaming.

Oxford raised his mug. "My congratulations to you both."

"Aye, aye," Robin said.

"To whatever ye are," Falstaff said, touching his mug to Robin's

Peaches looked at Falstaff. "'You're whatever ye are?" Running the Boar's Head had given her the ears of a cat.

"It's complicated," Oxford said.

"Yes," Robin said, making it clear she didn't want to talk about what had just happened at Oxford Court.

"Jack and I have more news. We are moving to Southwark."

"What?" Oxford exclaimed. "Getting married *and* moving? And Robin … What is going on today?" He looked bewildered.

Falstaff laughed. "It's like a day at sea, my lord. One day nothing happens and then people get married and move and change and die."

"Spare me the last one. Tell me about Southwark."

"We've bought the inn next door to *The Tabard*, where High Street comes off the Bridge."

"The Boar's Head is going to close," Peaches added.

Oxford blinked. "I did not know that. *Another* massive event."

Peaches explained. "The generous spirit who underwrites shortfalls for the inn has a debt problem himself. His creditors have secured a writ to catch any funds that come into the inn. Consequently, the Boar's Head" will close."

Falstaff grumbled. "It's the change come about from wot's going on in the City. No one lives innit anymore. They've moved out. They only come to the City during the day, my lord. They work as agents for shipping companies, insurance brokers, lawyers, printers, or whatever trade still remains here but they don't go out for a pint or a bit of food like they used to. They work all day and run for home."

"It's the Puritans, if ye ask me," Peaches said, "them who frown on those who come in for a pint and a meat pie. So, Jack and I are going to open a new Boar's Head over the bridge."

Oxford shook his head. "But next to The Tabard? The Tabard is famous. Ever since Chaucer wrote *The Canterbury Tales*. His pilgrims start out from there."

Peaches laughed. "Ye think people who drink beer care about where a bunch of pilgrims started out in a story? Characters who weren't even real?" She put her hands on her hips. "Ye think they can even read!"

Oxford had to acknowledge she had a point. "It must be hard." He meant all the change.

She shrugged. "If the river cuts a new bed, my lord, you go with it." She went back to the kitchen.

Oxford looked at Robin. "And you, my faithful Robin. How are you taking this? Was it a burden to masquerade as a boy, to be someone you weren't."

"Not at all. I loved it."

"And what will ye do now?"

"Keep writing plays and putting them in front of Henslowe and Burbage. They'll take something soon."

"As a girl?" Oxford asked. "Excuse me. A woman?

Robin laughed. "Have you seen any women bringing plays to the playhouse? Or women lawyers in the courthouse? I am John Webster, my lord. I have been John Webster this past year. I'd appreciate it if ye didn't tell anyone what Lady Elspeth just did to me now. As John Webster, I have a chance to be someone. As a woman, I am nothing."

Oxford looked at Robin with new appreciation. "So, when you met me for the first time at Greenwich Palace, you had already decided to present yourself to the world as a man."

"It worked, didn't it?"

"And I thought I was hiring you."

Robin shrugged. "A lady must be creative."

"Or lie, my lord," Falstaff couldn't stop himself from pointing out. "The truth would have sent her back into servitude. A little bit of theater here, and our dear little friend, Robin, gets to write plays with the 17th Earl of Oxford. No harm done, eh?" He winked at Robin.

Oxford wanted to protest but couldn't. Robin's deception had gotten her to where she wanted to go.

Falstaff took a pull on his beer. "Ye know, my lord, I knew she was a girl way back. She couldn't fool me. Before her 'mustache.'"

"Which you didn't pull off when you could have," Robin said. "For which I thank you. But why did you not?"

"I wanted to see how long ye could carry on."

"Surprised ye, didn't I?" Robin said. Falstaff acknowledged she had. She looked at Oxford. "And you, my lord? When did you figure I was not who I said I was? Or, did ye never find me out?"

"I was suspicious from when I met you at Greenwich Palace."

"What?"

Oxford nodded. "There was something about your neat appearance, your duck fat slicked down hair, your polished shoes. I wondered who you were."

Robin glowered. "Duck fat has never touched my hair, my lord. I use only capon grease."

"Duck fat or no, I knew for sure when we were about to go off to see Shackspear's first play - *The Poacher of Arden Forest* - and I mentioned that John Lyly could never say the word 'tits:'

If the word 'tits' could have passed John Lyly's lips, the little man would never have written, "hills and mountains crowned with castles whose locks can be picked with a tongue!'

"To which you, Robin, went 'Oooo,' disgusted at Lyly's words. That's when I knew. I sat back to see how long you'd last."

"I thought I had ye both." Robin was disappointed. "Still, no one else has discovered me. I was pretty good, if I say so myself."

"You were." Oxford raised his mug. "To the longest running cross-dressing hidden-female player in English theater history."

"That we know of," Robin added. They all laughed. "But this means you knew who I was when you threatened me with playing female parts. You were testing me."

"Yes. Except for Puck. I knew you'd play Puck."

"I had fun with Puck. But what about you, my lord? What will ye do in Hackney?"

"I am never busier than when I am alone. Don't worry about me."

"When do you go? Her ladyship is already out the door."

"Soon. Soon."

"*I'll be there, dearest,*" Falstaff sang out. "*Just a few days more.*"

They laughed.

"In that case," Robin said, "I'll stop by the Court and see if you're in. If you're working on something, maybe I can help. Like old times."

A silence fell over the table. Falstaff looked off. Oxford looked at the table, trying to make sense of all that had happened that day.

"No," he said softly. "It won't be like old times." He looked lost and sad at the same time. "What am I going to do without my Robin?"

Robin leaned into Oxford. The air seemed heavy with weeping though no one was crying. "Oh, brave new world," she said quietly.

~ 138 ~
An Empty House

Anyone here?"

Oxford looked up. Shackspear stood in the doorway. He looked sheepish, if that was possible for someone who was never aware of how he came across to other people.

"What are *you* doing here?"

Nigel appeared. "My apologies, my lord. I was in the kitchen with the cook who's going to take Frangellica's place, when this ... this ..."

"Gentleman," Shackspear volunteered.

"Gentleman," Nigel forced himself to echo, "entered the house."

"And where is Tobias?" Oxford asked.

"Gone to Hackney with the others, my lord. My lady thought I should stay behind during the transition to Hackney."

"Oh. Yes."

"And so, I came right in," Shackspear said breezily, "given that we should be putting the finishing touches on *Henry V*. Her Majesty expects it on Boxing Day." He gave Oxford a happy smile.

Oxford looked away. Shackspear in the house was bad enough. Being reminded that Elspeth had gone to Hackney, that Frangellica was returning to Italy, that Robin was, well, no longer Robin ... "Not now, William."

They heard the front door open. Nigel ran into the Hall to see who had come in. "Your ladyship!" he exclaimed. Oxford and Shackspear froze. "Let me escort you into the Day Room," they heard him say.

A mountain of furs topped by a profusion of thick lustrous dark-red hair passed across the open door to the library. Shackspear crouched; Oxford, at the end of the table, froze. "I will see if his lordship is in," they heard Nigel say.

Oxford and Shackspear both knew Oxford's newest guest was Lettice Knollys, Countess of Essex and Leicester

Shackspear looked across the table at Oxford. "She knows you are the author," he said in a hushed voice. "She came up to me after *Merry Wives* and said loudly; *you, sir, are a fraud!* I would rather not have to deal with her again, my lord. Do ye have a back door? Everyone should have a back door."

"The front door will do."

Shackspear bolted. Oxford went across the Hall to the Day Room where he found England's only double countess arranging herself like a queen in the biggest chair in the room. Her perfume filled the air.

"Edward," she greeted him, in a baritone that was surprising in a woman. Those who disliked her said it was a voice that had never been spoken in daylight. "Where is everyone?"

"Elspeth and the servants have removed to Hackney."

"Where in Hackney?"

"King's Place."

"Oh, how fitting. Henry VIII's, then Hunsdon's. The Countess of Lennox lived there for a while, I believe. Died there too, after supping with my Robin, which only added, of course, to the belief that he had poisoned his first wife, Amy Robstart. Does anyone believe she fell down the stairs?" She glanced up at the ceiling before returning her gaze to Oxford. "From there, he was credited with causing my first husband to die on his way home from Ireland, but that was God's work. He was so near so many deaths that he became known as the Earl of Poison. He would have added me to his list of victims had I not switched the cups when he came home on his last visit. One could almost say he died by his own hand, if you leave mine out of it." She looked at Oxford mischievously before glancing away again.

Oxford had no interest in how the Earl of Leicester met his end. He had never been attracted to gossip, even if it was presented by the person who must have known what had truly happened. He presented a pained expression to his guest. "I had naught to do with choosing King's Place, my lady. Elspeth has all the money, you know."

"But you have not left yet," the Countess said, looking around. "But this is not why I have come. I need to speak to you about my son. You'd think he'd listen to his mother, particularly when his mother has the experience and connections I have, but no."

"You are, I assume, here to talk about his dalliance with my daughter, the Earl of Derby's wife."

Lettice sniffed. "No, my dear man. I don't care where he wets his wand. He's young, male, and full of himself. He writes poetry. He wages war. He thinks he can have any woman he wants. And how does he get so many into his bed? They willingly climb in, my dear man. They want to be bad. This includes your daughter, Lisbeth."

Oxford thought of defending Lisbeth but couldn't.

The Countess took his silence as disbelief. "Don't look at me like that. Should there be different rules for her because you are her father?" She laughed. "Every woman is the daughter of some man, my lord. Even I am, although I've heard some doubt it. If a man looks at a woman and sees her as his mother or daughter, he looks at her one way. If he doesn't know her, he sees her quite differently. But I'm not here to talk about what my son does with your daughter; I'm here to ask for help with how he acts with the queen. He is going to go too far. If he does, she will swat him down, or worse."

Oxford thought the Countess was going to ask him to speak with the queen but she had a different idea.

"She loves your plays. Write one that shows the danger he poses to her. Something from ancient history. QuiCaesar. That'd be a good one. Knifed in the marketplace."

Oxford was surprised to hear this. "You want your son knifed in the marketplace?"

"Of course not. I want to scare Bess enough so *she* thinks might be knifed in the marketplace. She treats him like the son she never had. At first, I thought it was because he was her latest toy, like you were years ago, but she doesn't treat him like that."

"Maybe she favors him because she thinks he *is* her son."

This thought had never occurred to the Countess. "*I* am his mother!" she barked, glaring at Oxford.

"Of course, you are. But she always wanted to marry and have children. She came closest with 'your' Robin. Perhaps Essex is the son she thought she would have had?"

She frowned. "No. She is old now and dotters, and must have men who praise her. My son is at hand. Who else competes with his position as royal hand-kisser?"

Oxford couldn't think of anyone.

"When I was younger, I could wiggle a hip or lower an eyelid and men would eat out of my hand." She glanced at Oxford. "And don't say age has staled me," she said, looking at him closely.

"And are you wiggling now?"

She laughed. She *was* wiggling him. Oxford thought she looked like a mountain lion stalking its next victim. But the flare in her eyes faded. "Once, maybe," she said, more to herself than to him.

"'*Make sure you spell 'bitch' with a capital 'B,'*'" Oxford said.

She laughed. "Oh, I had fun bursting into your trial."

"And saving me."

"No. I only delayed matters till Yorick got to London."

"For which I thank you."

The Countess shrugged. She wasn't interested in reliving Oxford's trial and how she had been thrown out. She returned to Gloriana. "The queen thinks I languish in Drayton Bassett. Gaaad," she said, in the broad dialect she had acquired growing up in Oxfordshire. "Staffordshire is in the middle of nowhere! I'm never there. I'm at Leicester House on the Strand nine days out of ten. A large forecourt, windows that let in the breeze off the Thames. With a scarf over my head, I can go out unnoticed."

Oxford doubted this.

"I am thinking of going to Cambridge to see the plays this season."

This surprised Oxford. "What plays?"

"*The Pilgrimage to Parnassus.* The students are always so raw, so willing to stage shows that horrify those in authority. I expect it will be worth the trip."

Oxford smiled.

"What are you smiling about?" Lettice asked, casting a sideways glance at him. She was a mountain lion again, her look menacing.

"You? In Cambridge?" Oxford scoffed. "Everyone will know who you are."

"I would disguise myself."

Oxford laughed again. "If you fell into the water off Cornwall, the fishermen pulling you into the boat would know who you were." Oxford leaned to his right, like he was in a small boat. He switched into the character of a boatman, Cornish accent and all. "Blimey, the Countess of Leicester!" He leaned to his left, becoming a second fisherman. "Naw; it's the Countess of Essex!" He leaned back to t'other side; "Naw: *The Countess of Leicester!*" He leaned left again; "*Essex!*"

Lettice laughed heartily. She clapped. "A play for me, in which I drown! I love it."

"Naw," Oxford said, returning to the Cornish accent. "As the only double countess in England, you would survive. Because *Once a knight, always a knight, and once a night's enough! But if you are a double countess, ye can have a double life!*"

She laughed more, her merriment interrupted by a noise in the garden. Oxford got up to look. He returned with Falstaff.

"Yer ladyship." She held out her hand. Falstaff bent to kiss it.

"You were marvelous in *Henry IV*, Sir John, and *so* right not to return in *Merry Wives*." She sniffed. She looked at Oxford. "Awful, what you did to this man."

She got up and headed out of the room. Oxford rose. "Don't let me down, Edward," she called back as she went out the front door.

"A remarkable woman," Falstaff said, lowering himself into the chair the Countess had just vacated. He paddled the air in an effort to push away the perfume she had left behind.

"Yes, but a woman who is more enjoyable the farther away she is, whether in time or space." Oxford sat back down. "And you?"

"Malfis is working on the papers for Peaches and me to open the Boar's Head."

"Yes, useful things, lawyers. I spoke with him recently myself. He sensed how little I wanted to move to Hackney and suggested I lease the Court to a man who died in Devon last year. This man, though dead, will lease the Court back to me.

"Oooh," Falstaff. "I'd have made a wonderful lawyer. And when will the 'lease' be done?"

"Who knows? Negotiations will keep me here longer than expected."

"God be praised," Falstaff said. He leaned back and looked around. "But it's so quiet now, innit? It's voices and movement make a place a habitation. They go unnoticed until everyone's gone."

Oxford looked away. "Yes. The Court is empty. I've no one to work with. Robin is gone. I can't turn to Shackspear for help. I got up yesterday and started to walk out to ask Nigel what he thought of a line." He shook his head. "Asking Nigel about a line. Imagine that." He drew himself up. "Enough of that. Last time we talked, I asked if you could find me a clerk to help me. A new Robin."

"Aye. No luck."

"Have you been to Bacton?"

Falstaff sighed. "The Boar's Head is taking up me all my time, my lord. So much to do." He saw the disappointment in Oxford's face. "But I'll get there. Do na worry." He stood up. "Life's not a straight line, you know. It's a crooked one, full of zigzags." He headed out the door.

~ 139 ~
Lisbeth

The Countess of Southampton hosted a party to celebrate the new Garter knights. Oxford attended, hoping to see Southampton but the young earl did not appear. Lisbeth was there, however.

"Lisbeth," he said, coming up to her.

"Yes?" She thought her father was going to abuse her about Essex. "My lord, I am done with Earl Robert." She flicked her eyebrows and threw out a hand. "He woke me in the middle of the night to ask *if I was dreaming about him! Can you imagine? Dreaming about him? Hah! He should be so lucky!* Who was that Greek god who was always looking into a pool to see his image?"

"Narcissus."

"Yes. Well, the Earl of Essex is Narcissus. He's a book that contains one page - *a picture of himself!* I need someone who sees *me!*"

"I approach about Southampton, not Essex."

"Southampton?"

"I thought you might have dallied with him since you've bedded so many other men."

She laughed. "Oh, I tried. I thought it would be fun to find out what he was like since Pee-Pop had tried to get him to marry me, but," here her face went dark, "he refused me *again!*"

"Thank God," Oxford said, surprised at how strongly he said this. But then, how could Henry turn Lisbeth down? "Did he say why?"

"He says he loves Elizabeth Vernon." She was not impressed.

"But, knowing he was in love, you still pursued him."

"*He turned me down twice!* Pee-pop fined him £5,000 for refusing to marry me. How could *any* man agree to pay £5,000 *not* to marry me? His refusal was humiliation of a permanent nature. I should have left it at that. I don't know what I was doing. I guess I thought I would gain the upper hand over him if he slept with me now that I am married to the doddering 6th Earl of Derby *but he turned down again!*"

She saw the look on her father's face. "And why *can't* I chase him?" she went on. "You chased women when you were young?"

She didn't wait for an answer. She looked around at all the people in the room. "I can have anyone I want," she sniffed, ignoring that Southampton had rejected her twice. "I have power you never dreamed of." Preening like a swan on a summer day, she walked away.

The Countess of Southampton, another swan, floated up to his elbow. "My dear Edward," she purred. "Is your eldest daughter treating you the way you treated everyone when you were her age?"

"Touché. But I hate to disappoint you, your ladyship; we were talking about your son."

"Not my son, my lord." She gave his arm a squeeze. "We settled that at my wedding to Sir Thomas, may he rest in peace."

Sir Thomas had recently died, less than a year after Lady Mary had married him. "My condolences, your ladyship."

"A rum deal that was" she said, showing how up-to-date she was on the latest slang. "Older than Caesar's tomb, Old Tommy was. He didn't last long. Unfortunately, he owed the queen a mountain of money she'd given him as Lord Chamberlain to organize the entertainments. The old boot has demanded receipts to show how Tommy spent the money. She wants receipts? I give her receipts. My chambermaid and I spent a weekend in the kitchen dreaming up events and the cost to erect tents and feed the multitudes. You'd be amazed at how expensive it can be to entertain." She gave him a knowing look, squeezing his arm again. "We even added a few plays by the Lord Chamberlain's Men."

"But you'd have to make sure they matched Tilney's records."

"Oh, he won't check. It's like printing money. We write a receipt, send it over to the Exchequer, and the debt goes down."

Oxford sympathized with her. She might have been a victim of Heneage's attempt to use her money to pay off what he owed the queen. Didn't people marry to get their hands on money? On the other hand, everyone knew the Countess had spent money like water between her marriage to 'Tommy' and his overdue death. Heneage might have set money aside to pay the queen and the Countess had spent it. If so, the queen would know it. Not knowing these details, the ladies at court thought the queen was being unjust to squeeze the Countess for debts her deceased husband had incurred. Having no concept of money themselves, they worried about having to pay the queen outrageous amounts when their aging husbands died.

"Back to Henry, my lady. How was he smuggled out of the palace? How did he come into your house?"

"Ask Thomas Dymock," she said curtly.

"A bit more would be helpful. I doubt he will be forthcoming."

She frowned. "I suppose you have a right to know. The child I gave birth to in October 1573 was the result of seeking companionship elsewhere while my husband was in the Tower. The queen had locked him up for his declarations of Catholic faith."

She took her hand off his arm.

"No one could say when he might get out, if ever. I was thirteen when I married him, eighteen when he went into the Tower. He and I lived in separate houses before he disappeared into the Tower. My dalliance while he was gone was all well and good until I became pregnant. The potions and simples my physician gave me didn't work. I was faced with carrying the child to term, but this was of no great concern as a pregnancy on a remote estate is easily concealed, the baby being given away to a family that wants children and can't have them. I was four or five months along when my husband suddenly came riding into the courtyard, unannounced, like when he left."

"What did you do?"

"I greeted him as his wife. He immediately demanded his marital privileges, which I gave him, making him the father of my child."

"He didn't notice you were pregnant?"

"He made no verbal comment when he mounted me. To give him an excuse for his lack of awareness, I had presented myself under comforters and blankets despite the fact it was May. He probably thought I was trying to be modest. *Hah!* He should have seen me when 'his' son was conceived!"

She looked mischievously at Oxford, who was shocked to hear the Countess tell him how much she had enjoyed cuckolding on her husband. But he still could not believe the earl had not noticed she was pregnant. "How could he *not* have known?" he asked.

The Countess laughed. "Because he only wanted one thing. I gave him that and he immediately lost interest in me. When I told him a few weeks later I was pregnant, he was elated."

Oxford couldn't believe this. "He knew."

"No, he didn't. He was as dumb-as-a-post, my lord. He was thrilled to tell the world he had an heir. I was happy to let him think so. I had my revenge for the indifferent way he treated me: his son was not his. We never touched each other again. He disappeared into the great house and I went back to mine. When I gave birth, the child went off to a wet-nurse and I went back to sharing my afternoons with someone I was not married to."

"But this happy state did not last."

"No. The next summer, he ran to Spain."

"To Spain?" Oxford had run to the continent at the same time. The queen's indifference to the loss of their son had caused them to argue. He was so enraged by her coldness that he ran for the ports. He returned a few weeks later. She forgave him.

"He wasn't away long," the Countess said. "He never explained to me why he had run. A man named Dymock was with him when he came back. Dymock took over running the house. My husband went off into his quarters again and I went back to mine."

"What about your baby?"

"No one said anything. There was no reason to. He was somewhere on the estate with a wet nurse. I rarely saw him. What mother does, with all the mewling and puking they do all the time."

"But you came to suspect the babe might not be yours."

"That happen the following spring. We all came together in the great house dining room - the 2nd Earl, my father, Viscount Montague, his new wife, the baby, other relatives, and me. We were all seated at the table when the nursemaid thumped the baby's carriage into my chair. I was startled. I looked up at the nursemaid whose eyes were on the carriage. I looked down and knew instantly the child was not mine. His hair was lighter. He was longer. I looked up at the nursemaid again but she wouldn't look at me. Out of the corner of my eye, I saw Dymock studying me. I hid my reaction but apparently my performance was not good enough. He accosted me on the landing that night. 'Say nothing,' he hissed. He did not explain, but I had no doubt something horrible would happen to me if I did not keep my mouth shut."

"So, you did nothing."

"Who could I talk to? What could I say? My boy has disappeared? He's in the carriage, isn't he? My lord, it takes very little to commit a woman to Bedlam when those around her begin to think she has become irrational. I was completely defeated. My boy had disappeared and a new baby had taken his place. All kinds of theories flew through my head. Had my husband found out I had cheated on him? If he had, why didn't he confront me? And why substitute a new baby for mine? I began to have all kinds of wild thoughts. Maybe the baby *was* my boy. I finally got control of myself. I had no doubt the baby in the carriage was not mine. I swore I would find out what happened."

"Have you?"

"No. I don't know where he is or even whether he is alive."

"I am so sorry," Oxford said. He hadn't thought his questions would force Lady Mary to revisit the painful loss of her son. The clever adulteress had been replaced by a sad, grieving mother. "Perhaps we should continue this conversation another time."

"No. If I tell you all I know, perhaps your search for *your* son might help me find *mine*." She looked around to make sure no one could hear her. "I cornered the nursemaid a few days later but she refused to talk to me. This confirmed my suspicion: my son had been replaced with someone else's. Dymock was the key, of course, but I knew I could never approach him."

"What about the father of your son? Could he help you?"

She laughed. "He never even knew I was pregnant. He was good for an afternoon tumble but nothing beyond that. No, to this day he knows nothing of what happened. In desperation, I turned to a chambermaid I thought I could trust. Instead of asking her what she knew about my son, I asked her to find out what she could about Dymock. Given his sudden appearance and mysterious control over my husband, I thought my question would not raise any suspicion that I was asking about my son. She agreed to help. She found out that Dymock had been in service to the queen before he came to Titchfield but nothing beyond that. I have learned nothing more since. I find myself today, my lord, no closer to knowing what happened to my son than when the baby carriage was pushed into my chair."

"This has been very trying, I'm sure."

"Very trying. I believe my son has been taken from me to punish me for violating my marriage vows and for creating a world based on lies: giving birth to a son who was not my husband's and telling him it was his, made worse by my gloating over it."

She sighed. "The arrival of Dymock and the baby showed me that I was living in a prison I had built, with no way of finding out where my son was or whether he was even alive. In the meantime, I was forced to treat the new child as my own who became a constant reminder of what I had done and how much I was suffering."

"You have paid a heavy price."

"I have. To escape from wondering what had happened to my son, I diverted myself by taking other lovers, but my husband found out and shut me away from him. I had the boy at my house at the time. He was about six. I thought if I sent him over with a letter of reconciliation we could patch things up, but the earl tore up the letter and kept the boy."

She paused. "I didn't care he kept the boy from me. In fact, he did me a service. The boy's presence constantly reminded me of my loss. In any event, the earl died shortly after he took the boy."

"And did the boy come back to you?"

"No. The queen sold his wardship to the Admiral for £1,000. The Admiral assigned it to Burghley and the boy went to Cecil House. I had a few moments with him at the funeral, but it was enough to confirm he was not mine."

"And is it this boy who is the 3rd Earl of Southampton?" She nodded. "And who is his mother?"

"The queen, obviously. Dymock had worked in the palace. He came to Titchfield at the same time as the child. If a lady-in-waiting gives birth in the palace, the mother and child are shown the door, but if it's the queen's, it's placed in a household far from London. This child came with a full-time attendant to watch over him and to tell my husband what to do. I have little doubt Elizabeth is his mother."

"But why farm the child out to a potential rebel and Catholic sympathizer."

"Who better? He knew she would stick him back in the Tower if he didn't cooperate. He had a son who was only a few months older than hers but it seems apparent he didn't think the boy was his. Was he already suspicious and volunteered our house? I don't know."

The distress in her face was visible. "With all due respect, my lord, and forgive me for saying this, but I don't give a fig about the 3rd Earl of Southampton. I want to know what happened to my son. Is he alive? As I travel in my carriage I search the faces of young men who would be the same age he is now. If he is alive somewhere, maybe I could see him." Her face darkened. "If he has died, I could put flowers on his grave. It would help me sleep, for the nights are long, my lord."

Oxford felt sorry for making Lady Mary relive her memories.

"I have taken up too much of your time, your ladyship."

"Ye have," she replied. She walked away.

~ 140 ~
King's Place

Hackney had been an important crossroads on the way
to the north of England for centuries. It was far
enough north of London that city-dwellers thought it
too far to justify a house in the country. This changed when
Henry VIII purchased King's Place and made Hackney
fashionable. Other courtiers and members of the rising
merchant class built homes nearby but King's Place remained
the jewel in Hackney's crown.

Oxford stayed on in London. Something about working
out a lease, he told Lady Elspeth. And then he became
involved in the next play, a month hence. Elspeth had begun
to think he might never make the move when he rode into the
outer courtyard in early December.

Tobias came out to greet him. "My lord," he said warmly,
taking the reins to Oxford's horse. He was obviously pleased
to see his master. Oxford was comforted to hear Tobias' deep
voice. It was a touch of the Court transplanted to Hackney.
He dismounted.

"Gethsemane will bring you something warm in the
parlor, your lordship."

"Gethsemane?"

"Our new cook. Excellent, my lord, despite the name.
Her parents were avid churchgoers. They thought her name
would make her a devout believer but it has had the opposite
effect; she will have nothing to do with religion."

"And my lady?"

"At her devotionals in the chapel."

"And my lady hired Gethsemane thinking the cook was a
devout Christian."

Tobias glanced over his shoulder. "It would seem so."

Oxford looked at his new home. It was two stories in
height and well-built of brick. The front slanted away from the
road to the right. An open arch on that side showed where the

horses were stabled. The main door was flanked by a guardhouse Tobias had adopted as his own.

"I am able to show your lordship King's Place, if you wish, my lord," Tobias said. He was obviously pleased to be guarding the house where Henry VIII had slept. Oxford could sense Tobias' pride. He was fast becoming an Englishman.

"This is not the first time I have been here," Oxford said.

Tobias was surprised to hear this. "Does her ladyship know?"

"No. And, if you would, please, let it remain that way"

Tobias moved off toward the front door. Oxford began to follow him when Socrates wandered out of the stables. He ambled over to Oxford and rubbed himself across the front of Oxford's legs. "

"The cat remembers me," he said, surprised, but Socrates did not stop or make any other acknowledgement that he might know Oxford. He continued on toward the left side of the manse. "Still not saying much," Oxford commented.

"He never does," Tobias said, as he mounted the step to the foyer. "As anything from Egypt." He took Oxford into a large hall. He pointed out the kitchens to the right and a wide set of stairs to the left that led to the second floor. A large open courtyard lay ahead. It was enclosed by a second floor that ran around the courtyard with arched openings to admit light and air.

Tobias took Oxford up the stairs at the left end of the house. A hallway at the top continued along the left side to the gallery that ran across the rear. The arched open windows that Oxford had seen from below looked into the courtyard. The wall to Oxford's left was pierced by a series of doors that led into rooms along the rear.

The ceiling of the gallery was decorated with bas relief reproductions in shining plaster of emblems Oxford recognized as Baron Hudson's. The rooms along the rear had obviously been constructed after Hunsdon's emblems had been added because some of them disappeared into the top of the wall that closed off the rooms on that side of the gallery.

Hunny had been good to him, Oxford thought as they proceeded, even if the crusty old soldier had never been close enough to share Aemilia Bassano with him. This thought transformed the emblems over his head into memories of the dark lady who had bewitched them both. He wondered where she had laid her head while staying at King's Place, for surely Hunsdon must have brought her here.

"Your room, my lord," Tobias announced, breaking into Oxford's thoughts about Hunsdon and Aemilia Bassano. Tobias opened a door at the end of the gallery. He handed Oxford a key. Oxford walked in and saw a bedstead to the right. Unglazed windows ran along the rear wall. Oxford walked over to them and looked out them into a garden. There were shutters that could be closed in the heat of a summer day. A door to the left, also with lock and key, opened into a library which had windows along the rear wall that were glazed. A bench and table sat against the wall to the left. There were empty shelves above it.

Oxford crossed to an open window and looked out. A broad ditch ran behind King's Place. A fair garden on the other side was fenced. An orchard extended beyond it to a copse of silver beech trees that banded the horizon. He could hear muted conversation. He put his head out and saw two servants below him, an older man and a young boy, working in the ditch.

"I say I'm just as good a man as he is," the older man said. "Just cause he's an earl doesn't mean the violet smells differently to him than it does to me."

"How can that be, Mr. Bates. He's of the nobility, up high; we are the ground 'neath his feet. He is the flower; we are the earth that supports him."

"True. But if his ceremonies be laid by, in his nakedness he appears as a man, though his affections are higher mounted than ours. If the queen called us to serve, we would pick up our swords and pikes and march out to defend England, wouldn't we?"

The younger man agreed.

"But how much greater the burden he must carry because he is charged with leading us with bravery and wisdom. We only have to follow orders, Michael. Think on that. While you sleep, your belly stuffed with bread, your mind empty of care, he lies awake worrying about things we've never thought of."

"Oh!" Oxford said involuntarily, causing the two men to look up, but not quick enough to catch him before he pulled his head back in. He turned to find Tobias holding a small flat board in front of him. A piece of scrap paper lay on it. Tobias held out a pen in his other hand. Oxford looked at him, puzzled.

"I know that you sometimes call for paper and pen when ye want to capture an idea ye've had. I watched Robin help you."

"Did you do this for me whilst we were at the Court?"

He nodded. "When Robin was in the kitchen or out on an errand."

"I didn't notice."

Tobias made no comment.

"I thank you for this."

Tobias tilted his head toward the open window. "Like any loyal subject, my lord," referring to the two servants outside, "they like to be taken care of. In return, they are there for you."

Oxford sat down and began to write furiously.

First Soldier:	*We see yonder the beginning of the day, but I think We shall never see the end of it. Who goes there?*
King Henry:	*A friend.*
First Soldier:	*Under what captain serve you?*
King Henry:	*Under Sir Thomas Erpingham.*
First Soldier:	*A good old commander and a most kind gentleman: I pray you, what thinks he of our estate?*
King Henry:	*Even as men wrecked upon a sand, That look to be Washed off the next tide.*
Second Soldier:	*He hath not told his thought to the king?*
King Henry:	*No; nor it is not meet he should. For, though I speak it to you, I think the king is but a man, as I am: the violet smells to him as it doth to me: his ceremonies laid by, in his nakedness he appears but a man;*
Bates:	*He may show what outward courage he will; but I believe, as cold a night as 'tis, he could wish himself in Thames up to the neck; and so I would he were, and I by him, so we were quit here.*

King Henry:	*I think he would not wish himself any where But where he is.*
Second Soldier:	*Then I would he were here alone.*
King Henry:	*I dare say I could not die any where so contented as in the king's company; his cause being just and his quarrel honourable.*
First Soldier:	*That's more than we know.*
Second Soldier:	*Ay, for we know enough, if we know we are the kings subjects: if his cause be wrong, our obedience to the king wipes the crime of it out of us.*
First Soldier:	*But if the cause be not good, the king himself hath a heavy reckoning to make, when all those legs and arms and heads, chopped off in battle, shall join together at the latter day and cry all!*

Oxford stopped writing. "The balance of fault twixt king and subject? Good. *Legs, arms and heads chopped off in battle* crying out at the end of day? Wherefore?"

"Because ye care for those who bleed for the king," Tobias said.

Oxford had forgotten Tobias was there. And he must have been talking out loud.

"Shall I inform her ladyship you have arrived?" Tobias asked. He was gently suggesting Oxford should visit his wife.

Oxford frowned. He wanted to keep on writing but something told him he should follow Tobias downstairs. "Damn," he said under his breath. Uprooted and interrupted. This did not bode well.

He got up and followed Tobias back to the top of the staircase. The door to the chapel lay the other side. Tobias could tell Oxford wanted to know what was inside. He went over and opened the door.

Oxford stepped in. The chapel was empty. Malfis had told him there should be a set of stairs to the outside in the north wall and a priest hole hidden by a painting. Oxford pulled the painting aside and saw the door to the priest hole. It looked too small to hide someone but Oxford knew that Lord Vaux had hidden Catholic priests in there, including Edward Campion. Vaux's efforts to help Catholics landed him in the Fleet. Campion was eventually captured elsewhere, cruelly tortured, hung, drawn and quartered. He must have been a small man, Oxford thought, as well as unlucky. Oxford repositioned the painting and stepped out into the hallway where Tobias waited.

They went down the stairs. Tobias took Oxford to the parlor where Lady Elspeth was sitting at a long table. A place had been set for Oxford at the other end. The parlor was hung with a blue and yellow banner with the Oxford mullet in the middle. There was a cupboard opposite it with a picture of the story of Mount Syon over it. Another picture along the other wall displayed the story of Moses and Aaron.

"My lady," Oxford said, bending over to give her a peck.

"My lord," she replied. She gave him a cheek to aim at, held at the precise distance that would prevent his lips from touching her. Bona Fortuna stood to her right, holding a white linen cloth to shield her mistress when she spit into an enameled bowl on the floor.

Oxford walked to the other end of the table. Tobias pulled out his chair; Oxford sat down. He froze for a moment. Lady Lennox must have been sitting in this very chair when Leicester poisoned her.

"My lord?" Elspeth asked, wondering why Oxford was silent.

"How is Henry?" he quickly asked.

This pleased Elspeth. "Very well, my lord. He's taken to his new surroundings like he's always lived here. He's grown half a foot since we got here."

"And he is where?" Oxford asked, looking around.

"Asleep, tired from his activities of the day. He has fallen in love with a puppy who adores him. It's from a breed Great Harry established whilst he lived here." She looked positively beatific. Oxford thought the glow was more from feeling close to the great king than how happy her son was, although it could be the reverse.

"Who would have thought."

"Yes."

A servant brought in a tureen. She put it down in the middle of the table. She ladled soup into a bowl and took it to Oxford. She did the same for Elspeth. Bona Ventura remained standing next to Elspeth.

"I very much like the move," she said. "The servants are more obedient here and less expensive." She seemed oblivious, or possibly not oblivious, to the fact that servants were listening to her as she spoke. "The quiet has done wonders for me. I will show you the chapel. I adore it. It is just the right size. I can invite neighbors in for a prayer or two and, when alone, commune with My Lord."

"Ah," Oxford said. If she had asked him, and she didn't, he thought the house was dark and dank. It reeked of prior owners: Great Harry and his disinherited daughter; Lord Vaux and the priests he hid here; Lady Lennox, dead within hours of dining with the Earl of Leicester; and Baron Hunsdon entertaining Aemilia Bassano upstairs! Ghosts lined the walls. He thought they were looking at him, smiling demonically. They knew those now at the table would soon be joining them, poisoned or not, to intimidate the next owners and guests.

"You have finished your business in London, my lord?" Elspeth asked.

"No." He looked down the table at her and realized she had changed a great deal since she had captivated him with her long legs and studied elegance. She had taken to her role as wife with the thoroughness she had brought to their courting. She came naturally by this, having been ten years a lady-in-waiting to Her Majesty and the executor of her father's estate despite having two brothers who should have performed this office. As Oxford's wife, she had bought King's Place and was now raising the son she had given him. All of this left little time or affection for anyone else. Having given Oxford an heir, there was little need to give him access to her, although none of this, Oxford was sure, was the result of any conscious thought. Like the way bark appeared on trees, it just happened.

He watched Elspeth finish her soup and wondered what had happened. Was she someone else when she seduced him? Or had their marriage transformed her into a sexless and efficient matriarch, like the way apples slowly change in a cool cellar? Her embrace of religion hadn't helped.

He smiled. Maybe she had a twin sister. He had bedded the hot-blooded one high in Hedingham Castle but her dried-up twin became the Countess of Oxford. Was there a play here? *Two Ladies from Hedingham? Comedy of Errors,* as written by Elspeth de Vere, Countess of Oxford?

"My lord," Elspeth said, breaking into his reverie.

"My lady?"

"You arrived with no baggage. I take it you will be returning to London."

"Only to close up the Court, your ladyship." He waved a hand. "Years of living in one place, boxes to go through, papers to be organized." He let his voice trail off.

"How long before you return?"

"Actually, I am to London in the morning. Prince Hal is now Henry V and Her Majesty expects me to show him in all his glory, Agincourt and all. I have to finish it. She wants it for Boxing Day."

"Will you stay to see it staged?"

"No. I'm tired of Hal. And the queen." He looked around. "The quietness of this place draws me in."

Elspeth was pleased to hear this.

Oxford was not being entirely truthful, however. Given his freedom, he would get up from the table and ride back to London that evening. It was quiet; *suffocatingly, boringly, quiet.* But she held the purse strings. He must stay. At least for the night.

This thought made him realize that being unable to say what he really felt had forced him into lying to her. This added to his discontent. True, it was a white lie, justifiable on the ground that it made her happy while the truth would make her sad. Still, how much more proof did he need that his marriage had changed? This thought led to a very dark place. He decided some truth was needed.

"Actually, I will be in Cambridge on Boxing Day," he said.

"Cambridge?"

"The students are putting on their annual plays. Finley has talked me into attending. He thinks my presence will help convince the board of governors they should make him professor of a new theater department and allow students to study plays."

Elspeth had no idea who Finley was. As for plays, she had no room for such frivolous pursuits in her new faith. 'Foolishness,' was all she said when asked if she would like to see a play shortly before she moved to Hackney. This was in contrast to the excitement she greeted Lisbeth one day at the Court. They were off to see a play by Marlowe!

"I am sorry you won't be here. But, if you are returning to London, there is one thing I would like you to do while you are there."

"What is that, my lady?"

"Visit Marcus Gheeraerts and have your portrait painted. I understand the only portrait of you was done in Paris on your way out to Italy."

"By Jean Cousin the Elder, court painter at the time," Oxford said. "His mastery of the gold weaving on the jacket I wore for the sitting, the opulence of the black beret with gold buttons he made me wear, the ruff that ran up and down around my neck," his hand fluttered as he recreated it in his mind, "even the reproduction of my right ear, mashed to a pulp by a hog that slammed me into a stable wall when I was a boy at Hedingham."

Oxford went on. "I thought I could convince the beast to come peacefully along with me but it sensed it wasn't being *invited* to supper, it was going *to be* supper." He reached up and touched his ear which still looked like a fold of flesh that had started life as bread dough that had never been given a chance to rise.

"I've never seen that portrait," Elspeth said. "What happened to it?"

"I sent the original to Nan as a gift. Burghley had a copy made for the queen. He told her, of course, it was the original. I don't know what happened to either one. Burghley probably burned the original. Given how apart the queen and I became, I would not be surprised that she burned the copy she had as well."

"All the more reason to have a picture of yourself made for your son and your descendants."

Oxford did not share her enthusiasm. *My name will be buried where my body lies,* he almost said aloud.

"I've spoken to Marcus Gheeraerts. He has agreed to paint you."

"Oh. Is his studio still at the back of the Savoy?"

"It is."

The Savoy was a rambling collection of buildings and apartments across the Strand from Cecil House. The studio was in the rear yard that ran along the Thames. Patrons would visit by boat and bring friends and hangers-on. The number of boats was never as many as those that crowded the waterfront in front of Titian's studio in Venice but the party atmosphere was a pleasant alternative to the bullfights and bearbaiting across the river, not to mention the plays, which were rarely the works of genius expected of Marlowe or Shakespeare.

"You will visit Marcus?" Elspeth asked.

"I will."

Elspeth's use of the painter's Christian name made Oxford's pulse jump a bit but he didn't think she would ever violate her oath to him and God, particularly now that she was a Foot-Washing Baptist. *Or would she?* he wondered. Oxford listened to himself. *Ridiculous.* Still, the frisson of being cuckolded ran up his spine. He liked the way it made his eyes open wide.

Elspeth smiled contentedly. Having convinced her husband to have his portrait painted, she moved on to a topic closer to her heart. "You will see Henry before you go?"

"Of course. On the way back, too."

141

In Arthur's Bosom

Falstaff came into the library. "My lord," he said, going over and sitting down in the large chair he had appropriated for himself along the right-hand wall.

Oxford thought Falstaff might be the bearer of good news but the big man's face revealed nothing.

"And?"

Falstaff stirred. "A few dead ends cleared of possibilities, my lord, which is a necessary step to answering your question. Not every hunt ends with game on the table."

He eyed Oxford to see if that helped. It did not.

"And the reason for your visit?"

"You said you needed a clerk to replace Robin."

"Yes."

"I found out Kit Marlowe had a son."

"He did?" Oxford immediately thought the boy could be Aemilia Bassano's. "How old?"

"Twelve, I think."

Oxford did the math. The boy was not Aemilia's.

"Kit went over to Dover during his summer break from Cambridge first year and popped one in the oven of a young lady there who was his cousin. The two of them went for a walk that turned into a roll in a field. Sam was the result."

"He told me he didn't like women."

Falstaff shrugged. "Maybe he didn't because of what happened with his cousin? In any event, he never knew she was pregnant. She never told him. She hid her shame, gave birth at home, and raised 'Sam' in Dover."

Oxford was intrigued. "Have you met the boy?"

"Aye. His mother recently told him Marlowe was his father. He came up to London. He wants to write plays."

"Has he any schooling?"

"No. He says he doesn't need any. He's the son of Christopher Marlowe, he says, and that's all he needs."

Oxford was puzzled by this. "Should I interview him?"

"I don't think so. He says he's read all his father's plays but I don't think he knows how to write. I put a piece of paper in front of him and told him to take down my words. He couldn't."

"*He can't write?*" Oxford was amazed. "How could he not know how to write?"

"He said he didn't need to because he was going to dictate his plays."

Oxford whistled. "Who would've thought Kit Marlowe's son couldn't write?"

"To be fair, my lord, Kit didn't know he had a son."

"Well, he can't write, that's for sure, but his arrogance shows that he is certainly Kit's son."

Falstaff agreed. But his face had gone low tide, Oxford saw, with a hint of anger.

"What?"

"Jonson's out of the Marshalsea."

"I need a secretary, Jack, not a competitor."

Falstaff grumped. He was about to say Jonson could at least write but Oxford realized something else was going on.

"What, Jack?"

"I just looked at a draft of *Henry V*. Ye promised I'd be back but I never thought I'd come back *dead!* And my death would be reported third hand! *Off-stage!*" He ran his eye around the room. "God's blood!" he cried. "I should've died onstage where everyone could see me expire. I could have played myself rarely. My death would've been the talk of the town!"

"I couldn't bring you back, Jack. You stole *Henry IV* and refused to play yourself in *Merry Wives.*"

Falstaff made a grumbling sound, like a bear dreaming of dogs baying him in the pit.

"You went out as Socrates, Jack."

"Who?"

"Socrates. The Greek philosopher who died from drinking hemlock. It's a poison." Falstaff looked away, with a 'so-what' expression on his face. Oxford went on. "The hostess describes you as lying down, then your feet got cold, and then your legs. She says you went to 'Arthur's bosom:'

> *He's in Arthur's bosom, if ever man went to Arthur's bosom. I saw him fumble with the sheets and play with flowers and smile upon his fingers' ends. He were cold and bade me lay more clothes on his feet: I put my hand into the bed and felt them, and they were as cold as any stone; then I felt to his knees, and they were as cold as any stone, and so upward and upward, and all was as cold as any stone.*

Falstaff thought about this. "Arthur's bosom," he said, listening to how it sounded. "Might be a few tears."

He heaved himself erect. The anger on his face had cleared. "But I was done anyway. I have too much respect for the players to continue my career as an actor. It's the tavern for me, my lord, a tankard of ale and a bottom to pinch. Miss Peaches will provide all three. Malfis has given us the papers to purchase the Boar's Head and I, God willing, will become a tapster. We open before Christmas. Ye comin'?"

Oxford marveled at Falstaff's ability to sail past a disaster and pay it no mind. Oxford had readied himself to do battle with the fat knight but Falstaff had let him off the hook. "No, I won't be coming. I'm to Cambridge."

"Not going to see *Henry V*?"

"I'm tired of Hal."

"And me, apparently." He sniffed. "No place for me on the stage. No place for me in Hackney." He sighed. "After so many years of service." Then his head came up. "Well, t'is to be expected, innit?"

He began moving toward the door. He cracked an eye at Oxford. "Oh. By the way. I'm to Bacton tomorrow. If I find anything out about …" he said, not finishing his sentence before he disappeared out the door.

This at least made Oxford feel better. He had begun to think Falstaff had abandoned him, like he had abandoned the fat knight on the stage. Apparently not.

142

The Return to Parnassus

ambridge was a day's ride from Hackney. Oxford kissed his son goodbye and went out to find Tobias holding a fine gelding for him. For a moment, Oxford imagined himself leaping into the saddle like he had at the Accession Day Tilt in 1571. He won it that year, beating the likes of Sir Christopher Hatton, Oxford's competitor for the queen's favors at the time, Charles Howard, 1st Earl of Nottingham, soon to become Lord Admiral and defeat the Spanish Armada, and Sir Henry Lee, the queen's champion, who was now living with Anne Vavasour and raising Oxford's son, Edward.

Oxford had also won the Tilt ten years later, this time against younger men, but the athleticism he displayed then had been eroded by age and the wound Thomas Knyvet's sword had carved into his thigh in Pudding Lane. 'Every day he stabs me back,' Oxford said to himself. Bright sunlight coming through the trees dappled Oxford and the horse, causing him to pause at the surreal sight and reconsider how he should mount the horse. Tobias held out his clasped hands. With a wry smile, Oxford accepted his help and swung himself up into the saddle. He took the reins and turned the gelding out of the gate to head north.

Hedingham was not on the way to Cambridge but Oxford found himself veering off toward the castle. The closer he got, the stronger he felt an urge to climb to the top of the Keep. He had a vague feeling he wanted to stay there and live a hermit's life at the top.

As the Keep came into view, he sensed the gelding telling him not to dismount. He realized that if he did, he might not leave again. He stopped anyway.

Digby came running up. "My lord," he called out.

Oxford looked down at him. "I am to Cambridge, Digby. I would like to stay but can't." Without further explanation, he rode back down the hill and on to Cambridge.

Digby watched him go. Something had changed, he thought, but was his master merely immersed in the writing of a new play, or was it something more sinister? A new play, Digby decided.

Oxford headed north, the melancholy that enveloped him falling away as he rode. He arrived to find Finley waiting in the entrance to the college, its double towers rising high above him. A servant took the gelding. Finley took Oxford into the dining hall where they had something to eat before they headed out.

"We are off to Parnassus," Finley said. He took Oxford through the Queens' College yards and across the Mathematical Bridge. On the other side, he climbed a hill to a squat building that was in very poor condition. "This building," Finley explained, "is outside the control of the wardens because of a dispute over a deed. The prior owner died without a will and his relatives are fighting over what he owned. In the meantime, we have taken over the building as squatters and converted it into Cambridge's first theater."

They walked in. A stage could be seen at the far end with an assortment of chairs arranged in front of it. A dozen people were dragging objects about the stage; the sound of hammers could be heard in the back.

"And what is the play?" Oxford asked.

"*The Return to Parnassus*. Part One was presented last year at St. John's but the school has declined the honor of presenting Part Two."

"What was the first part about?"

"*The Pilgrimmage to Parnassus* told the story of two students going through their education here known as the trivium. Mount Parnassus represented their goal: graduation. *The Return to Parnassus* will show how they fared in London."

The building filled and the play began. The two original students - Philomusus and Studioso – were joined by Luxurio and Ingenisio. The four of them journey to London to try their luck but find only menial jobs. Philomusus becomes a sexton and work as a gravedigger. Studioso ends up working as a tutor. Luxurio and Ingenisio fare little better, although Ingenisio finds a patron named Gullio, who agrees to support him. In return, Ingenisio promises to write poetry that will make Gullio immortal.

"Their names tell the audience who they are: Philomusus is a philosopher; Studioso is a scholar; Ingenisio is, well, clever; and Luxurio likes to lie around and do little."

"Do the characters represent anyone?"

"Some think Studioso is Shackspear," Finley said, "while most people think Ingenisio is Thomas Nashe. Philomusus is Thomas Kyd. Gullio is the Earl of Southampton. He attended St. John's, which is the reason it hosted the play last year."

Oxford listened as the play unfolded but the plot was too thin to hold his interest, even when Ingenisio composes verses he stole from others for Gullio to give to his lover, Lesbia. 'Lesbia,' Oxford thought; 'good name.' But Oxford sat up when a character criticized Shakespeare – him – by making reference to *Venus & Adonis*:

> *Who loves not Adons love, or Lucrece rape?*
> *His sweeter verse contaynes hart throbbing line,*
> *Could but a graver subject him content*
> *Without loves foolish lazy languishment.*

The character on the stage was onto something. The queen had urged him to write about 'graver subjects.' Maybe they had heard her. 'Let others write comedy,' Elizabeth had told him. 'You, my lord, have been bred to hunt big game, and a fat man in a basket is not it.' Apparently, there were some who agreed with her.

The play ended with the four graduates going off in different directions, no more successful than they had been at the beginning. A player who spoke the epilogue promised a third play the following year.

Oxford and Finley were leaving when a tall gangly young man came up. Oxford thought a sneeze from a Norfolk sheep could knock him over. The student smiled. His front teeth stuck out. He looked look like a giant rabbit who had been forced to wear an ill-fitting suit of borrowed clothes.

"Thomas John Fletcher," Finley announced proudly.

"At your service, your lordship," Fletcher said, bowing.

"Thomas John is one of my prize students," Finley continued. "He has contributed much to the play you have just seen. I expect great things of him."

Thomas John thought Oxford would be interested in his ideas. "I believe the playgoers are ready for dramatic presentations, my lord," he said. "Plays about kings and knights are *passé*. They want to see something modern."

Oxford nodded. "Like the play we just watched." Fletcher agreed. "Studioso and Philomusus. Ingenisio and Gullio." Fletcher kept on nodding. "Hmm," Oxford said.

Finley cut in. "My lord, what better person to become your assistant than a young man who has already cut his teeth on an actual dramatic production?"

"Indeed," Oxford said, still looking at Fletcher. "And, perchance, your efforts will no doubt produce a 'graver subject,' *n'est pas?*" He couldn't help slipping in some French to counter Fletcher's affected use of 'passé.' Oxford did not like hearing his plays were passé. Or nothing more than 'foolish lazy, languishment.'

Fletcher realized Oxford had not liked the comment about Shakespeare. "I didn't write that," he quickly said. "It was a collaboration, you know."

"I will consider the offer, Mr. Fletcher."

Fletcher could tell Oxford would do no such thing. The young man had wasted his chance to work with the Poet Earl. But how? Finley had said Oxford would surely choose him to be his new secretary. He found himself humiliated. He found himself hoping the floor would open up and swallow him. Failing that, he bowed to Oxford and left.

Oxford spoke to Finley. "I'm sure he will turn out well. Unfortunately, Mr. Fletcher is not what I need." He didn't say that he could never work with a man who reminded him of a giant rabbit. He could see himself waking in a cold sweat as giant teeth bit into him, or a massive carrot came out of the darkness to bash him. This bizarre thought startled him. He was apparently more unmoored than he thought.

"I will return to Hedingham. Come visit me at Hackney."

"I will, my lord. And, if I may say so, I hope and pray you will shed this terrible melancholia that now enwraps you."

Oxford was surprised Finley had noticed. Yes, *melancholia, but from what cause?*

~ 143 ~
Hedingham and the Joy of Eating Small Birds

Hedingham came into view as the sun was setting. It had been a long day. Digby bundled Oxford into bed and gave him a posset of eggs, milk, and ale, spiced with nutmeg and parsley. Oxford slept like a hunting dog who had spent the day chasing foxes he never caught. He awoke refreshed.

Digby mounted Oxford on a dark bay the next morning and collected a hawk from the free-loft mews behind the stables. From there, they rode out with the dogs to hunt geese. Digby thought they were due but they did not appear. Oxford wondered whether Digby was imagining the sky full of geese in the hope it would bring his master around. The lassitude displayed by the dogs, even the son of Tater, reflected their belief that the geese would not be arriving that day.

Digby sat his horse alongside Oxford, scanning the sky and finally decided the dogs knew better than he did. "The geese being uncooperative, we will return to the castle and lime the bushes to catch thrushes. I have seen them at the feeders. I have a tub of lime that has been well-pounded and washed. It only needs a bit of nut oil and an hour on the fire to make it ready. We'll warm it up whilst we eat some lunch. Afterwards, we'll get us some songbirds."

Oxford, in a trance-like state, nodded. He had heard this description many times. Liming tree branches and waiting for the birds to get stuck was not as thrilling as launching hawks into the air but Oxford was vaguely content to follow Digby around like old times.

They spent the better part of an hour that afternoon liming branches on the other side of the castle. They sat back at the top of the slope to give the birds time to find the lime. They didn't talk. They were getting older. They both knew was more and more unlikely with each passing day that Oxford would come back to Hedingham to stay, even though Lady Elspeth's ploy to put Hedingham into a trust to save it from Oxford's creditors had been successful. The 500-year home of the Veres had been saved for Henry and his descendants.

Oxford imagined his son riding up the hill to the castle, the Vere banner streaming out behind him. Digby imagined no such future. He knew Oxford's pension would end with his death. The estates Oxford had inherited had been sold off for him to see the lands of others. There were few rents coming in, which was one reason repairs had been put off. Henry, growing up in London, would likely be drawn to the court when he grew older and sell Hedingham to some parvenu who had found a way through monopolies or trade to buy his way into England's upper class.

Whatever the future, Digby knew enough of Oxford's doings in London to realize his master's move to Hackney had uprooted him in more ways than simply changing where he laid lay his head at night. The earl's move to Hackney had 'evicted' him from the creativity that was London. Fisher's Folly had been a hothouse of wits that Oxford had traded for Oxford Court, but poets and playwrights still came to the Court. The move to Hackney was different. Visitors were rare. Digby could sense his lordship would never again be rooted hip-deep in creating plays, cobbled together in sweaty rooms populated by the likes of Thomas Nashe, John Lyly, Anthony Munday, Robert Greene, Christopher Marlowe, and, yes, little Robin.

The thrashing of the birds captured by the lime roused the two men from their drifting slumber. They pushed their way into the brambles and grabbed the startled birds, putting them into tight nets. The two 'hunters' descended to Digby's cottage where a pot of water was bubbling on Nell's stove. The table was set. Oxford sat down.

Digby was now in his element. "A French gourmet, Canon Charcot, came with the French who brought the head of the boar your grandfather killed in France," Digby recalled. He was referring to the one that hung in the Great Hall at Oxford Court. "While he was here, the Canon taught my father how to prepare songbirds. My father taught me. I usually follow the Canon's recipe exactly. I keep the birds in a closed box filled with millet seed where they gorge themselves and double in size, at which point I throw them into a container of Armagnac to drown them, warbling and singing happily to the end. I let them marinate for a week and bake 'em in the fire."

"Hmm," Oxford muttered half-consciously.

"The better course, however," Digby went on, "and the Canon's second way to cook them, is to roast them in the fire tout suite." He reached into the bag and took out a peeping ortolan, its gray-green head looking wildly around as Digby thrust it into the boiling pot. The others quickly followed. It only took a minute for the feathers to become loose. Digby reached into the pot with fingers long hardened by hot stews and sauces and plucked out the birds. He lay them in a row and rubbed the feathers off them. He coated each with a bit of sweet butter and laid them in the ashes of the fireplace.

Oxford watched. It had been a while since he had enjoyed roast songbird but he had no difficulty remembering how wonderful they tasted. He watched the tiny birds twist and pop in the coals as they turned a lustrous chestnut brown.

Digby took two out and put them on a plate. He dusted them with salt and held the plate out to Oxford. He swept one to his mouth. Digby took the second bird and followed suit. He held the bird by its beak and bit off the curled legs, which he spit into the fire. The head quickly followed, after which he tossed the bird's now crisp body into his mouth and bit into it, the juices from the bird's body exploding into his mouth.

Digby looked at Oxford. "Eh?"

Oxford closed his eyes and nodded. "No pen could describe this, even if it were filled with the juices that now fill my mouth." This flight into ridiculous analogy seemed to revive him. His eyes opened; his face brightened. "Nor is there enough paper in the world to set down what I am experiencing, nor marble to serve as monument."

Digby was happy to hear this. The ortolans might be the cure for his lordship's melancholia. He reached for more. In minutes, they were all gone, leaving the earl and his steward floating happily in a state usually brought on only by a warm afternoon sun on a day that had started out cold and damp.

When the sensations brought on by the tiny birds had begun to fade, Digby decided to see if he could right his master and send him back to London with some purpose. "Ye say Robin has left your service, my lord. I thought that would never happen."

"Yes. So did I." He did not explain. Digby didn't ask. He was not fishing for information. He was a plain-spoken man who only dealt in words that carried meanings, not hints of hidden meanings or trips into airy fantasy. As a consequence, he had never been able to appreciate the art Oxford created, although he would have nodded approvingly had he had seen a production of *Henry VI - Part Two* and heard Jack Cade harangue Lord Saye for having 'men about thee that usually talk of a noun and a verb, and such abominable words as no Christian ear can endure to hear.'

But Digby knew nothing of *Henry VI*. He was focused on helping his lordship regain his old self. "I thought you went to Cambridge to find Robin's replacement but it seems you have been unsuccessful."

"Yes."

"What about John Lyly?"

"Lyly?" This surprised Oxford. "Lyly? I hadn't thought of him."

"He used to be your secretary, didn't he?

Oxford nodded. The image of the little man and his furtive, darting eyes and round pate ringed by thinning hair floated into Oxford's mind. He remembered him skittering crab-like across the Hall at Oxford Court, calling up to him: 'I came as soon as I heard, my lord. As the doves coo when the sun is warm, friends flock together to hear your dulcet tones.'

"John Lyly." Oxford nodded. "Yes. John Lyly. A capital idea." He rose.

Digby rose with him. "So soon?"

Oxford nodded. He was already at the door. "Bid the ostler bring the gelding out of the stable. I must to London, Digby. Thank you."

~ 144 ~
John Lyly

J ohn Lyly came flying into the Great Hall. He was heading
for the library when he saw Oxford at the top of the stairs.

"My lord," he called up. "I have received great news: you have
need of my services." He bowed deeply. "Tell me this news is true. I
don't know much, but what I know I know at great length …"

"Yes," Oxford called down, cutting off the little man's speech.
"The library," he said, pointing to the door.

Lyly skittered into the library. He had not worked with Oxford at
Oxford Court. He was unfamiliar with the library.

"Ah," he said, But Digby knew nothing of. He opened it. He
loaded his pipe-stem arms with ink pots and quills. He laid them into
an inlaid ebony tray that contained a special knife, small and bone-
handled, used to shape quills into pens. He riffled through the quills.
"None from a right wing?" He looked at Oxford. "I am sure you
remember I am left-handed."

"Yes. But all my secretaries after you have been *right-handed* and,
thus, only wanted primaries from the left wing."

"Taken, I hope, from a bird's annual moult," Lyly said sternly,
holding a clutch of quills in his hand. He looked at them. "These
should not be used by someone who is left-handed, of course. I need
quills made from the primaries of a right wing. They curl away and
thereby aid in the accuracy of what I write, particularly if a working
session continues into the night." He eyed Oxford, who had kept him
up many nights when Oxford had been bitten by the Muse.

"Pen a note to Digby to send up some primaries from a right
wing."

Lyly nodded. "And how is old 'bristle-head'?"

"He has, not surprisingly, been dusted with a touch of gray, but
his bristles stand as tall as ever."

Lyly was disappointed. He had hoped that Digby had become
bald, as he was doing. Lyly had lost hair on the top, making his
remaining hair a monk's tonsure. He had taken to applying black dye
to what remained but this did not stop the growth of new hair which

created a black ring at the tips and white underneath, giving his head an odd halo-like effect.

He took a seat at the table. He made like he was throwing salt over his shoulder before he began to scribble the note to Digby.

Oxford chuckled. He had never been religious, or even a churchgoer, but he did knock on wood to avoid bad luck. He also kept in an upstairs closet the horn of a narwhal that had been sold to him as a unicorn's. He would rub it for good luck when he felt the muse had left him. And then there was London Stone in the street outside. He touched that on occasion. He and Lyly had a lot in common.

Lyly finished the note to Digby. He folded it in four. "I slipped into *Henry V*, my lord. The queen was not pleased. She wanted to talk to you after it was over but you were not there."

"Abusing me is her favorite recreation after a play, John. I used to find it amusing." He looked at Lyly. "What displeased her?" he asked.

"Something about 'tennis balls.'"

"Ah. You came in late." Lyly was *always* late. "God, I hate it when people come late to my plays and miss the first act only to complain that they could not understand what the play was about. If you had arrived on time, you would have witnessed the French ambassador delivering a set of tennis balls for Henry to play with."

"Tennis balls?"

"Henry is still Hal in the eyes of the French. They do not know the playboy will become our greatest king. The audience, of course, knows exactly what will happen. They love nothing better than watching the French make mistakes and then get bashed about on our stage. The playgoers who arrived on time were primed to see Hal become Henry V. He says to the French ambassador:

> *We are glad the Dauphin is so pleasant with us;*
> *When we have march'd our rackets to these balls,*
> *We will, in France, by God's grace, play a set*
> *Shall strike his father's crown into the hazard.*

"And so on."

"But tennis balls?" Lyly asked. "Did France actually send Henry tennis balls? Is that in Holinshed?"

"No, of course not. Henry's angry reply is only a slightly altered account of what happened between me and Sidney during our 'tennis court' argument. Philip - he was not yet *Sir* Philip - was playing tennis at Whitehall when I came in and told him to leave. He refused. He said I had no right to take his place. I told him I was the 17th Earl of

Oxford and could make him do anything I wanted. I then struck a ball at him that knocked the hat he was wearing off his head. It was a silly little hat. He was enraged. He charged me, but his retainers dragged him off before we came to blows."

This was shocking news to Lyly. He had heard Oxford had been the victim in this argument. Apparently, Sidney was the victim.

"Yes," Oxford said, recognizing why Lyly was taken aback. "T'was not one of my better moments." However, the slight smile Lyly saw showed Oxford had no regrets. "The queen had to dress him down about the differences between an earl and a commoner, although being Leicester's nephew and possible heir at the time probably gave him more power than I had."

Lyly knew how Oxford and Leicester had gone at each other before Leicester died in September 1588.

Oxford went on. "The queen has told me she is tired of seeing Sidney in every play. I can imagine what she would have said had I been there for *Henry V*. *Again? He's dead ten years. Haven't you skewered this man enough?* Had I been there, my answer would have been: *Never!*"

"Because he was to marry Nan?"

"No. I married her, didn't I? Check … and … mate." Here Oxford stopped to admire how he had slipped 'married' and 'mate' into the same paragraph. He returned to Sidney. "No, it was his poetry. His ideas about poetry would have crippled the English language. Accent and rhythm would have died away. I told Elizabeth after he died that every poet alive should thank God for calling him home. It may have saved the English language."

Shackspear could be heard entering the Court. Nigel was apparently somewhere else.

"My lord," he said, sweeping into the library. He saw Lyly at the table and stopped. "Mr. Lyly," he said in a different voice. He immediately assumed Lyly had been hired to take Robin's place. He then leapt to the further conclusion that Lyly had replaced him as author. "Will Mr. Lyly be taking my place?" he asked, never reluctant to give immediate expression to whatever floated into his mind.

"You mean, will his name appear on the plays instead of yours?" Oxford was enjoying Shackspear's fear of having his name removed from the plays. He could tell Lyly knew what Oxford was about. Wits love nothing more than out-witting witless fools; Shackspear, as witless as anyone, was a tempting target, but Oxford realized he had little stomach for such foolishness, particularly since it only exacerbated the wound that festered within him because Shackspear's name appeared on the plays and not his.

"No one would believe that Mr. Lyly has taken your place, Willum. John's style is completely different from mine. He is well-known for *Euphues* and *Endymion*, as well as other works. No, unfortunately, *my* plays will continue to have *your* name on them," Oxford said, followed by "God blast it."

Shackspear cringed. Then a smile crossed his face. He had news he thought might calm the waters. "Old Bess, my lord, is in a frightful mood herself today."

"How could you possibly know that?"

"She's in high dudgeon over what King James said to the Scottish Parliament last month. It's all over the City."

"Which was?"

"James said he has suffered much from the execution of his mother, Mary, as well as the delay in the payment of his pension."

"She gives him a pension?" Lyly asked.

"She's been paying him for years," Oxford said. "James is obviously short of cash. Interesting that he lumps in his need for money with the loss of his mother. Is he a loving son, short of money? Or a spendthrift who cares nothing about his mother."

Oxford did not like James; he wanted Southampton to succeed the queen. Sir Robert was promoting James because it gave him his best chance of staying in power once Elizabeth died. Therefore, Oxford thought, anything that dimmed Elizabeth's view of James might help Southampton. But only if Falstaff came up with something to show Southampton was Elizabeth's son.

Shackspear had more. "She didn't like James going public like that. A letter is on its way to him as we speak, and he is not going to like it."

"Why is that?"

"She wrote: '*Look you not, therefore, that without large amends I may not slupper-up such indignities.*'

"'*Slupper-up*,'" Oxford said. He looked at Lyly, who smiled. They thought this a wonderful word. "Oh, she is *still* so clever. 'Slupper' is an old Scots word that can mean many things, such as 'tolerate' or a wet mess, wet snow or slush, *as well as a person who makes loud noises whilst eating!*"

Shackspear and Lyly laughed. "He won't like her using a Scots word to reprimand him," Lyly said, "particularly one that sounds disgusting." He sighed appreciatively. "She's not lost her touch."

But Oxford's laughter was cut short by memories of his part in the trial that convicted James' mother. Oxford had begged Elizabeth to leave him out of it but she had insisted he, as her senior lord, must sit as one of the jurors.

The trial was held in the Great Hall at Fotheringhay Castle, a cold, damp place in the middle of England. A large table took up the middle of the room behind which prosecutors sat in a row facing the dais. Oxford and the other lords sat along the left wall. Burghley sat next to Oxford's left; Lord Chancellor Thomas Bromley sat next to Burghley. Bromley was famous, at least among lawyers, for his decision in *The Rule in Shelley's Case*, but he was enjoying far broader fame at the time for shepherding a law through Parliament that allowed an English jury to try a foreign queen, for Mary, Queen of Scots, was not English; she was a Scot. The other barons sat along the right wall.

Oxford remembered Mary coming into the Great Hall through a door in the far corner and immediately protesting that the court had no jurisdiction to try her on any charge. She refused to participate. She started to leave the room when she was somehow convinced to sit down and take part, thereby losing any right to complain about jurisdiction.

But legalities were the least of her problems. She knew the English judges and lords had decided they had to get rid of Mary. But Mary was an anointed queen. Can words written on paper approved by no higher authority than politicians elected to a parliament provide a basis for beheading a queen? A queen from another kingdom? The image of Richard II on a cold beach in Wales rose in Oxford's mind: *The breath of worldly men cannot depose / A deputy elected by the Lord. / Not all the water in the rough rude sea / Can wash the balm off from an anointed king.*

Nevertheless, he, along with the other lords save one, voted to convict Mary. Elizabeth, however, could not bring herself to issue the death warrant. Months passed. Her ministers finally got tired of waiting and sent the warrant to Fotheringhay without telling her. It took two strokes to cut off Mary's head, an ominous sign, but Mary, Queen of Scots, was finally dead, her little dog found entangled in the enormous blood-red dress she wore to her execution. It was a period in Oxford's life he would rather not revisit.

Shackspear was the bearer of more news. "Cecil is to France on a diplomatic mission in February and the Earl of Southampton is going with him."

"He is?"

"The queen has given the young lord license to travel beyond the seas for two years with ten servants, six horses, and £200."

"To Italy, no doubt," Oxford said. This pleased him. He immediately began to wonder how he could help.

"So, my lord," Shackspear asked, "what is the play?"

Oxford did not like being reminded that he had *another* play to write for the queen. He said nothing.

Shackspear looked at Lyly.

"My lord," Lyly said, bringing Oxford's eyes around to look at him. "I would also like to know. What *is* the play?"

Oxford wanted to announce that he was done with plays but found he could not utter the words. John Lyly's bright face showed how much the little man wanted to work on a new play. "*Julius Caesar*," Oxford said, surprising himself. Where had that come from? Oh, yes - Lettice Knollys.

"*Julius Caesar*," Lyly repeated. He sounded like he was giving voice to a magic spell.

"*Julius Caesar*," Shackspear repeated in a different voice. "My lord, the theater is done with Julius Caesars and King Henries. The university wits and the lords and ladies who fancy their Latin and Greek enjoy your plays, Ovid this and Plutarch that, but the paying public want stories about them."

"I don't write for the 'paying public,'" Oxford said, now thoroughly disgusted that he had to write another play *and* put up with *His Feebleness*, as Falstaff had taken to calling Shackspear. He got up. "I write for the queen. Let the other playwrights pander to the mob. It's *Julius Caesar*, gentlemen. Be here or be unknown." He walked out of the library.

145

A Bone in Shackspear's Throat

Shackspear and Lyly were waiting for Oxford the next morning. Lyly's face showed he was ready to work on *Julius Caesar*, the sour look on Shackspear's face showed he was not.

Oxford sat down at the head of the table. "Got a Roman stuck in your throat?" he said to Shackspear.

Shackspear didn't know what to make of this.

Lyly did. "As in *Julius Caesar*, my lord?"

Shackspear caught on. "Yes. Yes, I do. As in *Julius Caesar*."

"Would a different play dislodge it?"

"Yes," Shackspear immediately said. He and Lyly looked at each other. They had never heard Oxford sound so reasonable.

"And the play is?" Oxford asked.

Shackspear's contorted face showed he didn't have an answer.

"Something magical," Lyly volunteered.

"Magical?" Oxford asked. He wasn't dismissing Lyly's suggestion. He was pondering whether Lyly's suggestion might fit in with something rolling around in his mind.

"There is nothing magical in *Julius Caesar*," Lyly said into the silence that had descended over the table.

"No, there isn't. The queen has sent word she wants another play about English history, so *Julius Caesar* will not do. As best I can recall, he was not an English king."

Shackspear and Lyly nodded. And waited.

"The bone, as always, in *my* throat has always been Philip Sidney. In *An Apology for Poetry*, he took sledgehammers to poetry but he also ridiculed plays that showed two armies represented by 'foure swords and bucklers, and then what harde heart would not receive it for a pitched battle?' Or, 'two young princes who fall in love, she is got with childe, delivered of a faire boy who is lost, growth a man, falls in love, and is ready to get another child, *and all this in two hours space!*'"

They could hear the disdain in his voice. They didn't know where Oxford was going with this. They waited.

"Sidney said I wrote plays that didn't follow Aristotle's rules *because I couldn't. A Comedy of Errors* put the lie to that canard. I have not written another because Aristotle's rules are a *corsage de force*; they limit what a playwright can do with his genius." He turned to Lyly. "*Videlicet*," he said, using Burghley's favorite phrase for no apparent reason, "your suggestion that I consider 'magic' has fallen on fertile ground."

This said, he went silent again, his mind running off somewhere.

This outburst made Lyly realize that Sidney, to Oxford, was still alive because Sidney's words continued to live on the printed page and were available to any person who could read. This included the queen, who liked to praise the dead poet, and not just when she wanted to needle Oxford. As a result, Oxford's animus toward Sidney was as high as ever: for being Nan's first suitor; for being a nephew of Leicester, a rival of Oxford's for the queen's affection; for the embarrassing incident at the tennis court at Whitehall; *and for being a terrible poet people are still reading!*

"And for being an upstart," Oxford said aloud. "His pathetic attempts at poetry forced *me* to turn to poetry: "*Fain would I sing, but fury makes me fret,*" he began to recite, "*And rage hath sworn to seek revenge of wrong.*" He stopped. "But he is dead, gentlemen, and I am alive, so why do I rant at him? Far better," he said, a gleam in his eye, "to make him roll over in his grave."

Lyly and Shackspear still said nothing. Oxford went on.

"How bad can I make a play, at least in the eyes of Philip Sidney?" He chuckled. "Listen. I have a story in my mind that will make our stage leap to Rome and back, to Wales and back. I will so twine up the different plots that the audience will shake their heads as they listen to it unravel, believing no resolution is possible at the end. Philip will cry out from his grave but, *surprise!* Everything will turn out well!"

Lyly cleared his throat. "What if we start with *The Countess of Pembroke's Arcadia* - Sidney's most ambitious work?"

Oxford's face lit up. "Oh, yes. A capital idea. I will beat him with his own pen. Oh, yes, t'will do. Thank you, John."

Lyly and Shackspear didn't know what this meant. Oxford got up and headed for the library door.

"My lord," Lyly called after him. "We despair to know how to help you."

"Particularly," Shackspear added, a touch of sarcasm slipping into his voice, "if you continue out the door and leave us alone."

"Yes. Point well taken. But I should have said I was on my way to retrieve my copy of the *Arcadia*, which contains extensive notes I made whilst reading it. I shall return immediately."

He continued out the door where he ran into Robin, now known to all and sundry as John Webster. She had quietly slipped into the Court. Tobias was in Hackney and the door was unlocked. "Uh, John. John Webster." Oxford said this in a voice loud enough to carry into the library.

"Your lordship," Robin replied, bowing low. She did not curtsy; instead, she bent forward and scraped her right foot backwards across the stone floor, the way a man would act in 'giving the leg' to a lord.

"Well-done," Oxford said. Then, in a lower voice. "How goes it?"

"Well, my lord." She held out a small leather-bound book with a red ribbon hanging from it. She lowered her voice further. "Forgive me, my lord, but I have taken the liberty of transcribing your sonnets into this book. They are all here, rescued from the leaves you scribble them on." She had a large folder in her other hand. "These are the foul papers." She handed both to Oxford. "I did not ask for your permission to do this because I knew you would tell me not to. I have collected them over the years but, since I am now no longer living here," she gestured toward the stairs at the far end of the Hall, "I worry they will be lost."

Oxford hadn't realized how much he missed Robin. "My loyal servant, my friend," he said.

Robin ignored him, although he could see the visit was difficult for her as well. She touched the book. "You may think it small, my lord, but it is appropriate for your poems, which are rarely longer than a page. There are clean pages in the back for poetry not yet written."

"Thank you." He looked at her affectionately. "Elspeth has scheduled me to sit for Marcus Gheeraerts. I will clutch your gift thus, as he paints me." He clasped the book in his right hand with the ribbon falling away from it

"And, if I may be so bold, my lord, I would suggest wearing the gold ring your father gave you, the one with the boar's head on it. This would balance the book of sonnets in the picture."

Oxford nodded. "He gave it to me after seeing how excited I was to watch John Bale's *King Johan* at Hedingham. I was eight. He had a troupe of actors at the time."

Robin nodded. She bowed and turned away. In a moment, she was out the door and gone.

It was only after Robin had gone that Oxford remembered what the book reminded him of; the book in which the queen wrote her prayers. Beautiful script, Oxford remembered. In Latin, Greek, French, Italian, and English.

"My lord," Shackspear called from the library.

Oxford did not reply. He went up the wide staircase to the second floor. He went into his bedroom. He put the little book on the bed, promising himself he would read it once he found his copy of the *Arcadia* but he couldn't find it no matter where he looked. He went back to the bed and picked up the little book. He opened it and began reading Robin's graceful Italic script. Just a glance, he promised himself. He read the first poem, but the first one was so good he read another. And another. Some he had quite forgotten. 'Could I read a better writer?' he asked himself, chuckling silently. Of course not, and so he turned to another page.

Lyly and Shackspear finally gave up waiting. They headed out the door into Candlewick Street.

"There must be a phrase in Latin," Shackspear said, "to describe what Oxford has just done to us. Like *sic transit clodpoles* to describe how those of us without titles and money are treated by those who have both."

"Well, he hasn't got any money, that's for sure," Lyly said, "but we'll be here tomorrow, you and I, because he is a genius. We both know that he is the best writer *who ever lived*." Lyly was excited. "And we get to work with him!"

"Yeah," Shackspear replied, "when he's around."

146

A Chattering of Plots

A chattering of plots?" Shackspear asked, as he trooped into the library with Oxford and John Lyly. Oxford had given them a copy of *The Countess of Pembroke's Arcadia* to read 'to get the flavor of where I want this play to go.' He described what he planned as 'a chattering of plots,' which was of no help to Lyly or the man from Warwickshire.

Lyly knew of *The Arcadia's* complicated plot about jousts, political treachery, kidnappings, battles, and rapes. He sensed that Oxford wanted the play to be more fantastical than Sidney's gift to his sister.

Shackspear had been unable to get through it. He complained to Oxford as they met in the hall: "A woman locked into her family's home to keep her pure? A lover who disguises himself as a woman to get inside and, when he does, his love thinks he is a woman? Her father also thinks he is a woman and tries to seduce her/him, while the mother figures out he is a man and tries to bed him as well?"

"A chattering of plots," Oxford said, sitting down. "St. Albans lists the names of flocks of birds: an exaltation of larks; a siege of bitterns; a murder of crows; a clattering of jackdaws. Why not a chattering of plots?"

Lyly and Shackspear were lost.

"Did you know Sidney was knighted so he could escort John Casimir to the Order of the Garter ceremony?" Lyly and Shackspear looked at each other. Oxford went on. "A knighthood should only be awarded for acts that benefit the queen, such as bravery in action. But knighted for being an escort?" Oxford laughed. "No one gave it any regard. Even Walsingham, whose daughter married Sidney *after* he had been knighted, called him 'Mr. Sidney.' He was a 'carpet knight.'"

"You didn't like him," Shackspear deadpanned.

"I still don't."

"And the 'chattering of plots'?"

"They are all up here." Oxford tapped the side of his head. He looked positively maniacal. The other men could tell he was back in harness. The plots, like snakes, were writhing in his head.

"I wrote a play years ago called *The Wicked Stepmother*. It was well-received but only a bare pole compared to what I can do today."

He looked toward the window where Socrates had positioned himself. Oxford thought he looked like a lion guarding the entrance to an Egyptian tomb. His mind began to wonder what was inside the tomb but pushed this aside. "*The Wicked Stepmother* was based on Marie de Medici, the Queen Mother of France. Elizabeth had gotten the idea of marrying one of Marie's sons to fend off the Spanish. I wrote *The Wicked Stepmother* to urge her not to but we needn't have worried; she never intended to marry 'her frog,' as she called him. She was, of course, playing a better part than we gave her credit for."

Shackspear sighed. Oxford's speech reminded him why he had never finished grammar school. 'Can we get to the play?' he asked.

Oxford, of course, was unaware he was losing his audience, or, at least, half of it. He went on.

"I will take *The Wicked Stepmother* and add to it. My new effort will tell the story of one of Britain's first kings: *Cymbeline*. The king will be married to 'the wicked stepmother' when the play opens."

"What's her name?" Lyly asked. He had been taking notes. "I assume she won't be called 'Marie.'"

"Queen," Oxford said.

"No, her first name"

"She will have no first name. We need spend no time explaining what happened to her first husband or how she ended up marrying Cymbeline. Nor what happened to Cymbeline's first wife."

He continued. "The queen will have a grown son by her former marriage. She wants to marry him to the king's daughter, Imogen. The queen's plan is to have her son become king when Cymbeline dies."

"Which won't be very long," Shackspear chuckled, "from what I know about wicked stepmothers." Oxford didn't say anything. "Cymbeline's going to die, isn't he?" Shackspear asked. "This is a tragedy, isn't it?"

"Maybe not."

"Maybe not?" Shackspear wondered. "What kind of play is this?"

Oxford held out his hands. "I don't know."

Shackspear looked at Lyly who was looking at Oxford. Lyly sensed his lordship was striking out in a new direction. "And?"

"Cymbeline will have two sons in addition to Imogen. The two sons were kidnapped when they were babes. A once-beloved, unjustly banished courtier in Cymbeline's court named Belarius took them. He has raised them in a cave in Wales."

"A cave in Wales?" Shackspear asked in disbelief. "The heirs to the throne of Britain growing up in a cave in Wales?"

Oxford glared at him. So did Lyly. Shackspear harrumphed and sat back.

"Imogen has fallen in love with a young man named Posthumus," Oxford went on, "who is an orphan raised at court."

Shackspear laughed. "Posthumus. Good name."

"Oh," Lyly blurted out. "You and Nan." Oxford looked at him. "Well, you *were* sort of an orphan ..." Lyly's voice trailed off. He looked back at the paper in front of him.

"Not long for Posthumus," Shackspear announced. "The wicked stepmother will take care of him."

Oxford ignored him. "Posthumus and Imogen will marry without her father's permission. When he finds out, he will banish Posthumus to Rome."

"Rome?" Shackspear asked. He was lost.

"Cymbeline ruled during the time of Jesus."

"Jesus," Shackspear said, using 'Jesus' in a different way. He was convinced Oxford was playing with them. *The Wicked Stepmother* would soon turn into *Julius Caesar*.

"What happens in Rome?" Lyly asked.

"Posthumus will meet a man named Iachimo who listens to Posthumus praise Imogen. Iachimo doesn't believe women can be faithful. He plants a seed in Posthumus' mind that Imogen is cheating on him while he's in Rome. Iachimo will say, *strange fowl light upon neighboring ponds*, and other such stuff. Posthumus will not be concerned. He has complete faith in Imogen. Iachimo bets Posthumus that he can go to England and seduce Imogen. The two men decide to bet on the outcome. If Iachimo wins, Posthumus will give him a ring he got from Imogen; if Posthumus wins, Iachimo will deed over his estates."

"Hah!" Shackspear burst out. "Of course, she's cheating on him. He's in Rome; she's in England?" He grinned.

"Maybe not," Oxford said. "Iachimo goes to England and tells Imogen how much Posthumus misses her. Then he tries to seduce her. She rejects him utterly. Iachimo, the clever dog that he is, immediately tells her that he was merely testing her for Posthumus. He will happily report her faithfulness when he returns to Rome."

Shackspear was not impressed. "One attempt and Iachimo goes back to Rome? Not much there, my lord."

Oxford was losing patience. "William: a woman who says yes is as common as paving stones along Fisherman's Wharf. Imogen says no. You end your interest there. But what if Iachimo convinces Posthumus Imogen said yes?"

"This I like," Shackspear said. "How does he accomplish that?"

"By asking Imogen to keep a trunk in her room that he says will be filled with gold plate and gifts he is taking back to Caesar. He tells her he will retrieve it the next day when he departs. She agrees and the trunk is brought into her room."

"And?" Lyly asked.

"In the middle of the night, while Imogen is sleeping, the trunk will slowly open and Iachimo will stand up!"

"Oooo," both men said.

"And then Iachimo goes all Tarquin and rapes her," Shackspear said, referring to *The Rape of Lucrece.*

Oxford sighed. "Of course not." But then they could tell he was rolling Shackspear's suggestion around in his mind. "But a hint that he might violate her will add spice to this scene. Let's have Iachimo linger over the sleeping Imogen to make the audience *think* he is going to go '*all Tarquin.*'"

Shackspear was pleased. The Poet Earl had accepted a suggestion from him. Sort of. "But how will Iachimo convince Posthumus he seduced her?"

"By cataloguing what's in the room to show Posthumus he was actually inside Imogen's bedchamber!"

"But that is no proof Imogen violated her marriage vows," Lyly said. "Iachimo could have gotten into her room when she wasn't there."

Oxford agreed. "So, we will have Iachimo take a bracelet from her arm and note a mole under her left breast."

The two men went 'oooo' again.

"Iachimo will go back to Rome and, with the bracelet and the description of the mole, convince Posthumus he has won the bet. Posthumus will give Iachimo the ring and imagine how Imogen gave herself to Iachimo:

> *This yellow Iachimo in an hour, was 't not?*
> *Or less? At first? Perchance he spoke not, but,*
> *Like a full-acorned boar, a German one,*
> *Cried "O!" and mounted.*

Lyly and Shackspear took this differently. Lyly was disgusted; Shackspear thought it one of the best descriptions he had ever heard. "A full-acorned boar," he said, relishing the image of Iachimo mounting Imogen. He forced himself to return to the play. "So, what happens next?"

"Posthumus sends a message to Pisanio, his faithful servant in England, to kill Imogen. In the meantime, Cymbeline has decided to stop paying tribute to Rome. As a result, the Romans begin putting an army together to invade Britain. Posthumus is so distraught he joins the Roman army."

"What an arsehole," Shackspear said, referring to Posthumus. "And the wicked stepmother?"

"She is gathering poisons."

Shackspear nodded his approval.

"She tells a doctor she needs some poison to experiment *'on such creatures as we count not worth the hanging.'* In fact, she wants to poison Imogen and Cymbeline. The doctor suspects she's up to no good and gives her a sleeping potion instead."

"*Juliet,*" Shackspear exclaimed. He looked at Lyly. "At least we're not in Verona." Out of the corner of his eye he could see that Oxford's face had clouded over. "And it's not a tragedy."

"Because no one dies?" Oxford asked. Shackspear nodded. "Too soon to know that, don't you think?" Oxford rearranged himself at the head of the table. "The queen will try to get Pisanio to feed what she thinks is the poison to Imogen, telling him it's a potion that *hath the king five times redeem'd from death.*'"

Lyly blinked. "So, the queen, deceived by the doctor into thinking she has poison, will deceive the servant." He thought for a moment. "And we've already got Iachimo deceiving Posthumus."

Shackspear didn't follow. He was stuck on the wicked stepmother and her son. "And the wicked stepmother's son? He needs a name."

"What do *you* think we should call him?"

"I see him as stupid and arrogant," Lyly said.

"Aye," Shackspear agreed. "How about 'Cloten?'"

"Cloten," Oxford said, repeating the name. He liked it. He wanted to call Shackspear Cloten but stifled the urge. Thank God Falstaff was not in the room. "Cloten it will be, then. He wants Imogen for his bed. He will court her."

"How, my lord," Lyly asked, without taking his eyes off the pen scribbling all this down.

"By hiring musicians to go to her house and sing."

"Really?" Shackspear asked.

Oxford put a finger to his lips. "Listen:

> *Hark, hark! the lark at heaven's gate sings,*
> *And Phoebus 'gins arise,*
> *His steeds to water at those springs*
> *On chaliced flowers that lies;*
> *And winking Mary-buds begin*
> *To ope their golden eyes:*
> *With every thing that pretty is,*
> *My lady sweet, arise:*
> *Arise, arise.*

Lyly was confused. "*Hark, hark, the lark?*" he said. "*His steeds to water at those springs / On chaliced flowers that lies?*" He repeated the last line. "*On chaliced flowers that lies?*" He looked at Oxford.

"Who has asked for this song?" Oxford asked.

"Cloten."

"Is he capable of bringing a beautiful song to Imogen? No. The song, therefore, must be 'Clotenesque.'"

"Which it certainly is," Lyly said. Then he stopped. "I hear Philip Sidney." He looked intently at Oxford's face. "*Hark, hark the lark,*" he said, and then *"Sweet swelling lips well maist thou swell."* Lyly sounded like he was trying to wake a sleeping man by trying different languages on him. Oxford sat there unresponsive. "*But God wot, wot not what they mean,*" Lyly added.

In despair, he turned to Shackspear. "Our master deceives us, William, if he denies this song is not a parody of Mr. Sidney."

Shackspear was uninterested. "Who cares? Does Imogen find out Posthumus is on his way back to Britain?"

"Yes. He's with the Roman army. It's on its way to Milford Haven."

"Which is in Wales," Shackspear said, pleased to contribute this.

Lyly one-upped him. "Which is where Henry Tudor came ashore to take the crown from Richard III." He looked at Oxford. "Nice touch." He meant adding two words to the play that the queen would recognize as a nod to her grandfather, Henry VII.

What Lyly didn't know was that Milford Haven was the port Arthur Dudley ran to when he was told he was Elizabeth's son by Leicester. Elizabeth would know Oxford was referring to more than her grandfather when he has the Romans invade Britain through Milford Haven.

Shackspear still didn't care. "Does Pisanio kill Imogen?"

"No. While he is faithful to his master, he knows Imogen would never violate her wedding vows to Posthumus. He won't do it."

"It takes one to recognize one," Lyly said.

"Meaning?" Shackspear asked.

"It takes a faithful person – Pisanio – to see that Imogen is faithful."

Shackspear rolled his eyes. "What does Imogen do when she finds out Posthumus is on his way to Milford Haven?"

"She will be frantic to meet him there."

"But how can she get there? She's a woman."

"By becoming a man."

Lyly and Shackspear drew in their breaths. "A new deception," Lyly announced.

"Yes," Oxford said. "Pisanio will help Imogen by giving her men's clothing and telling her how to be a man:

> *You must forget to be a woman; change*
> *Command into obedience: fear and niceness--*
> *The handmaids of all women, or, more truly,*
> *Woman its pretty self--into a waggish courage:*
> *Ready in gibes, quick-answer'd, saucy and*
> *As quarrelous as the weasel.*

"She gets it:

> *Nay, be brief*
> *I see into thy end, and am almost*
> *A man already.*

"She puts on her new clothes and heads for Milford Haven. Before she leaves, Pisanio gives her the medicine the queen gave him and tells her *'if you are sick at sea, / Or stomach-qualm'd at land, a dram of this / Will drive away distemper.'*"

"Wait!" Shackspear said. "Is this poison? I'm confused."

"No, it's not. It's a sleeping potion."

"But the audience will worry it might be, won't they?" Lyly asked.

"Like in *Romeo*," Shackspear added. "Juliet worried the sleeping potion was poison." He looked at Oxford. "I like this." Oxford groaned. "What about Cloten?" Shackspear rambled on. "What does he do when he finds out Imogen has disappeared?"

"He will force Pisanio to tell him where she has gone. When he finds out she's trying to reach Posthumus in Wales, he will decide to run after her. He wants to kill Posthumus and rape Imogen."

"Oh, my goodness," Lyly exclaimed.

"Well, that's short and sweet," Shackspear said.

Oxford continued. "Cloten forces Pisanio to give him the clothes Posthumus left behind. He wants to dress like Posthumus."

"Why would he want to do that?"

"Because Imogen told him Posthumus' 'meanest garment' was more valuable to her than Cloten could ever be. This has enraged him. '*I'll be revenged: 'His meanest garment!' Well!*'" He imagines himself wearing Posthumus' clothes while he takes his revenge and rapes her:

> *With that suit upon my back, I will ravish her: first kill him,*
> *and in her eyes; there shall she see my valour, which will then be*
> *a torment to her contempt. He on the ground, my speech of*
> *insultment ended on his dead body, and when my lust hath*
> *dined, - which, as I say, to vex her I will execute in the clothes*
> *that she so praised, - to the court I'll knock her back, foot her*
> *home again. She hath despised me rejoicingly, and I'll be merry*
> *in my revenge.*

Lyly shook his head. "My lord, Cloten is one of the worst characters you hath ever conceived."

"Marvelous," Shackspear purred. "And what happens when Cloten gets to Wales?"

"First, let me tell you where Imogen goes." The two men stilled themselves. "She arrives at a cave where the two princes have been living. They are away hunting. They come back and find her, but remember, she is dressed as a man. They will assure her they mean no harm."

"Dressed as a man," Shackspear said. His face took on a sly look. "And won't know these two young bucks are her brothers."

Lyly was nodding. "Nor will the princes realize she is their sister." He had a suggestion. "Imogen should tell them her name is Fidele. She is so faithful. That would be a good name for her."

"Accepted," Oxford said.

"And they all live happily ever after in Wales?" Shackspear asked. He was worried. He saw a perfectly good play wandering off into ridiculousness.

"Until Cloten shows up."

"Dressed in Posthumus' clothes," Lyly reminded them.

"Oh, boy," Shackspear said. He and Lyly looked at Oxford.

"Cloten will run into the oldest boy, *the heir to the throne*, don't forget, and treat him with contempt. They will fight; the prince will kill Cloten."

"Finally!" Shackspear exclaimed. "Someone dies."

Oxford ignored him. "The prince, who doesn't know he's a prince, or that he has just *killed* a prince, cuts off Cloten's head and throws it into a river."

This surprised Lyly and Shackspear. Shackspear had what he thought was a better idea. "He should bring the head back to the cave. Imogen will boil it in a pot and feed it to her brothers." It was the others' turn to be speechless. "No?" Shackspear asked. "Wrong play? It worked in *Titus Andronicus*, didn't it?"

Oxford was amazed how Shackspear could bring up bits and pieces from the bottom of his mind like something one might find in a pot that had been left on the fire three days. Shackspear had confused Procne in Ovid with *Titus Andronicus*.

"No," Oxford said. "The head goes off down the river. The prince leaves Cloten's body lying in the forest. While the prince is killing Cloten, Imogen/Fidele begins to feel poorly. She takes the potion Pisanio gave her and falls asleep. Belarius and the brothers come back and discover Imogen/Fidele lying on the ground. They think she is dead. Belarius decides they should retrieve Cloten's body and lay it next to her."

"Next to her?" Lyly asked in disbelief. *"A headless body wearing her husband's clothes? Next to her?"*

Oxford was trying not to grin.

"She's going to think it's Posthumus!" Shackspear said.

"Yes. Belarius and the two brothers lay Cloten's body next to her and go off to fight the Romans. Imogen wakes and sees Cloten's headless body lying next to her. She will think it's Posthumus because the body is dress in his clothes. She will say:

A headless man! The garments of Posthumus!
I know the shape of's leg: this is his hand;

His foot Mercurial; his Martial thigh;
The brawns of Hercules: but his Jovial face
Murder in heaven? - How!

Shackspear protested. "But she's looking at Cloten's body! How could she make such a mistake?"

"They married quickly," Oxford said. He didn't look at Lyly who was figuring out that Imogen's failure to recognize who was lying next to her was a reworking of Oxford's failure to recognize Nan when he climbed into bed with her the night before he left for Italy. "Posthumus left their marriage bed before she could acquire a goodly image of his foot or thigh," Oxford added.

Shackspear was buying none of this. Lyly was studiously looking out the window. This *was* about Oxford's departure to Italy, he was thinking.

"Which raises the question," Oxford said, "of how people recognize each other." This got a blank look from both men. "Do we rely on *garments* in judging others?" Blank faces turned to frowns. "I saw a sparrow once sitting on a branch next to another sparrow," Oxford said, "*and they knew they were sparrows.*" He was amazed. Shackspear and Lyly were not. The frowns on their faces deepened. "How did they know each other?" Oxford asked. "By their feathers? But how could they even know they *had* feathers?"

Shackspear shook his head. Lyly was starting to look dazed. "Where is this going, my lord?" he asked.

Oxford forced himself to stop playing with the two men in front of him. "Fear not, *mes enfants*. We will wrap this up. *Fortune brings in some boats that are not steered.*"

"But this harbor is very crowded," Lyly said.

"It's even worse when you find out what's going on in the *wings*." This was said mysteriously. Shackspear and Lyly looked at each other.

"Imogen/Fidele, up now and feeling better, goes off to offer her services to Lucius, the commander of the Romans. Why? Because she thinks this will get her closer to Posthumus. But what she doesn't know is that Posthumus is no longer in the Roman army. He has had a change of heart and defected to the English to help his countrymen. He thinks Pisanio has killed Imogen and wants to die in combat. He changes his Roman clothes for British weeds and joins Belarius and the princes. They defeat the Romans and save Cymbeline but Posthumus is distraught: he hasn't been able to get himself killed. In the confusion after the battle, the English capture him but think he's a

Roman. Lucius and Imogen are also captured. Everyone is brought before Cymbeline."

"The finale!" Lyly cried out.

"Oh, there's so much more. Lucius, the Roman general, asks Cymbeline to spare Fidele, his page. Cymbeline agrees."

"Wait!" Shackspear said. "Fidele is Imogen, Cymberline's daughter. He doesn't recognize her?"

"No. She's disguised as a page. Also, the king thinks Imogen is in London. Belarius and the princes don't recognize her because they only know her as Fidele and they she is dead."

"And lying next to Cloten's headless corpse," Shackspear muttered.

Oxford put a finger to his lips. "And where is Iachimo?" he asked. The two men froze. "He was also at the battle and has been captured by the English. He is brought before Cymbeline as well."

"And Iachimo is *not* in disguise," Lyly said. His eyes got big. *"Imogen will recognize him!"*

"And see the ring she gave Posthumus on his hand. She will demand Iachimo explain how he got it."

"And?" Shackspear asked. He had no idea what was going on.

"Iachimo confesses all."

"But wait! Posthumus is watching? Won't *he* recognize Imogen?"

"And she *him*?" Lyly added.

"Posthumus will not recognize Imogen," Oxford said, "because he thinks she is dead. Also, she is still dressed as Fidele. Posthumus will rush up to Cymbeline and cry: *'I am Posthumus, that kill'd thy daughter, O king. / O Imogen! My queen, my life, my wife!'*

"Ta da!" Lyly sang out.

Oxford scowled. "No. Too soon. There's much more here. Imogen will recognize Posthumus. She will run up to him but he will knock her on her bum."

"What?" both men cried. "He strikes Imogen?"

"He strikes Fidele, not Imogen," Oxford said. "He will exclaim:

> *Shall's have a play of this?*
> *Thou scornful page, There lie thy part.*

"Oh, my goodness," Lyly said.

"How will you rescue *this*?" Shackspear asked.

"Pisanio, the loyal servant, has been watching. He will run forward and say: '*O my lord Posthumus, You ne'er killed Imogen till now!*'"

Lyly raced to get this down. "Finally!"

"No," Oxford said again. "Imogen will recognize Pisano and think he tried to poison her. She attacks him. '*Thou gavest me poison. Breathe not where princes are.*'"

"Oh, nice," Shackspear said.

"Pisanio explains that he gave her a harmless sleeping powder, which was why she did not die. This exchange allows Belarius and the princes to recognize Imogen as the page they thought they had left behind at the cave. They thought she was a man. They thought she was dead. Instead, they find out *she is a woman who is alive!*"

"Not dead, and not a man," Shackspear said, admiring where Oxford had taken them. There were moments, he thought, when being allowed inside Oxford's head made all the abuse worthwhile.

"The king will now recognize his daughter: '*The tune of Imogen!*' he will cry out. Posthumus will realize the page is his wife and take her in his arms: '*Hang there like fruit, my soul, till the tree die,*'"

Lyly scribbled away, a wide grin on his face. But he did not go ta-ta and say the play was over.

Shackspear thought there was something missing, though. "Where's the wicked stepmother, my lord. Ye haven't mentioned her in a while. She should die a horrible death whilst confessing all the evil she has committed."

"Yes. Excellent. We will have the good doctor report her death and confession."

"Which should include how she hated the king *and deceived him,*" Shackspear said. "I'm getting this."

Oxford thought otherwise but resisted the urge to tell Shackspear how far he was from understanding what Oxford was doing. "The good doctor will explain to Cymbeline that the queen confessed she never loved him:

> *First, she confess'd she never loved you, only*
> *Affected greatness got by you, not you:*
> *Married your royalty, was wife to your place;*
> *Abhorr'd your person.*

"And this comes as news to him?" Shackspear asked.

Oxford nodded. "'*New matter still?*' he will say.

"Another man amazed," Lyly commented, writing this down.

"Wot's in every play," Shackspear said.

"Hearing that the queen is dead will move Cymbeline to wonder where Cloten is. This will bring Belarius and the two princes in front of him. The oldest boy will step forward and tell Cymbeline how he killed Cloten. Cymbeline, not knowing he is talking to his own son, will beg his son to withdraw his confession because he has admitted to killing a prince, which means he must die. The heir to the throne has no problem with this, of course, because he would rather die than tell a falsehood. Cymbeline thereupon says: '*By thine own tongue thou art condemn'd and must / Endure our law: thou'rt dead.*'

Shackspear was incredulous. "His own son?"

"He doesn't know the boy is his. Belarius will save him, however, by confessing to the kidnapping of the two princes when Cymbeline unjustly banished him. Cymbeline, of course, will immediately sentence Belarius to death: '*Take him hence. The whole world shall not save him.*'

"Good lord," Lyly said. "Does he ever get anything right?"

"Do not worry," Oxford said. "Belarius will show Cymbeline the two boys are his sons."

Shackspear had a thought. "But before we get to that, my lord, I think the boys should sniff around Fidele when they think she is a boy, you know, like dogs checking out a new arrival."

Lyly protested. "My lord. They are sister and brothers. *Royal sister and brothers.*"

Oxford looked at Shackspear. "You're thinking incest?"

Shackspear shrugged. "An audience loves a touch of something forbidden, but it must be very subtle, my lord. Too apparent and they will go all Puritan, claiming they are shocked, when it's exactly what they wanted. We know she's a girl. The princes think she's a boy. Is there interest because she's a boy? Or is it because they can sense something that makes them think she's a girl?"

"You are disgusting," Lyly said. Oxford agreed. Shackspear had a mind that went to places other people didn't know existed. But he had touched on something that might be worth looking into further.

Lyly thought Oxford was inciting Shackspear to suggest they do something outrageous. After all, Oxford had written *Pericles*, which opens with a riddle about incest. Lyly decided it was time to 'steer' Oxford away from inflaming Her Majesty and offending everyone else. "Let us not lose sight of the fact that we are dealing with a king and a royal prince in the time of Caesar."

"Hmm," Oxford said. "The "sniff,' as you put it," he said to Shackspear, "will have to be very delicate."

Lyly's face fell.

"Ye think? Shackspear said this hopefully. Then he had another thought. "This play is about as far from Aristotle as ye can get, my lord. Does that mean we are done with Aristotle?"

"Very probably so. Particularly if this play shows everyone how a play can succeed even when it violates every rule he laid down."

Oxford got up. He suddenly looked tired.

"And how shall we continue working on this play, my lord?" Lyly asked.

"You shall write the parts for Belarius and the princes. I shall write Imogen. She's so pure."

"And me?" Shackspear asked.

"You shall limn Cloten. Make him as bad as you can."

"And Iachimo?" Lyly asked. "What does Posthumus do when he finds out Iachimo lied to him about Imogen."

"He forgives him."

"Forgives him?" Shackspear asked.

"'*Live, and deal with others better,*'" Oxford said. "This will cause Cymbeline to declare: *We'll learn our freeness of a son-in-law; / Pardon's the word to all.*"

"Forgiveness," Lyly said.

"Yes," Oxford said.

Lyly sighed. "After so much deception."

"And a 'chattering' of plots," Shackspear reminded them.

"Maybe we should call it a *reworking* of plots," Oxford said. He was suddenly tired. "You sketch the threads; I will separate and rearrange them. Tomorrow."

He got up and headed out of the room.

147

Lilah Stanhope

L ilah Stanhope, my lord," Nigel announced from the door to the library.

"Lilah Stanhope?"

Nigel nodded. "I have ushered her into the Day Room." His face showed that he had no idea who Lilah Stanhope was.

Oxford did, however. He got up and followed Nigel across the Hall where he found a woman of approximately fifty years standing primly in the Day Room, her hands folded around a small purse she clasped firmly to her bosom. She smiled wanly at Oxford.

"Lily," he said warmly, coming up to her.

The smile immediately disappeared. "Miss Stanhope will do," she said.

Oxford had not seen 'Miss' Lilah Stanhope since he had left Cecil House. He had known her as 'Lily', an upstairs maid. He had chased her around the House trying to get her to let him touch her in inappropriate ways. He succeeded with some of the other maids but not with Miss Stanhope. She had successfully resisted him.

He remembered little of her. She, on the other hand, had vivid memories of the dazzling young lord catching her on the back stairs, running his hands up her leg and trying to kiss her. She had enough sense to know that a tryst with a young lord would likely result in her dismissal or, worse, an unwanted pregnancy. She managed to fend him off but this did not mean she had not entertained fantasies about being countess to the 17th Earl of Oxford.

These dreams faded in the years after Oxford left as she was forced to recognize she would never rise above being a servant in someone else's house. She accepted her fate and devoted herself to being a loyal servant to Lord Burghley and a friend to the other staff members at Cecil House. This diligence and loyalty secured her promotion to her current position as Lady Susan's personal maid. When Susan asked her to deliver a message to her father, Lilah Stanhope accepted the task, even though she trembled at how she would react when she saw the earl after so many years.

Oxford turned to Nigel. "Nigel, something cool to drink for Miss Stanhope, if you would, please." He turned to his guest. "Please, have a seat." He gestured toward one of the chairs in the room.

She hesitated for a moment and then sat down. Oxford took the chair next to her. Nigel brought in two glasses of mint water. He put them on a table between them and withdrew.

"Miss Stanhope," Oxford said.

"Aye, miss. Not missus. I never married."

It was clear she thought this a great loss. Oxford asked why.

"You killed the man I was to marry," she said.

"*I did?*"

"Thomas Brincknell. Undercook in the kitchen where you tried to have me."

Oxford was astonished to hear this. He had never connected 'Lily' Stanhope with the undercook.

She had never intended to tell him. She had said nothing to anyone for how many years? But seeing the man who had destroyed her dreams gave her the strength to speak. She sensed Thomas nodding his approval.

"He offered me marriage and I agreed. We waited to save money so we could leave Cecil House and set up our own home. Thomas had promises of employment. The great houses between the Strand and the River - Arundel House, Leicester House, even Essex House - would have been glad to have him. He was a gifted cook. You, however, saw fit to take him from me."

"He was spying on me," Oxford said weakly.

"And doing it willingly. He knew who you were. He knew you would accost me if given the chance. Thomas agreed to spy on you because he was eager to show Lord Burghley how little you deserved his favor, but you stabbed him through a hedge and killed him." She paused, the spilling of her secret leaving her spent. She thought she might burst into tears but was surprised to feel strength rising in her. "We thought that

you were done but the coroner's inquest concluded that
Thomas ran upon the end of your sword and killed himself?' She
laughed aloud. "*He killed himself?* When he was to marry me?"

Oxford did not know what to say. He had never thought
of the undercook as someone with a fiancé, or a mother or a
father, a sister or brother. Thomas had simply been a 'spy'
working for Lord Burghley and, therefore, someone without
form or substance, a nobody. *A creature we count not worth the
hanging.*

But to Lilah Stanhope floating in her grief in front of him,
Thomas Brincknell had been her fiancé, her future husband,
the father of her children, all taken away from her with the
thrust of Oxford's sword. How could he write Jaques
shedding tears over a fallen stag in *As You Like It* and not feel
half as much for her or the fiancé he had killed?

> *The wretched animal heaved forth such groans*
> *That their discharge did stretch his leathern coat*
> *Almost to bursting, and the big round tears*
> *Coursed one another down his innocent nose*

Michael Lok appeared before him. Silently, he mouthed the
words *If you prick us, do we not bleed?*

Oxford shuddered. He felt dizzy. Like López, Thomas Brincknell
had been swept away. A living human being, unlike the phantoms of
Oxford's mind who were nothing more than 'airy spirits' Oxford had
created to populate a world of plays.

Lilah Stanhope watched Oxford floundering. She came to
life. "After it happened, the kitchen staff, the upstairs parlor
maids, the butlers, the grooms, the gardeners, *everyone* realized
your escape from justice was preordained, for how could them
that hold the levers of power and wealth the 17th Earl of
Oxford to the courts for the killing of an undercook? Of
course not. Thomas was just another servant in the basement
of a great house, cast out with the other dead carcasses killed
to feed the upstairs table and forgotten. But not by me."

She rose. "My instructions, my lord? As to your visit with
Lady Susan, your daughter?" she said sarcastically. She stood
in front of him, her face full of loathing.

Oxford sat up in his chair. "I am so sorry, Miss
Stanhope."

She said nothing. She was done talking.

"I will send Nigel to Cecil House to confer with you about a convenient time and place for Lady Susan and I to meet."

Lilah Stanhope gathered up her skirts. "My lord," she said as she retraced her steps to the front door.

Oxford listened to the door close behind her. He looked around. A ghost had entered the room: *Thomas Brincknell*. In all the years that had passed since Oxford had stabbed blindly into a hedge and took a man's life, he had never asked who he had killed. How little he knew about life, he thought, or himself.

Nigel found him sitting in the dark hours later, staring into the darkness. He left him there.

148

Boxes and Trunks

Boxes and trunks," Lyly said, seated at the table as Oxford came into the library. Oxford threw his coat and muffler onto a chair and took his seat at the end of the table. Shackspear was at the other end, looking sleepy.

"On Boxing Day," Oxford said. It was the only thing he could think to say in response. He had just returned from Hackney. He was exhausted from the trip. He had not learned yet how to sleep there. He had fled there to escape Lilah Stanhope. Her visit had shown him how poorly he had treated people in his life. Nan, his first wife. Anne Vavasour, partaking of her earthly pleasures and then leaving her with the care and upbringing of the son he gave her. Or was it the son she gave him? Then there was Aemilia Bassano, who may have had the sense to know she was nothing to him more than Anne Vavasour with dark hair. And his daughters. And Elspeth, of course.

Floundering under all these memories, he sought distraction by fleeing to Hackney. He took Henry for walks in the fields and dined with Elspeth but nothing gave him relief.

He had expected life to become simpler as he got older. It had not. A headless Cloten in Posthumus' clothes may have been a wry way of reworking how he could have slept with Nan without knowing she was his wife, but Lilah Stanhope's appearance showed him there were more ways than one to mask someone. Or oneself.

"Boxes and trunks," Lyly said again, to get Oxford to focus attention on the play they were working on. "First, there is the box the doctor gives the queen, which she thinks contains poison."

"Which it doesn't," Shackspear said from where he was sprawled.

"And then there is the trunk in Imogen's bedroom Iachimo climbs out of." He raised his arms like he was summoning a ghost from the grave.

"And then there is the cave," Shackspear said. "The *womb!*" he cried out, waving his arms in imitation of Lyly.

The two had been infected with the absurdity of the play.

"Let me see," Oxford said, reaching for the scripts. He gathered in the pages and started to read. The drone of the carpenter bees began.

"Pen!" he called out. Lyly handed him one. Oxford scratched something on the page and put it aside. He began reading the next page. The sound of the bees returned.

Shackspear got up and wandered off to the kitchens for something to eat when Ben Jonson announced himself from the entryway. Lyly went and let him in. Jonson came in and dumped his coat on top of Oxford's.

"My lord," Jonson said, making a perfunctory bow.

"Mr. Jonson," Oxford said, not looking up. Jonson made a gesture to sit at the table. Oxford waved a hand. Jonson sat down. "Any of this yours?" Oxford asked.

"Very little. I have read it, my lord. It's very different."

"Of course, it is." Oxford looked up. "But does it work?"

"The last scene is a bit crowded."

"How would you correct it?"

"By adding Jupiter."

Shackspear had returned from the kitchen with a piece of jam-encrusted moldy bread in his hand. He hadn't flicked all the mold off and the edge showed flecks of green. Maybe he *likes* mold, Oxford thought, looking at him.

"Jupiter?" Shackspear asked, wiping his hand on his sleeve.

"Yes," Jonson said. "T'would add another layer of ridiculousness to this heap of parodies."

Oxford didn't like hearing his work described as a 'heap of parodies,' but Jonson was right to want to add something like Jupiter to it. Jonson had sensed what Oxford was doing - having fun at the expense of the playgoers who would come to see *Cymbeline*. The patrons in the pit would love to see a Jupiter coming down out of the roof beams. Oxford had no knowledge of mechanics and gave no thought to how Henslowe or Burbage would be able to lower a god from the rafters, but he liked the idea. "Tell me about Jupiter," he said.

"This is a play about the beginning of the kings of England, is it not?" Jonson asked.

"And how they descended from Rome," Lyly added.

"Did they?" Shackspear asked. This was apparently news to him. The last piece of crusty bread and jam disappeared into his mouth, mold and all.

Jonson continued. "I would have Jupiter descend amidst thunder and lightning, riding down on an eagle, throwing thunderbolts!" He added the eagle and thunderbolts to see how far Oxford was willing to go with this play.

"Ouch!" Lyly said. He wasn't worried about being hit by a thunderbolt; he was worried about how much an eagle throwing thunderbolts would cost.

"And where would you insert Jupiter?" Oxford asked, apparently willing to accept Jonson's outrageous suggestions.

"In a prison scene we've not yet written."

"And who is Jupiter visiting in prison?"

"Posthumus." Oxford and Lyly were surprised to hear this. "Posthumus has been captured, hasn't he?. The English think he is a Roman. Cymbeline will condemn him to death."

"Why not?" Shackspear said, coming to Jonson's defense. "Cymbeline is condemning everyone, isn't he? Lucius, the Roman general; Belarius at first; his own son for killing Cloten. Iachimo was going to get it in the neck if Posthumus hadn't pardoned him. I love Cymbeline. He's always getting it wrong. He even made a mistake banishing Belarius twenty years before the play begins! He never knew the queen hated him! He's a never-ending babble of amazement at the end: *'Does the world go round?'* and *'New matter still?'* and *'This hath some seeming!'*"

"So Posthumus is in prison," Oxford said, tired of Shackspear's babble. "How do we get Jupiter to visit him?"

"His dead parents and brothers will return to sing prayers to Jupiter. They will stand around Posthumus who, calm lad that he is, has fallen asleep. They think he is dead. Maybe he is; maybe he isn't. They will invoke Jupiter's help:

> *No more, thou thunder-master, show*
> *Thy spite on mortal flies, ...*

when the god himself will descend, throwing bolts of lightning. Jupiter will complain:

No more, you petty spirits of region low,
Offend our hearing; hush! How dare you ghosts
Accuse the thunderer, whose bolt, you know,
Sky-planted batters all rebelling coasts?

"Good lord," Lyly mumbled.

"Yes. Good," Oxford said. He shot Lyly a glance. "We will have the prayers of the dead parents mirror the lamentations Belarius and the two princes have made over Imogen's body, thinking she is dead."

"Oh," Shackspear said. "This is marvelous! In neither scene is the person dead! Imogen sleeps under a potion; Posthumus, well, Posthumus *sleeps!*" He didn't ask how Posthumus could sleep while awaiting his execution, a very good question in every other play he had watched or worked on, but *this* play was different!

Jonson had more: "Jupiter will leave a tablet on Posthumus' chest that will contain a riddle."

"Which is?" Oxford asked.

"I don't know."

Oxford did. "Posthumus will wake up and read the tablet:

> *'When as a lion's whelp shall, to himself unknown,*
> *without seeking find, and be embraced by a piece of*
> *tender air; and when from a stately cedar shall be*
> *lopped branches, which, being dead many years,*
> *shall after revive, be jointed to the old stock and*
> *freshly grow; then shall Posthumus end his miseries,*
> *Britain be fortunate and flourish in peace and plenty.'*

Lyly was exasperated. "What means this, my lord?"

"The true heir," Oxford said. "'*When as a lion's whelp shall ... be embraced by a piece of tender air*, 'heir.' Do you recall the little changeling boy in *Midsummer* in the 'tender Indian air'?"

"Which means Guiderius," Shackspear said. "He's the true heir."

"No," Lyly said. "The 'lion's whelp' can only mean Posthumus. His full name is Posthumus Leonnatus." He glanced at Oxford. It suddenly hit him: Oxford was Posthumus!

"But Posthumus is not royal," Shackspear pointed out.

"But he is the hero of the play, isn't he?" Lyly asked.

"I thought Imogen was," Shackspear countered. "No?"

"What does *she* do?" Lyly asked.

"What does *Posthumus* do?"

"It's a strange play," Jonson admitted, looking at Oxford.

Oxford had one more thing to add. "Posthumus is not of royal birth, I grant you that, but he is married to Imogen, isn't he?" Everyone agreed. "If Imogen becomes queen, he will be her consort."

"But that will only happen if both her brothers die before Cymbeline," Shackspear said.

"Stranger things have happened," Jonson said.

"So, the riddle points to Posthumus, not Imogen's brothers?" Lyly asked

"Yes," Oxford said. "When Posthumus - the 'tender heir'- couples with Imogen - she of 'the old stock', he of the new - Britain will flourish in peace and prosperity."

"Sly," Shackspear said. He liked Posthumus coming out on top, but he liked even more the hint that Imogen's older brothers were going to meet an untimely end. "The two boys in the Tower," he said, almost to himself.

"What" Oxford asked.

"We can repeat what Richard III did who, acting as protector of his brother's two sons, sent them to the Tower from whence they never returned."

"The two brothers here, William, are grown men. No one's going to herd them into the Tower."

"Oh," Shackspear said, disappointed.

Lyly was looking at Oxford. If the Poet Earl was Posthumus, as he almost certainly was, why had he made Posthumus the father of kings? Why hadn't he written himself king? It would have been easy to do. No one knew what happened in Cymbeline's time or even who succeeded him. Lyly realized there was a piece of the puzzle here that hadn't been explained yet. Or was the character named Posthumus because of what would follow *after* he died, not just that he had been born after his father died? Lyly thought it possible Oxford was layering meanings under the name 'Posthumus.' The way Oxford had set up the plot, with the princess marrying Posthumus, the kings of England would come *after* Posthumus, and would all be Posthumus' descendants if Imogen survived her father.

"I'm done with *Cymbeline*," Oxford said, getting up. "John, weed out the mistakes, have a fair copy made, and give it to William to take to the playhouse."

Lyly nodded.

Oxford went out into the Hall. 'And,' he said to himself, 'if Jack gets me proof Southampton is the queen's son by me, I am Posthumus and the kings of England will have my blood in them for as long as the sun sets on this emerald isle.'

1598

~ 149 ~
A Visit with Lady Susan

I suggested the Savoy, my lord," Nigel was saying to Oxford, "and she accepted immediately." He was brushing Oxford's coat. The Savoy was across the street from Cecil House where Lady Susan was being raised by her grandfather, Lord Burghley. "Being so young, she will need to be escorted. Setting up your meeting in the Savoy will make it difficult for Lord Burghley to find a way to prevent Lady Susan from meeting with you."

"And where in the Savoy?" Oxford asked.

"The same tenement you rented when you moved out of Cecil House. You were seventeen at the time, I believe. The manager thinks you still control the lease. Whether this is because you are the 17th Earl of Oxford or their records are so poor, I cannot tell. For whatever reason, it is available."

Memories flooded into him: assignations with women he couldn't recall, weeks lost in drunken stupors when he felt the world against him, endless days spent crafting a play or a poem. Seeing his youngest daughter in the Savoy would be a curious twist on what had gone on there before.

—————◆◆◆◆◆—————

He had no difficulty finding the room. Nigel had refurbished it with furniture and wall hangings. He had barely laid his jacket over a chair when a knock was heard. He opened the door and found Miss Stanhope in the hallway. Susan was standing behind her.

"Please come in," he said, ignoring Miss Stanhope. Susan walked into the room. "Mi'lord," she said.

"I'll wait out here," Miss Stanhope said.

Oxford nodded and closed the door. "Please," he said to Susan, gesturing toward one of the chairs in the room. Susan sat down. He took the chair opposite her.

"You look well," he said. In fact, he was surprised at how much older she appeared. She was only twelve but already as tall as he was, which wasn't saying much since he was not a tall man himself. Her face was a pleasing combination of her

311

mother's and Oxford's. Her eyes were gray, her sister, Lisbeth, having gotten his hazel eyes. She was dressed in a frock that covered her arms and legs. Her head was bare.

She took off her gloves and laid them carefully on the arm of the chair. "Father," she said. "Thank you for accepting my request that we meet. I have not seen you in some time."

"Too long," he said.

"Congratulations on having a son, my lord. Please convey my congratulations to Lady Elspeth."

"I will."

"I trust you had a pleasant Christmas with Lady Elspeth and Henry?"

"I did. Thank you for asking."

In truth, he had stayed only Christmas night. The following morning, he had fled back to London.

"I will be thirteen in March," Susan continued, "and am told I will be going to court this spring to be presented to Her Majesty. Balls and dinner parties will follow, all with the purpose of inducing a young man to marry me. Pee-Pop will intervene, if he stays alive long enough. He is not doing well. He has already told me young girls do not have enough experience to know who to marry, so he will make the choice for me."

She did not mention that fathers usually decide who their daughters married but Oxford had lost that opportunity when he abandoned Susan and her sisters to Lord Burghley after their mother died. Nan, who grew up in Cecil House, rarely left there, even after Oxford married her, which meant that Oxford's daughters were raised there. Nan's death changed little. The girls stayed on with their grandparents. Lord Burghley and Lady Mildred were content with this, being more interested in controlling their granddaughters than giving their father a chance to resume his fatherly duties. But, in truth, Oxford had made no effort to take Nan's place. Indeed, it is doubtful he even considered the idea. He couldn't recall.

Oxford had visited his daughters only once since Nan's death. The visit had not gone well. Lisbeth claimed her mother had killed herself because of how Oxford had treated her. Because of this Oxford never returned. Burghley and

Oxford's daughters apparently preferred it that way. No one asked him to visit.

Susan had accepted the fact that her father would be unable to provide her with a marriage portion when she married. Other than the £250 Nigel received quarterly from the Exchequer, Oxford had 'nothing' from which he could take 'something' to give to Susan.

"Do you remember being twelve?" Susan asked, surprising her father.

"Yes. I was twelve when my father died. We buried him and I was whisked off to Cecil House."

"Where I live."

"Yes."

"But your mother was still alive when your father died. Did she not make arrangements to keep you?"

"No. My mother … made no objection to my transfer to Cecil House. She never came to visit me there. I never saw her again. She married quickly and died a few years later."

It was obvious to Susan that the memory was painful.

"But you have *some* memories of your mother," Susan pointed out. "I have *no* memories of mine. I was only two when she died."

She sounded sad, but Oxford heard no whinging. She turned to him, a brighter look on her face. "And you may have lost your mother *and* your father, my lord, but I still have you. Perhaps we can make up for early losses."

He didn't know what to make of this. She was clearly reaching out to him. "But your sisters are your companions, are they not?"

Susan laughed. "Lisbeth is no longer living at Cecil House, of course. She's not been back since her wedding. Bridget is an odd duck who quacks to a different drum." She put a hand to her mouth and laughed. "Oh, my goodness! How awful!"

Oxford laughed with her, cheered by seeing that his daughter was so comfortable with herself that she could laugh at something foolish she said. And, in front of her father.

She rearranged herself. "And how did you fare when you went to Cecil House?"

"Very well, I must say. I thought the world would come to my door. I expected the queen would summon me to visit so she could benefit from my wise counsel."

Susan guffawed, a deep, happy laugh. "An expectation that didn't last very long, I'll wager."

"No, indeed."

"But, having lost your father *and* your mother, how did you not sink into melancholy?"

Oxford had never been asked this.

"Well, my father and mother spent little time with me while he was alive, so being sent to London after my father's death did not deprive me of much. The tutors and servants I had there came with me. And Cecil House turned out to be every bit as good a school as Cambridge or Oxford. It was a beehive of activity from dawn till dusk, as I expect you have learned. I was roused before dawn to learn Latin and Greek, followed by dancing lessons, French, history, natural philosophy, and more. I loved it. *I loved it!* I imagined myself flowering into *un homme érudit.*"

"Oh, mon père, tu l'a fait!"

Her answer delighted him, particularly the familiar 'tu' instead of the impersonal 'vous' he would have expected. Maybe she felt closer to him in French? Maybe they should switch languages?

This made him realize he had thought Susan wanted to meet with him to ask for money or abuse him over Nan's death but instead the daughter he had never known had grown into a young woman wise beyond her years. He *liked* her!

"Et j'ai fait quoi?" he asked.

"Les poésies, *Seigneur, les drames."*

"Ah. plays. You know I write plays. Do you know I cannot put my name on them?"

"Tant pis," she said, tossing her head. "Time will wash away the mask, like a craftsman who rubs away the dirt on an old painting to reveal the artist's signature underneath."

"Now, that is a very nice metaphor," he said. "Unfortunately, I do not share your optimism, but I thank you for it nevertheless." He bowed slightly. She smiled, happily accepting his praise. "And please forgive me for not asking how *you* are faring at Cecil House."

"It is gracious of you to ask, my lord. I was three when Lady Mildred died. She oversaw the tutors for the royal wards and made them available to me. I am proud to say I have taken advantage of them. I have drunk from the Elysian Springs, my lord, and am thirsty for more."

Oxford was thrilled to hear this.

"I give Pee-Pop credit for my zeal, for he shared a letter Lord Zouche wrote him. In the letter, Lord Zouche, a ward after you left Cecil House, regretted misspending his patrimony and not 'searching for knowledge.' Pee-Pop didn't want me to waste my time and regret it, like Lord Zouche."

"But you did not need the encouragement."

Susan smiled. "No."

"You are a very unusual lady, Susan Vere," Oxford said, with a mixture of wonder and pride.

"I cannot claim much Latin and little Greek, my lord, and do not have the skills to write poetry or plays, but I have a wisdom my peers do not possess. Of that I am sure."

She looked at him. "Your genius is the ability to mine the souls of men and women and present them in dramatic fashion. My bent, if I have one, is to reach out to people and find out who they are. What do they want? How can I help them? We all want to be loved. In order to love everyone, I have to accept everyone, including a father who rejected my mother and left my upbringing to my grandparents."

Oxford didn't know how to respond to this.

"I do not say this to bring grief to your mind, my lord, only to explain where I am in my thoughts, which must be piddling indifferent to your years and experience. My prospects are not great, being the third daughter in a line of girls. I also have no mother. But I think I may have found my father."

Oxford had never experienced such love. Susan went on.

"I have read your plays and marvel at what you have created, particularly the women seeking to make their way in this world of men."

Susan had read his plays? More surprises. At twelve? But hadn't Oxford been writing plays and poetry at twelve? "Such as?" he asked.

"Well," she said, flattening a wrinkle in her lap, "I have been more taken with your characters than your plots. To me, plots are like branches on a bush, which are not as interesting as the flowers they support."

"Then, what *do* you think of the characters I have created."

"Most go no further than reporting action or arguing with each other. Falstaff and Prince Hal, for example. Falstaff is the wit and child we would all like to be. Hal plays the audience and not honestly, I may say. What did all their clever words reveal about themselves? Not much."

Susan checked to see her father's reaction. "Go on," he said.

"The same is true of the beautiful people in *Love's Labour's Lost*, or *Much Ado*, or *The Winter's Tale*. Didn't one say another was nothing more than the suit he was wearing?"

"Hmm," Oxford said.

"Which is true about most characters I have read about, yours included. Portia dazzles, but she exhibits little more than cleverness. Juliet limits herself to managing Romeo, who needs a good woman to tell him what to do, but she reveals little about herself. I thought Rosalind was going to show more, but she only hinted at unfolding herself; she never did."

"Well," Oxford said. He was dazzled. Susan understood what he does? "Have any of my characters met your standards?" This was said without sarcasm or innuendo, which is how she had made her comments. They had become comfortable with each other: Susan, upfront and without guile from birth; her father, relaxing in the warmth of their conversation.

"The two Richards," she said. "I think they are the closest so far to what I think you should write. One a man who should never have been king, the other a man who could never be anything else. They were alive in all dimensions. I felt I *knew* them. The Bastard in *King John*, too."

She leaned toward him, as if she were a kindly aunt come to visit and was relating news of relatives who lived far away.

"You've shown hints of what you can do, my lord. Shylock, for example, but he is a Jew and an outsider. Antonio: no one cares for him even when you make us think his heart might be cut out! Proteus and Valentine, two fools on a fool's errand."

"Well, it seems you have spent considerable time sifting through my plays."

"Is there anything better to do? People are complex, my lord. Their motives even more so. I sense that you have grasped this and are moving toward creating characters we will recognize as part of all of us."

"Like Faust," Oxford said.

"No, Faust is Antonio, with eternal perdition hanging over his head, but he is not us."

They were both enjoying their back and forth.

"You got close with Mercutio," she said. "I agree you had to get rid of him. Bottom started out in a promising direction but you didn't let him expound his dream. You sent him back to the mechanicals, just another extra in a play within a play."

Oxford had sent Bottom back to the mechanicals because Bottom's dream was a mystery to him.

"Is this why you asked to meet with me? To criticize my work?" He laughed as he said this.

"No. I really only wanted to re-meet you." She smiled at him. "I think I've done that." This was followed by a worried look that crossed her face. "But, forgive me if I have overstepped. I live alone. I have no friends. Steeping myself in your plays takes me away from my barren room at Cecil House." She smiled again, a bit sheepishly this time. "And they make me feel closer to you. It's a connection."

Oxford was moved. "I am flattered. I will take your comments to heart. But, pray tell, how have you been able to read my plays? They are rarely published and any scripts in the playhouses are jealously guarded."

"Robin, your page, visited Cecil House one day. Because of my interest in you, I talked to him. He told me he kept copies of your plays in his cubbyhole under the grand staircase. I begged him to make copies for me, which he did, and which *I* jealousy guard."

"The cheeky little bastard," Oxford said, with more affection than irritation.

"Someone has to save them," Susan said matter-of-factly.

"A waste of time."

"You do not you care if they are lost?"

"They are not mine!" he said, irritation slipping into his voice for the first time. He calmed down. "Besides, who reads plays? They are dead on the page. They only come alive when someone brings them to the stage." His face fell. He was suddenly sad. He looked an old man, Susan thought.

"You fail to recognize, *mon père*, that once your thoughts are captured on paper, they are no longer yours. They have become the property of others."

"I detect a library somewhere."

"A good one, my lord."

"But Robin has left my service. You have lost your source."

"Have I?" She gave him a sly look. She rose.

"Wait!" Oxford said, rising with her. Miss Stanhope appeared in the doorway. Oxford put a hand up to keep her in the hallway. "Who *has* been giving you my plays?" he asked. "Nigel would never …"

"I so enjoyed our visit," Susan said, gliding out the door past Ms. Stanhope. She paused in the hallway. "We'll talk again?"

"Of course."

He watched her go, Miss Stanhope behind her. And then he realized he had not asked her about Southampton. He ran into the hallway. "Susan," he called after her. "What think you of Henry Wriothesley?"

Susan stopped. "I found him ill-tempered, my lord. No, *hot*-tempered. Profligate with money, whether it's his or someone else's. A ward who suffers from an excess of *noblesse d'épée*. He fancies himself royal, my lord." She disappeared around the corner.

'Royal,' Oxford said to himself. "Lineage will out."

150

Bacton and Back

Oxford was in the library. He looked up and saw Falstaff standing in the doorway. The big knight shook himself, showering the entrance with snow. He slipped off a mammoth cape and draped it over a chair in the corner.

"Do you mind?" Oxford said testily. He pointed at the snow soaking the floor and the Turkish carpet James Lancaster, captain of the *Bonaventure*, had brought back as a gift from India. Oxford had been amazed to learn there were Muslims living there. He had thought India a Hindoo country.

Falstaff took affront. "Is this how ye greet a long-lost friend, returned from the provinces with news?"

"Yes, when he comes in like the untrained dog he is."

Falstaff harrumphed. He took his accustomed chair along the wall. With the formalities out of the way - how long had they been apart? Six months? A year? - he settled back to await the question he knew was coming. Why waste words, he once said, when ye've hung your listener on a petard, the grenade being the pent-up question the other person is dying to have answered.

Oxford knew what Falstaff was about. He went back to working on the pages in front of him and said nothing. Silence filled the room. Neither spoke.

Lyly came bounding in later, sliding across the wet floor into the chair with Falstaff's cape hanging over it. "*Well, Dip my Wick!*" he cried, grabbing the chair to keep from falling.

Oxford and Falstaff took no notice. Lyly's remark was the little man's latest faux curse. Lyly thought he could save himself time in Purgatory, if there was one, by crying out nonsense words when vexed instead of real curses. A cautious man, growing more cautious as he grew older, he steadied himself and looked at Oxford, head down at the table, and then at Falstaff seated in his customary chair.

"My lord," Lyly said. Oxford slowly looked up. Falstaff didn't move. "Sir John," Lyly said in a lower voice. Falstaff cracked an eye. Lyly looked from one to the other. "Shall I leave?" Oxford dipped his head, which Lyly took as a yes. He left.

He came back after lunch and found the two of them in the same position. He had imbibed a glass or two - maybe more - of Les Plantagenets at The Bell Inn. The chenin blanc gave him the strength to return to the Court and find out what was going on. "I say, my lord," he announced loudly as he came into the room. "What villain, what witch has wafted such a vile sleeping potion over my master and Sir John that I find them speechless and without movement?"

Oxford cringed. He regretted *once again* helping Lyly develop the verbose style that became known as *Euphuism*, a disgusting word in both sound and meaning. There was universal agreement that Lyly's invention had cluttered England's fair speech with an excessive use of balance, antithesis, alliteration and similes. *Euphues: The Anatomy of Wit*, had made Lyly famous when published in 1578. A sequel in 1580 continued the story and made Lyly more money. Lyly described Euphues as a "young gallante, of more wit than wealth, and yet of more wealth then wisdome." As a result, Oxford had to spend time on occasion denying he was Euphues.

But Lyly's fame faded, along with his money, which was why Oxford had offered him a job as Robin's replacement.

"Do spare us, John,"

Lyly nodded, then pointed to Falstaff. "And ... this?"

"Sir John," Oxford said, not looking at Falstaff, "is a neap tide that comes and goes in unpredictable ways."

"But he is here now," Lyly said. Strengthened by the chenin blanc, he asked Falstaff how he was. "Sir John. How fare thee?"

"Well," Falstaff said, opening both eyes.

"Pray, tell us where ye've been."

Falstaff pulled himself up. Oxford's pen paused.

"I been to Chartley Castle in Staffordshire, my little friend. The Earl of Essex hired me to bell his hounds."

Oxford's head came up. "Bell his hounds?"

"Ye know I am a renowned tuner of hounds." Oxford groaned. Lyly didn't know what Falstaff meant. Falstaff explained. "It's not enough that a pack of hounds can follow the scent of a fox; the hounds must be matched in mouth like bells, each onto each so that the cry they send up fills the sky with music as they course the hills.

"And how do you 'bell' them?" Lyly asked.

"I take a pack into a stable yard where I serenade them. This incites them to howling which allows me to identify the ones that need to be weeded out. One rough voice, one squeaker, can ruin the entire pack. Would you like to hear me?"

"No!" Oxford exclaimed.

"Actually," Falstaff went on, unruffled by Oxford's outburst, "I was there to use the occasion to train the Earl's dogs to kill him when they heard a whistle sounded from behind a tree.".

"Kill him?" Oxford asked in disbelief.

"Aye. Like Acteon, the hunter who stumbled onto Diana having a bath in the forest. For his impertinence, she changed him into a stag; his dogs ran him down and killed him. Ye love that story."

This rendered Oxford speechless.

"Have ye done it yet?" Lyly asked. He sounded worried. Oxford realized he was hoping the answer was yes.

"Nay. He's never there. If he isn't at court, he's sulking somewhere near London, Wanstead, usually, ready to come back when Her Majesty 'forgives' him for his latest outrageous act. How can ye train a pack of dogs to kill someone if the victim is never there?"

Oxford and Lyly realized they didn't know whether they had just listened to another tall tale from Sir John Falstaff or the fat knight was telling the truth. Either was possible.

"So, what *have* you been up to?" Oxford asked.

Falstaff kept his eyes on Oxford but made a gesture with his head in Lyly's direction.

Oxford saw it. "John, if you would, please." He waved him out of the room. Lyly left. Oxford turned to Falstaff.

"I've been out and back. Here and Bournebridge."

"Bournebridge? Bournebridge is ..."

"Aye. Just over the hill." Falstaff hooked a thumb in the direction of Epping Forest. "As I told you earlier, Blanche Parry's maidservant is living in a cottage behind the church in Bacton. Now, that's in that direction," he said, hooking a thumb in the opposite direction. "A *long* way away."

"I know where it is. Get on with it."

"She's in a nice little cottage, stone walls, built into a south-facing hill. I could live there, and she made it clear she wouldn't mind if I stayed, but, well, I was too young for her, ye see."

"And married."

"That too." He looked like he had more to say about the maidservant from Bacton. "Her state of age, …"

"Could she remember anything?" Oxford asked, cutting him off.

"Aye. Although it tended to range around a bit. All I had was a month and a year: June 1573. It took me a while to make sure she was in service to the queen then - she was - and where the court was in June. Then I had to get conspiratorial with her and talk about a missing baby."

"How did you do that?"

"I brought a bag of buttons with me I bought in Three Needle Street. No buttons in Bacton." He stopped to listen to how poetic *no buttons in Bacton* sounded but, seeing the look on Oxford's face, decided not to linger in his report. "She made a meal and we settled into two chairs side-by-side in front of a very nice fireplace, made of firestone, it was. I leaned toward her and lowered my voice. I looked around as if worried someone might hear us - this brought her head toward me - women love a tale that has to be told in a hushed voice - and I asked her if she knew about any babies that might have been smuggled out of a palace. 'I do,' she said in a hushed voice that matched mine. 'Havering,' she said."

"Havering-atte-Bower?" Oxford asked.

Falstaff didn't know. "She said Havering Palace."

"Good lord!" Oxford said. "My family has had the keeping of Havering from time immemorial. The Palace was built in 1066. It's older than the Keep at Hedingham. This woman went to Havering with the queen?" Falstaff nodded. "No one goes there. It's falling down, abandoned most of the time. Ah. But what better place to have a child! A short boat ride from Greenwich, up River Roding to Barking and over to Havering. Probably at night." He shook his head. "So that's how Elizabeth did it."

"Mary - for that's her name - said she and the ladies-in-waiting all got in a boat and went downriver. This was at night, as you guessed. She didn't know where it went in the dark but she learned from others that they went to Havering.

No one explained why they went there and when they did, only Kat Ashley was allowed into Elizabeth's presence. They were told the queen was not feeling well."

"There was nothing for them to do there. Late in the afternoon of the second day, they were suddenly ordered out of the Palace. It was cold outside, with a misting rain. No one explained what was going on. Mary decided to go around to the side to find a way to get back into the Palace. She was freezing. She found a servant's door and tried to get in, but it was locked. As she fiddled with the door, she saw a woman come out of a side door. She was carrying a bundle in her arms. A yeoman of the guard was guiding her. They walked across the grounds to the North Road where a horseman waited. The woman handed up the bundle and the horseman rode off towards London. She and the yeoman returned to the Palace."

"Could she see what was in the bundle?"

"No. Mary went back to the front entrance where she and the others were allowed back into the Palace."

"But she learnt more."

"Aye, but not from the woman who came out of the side door. That woman was nowhere to be seen the next morning. Later that day, they all returned to Greenwich. In the cart on the way back, Mary heard someone say that the woman she had seen the night before had been brought in from Bournebridge as extra help."

"Ah! So, you've been to Bournebridge."

Falstaff nodded. He then paused and coughed.

"Yer thirsty."

"This is taking a lot of talking, my lord."

Oxford got Nigel to bring Falstaff a beer. Falstaff tossed it off, wiped his whiskers, reinvigorated, went on.

"What I haven't told ye is what Mary told me about the woman from Bournebridge. Din't ye wonder why the woman needed an escort?"

"To make sure she didn't run off with the bundle?"

"That's what I thought, but nay: it was because she was blind. *She couldn't see!*"

"Ah. But that made it easier for you to find the woman when you got to Bournebridge."

"*Precisement!*"

"Precisement?"

"Practicing my French, my lord. For because of where I'm going next." He looked conspiratorially at Oxford, whose face showed he didn't want Falstaff to wander off subject, not at this point.

"So, you immediately returned to visit the blind lady in Bournebridge."

"Nay," Falstaff said, "I went to Titchfield."

"Why ever for?"

"Because Mary suggested I stop there and talk to a man named Cyril."

"But Titchfield is not on the way back from Bacton."

"No, it isn't, but I went there. Dooty, and all that, my lord." Oxford waved a hand, indicating Falstaff should get on with it. "I found Cyril still alive, though barely. He had been servant to Southampton's father when the earl was released from the Tower and Thomas Dymock took over."

"Lady Mary told me about him."

"Cyril ran the estate with an iron fist. He was a deep cove. He was a harder nut to crack than Mary."

"You had no buttons."

"I had better than buttons." He paused again. He started to think how 'better than buttons' sounded.

Oxford knew why he had stopped. "We've no time for poetry, Jack."

Falstaff frowned but went on. "As I say, I had better than buttons." He did this to roll the words around in his mouth again and to stick his finger, metaphorically, in Oxford's ear. A wet one. "What I had that was 'better than buttons' was news of Henry, the 3rd Earl of Southampton. Dymock's arrival had put Cyril out to pasture, but Cyril still got to work on the estate. He watched Henry grow into a young man and took a shine to him. Then, the 2nd Earl died and Henry went off to Cecil House. Since then, no had told him how Henry was doing."

Falstaff paused and made it clear he was thirsty again. Nigel was ready with a fresh one. Falstaff tossed it off.

"Cyril told me there were two sons, not one. When I suggested this might be confusion between the 2nd Earl of Southampton, Henry's father, and the 3rd Earl because they both had the same first names, he laughed. 'Who confuses a son with the father?' he asked, giving me a look that showed only an idiot would believe such a story."

Oxford wondered who the idiot was in the conversation but was struck with a sudden thought. "Burghley almost got Henry to marry Lisbeth. Do ye think he knows they might be brother and sister?"

Falstaff snickered. He began to sing, "Incest's the best, the game the whole family can play," repeating some doggerel he had heard in a pub.

Oxford put up a hand.

"What?" Falstaff protested. "Ye wrote *Pericles*, didn't ye, where the king is doing his daughter? And didn't Elizabeth translate *The Glass of a Sinful Soul* and give it to Katherine Parr, her stepmother at the time, as a gift? That was about incest." He pursed his lips. "And did Elizabeth's mother sleep with her brother? Is Elizabeth a child of an incestuous relationship?"

Oxford's hand shot up again. "Enough!"

"Her father thought she might be. I wager Burghley knew. He was steeped in the classics - didn't Cleopatra marry her brother? Didn't Oedipus marry his mother?"

"*Enough!*" Oxford shouted.

Falstaff ignored him. "Burghley would have thought the mix good. Brother and sister, marching off into England's future, shedding little heirs down the years to rule Britannia. It would have been his line, *your line*, on the throne!"

"But do ye think Lisbeth knows Henry is her brother?"

Falstaff laughed. "Not a chance. If she thought he was her brother she'd have made a bee line for him. She couldn't have resisted that."

"Enough! What about Bournebridge?"

"Aye. Bournebridge. The blind woman was dead when I got there, of course, but I found a granddaughter who had cared for her during her last days. It was no secret the grandmother had helped out at Havering Palace. It was an honor for the woman and the town as well. The granddaughter said her grandmother confided on her deathbed that she had been summoned to the queen's chambers one night and given a package wrapped in a blanket. She was taken out to the North Road where a horseman took the bundle from her. Before he rode off, she heard a baby cry."

"So, he lived!"

"But, being blind, she couldn't say whether the baby was a boy or a girl."

"Right. Right. What else had she remembered?"

"A man slipped a gold coin into her hand and swore her to silence. This was easy for her to do since all she had done was carry a parcel out of the palace."

"But it was a baby."

"Aye. She never heard whose baby it was, except it must have been the child of a very important person if Kat Ashley supervised the transfer."

"Bravo, Sir John. You have confirmed that Elizabeth had a baby, that it didn't die, *and that it must be mine!*" But then his face fell. "But has the trail gone cold."

"*Pas encore*," Falstaff said. "The grandmother remembered a French servant handing her the baby."

"A French woman! Ah. That's why you're practicing French. You're going to France."

Falstaff put up a hand to indicate he would not be rushed. "The French woman was from Calais. She had come over with Anne Boleyn and stayed after Anne's execution. When Kat died in '90, she went back to Calais."

"Is she still alive?"

"God willing, I will find out. Calais is only a day's sail from Gravesend. I embark tomorrow."

"God speed you, Jack Falstaff."

151

A Clash of Wits at the Mermaid

Oxford was regretting that he had let John Lyly talk him into going to the Mermaid with him. "A meeting of those who rule the theater today, my lord. There will be much throwing about of brains. Ben Jonson and John Marston will be there, and many others."

"John Marston?" Oxford had not seen John Marston since he had fled Oxford Court years before. The young man couldn't take Oxford's irreverent gibes. Joan of Arc as Jesus dying on the cross? Heavens full of different gods, waiting to welcome different worshipers? Marston ran away to university. Had school or his fellow students scrubbed away his Puritanism, Oxford wondered?

They found Marston, Jonson, Anthony Munday, and others seated around a table at the far end of the inn. Jonson had his back to the door; Shackspear was seated along one side; Anthony Munday, in a new Spanish hat and long matching curly cut, next to him; a taller but still slender John Marston sat on the other side; and Oxford quickly recognized a young man as his former clerk, his former *female* clerk, who was now masquerading as John Webster. They were talking over each other and didn't notice Oxford and Lyly come up.

"Gentlemen," Lyly said. "We would like to join you."

Jonson peered around at them. "What could *you* possibly add," he said. This was directed at Lyly.

Shackspear agreed. "We've already discussed all *you* know."

The others muttered and jostled each other. Marston stood up. "My lord," he said to Oxford.

"Milord," the other men now said in unison, turning to welcome Oxford.

"John Marston," Oxford replied. "I had thought university would have put flesh on your bones."

"Or learning in his head," Jonson said.

Marston made no response. He sat back down. Oxford and Lyly sat down opposite him. They had interrupted an argument about the purpose of theater. "But how will those who benefit from your education pay for their supper?" Marston asked Jonson. I cannot feed my appetite with aire. I must pursue my pleasures royally, / And leave this Idle concatenation, / To rugged Stoicall Morosophists."

Jonson growled. "I be no morosophist!" He pointed to Shackspear. "He is!"

"*I am not*," Shackspear protested.

Oxford spoke, looking at Jonson: "You seek poetry to make men artists," he said, quoting a line from Jonson's play, *The Case Is Altered.*

"We wrote that," Munday said, leaning forward. "We wrote it together, you and me." He was now looking at Jonson. "But that line was my particular 'polish.'" He was pleased with himself; the Earl of Poetry had liked something he wrote.

"Naw," Jonson rumbled. "I ne'er wrote that." He meant the play.

"Yes, you did," Munday said. He turned to Oxford. "Ask him, my lord. Henslowe paid us 12 and 6 for *The Case.*"

Oxford was puzzled. Why would Jonson deny writing *The Case Is Altered?* It was not a bad first pass at a play. But maybe Jonson didn't want to work with Munday anymore. If so, he was bucking the trend. Collaboration was all the rage. Playwrights were bringing in help to speed up the writing so they could earn more fees. But collaboration could get you in trouble. *The Isle of Dogs* was put together by a group that included Jonson and Tom Nashe. For their efforts, Nashe had to run to Great Yarmouth; Jonson - 'naw, they won't come after me' - ended up in the Marshalsea.

Munday, in the way he inveigled Jonson, sounded desperate. His novel *Palmerin of England* was not selling well. He was shopping a play to everyone about Robin Hood called *The Downfall of Robert Earl of Huntingdon* but everyone knew the censors would never let it see the light of day for fear it was somehow related to the Earl of Essex, known popularly as Earl Robert. This amused Oxford because it proved the title to a play *could* spell the death knell for it.

Jonson drained his mug and turned to glare at Marston. Oxford had heard Big Ben practiced scowling before a glass, thinking an angry visage would persuade a listener to agree with him about whatever he was telling them at the time. He was a big man, and he'd killed two men in hand-to-hand combat. Plus, he always came across as slightly unhinged, as if he was about to burst into violence at any moment.

"Ye like to rail, young Marston," he growled, "and give the unwashed a way to avoid becoming learnéd, which they so greatly need. *What better recreations can you find, / Than sacred knowledge in divinest things?*" he asked.

"And how do you expect to impart your 'sacred knowledge' when you lard your plays with Latin phrases no one understands! God, man; most of them that go to the theaters can't even read! *How ill it is when gaudy monkeys mow o're sprightly rimes!*"

"Monkeys!" Jonson cried out.

"'Ape' is more t'the point," Marston said. "Ye patch your poetry with a crooked eye and borrow what ye need from someone else!"

Jonson started to get up.

"*Pace!*" Munday cried out. "It'll be pikes and pistols next!"

Oxford had had enough. He stood up.

"Gentlemen. If beer were ink, and words could be printed onto paper by no more than breathing them out, ye'd be the most prolific writers the world has ever seen. Until then, I will return home, where I am never less idle, lo, than when I am alone." He headed for the door, humming "*My mind to me a kingdom is.*"

Marston ran after him. "My lord. My apologies. What ye see between Ben and me is nothing but show. We have agreed to go at each other in public. Good for business, he says. Maybe it is, but I don't think he's acting; I think he likes to bully everyone."

"*Caveat histrio,*" Oxford said. He turned to continue on his way.

Marston plucked his sleeve. "My lord, unlike Monsieur Jambon in there," he said, jerking a thumb over his shoulder at the Mermaid, "I have ever honored your true judicial style. I was but a boy when I had the privilege of being your clerk. I was filled with delusions about many things, including religion. I ran from you. At university, I realized that what little I know was learned in the library at Oxford Court. I would like to redeem myself by resuming my position as your secretary. I have no doubt that, though your worth is hidden now, it shall mount to its rightful place when apes," he meant Shackspear, of course, "are turned forth."

"Thank you, John Marston." Oxford was smiling at 'Monsieur Jambon.' That was clever. Jonson *was* a large slab of pork. John Marston had a way with words. "It so happens that I may have need of your services. Do you remember the play we worked on where the question was whether sin resided in the heart or in what a person does?

"*All's Well That Ends Well,*" Marston said immediately. "Bertram, thinking he's about to, you know, have relations with Diana, when he was climbing into bed with *his own wife!*"

Oxford smiled. The boy-cum-man in front of him still couldn't say the 'f' word. Marston was still '*a Puritan on his way to a Priesthood,*' as some wag had said of him recently. He had missed more than food at university.

"I have an ancient play in the trunk of plays," Oxford said.

"I know about the trunk of plays, my lord.".

"No, you don't," Oxford said, giving him a look.

"No, I don't," Marston quickly agreed.

"However, in that trunk of plays is a play I am thinking about taking out and finally finishing. It is based on a story I heard while I was in Venice."

"Has it been translated?"

"No. The story is about a man who is given authority over a large city. He thinks himself holy. A woman comes to him with a request."

"She is beautiful," Marston immediately said, "and her appearance tempts him."

"Mightily."

Marston's face brightened. "Is this her fault?"

"Who? The woman's?"

"Yes. Who sins most: the tempter or the tempted?" He liked the question.

Oxford was about to ask him in round terms *how the victim could be the sinner* when he realized Marston, without knowing anything about the woman in Oxford's play, had immediately blamed her for what would follow. Oxford thought this bizarre, but his instinct as a playwright made him realize that Marston's fixation on evil, and how the victim could be the sinner, might fit hand in glove with what he wanted to write. Marston would do. Yes, he would do.

"Be at Oxford Court tomorrow, John Marston. Nine O'clock in the morning. Do you remember where it is?"

"I do, my lord."

"Bring your own quills. John Lyly is left-handed."

152

Wicked Meaning in a Lawful Deed

M y lord," Nigel announced from the door to the library. "It is with great pleasure that I announce the return of Mr. John Marston to Oxford Court, former impubes of this illustrious seat of learning and now newly minted university graduate." He stepped aside with a flourish to let John Marston enter the library.

Oxford smiled. Nigel sounded like he admired the 'newly minted university graduate' more than he had dear Robin.

"My lord," John Marston said. He clutched a dozen goose feathers in his hand. Oxford waved him to the other side of the table.

John Marston folded his thin, gangly frame into the chair. He had, unfortunately, not pulled it out far enough, being much longer in frame than the last time he had sat in it and banged a knee painfully against the underside. "Ah!" he cried out, but still being the Puritan that he was, had no need of John Lyly's faux curses to keep him from blasphemy. He gripped his knee and grimaced in silence.

Oxford recalled Marston's discomfort as a boy when he last worked as his secretary. He had changed little since then. He had the same dour face. A Puritan then and a Puritan still, Oxford thought. For this reason, Puritans made excellent servants and government officials for they were rarely foolish. They avoided temptation by keeping their eyes focused on what awaited them behind death's door.

Some Puritans fell away as they realized they missed the cakes and ale others enjoyed, but they never gave up telling others how to live their lives. Oxford wondered which way John Marston would go, *so drest in certainty now, most ignorant of what he's most assured.* This was a thought that snapped Oxford's head up. He grabbed a quill and pulled a piece of paper to him. '*A good line,*' he said to himself, scribbling it down.

"You missed Frances Meres," Marston said. "He came in later."

"Who is Frances Meres?"

"A man who would love to write poetry or plays but can't, so he wanders about collecting information from those who can. He's putting a book together to list those who are great and those who are …, well, less than great."

"Should I purchase a copy?"

"No need, my lord."

"A guidebook, then, like the pamphlets sold to provincials come up to London to see the big town."

"Aye. After you left, Meres questioned Shackspear about your plays, my lord. He obviously thinks Shackspear is their author but he has his suspicious. He asked Shackspear questions about why he wrote this or why he wrote that. We all stopped talking to listen to how Shackspear responded."

"And how did he do?"

"Just enough, my lord. He's gotten very good at answering questions without saying anything. Meres thought his difficulty in understanding Shackspear was his fault, for wasn't he talking to the author? Didn't the plays show Shackspear was a genius? He never suspected he might be talking to the wrong person. After all, isn't Shackspear's name on the plays? Does anyone question whether Marlowe wrote *Tamburlaine* or Chaucer wrote *The Canterbury Tales*? If it's on the title page, that's good enough for most people."

"So Shackspear never gave himself away."

"No."

'Damn,' Oxford said to himself.

"But then Meres asked him about his 'sugared sonnets.'"

Oxford blinked. "What? How can this man know anything about my sonnets, sugared or otherwise?"

"He didn't say. He wanted to know if they had been written to a man or a woman. He thought they were salacious."

"*Salacious!*" Oxford exploded. "They are *not* salacious!"

"He thought they were. And so did Shackspear. 'Indeed,' he said to Meres. 'I have been assaulted in the street by a man who thought them abominably foul. He called me besotted and a buggerer to boot.'"

Oxford was amazed. "And in what way did Shackspear communicate this to Meres, or whatever his name is?"

"Like I just described. In truth, he sounded pleased to have written something someone thought 'salacious.'"

"What did Meres do after hearing this?"

"He wanted to know who Shackspear had written them to. Shackspear got all huffy. He said that was a private matter. Meres, not getting what he wanted, closed his notebook and left."

"So this man Meres got nothing."

Marston nodded. "You could say that."

"And despite his opinion that my sonnets are 'salacious,' you still want to work with me."

"I'm here, aren't I?"

Oxford accepted this. "Let us proceed, then, to why I asked you to come today." Marston picked up a quill. "The play we will work on is set in Genoa. The Duke of Genoa will announce he is going to leave the city. He does not say why he is leaving or whether he will return. He chooses a man named Angelo to govern while he is gone. He leaves but immediately returns disguised as a priest. He wants to see what happens while Angelo and the citizens of Genoa think he is gone.'

Marston looked up. "A Duke who sees all? A man named Angelo?"

"You can see the possibilities here."

Unfortunately, Marston could. "I warrant Angelo is perfect."

"At first."

John Marston had hoped for a different answer.

Oxford had begun work on this play while he was in the Tower in 1581. He needed John Marston to help him finish it. Marston would be the 'Puritan' spice that would lend verisimilitude to what would be Oxford's attempt to show onstage the frailties of the human condition.

"Do not pass judgment, John Marston, till all is done." Marston nodded, but he didn't look convinced. "The laws of Genoa have slept unenforced," Oxford said, "including the proscription against fornication. The first matter brought before Angelo involves a man named Claudio who is arrested for committing the crime of fornication."

"Oh, good," Marston said.

"Claudio appears onstage being dragged to prison, but the street he's being dragged along is not on the way. Claudio complains:

> *Fellow, why dost thou show me thus to th' world?*
> *Bear me to prison, where I am committed.*

The guard replies:

> *I do it not in evil disposition,*
> *But from Lord Angelo by special charge.*

Marston took this down. "*Why dost thou show me thus to th' world,*" he wrote. He looked up. "Claudio objects to being paraded through the city. '*Bear me to prison,*' he tells the provost."

Oxford nodded.

"But why is this important?"

"Because it's by the '*special charge*' of Lord Angelo."

"So, Angelo, *Lord* Angelo, has assumed the reins of power to the extent that he's giving special instructions to the guard to humiliate a prisoner. Marston's eyes widened. "You were taken to prison, weren't you?"

Oxford nodded again.

"To the Tower," Marston said. "For fornication. Oh, this play is about you. You are Claudio."

"And the Duke."

Marston tried to take this in.

"Let us continue. Angelo has ruled that Claudio shall be executed three days hence."

"Oh," John Marston said.

"A friend of Claudio's will go to his sister, Isabella, for help. She is about to enter a convent. The friend will ask her to go to Angelo. He will describe Angelo as:

> *a man whose blood*
> *Is very snow-broth; one who never feels*
> *The wanton stings and motions of the sense,*
> *But doth rebate and blunt his natural edge*
> *With profits of the mind: study and fast.*

Marston took this down.

"Isabella will learn that the woman her brother has committed fornication with is her cousin, Julietta, and he has gotten her with child."

"Uh, oh," Marston said, writing this down.

"She goes to Angelo. What do you think he will say when Isabella asks him to spare her brother?"

John Marston thought for a moment. "*His blood is very snow-broth,*" he said to himself, and then looked up. "He will say: *Your brother is a forfeit of the law, and you but waste your words.*" He could tell Oxford was pleased with this.

"Isabella will respond:

> *Authority, though it err like others,* she will tell him,
> *Hath yet a kind of medicine in itself*
> *That skins the vice o' th' top. Go to your bosom,*
> *Knock there, and ask your heart what it doth know*
> *That's like my brother's fault. If it confess*
> *A natural guiltiness such as is his,*
> *Let it not sound a thought upon your tongue*
> *Against my brother's life.*

"Oh," Marston said. "That will put him in a pickle. What does he respond?"

"Come tomorrow."

"Good. A day of reprieve."

"But not before she offers him a bribe."

"*She offers him a bribe?* Oh, my lord, Isabella is holy."

"Angelo is also surprised: *How? Bribe me?* Isabella replies:

> *Ay, with such gifts that heaven shall share with you.*
> *Not with fond sicles of the tested gold,*
> *Or stones whose rate are either rich or poor*
> *As fancy values them, but with true prayers*
> *That shall be up at heaven and enter there*
> *Ere sunrise, prayers fasting maids.*

"Not much of a bribe there," John Marston commented.

"No. But Angelo sees how beautiful Isabella is. He has begun to feel temptation. Isabella leaves and Angelo begins to wonder."

"About what?"

"You tell me, John Marston."

John Marston lowered his gaze. His face clouded over:

> *What's this? What's this? Is this her fault or mine?*
> *The tempter or the tempted, who sins most, ha?*

"Oh, wonderful," Oxford exclaimed.

"Yes?" John Marston asked. His beaming face showed he was pleased to hear Oxford liked his effort. "I have more:"

> *What, do I love her*
> *That I desire to hear her speak again*
> *And feast upon her eyes? What is 't I dream on?*

O cunning enemy that, to catch a saint,
With saints dost bait thy hook. Most dangerous
Is that temptation that doth goad us on
To sin in loving virtue. Never could the strumpet
With all her double vigor, art and nature,
Once stir my temper, but this virtuous maid
Subdues me quite. Ever till now
When men were fond, I smiled and wondered how.

Marston wrote this down as he spoke. He gazed up at Oxford, who was now the one beaming.

Oxford handed him some papers. "Here are notes showing the scenes in the play. Review these as you list. I have other matters I must attend to."

"But I know not the plot, your lordship."

"It is simple. Isabella is the one whose blood runs as white as snow, not Angelo's. His is red and heating up. He has tried to make himself pure. In fact, he will now obsess over Isabella."

"I think she is like him."

"Indeed, John Marston. All praise for seeing they are twins."

"But how can this be resolved? He now lusts after her and must have her, but she cannot give herself to him, can she?"

"Of course not. Angelo will twist himself around to the point where he will promise Isabella to spare her brother if she gives herself to him. She will be horrified, of course, and refuse."

"And go to her brother and say, 'prepare thyself for death,'" John Marston said."

Oxford was surprised by this. "Yes," he said. "To which, *he*, the brother, will be horrified. He has an entirely different view of fornication, of course, and will not believe his sister would let him to die."

John Marston like this. "There is much meat here," he said appreciatively. "Isabella will call her brother a beast for asking her to give up her virginity. *I'll say a thousand prayers for thy death, but not a word to save thee!*"

Oxford was very pleased. Marston was turning out to be the perfect vessel from which Oxford could pour out his play

"But how can this be resolved, my lord, if she refuses to let Angelo into her bed."

"The Duke loiters, does he not?"

"Ah, yes, disguised as a priest." John Marston was not comfortable with the Duke being God. Or going about in disguise.

"I've not told you all. Angelo was once contracted to marry a woman named Mariana but the ship carrying her dowry sank and he refused to marry her. He will say: *her reputation was disvalued in levity*."

"Oh, foul man," John Marston said.

"Indeed. But the Duke will make Angelo marry her."

"And she will take him back?"

"On bended knee, begging for his life." John Marston was now truly amazed. "It's been known to happen," Oxford said.

"And Angelo?"

"Angelo's *intention* to have sex with Isabella will be thwarted by the Duke, who will be helped by Isabella and Mariana. They will trick Angelo into believing he is climbing into bed with Isabella when, in fact, he is bedding down with the woman he had contracted to marry."

"Not again," John Marston said.

"Not again? It worked with Bertram and Helena, didn't it?"

John Marston did not want to recycle the bed trick from *All's Well* to save this play. "But isn't Angelo's heart full of sin? He wants to force Isabella to give up her virginity to him. Bertram's situation was different. He was a soldier in Florence who thought he was going to sleep with a woman he'd met there. The woman – her name was Diana, I think - had agreed to go to bed with him. There was no deceit in his heart. If anything, it was in Diana's heart, for letting Helena take her place and not telling Bertram."

"Bravo," Oxford said. "So, you agree the situation with Angelo is a step up from Bertram's?"

Marston agreed. "A step down," he said.

"But both characters are *intending* to commit fornication."

"But Angelo is using his office to force Isabella to commit fornication, while Bertram only inveigled Diana into his bed."

"Degrees of fornication then?"

John Marston groaned. His lordship still liked to impale him on a thorny question. "How will the Duke fix this?"

"He will pardon Angelo because Angelo's act of sleeping with Mariana was not what he intended, which was to sleep with Isabella. Therefore, *his bad intention* - to sleep with Isabella - *perished on the way to sleeping with Marianna because he did not sleep with Isabella*."

"His bad intention *perished on the way?*" John Marston asked in disbelief. He hadn't thought of this. This also disappointed him because he wanted Angelo to be punished.

"The Duke will explain that *intention is never more than mere thoughts, and thoughts can never be the subject of sin.*"

John Marston had not heard this. "So, Bertram did not sin because his *intention* to sleep with Diana was never carried out?"

"Yes. You feel better?"

"No. Sin resides in the heart, my lord. Paul said that. The law says that. The Fisherman's Case says that."

Oxford groaned. "The man who took a fish from a fisherman and was found not guilty of theft because he threw a coin into the fisherman's basket to pay for it?"

"Just so. Or the men acquitted of rape because the woman's husband told them she loved it."

"Good grief."

"She was the husband's property, wasn't she?" John Marston said. "Didn't Petruchio tell us he owned the shrew? I know the result sounds awful, but the logic is sound, so the result must be just."

Oxford didn't know what to say. Another Puritan, Oxford thought, whose heart and the effects of his actions would be overruled by impeccable logic, no matter the disastrous result it caused. How could John Marston think it just that the men should be acquitted of raping a woman because her husband said she loved it? Didn't she have any say in who had access to her body? Oh, but John Marston had bought Petruchio's description of his wife as his goods, his chattels, *his anything.* That being said, the rapists were sinless.

Oxford wanted to grab John Marston by the throat and shout *'What are you thinking?'* but restrained himself. Marston's logic-driven saintliness was what Oxford needed to show how cruel and cold Angelo was. The play, he said to himself: *toujours la pièce!*

"All right. Good for you, John Marston. Take the scraps I have given you and show us how Angelo treats the other characters."

"Aye, aye," John Marston said, enthusiastically.

Oxford left him pawing through the papers in front of him. "Lord, lord," Oxford heard him saying in a low voice as he went into the Hall.

~ 153 ~
# Timson

Nigel came into the library. "Your lordship, a man named Timson has presented himself with a card from her ladyship. Shall I show him in?"

"From her ladyship? Yes. By all means."

A tall man of thin build and narrow face entered the room. His mustache was neatly trimmed, his pointed beard carefully shaped. His hair was pulled back in a bun. He was wearing a long green cloak of quality fabric over a white shirt. A gold medallion suspended from a silver chain hung down his chest. He held his hat in front of him with both hands.

"Your lairdship," he said, bowing from the waist. He handed Oxford a card.

"Mr. Timson?" Oxford said, reading the card.

"Timson will do," the man answered, his eyes focused on the wall behind Oxford's head.

Elspeth's graceful Italic script told her husband that Timson had been referred to her by a neighbor in Hackney who spoke highly of him. He had served as manservant to Lady Lennox. She had sent him up to London in the hope he might be of use to his lordship, possibly as a replacement for Robin.

Oxford wondered if Elsbeth had sent Timson as a peace offering for barring Robin from coming to Hackney. No, he thought. Elsbeth did not back away from decisions she made. And Robin would have left in any event.

Oxford's interest in Timson was piqued by the tall, thin man having been in service to Lady Lennox. Lady Lennox had died at King's Place. Oxford had visited her there once. He looked up at Timson. "My countess writes that you were in service to Lady Lennox. Was that while she was living at King's Place?"

"It was, my laird. I came down from Scotland with her when she had to flee the whobub there."

Oxford knew what Timson meant. Oxford was seventeen when word came down from Scotland that Lord Darnley, husband to Mary Queen of Scots, had been murdered. Lady Lennox was Lord Darnley's mother. With her son dead, and the 'whobub' that ensued, she decamped to England, settling at King's Place.

Oxford was at Cecil House at the time. As ward to Lord Burghley, he was able to read the reports sent down from Scotland. He saw a drawing that showed where the dead bodies of Darnley and his servant had been found in a courtyard. What stuck in Oxford's mind was the drawing of a dagger floating over the dead men.

"But Lady Lennox has been gone some years now. Where have you been in the meantime?"

"I went back to Scotland after her death but found it so unsettled that I recently returned to England to seek employment here."

"How long were you in Scotland?"

"Fifteen yars, your lairdship, where I was in service to the noble family of Angus."

"That would be the 10th Earl, William Douglas," Oxford said.

This surprised Timson. "Aye, my laird." He hadn't thought Oxford would know anything about Scottish lords. "The earl was Catholic as a young un and supported Mary, may she rest in peace, but last year he became a Presbyterian, of all things." He made like he was going to spit to one side for emphasis, a form of punctuation for some in Scotland, but he restrained himself, being indoors and standing in front of the Earl of Oxford. "It was too much for me." He reached over unconsciously and straightened a book lying on top of the bureau next to him.

Oxford was not offended. A nervous habit, perhaps, but Timson obviously liked things to be in order. Oxford had need of such a man. "I am not Catholic, Timson."

"I am aware of that, my laird, but I hear yer a fair man. You were good to Lady Lennox. You were there when they buried her at Westminster. I were there as well, and a hundred poor women trailing her coffin."

Oxford remembered. He hadn't wanted to attend, but the queen insisted he go. That Timson would attend the funeral of a woman he served said something about him. Also, that he would remember seeing Oxford there.

"Can ye read, Timson?"

Timson nodded.

"Write?"

"English, French, Latin, Scots, and Gaelic, although some better than others. I accompanied the Earl to Paris during his exile. He is well-versed in the antiquities and history of Scotland. He has written a chronicle of the Angus earls, which, I may say without pride or judgment, is the fruit of my diligence as much as his."

"How long were you in Paris with him?"

"Three years, more than enough to know the French." He made like he was going to spit again but didn't.

"I will be going to Hackney in the future, Timson. Your service will be required there, not here, if we come to terms." Timson nodded. "Nigel is my steward. I need a manservant who can assist me with my literary endeavors. Do you believe you can help me in that regard?"

"Most assuredly, my laird. It would be returning home, in fact, since I was in service to Lady Lennox there."

"And where *is* home?"

"Wherever I am at the time, my laird."

"I mean, where in Scotland are you from?

"County Angus, my laird. A coastal village called Seacliff, a mile from Tantallon Castle, the ancestral home of the Angus earls. My family have served the earls since the first earl built the castle in 1346."

"You will do, Timson. Nigel will show you where to lodge. He will answer any questions you may have about Oxford Court. I look forward to hearing any Scottish tales you might recall."

Timson's eyes took on a brightness Oxford hadn't seen till then. "I will be pleased to oblige you, my laird."

154

Cymbeline at the Curtain

Oxford did not attend the performance of *Cymbeline* at the Curtain. Neither did the queen. Essex was having one of his tantrums and lay at Wanstead claiming he was ill.

Oxford had suggested Shackspear play Cymbeline. "He is right royally a king," Oxford had remarked, as he and Shackspear, John Lyly, and Ben Jonson finished the final draft. Jonson failed to hear the sarcasm in Oxford's voice. He also thought Shackspear should play Cymbeline. Lyly wasn't sure. He couldn't see Oxford's face in the darkened room but knew something else was going on.

"You are the man for the part," Oxford told Shackspear. 'You might even wear your turkey feather in your crown!"

Lyly looked away. Oxford was now clearly setting up the buffoon to make himself ridiculous on the stage.

Shackspear wanted the part, but he was ever wary of Oxford. "Did they wear turkey feathers back then?"

"They had turkeys in Caesar's time, didn't they?"

Shackspear looked at Ben for support. Jonson nodded gravely. He had been watching Lyly and had realized what Oxford was up to. He had no love for Shackspear. He viewed life as a bear pit and everyone else a dog trying to block him from what he wanted. A feather in Shakespeare's crown might put a feather in his.

"God," Lyly muttered. Oxford glanced at him. "Well, I do love 'crooked smokes'," the little man said.

The queen later expressed disappointment that she had not gone to see the play. Those who had trekked up the muddy road to the Curtain regaled her with descriptions of Iachimo rising out of the trunk in Imogen's darkened bedroom, the headless torso Imogen thought was Posthumus lying next to her, and the neat way all the plots were wrapped up at the end. And, yes, how regally Shackspear had played Cymbeline. He had found a pair of thick-soled shoes left over from one of Robert Greene's plays that allowed him to tower over the other players as he strutted about the stage with a turkey feather in his crown.

Burbage had objected to the feather. 'What king ever wore a feather in his crown?' he asked, but Shackspear sauced him by pointing out that a Roman god would descend at the end of the play, so what did it matter? Shackspear explained that all the rules for a play had been discarded in the writing of *Cymbeline*. He would wear his feather. The pièce de resistance came when a patron stood up during the applause and cried out: '*Some will say good Will / Thou hath made'st thyself a companion for a king!*'

Finley came down from Cambridge to see it. He left the Curtain to walk down to Oxford Court to talk to Oxford about what he'd just seen. He didn't know what to make of it. "Is it a fairy tale?" he asked. "Is it a history play? The handbill said it was billed as a tragedy, but no one dies in it, except the queen and Cloten, who deserve what they get. You open the play in England, take the story to Italy, and come back to Wales. Jupiter descends from the rafters to leave a message." He shook his head. "I am lost. Did Shakespeare and the impresarios rewrite your play after it left your hands, my lord, or is this yours?"

Oxford had an equally puzzled look on his face. "I don't know how to explain it. I wrote it. The others filled in where I told them to. No matter how many words they wrote, it's still mine. I am filled with a deep anger I cannot shape into words. I am slashing at plays. I am unsettled. The joy I felt whilst writing plays has fled me. It has become drudgery. I may be done."

Finley was horrified. "*Never* say that, my lord."

Oxford laughed. "It has to end someday, doesn't it?" With a dour look on his face, he went out the door, leaving Finley in the library.

155

By A Brand He Shall Be Known

Y er lordship," Falstaff announced, shattering the silence Oxford was enjoying as he worked over a sonnet. He looked up to see the big man striding into the library, moving, as always, at greater speed than necessary, looking like a ship that had just come in off the ocean with its topsails still set and would likely strike the quay in front of it, which, in this case, was the library table. But, as always, Falstaff slipped past the table and swiveled himself into his customary 'throne' along the wall without incident. He folded his hands over his immense belly and settled back.

A miniature version of Sir John appeared in Falstaff's wake. He was dressed in an identical broad-brimmed crowned hat, light brown in color, with an eagle feather sticking out of it. His jerkin and trousers were Kendall green. His boots were black and highly polished. His belly bulged out in imitation of Sir John's, an impossibility for a child the boy's age. His jerkin had obviously been filled out with bombast. He was towing an immense broad sword by its handle, the tip dragging on the floor. He angled his head back and announced: "Monsieur, I weesh you a veree gud day!"

Oxford looked in amazement at the boy, whose head barely topped the library table.

"My page, yer lordship. I need someone to carry my water, bear my sword and buckler, post letters for me, and pick up whatever I drop. I can't bend over anymore."

"Where, pray tell, did you find him?"

"In Gravesend, my lord. On the docks. He didn't say anything. I thought he was dumb. I asked around to find out who was responsible for him. A man claimed he owned him and said he couldn't speak. For this shortcoming, he was willing to sell him to me for tuppence. I flipped him a coin and 'Tupp,', as I named him, has been glued to my derriere ever since."

"But he just spoke to me. In English."

"Yes. I was very disappointed when I found out he could speak. I bought him because I thought he was dumb. I thought I was getting a silent servant who would never sass me or give away my business. Then, on my way to the ship, I went by a house of pleasure that was, quite naturally, staffed with ladies from France, so I said something to them in French and Tupp came alive. He's French, my lord."

Oxford looked at the boy. "*Ca va?*" The boy's face lit up.

"Oh, no you don't," Falstaff interrupted, putting out an arm. "He's my page! Ye can't have him."

"Fear not. I have no need of a French-speaking page. Tell me. You took ship and crossed over to Calais?"

Falstaff smiled. He pointed to his boots. Tupp ran over and pulled them off. "I had to travel across *La Manche*, my lord, *the Sleeve*, as it is called in French. Unfortunately, the French use the same word for a certain hidden part of a woman's body, eh? Ooo là là." He frowned mightily. "Poot etre, education may not be a good thing. Knowing what the Frenchies call the Channel has ruined my relationship with women forever. I can never again look out from Dover without …"

"Yes. And what did you find out when you finally got yourself and Tupp to France?"

"I found the French woman," Falstaff said. He paused to let Oxford digest this, but Oxford's slightly uplifted eyebrow let Falstaff know more was expected. "She has reached the age where she no longer fears rules, my lord. She didn't like the way Henry the Aith treated Anne, nor how Kat Ashley treated her."

"And?"

"She remembered all. She told me she had accompanied the queen to Havering Palace and was with her when the royal vagina went into labor." Oxford made a face. "She took the babe and handed it to Kat who passed it to the blind servant who took it to the horseman waiting out on North Road."

"Did she see anything?"

"No, but she did hear Kat Ashley exclaim when she opened the blanket and looked down at the baby: *Par un brand, il sera connu.*"

"*By a brand, he shall be known,*" Oxford said.

"Tupp said the same thing."

Oxford cast a baleful look at Falstaff, who said, defensively: "Best to get it *de source sûre*, you know; straight from the horse's mouth."

"And the brand is …?"

Falstaff shoulders went up and down in a perfect imitation of the way every Frenchman shrugs when asked a question he can't answer. "She didn't see what Kat Ashley was looking at."

"A mark of some kind, then. And Kat saw enough to know it was a boy. That's good. But what kind of a mark could it be?" He paused. "He's probably shed it by now." He sounded defeated.

"Maybe not. Maybe all we have to do is look at the earl's body …"

"And how would we do that?" Oxford asked. He was not comfortable imagining Southampton naked.

But not Falstaff. "You can ask the earl to undress, my lord."

Oxford's mouth dropped open.

"No, then." Falstaff continued. "How about asking the queen if the babe she birthed had any marks on him?"

This astonished Oxford even more. "She denies she ever had a baby. And, if she did, *she would never ever tell me anyway!*"

"No, again."

"We're talking about the next king of England, Jack! Some decorum, please!"

Falstaff kept going. "Then, what if you go to Elizbeth Vernon, the lovely young lady the earl is sporting with, and ask her what she's 'seen'?"

Oxford threw up his hands. "You want me to ask Ms. Vernon whether she's noticed any unusual 'mark' on the earl's body?" He shook his head in disbelief. "Ms. Vernon is a delightful young woman who will make Henry a wonderful wife, should they marry." *And queen,* he quickly thought, *should Henry become king.*

"Then there is the bed-switch," Falstaff calmly went on, as if he were discussing whether they should have beef or chicken for dinner. Oxford blinked. "We'll find a willing lass, my lord, the type of woman Bertram thought Diana was in *All's Well.* Our Diana will get Southampton into bed and make him show himself to her!" He opened up his arms like Jesus and beamed, showing his broken teeth. "All of himself."

Falstaff knew mentioning the bed-trick was waving a red flag in front of a bull but he thought Oxford might recognize the logic in his suggestion.

"Cheeky bastard," Oxford muttered. He looked away, trying to find something to hold onto while the fat, lying, mountain of corrupt flesh in front of him continued to stupefy and enrage him.

"Ye also used it in *Measure for Measure,*" Falstaff said, unaware that Oxford had collapsed inward, "which I dint see because I was on the road, trying to find a lost child." He glanced at Oxford who was scrabbling through the papers on the table.

"*Cymbeline,*" Oxford said aloud. "*How convince the king Guiderius is his son? A brand. A birthmark. Where to put it? On his neck?*"

He began to write, speaking the words as his pen flew across the page: "*Guiderius had upon his neck a mole, a sanguine star. He hath upon him still.*"

Falstaff sighed and rose. He retrieved his cape and went out the door, Tupp trailing along behind him, dragging the sword across the rough wooden floor, its tip bouncing over the splinters and gaps.

Oxford didn't notice them leave. Bent over the table, he continued speaking aloud, "Good: Guiderius' mole will match the one on Imogen's breast, tying them together. Sister and brother. I love it when one idea flows effortlessly into another. *Southampton would be known by a brand; so will Guiderius.*" He almost giggled. "A *sanguine star.* The Oxford star! *The Mollet!*"

He stopped. "But Guiderius will not show his neck to the king. This will leave the audience hanging. What if the two boys Belarius has raised are *not* Cymbeline's sons? He *says* they are, but maybe he has found two other boys and wants to get his revenge on the king for banishing him by tricking Cymbeline into accepting boys *who are not his long lost sons!* Hah, hah, hah!"

He kept writing. Then his head came up again. "Cymbeline can't look. If he looks and the mark *isn't* there, he loses a son as well as an heir. If he *doesn't* look, he gets both. One boy is as good as another, eh? Why tip over the fairytale when it's so close to the end? What's in a name? Hah! By these changes, Belarius may be the smartest man in the room. Cymbeline? He could be Cloten's father." But then he stopped. "Unless the king *knows* the boy might not be his. Hmm. Maybe he's *not* so dumb."

Oxford put his pen back down on the paper. He had scarcely finished a line when he paused again. "And Henry? What if *he's* someone else's?" He turned and noticed that Falstaff had left the room. "Damn. Why is that fat knight never here when I need him."

156

Every Man in His Humour

Shackspear and Billy Sly were bowing to the audience cheering Ben Jonson's new play.

"I should never have introduced him to Burbage," Shackspear said to himself. The audience had liked his performance of Knowell, an older character who worried about his son's adventures in London, but the applause had increased when Billy Sly came out to join Shackspear on the stage. Billy had played the part of Brainworm, a conniving servant who outsmarts his betters, a role the audience loved.

Shackspear liked the applause, but it meant Burbage would want another play from Ben Jonson. This was not good for William Shackspear, who had gained fame in London as the author of *Romeo & Juliet*, *Midsummer Night's Dream*, and *Henry V*. Now, he worried the plays Oxford gave him would be surpassed by Jonson's. Oxford wrote about kings and queens while Ben Jonson had just shown everyone he could write a play about common folk, city dwellers, people like those in the audience now clapping happily.

Jonson came out on stage. Shackspear and Billy Sly stepped aside, and the applause increased. Big Ben strode to the front and spread out his arms. Shackspear muttered 'Christ'. Billy said afterwards he couldn't tell whether Shackspear was referring to Jonson's increased fame or that Jonson was likening himself to Jesus.

Oxford was in the audience. Burbage had urged him to come see Jonson's new play. "Ben is good, your lordship," Burbage had told him when they ran into each other coming out of Bridge Street a week earlier. "His characters live in London. The plot engages them in a tightly woven mesh of action and reaction."

"No Jupiter," Oxford commented.

"No headless bodies," Burbage said with a wink. "No hidden ancestors or fumbling bedmates to tie up loose ends."

"I doubt he can do women," Oxford said, scowling.

"He doesn't have to. He presents deeds and language such as men do use."

"People will tire of his characters."

"Perhaps. Come see it."

And so Oxford had come to see *Every Man In his Humour*. He stayed to the end, as he always did, in respect of the author and the art form, much like an old man finishing his *Credo* despite interruptions. He descended the stairs to the side door that let him out into Holywell Lane. Shackspear, who had fled the applause by another door, was coming toward him. "My lord," he called out. Oxford stopped. "I should never have introduced Ben Jonson to Burbage."

"No, you should have killed him."

This shocked Shackspear. "My lord!" he exclaimed.

"How else could you have kept him off the stage? An army couldn't have done it. Do not discontent yourself; you are not the reason he is now famous."

"But his new style threatens to undo me, your lordship," Shackspear whined. "I mean you," he quickly added.

Oxford scoffed. "The violent, angle-eyed, pock-marked bear of man who has just seen his first effort applauded is no threat to me. His quibbling characters are of no importance. They are like acorns under a great oak. Time will sweep them away. His work will never displace what I have written, *or what is to come!*"

This last came out with some force, surprising both men. Oxford sounded like he was planting a flag in the ground, but he had no play in mind ready to be written down! He could not recall being so empty! Could *Cymbeline* be his last effort? Could he be done? If so, why was he saying something is to come when he had naught?

Shackspear was thrilled to hear Oxford announce he was not done. "What's the next play, my lord? What can I help ye with? I am in need of another play!"

So am I, Oxford thought. *So am I*. He walked around Shackspear without saying more, leaving a confused Shackspear behind him.

157

Hackney

Oxford finally realized that her ladyship had not sent Timson to be his new secretary but to pry him out of London. Timson kept up a steady drip of suggestions about moving to Hackney, describing what her ladyship was doing there and how much Lil Henry would love to see his father.

Oxford finally gave in. Nigel and Timson began to pack. A carriage was obtained. When they were ready, Nigel helped Oxford into it. As Nigel closed the door, he handed in Oxford's cane. Socrates appeared from nowhere and leapt onto the canvas that had been rolled down behind Oxford seated in the back. Socrates braced himself as the carriage began to roll away, squaring his body and legs while pointing his head forward to mimic the regal pose of a stone lion guarding the gates of Babylon.

Oxford glanced back at the cat; the nimble beast obviously knew their time at the Court was over. Otherwise, he would have stayed behind. He had first appeared the night Oxford arrived at Billesley Hall in Warwickshire, leaping onto Oxford's bed the way he had just leapt onto the folded-down carriage top. And then he suddenly appeared at Oxford Court when Oxford moved back to London. No one knew how he had gotten from Billesley to London.

Socrates' presence was also a sign that Oxford was not done with playwrighting. Socrates' 'arse' had become part of the process by which Oxford's scripts were written. Oxford would finish a page and push it down the table where Socrates would put his stamp of approval on it by sitting on it. 'The true author,' Oxford would mutter from time to time.

They had not gone ten feet when Nigel had Timson stop the carriage. "The Stone, my lord," Nigel said, opening the carriage door. London Stone, battered and begrimed with London soot, thrust up out of the pavement next to them, a shard of its former greatness. The Romans had planted it as Mile Marker One when they founded their new province *Provincia Britannia.*

Oxford slid out of the carriage and braced himself with his 'walking stick,' as he liked to call it, a 'cane' being too severe a term for a device that merely steadied him. He still thought he could do without it. He crossed the short distance to the Stone and brushed his hand over its top. He liked not the image that rose in his mind – a decrepit man beside a decrepit stone. The irony would have made him smile in his younger years, but not now. His world had turned inward. He was barely aware of the sea of humanity ebbing and flowing past him in the street.

He went back to the carriage and got in. Timson touched the reins, and the carriage continued down Candlewick Street toward Bishopsgate. The horses looked old and tired, Oxford thought, as did the carriage. It had had once been deeply lacquered, red, most likely, but little remained of it. A coat of arms would have been mounted on the door when new but nothing graced it now. Oxford's arms would have occasioned no remark had they been on the door. No one knew who he was. As far as Oxford was concerned, the arc of life that had started with his arrival at Cecil House at the head of eighty men on horseback and one hundred yeomen on foot had ended. The slow movement of the carriage down the street was a curtain being drawn across a stage.

They passed the Boar's Head. The front wall had been ripped away; they were rebuilding the inside. Oxford leaned out. The pub in which he had spent so much time looked like a whale being stripped on a beach, the studs and joists projecting into the air like ribs. He could see all the way to the back. The booths were already gone but he could still hear the laughter, the calls for the tapster, and the sound of knives and spoons striking trenchers and bowls. He remembered Falstaff baptizing Lil Henry with beer next to the fireplace and his mother storming into the pub to snatch him away before the devil took her baby and threw him into Limbo.

'Lil Henry,' he thought to himself. He'd have to start calling him 'Henry,' he thought. He won't put up with 'Lil Henry' much longer.

They passed Lombard Street. Oxford wondered if Sally was still selling turtle soup there but then remembered Sally was long gone. Swan Alley passed without a glance. Signore Baldini had returned to Venice. Frangellica too. Aemilia Bassano could have gone with her but had instead moved to Cooke-ham on the Thames to live with Lady Margaret Clifford and her daughter, Anne.

London had been a lush garden to him, full of excitement and perpetual promise, but it was now winter. He was folding up, like a flower that had enjoyed the day Nature had given it.

The carriage passed under Bishopsgate and the baleful eye that looked lifelessly up the road to the north. Bedlam was to the left; Fisher's Folly to the right. How many poems and plays had been hatched in that rabbit warren of rooms, Oxford wondered?

The Folly slipped away behind him as Holywell Lane opened on the left. The Curtain stood out midway down the Lane, the Theatre behind it. The first playhouse, Oxford thought. Empty now as the Burbages argued with the landowner over a new lease, but the Theatre was a playhouse no more.

The Curtain now hosted the Lord Chamberlain's Men, with its hidden box for the queen. She would have preferred a similar box at the Rose or the Swan but there was no way she could have gotten herself into either theater without being discovered. The Curtain, on the other hand, lay in the middle of a jumble of buildings and was accessible from many directions, which was why Burbage had been able to sell Hunsdon on a secret box for the queen. He offered it as a gift to her but knew it would cause the Lord Chamberlain's Men to perform there and increase his profits, for he was a hidden partner in the Curtain as well as the Theatre.

The Rose was also prospering, however. Jonson's *Every Man in his Humour* had just been staged there. The Swan, on the other hand, remained closed because of *The Isle of Dogs*.

The carriage was soon through Norton Folgate where the string of buildings straggling north from Bishopsgate began to run out. Garden plots, even farms, started to appear, for the City had not yet stretched this far into the 'country', as city folk called it. The fields that now lined the road were separated from each other by a narrow footpath or a lane and an occasional house. The sameness of the landscape put Oxford to sleep. The carriage finally arrived in front of King's Place. Nigel roused Oxford and helped him climb down.

Oxford straightened himself and surveyed the house Henry VIII had built. Despite visiting Lady Lennox when she lived there, and the few visits he had made to King's Place so far, Oxford felt like he was seeing it for the first time. Maybe it was because he had only been stopping by before; this time his arrival felt permanent. A stonemason has to start a gravestone with a chip from his chisel. Perhaps this was one of those chips, Oxford thought to himself.

Tobias came out to meet them. "My lord. Welcome," he said. He reached around Oxford to help Nigel and Timson carry the cases they had brought with them into the house.

Lil Henry burst out of the front door, pursued by a great full-feathered golden dog that began barking furiously. Lil Henry, now five, pulled on the dog's collar and came to a halt in front of his father. "My lord," he said, giving Oxford a leg. "As Lord Bolbec, I welcome you to King's Place!" He was so excited he fairly shouted this.

Oxford smiled. 'Bolbec' was a title the Vere family heir was entitled to bear. It descended from Isabel Bolbec, wife of the Third Earl of Oxford. For Henry to know this showed that someone had been taking the time to educate the future 18th Earl of Oxford as to his patrimony.

The dog strained to get closer to Oxford, who guessed the dog was the puppy Falstaff had given Henry in London. It had grown into an animal full of affection.

"His name?" Oxford asked, reaching down to rub the dog's head.

"Tater," Henry said.

"Ah," Oxford said. "You've met Digby."

"I have, my lord. He said he had a fine dog named Tater once that helped him hunt, but Tater passed away. He offered the name to me. I took it as an honor."

"It is, indeed," Oxford said.

"Did you know Tater, my lord?"

"I did. And Tater was a fine dog, particularly into the marshes to bring back a goose. You could not have chosen a better name."

This pleased Henry. Oxford rubbed the dog's head some more. "Have you been to Hedingham?"

"No, my lord. Digby said you'd bring me there."

"I will." Digby had obviously enlisted Henry to get Oxford to Hedingham "And, where is your mother? I should pay her a call."

"She's around the side," Henry said, pointing to the far end of the house. "In her garden."

"In her garden?" Henry nodded. He took his father's hand and began towing him toward the corner of the house, dragging Tater with them. Nigel, Tobias, and Timson were moving Oxford's baggage into the house. Socrates leapt off the carriage and headed for the stables.

The left side of the house provided Elspeth with a sun-filled plot of land she was busily raking. She looked up as Oxford and Henry came around the corner. "My lord," she called. She handed the rake to a servant and came across the garden, a beaming smile on her face.

Oxford hadn't seen her smile like that in years. And she hadn't gone near a garden since she had ripped up the one at Oxford Court. Something had changed.

"My lord," Elspeth said, coming up. "Henry," she added.

"My lady," Oxford said, bowing stiffly. He made like he was whisking a hat off his head though none was there. Henry giggled. He liked his father bowing to his mother. "Your garden looks, well, well-situated," Oxford said, not knowing what to say. The ground had been turned over but nothing had come up yet.

"Yes. Thank you. This represents my return to gardening, which is very recent. I hope I am not too late." She meant in the season. "However, we will plant and pray. That always works."

Oxford' nodded, the slight euphoria he had felt as she had come toward him disappearing when he heard the word 'pray.' She had obviously not abandoned religion.

The servants stood respectively around the garden. Human tools, they had stopped moving when their mistress stopped working. Oxford could sense they were not used to a lady who was married to the 17th earl of anything getting dirt under her fingernails. They obviously thought she should have been directing work from a carriage or a covered porch. But Elspeth had never cared for formality. She had always been direct and honest about what she wanted, as well as what she wanted from others, including her husband.

"I hope you have come to stay," she said. He nodded that he had. "Welcome, then, welcome, welcome. I have been very active in my little chapel, saying prayers for your safe arrival, and apparently someone has been listening." She looked up at the sky.

Oxford was pleased to see something of the Elspeth he had courted and wed, or rather, the woman who had courted him, including her seduction of him in the Keep at Hedingham before they married. Whatever remained of the heat and fun of those early days had burned out before Lil Henry came along, which only further increased the distance from Elspeth's room to Oxford's. They slept in separate rooms at Oxford Court, connected by a bridge. To make the distance even greater, Elspeth's maidservant slept in a cupboard off Elspeth's room. Elspeth's descent into religion - becoming a Foot-Washing Baptist - uprooted more than the garden at Oxford Court. But something had changed since then. Here she was now, covered with dirt, smiling happily. Miracles apparently did happen, Oxford thought to himself. Maybe more would follow.

Elspeth took him inside through a side entrance. It led directly into the hallway that ran across the west end of the house. "I will see to supper, my lord," she said, gesturing toward the dining room. "I trust you will need to settle in."

"Yes," he said. He remembered his rooms were on the second floor to the rear. "I will see how Nigel and Timson are doing."

"You like Timson?" she asked.

"Very much. I think he will do fine."

"But he is not Robin."

"No. Who could replace Robin?" he asked, giving her a sly look.

She laughed. "Indeed."

She went into the dining room while he climbed to the second floor. At the top, he went down the west side to the long gallery that ran across the rear. Lady Elspeth's rooms were at the corner; his were at the far end of the gallery. He could see Nigel and Timson moving items into his rooms as he walked down the gallery. He tried not to look up at Hunsdon's arms pressed into the ceiling above him. If they became an annoyance, he would have them removed.

"My lord," Nigel said as Oxford came up. He handed over a folder, which Oxford opened. In it was a letter from Lettice Knollys.

Oxford groaned. "I'm not here five minutes and she finds me."

"This was delivered as we were leaving the Court, my lord. I thought you would be better able to assay it once you arrived here."

"Thank you," Oxford said, passing into his rooms. A few chairs had been set up. He sat down in one and unfolded the Countess' letter. "*My good lord, etc. etc.,*" he read, appreciating the lacey Italic script that perfectly captured the woman who had written it. Her spelling was haphazard, and she obviously thought capital letters should be used to emphasize what she was saying, which was quite often. "*You need to Proceed Tout-Swuiet to do whatever you have to do to make the queen sit down and watch the assassination of Julius Caesar. The life of my Son and the kingdom Depends on it! The dear boy has been Blessed with everything except judgment. He frets and storms that She has blamed Him for the failure of the latest attempt to destroy Spain's Armada when Ralegh and Howard are at fault. But the expedition failed when he went off to sack a town in the Canaries and missed Philip's treasure fleet by only Three Hours! Two and half million in silver was on those ships, they say. Had he kept to his orders, We All would be rich!*"

Oxford shook his head. 'This was news? A play would right all?' He read further. She had foreseen his objections.

"*Do not think to wriggle and worble.*" Oxford looked up, 'worble?' he asked himself. 'Wobble? With an 'r' that wriggled in from 'wriggle'? He smiled. He liked her use of language. "*None of her courtiers can get through to her. She's Infatuated with the boy. She thinks she's Her twenty years ago and he's You!*" Oxford stopped to wonder whether this was intended as a compliment. Knowing Lettice, it was almost certainly not. "*A splash of cold water in the Face is what She needs. A dead Julius Caesar on the stage will do it. Put him there. A couple of Words pulled out of one of those Books you always have lying around. Otherwise, I lose either my Son or the Kingdom. Look at Your Son. He will be the 18th Earl of Oxford one day because I rescued Him and You from the Bitch and her spaniels, the Cecils, when they were scheming to make you Common. Don't Forget THAT!*"

'She does have a bit of a temper,' Oxford said, as he refolded the letter. He handed it to Timson. "Burn that, if you would, please."

He went into the other rooms. The trunk of plays was against one wall, the writing table from the second-floor room against the other. He went to the window. The same two men who had been sitting below it the last time were sitting there. "Good even," Oxford said.

They jumped up and doffed their caps. "Milord," they both said.

"Loyal servants, I presume," Oxford said.

"Aye, milord."

"And your names?"

"Ross," said one. "Angus," said the other.

"Good Scottish names, I wager."

They smiled. "As good as gets," the one called Ross said.

"Know you Timson?"

They both nodded. "We are from Seacliff, the same town as he," Ross said. "T'was his service to Lady Lennox that brought us down from Scotland," Angus added. "She died and we stayed."

"Timson is now my manservant," Oxford said.

"Guid man," Ross said. Angus agreed.

The sun had sunk behind the line of poplars to the west. "I crave a wee porch here," Oxford said. "Ten wide, four deep, with a railing and a roof over it. Can ye do that for me?"

"Certainly," they both said. "But not tonight," Ross added with a wink, casting an eye at the disappearing sun.

"I know ye have other tasks here, and I don't want to take you away from your customary werk," Oxford said. "When ye ken. I want to look out over the fields toward the forest yonder."

"A lovely view it is, milord," one of the men said.

"Good even, then," Oxford said.

"Good even," Ross said. Angus nodded.

Oxford pulled his head back in. 'Good names to add to a play.' Shackspear had suggested Peto, Bardolph, and Fluellen for three soldiers in *Henry V*. He said they were Stratford gents who had sued his father or sat on a jury that rendered a verdict against him. He knew Shackspear was always trying to salt the plays with names he could claim showed he was the author. Ross and Angus might offset this.

Timson put his head in. "Yer lady would be pleased to have yer company at supper, my lord."

"Please tell her that I will be there."

The long table was gone. In its place was a table that could sit six, Lady Elspeth was at one end; Oxford took the seat opposite her.

"Welcome, my lord. I trust you find this satisfactory."

"Very satisfactory," Oxford said. He was looking around at the walls, which were newly painted and hung with various banners and trophies collected by his ancestors. They must have been sent up from Oxford Court. Like Lil Henry's knowledge of the de Vere family, someone was digging through trunks and reading old papers.

They ate dinner in silence. When they finished, Elspeth picked up a glass of claret the departing servant had poured. She toasted her husband. "To our marriage, my lord, which, I am sad to say, has been neglected as I learned how to be a countess and raise a child."

'And gone off into hugger-mugger land,' Oxford thought to himself. Aloud, he said, "I have been as much at fault myself, what with writing plays and remaining away so much."

"But here we are now, without all those distractions. We have our son to raise. I have my garden. You, I am sure, have your literary pursuits. I hope we find time for each other."

Oxford nodded. "I am of like mind."

"To that end, I would like to invite you to visit my chamber this evening, if you are so inclined. You will find me at home."

Oxford was happy to hear this but realized she might be reaching out for him to get her with a playmate for Henry. She read his mind.

"My offer is for pleasure only, my lord. I am happy to leave having babies to other women. Henry's pregnancy was difficult."

"Oh," he said, giving away more than he intended. "Pleasure it will be, then." And so it was.

Henry and the Horseshoe

Yer lordship," Timson said quietly, standing in the doorway to Oxford's room. Oxford raised his head. Light was streaming in through the window. "Lord Bolbec has sent word that he would like to take you on a tour of the gardens behind the house, if you please."

Oxford had no idea what time it was. In London, he slept when he felt like it. He was still asleep and thought it was the middle of the night, yet the sunlight told him it was not. "Now?" he asked.

"Yes, my lord," Timson replied. Whatever Timson thought of 'Lord Bolbec' summoning his father from his bed before breakfast was served remained hidden.

Oxford groaned and pushed himself erect. Before he could swing his legs out onto the floor, Henry's face appeared, peering around Timson's long legs. "*Papa!*" he shouted.

"Oh," Oxford said. He forced himself to smile. "Good, my boy. How doth thou today?"

"Very well, my lord." Henry came out from behind Timson and gave his father a leg. Tater kept trying to crowd around him. Henry gestured dismissively toward Timson. "Begone, sir. My father and I have business."

Timson's face showed no reaction. He glanced at Oxford to make sure he was to leave, then pivoted out of the room.

"Allow me to dress for our excursion, Lord Bolbec," Oxford said, pulling his boots out from under the bed. He put a foot in one of the boots and pulled the bedpan out, into which he emptied his bladder.

Henry took no interest. His attitude, one of effected nonchalance, showed bedpans were not something worth his attention. He held Tater by the neck and watched his father dress. When Oxford had put on his clothes and boots, Henry took his hand and towed him out of the room, Tater excitedly following them.

They went down the back staircase and out into the garden behind the house. Servants were already working the ground. Oxford and Henry went by them, coming out onto the road that led to Epping Forest and the marshes along the River Lea.

Oxford was glad he remembered to grab his 'walking' stick as he went out the door. The surface of the road had been baked to the consistency of stone in the summer heat and the ruts would have been difficult to negotiate without it. Lil Henry was wearing substantial boots. He strode along next to his father, intent on his mission of taking them to wherever his destination was. Oxford decided not to ask what that was but to go along with his little boy and his decision to take his father in tow. Tater surged ahead.

The River Lea came into view. Henry knew of a sandbar that nearly blocked it off at low ebb. They forded the stream and continued on into the forest, as old as any in England. Great trees towered over them. Henry plunged deeper into the woods until they came to a clearing. Henry stopped and pointed to a horseshoe lying on the ground.

"Can ye dig 'im up?" Henry asked.

"Who?" Oxford asked.

"The horse."

"The horse? Ah, ye think a horse lies beneath the ground, with only the bottom of his horseshoe showing at the surface?"

Henry nodded.

"Well," Oxford said, not knowing what to say.

"Well?" Henry asked.

"Well," Oxford said again, bending down to use his walking stick to lever the horseshoe out of the ground, "things sometimes are not what they appear to be." He flipped the shoe over, revealing that there was no horse beneath it.

Henry stared at the ground. "Morder-forker," he said to himself. He kicked the horseshoe.

"What did you say?" Oxford asked.

"Morder-forker," Henry said. "It's not as bad as 'mother-fucker."

Oxford's jaw dropped open. "Where have you learned such words?"

Henry laughed. "From everyone. All you have to do is listen. There's 'shit' and 'damn' and …"

"That's quite enough," Oxford said. It sounded like Henry's list would be quite long. "You shouldn't utter such words."

"That's what Sir John told me. He said I needed to learn words that weren't bad, like 'morder-forker.' It would keep me out of trouble." Henry looked up to see if his father agreed.

"Yes, …"

"And save the bad ones for when ye're really mad." He frowned. He looked like he was about to tell his father what those words were, but Oxford put his hand up again.

"You're disappointed the horse wasn't under the shoe"

"I am, my lord. I would have sworn there was a horse under that shoe. I didn't touch it. I saved it to show it to you." His face got sad. "I thought you would be impressed and think well of me."

"I am," Oxford immediately said. "I do. It's a God-given talent to see things others don't. Imagining a horse underneath a horseshoe is, well, extraordinary."

"But things are sometimes not what they seem," Henry muttered to himself, repeating what his father had said to him.

"Well, yes. There's that too. But I'm sure you painted a scene in your mind of the horse rising out of the ground for you to mount."

"I did, my lord." The boy looked up at his father, his face animated again. "I would have leapt into the saddle, brushed off the dirt, and spurred him into a gallop!"

"Off to battle, I warrant."

Henry nodded. "Where I would strike down many an evil knight." The boy's face glowed.

"And so you created an adventure from merely seeing a horseshoe lying on the ground. Pretty good, I would say."

Henry nodded. "And so do I." His face brightened. "It's hot. Let's go swimming." This surprised Oxford again. He took Oxford's hand and towed him back to the river where they took off their clothes and splashed into the pool the sandbar had created. Tater charged in and out chasing butterflies and birds.

Oxford felt foolish sitting on his haunches in the cold water. What would anyone say if they came upon him? They'd say he was mad. Lords nearing fifty don't take off their clothes to go swimming in a river. Sane men don't even know how to swim. 'If God had intended us to swim, …' he heard someone saying to him when he was a boy. He wriggled around on the sand. Or was it 'worbled'? He laughed again. And, if Lettice could see him now, he thought, well, she might join them. But, upon further reflection, Oxford thought, probably not.

People thought the Countess mad but she was smarter than nearly everyone who came up against her. Besides, what would she do with her hat? Her feathers?

"My lord s'amuse," Henry said, splashing over to him.

"French now, eh?"

"Uh puh-tee," Henry said, squeezing his lips together. He was proud he could show his father something else he had learned. "Can we go to Hedingham?" he asked.

"Yes. When should we go?"

"Tonight."

Oxford smiled. "Not tonight, my little choux. Tomorrow, perhaps.

159

Caesar Becomes Brutus

Oxford began to settle into his rooms in King's Place. His books and writing instruments arrived and he busied himself arranging them on the shelves and setting up his desk with ink and quills when Henry appeared and reminded his father that they were to go to Hedingham that day. Oxford suppressed a groan, but realized he was looking forward to seeing Digby and the Keep.

"Run tell Timson to load up the carriage. We are going to Hedingham." Henry, thrilled, ran off.

Their visit lasted only two days. Henry was too little to ride to hounds or to understand all the stored-up wisdom Digby had been saving up to give him. By the second morning, he missed his mother. The two of them returned to Hackney later that day. Elspeth was glad to have Henry back. His duty done, Oxford could return to setting up his study.

Once all his books had been arranged to his liking, he pulled out North's translation of Plutarch's *Lives* and laid it on the table. This was followed by Appian's *Civil Wars*, Suetonius's *Lives of the Twelve Caesars*, and Tacitus' *Annals of Roman History*. The first had been translated into English; the last three were in Latin.

Oxford loved the way Latin washed though his mind, clearing away old English, the way the River Lea washed fallen branches and debris downstream. He reached for *Ovid* as well. Caesar would be warned on his way to the forum. There would be omens and portents. Oxford would have Caesar's friends speak them to him.

He went to the trunk of plays and opened it. He sifted through the manuscripts inside and found a first attempt at a play about Julius Caesar he had written shortly after he had come back from Italy. He had visited Rome and seen the Senate building on the Capitoline Hill, beautified by Michelangelo's magnificent plaza. Caesar had died down the hill in the ancient forum but a modern audience wouldn't know that and so Oxford had brought Caesar up to die in a location that hadn't existed at the time of his death. The irony of this intrigued Oxford. History changing what had happened to the extent that modern theatergoers would think Caesar had died in a completely different place from where Brutus and the other assassins had struck him down.

He began to write: 'The queen must see that Caesar is her. He had no heir; nor does she. He will be warned, as she is being warned." He wrote down some lines. "I will also add a clock that will chime." He smiled. "Shackspear will object: in a Roman forum? But this play is not about Caesar; it is about Essex. The chime will collapse the wall that separates the audience from what they are watching. They think they are in Rome in Caesar's time; the chime will instantly transport them to London in our time. Brutus will become Essex; Cassius, Southampton; Octavian, Robert Cecil."

Oxford nodded. "This will do good service for Southampton as well: he will see that he must free himself from Essex. And lest the queen think she is safe from Essex, I will have Cassius explain how Essex will remove her from power and claim it was necessary:

> *And, gentle friends,*
> *Let's kill him boldly, but not wrathfully;*
> *Let's carve him as a dish fit for the gods,*
> *Not hew him as a carcass fit for hounds:*
>
> *This shall make*
> *Our purpose necessary and not envious:*
> *Which so appearing to the common eyes,*
> *We shall be call'd purgers, not murderers.*

Shackspear's laughing face suddenly appeared in front of Oxford. His laughter at the chiming clock morphed into a vision of him taking *Julius Caesar* to the playhouse, laughing all the way at the foolish Earl of Oxford who continued to give him plays he could claim as his own.

Oxford threw down his pen. "How far have I come? From Poet Earl to mere scrivener, hidden away, serving up dramas for the Stratford hack to present as his and mount on high to a place that should be mine! No more! No more!"

160

The Death of Lord Burghley

Edward! Awake!" a voice cried out, shattering the stillness that filled Oxford's room. Oxford sat bolt upright. The Earl of Surrey, cradling his severed head, showed pale in the moonlight. A look of surprise was frozen on Surrey's face. The eye sockets were empty, full of dust. Blood dripped off the arm that held it. More blood obscured the coat of arms on the shirt Surrey was wearing.

"Lord Henry."

"Yes. I visited ye at Billesley and told ye to pick up yer pen, *and ye have!* I thank thee for that."

Oxford rubbed his eyes. "Has he died?"

"He has indeed. Despite the ministrations of soups and poultices, some given to him by Her Majesty herself, William Cecil, 1st Baron Burghley, has finally died."

Oxford knew Burghley had been at death's door for months, but the news still startled him. The old man's departure was overdue. "He has met his maker," he said.

"Not yet, milord. There be ceremony that must be attended to. His spirit perforce lingers whilst those alive fret and stew. There will be the funeral, a grand one to be sure, with thousands of mourners, some paid for. The cortege will be long. His casket will go into the ground in Westminster, but his body will not be in it."

"No?"

"Come with me, my lord." The Earl of Surrey beckoned with his free hand. He walked out of Oxford's bedroom onto the gallery. Oxford followed. The two of them, Surrey's severed head still dripping blood on the tiled floor, padded along the gallery to the front of the house where the earl stopped at a window that looked out on the north road. "List, list," he said, pointing out the window. "He comes."

A carriage came over the hill from London. Four horses in pairs pulled the wagon down the hill into Hackney. It thundered by King's Place and continued on into the night.

"He lies inside," The Earl of Surrey said. "They are taking him to Stamford where he will be buried in St. Martin's Church."

"Stamford and not Westminster?"

"The man spent his life hiding from view. A hand in a glove, he was, never seen. Well, I've seen him. He's seen me too. He knows I wait for him."

"But why will his body be buried in Stamford and not Westminster?"

"It's who he was, in'it? One last trick. He wants ye to think he's in Westminster when he's really in Stamford. I have been doomed to walk the night till he comes to join me. Perhaps he thinks I will be waiting for him at Westminster. No matter. I will be in Stamford when he arrives and there take my revenge."

"And what revenge will it be?" Oxford asked. The shock of seeing the earl again was beginning to wear off. He wondered if he was talking to a hallucination, a creation of his own mind.

"I shall escort him to St. Peter who shall send him down to Hell!"

Oxford shivered. "But why show me this, my lord?"

The sound of the carriage was dying away.

"The little Welshman beheaded you by cutting off yer hands, Edward. He whispered in the queen's ear to let Shackspear take the credit ye should have gotten. Ye gave up. I came to you in Warwickshire and ye began again. Ye gave us *Romeo* and *Venus* and Falstaff and Prince Hal, Titania and Shylock. But, Edward, ye've gone to sleep again. *Pick up your pen!*"

"No, my lord; I am done."

"*Nonsense!*" Surrey thundered. His entire being shook. The head in his hand seemed to be even more dismayed. "The man who denied you so much just went by us in a coffin! *Hamlet* must come out of the trunk of plays." He leaned in. "*The best is yet to come.*"

He turned the head to look out the window. Early light could be seen in the east.

"My hour has come. Beware of Jonson, my lord. He is jealous of yer genius and will do all he ken to deny you fame. He seeks it for himself. Unlike Shackspear, he can write. Beware Jonson, my lord. Every man is a moon and has a dark side he never shows to anyone."

He held out his hand. Oxford took it. It was warm and wet. As Oxford held it, the earl faded from sight.

161

John Florio and the Earl of Southampton

Nigel appeared in the doorway. "John Florio, my lord, has written that he would like to come to Hackney to meet with you."

Oxford turned around. "The little Italian? He who thinks he was Holofernes in *Love's Labour's Lost?*"

"The same, my lord." Nigel fanned a piece of paper he was holding. "*My request is to ask you about two matters that are of the utmost importance to me, and, I believe, to you.*"

"He seeks money and a patron," Oxford grumbled.

"'*Which,*'" Nigel went on, still reading from the paper, "'*does not include either a request for money or patronage.*'"

This surprised Oxford. "And?"

"That is all he writes. Aside from 'your most affectionate servant, etc., etc. ...'"

Oxford paused. "Reply that we would be pleased to entertain him. You select the date."

"I will, my lord."

"It's so quiet here," Oxford said. "I miss the Court. Falstaff sleeping in the library, Shackspear barging in at all hours, Frangellica banging pots in the kitchen; Robin hurrying in and out." He sighed.

"Yes," Nigel said. "The hustle and bustle. The interruptions."

"The 'whobub,'" Oxford said. "And you?" Oxford asked, looking at Nigel. "Do you miss the 'hustle and bustle;' the 'interruptions?'"

"I find the quiet here most salubrious, my lord."

Oxford frowned. "Well, I don't. I miss the fat man, even Shackspear, oiling himself, hat in hand, as he loiters in the entryway." He looked at the paper in Nigel's hand. "But tell Florio he can come. We will talk about Giordano Bruno, locked in a dungeon in Rome. An amazing man, Bruno. He told me one night that each of the stars was a sun around which planets revolved! How extraordinary? He should have stayed in England."

"In which case, my lord, he would be sitting in a dungeon here."

Oxford was not surprised to hear Nigel's disapproval of Bruno. The Puritans were getting to his faithful steward. All of them, Oxford included, were getting older, and the closer everyone got to Heaven or Hell, the more religious people became. No one gifts their property to the church when they are young, Oxford mused, only when they see the sun setting. Nigel sounded like he was drifting in that direction. For Oxford, death was a door that led to nothing.

"Next Tuesday, my lord?"

"Do we have anything on?"

"No, my lord."

Oxford knew Nigel's answer would have been the same for any other day in the coming weeks but asking made him feel important. No one came to visit. Not even Falstaff. A visit from John Florio would be a welcome change, if only because of the news he would bring from London.

----------◆◆◆◆◆----------

"Master John Florio, my lord, waits in the Day Room," Nigel announced.

Oxford followed Nigel down to the first floor and walked into the where his guest awaited him. "Mr. Florio," he said, extending his hand. Florio shook it vigorously.

"So good of you to see me, your lordship."

"Yes," Oxford agreed. He gestured to a chair. Florio sat down. Oxford sat down opposite him. "And what brings you so far, if I may ask."

""Two reasons. I am finishing a dictionary of Italian and English words. I would hope you will grant me the favor of running your eye over it, given your vast knowledge of my native tongue."

Oxford pursed his lips. He looked to Florio like he had just tasted a pear compote with too little sugar in it. "And what need would I have of a dictionary of Italian and English?"

"Oh, it's not for you, my lord. It is for those who wish to emulate your knowledge of my native tongue."

"Hmm," Oxford said. He could understand the need for an Italian dictionary but reading Florio's effort would be absolute drudgery. "And your second reason for coming here?"

"The Earl of Southampton." Florio could sense that his lordship would not be reviewing his dictionary. He hid his disappointment. Unless the dictionary was not the reason Florio had made the trek to Hackney.

He continued. "I have been residing at Titchfield for some time now, my lord, advising the earl on all the subjects he should learn so that he will rise to the level of his birthright, and I am happy to report that he has been an attentive student."

"And?" Oxford asked.

"However, he has lately come under the influence of a certain gentleman at court, recently risen to high levels of power in the Queen's eye, ..."

"Robert Dudley, 2nd Earl of Essex," Oxford said.

"You speak it. Not me." Florio looked around. It was clear that he did not want to say anything to offend the Earl of Essex.

"Proceed, Master Florio. There are no ears in this room save yours and mine. The Earl of Essex and I are not close."

"Be that as it may, my lord" Florio said, sailing away from any confirmation on his part that he was trying to communicate something unflattering about Essex.

"Please," Oxford said. "I have no interest in the Earl of Essex. The Earl of Southampton, however, is another matter."

This made Florio feel better. "Yes, I know your love for him. He is young, my lord. He has greatness in him, but he is ill-equipped to deal with the likes of the earl I refuse to name and the courtiers who surround him. It will not end well."

"And why does this concern me?"

"You have shown much love for the Earl, my lord. Your sonnets; your dedications to him in *Venus & Adonis* and *Lucrece*."

"Shackspear wrote those. Not me."

"Yes, of course," Florio quickly said. "But you have a close relationship with Master Shackspear. He's written many plays that have pleased the queen. Perhaps you could suggest to Shackspear that he pen a play about a tyrant to show the Earl of Southampton how he may be risking himself by his close dealings with, uh, with the earl I have not named."

"And which tyrant would you suggest?"

"Julius Caesar."

"Julius Caesar?" Had Florio been dining with Essex's mother? But that was impossible. Was it an omen? Were the fates joining hands to urge him to write a play about Julius Caesar? Florio was waiting for Oxford to say something. "You want Essex assassinated?" Oxford asked.

"Oh, no, your lordship. I only suggest a play to show the man I tutor that he should not hitch his star to someone who is certain to fall."

"He is your best pupil, is he not?"

Florio nodded.

"He is perhaps more than that? A son to you?"

Florio nodded again, albeit somewhat reluctantly. "His father paid no attention to him, my lord, and then died when the earl was only eight."

"But Lord Burghley surely acted as his father while the earl was a royal ward in Cecil House, didn't he?"

Florio's face went into contortions. He might be willing to speak poorly of Essex but would not risk offending Lord Burghley under any circumstances, even though he was dead. His son, Sir Robert, now ruled.

Oxford smiled. He knew why Florio had suddenly gone silent. "I will speak to Master Shackspear."

"Thank you, my lord." He got up. "Until next time," he said.

"Arrivederci," Oxford said.

"Arrivederci," Florio replied.

Oxford's use of the Italian was a gentle hand on Florio's shoulder. Taller than when he came in, the little man went out the front door.

Oxford sat back. Surrey had urged him to pick up his pen again. Now, Lady Lettice *and* John Florio had urged him to write *the same play!* "A pity I do not believe in the gods," Oxford said into the empty room, "be they Christian or Roman. But perhaps I should imagine their existence. After all, I have now twice been visited by a dead earl. Imagining the gods urging me to return to writing plays should be easy. I'll write a scene or two and see how it goes down.'

~ 162 ~
Finley

"Yer lordship," Nigel announced, coming into Oxford's study. "A boy has brought a message from a man named Finley which states that this Finley is within a few miles of Hackney and he would like to stop by and meet with you."

"Finley!" Oxford exclaimed, getting up from the table where he was working on *Julius Caesar*. Things had been very quiet since John Florio had visited King's Place. Weeks had passed with nothing more than the slow passage of the sun to mark them. Her ladyship labored away in her garden; Henry had found friends in the village and busied himself with building castles of mud and bricks. Oxford had withdrawn to work on his latest play. In short, it was *very* quiet. All good for the writing of plays and dozing on the porch Ross and Angus had built him off his study, but Oxford was hungry for news. Finley would surely bring some. "But why a messenger?" Oxford asked Nigel. "Finley does not travel in such state that he would have had a messenger precede him."

"Perhaps because his form of transportation is a mule. The boy said as much."

"A mule?" Nigel nodded. Oxford smiled. "Have him into the Day Room when he arrives, if you would, please."

<hr>

It was not more than an hour before Nigel brought news Finley had arrived. He had placed him in the Day Room. Oxford went downstairs and found the tall, gangly man waiting of him.

"My dear Finley," Oxford said, coming up to him.

"My lord," Finley said, bowing stiffly.

"My steward tells me you travel by mule now."

"I do, my lord. I visited Cecil House on one of my earlier trips to London where I found Lord Burghley surveying his extensive gardens from a mule. I asked him about it to be courteous and he launched into an animated explanation of why he preferred the mule to a horse. He told me it never complained and it cost him little to maintain. He also said it was low to the ground so that he could slide on or off with ease, something he appreciated as he aged and his joints became stiffer. Being long-legged myself, and without a great deal of money, I found his observations valuable. I thought a mule would do me well in my travels back and forth to London and bought one before I left. I must say, it is carriage suitable for one such as myself, an academic prone to dreaming as I travel up and back to Cambridge."

"And which direction are you now headed."

"To Cambridge, my lord."

"Oh, good. Have you news of London, then."

"I do, my lord."

"Seat thyself and stay." Oxford pointed to two chairs over against a wall. Nigel brought a lemon drink in for them as it was an uncommonly hot day. He placed it on a small table inlaid with different exotic woods.

Finley picked up his drink and took a sip. "Oh, that's jolly good," he said, putting it back down. "The road is dusty."

"And the news?"

"A book has been published by Frances Meres called *Palladis Tamia*. In it, he describes authors who have written works recently. Its subtitle is: *'A Comparative Discourse of our English Poets with the Greek, Latin, and Italian Poets'*.

"How good is it?"

"He steals from others and presents it as his own. He praises the queen as a patron and poet but his honeyed words are taken whole cloth from Puttenham."

"His *Arte of English Poesie*."

Finley nodded. "You would be interested in knowing he lists twelve plays as Shackspear's, as well as 'sugared sonnets among his private friends.'"

"Twelve plays," Oxford repeated. "And sonnets!" He frowned. "I heard he knew about them. He tried to get Shackspear to talk about them, but Mumblemouth couldn't, of course, because he's never even seen them. Does this Meres explain how he knows about them?"

"No. However, Meres is John Florio's brother, my lord." Oxford hadn't known that. "And connected through marriage to Sir Robert."

Oxford exploded. Robert had sent Florio to Hackney to spy on him. "Of course! The bastards time their entrances to drag out my suffering and make my humiliation complete!"

Finley disagreed. "My lord, it is but temporary. The world will soon realize Shackspear did not write your plays."

"I do not have your optimism, my friend. In fact, I am becoming more and more certain I will never be recognized as their author. Sir Robert has made it clear he will continue his father's vendetta against me. He intends to fill books with lies and grind me down, so that when I die, nothing will be left of me."

"Oh, no, my lord. The truth will out!"

"No, it won't, because those who know I wrote the plays will die, leaving behind lying books, resting smugly on library shelves, waiting for virgin eyes to open them and exclaim 'oh, Shackspear wrote this!"

Finley was alarmed at Oxford's state. He decided he should change the subject. "You might better appreciate news that the Earl of Essex has agreed to go to Ireland to resolve Her Majesty's problems there."

Oxford looked at Finley in amazement. "How stupid can that man be? Doesn't he know Sir Robert is the one urging his 'advancement' whilst hoping Essex never comes back from Ireland? I, at least, know who's stabbing me in the back."

"At least he will be away."

"Yes. That will have some value. What else can ye report?"

"A woman has been arrested for slanderous words about the queen and will no doubt be hung at Tyburn before Christmas."

"For saying what?"

"That the queen had three bastards by noblemen of the court, and that Her Majesty was herself base born."

"No."

"Yes. The woman claims she was merely repeating words she heard spoken by a man who, of course, has denied he ever said them. He has also fled. His friends object that women are base creatures and of no credit. She's in the Counter. No one is willing to wait till the man is found and can be confronted. She is to the gibbet."

"Good lord," Oxford said.

"And Southampton has been sent to the Fleet."

"Wherefore?" Oxford asked. "He went to France with Sir Robert, didn't he?"

"He did, but stayed in Paris when Sir Robert came back. He returned secretly in August to marry Elizabeth Vernon, who is carrying his child."

"*No.*" This was almost a cry.

"Yes. After which, he immediately returned to Paris. Someone told the queen, of course. She ordered him home. He dragged his feet but has finally come back. She immediately put him in the Fleet."

Oxford groaned.

"He's done the honorable thing, my lord. Ms. Vernon complained not of foul play and said the earl would justify it, and he has."

That may be true, Oxford thought, but he was saddened that 'his son', like so many hot-blooded young men before him, had let his choice of who he married be determined by an act of lust. Perhaps Oxford, thought, he was better off sitting in Hackney ignorant of what was going on in the world.

Finley had more. "Philip, King of Spain, died September 13."

"No. May he rest in peace. He was Bloody Mary's husband and did England a great service when he recommended the Privy Council accept Elizabeth as Mary's successor, even though Elizabeth was Protestant and not Catholic."

"I didn't know that."

"Not many people do. He didn't care much for religion while he was here. He was only a prince at the time, with no idea of whether or when he would become King of Spain. Had he not put a word in for Elizabeth, a lot of people would have died in the struggle to determine who should succeed Mary."

"But he sent the Armada to unseat her when he became king, didn't he?"

"He became more religious as he got older. The Pope convinced him he owed God for giving away England. I was eight when Mary died but I met Philip twice, once at Hedingham, when he visited my father, and once in St. James Palace on the Mall. When I visited him at St. James, he had a painting of *Venus & Adonis* in his chambers. He took it with him when he returned to Spain. I saw a copy of it in Venice. The copy had a bonnet on Adonis' head."

"Ah," Finley said. "The poem you wrote about Venus' pursuit of Adonis:

He sees her coming, and begins to glow,
Even as a dying coal revives with wind,
<u>And with his bonnet hides his angry brow;</u>

"I thought you were devoted to plays, my friend," Oxford said.

"To poetry, my lord. Aren't your plays poetry? But thank you for this. The bonnet has been much discussed at Cambridge. I didn't know about the copy in Venice having a bonnet. The original in Spain lacks it. This detail, although about a poem, shows us that each and every word is important. Thank you, my lord."

Oxford smiled.

"And there is news about Ben Jonson."

Oxford's eyes narrowed. "What about Ben Jonson?"

"He has killed another man."

"Another? Who was the first?"

"He killed a Spanish soldier in single combat, I am told, whilst serving in the Low Countries."

"And now?"

"Gabriel Spenser."

"Gabriel Spenser? Oh, no. Gabriel was gifted. He didn't play kings and dukes; he played servants and hangers-on. It is a special craft, needed to flesh out a story but not upstage a Burbage or an Alleyn. How did he die?"

"Jonson ran him through. They got into an argument in a pub and took the dispute to Hogsden Fields, where Jonson killed him."

"What happened then?" Oxford asked. He was hoping Jonson was dead, killed by Spenser or executed for murder. He recalled the Earl of Surrey warning him about Jonson.

"He pleaded benefit of clergy and avoided the gallows."

"By reciting the neck verse," Oxford said dismissively. "*Miserere mei, Deus, secundum misericordiam tuam.* Anyone recites it walks free."

"Fewer than before, my lord. Some have learned to memorize it before they appear in court. They run the risk of being taken before a suspicious judge who may ask them to read a different verse."

Oxford laughed. "Pray tell me this happened to Jonson."

"It did, my lord. He was enraged that someone might think he could not read. He grabbed the clerk who was holding the Good Book and tried to tear his head off. The bailiffs had to restrain him. Insulted, he read an entire page and then tried to throw the Bible on the ground.

For this, he was rewarded with a *very* black 'M' burned into the back of his thumb."

"He was, perhaps, '*out of his humour*,'" Oxford suggested.

"Oh, well said, my lord," Finley chuckled. "And you, my lord? Who takes down your words? I don't see anyone who has replaced Robin."

Oxford shrugged. "I have no one. John Marston worked with me for a while but he has his own works to present to the world. John Lyly too but, as you can tell, little of the theater world comes this far from London."

"John Lyly is very busy, my lord, that is true. He has obtained a commission to organize an event at Chiswick for the queen on her progress through Kent. He has funds and control over what the entertainment will be. He intends to write a masque for it. He finally feels appreciated by Her Majesty."

"Good for him," Oxford said.

"Yes. But, without Robin, how do you get on?"

"Very well, thank you. I am my own audience. I ask questions aloud I would have asked Robin; I answer them myself. Nigel must think me daft. Timson takes no notice."

"How is it working out?"

"Surprisingly well. I like myself. I like my answers. The plays I am working on do not call for clever plot twists or outrageous characters. They are bones stripped of flesh. I know what I must write from here on out."

"More plays," Finley said, nodding hopefully.

"And your efforts at Cambridge? How is that getting on?"

"Ongoing, my lord. Ongoing."

"Stay the night, Finley. It is coming on dark. Your mule will be well-taken care of."

~ **163** ~
Christmas

Christmas was quiet at King's Place. Lady Elspeth had taken Henry and Tater to her brother's estate in Staffordshire. Oxford declined to go with them, claiming he had work to do but, truth be told, he was like a ship back from a long voyage who, left unmoored, had drifted up onto a sandbank. A cook borrowed from a nearby house fed Oxford and the servants who remained.

In the stillness, Oxford thought he could hear the two-hundred-year-old mortar in the stable walls cracking as it dried. To escape, he had taken to having a horse saddled for him in the afternoon and riding out toward the east. It was while walking the horse out of the stable that he first thought he heard mortar drying. He would pause to listen, but the breath of the horse obscured whatever he was trying to hear.

He rode toward Waltham and Epping. He forced himself to look into the distance to exercise his eyes which had begun to bother him from so many years spent peering at papers lit only by candlelight. The papers his quill scurried across were reused butcher papers because good paper was too expensive for all the drafts it took to come up with a script. Foul papers, indeed, he had thought more than once, as he tried to write across a smear of fat left on a wrapper from the bacon it had carried into the kitchen.

The drying mortar, or whatever he thought he was hearing, contributed to his sense that something was awry and why he had stayed behind to be alone in King's Place over Christmas. He began to wonder if it might be the barrier that separated the living from the dead. Was there a barrier, he asked himself. Could it leak? Oxford had been convinced the Earl of Surrey was alive when he appeared in Billesley, head in hand, and more recently in Hackney after Burghley died, but was he? How could a headless man be alive? Or even *seem* to be alive?

Oxford knew he was not sure of what he had seen because he realized immediately that he could not tell Elspeth about Surrey's visit. He didn't think she would laugh at him; he worried she would think him mad. Was he?

He had never given any credence to stories about people coming back from the other side. When yer dead, yer dead, he liked to say. He

377

had used the fear others felt to taunt them. Arundel and Howard were horrified when Oxford told them he had been visited by his stepfather one night, whip in hand. The man who had taken over his father's duties in his mother's bed had been dead nine years when Oxford told the tale, standing in front of a flickering fireplace, snapping a whip over his head. But Oxford knew he had made up that story.

The horseback rides invigorated him and restored some sense of balance but Christmas was lonely. It was the dark time of year. The loss of light affected him, and when night descended over the house, the candles lit by the servants did not offset the darkness.

The next day, Boxing Day, was no better. Nor the next, except that Falstaff suddenly appeared in the forenoon. The big man had arrived in Hackney in a dog cart, legs splayed, arms akimbo, as if he were one of Marlowe's pampered jades inspecting his kingdoms. Tupp led the dog pulling the cart. He was wearing a scarlet jacket and matching hat, shaped like a round hat box.

All of Hackney was aware of the cart's progress as it came off North Street. The wheels were emitting a horrible scraping noise. It was so loud that people came out of their homes and shops with their hands over their ears. They were astonished that the big man in the cart and the boy leading it seemed to be unaware of the awful sound coming from the wheels.

Oxford and Tobias came out of King's Place to find out what was making all the racket. The cart came to a halt in front of them and the awful sound stopped.

"Yer lordship," Falstaff said, heaving himself out of the dogcart. A young man from down the road ran up with a bucket of pig grease. Falstaff made a vague gesture that the young man took as permission to grease the wheels, one of which was smoking slightly.

"Jack. I joy at seeing you," Oxford called out.

This was more than Falstaff had expected, considering that he had not sent word he was coming and hadn't seen Oxford in months. Falstaff bowed. "Tupp and I would like to spend the night, my lord, if you please, and," here he reached back into the dogcart to pull out a large hamper, "give you a present on Boxing Day."

"It is not Boxing Day," Oxford said. "It's the day after Boxing Day."

Falstaff showed no surprise at this. "And what of that?" he said. "Does Time make any difference to me? No. I live on Heavenly chimes. Others must have calendars and holidays and feast days to know when those days are, and so a perfectly usable day becomes burdened with being called Christmas or All Hallows Eve or Boxing Day, whilst all the rest are relegated to workdays. How does this affect me?" he went on expansively, still standing in the street, the villagers looking on from down the road who were trying to hear what he was saying. "On Boxing Day, all the pubs are full. The Boar's Head is full. Oh, excuse me, yer lordship, the *new* Boar's Head is full. This is good for us, my lord – us being Peaches and me – but it means I have to devote myself to my dooties at the inn on Boxing Day. And the holidays that crowd January are coming up, so I said to Peaches, you take care of the inn for a few days, honeybun. I need catch up with his lordship."

"Thank ye, Jack," Oxford said. He turned to Tupp. "And welcome, Tupp." Tupp gave him a blank stare. "*Bienvenue,*" Oxford added.

Tupp's face lit up. "*Merci, monsieur. Et grâce à vous pour nous donne un abrit pour la nuit.*" He glanced up at the sky, which looked like it was going to rain.

"*Pas de quoi,*" Oxford said. Tobias came out into the walled forecourt from his lodge. "Tobias, please take the dogcart into the stables and settle it for the night. Come," he said, gesturing to Falstaff and Tupp.

<hr>

Falstaff brought supper with him, a pot roast and a truffle pie, which Timson snugged into the coals in the fireplace. While the meal warmed, Oxford broke out a bottle of Carbonnieux and filled two glasses. Tupp made a face; Oxford got a third glass for him.

"His English hasn't improved since I bought him," Falstaff complained, as he tossed off the Carbonnieux.

"Jack!" Oxford exclaimed, shocked at Falstaff drinking off a wine that was made to be savored. Falstaff ignored Oxford and held out his glass for more.

"I think the little bugger is trying to get me to speak French! Moi!" Falstaff said. "Can ye believe that!"

Oxford refilled Falstaff's glass but put the bottle out of Falstaff's reach. "Peaches is doing well?"

Falstaff grinned. "Can't get enough of me. When she's not working."

"At the new Boar's Head?"

"Aye. She hires and fires and cooks and serves. She does it all. The woman never stops. I, on the other hand, need time for composition."

He nodded gravely, indicating Oxford understood. Oxford did not. "Even more so now that I'm famous," he added, tilting his head back to show what he thought was his leonine profile.

"Famous? How?"

"*As meself!*" Falstaff cried out. "Everyone loves me - *The Big Man!* They come from the provinces to engage me in dialogue."

"Part One, or Part Two?"

Falstaff frowned. "Part One, ye traitor. Ye set me down in Part Two and killed me in *Henry V*. And *Merry Wives?*" He snorted and twisted back and forth as if a fit was coming on. Oxford thought he looked like a bull about to break out of its pen.

"It must be so trying, being famous."

Falstaff came to rest, suggesting once again that what looked like a fit was nothing more than performance. "He's never not onstage," a woman had commented after seeing him in *Henry IV*.

"Not as long as it pays," Falstaff said, instantly calmed by the thought of how successful he now was. "They come into the inn with their money and leave without it. Peaches loves me for it."

The thought of being mobbed by people one didn't know, Oxford thought, would be horror for him. Perhaps there was some benefit in being anonymous after all.

"Can't say there's not much on the boards, my lord. The most recent is *The Triangle of Cuckolds* by Thomas Dekker, a retelling of a retelling of a story everyone has heard before."

"I was told the Theatre sits empty, the lease having run out and Burbage and Giles Allen being at an impasse. Can that be true?"

"Aye, true it is. And Giles has made a huge mistake. He has gone home for the holidays." He winked. "Word is that Burbage and the Chamberlain's Men are going to take down the Theatre and drag the pieces across the Thames to rebuild it in Southwark. They're going to call it the Globe."

"Can they do that?"

"Burbage says the lease entitles him to the timbers. His lawyers tell him he's exercising his right to self-help. He asked *me* to help with the move. I told him I only perform *on* the boards; I don't *carry* them." He laughed.

"And Shackspear?"

"Gone to Stratford. He wants nothing to do with moving the Theatre. Something about his family needing him, he said."

"Henslowe won't like a new theater next to the Rose.'"

"No. But he can't do anything about it. Judge Gardiner is dead and, with the Swan closed, the Privy Council won't care."

"What else?"

"Ben Jonson killed Gabriel Spenser and has been released."

"I heard."

"But not that Ben was visited by Sir Robert Cecil while he was in Newgate." Falstaff cast an eye at Oxford. "BJ, as some are calling him now, thinks very highly of himself. *Every Man In his Humour* did well enough that he's got a new play rehearsing at the Curtain. This one he's going to call *Every Man Out of his Humour*."

"*Out* of *his* Humour?"

"*In his Humour* was about city folk in a town in Italy. This one is to be about people we might know. He wants to be the playwright paramount. He's resentful of anyone who might compete with him. Marston is at the top of his list. They've been at each other. Throwing mugs across the Mermaid."

"And?" Oxford asked.

"And?" Falstaff asked, trying to look like he didn't know what Oxford was talking about. "Oh, aye," he said: "The Earl of Southampton. I was comin' to that." He drained his glass and held it out for a refill. Tupp was barely visible, his head just above the table, sipping the wine in his glass. He had seen Oxford's reaction to Falstaff emptying his glass and was lingering over his in case Oxford decided not to refill it.

"Truth is," Falstaff said as he retrieved his glass from Oxford, "ye must now mention Essex in the same breath as Southampton, for the boy has affixed himself to the earl's arse. Essex will be leaving for Ireland soon and Southampton'll be going with him."

"But what about whether he's the queen's son?" Oxford asked.

Falstaff sighed. "Still nothin. I've bought many a pint for a sailor who said he was with him on *The Garland*, or for a soldier who fought with him in the Lowlands. Even prisoners in the Counter when the queen sent him there for marrying Elizabeth Vernon! Do ye think any of 'em saw his excellency in his raw onions? Huh? Do ye know how delicate ye have to be to inquire about whether a member of the noble class has anything unusual on his body? When ye don't even know *what* it is or *where* it is? In Portsmouth, I had a bailiff with the gimlet eye of a Puritan asking me what I was up to. Ye've given me an impossible task."

"What about his doctors?"

"He doesn't go to any."

"Has he been to Bath to take the spa treatment?"

"Ye want me to give him something that'll make him go there?"

"No. No." Oxford was blocked. "Ye'll keep tryin', though?"

"Aye. Aye. For the love of Michael, or some other sort."

1599

164

The Theatre Tiptoes Away

Christmas for the lawyers came in January. That's when the lawsuits were filed over the removal of the Theatre to Southwark. Pried apart and muscled onto sleds, the bones of the first theater in London were slid down to the frozen Thames and rebuilt across the river next to the Rose. *They took my theatre,'* Giles Allen's lawyers thundered. *'We took the timbers!* Burbage's replied. The case, with its demurrers and motions, moved off into the future like a thunderstorm that had expended all its lightning and noise.

The demise of the Theatre pleased the Privy Council, which could finally report that a theater in the City had been closed. They ignored its replacement rising across the Thames in Southwark. One was gone; the other, well, it had a different name, didn't it? And was it really going to be a theater? It must be something else.

In all this confusion, the death of Edward Spenser, Britain's poet laureate to those who didn't know Ben Jonson, went almost unnoticed. Spenser was buried in Westminster Abbey. Oxford claimed lameness to avoid the service, but he wouldn't have come if he'd been healthy. He had fought Spenser to prevent English poetry from being turned into a rigid, clunking hexameter dead-end. Spenser himself had described his poetry as *cloudily enwrapped in allegorical devises*, a form of art that was so dull his death was almost lost in the vitriol being exchanged between Jonson and Marston.

The queen hardly mentioned Spenser's passing, despite his years of toil in writing *The Fairy Queen*, an homage to her. Ben Jonson said Spenser had died for "want of bread," which was a scurrilous remark to make, considering that the queen had granted Spenser a pension. This type of cutting remark was becoming typical of the new Jonson, who was intent on denigrating anyone who might be compared to him, dead or alive. Someone, possibly John Marston, claimed that the other poets threw their failures and unedited foul copies into Spenser's grave in the hope that it might cleanse their writings of shortcomings. It was the time of the biting epigram.

Shackspear – a sharer in the Globe – talked Burbage into staging *Julius Caesar* as the first play presented there. The premiere was an enormous success. It didn't rain. Everyone turned out, including the Earl of Essex and his ever-present companion, the Earl of Southampton. They and their followers were wallowing in the attention they were receiving as they prepared to cross over to Ireland and put an end to the 'Irish Problem.'

The audience appreciated the battles and great writing but began to wonder what was going on when Caesar was assassinated midway through the play. What had begun as a play about Julius Caesar turned into a play about Brutus and Cassius.

"What were you trying to do here, Master Shackspear?" the puzzled theatergoers asked Shackspear as they streamed past him toward the boats bobbing on the Thames a short distance away. Shackspear had no idea, of course, not having written the play. In fact, he had not even *helped* write this one. The script had arrived from Hackney a week before in a leather pouch embossed with a boar's head. Shackspear and Burbage immediately realized that Caesar could not die in the middle of a play entitled *Julius Caesar* but did not have the time to rewrite it. 'Improving' *The Jew of Venice* had only required heaping ignominies on Shylock at the end. *JC*, as Burbage nicknamed it, could not be reshaped in the short time they had.

Oxford thought everyone would recognize Caesar as Elizabeth and Brutus as Southampton and Cassius as Essex, but no one came away with that message. Elizabeth had not attended the play, of course, there being no secret box in The Globe. She stayed at Richmond and missed Oxford's warning. Essex, for his part, fell in love with Caesar straight away, despite Caesar dying in the middle of the play.

Oxford was amazed when he heard how *Julius Caesar* had been received; but then, he had to remind himself how surprised he had been when *Titus Andronicus* had become Shackspear's first triumph instead of sending him back to Stratford.

"Too bloody subtle!" Lettice Knollys announced as she came out of The Globe, her remark being uttered loud enough for her son to hear. He knew his mother was trying to bank his fires but could care less. He strode past her towing Southampton, Blount, Mountjoy, and a growing band of earls and knights who thought they were hitching themselves to a star. Essex and his followers headed off to celebrate their impending glory in the new Boar's Head on Canterbury Road. His mother repaired across the River to Essex House where she wrote a scathing letter to Oxford that was delivered the next afternoon.

⁙
ㄚ

165

Far Fly Thy Name

You were not aware?"

"No, Robert."

Sir Robert Cecil frowned. Oxford had used Robert's Christian name to remind him the status of an earl far exceeded that of a knight. "He was your secretary at one point, wasn't he?"

"He was, but John Marston left my service many years ago. As you know from the acrimonious debates he is having with Ben Jonson, he is no longer the timid, God-fearing boy who took Robin's place. He does not consult with me before he publishes something he writes."

Sir Robert wasn't convinced. "You had no part in *A Scourge of Villainy?*"

"I did not."

Sir Robert was intent on quoting from it nevertheless.

> *Far fly thy fame,* Marston claims *he* wrote,
> *Most, most of me beloved! whose silent name*
> *One letter bounds. Thy true judicial style*
> *I ever honour; and, if my love beguile*
> *Not much my hopes, then thy unvalued worth*
> *Shall mount fair place, when apes are turnèd forth.*

Oxford suppressed a smile. He thought the first line should have been *Far Fly Thy Name* but 'fame' was necessary given what followed.

Sir Robert squinted at Oxford. "*Most of me beloved! Whose silent name one letter bounds?*"

Oxford's face remained expressionless.

Sir Robert was convinced Oxford had something to do with Marson's poem. "Who is he talking about? Who does he - Marston - love most? Whose name *one letter bounds?*"

"*Whose silent name one letter bounds,*" Oxford pointed out.

"You!" Sir Robert said, solving the puzzle. "*Edward de Vere!*"

Oxford was becoming irritated. "Ask him, if you must"

"I will. The Council and the queen consider this flinging about of insults inappropriate. It must stop. And the not-very-well-hidden allusions to a certain lord, …"

"Who will *mount fair place, when <u>apes</u> are turnèd forth?*" Oxford said. This stopped Sir Robert.

"Shackspear?"

"And *fair?*" Oxford said. "Sounds like *Vere*, doesn't it?" Oxford had decided to have fun.

Sir Robert's frown deepened. "I do not regret having failed to master how to slip hidden meanings into poetry or normal discourse."

"You search for conspiracy, Sir Robert, where none exists. If authors are tongue-tied by authority, they will perforce slip in clues as to who the true author is, no matter what the Privy Council does. For example:

> *Thou, which deluding raisest up a fame*
> *And having showed the man, concealest his name.*
> *Whose good we praise, as being liked of all,*
> *Whose ill we bear as being natural,*
> *Thou which art made of vinegar and gall …*
> *Cease, write no more to aggravate thy sin.*

"Thomas Bastard," Oxford said, "in his collection of epigrams published as *Chrestoleros.*"

Sir Robert had never heard of Thomas Bastard. He was becoming exasperated with Oxford. "I must be blunt, my lord. There will be no 'mounting up' for you, no matter what the 'ape' does."

"And for those, like John Marston, who will continue to proclaim truth, no matter how hard Her Majesty's minions try to suppress it?"

"Marston's writings will be suppressed. The archbishop is working on it. Marston's diatribes constitute offenses against morality. His books will be publicly burned, as well as the writings of others."

"What others?"

"John Hayward."

"Ah. Sent to the Tower for *The Life and Reign of Henry IV.*"

"Yes. And, rest assured, he will remain there. There hath been much descanting about why he would write a story about Henry IV, with a dedication to the Earl of Essex, whom he praises highly."

"This 'descanting' includes the queen?"

"It does, my lord. She believes that Hayward, writing under the guise of creating a treatise on history was, in fact, hinting at what might befall the queen. Bacon is on it."

"A formidable hunting dog, to put on it."

"Aye. Order will be restored." Sir Robert missed the 'dog' reference, which tied Bacon to *The Isle of Dogs*. Oxford was trying to remember the type of dog that had represented Bacon. Sir Robert was still smarting from being represented by a mutt, a classification based on his father, Lord Burghley, a relatively recent arrival in the aristocracy, having been knighted and made baron during his lifetime.

"Yet *Richard II* has gone through three printings this year," Oxford said. "Why is it that Hayward is in the Tower whilst Shackspear is allowed to wander the streets of London? Indeed, why am *I* still walking around?"

Sir Robert glared at Oxford. "You know she can't put you in the Tower for writing plays. If she did, she would be admitting you wrote them."

Oxford, disgusted, lowered his voice. "Then let us talk about you and me. I urged you to seek out Colin Sanderson to confirm that he was never one of my retainers and I was not the reason you could not marry the woman you loved. Your father was the cause. He secured Sanderson a parsonage far from London to induce him to marry the maid."

"Port Isaac," Sir Robert said. "Yes, he confirmed what you told me. My father lied to me."

He went silent for a moment. His face flooded with grief, like an incoming morning tide running across the flats behind Mersea Island. Robert had worshipped his father. The scullery maid had faded to a dim memory, but the loss of faith in his father hurt him.

"He did what he thought was right for you, Robert," Oxford said quietly. "Perhaps you and I can put this behind us."

Sir Robert regained control of himself. His father may have tricked him but Oxford didn't know that he had knelt beside his sister's tomb and promised he would make Oxford pay for how he had treated her. His ardor for the maid may have faded, but not the loyalty he felt toward his sister, Nan. "Perhaps," was all he said.

They were standing in a large corridor outside the hall where Oxford's second daughter, Bridget, had just married Baron Rycote. Oxford had not wanted to attend because it forced him to admit once again that he had 'nothing' to give his daughter as a marriage portion.

Sir Robert also wished he were somewhere else but had to attend because he had become the guardian of Oxford's daughters when Lord Burghley died.

The ceremony in the hall ended. The wedding train came winding its way into the corridor. Bridget had her hand on the arm of her new husband. She stopped next to her father.

"My Lord of Oxenford," she said, pronouncing each syllable of her father's name clearly. "No play?"

The people in the hallway paused. Their eyes glazed as their ears strained. They stilled even their heartbeats lest they miss what was said by the new baroness and her father.

"I was not informed of the date of your wedding in time to write one," Oxford said lamely.

Bridget tilted her head back. The disdain in her voice was audible down the hallway. "I am made of the self-same metal that my sister is, my lord. You graced her wedding with *A Midsummer' Night's Dream*. You couldn't find time to grace my wedding with a play? No matter; it wouldn't have been for me anyway. *Midsummer* was written for the queen, as all your plays are."

The wedding party and the guests were scarcely breathing. Some wished they were elsewhere, but everyone wanted to hear more, inveterate gossips as they all were. Bridget did not disappoint them.

"T'was sweet when you were younger, my lord. She was only seventeen years older than you then. She's still only seventeen years older than you are." She smiled, a look usually seen only on the face of a cat as it is about to snatch a goldfinch off a feeder. "Better hurry up."

She turned to continue down the corridor. In a voice loud enough for all to hear, she said to her new husband: "'Tis not the infirmity of age, my husband: he hath ever but slenderly known himself."

The guests trailed off like smoke on a windy day. Sir Robert had disappeared as well, slipping into an adjoining room.

Elspeth came up and put her arm through her husband's. Oxford turned to her. "I wish you had never made me come," he said. Elspeth smiled. "Trust me; it would have been worse if you had stayed away."

Every Man Out of His Humour

The Earl of Derby stood up as the wherry carrying him approached the landing for Cannon Row. The Thames was full of boats in the late afternoon sunshine. A pair of swans, heads held back, hurried out from under the bow of Derby's boat with as much dignity as they could muster. Derby readied himself to disembark when another boat ran into his.

"I say!" he called out, holding onto the standing bar as the two boats rolled back and forth from the collision. A slim man leapt onto Derby's boat.

"Gudday, yer lordship," the man cried out, swiping Derby's arm with a roll of legal papers he dropped into the bottom of the boat.

"Oh, bother," Derby said, as the man jumped back into his boat.

Derby's boat reached the landing. Oxford was waiting for him. Derby reached up, took his hand, and stepped onto the landing.

"Apparitors, no doubt," Oxford said, as the two of them walked off the landing onto dry land. "And how does your garden grow, William? I speak of plants now, not lawsuits."

"Very well, my lord. I will show you."

They walked up a lane away from the river. Derby House lay to the right, one of a half-dozen houses on Cannon Row that had been built on the slight rise of ground along the Thames north of Whitehall. The earls of Sussex, Hereford, Lincoln, and Derby had their London homes here. Derby and Oxford went through a gate and down an allée lined by boxwood to reach a series of terraces that fell away to the river. The terraces provided a maze in the first one, vegetables in the second, and flowers in the third, which Lisbeth, Oxford's daughter and now Countess of Derby, had demanded she have at all times.

"My Lady Lisbeth is on the Isle of Man sorting business there for me. The apparitors are constantly after me because I inherited the island from my brother but his widow is contesting the will. Ergo, the lawsuits and process servers."

"Lisbeth agreed to leave London?"

"Not at first, but when she learned she would be unfettered in governing the island - it is a personal possession, my lord, not a Crown colony - she could not resist being queen of an island, even one located in the Irish Sea. I insisted she go. It gets her away from temptation here, if you know what I mean."

"I do. And the play?" Oxford asked. He was inquiring as to Derby's opinion of Jonson's newest play.

"Most extraordinary," Derby said. "Jonson's first play – *Every Man in His Humour* – was an attempt to create interest in uninteresting people. Setting the play in Italy did not save it for me."

"And this one?"

"Completely different. *Every Man Out of His Humour* is a play that attacks playwrights and poets here in London who Jonson doesn't like. The characters are thinly veiled and easy to identify."

"Such as?"

"Marston, for example. He's Clove, twin to a brother named Orange, inserted for what Jonson thinks is humor of the laughing kind, of which he possesses none, and to infuriate your former secretary."

"John will retaliate."

"He is already working on a reply."

"Indeed," Oxford said. "And the rest?"

"I took notes." Here Derby opened a slim leather folder and pulled out some pages. "Jonson's blast against Marston is nothing compared to what he says about Shackspear, Shackspear's brother, and others."

"How so?"

"First, a character named Sogliardo is described as *an essential clown, so enamoured of the name of a gentleman, that he will have it, though he buys it.*"

"And does he?"

"For £30, my lord. The amount Shackspear paid for his. Then there is Sordido, described as Sogliardo's brother, who is *a wretched hob-nailed chuff, whose recreation is reading of almanacks; and who never pray'd but for a lean dearth, and ever wept in a fat harvest.*"

This puzzled Oxford. "Shackspear's brother is a haberdasher on Three Needle Street. It's not his brother. It's his father. John hoarded grain and wears hob-nailed boots. He prays for a poor harvest to drive up the price of corn." He looked at Derby. "Am I in this play?"

"Very much so. Puntarvolo," Derby said. He read from his notes.

> *A vain-glorious knight, over-englishing his travels, and wholly*
> *consecrated to singularity; the very Jacob's staff of compliment;*
> *a sir that hath lived to see the revolution of time in most of his*
> *apparel. Of presence good enough, but so palpably affected to*
> *his own praise, that for want of flatterers he commends himself,*
> *to the floutage of his own family. He deals upon returns, and*
> *strange performances, resolving, in despite of public derision, to*
> *stick to his own fashion, phrase, and gesture.*

Oxford face turned dark.

"Sogliardo asks another character what Puntarvolo is like. *Shun him as you would the plague*, he is told. Sogliardo asks why: *Is he a scholar, or a soldier?*

> *Both, both; 'ware how you offend him; he carries oil and fire in*
> *his pen, will scald where it drops: his spirit is like powder,*
> *quick, violent; he'll blow a man up with a jest. Away, come not*
> *near him!*

"This could be anyone," Oxford said. "John Lyly, Marston."

"Not after you learn Puntarvolo talks to his horse." This caught Oxford's attention. In *Woodstock*, he had created a character who had a long conversation with a horse. "And when Puntarvolo comes home, he stands in front of his house and, when his wife comes to the window, Puntarvolo asks if the master of the house is at home. Mark, he's talking to his wife but acting like she's someone else. She knows he's her husband but pretends she knows him not. *Therein lies the syrup of the jest*, an onlooker says."

Oxford drew back. He had once, on a lark, tried to climb into Elspeth's window one night when he was imagining himself a knight errant and she a lady in distress. She knew who he was. Nevertheless, she pushed over the ladder he was standing on, sending him into the garden below. Jonson must have heard about this.

"So, what is this play about?" Oxford asked.

"A wager. Puntarvolo announces that he plans on spending £5,000 to voyage out to Istanbul with his dog and cat and safely return. He wagers that if he is successful, he will gain £25,000!"

Oxford blinked. "This is me?"

"The dog is very expensive, my lord. Puntarvolo gives him to a porter to hold for a while but the porter loses the dog."

"Loses him?" Oxford sat up. "That cheeky bastard. This is a send-up of Launce and Crab in *Two Gentlemen of Verona*. Launce was supposed to take a dog to Silvia but lost him!"

"Worse," Derby said. "In Jonson's play, someone *kills* the dog."

Oxford looked away.

"And *any* doubt Jonson is aiming at you disappears when Sogliardo returns with his new coat of arms." Derby shuffled the papers in his hands. "Sogliardo announces he can now write himself gentleman. He describes his coat of arms. Puntarvolo does not understand. Sogliardo says, *Marry, sir, it is your boar without a head, rampant.*

"A boar without a head? Rampant?"

Derby nodded, trying not to laugh. "One of the other characters says; *I commend the herald's wit, he has decyphered him well: a swine without a head, without brain, wit, anything indeed, ramping to gentility.* Another character says *'Slud, it's a hog's cheek and puddings in a pewter field, this.*

"And what is Puntarvolo's reaction, pray tell?"

"*Let the word be, 'Not without mustard': your crest is very rare, sir.*"

Oxford started to smile. "And how did Shackspear react?"

"He thought it was funny. After all, he did buy arms and does claim he is a gentleman. He thinks Jonson is making a sly allusion to him, which only puffs up his feathers. What he doesn't get is that Jonson is telling the world that Shackspear is nothing more than a swine without a head because you write the plays."

"So, why is Jonson doing this?"

"He thinks you wrote *Shackspear is Shakespeare; Johnson is Jonson.* Every time he walks into a pub, he hears it. He knows Shackspear couldn't have written it. Since you give Shackspear plays, Jonson thinks you gave him the poem."

"Marston must have written it."

"Aye, but Jonson thinks you're the author. He's a violent man, my lord. Be best to avoid him." Oxford bristled. Derby continued. "But Burbage is upset because he also thinks *Every Man Out* is saying that you wrote the plays Shackspear claims are his."

"Why would Burbage care about that?"

"He's worried Tilney and the Privy Council will come after him. He thinks they will come to the conclusion that *Every Man Out* was written by you and should be called *Oxford Is Out.*"

Oxford chuckled. "But Shackspear doesn't get it."

"He will, my lord. Everyone else at the Curtain did."

"They did?" Oxford liked hearing this. "Are you willing to work with me on *Coriolanus*?" he asked. Derby nodded, a smile spreading across his face. "You'll have to come to Hackney," Oxford said.

"I'm already there. But tell me about *Coriolanus*, my lord."

"A warning to the queen about Essex. Cicero, in his treatise *De Officiis*, worries about the tendency of great warriors to lust after power. Needed in times of danger, they have difficulty returning to being citizens when the danger passes."

"Essex, indeed, my lord," Derby murmured.

"Plutarch gives us the story we will stage. Caius Martius Coriolanus was the great Roman warrior who helped establish democracy by defeating Tarquin the Proud. But he only knew war and was utterly contemptuous of the people."

"Essex again," Derby said.

"Coriolanus will be a man-child, raised by an over-weening mother who wants him to be nothing but a warrior. She will wax eloquent over his wounds and boast of how his son is so like him:

> *I saw his boy run after a gilded butterfly: and when he caught it, he let it*
> *go again; and after it again; and over and over he comes, and again;*
> *catched it again; or whether his fall enraged him, or how 'twas, he did so*
> *set his teeth and tear it; O, I warrant it, how he mammocked it!*

"*Mammocked it!*" Derby exclaimed. "Like the butterfly was a piece of meat." He glanced at Oxford. "A new word," he said wonderingly, and a scene he could never have imagined. Listening to Oxford was like peering through a slightly opened door down a long hall filled with marvels.

"Coriolanus, being nothing more than an infant Mars himself, will throw off attempts to limit him."

"Essex," Derby said again.

"Indeed. Coriolanus' arrogance will get him banished from Rome. He will come back at the head of an army to sack the city that honored him."

"My lord!" Derby exclaimed. "Which is what Essex might do!"

"Shh," Oxford said, putting a finger to his lips. "Perhaps members of the audience might make the connection, but we are in Rome."

"Aye," Derby said. "How to stop Coriolanus? His mother will convince him to stay his hand," Derby said.

"Yes. Difficult, but his arrival outside the walls of Rome will provide his mother an opportunity. Thank you. She will speak to Coriolanus, her son, and avert bloodshed:

> *For myself, son,*
> *I purpose not to wait on fortune till*
> *These wars determine: if I cannot persuade thee*
> *Rather to show a noble grace to both parts*
> *Than seek the end of one, thou shalt no sooner*
> *March to assault thy country than to tread--*
> *Trust to't, thou shalt not--on thy mother's womb,*
> *That brought thee to this world.*

"And all will go off to dinner," Derby said, pleased.

"Nay. The people will tear him to pieces:

> *'Tear him to pieces.' 'Do it presently.' 'He kill'd*
> *my son.' 'My daughter.' 'He killed my cousin*
> *Marcus.' 'He killed my father.'*

"Well," Derby said. "He'll not displace Mercutio in the hearts of playgoers."

"He'll make Elizabeth see what will happen if she does not take action to curb the ambitions of the Earl of Essex."

167

The Burning of the Books

The earls of Oxford and Derby were on their way back to Derby House. They rounded St. Paul's and headed into Ludgate Hill. Ahead of them, a bonfire was burning brightly in front of the Stationer's Hall. Dignitaries and servants stood around the fire. Piles of books lay in the street. Servants were picking them up by the armload and heaving them into the fire.

Two bishops were supervising the work: Richard Bancroft, Bishop of London, and John Whitgift, Archbishop of Canterbury. They were looking into the flames, bright in the fading afternoon light. Sir Thomas Egerton, Lord Keeper of the Great Seal and judge of the Court of Chancery, stood next to them. All three were directing the servants to hurry up. It was a hot day and the fire made the air unbearable.

Sir Thomas saw Oxford and Derby first. "My lords," he exclaimed, doffing his cap. Bancroft and Whitgift quickly followed.

"You should be burning the authors, gentlemen, not their books," Oxford said to them.

The three book-burners didn't know what to make of this. "Ye don't see any copies of *The Isle of Dogs*, do ye?" Whitgift said.

"Did they print that?" Oxford asked. "I thought they only spoke it."

Whitgift growled.

Derby picked up a book. "John Marston, *The Scourge of Villanie*," he said.

"Aye," Whitgift said. "All his books. And Gabriel Harvey's too. There'll be no more *Satyres* or *Epigrams*." Whitgift motioned for Derby to throw Marston's book into the fire. Derby cast an eye at Oxford.

"I've one at home, William," Oxford said, waving his arm as if he were throwing the book onto the fire. Derby cast Marston's book on to the pyre.

Bancroft stepped forward. He thought Whitgift, though senior to him, was unaware the earls were playing with him. "This be about more than *Satyres* and *Epigrams*, my lords." He cast what he thought was a fearful eye at Oxford and Derby.

"Peace, Sir Thomas," Oxford said. "We all know the ban is about more than satyrs and epigrams. Ye've obviously had enough of hints that someone else is writing the plays William *Shake-spare* claims are his." Sir Thomas and the bishops tried to look like they didn't understand what he meant. "Sir Robert gets Meres to praise William: *The sweete wittie soule of Ovid lives in mellifluous and honey-tongued Shakespeare.* But who is Ovid? Perhaps Marston's beloved poet *whose silent name one letter bounds?*" Oxford reached down and picked up a book. "Not Weever's *Epigrams?* He's been exempted from the flames despite *his* praise?"

> *Honie-tongd Shakespeare, when I saw thine issue,*
> *I sware Apollo got them, and none other!*

"Is Shackspear now being fed plays by Apollo?"

The bishops were flustered by this. Not Sir Thomas. "You flout the law, my lord. Ye hide behind your titles. Ye should be setting a standard to follow instead of encouraging others to write drivel that points more and more to you."

This angered Oxford. "And point it should, Sir Thomas. Steam in a boiling pot will out!"

"Not if we can stop it," Bancroft muttered.

"Gentlemen," Oxford said, turning to look at the fire, which was starting to burn out, "you slack in your duties. More books! Quick! Save our countrymen from a fate worse than death: reading a book that may expand their minds."

He strode around the three men and continued down Ludgate. Derby followed.

168

Essex Returns

The earls of Oxford and Derby were bent over the library table when a kinsman of Derby burst into the room. "My lords," he cried. "The Earl of Essex has returned from Ireland."

Oxford and Derby looked up. "With Her Majesty's permission?"

"Apparently not, my lord."

"Where is he now?"

"He's passed Holborn. He's going to take a boat across to Lambeth. He may be on the river as we speak."

The three men went to the window and looked out over the Thames. An eight-man wherry was being rowed across it. Essex could be seen standing in the middle of the boat. The wherry reached the riverbank. Essex leaped ashore and ran up the hill to Lambeth Palace.

"He's alone," Oxford said. He was relieved. Perhaps Southampton's good sense had kept him in Ireland.

"I am told Earl Robert," Derby's kinsman said, "is on to Nonsuch where the queen lies. Lord Gray is ahead of him and determined to reach her before he does. It's the horse race of the century!"

Oxford was worried Southampton had not stayed in Ireland. He expected Southampton would soon appear at the riverbank.

"Permit me, my lord," Derby said, turning to the man who had burst into their rooms. "This is John Salusbury, my kinsman."

"Yer lordship," Salusbury said, bowing.

"And how related?" Oxford asked.

"I am married to Ursula Stanley, the 4th Earl's illegitimate daughter. William and I are related as brothers-in-law, although his begetting occurred on the lawful side of the sheets, mine on the other side. No matter, we are both loyal servants of Her Majesty."

"Indeed," Oxford said. "How fortunate she is."

"Thank you, my lord. Now, if you would both excuse me, I am to follow the earl to make sure he doesn't get into any mischief." He left the room.

"The queen made him Squire of the Body a few years ago," Derby said.

Oxford was surprised. "The only one, I believe."

"Aye. There were many under Henry and Edward. They helped with everything in the Privy Chamber, but, with a queen, her ladies-in-waiting are her squires."

"Still, she puts Salusbury in the Privy Chamber. She must trust him a great deal."

"Aye."

Oxford looked back out at the river. He was wondering where Southampton was. Hopefully, Essex had crossed his Rubicon alone. Perhaps Southampton had stayed in Ireland. Maybe he would be smart enough to take advantage of Essex's behavior to pull away from him.

"Shall we return to *Coriolanus*?" Derby asked.

Oxford didn't think he could work on a play now, but Derby wanted to keep writing. Oxford only agreed because he thought it might distract him from what was going on outside.

The two of them returned to the library. Derby wanted to make Coriolanus' mother as evil as possible. This would be his revenge on his brother's widow who, having given birth to a girl, was nothing more than a dowager countess subject to William's orders. But she had found a lawyer and challenged her husband's will.

Oxford wanted *Coriolanus* finished so he could convince the queen she must rein in Essex. *Julius Caesar* hadn't done it. But Essex just might have 'unearled' himself by returning from Ireland without permission. If the queen took action, which seemed very likely now, *Coriolanus* would end up being a wasted effort. As a result, Oxford lost interest in finishing it. It was a dreary story anyway, good for slowing down Essex, but of little interest beyond that.

Oxford gazed out the window, lost in thought. He turned to Derby. "William, my dear man, I'm going to leave the rest of *Coriolanus* to you. I know you'll do a good job. Avoid making the mother too man-like. The audience may think …"

"She is Elizabeth."

"Yes. I have a sonnet to write."

~ 169 ~

At a Frown, They in their Glory Die

The Earl of Oxford set out for Hackney the next morning. He was unsettled. He learned on the way that Southampton and many of Essex's followers had returned from Ireland as well. They had holed up in Essex House where they waited to find out what the queen would do with Essex.

How different Essex's departure had been the year before. The Strand had been packed with nobility and gentlemen of worth who had pressed in among the people gazing on Essex and his troops as they marched away. It had been a bright, sunny day that suddenly turned dark. A shower of hail and rain fell. The onlookers ran for shelter. The soldiers took it gaily, an opportunity to show how a little soaking was nothing to warriors on their way to glory.

After the storm blew away, the citizens debated whether the storm was a sign. *"He will return with rebellion broachèd on his sword,"* one onlooker called out, stealing a line from *Henry V*. Oxford had not been there. He frowned when he heard it. He had not written *Henry V* to praise Essex.

The Earl's ignominious return made it clear that the storm had been an ill omen. He returns with tail between his legs, Oxford mused. *"Let those who are in favor with their stars / Boast of public honor and proud titles,* because, *at a frown,* great princes can *in their glory die."*

He withdrew into himself as the carriage carried him out of the City. He worked on capturing the sonnet in his head. Pen and paper were unnecessary. He had nearly finished it by the time the carriage rattled down the hill into Hackney.

To Oxford, the sonnet's formal structure was like a jewel box crafted in a royal shop. Its symmetry gave him a feeling that all was right with the world, that order had been restored by form. The contents of the sonnet, the words when unpacked, however, was recognition that his beloved son was in peril. There would be those happy to see Southampton 'in his glory die' alongside the Earl of Essex. Sir Robert would do everything he could to eliminate Essex in the coming struggle. If Southampton stood too close to him, he would go down as well.

———◆◆◆———

Elspeth welcomed Oxford. She had missed him, and not only because she wanted him to become the father to his son that Earl John had never been to him.

The kitchen whipped up a plate of venison medallions with leeks and mushrooms grilled over an open fire, after which she took him upstairs to her bed.

Back in his own bed that night, Oxford realized he didn't miss London. It was not that he was becoming a country squire. It was that London had changed. The Boar's Head stood gutted. The playhouses were being torn down or closed. Even the world of plays was changing. Plays about Londoners? Poetry so acerbic you felt you'd been slapped when you read one aloud?

He lay under the covers and felt small. The world was changing, and he was not finding himself capable of going with it. Was he becoming a *minimis?* Were there no more great plays left in him? No poetry? This reminded him of the sonnet he had composed on his way to Hackney. He ran it through his mind. He would capture it in the morning. It was good, he knew. This made him smile. Sleep, Bruno had told him, ravels up the sleeve of care. The world would look better on the morrow with the sun pushing the darkness away.

170

How Rare a Phoenix

How rare a Phoenix the Queen of England hath been," Dr Thomas Holland, Regius Professor of Divinity, proclaimed into the frigid air that filled St. Paul's Cathedral. His breath came out in well-defined clouds. It was Accession Day. Dr. Holland was beaming, his voice booming. He was giving his first sermon at Paul's, which presented him with an opportunity to show the queen that his talents were being wasted in the provinces.

Elizabeth was scarcely paying attention. She was bored. Holland had already declared her Solomon's bride as well as Queen of Sheba. Elizabeth dreamed of hearing something new for once.

The Earl of Oxford was sitting in the front row a few seats to her right. He had resisted coming but Elspeth had dangled the prospect of spending a few days at Derby House, a short distance away from where they now sat. Lisbeth would not be there. Elspeth and Derby were seated further back.

Oxford had come to like Derby. They found they shared many interests. Plays, for one. They had both traveled on the continent and had much to discuss, particularly Spain, a country that Oxford had not visited. Derby had spent considerable time there. He had defeated a Spanish knight in a duel in Madrid and had to flee the country disguised as a monk. He claimed he had visited Egypt and Jerusalem and gone on to Istanbul. He regaled Oxford with stories of ardent women in Turkey and killing a tiger in Egypt.

"But there are no tigers in Egypt, William," Oxford had gently reminded him. "Make it a lion, perhaps, or a hippopotamus."

"I liked killing the tiger, my lord," Derby protested, quietly admitting he was having everyone on. "I'll change the continent; not the animal."

Oxford had laughed at his son-in-law's wit. This cemented their relationship. "India, then, my friend," Oxford said. Thereafter, the two of them began seeing plays together and eventually began to write plays when Oxford came up to London.

Oxford had been working on a court drama about the Trojan War when the invitation came to attend the Accession Day celebrations. He was not pleased how it was coming along and, therefore, agreed to accompany Elspeth to the annual celebration honoring the queen.

As he listened to Dr. Holland drone on, Oxford recalled participating in the tilts, winning them in 1570. The queen was in love with him at the time and gave him a tablet of diamonds that resembled the board used to keep track of hits and passes. He eventually gave it to Anne Vavasour. In the madness that descended over the palace when Anne gave birth to Oxford's child in a bedroom next to the queen's, the tablet of diamonds was discovered in Anne's room. This discovery further enraged the queen. Sleeping with Anne was one thing; Oxford giving Anne a gift the queen had given to Oxford was quite another.

Oxford used his time in the Tower to pen a sonnet expressing his dismay that she would think the tablet so important he would forget her because he had given it to someone else.

> *Thy gift, thy tables, are within my brain*
> *Full character'd with lasting memory,*
>
> ...
>
> *To keep an adjunct to remember thee*
> *Were to import forgetfulness in me.*

He had the sonnet smuggled out of the Tower and delivered to Elizabeth, who was not pleased that Oxford had twisted her anger into faux dismay that she would think he would need it to remember her. The tablet of diamonds never resurfaced, of course, lost to sticky fingers and scheming maids, but Oxford knew Elizabeth would eventually appreciate the sonnet because it would live on forever, long after the gaudy object she had given him was broken up to make rings and broaches for others.

These memories warmed him. "*How rare a Phoenix the Queen of England hath been,*" Oxford repeated to himself. 'If she be the Phoenix, I am certainly the Turtledove.' He smiled. 'I can make something of this.' His mind began to churn as the good Doctor droned on.

⎯⎯◦✦◦⎯⎯

The music woke Oxford. All rose; the queen stood. She crossed in front of him as she headed for the door and the windy day outside. "I will be in Whitehall, my lord," she said out of the corner of her mouth. "Come to me."

She swept out the door to a waiting carriage. Oxford got up and followed, stopping next to Elspeth and the Earl of Derby.

"To Derby House for an early supper, my lord?" Derby asked.

"I'm afraid not. Her Majesty has asked me to visit her."

"When?"

"She didn't say. Which means now. I shan't be long. She never is."

"Of course."

<hr>

The palace was beyond Canon Row. Oxford leaned into the biting wind that struck him in the face. He was excited. He had no idea why she wanted to see him. He had done nothing of late to merit censure or praise. He had taken to lounging on the porch at Hackney and scribbling plays with the Earl of Derby when he came down from London, or riding with Henry, now seven. The boy could sit a pony, making Oxford and his mother proud.

Word had been left at the north portal that he was expected. A guardsman with a halberd - a sign the queen was perhaps taking Essex seriously - took him to a second floor sitting room overlooking the Thames. Refreshments were laid out on a table. Elizabeth came into the room.

"Edward," she said, coming over to take his hand. "How nice of you." She sat down. He followed suit.

"I trust you are aware of the difficult situation the Earl of Essex has placed us in," she said. "He has returned from Ireland unannounced and without our permission."

"Such news reaches even Hackney, Your Majesty."

"We have restricted him to York House whilst we decide what to do with him. The army he took with him is melting back, filling the streets and taverns with vagabonds, itching to support him if given the chance."

This was also not news to Oxford. Everyone knew the pot was on the boil.

"I appreciate what you've done to show Earl Robert examples that should pull him up but, alas, he has, in all his blockheadedness, mistaken your efforts for encouragement. He sits and broods. He claims he only wants to replace Cecil as my advisor but everyone, including me, thinks he may want more. We fear he may already see himself as Bolingbroke and me as Richard II."

Oxford said nothing. She wasn't used to this. "Why the silence?" she asked. "Are you writing a play about the Spartans, my lord? Three acts in five words? I would not think anyone would ever describe you as laconic, yet here you sit saying nothing."

"J'attends," he said, making it clear that he was there to listen.

Elizabeth liked this. "Your silence commends you. We have need of counselors who do not fill our tired head with advice before they hear what we need. I have Cecil, who is my right honorable adviser, as good as I'm going to get now that his father is no longer with us, but half the council, to my mind, has gone over to Essex. The Admiral steers down the middle, of course, but he is a Howard, and all the Howards chart their own courses. Bacon and Popham are lawyers, and lawyers are useless if the action that is needed does not comport with their reading of the law."

"Your Majesty needs advisers who can rise above petty entanglements and see the course of English history."

"Just so. It is for this reason that I am appointing you to the Privy Council." This surprised Oxford. He had long ago given up any hope that she would appoint him to a position of importance. Elizabeth took his reaction as reluctance "You need not attend unless I send word but shift yourself to Derby House for the time being so that we may avail ourselves of your counsel, if need be."

Oxford bowed. "I am honored."

"Thank you, Edward."

He rose. Their eyes met. She looked over him, but only to assess how he was faring, seeing the cane he was leaning on.

He went out into the hallway where the guard waited to escort him out of the palace. His mind was in turmoil. She recognized she needed his help, but their meeting had been business only, nothing personal. She had reached out to him as his sovereign, not as her former lover. Or mother of their son!

The guard opened the door to let him out into The Street. He walked away toward Canon Row. She had said nothing when she learned Southampton had married without her permission. She sent him and his new wife to the Tower, of course, but she would have done that if any of her senior lords had married without royal consent. What was missing was the usual tirade that should have followed the slamming of the prison gates. Did that mean she didn't care? Or that she did?

Oxford broke into a broad smile. Why else put him on the Council and ask for his help? 'To save *our* son, of course. Now, where is Falstaff?'

171

Christmas at the Boar's Head

"The *new* Boar's Head, my lord," Falstaff announced, ushering Oxford and Derby into the tavern Falstaff and Peaches had purchased off London Bridge. The two earls surveyed a room full of tables. Patrons were arguing as servers ran back and forth with beer and meat pies. Peaches came up.

"Yer lordships," she said, curtseying.

"Most impressive," Derby said. "The food must be wonderful."

"Not likely, yer lordship." She saw Derby's reaction, which was a mix of disappointment and why ever would she say such a thing? "Don't get me wrong, your lordship; we serve a very good figgy-dowdy, and our eel pie is the best this side of the Isle of Sheppey, but our patrons don't come here for the food. Food to them is like wood to a stove; in it goes and the smoke goes up the chimney." She laughed. "Well, maybe not up. No matter. We sell beer, my lord, with food to go with it."

"And fame, my lordships," Falstaff said, tipping his head back.

"Jack!" a man called out, who had just come into the pub.

Falstaff put up a hand. "Bar first, sir," he said, pointing to a bar along the far wall. "Stories after."

"And I to the kitchen," Peaches said, running off.

"Follow me, my lords," Falstaff said. "We have a screened-off area in the back where you can hear each other." He took them around a corner. "And, out of sight from the front door to keep the apparitors at bay. A feature some of our patrons appreciate."

Oxford and Derby didn't know whether they were included in this category or Falstaff was just showing off the inn. "I'll have some beer brought over," he said, and headed for the bar. A moment later, a thin, tall man arrived with two tankards of beer. He put them down.

Oxford looked up at him. "Do I recognize you?"

The tall man touched his forehead. "Milord," he said, not answering Oxford's question.

Falstaff came up behind him. "Recognize Long Tom?"

Oxford nodded. "Yes, I do."

Derby couldn't imagine how Oxford was connected with the gangling man standing next to them. Oxford explained.

"T'was this very season – Christmas - that Thomas Knyvet attacked me in Pudding Lane. He was one of Anne Vavasour's cousins and thought I had brought shame on his family by getting her with Edward. He stabbed me in the leg to somehow right the score. Jack fought him off and took me to his apartments in Cheapside where Long Tom, here, nursed me back to life."

"And Armado," Falstaff said. "Let us not forget Armado."

"Aye, and Armado. He who lost his legs when a cart ran over him. How is he doing?"

"You can answer that question yourself," Falstaff said, hooking his thumb over his shoulder at the bar.

Oxford looked across the room. Armado waved casually, like he waved to earls every day.

"But," Oxford began, "how …" He looked at Falstaff. "He has no legs."

"And doesn't need' em," Falstaff said, "oncet we build a shelf behind the bar he could slide back and forth on." He frowned. "Course, it was Peaches idea to bring him here. Legless but reliable, as ye know."

They watched Armado slide a pitcher of beer down the bar, coming to a halt in front of a patron who waved back to show his appreciation of Armado's skill.

"Well, I never," Derby said.

Shackspear came in. It had started raining. He saw Oxford seated in the booth and immediately came over.

"My lord," he said. When he got closer, he saw Derby across the table. He bowed again. "My lord," he repeated.

"What are *you* doing here?" Oxford asked.

"I live in Southwark now," Shackspear said. "Silver Street was no good for me anymore. The bailiffs had figured out where I was living. They say I owe some kind of tax. And a whole row erupted in the house where I was living about whether the master had promised a dowry to the man who had married his daughter. Now, seeing as I am a gentleman, I don't pay taxes. And I ain't no witness for anyone, neither." He looked pleased with himself. "Plus, the theaters are mostly on this side of the river now. The Rose. The Globe. The Swan is about to reopen. No need to live elsewhere."

"And *Coriolanus?*" Derby asked. He had missed the opening, which had taken place at the Curtain. "How did it fare?"

Shackspear made a face. "Like all his lordship's Roman plays: not well. *The Shoemaker's Holiday* outsold it. Now, there's a play. A city comedy. Dekker is on to something."

"Yes, yes," Oxford said, irritated at Shackspear and himself for asking about *Coriolanus.*

"But this ye may like. Master Edward Peers is going to allow Paul's Boys to start performing again at Blackfriars. They'll need plays. They'll want fairies and what-not there. Romans and Greeks too, I'll wager."

"Lyly wrote for Paul's Boys last time Blackfriars was allowed to put on plays, didn't he?" Derby asked.

"He did," Shackspear said. "There's a renewed interest in theater. The Puritans are stranded at low tide. People are tired of them telling everyone what to think while they walk around clanking on about freedom."

Derby turned to Oxford. "This may be an opportunity for me to try my hand, my lord. What do you say?"

"Why not?" Oxford said. "London can always use a new play, right William?"

Shackspear agreed, but his enthusiasm was beginning to fade when he couldn't figure out how a play by Derby would benefit him.

"And how is Mr. Jonson faring?" Oxford asked.

"He's working on a new play."

"*Every Man Inside His Humour?*"

"No. A new one. *Cynthia's Revels, or The Fountain of Self-Love.*"

"*Cynthia's Revels?*" Oxford chuckled. "Well, we all know who Cynthia is. Who is he going after in this play, other than the queen?"

"John Donne, I think."

"Donne?" Derby sat up. "Donne was one of my servants on my trip to the continent."

"To Egypt and Turkey?" Oxford asked.

"No. Not that far. And, I must confess, my lord, I never got to Egypt or Istanbul. I spent most of my time on a small island off the north coast of Sicily"

"In the arms of a woman."

"Oh, yes. And what a woman. My Circe." He sighed. "I was her captive."

This confession surprised Oxford. Derby *hadn't* gotten to Istanbul, then. Or Egypt. Oxford wondered how much *else* about Derby' trip was untrue. No one believed he shot a tiger on *any* continent. Fixing the hole in his story by changing the continent was merely being witty, wasn't it? But did that mean he had made up the rest of his trip?

Shackspear had no such thoughts. "Do I hear a play here, my lord?" This was asked of Derby, not Oxford.

"Perhaps," Derby said. They could tell he liked the suggestion.

"Do you bring any other news?" Oxford asked Shackspear.

Shackspear squared his shoulders and assumed a look of shock. "The Earl of Southampton, my lord, approached *me* for a loan." He hooked his thumbs into imaginary pockets on his nonexistent belt. "Me!" he repeated. It was obvious Shackspear thought Southampton's request was an acknowledgement of how important he had become.

Oxford couldn't believe Southampton would ask Shackspear for money, but Shackspear didn't have the creativity to dream this up.

"And, did you?"

"Of course not!" Shackspear said. "Money loaned to a nobleman is money lost, my father always said." He quickly bowed to Oxford and Derby. "Your lordships excepted, of course."

"How much did he want?" Oxford asked.

"£1,000. He said he had to finance his own expenses in the Irish wars and his new wife and baby were draining his coffers." Shackspear laughed. "He's got money. He doesn't need a 'loan.'"

"And did he say why he approached you?"

"*Venus & Adonis*," he said. I told him I didn't owe him anything."

"Did you tell him you didn't write *Venus*?"

He snorted. "Cut off my legs if ye want me to say that. I'm the author, ain't I? I ain't givin that up."

Oxford sighed. "Yes," was all he could manage to say. He gestured to Derby. "We need to be somewhere else," he said to no one in particular. He and Derby got up and walked out of the pub.

1600

172

The Metamorphosis of a Maid

I say, my lord; what think you of a plot in which a girl and boy fall in love and want to marry but the boy's father objects." Derby was standing in front of Oxford with his head cocked.

Oxford sighed. "I think it's been done before."

"The father objects because the girl is beneath him."

"*All's Well.*"

"But in my play, the father orders two servants to take the girl into the forest and kill her."

Oxford sat up. "Well, that's different."

Derby took this as praise. "But they don't, of course, because she is beautiful and sings well."

"Of course. The only things expected of a woman. I will hazard a guess that she escapes from them."

"She does, my lord. Apollo, weeping over the loss of Hyacinth, will come down to have his way with her."

"*That's* not good. Escaping from men is one thing; getting away from a god who wants to rape you is quite another." Oxford was intrigued.

"She avoids being deflowered by Apollo by asking him to change her into a boy."

Oxford shrugged. "Greek gods liked boys as well as girls."

"Yes, but in my play, the gods will refrain from pursing boys. People will like that."

"Perhaps. Go on."

"So Apollo changes her into a boy. As a boy, she convinces the shepherd she has been living with that she is the girl's brother."

Oxford shook his head. "He accepts this?"

"It's a play," Derby said, as if this absolved him of all faults.

"But you have turned the girl into a boy. How will you reverse this at the end of the play so she can marry the young man her father objected to? The audience will expect them to marry."

"I know, my lord. Will ye help?"

Oxford thought for a moment. "I'll be too involved in other projects to help you with this play. But Shackspear is right: Paul's Boys will want fairies and songs. Let's get Lyly involved. He'll love working with them again. He's an experienced playwright when it comes to fairies and music."

"Oh, my lord, that's wonderful. Thank you. I shall find out where he is and he and I will finish this for the Boys."

"What are you calling this new play you're working on?"

"*The Metamorphosis of a Maid.*"

"Oh, good that. And the play about your Circe?" Oxford asked.

"I'm working on that, my lord."

~ 173 ~
A Summons from the Queen

The guard at the gate recognized Oxford. He led him to a different room this trip, one that took them through the depths of a warren of tiny rooms filled with clerks scurrying about carrying documents. It was where Walsingham had started his spy network. Oxford had been invited in once, the invitation clearly not a request.

The guard continued through the offices to emerge into a hallway that led upstairs to an ornate conference room. Various impresa lined the walls. The queen was seated at one end of a small table; Sir Robert Cecil sat at the opposite end. The queen gestured for Oxford to take a chair to her left.

Oxford bowed to Elizabeth, dipped his head in Cecil's direction, and pulled out a chair to sit down.

"I want to strip Essex of all his powers," Elizabeth said. She was angry. "But Sir Robert says I must be careful because Essex has many followers. We do not know their number or loyalty to him. What do you advise, my lord."

Oxford took in Sir Robert. "I agree with my brother that we must tread carefully. However, if you take no action, your people may begin to believe that you have forgiven him for Ireland as well as returning without permission. Inaction may also encourage Essex to take action himself."

"Doing nothing is doing something, Your Majesty," Cecil intoned.

"No, it's not," she snapped. "Tell me what you think I should do." This question was directed at both men.

Cecil deferred to Oxford

"I think Your Majesty must take some action against the earl that will show you are in command. Perhaps you could move him from York House to Essex house. This will give him the illusion Your Majesty is in the process of forgiving him."

"But his family and friends are there."

"Clear Essex House first and then let him come home. It may be only a short distance, but the move will be viewed as significant by everyone, including him."

"And then what?"

"Hold out the prospect of a fair hearing where he can present his complaints. Let him know it will be held before a special group of his peers. In the summer. June perhaps. The start can be delayed, of course, and once started, adjourned as the temperament of the people is assessed. This will bleed off Essex's support. His followers cannot remain in London without a source of income. They will have to go home."

"Issue an order for them to go," Cecil said. "Not all will leave, of course, but many will."

"And your command will give those who want to return home an excuse to leave," Oxford pointed out.

"He must be without funds," Elizabeth said.

"His sweet wines monopoly is up for renewal," Cecil said. "I suggest not renewing it."

Oxford agreed. "But not telling him."

"A carrot, then." They nodded. "Thank you, gentlemen."

174

A Visit from the Countess of Southampton and Her Son

Nigel came into the rooms Oxford was using in Derby House. "My lord, her ladyship, the Countess of Southampton and her son, the Earl of Southampton, are in the parlor below. They wish to speak with you."

"And her son?" Nigel nodded. "Please show them up."

Nigel went to get them. 'What can this possibly mean?' Oxford asked himself. It was the Countess who had told him she was not Southampton's mother. What was she doing now in London traipsing around as if she were?'

Nigel returned with them. The Countess, somewhat less rotund than when Oxford had last seen her, came into the room hurriedly. Southampton followed.

"My lord," the Countess said, taking Oxford's hand and bowing.

Southampton nodded as well. Oxford waved them to chairs in the room. The Countess swiveled herself into one; her son took the other.

The Countess leaned forward and put her best smile on her face, which made Oxford recall a remark Lettice Knollys made about the Countess once: 'A bit too much crocodile, for me,' she had said behind her hand.

"My congratulations, my lord, on your elevation to the Privy Council, which is long overdue. You are aware, my lord, that Her Majesty has misinterpreted efforts by the Earl of Essex to gain access to her as threatening her royal authority. Nothing could be further from the truth. Earl Robert only wants to offset the insidious influence of Mr. Secretary, Sir Robert Cecil, who has convinced Her Majesty to confine Earl Robert to Essex House like a common criminal."

"I am aware that he has been restricted to his House, your ladyship. She was gracious to let him shift from York House so he could be in his home."

"But threw out his family before he got there!" She looked around, exasperated. "However, I am not here about Earl Robert. The shade cast over Essex shades Henry as well." She cast an arm in the direction of her son. "Someone must show her how she is being ill-served by that little man before he convinces her to take more serious action that will reflect unfavorably on her legacy. And on my Henry."

'Her Henry?' Oxford asked himself. He turned to Southampton. "And Henry, how dost thou?" Southampton was surprised to be asked. Knowing that Oxford and Essex were sworn enemies, he had not expected Oxford to be concerned about him.

"Well, my lord."

"Has the queen taken steps to confine you or otherwise affect your liberty?"

"No, my lord. But one of Sir Robert's minions, Thomas, Lord Grey of Wilton, has attacked me in narrow lanes. One of my servants lost a hand in the most recent encounter, but I forced Grey to retreat. He now demands I meet him in a remote location, weapons to be chosen by me."

"But dueling is forbidden by the queen."

"No matter. We will find a place outside England, then - Ireland, perhaps - and settle the matter."

Oxford was disconcerted to hear this. Could Southampton shrug off his loyalty to the queen so easily? It was not an attitude befitting the son of a Vere, or the next king of the realm. This turn of events made wonder if the young man in front of him was indeed his son. Southampton felt Oxford examining him closely. He glanced at his mother.

"My lord," she said, "Henry's contretemps with Lord Grey is beside the point. What can you do to help my son?"

This surprised Oxford as well. 'Her son?' What game was the Countess playing? Had she lied to him at her wedding? Or was she lying now? Had Elizabeth understood the Countess better than he had? Was he nothing more than the butt of an elaborate joke? He remembered Elizabeth laughing when he told her the Countess said Elizabeth was Southampton's mother. His choler began to rise.

But what the Countess had told him at her wedding was not something he could discuss in Southampton's presence. He had to get rid of Henry, fidgeting now in his chair.

"I will speak with the queen," Oxford said, eliciting a grunt of satisfaction from the Countess. Southampton rose. The Countess began to rise as well.

Oxford put up his hand. "If you would please stay a moment, your ladyship."

She knew exactly what he wanted to talk about. She raised her hand to let Southampton know he could go. He fled the room. Oxford got up and closed the door. He pulled his chair closer to hers and sat down.

"Now, the small business of you referring to Henry as 'your son.'" He looked at her intently. "Did you tell me the truth at your wedding?

"My lord, I spoke the truth as I knew it at the time, but it's been years since I told you he was yours by the queen and, as far as I know, you've done nothing to answer the question: Who is his mother? Who is his father?"

This almost came out as a wail. She went on.

"I have returned to God, my lord. I have been 'awakened.' I now believe the Devil tricked me into believing Henry was not my son. This was to punish me for my sins, which punishment I richly deserved. But I now believe Henry is my son. I want you to stop trying to prove he is your son. If you are successful, you will 'unmother' me again." She reached for a handkerchief. "Worse; you will put him in danger if word gets out that he is the queen's son. He's already in enough danger for coupling himself to the Earl of Essex! Let him be!"

She sat back, burying her face in her handkerchief.

Her speech unnerved Oxford. 'Unmothered?' How much worse than being 'unearled,' which only meant a man went back to being common; a mother who was 'unmothered' lost a child.

He couldn't agree to give up his claim that Henry was Elizabeth's son. If he did, he would be 'deposing' Henry before he had an opportunity to become king. He couldn't do that. He had a duty to Elizabeth, and to Southampton as well, if he was their son, as well as the generations of Englishmen who would follow them. He could not give up until he knew for sure whether Southampton was his son and the next king of England.

He stood up. "I'm afraid, your ladyship, I must continue my quest to find the answer to the question we both want resolved."

She rose from her chair. "Well, then, thou art a fool, Edward de Vere, for only a fool would risk Henry's life in the hope that he will be crowned Elizabeth's successor." She stormed out.

175

By A Mark He Is Known

"*astaff!*" Oxford cried out, jumping out of the chair he was sitting in. T'was not a greeting; it was a curse.

Sir John Falstaff was entering the small chamber that Oxford had been using at Derby House. He came to a halt in the doorway. "My lord! Why dost thou greet me thus?"

"Because ye have disappeared to India, or Muscovy, or wherever, *without satisfying my command to find out if the Earl of Southampton is my son!*"

"Oh," Sir John said, continuing into the room. "That."

"Yes, that. You promised me you would find out."

"Oh," Sir John said again. He sat down in a chair without asking permission to do so. Tupp came in behind him. The page leaned the sword he was dragging against the chair Falstaff was sitting in.

"What do you mean 'oh'?" Oxford asked, still angry. "Do ye bring me news or not?"

Falstaff leaned over and winked at Tupp. "He'll make a play of this, I warrant." He sat back, composed and confident.

"*I will not,*" Oxford almost shouted. "Answer me: do ye know? Or not?"

Before Falstaff could speak, Tupp stepped forward.

"Seigneur," he said, "the answer to your question lies there." He pointed to Oxford's feet.

Oxford looked down at his feet, then at the page. "What does?"

"If you please to take off your boot, Seigneur, you will find somezing on the inside of your right angle."

Oxford looked at Falstaff, whose face was blank. Oxford sat down. He pulled off his right boot. He and Falstaff bent down to look. They could just make out some kind of birthmark.

"It's a boar's head," Falstaff said, trying to muffle his surprise.

"It is?" Oxford twisted his leg to see his ankle. "So?" He looked at Falstaff, dropping his foot. "What meanest this, Jack? What are you and this miniature Frenchman trying to tell me?"

Tupp spoke again. "Your son, Seigneur, has the same mark on his angle."

"My son?"

Tupp nodded.

Oxford looked at Falstaff again.

"My little page," Falstaff said, smiling beneficently, "has shown you the answer to your question. *Southampton is your son!*" He made like he was blowing a trumpet.

"Why not just come out and tell me?"

Falstaff gave a Gallic shrug, which Tupp imitated. "My lord," Falstaff said, "you know how quickly good news flies away. We thought we would stretch it out a bit to increase your pleasure when you learned Henry has the same 'boar's head' mark on the inside of *his* right ankle that you have on yours."

Oxford sat back. He didn't believe Falstaff. "How do you know?"

Falstaff shrugged. "That, I cannot tell you."

"Oh, yes, you can."

"No, I can't, my lord. There are some matters that are best left to one's servants. As your servant, I undertook the task of finding the answer to your question, but I did not promise to tell you *how* I fulfilled my duty. It should be left unspoken."

"*No, it should not.* How do you expect me to believe you when you will not tell me the source of your information?"

"Well, you have a mark on your ankle that looks remarkedly like a boar's head. So does your son, Southampton. That should be enough."

"But how do you *know* he does?"

"Tupp, here, is the key to the mystery. He noticed the birthmark on your ankle. He is shorter than I am - as is most of the world - and brought the mark to my attention. With this information, I was able to refine our search. Knowing that you had a birthmark on the inside of your right ankle helped me figure out a way to find out if Southampton had the same mark on his ankle."

"*Et voila!*" Tupp said: "He does."

"*But how do you know?*" Oxford demanded. He was losing patience.

Falstaff looked away. "I am not at liberty to say, your lordship."

"You won't tell me?"

"You must trust me on this, my lord."

"Trust you? *You? Of all people?*"

Falstaff shrugged. "I admit it is difficult."

Tupp stamped a foot. "Just tell him," he said, muttering something in French. "He's going to find out anyway."

Oxford turned to Falstaff. "What am I going to find out anyway, Jack?"

Falstaff rearranged himself in his chair, looking very uncomfortable. He gave out a deep sigh. "Very well, my lord. You have pressed me to the end of my honor. It is only under such duress that I will tell you how I know your son has the same birthmark on his right ankle that you have on yours." He glanced at Tupp, who was looking very pleased with himself.

"Some time ago, my lord, you and I talked about ways to find out if the Earl of Southampton had a mark on him that would identify him as your son."

"Yes. I know all that."

"My efforts to find out whether he did came to naught. I buttered up his colleagues, bought drinks for his fellows-in-arms, pinched tavern maids, listened to stories from his shipmates, and strong-armed servants who may have been in his service. Desperate, I decided on a plan you would never approve."

"You're making me nervous."

"Only because you are forcing me to tell how I know Southampton has the same mark on his ankle that you have. Avast, my lord. Let this secret rest in Jack's deep soul. We will all be better off."

"Never!" Oxford shouted. "Continue."

Falstaff sighed again. "All right. Here we go. Hold onto something solid." He took a deep breath. "I went to the Countess of Derby and asked her to seduce the Earl of Southampton."

Oxford's jaw dropped open. "You didn't."

"I did. With proper instruction, of course, as to what she should be looking for whilst … she was … you know."

Oxford was unable to say anything for a moment. "*You went to my daughter and asked her to sleep with my son?*"

Falstaff shrugged. Tupp imitated him.

"She rejected the idea out of hand, of course."

"Fortunately, my lord, she did not. In fact, my proposition intrigued her. She had been encouraged to marry Southampton, you will recall, but he turned her down. She wondered what it would have been like to sleep with him, now that she as she had slept with Essex and Raleigh, and, of course, her husband, the Earl of Derby."

The room went silent. Oxford was speechless.

Oxford finally spoke. "So, your source is Lisbeth, who says Henry has a boar's head birthmark on the inside of his right ankle?" Falstaff nodded gravely. "And she knows this because she went to bed with him." Falstaff nodded again.

Oxford was still trying to take this in. He looked out the window. "She must have done this for me. To put a Vere on the throne of England. To make Henry our next king."

"I wouldn't go that far, my lord. Getting him into bed was what lit her up. 'I'll trick him into thinking I'm Lady Rich,' she told me. 'He's always making cow eyes at her. I'll send him a message to meet me - her - at the Savoy, but he'll find himself in my bed, not hers.'"

Oxford exploded. "She tricked Henry into sleeping with her by claiming she was Lady Rich? And he stayed, even after he found out he was in bed with Lisbeth and not Lady Rich?"

Falstaff shrugged. "Didn't Bertram?"

"That was a play!"

"Ye see why I begged you to leave this alone?"

Oxford was beyond words again.

"Let us ignore how this intelligence was obtained, my lord, and celebrate the good news that Southampton is your son."

Oxford forced himself to calm down. "Yes. It is." He looked at Tupp, standing tall beside Falstaff. *"Merci bien, monsieur."*

Tupp smiled back. *"De rien. Et maintenant, allons-y à la portraitiste, n'est pas?"*

"What?" Falstaff asked.

Tupp explained: "Eet is time to go to Monsieur Gheeraerts."

This made Oxford smile. "Oh, yes. For a portrait of a very pregnant queen. *Enceinte*, eh, my little friend?"

"Enceinte, Seigneur; enceinte." He rubbed his hands over his tummy. "She weel not like it."

"No, indeed." Oxford knew Tupp was referring to the queen. "No indeed. But it will be well worth it."

176

A Portrait of a Pregnant Lady

"My lady!" Oxford cried, coming out into the sunlight and seeing Lady Rich, arm outstretched, posing for Marcus Gheeraerts against a background of boats on what had turned out to be the first sparkling day of the year. Clouds of Egyptian cotton hung in a calm blue sky.

"Marcus," Oxford said to the man trying to capture Lady Rich, who was dressed all in white except for a blue ribbon that hung over her left shoulder. She tilted her head to acknowledge Oxford.

"My lord," Gheeraerts said, turning to acknowledge Oxford. His portrait of the earl had only recently been completed. Spinoza had released the money Lady Elspeth had deposited with him and, with that news, Gheeraerts had lost interest in the Earl of Oxford who was now interrupting him on the first day of the year that allowed him to paint en plein air. His irritation, however, began to fade as he noticed that Oxford's man, Timson, was carrying a roll of paper and a purse that looked suspiciously heavy. He realized Oxford might be bringing him a new commission, along with the gold to pay for it. His good humor returned.

Oxford now saw the Countess of Leicester seated to the right in the shade afforded by a wall covered with roses. The Countess was Lady Rich's mother. She was obviously present to squelch any rumors that Lady Rich was there for any purpose other than to have Marcus paint her. "My lady," Oxford said, going over to her.

"Edward, my dear."

Oxford looked over at Lady Rich, who had not moved since Oxford's arrival. Gheeraerts had gone back to work.

"And who is the painting for?" Oxford asked.

"The queen," the Countess said.

"Her Majesty needs *another* painting of fair Penelope? Sidney has made her immortal as Stella."

"He has. But Her Majesty persists in abusing my son, Essex, and keeping him in disfavor. You, of all people, know better than most that royal favor is the water we swim in, the air we breathe, the wind that keeps the birds aloft. Take it away and we die."

"And how will a new painting of Penelope help her brother?"

"The queen likes Penelope. A new painting will stir her memories of my daughter and help our efforts to restore her brother to royal favor."

"Indeed," Oxford said.

Gheeraerts took this moment to put his brush down. "A break," he said. "My hand tires." He picked up a rag to wipe his hands while looking at Oxford, a look that told Oxford Penelope could wait until Gheeraerts learned what his lordship had come for.

The Countess of Leicester understood. She and her daughter went inside.

Oxford went over to Gheeraerts. He had Timson unroll the paper across a table. "Here, Marcus, is a sketch of what I want you to do for me. I want a full-length portrait of a lady in a fancy dress." He reached out to Timson, who produced a sack he had been carrying. Oxford reached into it and pulled out a magnificent dress made of a fabric from India that was so diaphanous it appeared to be made of nothing more than morning mist. It was covered with swirling lines that surrounded multi-colored flowers and elegant birds. Oxford pulled out a pair of tiny slippers whose soles and straps were sewn of gold thread. They offset and framed the upper part of the slippers with a mesh of blue threads darker than the sky above. The slippers were sprinkled with tiny pearls; rubies studded the straps where they crossed over the top of the foot. Timson handed Oxford the last thing in the bag, a hat in the shape of an elongated dome made of grayish-blue silk taffeta.

Gheeraerts picked up the dress and ran it through his fingers. He whistled. "I have heard of this fabric but never seen it." He held up a panel to the sun. "Three hundred threads to the inch, I am told." He put it down and picked up the shoes. "Marvelous," he said. He put them down and turned to Oxford. "And how can I help, my lord?"

Oxford pointed to the sketch that lay on the table. "I want you to paint a portrait of a lady wearing this dress, hat, and slippers standing in front of a walnut tree next to a sobbing stag."

Gheeraerts looked down at the sketch. "Sobbing?"

"Yes. Her hand will be on the stag's head. I have provided the three Latin phrases I want you to paint amongst the leaves of the tree. A cartouche in the lower right-hand corner will contain a sonnet you see inscribed here." Oxford pointed to the sketch.

Gheeraerts remained hovering over the sketch. He finally looked up. "And the lady is your Countess?" Oxford shook his head. Gheeraerts' face darkened. "Who is she, then?"

"She who rules England."

Gheeraerts blanched.

"And you will paint her in the last months of her pregnancy," Oxford said.

Gheeraerts stepped back. "No, my lord. I could not possibly …"

Oxford gestured for Timson to pour the gold out onto the dress, which lay draped over the sketch on the table.

"Mon Dieu," Gheeraerts exclaimed.

"The Ditchley Portrait redux, Marcus, with a flowing dress and poetry."

"Mon Dieu," Gheeraerts said again. He turned to look at Oxford. "Why, my lord, do you do this to me?"

"Who else can paint grapes the birds come down to eat?" He gestured to the dress on the table. "Only you can paint Her Majesty in the dress and slippers sent to her by the Sultan's wife, which she wore when she was pregnant with our child."

Gheeraerts shuddered to hear this. He instantly recognized how dangerous it was to hear what Oxford had just told him. "No, my lord. She will disembowel me if I do what you ask of me."

"No, she will not disembowel you; she will disembowel me. You will not sign it, of course. That way, you can deny you painted it. And, if you repeat what I have just told you, I will sue you for slander. My man, Timson, here, will vouch that I never said any such thing, won't you, Timson?" Timson nodded. "And who would believe a foreigner over a lord who has a witness?"

Gheeraerts gasped.

"Forgive me, Marcus, for asking you to do this, but I had to tell you why I need the portrait to convey everything possible to Her Majesty when she sees it. I regret the threats, an unfortunate necessity in this circumstance, which I hope you understand and will forgive me for. But there are advantages to you here as well." Oxford tapped the pile of gold glittering in the sunlight on top of the dress. "Whilst you painted my portrait, you said you had not seen your family for many years. I'm sure they miss you. I'm sure you would like to see them before you get too much older and something happens that prevents you from seeing them again. Perhaps a trip home is what you deserve, once you complete this portrait for me."

Gheeraerts had been looking at the gold while Oxford spoke. "Yes. It would be good to be somewhere else when you present it to her."

"Of course. And what an opportunity to add to your collection of royal paintings. And a pregnant queen, at that!"

Gheeraerts did not share Oxford's enthusiasm, but he had decided to take the money. "I will do it, my lord."

"Good man," Oxford said. He motioned for Timson to hold open the bag for Gheeraerts to shovel the dress, the slippers, and the gold, into it before Lady Leicester and her daughter came back out.

Lady Leicester caught a corner of the dress disappearing into the bag as she came into the sunlight. "How extraordinary," she said, coming up to the men at the table. Gheeraerts passed the bag to a servant who quickly took it away. He and Oxford acted as if nothing had happened.

"My lady," Oxford said, bowing. He turned to leave, gesturing for Timson to come with him.

Lady Leicester watched them go. She settled into her chair, giving a glance at Gheeraerts, who was repositioning Lady Rich for the next session. "Hmm," she said, looking out over the river.

~ 177 ~
A Visit with the Queen

The queen toddled into the room, leaning on a cane. Oxford, who was also leaning on a cane, bowed to her. She looked away, a royal sweep of her head that made it crystal clear there would be no talk of how they had arrived at this point in life where they needed a third leg to remain upright. She made her way to a straight-backed chair and sat down, hanging the cane on the arm. "Begin," she announced.

"I bring a gift, Your Majesty."

"I love gifts, particularly when they are unusual. This past Christmas, Sir Thomas Tasburgh gave me three shovelers. He knows I love them roasted over juniper and chestnuts." She looked at him. "I don't remember receiving anything from you."

"Not at Christmas, Your Majesty."

"What doth thou bring me now, Edward?"

"If it please Your Majesty, I would prefer if we could speak in private." There were a half dozen servants in the room.

Elizabeth waved a hand; the room emptied.

Oxford walked over to an easel covered with a sheet. "We have oft times discussed whether you and I are the parents of the 3rd Earl of Southampton."

"Not at my request."

"I have obtained information that we are."

Elizabeth glared at him. "We have been over this. Leave the boy alone. Leave *me* alone. I am tired. I won't hear anymore of it."

Oxford waited.

"What?" Elizabeth said.

"You don't want to know?"

"No."

"Liar," Oxford said, a smirk on his face. This shocked her. "You were never a good liar," Oxford went on. "Of course, you want to know." He paused again. This time she remained silent. After a moment, he walked over and sat down on a footstool next to her. He pulled off a boot. She drew back. "Look," Oxford said, grabbing his foot and pulling it around so she could see the inside of his right ankle. "A boar's head birthmark. It runs in the family." He looked up at her. "In the family," he repeated. "Guess who has the same mark in the same place?"

"I never guess."

"Of course not. So, I'll provide the answer: Henry Wriothesley, 3rd Earl of Southampton."

He let his foot drop back. She didn't say anything. Oxford couldn't tell if this was news to her or she already knew. He guessed the latter and that she didn't want to risk speech until she was sure she was in control of her faculties.

Oxford didn't wait. "You are aware that there are learned scholars and ancient traditions that recognize birthmarks as proof of royalty?"

"Of course, I do. Russia is being torn apart by such claims as we speak. A little soot rubbed into a cut, and - poof! - I present the next czar of Russia!'"

"Or the next king of England."

"No. That's not going to happen. We are not Russians. You must let go of this madness."

"How can I when there is *proof* he is our son?" He paused. "In your heart, you know I am right."

"*I do not.*" She glanced away. She looked cornered. She turned back, her head held back. "Let's get this over with, shall we? What have you brought me?" She pointed toward the covered easel. "Proceed and we will bring this to an end."

Oxford left his boot next to the queen and hobbled over to the easel. He pulled off the sheet, revealing Gheeraerts' painting of a pregnant Elizabeth. Her jaw dropped open. She knew instantly who the subject of the painting was, and who the artist was. "How did he ever see that dress?" she asked, pulling herself forward in her chair to squint at the canvas. "The Sultan's wife gave me that dress, and the hat and shoes." Clutching her cane, she stood up and took herself across the room, stopping in front of the painting, which, being twice life-size, towered over her. Gheeraerts had made her far younger than she was and Elizabeth was, for a moment, dazzled by her far larger and younger self. The brilliant colors of the dress and slippers shocked her as well. She ran her eyes across the painting, merging into it for a moment. She was young again.

She had worn the Sultan's dress and slippers as her baby grew larger inside her. Gheeraerts had created an image that transported her back in time. It was the summer of her romance with Oxford. She wobbled slightly on her cane. Oxford reached over and steadied her. She let him. The two of them gazed into the portrait, young again, happy again.

She finally stiffened. He took his hand off her. She walked back to her chair. She sat down and gestured toward his boot. He came over and picked it up, slipping it on.

"You always surprise me, Edward. I shivered when I learned you were bringing me a gift, but I must admit it is wonderful." She straightened the dress she was wearing.

Oxford was thrilled. "You remember the slippers?" he asked. "You loved them. You wore them to bed at times. Fairy slippers, you called them."

She was looking at the painting. "But the baby died, Edward. Your dream, our dream, ended there."

"Servants say otherwise."

The dreamy look on her face disappeared. Her face hardened. "What servants?"

"Those who may be dead now, Your Majesty, but who told their loved ones and families that the boy you gave birth to at Havering did *not* die. He was spirited off to London by a horseman waiting outside. The servants said the baby had a mark on his ankle." Oxford pointed to his right ankle. "The same mark that is on my ankle."

"Not in my world," Elizabeth said in a husky voice. She stamped her cane. A servant came in. "Take that," she said, pointing to the painting, "and burn it." She stood up. "Good day, my lord."

"Your Majesty!" Oxford said, as the servant flipped the sheet over the painting. A second servant joined him. They picked up the painting and began to carry it away.

Elizabeth had gotten up, needing her cane to steady herself. "You fool," she said, as she disappeared through a door behind her.

~ 178 ~
The Duke of Orsino

My lord," the Earl of Derby said, putting his head into Oxford's rooms at Derby House. "The queen has commanded that I meet the Duke of Orsino at Dover tomorrow and conduct him to London where he is to be housed here, in Derby House."

"But what rooms are there for him?" Oxford asked. "I have taken the … Oh. Of course. Timson and I will return to Hackney."

"She has put me in a most awkward situation, my lord. You are most kind."

"I have suffered her whims more than once. How goes *The Metamorphosis of a Maid?*"

"John Lyly has added fairies and songs. It's coming along well."

"How is John?"

"He is thriving. He's just finished an entertainment at one of the grand estates and he's working with Jonson on *Cynthia's Revels*. I'm hopeful of putting *The Maid* on with Paul's boys; Lyly and Jonson are working to have the Children of the Chapel put on Jonson's *Revels*. They're going to use Blackfriars. Burbage has agreed to rent it to them because he can't get permission to put plays on by adults. Maybe I can get Paul's Boys in there as well. They are all little eyases that cry out on the top of a question."

Derby was holding something in his hand. "This is for you, my lord."

"From 'Cynthia'?"

"I'm afraid so." He handed the paper to Oxford.

"God blast! I am to provide a play for Christmas. To entertain the Duke. A comedy! I am *done* with comedies!"

"Her wish is our command, isn't it?" Derby was hoping Oxford would let him help. "We can work on it together!"

"Not if you're here and I'm in Hackney. No matter. I'll pull out something stale. She won't notice."

"Such as?"

429

"Not *Troilus and Cressida*. I wrote that to curb Earl Robert. A dour piece on the Trojan War but, according to Jonson, no one wants to hear about the Trojan War again."

"So, what 'stale' work are you thinking of, my lord?"

"An earlier piece about the rise of a mean gentleman at court."

"Who?"

"Christopher Hatton. A Puritan before there were Puritans. He shall be Malvolio, steward to a countess who will be mourning the death of her brother. The queen will recognize the countess is intended to represent her. Another character, Aguecheek by name, will represent Sidney."

"Sidney? He's dead!"

"Not as long as the queen keeps praising his poetry and Penelope Rich, Sidney's muse, sits for portraits to give the queen."

"How will you bring in the Duke of Orsino?"

"I will demote him to count. You realize I don't want to write this. The count will be lovesick when the play opens: *If music be the food of love, play on.* The queen will recognize him as one of her former lovers, François, duc d'Alençon." He stopped and looked at Derby. "In fact, I will add a maid – Viola - *metamorphosized* into a lad named Cesario."

"By Apollo?" Derby asked, looking pleased and worried at the same time.

"No. By taking off her clothes and changing into her brother's."

"Oh. Like Rosalind in *As You Like It*."

"Ah! Yes. Thank you, William."

Oxford immediately thought Robin, now John Webster, would love to know what he was working on. Even better, Oxford thought; why not press her to play Viola? She'd been acting a young man for years. She played Puck in *Midsummer*. She won't be able to turn it down. He could hardly contain himself.

A Surprise Visitor

Oxford looked out from the balcony Angus and Ross had built for him. The fields were heavy with grain. Cutters moved through them. Lady Elspeth sat a horse to one side, directing the men, pointing this way and that. She was too far away to be heard but the men were moving as she directed.

"How far from directing maids to plucking flowers," Oxford said to himself, as Timson handed him a plate of pickled herring and beets for breakfast. "Thank you, Timson." Oxford put the plate on his lap. "How goes the harvest?"

"Well, my lord. She has most of it in." He stood there, hands behind his back, gazing out over the fields.

"Strange, isn't it," Oxford said.

"Milord?"

"Her ladyship turning into a field boss."

"No stranger than my aunt running the kitchens at Tantallon Castle. There was a job, my lord. Feeding the lords at one hour, the staff the next, guests amongst them, and then do it all over again, all the while trying to keep the larder full, what with vegetables going bad and vermin in the cold rooms."

Oxford had no sense of what went into running great houses, including King's Place. "Is it early for the harvest?" he asked, trying to find something he could talk to Timson about.

"Oh, no, my lord. Ye can't cut grain that ain't ready. It ain't food yet. But ye can cut wot's early if the grain is only a little early and you need the money, which is what her ladyship is doing."

"Why would she do that?"

"Because we dint have the money she thought we'd have. That's because wot she thought was there went to a painter in London. She knows about the bag of gold ye took to the portrait painter."

"How did she find out about that?"

"She put the boots to Nigel when she went into the strong box and found it missing. Ye'll recall ye asked me to get it; Nigel had to open the box to give it to me. I told Nigel it was for you, which it was. He didn't think she'd notice it was missing, but she did."

"Oh."

"The disappearance of the gold has her worried, yer lordship. She knows ye took it, but not why. She's complaining that she might not be able to pay bills and wages. That's why she's out there, sittin a horse before breakfast."

"Has she asked you about it?"

"No, yer lordship, but I fear she will. With yer permission, I would like to claim I gave it to ye but have no idea what ye did with it. Which is the truth."

"Yes. Leave it to me."

"Thank you, my lord." Timson nodded and left.

Oxford went back to looking out at his wife and the workers clearing the grain in the distance. 'Money,' he said to himself. 'Why is it always about money? I'm the 17th Earl of Oxford. Money should never be a concern for me. My father never cared about it, but Burghley did. Mr. Tightwad, he was. So tight you could hear him squeak as he walked across a room. And the moneylenders! Oof!' Oxford sighed. 'Spinoza here, Spinoza there; Minola in Padua, Spinola in Venice, and a wife now who could school them all. I had gold; I wanted a portrait of the queen. I swapped one for the other. So be it.'

His herring, dead before it was brought to port, pickled to give it a new life, had died a second time in his lap. He threw it over the railing. He pushed away the blanket Timson had put over hm to ward off the morning chill and got up, only to be met by Timson coming back in.

"My lord, the Earl of Southampton has arrived. Nigel has put him in the Day Room."

"I'll go right down. Help me put on a clean shirt."

⸺⬥⬦⬥⬦⬥⬦⬥⸺

Oxford found Southampton lounging in one of the armchairs. He immediately got up. "My lord," he said.

"What a pleasant surprise," Oxford said. They shook hands. "I have so few visitors. Your visit is most welcome. Can I prevail upon you to stay for lunch?"

"I'm afraid I can't, my lord. I am on my way to Wanstead. You know how ill the queen treats my Earl Robert. She has thrown everyone out of Essex House and confined him there. His mother and wife, Lady Rich and her family, and the others with them have been banished to other quarters. We thought the show trial he had to suffer in June would be enough. He admitted his guilt; he gave her a 'pound of flesh,' but it hasn't made any difference. I'll meet with Lord Mountjoy and others at Wanstead who favor Robert. We're to decide what to do next."

"Henry," Oxford said, motioning for Southampton to sit down. "I am worried about you."

"I can handle Cecil. I know he will do anything to keep Robert away from the queen."

"Including taking action against his confederates, which has to include you."

"I care not. Gray ambushed me again. There will be more ambushes. Cecil must be defeated."

"But that is becoming more difficult as his power grows. Perhaps some time abroad would be good until things calm down."

"I do not run from fights."

"Of course not. No one is saying you do. But there are times when even the best general decides to withdraw from the field so he can return later and gain victory."

Southampton looked away. "I'll not be withdrawing, my lord."

Socrates came ambling out of the shadows and crossed Southampton's legs, rubbing against him.

"He likes you," Oxford said.

"I have no time for cats," Southampton said, pushing Socrates away with his foot. It was his right foot. His boot slid down as he stretched out to steer Socrates away from him. Oxford leaned over to see if there was a birthmark on Southampton's ankle but he pulled his foot back and his ankle disappeared.

"What do you hope to accomplish at Wanstead," Oxford asked.

"I don't know, but we have to do something. It's been a year since Robert came back from Ireland. He has sent a messenger to James in Scotland asking for help but James has dithered for so long that it is unlikely any help will come from the north."

"Cecil knows about the messenger, Henry. He was intercepted on his way back."

"I didn't know that."

"That's why I suggest you absent yourself for a while. I'm sure Her Majesty would give you permission to go over to the continent. If things go well for Robert, you can come back when it would be prudent to do so. He will always welcome you, given the history you two have together. On the other hand, if things go poorly, you will avoid being pulled down by him. Think of your lovely wife and child. They need you."

Southampton's face was set. "I cannot, my lord. Honor is everything to me. It is like virginity; you only lose it once."

"With all due respect, Henry, virginity is a fact, determined by a doctor's examination; honor is an opinion that lives off shame. To take steps to preserve yourself for your family is not shameful; it is honorable. Essex is the cause of the problem you find yourself in. There is no obligation on your part to follow him blindly over a cliff."

"It is too late for me to reverse course, my lord. I must respectfully disagree."

He rose, stepping into a pool of sunlight that flooded the room, brushing his hair with highlights of reddish gold. Oxford instantly recalled the setting sun burnishing Elizabeth's hair one afternoon at Nonsuch.

"I hear you are now on the Privy Council, my lord," Southampton said as he pulled on his gloves. "Congratulations. If need be, please put in a word for me."

"I certainly will."

"I must go."

"God be with you, my son."

"Thank you." He left, without noticing that Oxford had called him 'son,' or that Socrates had arranged himself, tail over paws, beneath his chair.

~ 180 ~
What You Will

Shackspear was in his element. He and Burbage were standing outside the door to the Globe accepting accolades from happy theatergoers. The throng streaming by them had just watched a countess fall in love with a girl dressed as a boy thinking she was a boy, and a count fall in love with the same girl thinking she was a boy.

"Or," a puzzled theater-goer asked his companion as they went by Shackspear and Burbage, "did he love the girl because he thought she was a boy?"

"Keep 'em guessin," Burbage said to Shackspear.

"Aye," Shackspear said. He wasn't paying attention. He was busy trying to figure out how much he had made that night.

"I love it when the people you defame in a play are dead," Burbage said.

"Eh?"

"Aguecheek is Sidney, right? Malvolio is Christopher Hatton. And they're both dead. So, they can't sue us."

"Ye think Malvolio is Hatton?"

"Of course, I do. Rascally sheep-biter, and all that."

Shackspear didn't understand.

"Sir Toby Belch made it clear, didn't he?

> *Wouldst thou not be glad to have the niggardly*
> *rascally sheep-biter come by some notable shame?*

"You torched him as a sheep-biter in *Two Gentlemen*. Don't worry; they get it."

"Ye didn't think it was Jonson?"

"No. Jonson's not a Puritan. Hatton was. 'No more cakes and ale.' Hah! You were'n good on that one, William."

Shackspear was disappointed that Malvolio had not been taken as Jonson. "Well, a few more shows and we'll be ready to take Viola and company to Whitehall. The queen wants it presented in the Great Hall on Twelfth Night.

"She'll like it," Burbage said.

"How can you be sure?"

"Viola is another name for the pansy, the queen's favorite flower." Burbage looked more closely at Shackspear. "I think it's time you stop playing the fool."

"I play the fool?"

"A role more difficult than people think. You should take more credit for your asides, your puns and innuendoes. The public loves them."

Shackspear was getting irritated with Burbage. "Enough of that. The Duke of Orsino will be the queen's guest on Twelfth Night."

"Aye. T'is why he's named in the play."

"It will have to be a fine performance, with such a distinguished audience. I'm glad we got John Webster to play Viola. The queen will love seeing her."

"Him."

"Yeah. Him."

1601

181

Twelfth Night before the Queen

The queen came through the door into the Great Hall which had been cleared of the law courts. She was dressed in white, her gown encrusted with pearls, embroidered designs, and diamonds. She was escorted by Orsino, Duke of Bracciano on one arm, and Grigori Mikulin, Russian Ambassador, on the other. Various and sundry other gentlemen trailed them to their seats in front of the temporary stage at the far end of the Hall. Other dignitaries and nobles, English and foreign, followed, filling the chairs behind the queen.

The Earl of Oxford came in with his wife, Elspeth, accompanied by the Earl of Derby and his wife, Lisbeth. The queen had ordered Oxford to attend. Orsino had shifted his lodgings to those of Filippo Corsini, a wealthy merchant and agent for the Duke of Tuscany, opening up Derby House for Oxford and Elspeth to stay there.

Essex and his followers were not present. Essex remained under house arrest at Essex House. His followers stayed away because they did not want to offend him by appearing in public with Sir Robert Cecil, who would almost certainly appear. The celebration of the New Year, the feasting of the Duke and the Ambassador from Russia, and the play they were looking forward to floated eerily above the tension that could be felt throughout the City.

Twelfth Night went off without incident. The queen and the Duke loved it. The queen easily imagined herself as Olivia and liked it even more when she sensed that the audience made the connection as well. Oxford was the Fool, no doubt. She frowned mightily when the Fool tricked Olivia into admitting she was a fool. The Fool asked Olivia why she mourned the death of her brother:

Fool:	*Good madonna, why mournest thou?*
Olivia:	*Good fool, for my brother's death.*
Fool:	*I think his soul is in hell, madonna.*
Olivia:	*I know his soul is in heaven, fool.*
Fool:	*The more fool, madonna, to mourn for your brother's soul being in heaven. Take away the fool, gentlemen.*

This, she knew, was vintage Oxford. He had pressed her to accept Southampton as her son and successor. She had rejected the idea and called Oxford a fool. In *Twelfth Night,* he took her comment that *he* was a fool and put it into a play where *she* became the fool.

She couldn't react. She smiled wanly as Orsino took her hand to escort her from the room. "C'était merveilleuse," he said.

'More than you know,' she replied.

182

The City Knows Him Not

Derby came into Oxford's apartments. "Come, my lord." He gestured toward the window that looked out on the Thames. "Something is going on at Essex House."

Oxford got up and came to the window. They opened it and looked out. Boats crowded the river. Crowds could be seen surging toward Ludgate in the distance. Smoke rose from various chimneys at Essex House, which lay between Derby House and the City.

"It's started," Oxford said.

"Aye. They're burning papers that would incriminate them. It's too warm for a fire."

Oxford strained to see if he could identify Southampton. "Is that Essex at the head?"

"It looks like him."

The crowd had acquired a spearhead of men, some of whom had put on breastplates and arm guards. Pikes and swords could be seen. The crowd, now a mob, began to roar as it disappeared into Ludgate.

"He should have gone to Whitehall," Oxford said. "The City will close its doors to him."

Derby looked at him, surprised.

"I only remark on it because it shows Essex is not thinking strategically. He might have overwhelmed the guards at Whitehall if he had gone to the palace. The City will not respond to his pleas for help. Sir Robert has had his men urging Londoners to leave and bribing those who want to stay. Essex lives on hopes; Sir Robert lives on intelligence. The City will eat him up and spit him out, if he is not taken down inside the walls."

He could not stop imagining a bad end for Southampton. The two earls continued at the window, searching in the distance for anything that would tell them what was going on.

"Essex had *Richard II* put on last night at the Globe," Derby said.

"Did they play the deposition scene? Where Richard hands his crown to Bolingbroke?" Derby nodded. "Was Southampton there?"

"He was. They were all there."

From this, Oxford knew Southampton was in the group that had just passed into Ludgate. Smoke from inside the City could now be seen. The boats on the river were schooling like fish downstream along the north bank near Baynard's Castle.

"What can we do?" Derby asked.

"Nothing, except watch a day unfold in English history that will be remembered long after Agincourt is forgotten. I should proceed to Whitehall. The queen is there."

"If he comes back from the City with a bigger mob, my lord, he will no doubt proceed to Whitehall. It may be prudent to stay here and avoid further confrontation. What can we do, ancients ourselves?"

Oxford hesitated. 'Ancients, indeed.' Derby was right. What could they do? He heard Falstaff telling him to lie down behind a sofa. A part of him liked the suggestion but could not act on it. He should go to Whitehall, he knew, but realized he had no interest in sacrificing himself to save the queen. Honor, he smiled sardonically, was apparently a young man's burden. Whatever the killing of the undercook had done to him was confirmed: of honor he had none. What was there to live for, then? Not plays, he thought. Southampton! That was worth living for.

"I am to Whitehall. I owe that much to the queen."

'And to Southampton,' he muttered to himself as he went out the door.

———————————

Essex was indeed rejected by the City. An edict branding him a traitor had been distributed before he entered. He had to fight his way back out, taking boats to avoid angry citizens who blocked his return by land. He barricaded himself and his companions, including Southampton, in Essex House. Shots were fired; a few were killed, but by midnight Essex and his men were in custody. He and Southampton were in the Tower the next morning. The rebellion was over.

183

Malfis

"Malfis!" Oxford exclaimed. "What brings you here? I haven't seen you since you abandoned me to Sir Robert when he tried to 'unearl' me."

"I never abandon anyone, my lord. I had no way of preventing Sir Robert from taking your titles and lands away from you. Ergo, I did not waste my time trying."

"You could have done something."

Malfis looked pained. "The outcome would be determined by facts. I have no control over them."

"Whether they be true or false?"

"Facts are *always* either true or false, my lord, depending on how one views them. God be praised that Falstaff found Yorick and Joan Jockey. Although," he continued before Oxford could interrupt, "your lordship might be interested to know that Lord Ellesmere wanted to pursue the case even after Joan Jockey's open face sent the jurors running from the courtroom."

"He did?"

"Sir Robert told Ellesmere to continue the trial, which Ellesmere was more than willing to do because he was embarrassed that Yorick had taken over his courtroom."

"But the trial was not continued."

"No."

"Why not?"

"I had some title searches done and presented my findings to Lord Ellesmere. I couched it as a favor to him to show that, if the trial was reopened and a verdict returned declaring you illegitimate, titles to properties he owned would be in jeopardy."

"My God! T'is true! I spent my early years selling off properties inherited from my father. I was always in your office signing papers or sending you instructions to sell this or that."

"You see the scope of the problem."

"I do."

"So, Falstaff didn't save me. You did."

"I wouldn't say that, my lord. Falstaff got the legal cart, as it were, to the top of the hill. I pushed it over by showing Lord Ellesmere how a verdict against you would rebound against him. It worked; the case was not revived."

Oxford didn't know what to say.

"But, if I may add, my lord," Malfis went on, "I would resist the urge to pass this information on to Falstaff. He will not take kindly to being told he is not the hero he thinks he is. Discretion is the better part of truth, my lord, if I may twist Sir John's words to say so."

Malfis apparently thought he was being clever by quoting Falstaff, but was Malfis being truthful? Was he making up his research in the land records? Was everything tricks and mirrors? "How often do we learn that something has happened for reasons we never understood?"

"All the time, my lord."

"Or that what we are told is not what happened anyway?"

"Not quite as often."

"And you speak truth to me now."

"I do."

"But you have waited a long time to tell me, so what is the purpose of your visit today?"

Malfis shifted his weight from one foot to the other, causing Oxford to realize he had not asked his guest to sit down. Oxford gestured toward a chair. "Please." They both sat down.

Malfis eased himself into the chair. Oxford noticed his lawyer had aged since the last time they had been together. He was a bit grayer and had lost enough weight that his clothes were beginning to hang on him. Malfis finished arranging himself in his chair.

"Forgive me, your lordship, for coming unannounced, but time is of the essence. The trial of those who revolted against the queen will begin soon. The City is aware that Her Majesty has had enough of Essex. She intends to finish this business as quickly as possible."

Oxford immediately thought Malfis had come to ask him for something inappropriate, now that Oxford was a member of the Privy Council, but Malfis quickly disabused him of this.

"It is no secret you will be on the jury that will hear the charges against Essex and Southampton. You are not a friend of Essex but I believe you have a particular interest in the wellbeing of the Earl of Southampton."

"I do."

Malfis continued. "Essex will be charged with trying to overthrow Her Majesty. Southampton and the others will be charged with conspiracy to help him do it. The facts are not in dispute. The verdict will be guilty. The judgment will be death."

Oxford knew this would almost certainly be the outcome but he was shocked to hear Malfis say it.

Malfis was not finished. "There is a concept in the law called 'misprision of a felony.' A person is guilty of this crime when they learn that a felony is being committed or has been committed and do nothing about it."

"But Southampton backed Essex to the hilt. He can't possibly claim he was not part of the conspiracy."

"No, he can't, but he may be able to put some daylight between himself and the earl by throwing himself on the mercy of the court and confessing how wrong he was to follow the earl."

"That won't make any difference. The jury is still going to convict him."

"Of course. The verdict will be guilty and the sentence will be death. But what happens then? I think she will sign the warrant to execute Essex immediately, but we may be able to give her reason to pause when she comes to Southampton?"

Oxford certainly hoped so.

"Sometimes a judge wants a result the facts do not support and will look kindly on a plea that, while it may not agree with every fact, will allow the case to be resolved to everyone's benefit. A 'wink' plea, we call it."

"Meaning everyone knows what's going on but they just wink and proceed to the result they want."

"It doesn't take much clothing to garb the emperor in cases like this if that is what everyone wants. Treason is the felony, my lord. The earl might be able to deny treason if he admits to not doing enough to prevent or report it."

"Which, if everyone 'winks,' will serve to avoid the axe."

"You begin to understand me. If the trial results in a verdict of guilty, you might find this information useful."

"Indeed, I do, Malfis. Thank you. How can I compensate you for your efforts in helping me with this?"

"Reward is not expected, my lord. 'Tis enough that I am able to find something of value in the great rubbish bin of my mind to help some other, such as yerself, or the young lord."

"That you have done. I thank you once again for all the service you have rendered me over the years. Stay well and go in peace."

"T'would be good if the young man knew what words would help his cause, and what he should not do or say."

"I will not be admitted to his presence."

"They're be others, my lord." He winked. "Yer lordship," he said, touching his forehead. He got up and went out.

~ 184 ~
The Tryall

hou shalt attend!" Elizabeth shouted. She and Oxford were alone in one of her private rooms at Whitehall. "You are my most senior lord; you sat on Mary's jury; you will sit on this one. My people need to know I mean business!"

"Your Majesty," Oxford pleaded. "I care nothing about Essex. But you know that I believe with all my heart that Southampton is my son! How can you make me sit on a jury that will make me *judge my own flesh and blood?*"

"Very easily: he is *not* your flesh and blood! I need you front and center to make it clear that this trial will be conducted by my most trusted advisors and not those carpet knights who sniggered last summer and gave Essex a pass."

"I cannot do it."

"You *will* do it. Go home and read your latest attempt to mix Troy and lust together, for while there are pearls in oysters, you find none in a thousand. Listen to your Ulysses – *you!* - lecturing Agamemnon – *me!* - about how *the specialty of rule hath been neglected*:

> *Take but degree away, untune that string,*
> *And, hark, what discord follows! each thing meets*
> *In mere oppugnancy: the bounded waters*
> *Should lift their bosoms higher than the shores*
> *And make a sop of all this solid globe:*
> *Strength should be lord of imbecility,*
> *And the rude son should strike his father dead.*

"I treated Essex like a son and what did he do? He attempted to strike me dead!"

Oxford was shocked Her Majesty knew *Troilus and Cressida* so well she could quote parts to him. But how? He had written it to persuade her to rein Essex in but hadn't finished it before she confined Essex to his house. It lay in draft form on a shelf. Shackspear had 'borrowed' the manuscript to stage it at Gray's Inn because he needed money. He thought the lawyers would love the classical elements in it as well as the 'pander' who put the two lovers together. Shackspear reported back that the story was so bad that Henslowe *and* Burbage had turned it down.

How did she get her hands on it? Shackspear wouldn't have given it to her. How would he ever be in her presence? It could only have been Derby, Oxford thought.

Elizabeth took Oxford's silence to mean he would cooperate with her. This calmed her down. "Being the 17th Earl of Oxford, my lord, comes with duties as well as privileges. One of your duties is to sit on a jury to hear charges of treason brought against a fellow earl. And damn your belief that you might be related to him! *Now get out!*"

The trial was held at Whitehall on February 19, eleven days after the rebellion. Essex and Southampton were barged up the Thames from the Tower surrounded by boats carrying soldiers and Household Guards, their halberds facing outwards. Oxford and Derby had to walk only a few blocks from Cannon Row to reach the palace. They and twenty-three other earls were seated by 9 a.m. They would serve as the jurors. Lord Buckhurst, appointed Lord High Steward of the trial by Elizabeth, took his seat beneath the canopied chair of state at the end of the Hall. Eight justices sat in chairs in front of him. Oxford and the other lords were seated along the side walls facing each other. Queen's Counsel and the prosecuting attorneys were arrayed across the near wall. Sir Walter Ralegh, Captain of the Queen's Guard, stood in the back with forty of his yeomen.

The prisoners were brought in. They embraced each other. Essex was dressed in black; Southampton wore a dark-colored suit. He wrapped himself in a cloth gown with long sleeves in which he kept his hands throughout the day. Essex appeared cheerful and confident; Southampton looked sad, but not dismayed.

The indictments were read. The first prosecutor likened Essex to Catiline. The second, Attorney General Coke, laid out the law and proceeded to upbraid Essex and Southampton for their ingratitude to the queen. "Ye sought to be Robert the First of England," he concluded, "but will end as Robert the last of yer earldom."

Essex couldn't take this. "Mr. Attorney general playeth the orator," he said, turning to the jurors, "and abuses your lordships' ears with slanders against us. These are the fashions of orators in corrupt states, and such rhetoric is the trade and talent of those who value themselves upon their skill in pleading innocent men out of their lives."

No one reacted to this. The silence that followed Essex's outburst was more telling than if they had all stood up and cried '*Guilty!*'

The Attorney-General had various members of the law in front of
him read statements that had been taken from other conspirators who
had been arrested and put in the Counter, the Clink, Newgate, and the
other prisons sprinkled across London. The statements spoke as one.
Everyone in the room knew that this was because the words had been
carefully tailored and edited. There was no right to confront witnesses
in person, nor were the accused entitled to counsel.

The reading of the statement of Lord Gray caused the Earl of
Essex to laugh and pluck Southampton's sleeve, but the statement of
Sir Ferdinando Gorges caused him to object out loud. "I beg the court
to be allowed to confront Sir Ferdinando face-to-face."

"Very well," Lord Buckhurst agreed, in a mild voice, as if her were
hosting a banquet and Essex had asked to leave the table early. "Fetch
Sir Ferdinando," he ordered.

Lord Buckhorst's willingness to grant Essex's wish conveyed to
everyone that nothing was going to alter what the verdict would be.
Essex recognized this. He hardly listened as Sir Ferdinando testified to
the various conferences at Essex House that led to the assault on the
City.

Oxford had purposely chosen a seat in the jury box next to the
Earl of Shrewsbury rather than sit next to his son-in-law, the Earl of
Derby, for fear Derby might discover in Oxford's face a special
connection with Southampton. But Oxford soon realized he needn't
have worried. Derby had proved himself a thin salver when it came to
writing plays. He now looked out of his depth as a juror on the
greatest trial of the century. It was the first time he had been asked to
exercise his feudal obligations and sit in judgment on a fellow earl.

Oxford recalled how he had felt when summoned to sit on the
jury that tried Mary, Queen of Scots. The pomp and circumstance of
sitting amongst nobles who were rarely in each other's company,
coupled with the heady feeling of power after the Attorney-General
had charged them with the duty they would undertake was as
memorable as one's first kiss, as the first silver hair seen in the glass,
the first crack in the back when picking something up. Derby, goggle-
eyed, caught up in the trial, had no room left in his imagination to pay
attention to how Oxford may have been reacting to Southampton.

Oxford, on his side, kept his eye fixed on Southampton. He
gripped the rail in front of him as if he were about to leap into the
room. He scarcely glanced at Essex, who had captured everyone's
attention by bursting out with comments or making faces each time a
new statement was read. Southampton stood to his left, separated by
just enough distance to make clear that he did not concur with

everything Essex was saying. Silently, he was letting everyone know that he should not be treated the same as the man he had followed into rebellion against their sovereign queen.

Oxford wondered if Southampton knew he was in his father's presence. He watched carefully for a clue. Southampton's eyes finally wandered away from Essex and Lord Buckhurst, now arguing over some arcane rule of evidence, and ran his gaze over the jurors. Oxford acted like he was looking beyond Southampton but watched the young man closely. He hoped he would see something that would suggest a connection when Southampton's glance ran over him. Unfortunately, the young man took no more notice of Oxford than he did of the newel post Oxford was hanging on.

Essex had been bullying Lord Buckhurst with his comments and questions. He began to argue that he had acted on the day of the rebellion to save the queen because he had been told by a member of the Privy Council that Sir Robert Cecil thought the claim by the Spanish Infanta to inherit the English crown was as good as any other's.

Oxford saw movement at the edge of an arras hanging to his right. The movement had gone unnoticed by the others in the courtroom. Oxford's hand went for his sword but, of course, weapons had been forbidden and he had none. A moment later, a hand pushed the tapestry aside and Sir Robert strode into the room. Oxford realized he would have skewered him through the tapestry if given the chance to do so, striking him dead for all the oppugnancy he had shown Oxford over the years.

"Who told you that?" Sir Robert called out.

Essex refused to name his source.

"Then it is fiction," Sir Robert said dismissively.

"No!" Essex shouted back. He gestured to Southampton by his side. "For this nobleman who standeth next to me heard it when it was jointly told to us both."

Sir Robert, having taken over the courtroom, turned to Southampton. "My lord," he said, "I hold you severed from him in impudency and urge you by whatever you hold honorable, by the love and friendship that hath been betwixt us, that you name the man who spoke to you thus."

Southampton glanced at Essex but spoke to the court. "My Lord Buckhurst," he said, "I refer me to yourself, sir, and, if you will say upon your honor that it were fit for me to name him, I will do so."

Buckhurst nodded. "It is fit for you to do so. Name him."

Southampton looked at Sir Robert. "Sir William Knollys, my lord."

Sir William was sent for and presently appeared. Being sworn, he testified: "Sir Robert hath never expressed to me an opinion that the claim by the Spanish Infanta to inherit the English crown was as good as any other's. Sir Robert spoke to me about a seditious book written by a certain Doleman in which the author wrote that the claim by the Spanish Infanta to inherit the English crown was as good as any other's, but Sir Robert dismissed the claim as Catholic falsity."

Essex slumped.

Lord Buckhurst waited to make sure Essex did not want to say anything else before dismissing Knollys. Essex looked away and Knollys left the courtroom. Sir Robert, with a glare at Essex, slipped back behind the arras.

"My lords," Lord Buckhurst said, addressing Essex and Southampton, "the charges have been stated against you. What say ye in defense?"

"My lords," Essex said to the assembled courtroom, "I am subject to three laws, those of Nature, Reason, and God. In defending myself from my enemies who were set to destroy me, I defended myself in keeping with the law of Nature. I locked up the four lords sent to negotiate with us to protect them from my followers. Finally, I refused to comply with the proclamation read out by the Garter King of Arms because he is a man noted for his dishonesty and was once burnt in the hand."

The silence that greeted this statement showed how weak Essex's defense was. Lord Buckhurst turned to Southampton. "And you, my lord?"

Southampton stepped forward. "My lords, I belie Lord Rutland's statement that I stirred up the Earl of Essex. I have been loyal to him as my kinsman as I am duty bound to do. I am related to him by marriage and beholden to him for the many benefits he has conferred upon me. I admit I was present at the conferences held at Drury House, and, had the plans discussed at those conferences been acted upon, we would have been guilty of treason. But those plans were not carried out. As explained by Attorney-General Coke in his remarks to you, the law takes cognizance of deeds, not intents."

Oxford and the others could sense the wind changing. Southampton was not disrespecting the proceeding as Essex had done or acting like he was guilty and should be punished.

Coke, an experienced trial attorney, realized Southampton might be slipping his tether. "And yet you went to Essex House with your retainers Sunday morning to take part in the uprising."

"I knew nothing of any plan to march on the city, Sir Edward, and only brought with me ten or twelve of my usual attendants. I was unarmed, except for my sword, which I always wear. I went with the Earl of Essex when he sallied forth to defend him from his private enemies. I never heard the proclamation made that day because I was not near the Garter King by the length of a street."

"But you went into the city fully armed. You displayed a pistol!"

"I went into the city carrying only my sword, which I never drew that day. As the events turned violent inside the walls, I spied a man with a pistol and asked him for it, which he gave me, but it had no flint and couldn't hurt a fly. Upon my return to Essex House, I sent Captain White about the House to prevent any attempts to fire on those outside. I therefore beseech you, my lords, to censure me not according to the strict letter of the law but as in your consciences you are persuaded."

Southampton's hands never came out of the cloak that was covering him. He stopped talking. Again, the room fell silent.

Oxford was aglow. Malfis had found a way to get to Southampton in the Tower. The Earl neither bowed nor kneeled before the jury, an act that would have stripped him of his dignity and given them a sign that he was guilty. Nor did he act in a capricious or fantastical way as he had been known to do in the past. Instead, he denied the charge of treason and confessed to a lesser offense – failure to prevent or report what Essex and his followers were up to. *Misprision of a felony*, Oxford muttered to himself. *Malfis, you clever fox, you have prepared the Earl of Southampton in such a way that a door has been left ajar for him to escape with his life.*

"My lord," one of the clerks said, standing on the other side of the rail Oxford was holding onto. The other lords were streaming through a door in the wall behind the Lord High Steward's chair. Essex and Southampton were being led out a separate door. Essex looked back. He laughed. "The Earl of Oxford: his brain frizzled out like a spent rocket. He doesn't know where he is!"

"Strike that from the record!" Lord Buckhurst ordered.

Oxford stood up. Essex's laughter had not erased the feeling that Southampton had a chance to live. Essex followed the clerk into a room where the other lords had taken seats around a large table. Other clerks brought in biscuits and beer. The peers drained the mugs and set to the biscuits with an eagerness that belied how rich they were, or showed how rich they weren't. One asked for more. A clerk said that was it.

The Earl of Lincoln, older than Oxford in age if not in title, rose and headed for the door.

"My lord," the Earl of Worcester said to Lincoln. Oxford was surprised to hear his voice. He had been so focused on the Earl of Southampton that he had not noticed the Earl of Worcester was on the jury. He and Oxford had been married in a double ceremony on the same day, Oxford to Nan, Worcester to his bride. In fact, the weddings had taken place in the Great Hall just outside the room they were sitting in! His head began to swim. And a play. Hadn't one of his plays been performed here? The paneled walls seemed to be exuding memories, like blood that comes out of walls in a nightmare.

"What?" the Earl of Lincoln said, having stopped in the doorway.

"We must deliberate on the verdict, my lord."

"There are no more biscuits and beer," Lincoln said. "I'm leaving."

"Please, my lord," Henry Windsor, 5th Baron Windsor, and son of Oxford's half-sister, Mary Vere, said. "It behooves us to render a verdict lest we besmirch these august proceedings."

"Here, here," a number of the other lords agreed.

"How have we found?" Lincoln asked, looking puzzled and belligerent at same time. "Guilty? Eh?"

"It's been a half-hour," Lord Hunsdon said. "Is that enough?"

The other lords thought it was. They rose together and streamed back out into the courtroom where they took their places. Oxford was last out and last to sit down. He was dazed.

"Take the verdict," Lord Buckhurst announced.

The Serjeant at Arms began at the punie Lord, Thomas Lord Howard, who stood up bare headed. "My Lord Thomas Howard, how find ye as to Robert, Earl of Essex: guilty or not guilty of treason?"

Lord Thomas Howard bent his body, laid his left hand upon his right side, and said "Guilty."

The Serjeant at Arms continued in this manner, asking each lord his verdict. He then returned to the punie lord and began again as to Southampton. All pronounced the earl guilty until he came to the Earl of Oxford. "My Lord of Oxenford, how find ye as to Henry Wriothesley, Earl of Southampton: guilty or not guilty of treason?"

Oxford was looking down at the scarred railing in front of him, wondering how many other lords had sat in his seat, forced to pass judgment on one of their own.

"My lord?" the Serjeant at Arms asked again. "How find you as to the Earl of Southampton: guilty or not guilty of treason?"

Oxford remained frozen. The other peers leaned forward to look at him. His was the last vote.

He did not return their gaze. His eyes came up to look at the slender stalk of a man standing in the middle of the room. Southampton did not return his gaze. His eyes were focused on the floor in front of him.

"My Lord of Oxenford," the Serjeant at Arms began a third time, a touch of asperity slipping into his voice.

Southampton finally looked at Oxford. The two locked eyes. Southampton was surprised to see in Oxford's face a grief that mirrored his own. Oxford rose.

"Guilty," he said.

~ 185 ~
James Decides Southampton's Fate

The queen was striding back and forth in her Privy Chamber thrusting a rusty sword into furniture, hangings, the curtains that stretched from ceiling to floor, and anything else within range. Oxford and Sir Robert Cecil watched her totter back and forth, barely able to wield the sword. "Captain Thomas Lee!" she cried, thrusting the sword into a high-backed upholstered chair.

"Your Majesty," Cecil said, "your realm is secure. You need fear nothing further."

"Oh? And if Sir Thomas should make a second attempt?"

"Ma'am, he was executed at Whitehall Gate this past Friday. Essex and Southampton will be beheaded on Tower Hill tomorrow. The others will soon follow."

Oxford, unlike Cecil, had seen the queen in a rage many times but Cecil had never seen her in such a state.

"Your Majesty," Oxford said in a soothing voice, trying to calm her down, "the rebellion is over. But there is still time to spare Southampton."

"No need," Cecil quickly said. "Let events take their course."

Oxford demurred. "James may not agree."

"I think he would."

Elizbeth dropped the sword she'd been wielding and walked over to Cecil. "How can you be so sure?" She looked at him closely. "Have you spoken with James about Southampton?"

Cecil looked away. Her question made him uncomfortable. "Yes."

"And when was this?" Her voice rose.

"On my visit to Scotland, Your Majesty."

"Without my permission? Do all my agents come and go as they please? Essex from Ireland, *without my permission*; you to Scotland, *without my permission?*"

"T'was *with* your permission, Your Majesty. You sent me north about his pension. He was complaining it was too little and too late."

He was right; she had forgotten. Her face told Cecil he was to say no more. "Did you talk to James about Henry?"

"Only my Lord of Oxford's outrageous claim that Henry is … that you …"

"You discussed this with James?" Her eyebrows shot up. "Why?"

Cecil waved a weak hand at Oxford. "Because his lordship's fantasy about Henry poses a threat to the succession."

She retrieved the sword. She dragged it behind her as she came closer to Sir Robert. "What exactly did you say to James, and what did he say in reply. Report!"

"I told His Highness that Lord Oxford believes the Earl of Southampton is his son by Your Majesty."

"And what was His Majesty's reaction?"

"He was shocked, of course, which is understandable, …"

"What did he say?"

"He asked if there was any support for the claim. I said no. Only his lordship and Your Majesty were privy to it."

"But if only his lordship and I were privy to it, *how did you know about it?*" She came closer to him. "Who else knows? For, as the prologue to a certain play I saw recently tells us:

> *Rumor is a pipe*
> *Blown by surmises, jealousies, conjectures*
> *And of so easy and so plain a stop*
> *That the blunt monster with uncounted heads,*
> *Can play upon it.*

Cecil was on the defensive. "I learned about it from you, Your Majesty. And him." He tipped his head toward Oxford.

Elizabeth leaned in. "Explain." She twitched the sword behind her.

"I arrived outside your chambers one day when you and his lordship were having … a discussion … about Henry."

"You were eavesdropping."

"No, Your Majesty. The two of you could be heard the length of the gallery. As soon as I understood what you were talking about, I walked away."

"And when you found yourself in Scotland, you told James what you had heard outside my door."

"His highness pressed me about who I thought would want to block him from succeeding you. We discussed Arabella Stuart, the Infante, and others, all of no consequence. Based on hearing you say James was your choice to succeed you, I thought I was duty-bound to tell him the Earl of Oxford believed the Earl of Southampton was your son."

"What did he say when he heard this?"

"He was shocked and surprised, of course."

"So," Oxford intervened, "you told James what you heard outside Her Majesty's chambers in the hope James would eliminate Henry."

"I did not," Cecil protested.

"Is Southampton in danger?" Elizabeth asked.

"No."

"How can you be sure?"

"Because James immediately told me his thoughts on the succession and Southampton."

"Which were?"

"He said that if Southampton was your son, he could succeed you under the Succession Act of 1571."

Oxford glanced at Elizabeth, whose face showed no reaction to this.

"Did he explain how he came to this conclusion?"

"He said the prior Act limited your successor to the issue of your body '*lawfully begotten*.' Since you have never married, there cannot be any 'lawfully begotten' issue. But the Succession Act was amended in 1571 to allow the '*natural issue*' of your body to succeed you. James said that if Southampton was your 'natural issue,' Southampton could succeed you under both statutory and canon law."

Oxford liked what he heard. "He believes in the divine right of kings, Your Majesty. He will step aside if he believes Southampton is your son."

To Oxford's surprise, Sir Robert agreed. "He said as much. He said if Southampton was your rightful heir, he would not touch a hair on his head. He quoted Richard:

> *Not all the water in the rough rude sea*
> *Can wash the balm off from an anointed king;*

> *The breath of worldly men cannot depose*
> *The deputy elected by the Lord.*

"And, if I deny Southampton is my son?"

"Then Southampton cannot succeed you and James has no interest in him."

No one said anything for a moment.

"Does he think Henry knows?" Elizabeth asked.

"He asked me that question. I told him, as far as I knew, Henry was unaware of my Lord of Oxford's claim."

"Thank you, Sir Robert," Elizabeth said, "You have helped Henry. As long as James thinks Henry is not my son, he will be safe."

"For there is nothing either good or bad, but thinking makes it so," Oxford murmured.

"Who said that?" Elizabeth asked.

"I did. Or will." He turned to Cecil. "In trying to have Henry assassinated, you have probably saved his life."

Cecil bristled.

Elizabeth put up a hand. "But for how long?" She gestured toward the warrants lying on the table, the gold and scarlet lettering glittering in the fading light. Seals hung off the table. "One is for Essex; the other for Southampton." She looked at Oxford, as if to ask him what he had to say about them.

"A piffle Your Majesty can safely ignore," Oxford said lightly. He had been trying not to sink into a depression as the queen raged about the room with the warrants lying in plain sight. But Cecil's effort to have James eliminate Southampton had obviously backfired. This had put Cecil on his back foot and greatly improved Oxford's mood. The queen was obviously looking to Oxford for advice. "Not as to Essex, of course," Oxford said. "Few will mourn his passing. Henry is a different story."

He turned to Cecil. "Robert, be aware that James will be very displeased if something untoward happens to Henry. He may conclude that you did not accurately report to Her Majesty the conversations he had with you."

Cecil, to Oxford, looked like a fox the hounds had driven into a corner.

"Ergo," Oxford said, looking at Elizabeth, "the warrant for Henry's execution should be stayed. If anyone asks, Your Majesty should say you are consulting with crown counsel about a related offense - misprision of a felony, for example."

He studied Elizbeth's face. She wanted him to go on. "It is also clear that James will step aside if you name Henry as your successor. Divine right of kings, and all that. Henry's succession is safe if you decide to go in that direction."

"That is not going to happen," she snapped, coming back to life. "He is *not* my son, so leave off with this foolishness."

Oxford thought this mere posturing, with Cecil still in the room. He was giddy: James had saved Henry's life. Oxford thought he might take advantage of the occasion. "Then there is the matter of allowing my name to appear on the plays I write. They are mine. Grant me this boon before you leave us so that I do not go unknown into that land from which no one returns."

This caught the queen and Cecil off-guard.

"This was settled long ago, Your Majesty," Sir Robert said. "Lord Oxford was allowed to write plays as long as his name did not appear on them. Nothing has changed."

"Everything has changed," Oxford countered, an edge in his voice. "Time has changed. I am presented to the world as William Shackspear!"

"Yes, a burden," Elizabeth acknowledged, "but my reasons for denying you fame have not changed. It ill-befits an earl to write plays. Besides, what would Henry say if he becomes king?"

This surprised Oxford and Cecil.

"I do not say he will," Elizabeth went on smoothly, "but what if he does? Being the son of a penny-a-page playwright will make his succession more difficult that it would otherwise be."

Oxford persisted. "Your Majesty, your subjects would be thrilled to find out their new king is the son of a playwright! They know you love the theater. You've supported playing companies. Your father too! Burbage even built a special box so you could attend plays!"

Unbeknownst to Oxford, mentioning the special box Burbage had built for her was a mistake. She was pleased to have a way to see plays but embarrassed at the same time because she could not stop herself from slipping in unannounced to enjoy a play. It had become an addiction! As bad as opium! she had complained to one of her ladies-in-waiting after the last play she saw. She didn't like things she couldn't control.

"No, my lord. Fame will have to wait."

She waved a hand. Both men got up. They were each disgruntled for different reasons. Cecil had lost an opportunity to rid himself of Southampton while Oxford would remain invisible. But, he thought, grabbing for another straw to keep alive his hope that Southampton would succeed Elizabeth, was Elizabeth still denying him fame because she planned to name Southampton her successor? A small price to pay if Southampton succeeded her. And there was time for her to change her mind.

As he turned into Canon Row, he realized Elizabeth had parked *their* son in the Tower to keep him from getting into any more trouble while the country recovered from the rebellion and the execution of the Earl of Essex. She would keep him there until she decided whether to name him as her heir. Yes, that must be it, Oxford thought. The *blunt monster with uncounted heads* will come every day to the Tower to see whose head falls but they won't see Henry's. They will finally tire and stop coming. And, while they waited, Henry would live.

He was positively grinning as he entered Derby House. But then he remembered how erratic Elizabeth could be. Witness her forgetting she sent Cecil to Scotland to meet with James. The image of her dragging the old sword around and stabbing chairs was fresh in his memory. The warrant for Henry's execution lay on her table. She could, rising on a dark morning in an ugly mood, sign it and send it on. Henry was not out of the woods yet. The door to his cell was still firmly locked. More work was needed. Reminders that Henry deserved to live. Perhaps James held the key.

The froth of excitement he had felt leaving Whitehall had not completely dissipated. Hope hung on.

186

When Jacks Go Up, Heads Go Down

The queen insisted Oxford remain in London until after Essex had been executed. She signed the warrant and sent it to Sir John Peyton, Lieutenant Keeper of the Tower. She then embarked on a series of dinners and soirées at Whitehall to show that nothing out of the ordinary had happened. She even had the Lord Chamberlain's Men present an old play to show she had forgiven them for staging *Richard II* the night before Essex began his insurrection.

The next day she hosted Cecil, Oxford, Sir Walter Ralegh, Derby, the Admiral, and others for a simple meal as everyone awaited word. Afterwards, she led them into an inner chamber where she sat down and began to play the virginals. She was in the middle of playing a tune when word came that Essex had been executed.

The news ran through the Queen's guests like a breeze ruffling sea grass at a beach but the queen took no notice. Oxford had positioned himself at the end of the instrument watching the keys rise and fall under Her Majesty's fingers. He muttered something to Ralegh, who laughed. When Elizabeth finished the piece, she turned to ask what had made Ralegh laugh.

Ralegh glanced at Oxford, who said: "When jacks go up, heads go down."

The room tittered. Elizabethan courtiers loved nothing more than wit, and Oxford had given them a quip to brighten their day and a story to pass on when they next wanted to appear witty at a dinner party.

The queen, however, was not amused. She scowled, but Oxford could see she was trying not to laugh.

"A loss to us all, ma'am," he said.

"A more foolish man never lived," Elizabeth retorted. "An excellent poet and a better soldier; would that he had been a better servant to himself and to me."

Her guests murmured agreement.

"What bothers me most is that he never sent me the ring I gave him after the Cadiz expedition. I told him to put it in a safe place and send it to me if he ever needed my help. He never sent it to me. This showed me he had no regret for what he had done."

No one commented. The silence made her suspicious. "Or, he sent it but it was intercepted?" She ran her eyes over them. Everyone acted as if they didn't know what she was talking about. She upped the pressure: "Do any of you know what happened to the ring?"

No one answered.

Disgusted, she waved them out of the room. Oxford pushed himself away from the virginals but Elizabeth let him know with a flutter of her hand that she wanted him to stay. He drifted toward the door, lingering. When the others had left, he came back to her.

"It wasn't you, of course," she said, searching the corners of his eyes. The ring's failure to appear had unsettled her. She was becoming more and more convinced that Essex had sent it to her.

"Essex and I were not friends, Your Majesty. He would not have sent it to me. Ask Penelope, or Lettice. They might know."

"Oh, I doubt that. Sir Robert withheld the warrant from Peyton to see if Essex revealed more about the plot. He did. He said Penelope was part of the rebellion."

"He named his own sister?"

"They were not close."

"More proof England is better off without him."

"For once, my lord, I agree." The events of the past weeks were beginning to weigh on her. Oxford was suddenly concerned that Elizabeth, out of exhaustion and fright, might take her anger out on Penelope and the rest of Essex's family.

'Your Majesty, may I suggest you leave Penelope and the rest of the earl's family out of this? They were all involved, for sure, but perhaps it is time to let your people know the Essex rebellion is over. Let Penelope and Lettice go home. Ignore whether Mountjoy was involved. You need him in Ireland. Take down the scaffolds at Tyburn. Their dismantling would send everyone a clear sign."

"Just as soon as Blount and Danvers follow Essex."

"But Blount is Lettice's husband, Your Majesty. She only recently married him."

"Ye think I don't know that? She should count her lucky stars I'm sparing her and her daughter. Now, go."

187

Like a Jewel Hung in Ghastly Night

Oxford and Timson descended to the waiting boat. Oxford was returning to Hackney, now that the trial was over and Southampton's life had been spared. The boat would carry them down to River Roding and up to Barking where Amos would meet them with a carriage.

Oxford stood holding onto the standing bar as the outgoing tide swept the boat downriver and under the bridge. He told the men to steer toward the Tower. They swept past Traitor's Gate, where those committed to the Tower were brought in by water. A rusting iron portcullis blocked access to the wharf. A raven lumbered by overhead, returning from Southwark. A good omen, Oxford thought. Everyone believed the crown would fall if the ravens ever left the Tower.

The boat swept past the Gate and continued on down the river. Oxford didn't glance at Greenwich as they went by it on his right. River Roding was soon off their bow and the rowers began to earn their keep, pulling against the tide coming down the river.

Oxford worked on a sonnet as the boat labored upstream.

> *Weary with toil, I haste me to my bed,*
> *The dear respose for limbs with travel tir'd;*
> *But then begins a journey in my head*
> *To work my mind, when body's work's expired:*
>
> *For then my thoughts--from far where I abide--*
> *Intend a zealous pilgrimage to thee,*
> *And keep my drooping eyelids open wide,*
> *Looking on darkness which the blind do see:*
>
> *Save that my soul's imaginary sight*
> *Presents thy shadow to my sightless view,*
> *Which, like a jewel hung in ghastly night,*
> *Makes black night beauteous, and her old face new.*
>
> > *Lo! thus, by day my limbs, by night my mind,*
> > *For thee, and for myself, no quiet find.*

In an hour they were at Barking where a carriage waited. They were in King's Place before midnight. Oxford, exhausted, went upstairs to his rooms. Lady Elspeth and the rest of the house was asleep. Timson helped Oxford into bed and put a blanket over him. Oxford lay in the dark and stared at the ceiling.

He brought up the sonnet he had been composing on the way back. He hoped that working out the rhyme scheme and the meter, sliding in a word here or there to replace one that didn't quite convey what he meant, would bring him sleep, but replacing *darkness* with *black night* to accentuate the rhythm of *sight* and *sightless* failed to bring him rest. He was still awake when a servant passed under his window the next morning on his way to milk the cows in the near barn.

He finally fell asleep. He woke later as the sun streamed into his room. Timson was waiting in the adjoining room. He brought him some breakfast beer. Oxford dictated the sonnet to him and wondered how Southampton was doing in the Tower. Scarcely a leaf moved on the trees outside. The air had gone to gaze upon some Cleopatra, he thought, leaving a gap in nature. A second sonnet began to form in his mind. He would finish it later. But what could he do to thank the queen for sparing their son? Cleopatra appeared in his mind, gliding by as if to suggest it was time to put together the scenes and glittering words he had been collecting about the Egyptian queen. *The barge she sat in, like a burnished throne, ...*

He smiled. Yes, it would do. She would like it.

~ 188 ~
# The Worm of Nilus

Oxford remained in Hackney while Essex and his conspirators were executed and their bodies given back to their families. Their heads were put up on poles at the south end of the London Bridge. The scaffolds came down and the country returned to normalcy.

Oxford spent the time writing sonnets to Henry, knowing, of course, that Henry would never see them.

> *When in disgrace with fortune and men's eyes*
> *I all alone beweep my outcast state,*
>
> . . .
>
> *Haply I think on thee, - and then my state,*
> *Like to the lark at break of day arising*
> *From sullen earth, sings hymns at heaven's gate;*
>
> > *For thy sweet love remember'd such wealth brings*
> > *That then I scorn to change my state with kings.*

Each sonnet took the greater part of a day to write. Oxford did little else. He rarely left his rooms. Timson brought him his meals while Elspeth stayed away. Nigel told her Oxford had suffered an unspoken loss from the Essex Rebellion but she was not to worry; this had happened in the past. He's a poet, etc. etc. Her husband would soon return to them. Events like these, he said, were like the passing of the seasons. He pointed to the dark winter sky outside and reminded her that winter would soon give way to spring.

Oxford had settled into a firm conviction that Elizabeth had spared Henry because he was, in fact, her son. There could be no other reason. All the other conspirators had been executed, punished, and fined. Henry, the sole exception, remained unharmed, safely put aside in the Tower, his family and fortune untouched. The farms and estates owned by the other conspirators were being auctioned off on a daily basis. The Earl of Cumberland, for example, put in a bid for Essex's favorite horse. Others sought title to odd lots he had acquired across England.

Oxford fantasized that Elizabeth would begin to wonder whether James was the right person to succeed her. The Scotsman was a foreigner, for goodness sake; he couldn't own land in England or

inherit property, so how could he become king? These thoughts fed
his hopes but he realized that, to save Southampton, he must stop
claiming Henry was Elizabeth's son and rightful heir. Left to her own
devices, he thought, she might become more open to having Henry, an
Englishman, succeed her.

In the meantime, he would write a play to show her that the book
she had been trying to get her hands on since Arundel and Howard
mentioned it in 1581 was no more. The two earls had been sent to the
Tower when Oxford told Elizabeth they were Catholic spies working
for Spain. In long scrawling statements, they denied Oxford's charges
and did their best to libel Oxford in return. They said Oxford had
boasted he could write a Bible in six days, that the Trinity was an old
wives' tale, that Joseph was a cuckold *and* a wittol, and, most
importantly, that Her Majesty had the worst singing voice anyone had
ever heard. None of this was news to Elizabeth, but what got her
attention was mention of *The Book of Prophecies*. The earls could not say
what was in it, only that Oxford showed it to them once and it had a
picture in it of a son of Elizabeth with a crown on his head. He had
denied he still had it but he could tell she didn't believe him.

Where had it gone? Oxford asked himself. He had lived his life
like a desert Bedouin, always shifting camp, sometimes day to day.
He'd started out at Hedingham, then went to Hill Hall in Essex at
seven or eight to study with Sir Thomas Smith, then on to Cecil House
when Earl John died, then across the Strand into the Savoy to escape
Lord Burghley and Lady Mildred, followed by a long succession of
lady's beds leading up to the Folly, Oxford Court, and finally, King's
Place. So much left behind each time, to be cleaned up by servants and
sold in Spitalfields.

The Book had disappeared somewhere in there. Dee would come
back from the continent someday and the queen would surely
summon him for a conference and ask him about *The Book*. Oxford
realized he needed to put Elizabeth's fears to rest. A magus in a new
play would announce that he would be '*drowning his book deeper than did
ever plummet sound*' and Elizabeth would know that *The Book of Prophecies*
had been destroyed and was nothing more to fear.

In the meantime, he would entertain her with *Antony and Cleopatra*.
He would use all the beautiful words he had been storing up to show
Elizabeth as the wily queen of the Nile. She would like being
Cleopatra, he thought, and seeing *Helen's beauty in a brow of Egypt*. He
grabbed a sheet of paper and began to write. A Roman general would
sneer that Antony had been *transformed into a strumpet's fool to cool a gypsy's*

lust. 'She will like being called a strumpet,' Oxford thought, as his pen sped on. 'But Antony will be the fool, Cleopatra his master.'

His face brightened. "I will add a clown who will bring the asp Cleopatra will use to take her life. He's not in Plutarch. The clown will call it a *worm*." He smiled. "By this she will know I am the clown, because 'ver' is 'worm' in French:

Cleopatra: *Hast thou the worm of Nilus, That kills and pains not?*
Clown: *Aye. But the worm's an odd worm.*
Cleopatra: *Get thee hence, farewell.*
Clown: *I wish you all joy of the worm.*
Cleopatra: *Farewell.*

"Yes. Yes," Oxford said, crouched over his desk. "Through these words she will see me peering out at her, like I looked at her through the eye holes of the ass's head I wore in *Midsummer*." He laughed. "By mastering her death, Cleopatra will show us how she mastered Julius Caesar and Mark Antony. This Elizabeth will also like.

"But I can't do a play about *The Book of Prophecies* and write *Cleopatra* at the same time. I will give the play about *The Book of Prophecies* to someone else, but who? Derby? Lyly? Marston?"

He shook his head. "Cleopatra beckons me now." He brought new paper in front of him.

"*The barge*," he said, his voice sounding husky in the empty room. Someone listening in, a Robert Cecil, for example, would have thought Oxford was about to write a steamy scene in which Cleopatra took Mark Antony into her arms. Instead, he was about to describe the vessel that brought Cleopatra up the Cnidus River to meet Antony in Tarsus. It was his love of the words he would write that made his voice suddenly deepen:

The barge she sat in, like a burnished throne,
Burned on the water; the poop was beaten gold,
Purple the sails, and so perfumed, that
The winds were love-sick with them, the oars were silver,
Which to the tune of flutes kept stroke, and made
The water which they beat to follow faster,
As amorous of their strokes. For her own person,
It beggared all description; she did lie
In her pavilion,--cloth-of-gold of tissue,--
O'er-picturing that Venus where we see
The fancy outwork nature; on each side her
Stood pretty-dimpled boys, like smiling Cupids,
With divers-coloured fans, whose wind did seem

To glow the delicate cheeks which they did cool,
And what they undid did.

...

A seeming mermaid steers: the silken tackle
Swell with the touches of those flower-soft hands,
That yarely frame the office. From the barge
A strange invisible perfume hits the sense
Of the adjacent wharfs. The city cast
Her people out upon her; and Antony,
Enthroned i' the market-place, did sit alone,
Whistling to the air; which, but for vacancy,
Had gone to gaze on Cleopatra too,
And made a gap in nature.

"*The air had gone to gaze on Cleopatra too and made a gap in nature.* She will love it," he said.

'*But not as much as you will*,' a voice said in his head.

466

The Phoenix and Turtle

Oxford did nothing over the next few days but write and rewrite *Antony and Cleopatra*, but a poem waited in his mind to be brought to life. The clean paper at hand, awaiting the stroke of his pen, was something novel for Oxford. Heretofore, he had scribbled on greasy scraps of paper thrown out by the kitchen, but Timson had decided that Oxford deserved better. Without asking permission, he veered off from a trip to London for Lady Elspeth to visit Richard Field in Blackfriars. Timson had heard Oxford speak of Field as a printer. Timson thought printers must have good paper. He went into Field's shop and explained who he was and that he wasn't leaving until he had good quality paper to take back to his lordship.

Fielding knew that a Scotsman with a bee in his bonnet and a gleam in his eye would not be put off. "He is writing?" Field asked.

"Aye. And I'll be back for ye to print it when he writes it down."

Field handed over an armload of paper and bade Timson convey his best wishes to Oxford.

Thus, Oxford had the pleasure of guiding his quill across clean white paper without a skip or a blot, a new experience for him after years of navigating around a smear of fat left over from last night's meal. Finding clean paper had never been a priority for him. Rather than fixing a problem, he put up with it. Even though a lord, Oxford endured left-over paper in quiet desperation, a typical English response, visitors from the continent had noticed. Timson's trip to Richard Field ended all that.

The poem would express Oxford's grief at Southampton being denied his rightful place as the next king of England. He was, in Oxford's mind, the queen's son by him. She being unmarried, what better father could the next king of England have than Oxford, England's last medieval knight. His family stretched back 500 years. Naming Southampton as Elizabeth's successor would be the culmination of centuries of loyal service by the House of Vere.

Poets and flatterers had hailed Elizabeth as a phoenix throughout her reign, but in every version of the myth the phoenix gives birth to a successor. Oxford's poem would end differently. A new phoenix would not be waiting to take her place. Elizabeth was refusing to name

Henry as her successor. Perhaps, Oxford thought, if she could see his grief and their loss, she might change her mind about Southampton:

> *Beauty, truth, and rarity,*
> *Grace in all simplicity,*
> *Here enclosed, in cinders lie.*
>
> *Death is now the phoenix' nest,*
> *And the turtle's loyal breast*
> *To eternity doth rest,*
>
> *Leaving no posterity;*
> *'Twas not their infirmity,*
> *It was married chastity.*

'She *beauty*; I *truth*; Henry, our son, *rarity*. *Beauty* for Betty, Elizabeth's nickname; *Truth*, for me, Edward de Vere; *Rarity* for Wriothesley, or 'Rosely,' as he likes to pronounce it." He chuckled grimly. "All three *in cinders lie*. T'was not from any infirmity: she and I *had* a son. But she cannot *acknowledge* him because of *married chastity*. She is fated to die a virgin. Our son in confin'd doom lies, stripped of his freedom. Though he yet breathes, he is dead to all the world."

"But who am I borrowing from?" he suddenly asked the silent room. He jumped up and went into the next room where his books were arranged on shelves. Shutting down his mind to reach perfect stillness, he surveyed the books in front of him the way a man uses a dousing rod to search for water, the mind asleep, the emotions free of restraint. His eyes fell on Sidney's *Astrophil and Stella*. "No," he said. He pulled it out and took it to a table.

> *In a grove most rich of shade,*
> *Where birds wanton musicke made*

"No, no, no," he said. "*Birdes wanton musicke made?*" He paged on. "Ah," he said:

> *But when their tongues could not speake,*
> *Love its selfe did silence breake;*
> *Love did set his lips asunder,*
> *Thus to speak to love and wonder."*

"Forced. So much better this." He took the book back into the other room and grabbed a sheet of paper:

> *Hearts remote, yet not asunder;*
> *Distance and no space was seen,*
> *Twixt this Turtle and his Queene;*
> *But in them were a wonder."*

"Better," he muttered. "Now for the beginning:

Let the bird of lowdest lay,
On the sole Arabian tree,
Herald sad and trumpet be:
To whose sound chaste wings obey.

He sounded out what he'd written, confirming the trochaic tetrameter, with stresses on the first and last syllables. "Ça marche," he said aloud. "Sidney in a higher key."

And thou treble dated Crow,
That thy sable gender mak'st,
With the breath thou giv'st and tak'st,
Mongst our mourners shalt thou go.

"Henry Wriothesley, triple-dated by being born, then by becoming the 3rd Earl of Southampton, and then being attainted and stripped of his titles by his conviction. Who else could the Crow be? Who else but Her Majesty could the Phoenix be? And Truth?" He cackled alone in the room. Then he wept. "All lies in cinders, is what Truth must say."

He worked to finish the poem. Sixty-seven lines, the words flowing out of him like honey being poured out of a warm cup. He had the poem finished by supper time. He stood up, dizzy, as he always was when his mind became a kingdom of verse. He went into the room where his bed lay and fell into it. Not more than a few minutes passed before Timson quietly came in and spread a wool blanket over him.

<hr>

The Earl of Derby stopped by the next day on his way to a meeeting of his college at Cambridge. "May I send Ben Jonson your way to discuss a book of poetry I am putting together with John Salusbury? You met John at my house. He was with us when we watched Essex cross the Thames on his way to Nonsuch. John was also the man who, the day after the Essex rising, captured Sir Thomas Lee outside the queen's Privy Chamber."

"And saved Her Majesty from certain harm."

"Yes. She promises to knight him. John would like to present her with a book of poetry to celebrate her escape. Chapman, John Marston, Ben Jonson, and others have agreed to contribute poems to the book. John will be the author of the book but remain, of course, for modesty's sake, anonymous."

"Anonymous I know. What will the subject be?"

"We haven't settled on that yet."

"May I suggest the phoenix."

"Oh, excellent. Rising from the ashes. Perhaps you could speak with Shackspear about making a contribution?"

"I already have. He has written an elegant dirge lamenting Her Majesty's passing."

"But she hasn't 'passed' yet."

"William likes to stay ahead of events. I will get Shackspear's *Phoenix* to you, William."

"We hope to have Fielding print it in time for John to give the book to her when she knights him at Whitehall. It's to be on June 15."

"I'll have my man, Timson, carry it to you next week."

"Excellent, my lord."

"Send Mr. Jonson to me," Oxford said. "I may have use of him."

"Splendid."

<hr>

The next weeks flew by as Oxford worked over *Antony and Cleopatra*. As a break, he would work on *The Phoenix and Turtle*. When he thought it was finished, he had Timson make a clean copy and take it to Derby to add to the book John Salusbury would present to the queen. Marston, Chapman, and Jonson added their poems. Richard Field published *Love's Martyr, or Rosalins Complaint* in time for it to be given to the queen when she knighted Sir John at Whitehall on June 15, 1601.

Elizabeth noticed, with her quick eye, that only Shakespeare's poem – Oxford's, of course – did not have a phoenix rising from the ashes at the end. Again, a message only she would understand.

She read through his contribution a second time that evening when she was alone in her chambers. She drank in the measured, stately verse, knowing full well who the phoenix was, the turtledove, and the third person – rarity. She closed the book and lay it in her lap. She looked across the room through the open windows – it was a warm June day. "I suffer as he does," she said aloud into the empty room, shaking her head slightly, "but suffer both we must."

She laid the book on the table next to her chair and got up, leaning on her cane. "Mary said being queen would be difficult, but some days are certainly harder than others." Her felt slippers scuffed across the heart pine floor filling the silent room with a sound John Dowd could have borrowed for the underlying bass for of one of his motets.

~ 190 ~
Antony & Cleopatra

The Garter ceremony was held on Friday, April 24 at Whitehall. The queen presided over a banquet to honor the new members that year. There were only two: William Stanley, 6th Earl of Derby, and Thomas Cecil, 2nd Lord Burghley.

Oxford had to attend. He was father-in-law to William through Lisbeth, his daughter, and brother-in-law to Thomas through Oxford's first wife, Nan. Getting older, he was learning, was giving him a new perspective on crotchety old men. They weren't crotchety; they simply didn't care what anyone thought anymore. Oxford tried to grouch his way out of attending but, given his family ties to both new members, had to agree to attend the ceremony. He sulked through the meal. The food was terrible.

The talk was all about the Earl of Pembroke. He had gotten Mary Fitton pregnant but refused to marry her. The queen thought this intolerable and sent him to the Tower. A stubborn man, he refused to change his mind. He waited in the Tower while Mary languished in an upstairs room someone got her in a tenement built over part of the remains of St. Mary Overy's Priory in Southwark. Mary finally gave birth but the baby died. The queen, exasperated, released Pembroke to Baynard's Castle, his London home on the Thames; Mary went home in disgrace.

Pembroke took time in the Tower to tell Mary why he could not marry her. In a poem entitled *To a Lady residing at Court*, he wrote:

> *Then this advice, fair creature, take from me*
> *Let none pluck fruit, unless he pluck the tree.*
> *For if with one, with thousands thoul't turn whore.*
> *Break ice in one place and it cracks the more.*

This disdainful dismissal of a woman who had given birth to his child should have earned him even more punishment but the earl's foray into poetry was greeted with lewd chuckles from men and women alike, the queen included.

Oxford felt sorry for Mary. He remembered her arriving late for the dinner party at Peregrine Bertie's house when he had met Aemilia Bassano for the first time. Mary had been a child then, no bigger than a bird's nest. Like so many young people, she saw herself as more

471

adult and important than she really was. She leaned around Gabriel Harvey, who had brought her to Peregrine's House, to flirt with Oxford, but Oxford was enraptured with Aemilia Bassano. Poor Mary – a child compared to Aemilia's dark, smoking beauty – had apparently left the dinner thinking she could play on the same field where earls and ladies gamboled. Maybe she wanted to get pregnant to snare Pembroke as a husband, but losing the baby meant she lost the game as well. Instead of becoming the Countess of Pembroke, she became the butt of a poem that fed the prejudices of the men who forced women, in various ways, to have sex with them while escaping the consequences of their assaults.

The women who laughed at the poem were unforgiving women who dreamed of liaisons themselves but publicly voiced disdain for any woman who slipped into the bed of someone to whom they were not married. Pembroke's poem may even have accelerated his release from the Tower. It was not an age that valued empathy. The queen herself loved bear-baiting more than plays and never expressed any concern for the wounds suffered by the bears or the dogs. Disease and death were everywhere. Most learned to avoid getting close to the misfortunes of others and sought relief from their own fears by attending cockfights, hangings and, of course, plays.

Would Cleopatra have been any different? She was a woman who had given birth to children by Julius Caesar *and* Mark Antony, a notable achievement in any age. Oxford wondered what Burghley's puritanical hag of a wife, Mildred Cook, would have thought of the Queen of the Nile. Probably not much. But Oxford's beautiful depiction of Egypt's last ruler and her decision to end her life with poison made all the carpet warriors in the room feel brave, while the women found enough of themselves in Cleopatra to feel good as well.

They had done their homework. They consulted their maidservants about what Cleopatra had used to preserve her legendary beauty. They were told it was a cream made from two new-laid eggs and their shells mixed with burnt alum, powdered sugar, borax, poppy seeds all finely beaten together and 'a pint of water that runs from under the wheel of a mill.' But no one knew whether she covered herself in this paste before or after her bath in ass's milk. The Admiral's wife confided she only used 'liquid pearl', whatever that was, to give her skin its translucent glow. The queen listened attentively as well for she was the biggest user of thick cosmetics of all. She arrived at Whitehall to watch the play looking like she had encased herself in thick plaster. It were a wonder she could move.

Oxford watched the ladies settle down as they eyed each other and, when the play caught them up, he considered his effort well-done.

The queen also found herself gawping at the stage. After all, wasn't she Cleopatra? Her amazement turned to frowning anger as she listened to the Clown bring in a 'worm' instead of 'snake.' Cleopatra put the 'worm' to her breast and died. She seethed while she waited for him to appear. "Still marking your plays, my lord, like a dog pissing on a stone as he trots down the street? I know 'worm' is 'ver' in French. As in 'Edward de Vere?' Edward the 'worm?' I think I like that."

"*Exactement*, Your Majesty. *Un chien, qui gambille en bas de la rue.*" He paused. "'*I geeve you all joy of the worm,*'" he crowed, repeating the clown's line but mangling his French accent to make sure Her Majesty knew he was reminding her of a time when they were lovers and 'worm' referred to something she liked to give 'all joy to.'

"God," Elizabeth muttered. "I would have thought Shackspear'd have cut that," she said, suggesting Shackspear should have cut Oxford's 'worm.'

"He's still not reading what I give him," Oxford said matter-of-factly, refusing to acknowledge her quip had hit the mark.

"Cleopatra dies at the end. Not good," she said. She didn't like being reminded of her mortality.

"She dies in Plutarch. She actually died in real life. But you will live on in this play as the noble, self-sacrificing sovereign that you are."

She harrumphed. She liked being compared to Cleopatra but not that she was mortal. At least he hadn't brought up Southampton. But then he did.

"Your Majesty, I have come to realize that my belief Henry is my son and your successor only places him in danger. I want him to live. I accept that James will succeed you."

This was a startling volte face. Perhaps his appointment to the Privy Council had brought out a wiser and more serious Earl of Oxford.

"I value these words, my lord. I will hold you to them."

Oxford made a short bow. "In return, I ask a simple boon: permission to visit Henry in the Tower."

Her eyebrows rose. "The reason?"

"I have a cat I would like to give Henry to help him pass the time in the Tower. Sir John Peyton can accompany me while I visit. I will not discuss politics, Essex, the Rebellion, Ireland, James, or anything else with Henry. His mother says he has been allowed no visitors. She worries about him. She would like me to visit Henry and report back."

"*His mother?* I thought I was his mother."

"Lady Mary has had an 'awakening,' Your Majesty. She told me she now believes the Devil tricked her into believing the earl was not her son. She says it was all part of God's plan to punish her for her transgressions. She grieves for Henry, convinced he is her son."

"Well," Elizabeth muttered, "God – or the Devil - certainly works in mysterious ways." Or, she thought to herself, Lady Mary is a lot cleverer than anyone has given her credit for.

Oxford continued. "I assure you I have also had an 'awakening.' I confess I still hope he is our son, Your Majesty, but I accept the fact that my dreams must remain in the playhouse. I will leave Henry to you and your world."

She studied him for a moment. "I will send a note to Sir John to allow you to visit Southampton on the terms you have laid out."

"Majesty," Oxford said, bowing. His daughter, Lisbeth, came up.

"Your Majesty," she said. She bent a knee. She acknowledged her father with a tip of her head in his direction but kept her eyes on the queen. "I think my father has given you a lovely present." she said. She was apparently referring to the play they had just watched.

"Indeed," Elizabeth murmured. "Congratulations on your husband being made garter knight."

"Thank you, Your Majesty. He well-deserves it."

"I thought you were unaware of his many fine qualities."

"I was, Your Majesty. But William and I have mended fences. I have recognized his qualities whilst he has acknowledged mine. I have just returned from the Isle of Man where, if I may say so, I ably represented him as lord governor."

Elizabeth reached out and took Lisbeth's hand. "I like the woman I see before me. It is not where one has been, my dear, but where one is going that matters. I like the course you have set. Now, if you will excuse me, I am tired."

She rose and tottered off.

"A moment," Oxford said to Lisbeth. He beckoned for her to walk with him into an empty corridor. Once around the corner he turned to face her. "It is difficult for me to ask this, but have you slept with the Earl of Southampton."

Lisbeth looked at him in astonishment. "I? Sleep with Henry?" She laughed aloud. "You and Pee-Pop tried to get me to marry him, remember? He refused me."

"But you said you tried to seduce him, and he rejected you again."

"That was only to stir you up, which is so easy to do. No, I have never slept with the Earl of Southampton. There is something about him that makes my skin crawl. Is it his long fingers? His 'sweetness?' I thought he would end up with a closet Ganymede but then he got Elizabeth Vernon pregnant so that put paid to that idea. I could never sleep with him, my lord. Never. Why do you ask?"

"An idle rumor, that's all." He could tell she was telling him the truth.

"A *false* rumor. I have been accused of many things, my lord, but I have never slept with the Earl of Southampton."

"I'm so glad."

"Milord," she said, and walked away.

'*Falstaff?*' Oxford muttered. He headed for the door.

 Derby intercepted him. "My lord."

"William." Oxford forced himself to come to a halt. "And how go your efforts, William?"

"Ongoing, my lord. I hope to have something to show you shortly. I find it extraordinarily difficult to find time to write when so much other business, the getting and spending, lies in the way. I was in Moscow when I heard that I had risen to the earlship as a result of the death of my father and brother. Not pleased about their deaths, of course," he hastily added, "but my elevation. I immediately came home to accept the honor and found that guardians had been appointed of my brother's estate and they had given everything to his widow. The resulting lawsuits will outlive us all. I have recovered some of my property but had no idea how much more work it would take to be the 6th Earl of Derby. It was so much easier when I was a second son with no expectations. How do you handle your affairs such that you can find time to write?" He looked desperate.

"Nigel takes care of everything for me at Hackney or, at least, whatever my lady has not taken over. Timson takes care of my personal needs." Oxford delivered this as if he were on a parade ground, barking orders. "You need a Nigel or a Timson, William. Hire yourself a Puritan who works all day and prays all night, someone who constantly finds himself short of what is expected of him."

Derby didn't know what to make of this. Oxford sounded like he thought Derby had done something wrong. He decided to change the subject. He asked about Oxford's son. "And your son, Henry, my lord. How goeth he? He must be eight or nine now."

"He is. A proper toff, he is. With all the airs and arrogance that come with it. He's not shy about ordering everyone around, which pleases his mum. She thinks this will help him as he grows older. It didn't help me."

"Is he to Cambridge?"

"Next year, perhaps. He has tutors now but is not driven to his studies the way I was. He's dragging his feet about French. 'Why do I have to?' he asks. 'I'll have translators if I go over.'"

"You can lead a horse ..."

"Aye. I need to show him there is so much to learn in the world."

"A week with Falstaff might do it, my lord."

"Falstaff! That would be the ruin of him." This reminded Oxford where he had been going when William intercepted him. "*Falstaff?*" he said in a different voice. "I must go," he said. "I'm to meet the devil himself, William. And I know just where to find him."

On that mysterious note, Oxford left.

~ 191 ~

The Devil Himself

He's in the back," Peaches said. She went by Oxford carrying trays of food to a nearby table. Oxford continued into the inn where he found Falstaff slumped over in a booth.

"Jack!" Oxford said.

Falstaff sat up. He spied the angry frown on Oxford's face. "Ah. Ye've finally seen her." They both knew he was referring to Lisbeth.

"Ye lied." Oxford looked as angry as Falstaff had ever seen him.

"Not exactly," Falstaff said. He straightened himself up. "It was Tupp who said the boy had a birthmark on his ankle, not me."

"What? Ye can't hide behind that minimus of a page to defend yourself."

"True. But that's what happened. Tupp got irritated with you and I going back and forth about whether Henry had a birthmark. I was going to ask Lisbeth to help but couldn't get in touch with her. She was off on the Isle of Man or somewhere. Tupp decided to tell you that Henry had a birthmark on his ankle to end it."

"But that was a lie!"

"*We don't know that, do we?*" He cocked his head. "Think about it. Does anyone know what's on the inside of the 3rd Earl of Southampton's ankle? Besides, I had to back up my liegeman, Tupp, didn't I? It would have been dishonorable not to do so.

"By telling me a lie?"

"A lie works, if you get away with it."

"How can you say that?"

"Thomas Brincknell."

"What? You rogue!"

"I told the jury what they wanted to hear." He put up his hand; *Under penalty of perjury I tell you Thomas Brincknell ran onto the end of the Earl of Oxford's sword, valued at £7 6, and committed suicide.* The truth would have sent you to the gallows." Falstaff folded his hands over his immense belly. "I gave you a second life. *I gave England its greatest poet!*"

"But the earl is not my son," Oxford complained.

477

"Who says he isn't? The mark on your ankle has distracted us. The queen should accept him as her son. He'll make a fine king."

Oxford looked at Falstaff. "You don't get it. A king must be of royal descent. If Henry is not Elizabeth's son, he's not royal. Ergo, he can't be king."

"*You* don't get it," Falstaff said, whirling his arm over his head like he was a magician bringing down a magic spell. "It's what people *believe* that matters, not what the truth is. Elizabeth may be a bastard herself! Wasn't her mother executed for adultery? Five lovers went to their deaths with her, didn't they? Henry didn't think she was his daughter. Neither did Parliament. Twice, in fact. But, to the people of England, Elizabeth is their lawful sovereign. Didn't I hear you say nothing is either good or bad but thinking makes it so? Put *that* in your next play. If Elizabeth recognizes Henry as her son, the succession will go down as easily as an eel slips down a heron's throat."

Oxford did not want to hear any more. 'You are indeed the devil,' he said, heading for the door. Peaches passed him again, her arms full of dirty dishes. "He's missed you," she said.

Oxford stopped. Peaches continued on into the kitchen, but her words had frozen him. He stood in the middle of the inn as patrons and servers swirled around him. Instead of continuing out the door, he turned around and headed back to where Falstaff was trying to get a pair of spectacles to sit on his nose. The script for *Henry IV* lay in front of him. *Part One*, of course. He looked up. He acted like he'd been caught out. "I have to keep up with me lines, my lord, what with everyone asking me to recite them." He took off his spectacles. "But, truth be told, my lord, me eyes are not what they used to be."

"Yes," Oxford said. He didn't care a farthing about Falstaff's jokes or how his lies may have saved the 17th Earl of Oxford from the scaffold. He saw for the first time that the fat knight lolling in a tavern booth fiddling with a pair of spectacles was going to be famous forever, while the man who wrote him into history would be rotting away in an unmarked grave.

Falstaff was waiting to hear why Oxford had come back.

"Thanks, Jack," Oxford finally said.

"Been a privilege, Nedward."

Another dig – his nickname – a reminder of who Oxford was and times gone past, another link between them.

Oxford didn't reply.

192

Helping Mister Wriothesley with a Poem

Timson brought the carriage down Tower Hill toward the river, stopping at the entrance to the Tower. Oxford got down clutching a box under his arm and walked under the arch beneath Middle Tower. A guard glanced at the paper in his hand and waved him on. Oxford crossed the now-permanent bridge over the dry moat that protected the Tower. A Barbary lion roared up at him from below. Oxford smiled. A good sign, he thought.

He went through Byward Tower into the outer ward where the next guard recognized him and waved him on. Oxford continued along the inner curtain wall to Bloody Tower, which guarded access to the inner ward.

Southampton had been housed on the north side in Flint Tower. The tower to the west was already being referred to as Devereux Tower because the 2nd Earl of Essex had spent his last days there. Essex had been beheaded in the open courtyard in front of the Royal Chapel of St. Peter ad Vinculo. Oxford walked past the church, possibly over the very spot where Essex had been beheaded. The inner ward was empty, but Oxford thought there were ghosts about. So many people had met their ends there. Anne Boleyn, for one. Her body lay buried inside the church.

Sir John Peyton met Oxford at Flint Tower. He glanced at the box Oxford was carrying but said nothing. Without comment or greeting, he took Oxford up two flights of stairs to a spacious room lit by a window that faced north. Southampton sat on the edge of his bed looking weak and wan. Oxford slipped a jewel into Sir John's hand. Sir John stepped into the hallway but left the door ajar.

"My dear Henry," Oxford said. "How glad I am to see you."

Southampton looked distressed. "To see me here?"

"To see you alive." Oxford put the box on a table and opened it. Socrates climbed out. Oxford picked him up and handed him to Southampton. "A gift to help you pass your time here."

Southampton leaned back slightly to look at Socrates. He didn't seem familiar with small animals. Socrates looked up at him with big eyes and promptly curled up in his lap. His new owner seemed pleased, if still somewhat apprehensive.

"He likes you," Oxford said, "an honor he rarely bestows. He has assisted me in the writing of plays."

"How so?" Southampton asked, running a hand over Socrates' back.

"He puts his stamp of approval on a page when I finish it. He sits on it. When I produce a new one, he moves over to sit on the new page."

"They must be warm."

"I hope there's more to it than that."

Southampton smiled. "What's his name?"

"Socrates. He never answers questions."

"Oh," Southampton chuckled. "We had a cat while I was in Cecil House. It died. I have vivid memories of Lady Burghley towering over me wanting to know why it died. *And why did it die?*" He imitated her high-pitched nasally voice. Oxford knew it well.

"And your answer?"

"'It didn't like the question,'" I replied. '*No,*' she cried, giving me a whack with a dried donkey tail she was always carrying around."

Oxford burst out laughing. "A donkey tail?" He laughed harder. "When I was there, she used to hit us with a rush from the floor. She must have gotten the tail off one of Burghley's asses."

"He was still riding them when I was there," Southampton said.

Oxford liked being able to share stories with Southampton about their time in Cecil House. While they talked, Oxford searched Southampton's face to see if there were any features Oxford might claim as his. He couldn't tell.

Southampton was beginning to like Socrates. "I have lots of questions too, and no one to answer them. Having someone I can ask but who never answers will be a boon to me. Thank you, my lord."

"My pleasure."

"But," Southampton continued, "if I may be so bold, you might be able to help me with something else." He reached for a piece of paper lying on the table next to the bed. "A poem I want to send to Her Majesty. I remember you sending me sonnets that urged me to marry Lisbeth. At the time, I was trying to learn how to be a poet. My efforts showed so feebly against yours that I was forced to ask you to stop. But now, perhaps, given my current circumstances, I feel less reluctant to ask you to help me." He handed the paper to Oxford. "It is the most important poem I will ever write. If I do it well, she may give me back my freedom. You are my first visitor. I have not been allowed any others. Not my wife and child, not my mother. Only a Doctor Paddy who covers me with plasters to fight the quatrain ague I suffer and the swelling in my legs."

"Say no more. I would be pleased to help."

Oxford sat down at the table under the window and began to review Southampton's poem.

Southampton continued talking as Oxford read the poem. "I am earl no more, my lord. I am 'Mr. Wriothesley.' The carrion pick over my possessions. The Solicitor-General is at Titchfield doing an inventory of everything I own. In the meantime, I must sit here, powerless. Oh, my lord, I am the most foolish man who ever lived. I have thrown away all and for what?"

"Rest easy, my lord," Oxford said. "Her Majesty has plans for you. I know it. I am doing everything I can to protect your interests and promote your release."

"I am grateful, my lord. She loves your plays and poetry. With your help, my poem can perhaps tip the scales."

Oxford nodded as he ran his eyes over the page. It needed help, but he dare not take out too much lest his help be seen in the words left behind.

> *Not to live more at ease (Deare Prince) of thee*
> *But with new merits, I begg libertie.*

"Not as artful as it could be," Oxford said aloud, "but she will know it's you. That's important. My help must not become visible or your effort will be for naught."

He read more of the poem aloud:

> *Let grace swim above all my crimes.*
> *In lawne, a stayne well taken forth,*
> *May be made to serve again;*

> *And a horse that stumbles in the morn*
> *May get up and go well all day.*

"And:

> *Prisoners condemned like fish within shells lie*
> *Cleaving to walls, which when they're open'd die.*

"Again good, but this implies you will die if the walls are opened. Still, it shows a poet reaching for stars just beyond his reach. I would leave it in. But you need to ask point-blank to be released. I suggest:

If faultes were not, how could great Princes then
Approach so near God, in pardoning men?
Wisdome and valour, common men have knowne,
But only mercy is the Prince's owne.

"Oh, that is very good, my lord. With these words, she will surely let me out. I will find someone to scribe this in elegant style and send it to her."

"No, if I may. Place no man between you and her. Dress your offering in your own handwriting. It is not the words that matter but your anguish. *Prisoners cleaving to walls like fish within shells* will appeal to her poetic sense, for she is an excellent poet. Appealing to her mercy is what she expects since, as you point out, *only mercy is the Prince's own.*"

"Oh, I see. I am so grateful, my lord. Why do you do this for me?"

'Because you are my son,' Oxford said silently. Aloud, he said: "Because your mother and I are close. I'm doing this for her."

Southampton took this as Lady Mary. Oxford did not tell him he was referring to the queen. He wanted to, but letting Southampton know what Oxford believed about who his mother was would only endanger him.

"I will see what I can do about allowing visits by your family," Oxford said. "Enough time has passed that a request should be received favorably."

"Thank you, my lord."

"You're welcome. One more thing." He stroked Socrates' head. "Never call him Sox. Promise?"

"I promise." Southampton ruffled Socrates' head. "Socrates," he said.

193

The Ambassador from Morocco

Abd al-Wahid bin Mas'ud bin Mohammed Anun," the herald called out, stepping aside to let the queen's newest visitor, the Ambassador from Morocco, step into the dining hall at Harefield. The lords and ladies, knights and gentlemen, and curious hangers-on applauded warmly. They all knew the Ambassador had arrived for talks about England and Morocco joining forces to end Spain's threat to English sovereignty and its Protestant religion. His country was rich in gold brought across the Great Desert from hidden mines in Mali.

The Ambassador strode across the room to greet the queen. The confidence with which he approached her left no doubt he was used to holding positions of power. He wore a long white gown of the richest silk. A black shawl was wrapped around his shoulders and hung to his waist on his right side. His sword, the handle of which was wrought in fine gold, hung in a scabbard on his left side. The wide strap, also worked in gold, looped over his right shoulder. A turban of the same material as the gown was wrapped tightly around his head before spiraling down around his neck and one shoulder. His dark eyes, beneath black eyebrows, looked out either side of a long prominent nose. His beard was neatly trimmed.

Oxford was in the audience. He had not wanted to come but the queen had made it clear his presence was required. Elspeth came with him. She looked forward to seeing people she had left behind when she moved to Hackney. Lisbeth was there as well. She never missed an opportunity to be seen. The queen allowed her husband to be elsewhere since Harefield had recently been purchased by the Dowager Countess of Derby with money the 6th Earl would undoubtedly claim was part of his patrimony.

Oxford was standing next to the long tables filled with roast venison, crackled pork, breaded plovers, smoked salmon sliced thin, and other culinary delights when he saw his wife gazing in rapt attention at the Ambassador. Her head was tilted back, her mouth was partially open, and she was barely breathing. He could almost hear her blood surging through her.

He moved closer. The sight of her gawping at the Ambassador caused a wave of jealousy to course through him. It took him back to when he was told Nan had cuckolded him! Or, so Rowland Yorke had whispered in his ear.

'*Yorke!*' Oxford almost cried aloud. The dishonorable son of an honorable father, Yorke had been a traitor of the first order. Oxford found out later that Yorke had lied to him to ingratiate himself with Leicester, who was angry at Oxford for having captured Elizabeth's eye. But Oxford wasn't the only one Yorke toyed with. He spread lies throughout the court. There did not seem to be any limits to who he would betray, including Leicester, who learned this the hard way when Yorke, under Leicester's command, went over to the Spanish and helped them take the Zutphen sconce. He didn't last long with his new employers, however. The Spanish didn't trust him either. Once a traitor, always a traitor. They poisoned him. When the Dutch recaptured the ground from the Spanish where Yorke had been buried, they dug up his body and hung it from a gibbet outside Zutphen. They put a sign on his body that read '*D'Iago – Traidor.*' 'Traidor' meant 'traitor,' but what did 'D'Iago' mean? Oxford subsequently learned the Dutch had misspelled 'Diablo.'.

Yorke's infamy was held up by scholars as the epitome of evil. Wasn't 'vile' made from the same four letters as 'evil?' Didn't those letters, with the addition of only one more, form the word 'devil'?

At least in English, Oxford wryly thought. But why *was* Yorke so evil? Why did he lie to everyone? Why did he help the Spanish?

Part of the reason Oxford wrote *As You Like It* and *Measure for Measure* was to purge himself of Yorke for tricking him into believing Nan had cuckolded him but, as he watched Elspeth gaze up at the ambassador, Oxford realized Yorke was still very much with him. Oxford had demanded 'ocular proof' that Nan had cheated on him but nothing was ever produced before Yorke went over to the Low Countries to continue his perfidy against the Dutch and the Spanish.

Over time, Oxford came to accept Lisbeth as his daughter and Yorke's claim a lie. But the shame Oxford felt never faded completely away. It still burned deep within him.

He now found himself wanting to fan those flames. He'd not written a play yet about Yorke, about a man who lies to those who trust him for no apparent reason. Here was unfinished business.

He looked at Elspeth staring at the magnificent man standing in front of her. Her fixed gaze fed fuel to his jealousy. Yorke would be the ensign. His name? Diago without the 'D': *Iago! Hah!* he said aloud.

This caused Elspeth to turn around. Oxford was still staring at her. "What fire burns in your eyes, my lord?" she asked.

He looked away, not because he had been caught but because he didn't want to lose the jealousy burning through him.

"How sweet," she said. She slipped an arm through his. "I thought I had lost all my charms, tending to King's Place and raising Henry. I have missed you, my lord; you have obviously missed me. And all it took was for me to glance at a handsome man to make you come running back. We should return to Hedingham so I can seduce you again on the roof of the Keep."

"My lady," he began, but stopped short.

She read his mind. "Ah. The rage is not about me but something about a new play, for that is what I see when you are transfixed like you are now. You may be here in body but you are somewhere else in spirit." She laughed. A gentle, understanding, laugh. She squeezed his arm. "Shall I make cow eyes at him? Would that feed your furnace?"

"No," he said. "We should go," he said, worried that all her kindness to him would burn up his rage toward Yorke, now Iago.

The image of Yorke greeting him in France was still seared into Oxford's brain. He could see Yorke's face leaning in toward him, eyes bright, carefully enunciating each word of his message.

'My lord. It is with great sadness that I must report that your wife has shamed you and your noble family whilst you have been gone to in Italy.'

Oxford still remembered the shock with which he heard this.

'How so?' he had asked.

'By making the beast with two backs, my lord," Yorke had replied slyly, "and much else.'

'What? How doth thou know this?'

'Tis the fable of the town. Everyone knows.'

Yorke had paused, enjoying Oxford's reaction to this.

'But what proof, man? Mere words oft turn out to be lies.'

Yorke smiled. 'She gave birth to a child in September, my lord.' He let Oxford do the math.

Oxford had readily accepted York's claim. *Too readily*, he later learned. Lisbeth had been born in June.

Oxford remembered Yorke's eyes as his manservant told him Nan had violated their marriage vows. They had been lit from behind, Oxford remembered. The Dutch saw them in Holland, as did the Spanish, apparently.

All this came back to him as he watched Elspeth gaze at the Moroccan. Oxford would set out in words what he had seen in Yorke's eyes, which had been empty of any humanity when he told Oxford about Nan. This would be the challenge in writing *Iago*, for that is what he would call the play.

~ 194 ~
# Ben Jonson

Oxford descended the stairs to find Ben Jonson standing inside the front door to King's Place. He was soaking wet from the rain falling outside. He looked like he had walked all the way from London.

"The Earl of Derby said I could stop by, my lord," Jonson said, holding a wide-brimmed hat in front of him.

Oxford nodded. Tobias closed the big oak door shut. Oxford gestured for Jonson to follow him when Lady Elspeth appeared.

Oxford stopped. "Your ladyship. Mr. Ben Jonson."

Jonson bowed. "An honor."

"And mine as well," she replied. "I so enjoyed *Every Man Out.*" This surprised both men. Oxford was unaware that Lady Elspeth had been to the theater. Jonson, who loved to watch from the wings and identify everyone who came to see his plays, had not spied her in the audience. She smiled. "So much good fun. Shackspear's brother, Sordido, hanging himself when a good harvest dropped the price of corn, and then abusing the peasants who cut him down because they could have unbuckled the belt round his neck instead of cutting it in two!" She laughed. "But, from what I know, Mr. Jonson, Shackspear's brother is a haberdasher in London. Perchance you were aiming at Shackspear's father? I've heard he's hoarded grain."

Jonson was pleased, of course, to hear someone like her ladyship praise his work. "And, pray tell, my lady, how do you come by such information? It is not in the script."

"After a play, everyone compares notes. Who was the author aiming at? Real names are never used. Fear of a suit, I imagine. Sogliardo, for example. *Sogliardo!*" she repeated. "Wonderful, Mr. Jonson. I commend you. Then there was Puntarvolo. I wonder who you were aiming at there?" She looked mischievously at her husband and then at Jonson before going back into the house.

Jonson turned to Oxford. "Her ladyship's question is one of the reasons I have come."

Oxford nodded. "Follow me."

He took Jonson into the Little Parlor. He gestured toward a chair, but Jonson, shaking with cold, went over to the fireplace and stood in front of it, opening his coat to warm himself up.

Oxford sat down. "So, Mr. Jonson, what brings you to Hackney?"

"I come to apologize for writing Puntarvolo into *Every Man Out of his Humour*, your lordship."

"And why would that be of concern to me?"

"Because Puntarvolo was intended to be you, my lord. Your wife got it right."

"Ah. And why put me in one of your plays, Mr. Jonson? Or, even better, come all this way to confess it?"

"I put you in the play because I was told you wrote *Shackspear is Shakespeare; Johnson is Jonson*. I was furious. I withdrew to my lodgings where in one long session over four days I wrote *Everyman Out of His Humour*, a screed against you and Shackspear. I hate Shackspear. He has you for his writing desk. I have only myself."

He sighed and made like he now wanted to sit down. Oxford gave a slight wave of his hand and Jonson seated himself.

"I thought at first I exceeded the other writers so much that my ascendancy to being known as *the* playwright in London and England's poet laureate was only a matter of time. Then, Shackspear began to produce art beyond mine. But how? I engaged him in discourse and soon realized he had to be fronting for someone else. It did not take long to figure out it was you! Armed with this knowledge, I vowed to catch up. *The Case Is Altered* was my first effort but it fell so far short of what you were writing that I disowned it."

He took his overcoat off and laid it over the chair next to his.

"*Every Man in His Humour* was my next effort. It did well, but Henslowe and Burbage took it as filler while they waited for Shackspear's *– your –* next play. So, I succeeded and fell short at the same time."

He glowered at the fireplace. Oxford let him ramble.

"If I couldn't best you, I would bring you down. I thought *Every Man Out* would showcase how much better I was than you and Shackspear and Marston and Nashe, …"

"But you aren't."

"No, I'm not."

"So, why confess this to me now?"

"Because I killed Gabriel Spenser."

Oxford shrugged.

Jonson leaned forward. "I killed Spenser so I could claim I had killed him with a sword six inches shorter than his! *Nothing more!*" He looked at Oxford. "Kill a man so I can boast of it in a tavern? What kind of a man had I become?"

"What kind of man had you become?" Oxford repeated. He had no patience with people sobbing into their beer, so to speak, but was there a play in here somewhere?

"All of this came to me while I was in Newgate. A priest there explained to me that if I became a Catholic, I could confess my sins and they would all be forgiven. I confessed, but the priest said that wasn't enough. I had to do more. I had to go back to those people I had sinned against and confess to them. The list was long: my son, for ignoring him. The boy's mother, a shrew, to be sure, but honest. You, my lord, for Puntarvolo."

"And Shackspear, of course, for Sogliardo."

Jonson hesitated. "Yes," he said, with great difficulty.

"Thank you, Mr. Jonson. I appreciate your apology." Oxford rose.

"My lord!" Jonson exclaimed. "I am not through."

"No?"

Jonson grimaced. "There is Sir Robert, my lord."

Oxford sat back down.

"Call me Ben, my lord."

"No, Mr. Jonson."

Jonson squirmed. Not because Oxford wouldn't call him Ben but because it was taking all of Jonson's self-control to apologize to Oxford - something he was not good at in any case - and toady up to the slight, balding, man opposite him. But he had decided in Newgate that he needed Oxford. He needed to learn from Oxford and steal whatever he could. After all, hadn't Shackspear gained fame by claiming Oxford's plays were his? Why couldn't he - Jonson - do the same thing?

"You mentioned Sir Robert," Oxford reminded him.

"Yes. He visited me while I was in Newgate. In disguise, as a monk, as a matter of fact. He had obviously planted the priest to smoke out Spanish spies and sympathizers. Why else would ye find a priest in an English prison?"

Jonson left out Richard Topcliffe trying to get him to do the same thing when he was imprisoned for helping write *The Isle of Dogs*. Jonson knew enough about English lords that Oxford would not be impressed that Jonson had resisted Topcliffe. Sir Robert was another matter.

"What did Sir Robert want?"

"He wanted me to spy on you."

Oxford was puzzled. "But what did Sir Robert say he gained by having you 'spy' on me?"

"He didn't say. He wanted reports about what you did when he asked for them. He didn't say when he would ask for them. Or what he wanted to know."

Oxford looked at him suspiciously. "So, why tell *me* this?"

"Because I am done with prevarication, my lord. I have recovered my soul through confession. The little crooked-back man – I refer to Sir Robert – is trying to steal it again by making me spy on you. I will not become an informant, my lord."

Oxford didn't believe him. He knew Jonson, all bluster in Hackney, would sing a different tune in London. But this stream of babble apparently satisfied Jonson's need to confess to Oxford. Jonson wiped his mouth on his sleeve. Oxford thought he looked like he was about to get up but he still wasn't done.

"One more thing, my lord. The Earl of Derby is helping his kinsman, John Salusbury, put together a book of poetry to celebrate Essex's demise. He's going to give it to the queen. He wants those of us who are poets to contribute poems about the phoenix rising from its ashes. He said you were aware of the idea and would help."

"I have already sent it over."

"Oh. Very good, my lord." Jonson started to get up, but Oxford put up his hand. Jonson sat back down.

"You were gracious to help me with *Falstaff in Love*. I would like you to perform a similar service for me."

"Of course, my lord."

"I will give you an outline of a play that you will use to prepare a draft. I will review it. This will allow me to work on another play."

"Two plays?"

"Yes. Both will have a connection to your first play, *Every Man in his Humour*."

"How so, my lord?"

"In *Every Man In*, you have a character named Thorello who is jealous of his wife, Bianca. You did little with Thorello, burying his jealousy under the other characters in the play. I will give him the moment he deserves."

Jonson's eyebrows went up. He had buried a character? He started to boil over but reminded himself bigger game was afoot. "Yes. Of course," he forced himself to say. He put a thin smile on his face. "I can't wait to hear how you improve on my Thorello."

Oxford heard the sarcasm but didn't care. In fact, he liked irritating Big Ben, pompous pedant that he was. "I would also like to borrow Prospero," Oxford said.

"You want to take Prospero as well?" Jonson's choler began to rise again. "Are you going to pillage all my characters?"

"No. Only Prospero. I like the name. He doesn't do much, but in the one you will write for me, he will be the lead character. If, of course, you agree."

Jonson didn't want to agree to anything, but if he could write a play in which Prospero would be the lead? Under Oxford's direction? He forced himself to look attentive. "Tell me about *your* Prospero, my lord."

"Gladly. Prospero is the Duke of Florence. He has been overthrown by his brother, Antonio. Prospero and his daughter, a babe at the time, are put out to sea in a small boat that is blown to a volcanic island where they have been living for twelve years. The daughter, Miranda, is now fifteen, when the brother's ship is driven by storms onto Prospero's island and the play opens."

Jonson came alive. "Prospero will capture his brother, reverse his fortunes, and return to Florence as its rightful ruler."

Oxford frowned. "T'would be a short play if that happened. Matters will be complicated by the presence on the island of a spirit of the air named Ariel and a monster named Caliban."

"Cannibal!" Jonson exclaimed.

"If you say so."

"How will they get along?"

"I have no idea. I leave this to you."

"I will open with a storm and a shipwreck," Jonson immediately announced. 'I will call it *The Tempest*."

"Excellent."

"St. Elmo's fire," he went on, but Oxford waved him silent.

"Two conditions," Oxford said. "You will not give your work to Shackspear. Write *The Tempest* in your own words, not in words you think would be mine."

Jonson nodded. "And the second condition?"

"I will provide a short epilogue for Prospero to speak, which you will append to the script."

Jonson nodded again.

Oxford glanced out the window. "The rain has stopped." He reached over for a sheaf of papers. "Here is the outline of your new play."

Jonson took the paper from Oxford. "Milord," he said, bowing. He gathered up his overcoat and headed for the door.

195

Nedward's Bowl

Lady Elspeth came back from Harefield resolved to be wife to her husband and mother to her son. This meant talking Oxford into going to Hedingham, which required loading everything into a train of carts and setting out across the River Lea. They went through Epping Forest and the towns that stretched away northeast till they reached the Castle. Digby greeted them at the top of the hill.

"Welcome, my lord, my lady," Digby called out as they came to a halt. Henry vaulted off the wagon and ran up the hill toward the Keep. Digby helped Lady Elspeth to the ground.

"Good day to you, Digby. You are looking well."

"Thank you, ma'am."

"Indeed," Oxford said. He shook Digby's hand.

But Digby did not look well. His bristle-topped head was now all white. The muscles he had used to string a bow or hold down a hog were as thin as vines on a tall oak. His clothes hung off him.

"Supper in the Keep, my lord," Digby said, his eyes still alive and bright. "Cooked it meself. A doe not more than a year. It'll be tasty."

Digby's wife, Nell, had died the year before. The horses and cattle that used to fill the paddocks and stables were gone. So were the servants.

They went up to supper. Digby served them roast venison and root vegetables, washed down with beer brought up from the town below. A game of noddy took an hour to play among the four of them, with Henry the excited winner. Digby took him outside to show him a new constellation, leaving Oxford and Elspeth alone. They huddled in front of the fire. "Ye kept your stockings on," Elspeth said after a while, bringing up how she had seduced him on the roof far above them before they married. "You said they were optional," Oxford said. "Indeed, they are," she agreed, but Henry came bursting in and all three went to bed early.

Oxford went off with Henry at first light. He didn't ask Digby to come with them. Digby was working on breakfast in the kitchen below anyway, but Oxford didn't think his old steward could hike around the castle grounds like he used to, at least not in the early morning air. Oxford described to Henry where the buttery had stood, the dovecote, the stables, and the outbuildings for the servants who had worked the Keep and the farms surrounding it. Only the bones remained of the buildings that had crowded the mount on which the Keep stood.

As Oxford and Henry came around one of the many low posts sticking up out of the ground, Oxford suddenly stopped.

"What?" Henry asked.

"I think I buried something here before I left for London."

"What was it?"

"I don't remember. It was something important, I think."

"Let's dig it up," Henry said excitedly. "I'll go get a shovel."

He ran off. Oxford took the time to look out over the Essex countryside. His heart ached. He had spent so much time here when he was young. Then his father died and he went off to Cecil House as a royal ward. He had promised himself then that he would come back, but he had ended up living in London and rarely even visited. Maybe it was time he came back?

Henry returned dragging shovels. Oxford took one and the two of them began to dig, laughing as they turned over the ground. On Oxford's third strike, his shovel hit something. He and Henry dropped to the ground and began scrabbling in the loose soil, the two of them laughing like the little boys they had become. Henry got his hand on something and pulled it up. It was a small bowl, blue with a tawny lip. A boar's head in the center looked up at them.

Oxford stood up. "Nedward," he said. He looked up at the sky. Without saying anything, he walked away.

"My lord!" Henry cried, still on his knees.

Oxford didn't answer him. He went down the hill into the town and didn't come back till supper time.

Henry dug the bowl out of the ground and took it to his mother. He told her what had happened. She didn't know what the bowl meant to Oxford. She suggested Henry let his father decide what to tell him. Henry took the bowl upstairs and put it on his father's writing desk.

When Oxford came back, everyone went into supper. No one brought up the bowl. Oxford never told Henry what it meant or why he had walked away.

196

The Green-Eyed Monster

Timson found his master sitting in the dark. The candles had burned out. Oxford had his hands in his lap, staring at the wall in front of him.

"My lord," Timson said, holding up a lantern.

"I am blind," Oxford muttered.

"Ah," Timson said.

"The candle went out. What is it like to be blind, Timson? Or, am I blind now and don't know it?"

Timson did not know what to make of this.

Oxford turned. He had placed circles of white paper over his eyes.

"Well, if ye want to be blind, milard, I can gouge out yer eyes, if ye want me to."

This surprised Oxford. The paper circles fell off his face. "You would gouge out my eyes?" he asked.

"Of course not. And ye'r not blind." Timson said. He was too practical a Scotsman to play along with Oxford's fantasies. "Supper awaits.".

Oxford nodded. "But blind I am," he said, getting up with some difficulty. He'd been sitting at his desk all afternoon. Timson held out a cane, but Oxford pushed it away.

"I thought you would need it, being blind."

Oxford acknowledged the putdown. "Well done. You serve me well, Timson. I thank thee for that."

"I do. But doonitt tell her ladyship yer blind. She'll not like that."

"She'll laugh at me," Oxford said, heading for the door.

"She'll worry. That's worse."

———◆◆◆◆———

He didn't tell her. She could tell he was different, though.

"How goes it, my lord?" she asked, as the plates were brought in. She handed one to Henry. "Is the green-eyed monster in residence?"

"The who?" Oxford asked.

"The green-eyed monster. Jealousy. I thought it grabbed you fiercely while I was looking at the Ambassador from Morocco."

Oxford started. He leapt up. "Forgive me," he said, hustling out the door and up the stairs.

"Lordy," Elspeth said.

"Where's he going?" Henry asked.

"Back to his study. The idea of a play is like a splinter in him; he has to pull it out before he can do anything else."

"I think he *is* blind, mother. He still has eyes but he doesn't see me or you. Will I end up blind like him?"

"Of course not. He is a genius when it comes to telling stories. In everything else, he needs help."

"But what if he is this way because he is the 17th Earl of Oxford? That's 500 years of ancestors, which is a long string. Perhaps the string is thinning? Will it break? Will I need help?"

She laughed. "No, my dear. Your father is extreme. If he lived alone, he might walk out naked if no one was with him to point out he needed to put on clothes first."

Henry sniggered. "Him, naked."

Elspeth glanced at him, eyebrows raised. "None of us look good naked, Henry." Henry hadn't thought of his mother being naked and didn't want to. "But you needn't worry about being too much like your father," she went on. "Ye've put yer toys behind you. Yer not writing stories about horses; yer riding them."

This puffed him up a bit. "I am," he said.

<hr>

"T'was so much I didn't see," Oxford said to himself as he sat down at his writing desk, lit this time with fresh candles. "Blind," he repeated. "Blind about Nan. Bind about Rowland Yorke. But I was a willing victim, wasn't I, believing the tales I heard about women cheating on their husbands. The ground was well-manured when Yorke whispered into my ear. And those words will be honey-sweet when Iago whispers them into the Moor's."

He pulled paper to himself and began to write.

1602

~ 197 ~
Finley

Nigel put his head in Oxford's study. "My lord," he began, "uh, Mr. Finley is downstairs."

"*Dr. Finley*," Oxford immediately said.

"Of course. *Dr. Finley*."

Nigel was relieved and upset at the same time. He was relieved because he had been unable to find out how he should present someone named 'Finley.' Was it a last name, he had asked Ross, thinking he might know from the last time Finley had been at King's Place? Was it a first name, he asked Angus? No one knew. Nigel had never heard of a person with only one name. As steward to a noble house, such matters were important to him. Not knowing how to properly announce the arrival of 'Finley' annoyed him 'Dr. Finley' would do very well, Nigel thought, his questions answered. He was back with 'Dr. Finley' in a trice.

"Finley, my good chap," Oxford said, with more vigor in his voice than Nigel had heard for some time now. "Just in time."

Finley was also surprised. His other visits had been met with various levels of irritation, his lordship being at those times in full-throated pursuit of a metaphor, or the perfect word to complete a poem. This usually only lasted a few moments but, this time, Finley could see that Oxford was truly glad to see him.

"I trust you bring me news from London and hope you can stay a while to help me work on a play that is slipping and sliding away from me. For, as always, I see it as already finished and want to work on something else!" He looked amazed with himself. He motioned to a chair.

Finley sat down. "As for news, my lord, Ben Jonson has put on a satire called *Narcissus The Fountain of Self-Love,* or *Cynthia's Revels.*"

"He seeks the favor of the queen."

"But didn't get it. Her Majesty pronounced the play paralyzed, repugnant, and stupefyingly dull."

"Where did she see it?"

"At Blackfriars. The Children of the Chapel put it on."

"Henry Evans?"

"Yes. By the way, he has been a wonderful help to me in my search for plays."

"A man of the theater," Oxford said. "I funded him in the 80s. Lyly too. At Blackfriars, in fact. I recall giving Evans a piece of property to help him put on my plays. 70 acres, I think it was, with a manse. '*He gave his property away for a song!*' the crows on the fence sang. But it was worth it. Evans has a way with children. He could get them to play women and old men like no one else. He sometimes made us marvel at the transformation he brought about more than the story the actors presented to us. I'm glad to hear Henry is still at work. But why did Jonson's *Cynthia's Revels* fare so poorly?"

"He modeled it on the works of John Lyly. In fact, he stole most of the characters from *Endymion* and put in lots of dancing and masques."

"I would have expected more from him."

"Yes. But it may be too early to expect much of him. *Cynthia's Revels* begins with three pages fighting over a black cloak that the actor who delivers the prologue will wear. In the middle of it, one of the pages turns to the audience and starts telling them what the play is about. The others try to stop him. The three get into a fight. They go on to criticize the author and then turn on the audience, at which point the fight spills off the stage into the pit."

Oxford shook his head. "Why would he write something like that? You can't be a successful playwright if you start a play by having a fight that spills into the audience."

Finley agreed. "He may have been inspired by Christopher Sly who you had sit on the side of the stage to watch *The Shrew* instead of being in it."

"That was a frame. He didn't get into a fight that spills into the audience."

"No. Too far. But Jonson'll make it, I think; just not with this play."

"I hope you're right. I have given him a play to write for me."

Finley was surprised to hear this. "Ye had a play, my lord, but gave it to Ben Jonson? Ye couldn't think of anyone else?"

"No."

Finley was crushed. He wanted to say, 'ye couldn't give it to yer old friend and colleague?' The Poet Earl obviously didn't think Finley capable of writing a play for him. No one, Finley thought, had ever received a lower failing grade.

"Forgive me, my friend," Oxford said, oblivious to what Finley was thinking, "but I need a play that would convey a message to the queen."

"Which is?"

"Actually, an explanation and an apology."

"About?"

"A prince banished by his brother to a deserted island."

Finley said nothing. He was trying to come to grips with Oxford considering him no more than a university don studying plays but incapable of writing them.

"The island is full of noises, sounds and sweet airs."

"Well, if you did not give Jonson strict instruction, he's going to fill his play with masques and song. But pretty ladies imitating goddesses walking back and forth do not supply a plot."

"No matter. I crave only to speak the epilogue, which I will write."

"Ah. The message."

Oxford nodded.

"If Jonson is working on a play about a banished prince, my lord, what was it that you wanted me to help you with?"

"A play about a man who thinks he's been cuckolded."

Finley was dismayed. "Again?"

Oxford was surprised. "Again?"

"My lord, if someone wanted to find a common thread that runs through your plays, cuckoldry would be it."

"It would?"

Finley nodded. "Think Hero, my lord, or Joan, or Lavinia. Not one woman ever turns out to be unfaithful. Ye need to do it again?"

Oxford nodded. "One more time."

Finley shook his head. "It all comes from Eve, ye know. Every man has heard the story about Eve, who tricked her husband into eating the forbidden fruit. It's a story about how women trick men."

"It is ever-present," Oxford said solemnly.

"Adultery?"

"No. The *fear* of adultery. It lies in the heart of every man. A glance can wake it. If a man steals my purse, he steals nothing, but if he steals my wife, he takes from me that which is mine, and leaves me poor indeed. Tis why I want you to help me." Oxford passed a handful of pages to Finley. "Retire, prithee, to the room Nigel has assigned you to use while you are here. It is yours whenever you need it on your trips twixt Cambridge and London."

"Thank you, my lord." He thought for a moment. "You want me to work on this now?"

Oxford nodded. His eyes were bright. He meant now.

"I was just passing through, my lord," Finley protested. Then again, he had always wanted to work on a play with Oxford. Maybe this was it. He held up the pages Oxford had given him. "Well, I guess I'll stay and see what I can do with this."

Oxford nodded.

Finley started to get up. "Oh, before I retire, my lord, I should show you a script Henry Evans gave me. It is of *Hamlet*, my lord."

"*Hamlet?*"

Finley reached into the sack he had brought with him and pulled out some rumpled pages. "Henry thought these were yours."

Oxford was alarmed that someone might have stolen the *Hamlet* he was working on. A glance put his fears to rest. "This is not my *Hamlet*. I never wrote this. This is a prompt copy put together from the recollections of one of the players."

Finley was disappointed. "I heard it graced the boards years ago before it was withdrawn."

"It was." Oxford did not explain why. He rifled through the pages and held one up. "Listen:

> *To be, or not to be, I there's the point,*
> *To Die, to sleepe, is that all? I all:*
> *No, to sleep, to dreame, I mary there it goes.*

Oxford frowned and looked at Finley. "Do ye think I wrote that?"

Finley smiled. "Well, if ye leave *Hamlet* in a chest, my lord, someone is going to finish it for ye. Cervantes says someone has written a sequel to *Don Quixote* he didn't write. He's rushing his version into print."

Oxford threw the script back to Finley but then immediately retrieved it. "No one must see this." He clasped the script to his chest.

Finley got up, took the pages to the play he would help Oxford write and headed for his room.

Stand and Unfold Yourself!

Finley helped Oxford ready *Iago* for the stage while Oxford worked on *Hamlet.* Years of adding scenes and changing a word here or there had ballooned the script to where the playing of it would take four hours. "Oh, well, Henslowe or Burbage will cut it anyway. I will leave it as is, subject to a few shavings and rewording that can always be done. Nothing is *ever* finished."

He plucked a quill from a jar and absent-mindedly shaved a new point on it. The *Hamlet* box lay to his right. Something in the box flashed a roseate pink. A flamingo feather! He pulled it out.

His face lit up. "A gift from Virginia Padoana," he said aloud, the Venetian courtesan for whom Oxford would have stayed in Italy if she had let him, but she didn't. She sent him home to his wife and daughter. The quill, plucked from the wing of a flamingo captured in the lagoons that surround Venice, was her final gift to him. He had brought it back to England in the bottom of a box. He buried it under papers and other objects lest his eye glimpse it and ignite bittersweet memories of his time with 'Ginia.' He had carried the box with him as he wandered from lodging to lodging. He put things he valued most in it. Over time, his notes on *Hamlet* went into it. Eventually, it became the *Hamlet* box. The flamingo quill lay forgotten in the bottom.

He gripped the quill and flipped it back and forth to relearn its weight and balance. Ginia had told him it was the best quill money could buy. He sharpened it now with a special knife and dipped it into a pot of ink. Gracefully, effortlessly, he put the tip to paper and wrote out his name:

Edward Oxenford

The quill was now an extension of his mind. It came up and hovered over the page, refusing to come down and make contact with the paper. It was almost as if it was asking Oxford for an explanation as to why it had taken him so long to begin writing *Hamlet* again.

"T'was Nashe who first put me off: *English Seneca read by candle-light yields many good sentences, as Blood is a beggar, and so forth; and if you entreat him fair in a frosty morning, he will afford you whole Hamlets, I should say handfuls of tragical speeches.*"

Oxford scowled. "Tom learned too well at the Folly. He shoots arrows now that skewer his target, which, in this case, was me."

"And Marlowe, damn him in his grave, I say, for calling it *Hoglet* when we had too much beer in the Boar's Head one night. Thank God, no one heard him."

He moved a box in front of him from which he began pulling papers, short cuttings, longer pieces, scraps of this and that with thoughts scratched over them in the middle of the night, like flakes of paint falling off a decaying ceiling while everyone slept.

"Thomas Lodge," Oxford said, taking out a strip of paper on which he had written notes: "Thomas Lodge describing a devil dressed in black who 'looked as pale as the ghost who cried so miserably at the Theatre, like an oyster wife, *Hamlet, revenge!*'"

Oxford balled up the note and threw it on the floor. "It was the actor who cried like an oyster wife, Thomas, *not the author! Tragical speeches?* I'll give you tragical speeches. But because of you, the ghost who appears in this version of *Hamlet* will not speak! Not at first. Masked in iron, glowering at the players and the audience, he will send them gibbering and squeaking from the playhouse."

He brought Ginia's quill down on the paper in front of him. It sped across the page. "*Stand and unfold,*" he said aloud, surprising himself. He turned to look at the balcony. The door was open. "I know you are there," he said, but no one appeared. "Murdered by poison poured into your ear, Father, whilst you slept in your orchard? Was it Leicester? Was it Burghley?"

He thought about what he had just said. "No. Leicester was evil, but he was never good at *planning* evil. It was Burghley. He is the one who arranged to do in my father. To make me ward and marry me to Nan so that he could put his grandchildren on the throne!"

He laughed. "But Nan let you down, didn't she?" He glanced at the balcony again. It was still empty. "She gave you only granddaughters." He smirked. "T'was not because of me. I had a son by Elspeth, didn't I? And one by Anne? *And a third by Her Majesty?*"

He drifted off, dreaming vaguely of Southampton as Henry IX. But then he remembered how angry the queen had been when she saw his first *Hamlet.* She had immediately recognized that Oxford was implying Burghley had poisoned Oxford's father! When it was over, she pulled Oxford's head down to her and hissed: "You will never stage this play again, my lord. Never!"

Hamlet disappeared from the stage. People who wanted to see it were disappointed. Oxford did not explain why he had shelved it. There was no buffer between him and a puzzled audience back then: Shackspear had not yet arrived in London.

"Maybe if I hadn't named him Corambis," Oxford thought, "she might have missed what I was up to." Burghley's motto was *cor unum, via una* - one heart, one life. Calling Claudius' meddling first minister Corambis changed Burghley's motto into *double-hearted or two-faced*, which left no doubt who Oxford's target was. Elizabeth's injunction meant that *Hamlet* would only be mentioned in passing after that - although not by Frances Meres – and never performed again.

But Burghley was dead. The queen had no reason to protect him now. Burghley's son was still alive, though. He would never let the play be staged with a character named Corambis. Like Oldcastle becoming Falstaff, Corambis would have to be renamed. 'Polonius,' Oxford thought. Everyone was reading *The Counsellor*, by the Polish courtier, Wawrzyniec Grzymała Goślicki. It had been translated into English and published in 1598. Goślicki's book railed against 'pratling Orators and witless Philosophers.' He proclaimed that princes should prefer counsellors who gave wise advice to rulers instead of mere noise. Burghley would become 'Polonius,' the Pole, 'a foolish prating knave.'

Pleased with having resolved the 'Corambis' problem, Oxford decided to add Burghley's homilies to the play. Everyone knew Burghley was fond of uttering homilies, an ever-growing list of do's and don'ts. Burghley would write them out and leave them on a table for younger eyes to see. He would repeat them at family dinners whenever he had a captive audience and the claret warmed his belly. He made a special set for his son, Thomas, when Thomas went to Paris. 'Neither a lender nor a borrower be,'" Oxford intoned, the flamingo quill gliding across the page as he wrote down the scene. "*To thine ownself be true, ...*"

The quill dipped into the ink pot and came back to the page like its former owner striding across a Venetian lagoon, dipping into the inkpot to gracefully distill *Hamlet* across the fine paper Timson had gotten Oxford.

Oxford recalled that Burghley claimed he was a man of the theater; Polonius would also claim he had been on the stage:

Hamlet:	*My lord, you played once i' the university, you say?*
Polonius:	*That did I, my lord; and was accounted a good actor.*
Hamlet:	*What did you enact?*
Polonius:	*I did enact Julius Caesar: I was killed i' the Capitol; Brutus killed me.*
Hamlet:	*It was a brute part of him to kill so capital a calf there.*

Oxford sat back. "Oh, I'm stealing from Shackspear, aren't' I. He likes to boast how he'd butcher calves and make a speech 'in high style' about it. Maybe he'll recognize the theft, if he reads the script."

Oxford kept the quill moving. "For this and other sins, Polonius will die when Hamlet stabs him through an arras, like Sir Robert popping out from behind a curtain at the trial of Essex and Southampton. You may say that Burghley is dead," Oxford said to the empty room, "and can only die once, *but Hamlet can kill him every night!*" He laughed aloud. He made a stabbing motion with his quill: "*Death by pen! Again and again!*"

Oxford shuffled the papers in front of him. "Polonius will die in Act III and be gone from the play. A good days' work. Hamlet will then be off to England where Claudius expects Rosencrantz and Guildenstern to kill him. He will save himself by forging a letter that will cause their deaths instead. But I can't have him go on to England; I need him to go back to Denmark." He paused. A smile slid across his face. "His ship will be captured by pirates. They will recognize him and take him back to Denmark instead of on to England."

He looked around the empty room. "*Incroyable,* you say? But wasn't I captured by pirates as I crossed the Channel and saved by a Scotsman who recognized me? Good enough for the high seas, good enough for me."

199

Falstaff and the Earl of Worcester

The Earl of Oxford was seated in front of a window that looked out on the Thames. Derby came into the room. "My lord, the Earl of Worcester would like a moment."

Oxford rose to meet him. "My dear Edward," Oxford said, taking his hand.

"My lord," Worcester said. "Would you be so kind as to help William and me secure permission from the Privy Council to put on plays at the new Boar's Head? Only two companies are allowed to stage plays in London at the moment: the Lord Chamberlain's Men and the Admiral's Men. One is monopolizing the Rose; the other, the Globe. This is preventing us from challenging them with new plays. We would like to combine our players with yours. Together, we believe the Privy Council will not turn us down."

"I will do what I can to favor your cause, Edward, but I have no players anymore. They have gone elsewhere."

"Your name will be enough."

"Aye," Derby said. "With your signature on our petition, we are sure to be granted approval."

"Where is the paper? I will sign it."

A clerk unfolded a large parchment and laid it out on a table. Oxford looked over it quickly, reaching for a quill as he did so. He signed it and stepped back. "And what says Falstaff?"

"He is all for it. He hath expanded the tavern to the rear and built a large stage. He is already putting on plays. We hope to share in his good fortune by putting on ours."

"You mean the plays the two of you have been writing since I moved to Hackney."

"Aye."

Oxford smiled. "I am happy for you both. I am told, Edward, that William's *The Maid's Metamorphosis* graced the marriage of your son."

"It did, my lord. William was gracious to let us enjoy it. Would that you and I had been given such entertainment at our weddings."

Derby was puzzled. "Your weddings?"

"Edward and I were married at the same time."

"Along with a third couple. Edward Sutton, 4th Lord Dudley, who married a daughter of the Admiral."

"A thrice-braided ceremony of England's finest," Oxford said.

The three lords murmured approval.

"Finley, a colleague of mine and professor at Cambridge, slipped into your son's wedding to see *The Maid's Metamorphosis*. He collects plays and studies them. He said you borrowed the story from Golding and that Lyly could have written it."

"He did?" Derby hesitated. "Is that good?"

"Of course, it is. When you want fairies and gods who transform mortals, Lyly paved the way for you. Finley said you wrote:

> *By the Moone we sport and play,*
> *With the night begins our day:*
> *As we dance the dew doth fall,*
> *Trip it little urchins all:*
> *Lightly as the little bee,*
> *Two by two, and three by three:*
> *And about go we, and about go wee.*

'Pure Lyly," Oxford commented.

The two earls took Oxford's words at face value and enjoyed what they thought was praise. They missed the sarcasm, for Oxford was ever unable to curb his tongue when confronted with what he thought was mediocrity.

"Take the young princess, for example, transformed by Apollo into a young man to escape death," Oxford continued.

"Yes," Worcester said. "Bring in the gods when you need them!"

"Yes," Oxford replied. "How much better than Viola putting on her brother's clothes when she finds herself stranded on a far shore with no one to defend her, not even Apollo."

"Yes," the two earls murmured, not understanding Oxford's reference to *Twelfth Night*.

'To be presented by apes and followed by dunces is a fate worse than death,' Oxford muttered to himself. 'Cannot they see how far short they fall? How blind they be? Falstaff's Boar's Head will be the perfect venue for the plays they will write."

200

The Tempest

Falstaff was greeting people coming into the Boar's Head. Most were streaming off London Bridge. A few had wandered over from The Tabard next door. Patrons who felt they had moved beyond *The Canterbury Tales* were enticed by word that a new play by William Shakespeare would be presented at the new Boar's Head.

"Milord," Falstaff said warmly, waving the Earl of Oxford in. Finley was right behind, followed by Ben Jonson, who had come up behind them. The three men went past Falstaff into the Boar's Head.

"Yer lordship," Jonson said, turning to Oxford.

"Mr. Jonson," Oxford replied. "I thank ye for taking my notes and writing *The Tempest*. I like what ye've done. The audience'll like the masque you've added. What sayeth the man from Stratford about 'his' newest 'invention.'"

"He understands it not, yer lordship, but likes the music and the aery creatures I've added."

"And Caliban?"

"Only that he utterly refuses to play him."

"I wonder who could have suggested that?"

George Carey, 2nd Baron Hunsdon and now Lord Chamberlain, came up, looking as small-eyed and round-headed as ever. And not well, Oxford thought.

"My lord," Hunsdon said to Oxford in a low gravelly voice. As Lord Chamberlain, of course, he had seen the script for *The Tempest*. He knew Shackspear was only a mask for Oxford but not that Jonson had penned the play. Hunsdon rarely attended plays. Oxford was surprised to see him.

"What sayest thou, my Lord Chamberlain, about *The Tempest*?" Oxford asked.

"A strange beast, my lord."

"How so?"

"Two people, an aery personage, and a cannibal on a deserted island. Very different. Few bones on which to hang any meat."

"Perhaps the man from Stratford is trying out a new form? Setting a challenge for himself?"

"But doing it, my lord, with long speeches in which the main character has to keep reminding his daughter to pay attention? *His only companion on the island for, what, fifteen years? Eh?*" He squinted at Oxford. "Is she short a few biscuits and can't remember what happened? Eh? Or is Shackspear at sea himself, my lord? Eh? It doesn't sound like him."

"Well," Oxford said: "There it is."

"Indeed."

"The play will end with an epilogue," Oxford said. "Prithee, my lord, when you present this to the queen, I would consider it a great favor if you would ensure the epilogue is spoken to her."

"A message?" he asked, looking sideways at Oxford. He didn't like being a messenger. He didn't like doing anyone's bidding, but Oxford outranked him by four hundred years. And the queen liked him. He nodded.

"My lord," Oxford said, bowing.

Hunsdon went off into the tavern. The Earls of Derby and Worcester went by on their way to prepare the players.

———◆◆◆◆———

The Boar's Head filled. The play went off without a hitch. Shackspear came out at the end as Prospero and voiced the epilogue:

> *Now my charms are all o'erthrown,*
> *And what strength I have's mine own,*
> *Let me not dwell*
> *In this bare island by your spell;*
> *But release me from my bands*
> *As you from crimes would pardon'd be,*
> *Let your indulgence set me free.*

The audience applauded.

Most of the audience lingered. Jonson buttonholed Oxford. "Thank you, my lord, but ask me no more for help. I'm done with magic tricks, fairies, books drowned in the deep. Let Shackspear take the plaudits." He said this through gritted teeth. He truly *hated* that Shackspear would get the credit for what he had written. "I'm not going to let them do to me what they've done to you."

He strode away. Oxford watched him go, realizing he resented Jonson for being allowed to write plays in his own name.

Finley came up. He had been scribbling notes during the play. "My lord!" he said. He looked at Oxford quizzically. "This is by you?"

"The epilogue, perhaps. Ye think not the rest?"

"No." Finley shook his head. "Prospero is as wooden a character as I have ever seen. He *lectures* people. He arranges for a masque to celebrate the marriage of his daughter to a young man. *A masque! Complete with Juno, Ceres, and Iris!*" He looked at Oxford. "Which is interrupted when Prospero remembers Caliban is plotting to kill him!"

> *[Aside] I had forgot that foul conspiracy*
> *Of the beast Caliban and his confederates*
> *Against my life: the minute of their plot*
> *Is almost come.*

"My lord, *Prospero forgets that Caliban was going to kill him?* And when the lovers are finally alone, they pour out their affection in a *game of chess!*"

Oxford was trying not to smile.

Finley was now in full gallop. "Could anyone imagine Romeo and Juliet sitting down to express their love *in a game of chess?* Worse still is the verse. There is no poetry in this play, my lord. There are weak endings galore, 'ands' and 'buts,' and a feeling that someone wrote prose and chopped it into verse:

> *If by your art, my dearest father, you have*
> *Put the wild waters in this roar, allay them.*

Finley wagged his head in disbelief. "And *I'll drown my book deeper than did ever plummet sound?* What's with books in this play?"

Before Finley could go on, a man came up who appeared to be prosperous and was well-dressed in all regards. "My lord," he said to Oxford in a pleasant voice. "Allow me to introduce myself. I am a new neighbor of yours in Hackney. Your son and mine have become friends. We should know each other. I am Edward Sutton." He held out his hand.

Oxford took it. "Mr. Sutton."

"An excellent play, my lord, but somewhat different from what I have come to expect from Mr. Shake-spear. Is he here?"

"In the back, I believe." Oxford said. He thought this would send Mr. Sutton away, but it did not.

"I must say, my lord, that I am amused at how your son, Henry, has taken to ordering my son around."

Oxford was surprised to hear this. "I will speak to him."

"Don't bother, my lord. Your son is the scion of an ancient family; mine is of more recent origin. It is no surprise, in this year of 1602, nay, *expected*, that the son of a noble lord would order a child around who is without a title."

Sutton said this matter-of-factly. He seemed sincere.

"How is it, Mr. Sutton, that you live in Hackney and attend plays."

"Because I am a made-man, your lordship."

"And how are you a made-man, Mr. Sutton?"

"I own the coal leases in Newcastle."

"Ah. You are, if I may say so without offending, the Coal Baron."

"I am, indeed. No offence taken."

"But you also have an interest in the theater."

"I do. But only from the standpoint of enjoying plays. I have no interest in investing in one. There are better places to put my money. The world is changing, my lord. Even the way power and money are acquired."

'Ah,' Oxford thought: 'we have reached his religion; money.' *'For in the fatness of these pursy times / Virtue itself of vice must pardon beg."*

"You, as a member of the aristocracy," Sutton went on, "have obtained money through the grants of land and monopolies from Her Majesty."

"As you have acquired coal leases."

"With a slight difference; I have paid for my leases."

Oxford did not disagree. Sutton thought this meant Oxford was following him; he was not. Oxford had never understood money. Where it came from and where it went, except in vague terms, was a mystery to him. Money was like water to Oxford; not in the sense that he spent money like water, which he had been accused of doing on more than one occasion, but in the sense that money kept everything afloat the way water keeps boats afloat. Oxford had a vague sense that if it ever ran out he would be hard aground.

"Lord Burghley understood this change," Sutton was saying. "He was no doubt the queen's greatest recipient of royal largesse, but he knew how to make money in other ways as well. His fish day, for example. A law that forced people to eat fish on Wednesday as well as on other days. He said it would increase the demand for fish and increase the number of ships and sailors available to Her Majesty in times of war. But it was the fishmongers who brought him the idea.

They paid him a handsome fee to get Parliament to pass the law requiring it."

He gave Oxford a knowing look. "Learning of this, I went to Burghley and pointed out that the growing need for firewood was stripping England of its trees, which were needed for our navy. If people burned coal instead of wood, England would be stronger."

"And if people bought more coal, you would benefit."

"Of course. Burghley saw the merit of my proposal. He immediately made it clear that, if I wanted him to urge people to burn coal instead of wood, I would have to pay him like the fishmongers had."

Oxford was surprised Burghley had gotten his fingers into coal, among so many other things. Sutton thought Oxford didn't believe him.

"How do ye think he built Stamford? Or Hatfield??"

"You paid him."

"Of course. One pound in his direction, five pounds in mine." He took Oxford's empty face as proof of his lordship's inability to understand modern business, which he believed was the common condition of any peer.

"Mr. Jonson, on the other hand, seems to understand our times. He may like to pontificate, as we have just seen in *The Tempest*, and he likes to lard his plays with Latin to impress those he thinks are above him. Someone said Jonson has never recovered from his education but his other plays show he understands how our world is being shaped by contact with the Islamic world, including Turkey."

"How is that?"

"In *Every Man Out*, he makes fun of you and your contemporaries." He stopped, thinking perhaps he had become too familiar. "You *are* Puntarvolo, my lord."

"Am I?"

"No doubt. But, as amusing as Jonson's effort may be to your fellow poets and playwrights, he recognizes the game has changed. Take the bet that you, as Puntarvolo, make that you can voyage out to Turkey and return, *without going Turk*. This expresses the fears the public has about the exotic changes that are occurring in England now, mostly from contact with foreigners."

"Fueled by the Puritans."

"Yes. What's also changing is that the new world will be built on trade and coal, not monopolies from the crown."

Oxford nodded. "How interesting, Mr. Sutton. I will speak with my son about how he treats your son. He can do better."

He walked away, the reference to their sons reestablishing the social order in his mind. The upstart! Oxford thought. Elevated to a lofty place through money, obtained by exchanging black rocks dug from the ground. What did Falstaff say about coal?

> *"Coal is made by the Devil. It stinks when ye burn it. Only what God grows with sunlight goes into my fireplace."*

Finley ran after him. "Now that *The Tempest* and *Iago* are done, what next?"

"*Hamlet*, perchance. He is awakening from the shadows that have beslubbered him all these years."

"Oh," Finley said. "I'm to Cambridge, my lord. Does your offer of a room still hold?

"It does.

He did not ask to help write *Hamlet*. He had the sense that Oxford might let Jonson write *The Tempest* but he would not share the awakening of *Hamlet* with anyone.

The two went back to Hackney. It was around this time, Nigel thought later, that Finley moved into King's Place permanently, rarely vacating the room given him to use on his trips between Cambridge and London.

An Invitation from the Queen

Your Majesty." Oxford leaned against the wind and levered himself out onto the covered porch that overlooked the Thames. A late October gale pinned him against the door a servant was closing behind him. Elizabeth looked up from the bearskin blankets in which she was buried. She motioned to a chair next to her. Oxford sat down, pulling another bearskin blanket around him that had been left on the chair. His left hand leaned his cane against the top of one Elizabeth was holding onto. He tapped his against hers. She smiled. "Together once again," she said, "if only in infirmity."

He settled back and reached into his coat to pull out a small bag, white in color, with two thin straps. He extended his arm. She took the bag and looked into it.

"Peewit eggs," she said, pulling one out. She held it up to peer at its light tan shell dusted with dark brown dots. She sniffed it before placing it on the arm of her chair and trying to spin it.

"Still fresh, Your Majesty, as you like them."

"Yes, I do. Thank you, my lord." She slipped the egg back into the bag. A servant appeared and took the bag back into the palace.

Oxford had thought Elizbeth would appreciate Digby's gift. "Your invitation was a delightful break in the dull existence I now endure in Outer Hackney," he said, suggesting that his home was as far away from London as the Outer Hebrides. "You write with such grace. The characters so delicately limned, a bit of gold in one place, a crimson rose in another."

She made no response to this, although he could tell she was pleased that he could recognize she had written the invitation herself and that he appreciated the calligraphic skills she still possessed.

He looked at the river. The sun was within a hands-breadth of the horizon. The wind continued to push into them, filling the skysails of a brig running down the Thames across from them.

"The *Edward Bonaventure*," Oxford said. "Still looking trim and spry. Outward bound on her way to India, no doubt."

Elizabeth snorted. "Her course we do not know, my lord, but she is *not* the *Edward Bonaventure* you sailed in against the Spanish; your ship was lost last year on the north coast of Hispaniola." He was trying to slide something past her she might not know. She couldn't resist slapping him down.

'Benedict and Beatrice to the end,' Oxford said, smiling. He had no idea where the *Edward Bonaventure* was but he liked Elizabeth's pushback. Some things hadn't changed.

"There are many *Edward Bonaventure* sailing under our flag," she said. "You are not the only 'Edward.' There is my brother, Edward. And many others. That anyone would name a ship after you defies odds."

They both knew the ship Oxford had sailed into the Spanish Armada had been named after him. He was entitled to the privilege, having paid for it. Of course, he did it with borrowed money, some of which he still had not repaid.

The ship going by them dropped another course to add speedas it went around the Isle of Dogs to the last bend in the river before it opened into the Channel and the open sea.

"Outward bound. Crammed with young men who know not what lies in store for them ..." Oxford began.

Elizabeth glowered, resentful of the adventure awaiting those on board and at her imprisonment in the body of an aging woman. "I nearly fell at Parliament this past week," she confided. "Had Norfolk not seized my elbow, I would have ended up splayed on the ground for all to laugh at."

Oxford tapped his cane against hers again. "First, on four legs, then on two, now on three," he said, referring to the riddle of the Sphinx, but Elizabeth was not ready to wax philosophical about having to use a cane, even if she took some comfort in seeing Oxford was falling apart as well.

"When thou dost feel creeping time at thy gate, my lord, these fooleries will please thee less; I am past my relish for such matters; thou seest my bodily meat doth not suit me well; I have eaten but one ill-tasting cake since yesternight"

"I am sorry to hear it."

She harrumphed. "As my fall and our canes show, our time here is growing shorter. I did not invite thee here for foolery. It is time to talk business."

This sounded ominous. He took his eyes off the ship, now moving away from them. He looked at Elizabeth. He set his face. He became her loyal minister, awaiting instructions.

"You have been my minister of wonder. A great poet. A better playwright. You have slain humorless Vice and given us the individual: Richard and Romeo; Viola and Rosalind. Falstaff! These are not stock figures. Hearts not yet born will swell when the statue of Hermione turns to gaze at them. It was for this that I give you your pension. I am pleased to say I think my investment has paid off handsomely."

Oxford was surprised to hear this. "I heard you say my pension was to maintain me as earl because I had wasted my patrimony. I was an embarrassment, you said, given my noble heritage and what I had done with it."

"I did it for the plays, my lord, nothing else."

Oxford didn't believe her. "To meld your people against the Spanish?"

She harrumphed. "And how did *Two Gentlemen of Verona* accomplish that? *All's Well That Ends Well? The Taming of the Shrew?* I didn't nag you to write *Romeo*; I nagged you to write them all! And I gave you the money to do it. If I wanted to send messages to my people, I would have hired Nashe and Greene and not had to dealt with the likes of you!" She looked at him obliquely, implying she had paid a heavy price. "No, my lord: I gave you a pension to give birth to your genius. T'was for art's sake and nothing else."

"But then why take away my name?"

"Because the Earl of Southampton is our son."

Oxford's mind came to a halt. He thought he had misheard her. "*Our son?*"

"Yes. Our son. And the father of the next king of England cannot be a common playwright."

Oxford sat up, stunned. "He will be king?"

"No."

"I don't understand."

Elizabeth reached over and took his hand, surprising Oxford even more. "I knew Henry was our son from the beginning, Edward." Oxford's mouth dropped open. "I lied to you to protect him. I lied to everyone to protect him. I was the virgin queen, wasn't I? How could I say I had given birth to a son? I hid him away."

"Moses in a basket," Oxford mumbled.

"Henry was a babe," she said, not hearing him. "I didn't know whether he would live. So many children don't. Would I live long enough to see him grow into a man? Would he grow into a man fit to be a king?"

She looked at him. "I couldn't tell you he was our son. Could you ever hold a secret? That you were the father of my child? *Hah!*"

He did not protest. She was right. He was a poet. A man of the theater. He could not have kept secret what she was telling him now. *The Earl of Southampton was their son?* He had no words to speak. He wanted to pick her up and dance across the balcony and give her a smack at the same time!

He was floating, like the gull riding motionless just a few feet above their heads. Questions rose within him. "Why did you send the babe to Titchfield?" he asked. "The 2nd Earl of Southampton was Catholic. You'd locked him up for speaking well of the Pope."

"What better place?" Elizabeth said. "Mary didn't fool him. He knew the baby Mary gave birth to after I let him out of the Tower could not be his. He may be slow, my lord, but he can count to nine!" She laughed, a bark that startled people who weren't used to her sense of humor.

"But Lady Mary says he said nothing."

"Of course not. He knew a row over whether he was the father of the child might land him back in the Tower. Lord Burghley, of course, learned that Mary had cheated on her husband. When I gave birth to our son some months after hers, Mary's son was quietly gifted out and Henry slipped into his place. Mary had misgivings, of course, but she was told Henry was hers and, seeing him so infrequently, said nothing."

"Perhaps she didn't want to know."

"Perhaps. She also knew her husband would throw her out if she raised a fuss. She liked being a countess. She made peace with the devil and carried on. At least, until, awash in wine at her wedding to old Heneage, she told you I was Henry's mother."

"Do you know what happened to her son?"

"No."

"I've spoken to her recently, Your Majesty. She told me she now believes Southampton *is* her son and the anguish she has suffered since his birth is punishment for her sins."

"Do you think she really believes this?"

"She wants to believe Southampton is her son, Your Majesty, but her mother's heart tells her he is not her son. Her son is somewhere else. If he has died, she told me, she would like to put flowers on his grave. If he is alive, she would like to see him from a passing carriage before she dies."

Elizabeth was unmoved. "Loyal servants of the crown die every day. How they die, who they leave behind, is something that does not reach my ears. Such is the fate of Lady Mary's son."

Elizabeth's callousness did not surprise Oxford. As queen, she had to learn early on that she could not put faces on those who died in her service or visit those who suffered loss from their deaths. Madness lay that way. Falstaff may have dismissed soldiers he led to their untimely ends as '*food for powder*,' but he too knew how to avoid knowing too much lest, like Oxford's knowledge of Thomas Brincknell, one ended up knowing too much.

Oxford's elation at being told Southampton was his son began to ebb away as he realized Southampton was not going to become England's next king. He began to wonder why she had told him Southampton was their son. He started to grow angry. "So, if you think him unfit to succeed you, why tell me he is our son? Why not leave me in peace?"

"Because you are his father and entitled to know. I will not be here much longer. James will take my place but James could falter. He is a Scot and not loved by my people. Some think he is a secret Catholic. If he fails, Henry can possibly step forward."

"James will not let him live to see that day."

"I think he will. James is a staunch believer in the rights of kings. If he slumbers in the belief that Henry is *not* my son, he will leave Henry alone. If he starts to believe Henry *is* my son, he will probably still leave him alone unless he feels threatened. That is why it is imperative that no one but you and me know he is our son."

"Sir Robert …"

"Is bound to me. I have plied him with gifts and hidden traps if he should turn against Henry. What de ye think I was talking to Falstaff about?"

"Falstaff?" Oxford said, surprised. "I would not rely on Falstaff, Your Majesty. I think it far better to declare Henry your son now before James comes south."

"If I did, I would be putting England's needs ahead of my own. I have given my life to England, Edward. I have not married. My people believe I am a virgin. Let them believe that. But I am Henry's mother, by God, and not England's. My son is as real as the oak trees in the park in front of us; t'other is a fiction. Henry may be my son, but he will not succeed me. I will not sacrifice him on an altar erected to England having a 'proper king. If I name him, he will die!"

Oxford was taken aback. Elizabeth had become the fierce mother bear who sounded like she would do anything to protect her young. She wasn't finished.

"You, who can never give birth to a child, have no qualms about risking Henry's life to obtain a reward *you will never see*, my lord, for you and I will both be dead when all this plays out,"

Oxford had no response to this.

"You also forget that naming Henry as my son would also strip him of his titles and wealth, for he would no longer be the 3rd Earl of Southampton. Didn't the Cecils try to do that to you?" She looked out over the river. "I tell you this to make sure you will never say anything about this to anyone, including Henry. Let him live, my lord; speak out and watch him die."

He had forgotten how commanding she could be. Her explanation shamed him into abandoning his desire to put Henry on the throne. But with that peeled away, his anger over being denied fame for his plays rose to the surface.

"And I," he said, "am consigned to suffer the humiliation of having my plays presented to the world as written by a country slow-wit from Warwickshire, when I am Edward de Vere, the 17th Earl of Oxford, *and father of the man who should be the next king of England!*"

"We do this for our son," she said calmly. She reached over and squeezed his hand. "Parents sacrifice for their children, Edward. This is our sacrifice. Yes, you will say, I will die queen of England and you will die unknown, but do not despair. Those who love your plays will cipher out who wrote them. Finley is working to get Cambridge to accept the theater as a subject worthy of study. He will be successful in bringing this about. They will study your plays. They will ask uncomfortable questions. The growth of the theater – your plays, your poetry in your plays – will be enough to tip the scales. And once exposed, the man who has been your mask will disappear from history."

"The Puritans are on the rise."

"The Puritans will *never* take the theaters away. Write something for James, my lord. He loves your plays. A Scottish play. The more he loves the theater, the more he will help you. And me."

Oxford wasn't interested in helping either of them. The greatest prize of his life had been given to him and snatched away. He was a Vere, a medieval knight through and through. His ancestors cried out from their graves: *put Henry on the throne! Give England kings that will stretch out to the crack of doom!*

But she would never let Southampton succeed her. Not now. He felt defeated. Blocked at every turn. And yet… And yet he found himself intrigued about writing a play for James. Perhaps James might be willing to reveal to the world what Her Majesty has kept secret — the identity of the man who wrote the plays James loves.

"*The Tragedie of the Kinge of Scottes?*" Oxford suggested.

Elizabeth looked at him. "Your play about the murder of James' father? You can't be serious."

"It was about Macbeth and how he murdered Duncan."

"It was about Darnley, James' father. You fell in love with the floating dagger, from the drawing sent to Burghley of the field in which Darnley's body was found. The knife floats in the air. You couldn't stop talking about it when we lay on a blanket in the park outside Nonsuch. Up and down with your hand, imagining the fatal blow was struck, whilst I was wishing for something else."

"Oh," Oxford said. He'd forgotten. He was surprised at how bawdy she could be. He had not knick-named her *Reginia Vagina* for nothing. "The drawing was remarkable, yes. The Children of the Chapel loved putting on *The Tragedie of the Kinge of Scottes* before you."

"I may have loved it then but, for God's sake, it was a juvenile effort."

"I could improve it."

"Anyone could improve it."

Oxford ignored her gibe. "I've read Stewart's *Buick of the Chronicles of Scotland.* There's good meat in there about the Macbeths.

She looked at him. "I thought the *Buick* was in Scotland."

"Lady Lennox had it. She gave it to me."

Elizabeth, a lover of fine books, was jealous that Oxford had gotten his hands on something she had always wanted. She almost asked him for it but realized it was too late for her to start reading something as difficult as the history of Scotland written in Scots.

Oxford, meanwhile, was already 'improving' his earlier play. "Much has happened since I wrote *The Tragedie.* The Massacre at Paris, for example. Catherine de Medici, the queen mother, murdering so many people. The ringing of the bell that gave the signal to begin."

His face was glowing. Elizabeth had seen him like this before. "Forget the murder of Darnley, my lord. James'll not like seeing his father murdered again. Show him *another* murder."

Oxford nodded. "I will. I'll fill it with omens and witches."

"He'll like that. Do ye have a copy of his *Daemonlogie*?"

"I do. Angus and Ross, Scottish lads in my service, have been filling my ears with curses and witches. They'll be my guides."

"Good."

He stood up. The sun was into the trees on the other side of the Thames. He took his cane and clicked it against hers.

"Your Majesty," he said, bowing slightly. "We are done here."

"We are, indeed."

He opened the door and entered the palace, closing off the wind behind him. He clattered along the stone floor sculpted by thousands of passing feet, his cane and sliding feet the only sound in the silent palace. Falstaff's lie had saved him from being hung for murdering Thomas Brincknell, but for what purpose? To die unknown? The gods were surely laughing at him, he thought.

The wound Thomas Knyvet had given him was suppurating again. It matched the one he had given Thomas Brincknell; in the groin, like the boar slashing Adonis in *Venus & Adonis*. This brought him to a stop. Did this mean he was the Fisher King? The Fisher King's wound had never healed either. And Oxford had been on a quest to gain *his* holy grail. In fact, *two* holy grails: acknowledgement that he wrote the plays Shackspear claimed were his, and that he was the father of Henry Wriothesley. But the knights Oxford he had read about as a boy never found the holy grail they were looking for, and Oxford now knew he would never find his either.

He walked out into the evening air and looked up at a pale, translucent moon. He understood now, the way the body understands something the mind has no words for, that his leg would never heal and the end could not be far off. But there was business to attend to, he told himself. "*Once more unto the breach,*" he heard Hal say into his good ear. "*Maybe more than once,*" Oxford replied, a wry grin spreading across his face. Of one thing he was certain: a new play would save him from whatever slippery slope beckoned to him.

~ 202 ~
Iago

Shackspear took the script for *Iago* to Burbage because he thought Henslowe had cheated him out of his rightful takings from *Twelfth Night*. Oxford had written *Iago* with Burbage in mind as the moor, but Burbage wanted to play Iago instead. "The moor is of no interest dramatically," he told Shackspear. "He's a block of wood. A dull, unimaginative captain, dutiful when it comes to his soldiers – *Keep up your bright swords, gentlemen, for the dew will rust them* - but completely unaware of what Iago is up to. I can't play him. Marlowe's Mephistopheles was a villain like Iachimo, but Iago is evil cut from diamonds. Black diamonds."

"Which is why you should play the moor. The moor is black. Ye'll love putting on the makeup."

"It's not about makeup, Will. It's about the character. Iago will chill hearts thirty rows back. I *must* be him."

Shackspear told Oxford that Burbage refused to play Othello. "I have no one else who can play Othello, my lord. Burbage would have made a grand Othello, but there is no one in the Lord Chamberlain's Men who can play the role. Alleyn won't help me. He won't work with Burbage after *Midsummer*. They took Demetrius and Lysander into the tiring hall. The cuts and bruises the audience saw at the end of the play did not take place off stage. I have no one to play the moor."

"Tobias," Oxford said. "He can do it."

"Your porter?"

"My whiffler."

"Whifflers are not players, my lord."

"No, but Tobias will know how to play Othello. Trust me: he'll *be* Othello."

Burbage played Iago; Tobias played Othello and stole the play. Burbage was chagrined that he was upstaged by a man who was African and not a player. To boot, he could have been the moor. The ladies drew back when Tobias walked out onto the stage, his immense fists looking like resting hammers. His voice left no doubt he was a commander:

By heaven, I saw my handkerchief in's hand.
O perjured woman! thou dost stone my heart,
And makest me call what I intend to do
A murder, which I thought a sacrifice.

No storm announced its arrival with a deeper voice.
Burbage, as Iago, was so taken aback he sometimes hesitated
in delivering his lines because he had become so engrossed in
watching Tobias. He couldn't comprehend how Tobias could
convey such threats of violence with no more than a
measured pace and a voice so low that the audience had to
lean forward and give up cracking nuts to hear what the giant
blackamoor was saying. It helped that his bare feet looked like
they were leather boots, thick and cracked from never having
worn shoes. When he placed his hands on Desdemona's
throat, countless hands in the audience flew to their own.

Burbage, in trying to overtake Tobias, overplayed Iago.
He made Iago hysterical instead of the cold Machiavelli
Oxford had intended.

When the play was over, Burbage realized he had made a
mistake thinking Iago would be the center of the play. Iago
was a study in evil but Othello would be who the audience
came to see. And, as much as the first audience loved seeing
an African man play the jealous husband, Burbage could tell
that a white man playing the moor would be even more
fascinating. He dismissed Tobias and assumed the part of
Othello.

Tobias did not object. He had only agreed to play Othello
out of loyalty to Oxford. "Too many words, my lord. Too
many people. Too far from where I want to be," which was at
King's Place, with a garden behind the manse where he could
see more birds in a day than flew over London in a year.

Oxford was surprised. He had thought Tobias would love
the applause and Burbage would revel in playing Iago. But he
had been wrong before. He wrote *Titus* to fail and send
Shackspear back to Stratford. Instead, it was Shackspear's first
hit. *Iago* made him realize his plays had lives of their own once
they left his writing desk and, like children, could become
something very different from what their author had intended.

1603

~ 203 ~
A Gift for James

Oxford was bent over his writing table. A candle sputtered on top of a pile of books to his left where Timson had placed it.

"Hah!" Oxford said into the empty room. "Hah!" he said again. He put down his pen and held up the paper he had been writing on, cocking it sideways to capture the light from the dying candle. "James will love this:"

> *Double, double toil and trouble;*
> *Fire burn, and cauldron bubble.*
> *Eye of newt and toe of frog,*
> *Wool of bat and tongue of dog,*
> *Adder's fork and blind-worm's sting,*
> *Lizard's leg and owlet's wing!*

"I am witch," he said in a low voice.

The curtain across the door to the balcony swelled open. A raspy voice spoke: "Thou canst not be witch sith thou art man and still alive."

Oxford didn't turn to look. "Lady Lennox," he said.

A woman in a flowing gown slipped past the curtain. She swayed slightly in vague acknowledgement of Oxford's statement.

"Welcum," Oxford said, turning to look at her.

"Ye fear me not."

"Only whether ye be a spirit of the night come to haunt me, or a spirit of mine own come to haunt me from my own fevered brain."

He could see her face.

She was smiling wanly. "Ye write a play for my grandson."

"Aye, my lady." He patted a thick loosely bound manuscript to his right. "From *The Buick of the Chronicles of Scotland.*"

"Ye still have it."

"And many thanks for it." He tipped his head back. "Listen. Here be Macbeth and Banquo comin into a wood:

Than hand to hand intill the forest greene
Three wemen met, their clothing very strange,
The first of them that to Macbeth came, said
"The Thane of Glames, gude morne to yew,"
The secund said, without ony scorne,
"The Thane of Caldar, Sir, Go yew gude morne!"
The hundmest, with plesand voce benyng,
"God save yow, Sir, of Scotland salbe king!"

"Ah, I love to heer it!" She came closer to him. "*Double trouble,*" she repeated. "These witchits beloved by James will be. But bring them back – theyer too good to appear only once, as they do in *The Buick*. The audience will crave to heer them speak again."

"Hecate will summon them."

"Good. Have them meet with Macbeth. Have them make him think he is invincible!"

Oxford spun around to pick up a quill: "They will tell him:

Be lion-mettled, proud; and take no care
Who chafes, who frets, or where conspirers are:
Macbeth shall never vanquish'd be until
Great Birnam wood to high Dunsinane hill
Shall come against him.

"Yes," Lady Lennox said, her voice coming out like a hiss. "Then troop apparitions of future kings by him to vex him, all descendants of Banquo."

Oxford was puzzled. "None such happens in *The Buick*."

"Add it," Lady Lennox said. "Ye haven't cared to stick to the stories ye found before. Make these apparitions appear like the woman who stands before ye enow, but make them wraiths only he sees. T'will add to his madness."

Oxford nodded. "You think of Catherine de Medici, who saw a parade of kings in her glass, I warrant."

Lady Lennox smiled. "Thou art adept. The Black Queen of France. She had to push the king, her husband, to begin the Massacre at Paris, as Lady Macbeth will have to urge Macbeth to slaughter his king:

Gratius God decreittit this thing,
Tarie nocht but speed thy hand,
Half done, for thow has all the riycht
Granted to thee by God of mycht.

Oxford turned back to his desk and began to write again.

What beast was't, then,
That made you break this enterprise to me?
I have given suck, and know
How tender 'tis to love the babe that milks me:
I would, while it was smiling in my face,
Have pluck'd my nipple from his boneless gums,
And dash'd the brains out, had I so sworn as you
Have done to this.

He turned to look at Lady Lennox, who was standing quite close to him. He passed a hand through her. She didn't react.

"How doth thou speak Scots so well, my lord?"

"Angus and Ross, thy servants when ye lived here, are now in my employ. I show them passages from *The Buick* and they translate it for me."

Lady Lennox murmured. "I remember them well. Guid men both."

She drew away from him.

"Send the play ye write to James in Scotland. No one heer will understand it. Let it be a gift for him only. Send it with *The Buick*," she said, pointing to the manuscript on Oxford's desk. "It should be in Scotland with him. He'll nair have a copy sith it's more than 40,000 lines."

"I will, my lady."

"He'll like it well. And you for givin it to hem."

She was now at the curtain, which the soft evening breeze curled open to carry her out of the room.

Oxford turned back to his desk. Sharpening the point on his quill, he took one of the clean pages Timson had brought him from Richard Fielding and began to write.

———◆◆◆◆◆———

It took fewer days than Oxford thought to finish a clean copy of *The Tragedie of Macbeth*. Ross and Angus read from James' book on witches and charms – *Daemonologie* – to give him the atmosphere of the witches. He had Timson bind it with a purple ribbon and place it in a wooden box. He then wrote a letter to James:

"My most learned, honorable, and just sovereign, James Rex, at Holliroode House," he wrote. *"Elizabeth Regina has settled the succession of the English crown on you. All of nature rejoices, myself most of all. I look forward to serving as Lord Great Chamberlain at your coronation and washing your hands as my ancestors have done for England's kings for 500 years.*

I am so bold as to speak thus because my health declines and, in the event death overtakes me before I am granted the honor and pleasure of serving you, I desire that you know my thoughts in case they are unspoken at your coronation.

Her Majesty, in her wisdom, suggested I present you with a gift — a play — which my servant will deliver to you in Scotland with this letter. This play -The Tragedie of Macbeth - has never been clapper-clawed with the palms of the vulgar. It is my personal gift to you. The script has not been copied. It is yours to do with as you wish.

The Tragedie of Macbeth is a reminder to all that peace and order flows from obeying one's obligations and doing our dooty. Macbeth violated Scotland's double trust — he slew his sovereign, and he did it whilst his king was a guest in his own house. A parade of apparitions show him that his line will end with his death and that the Scottish crown will descend to you.

With all due and humble respect, I am, Your Majesty, your faithful and loyal servant."

Oxford ended the letter with his signature and called for Timson. He handed him the letter. "Add this to the box in which you have placed *The Buick of the Chronicles of Scotland* and the play I have just finished. See Nigel to withdraw funds for you to travel to Scotland and back. Deliver this box to no one else but King James. His men will deny you entrance; instruct them that you come with a personal gift for His Majesty from the queen."

"The queen?" Timson asked, his eyes opening wide.

"How else get in?" Oxford said. "Now, off with ye."

204

The Mortal Moon Hath Her Eclipse Endured

James sent a note to Oxford to thank him for *Macbeth*. He and everyone else settled in to wait for Elizabeth's death. Like farmers waiting for the winter frost to end or the geese to return, the citizens of the four kingdoms of England, Wales, Ireland, and Scotland greeted each other every morning with a raised eyebrow, asking whether England's longest-reigning monarch still lived.

Oxford spent the time writing sonnets to mourn the loss of his son, confined in the Tower. He had high hopes James would release Southampton but no idea whether James would let him free or, if it happened, when. Such decisions moved at glacial speed. Elizabeth, for example, had been promising for years to return Epping Forest and Havering-atte-Bower to Oxford, long-owned by his ancestors before Henry VIII took them without law, but the conveyances remained marooned somewhere in a solicitor's office.

Oxford kept the sonnets he wrote in a box, along with the little book Robin had given him on her last visit to Oxford Court.

> *Your monument shall be my gentle verse,*
> *Which eyes not yet created shall o'er read,*
> *And tongues to be your being shall rehearse,*
> *When all the breathers of this world are dead.*

He sometimes wandered into more personal thoughts about how 'time doth crack my sinews and cake my brain:'

> *That time of year thou mayst in me behold,*
> *When yellow leaves, or none, or few, do hang*
> *Upon those boughs which shake against the cold,*
> *Bare ruined choirs, where late the sweet birds sang.*
> *So are you to my thoughts as food to life,*
> *Or as sweet seasoned showers are to the ground.*

And his lament that he had been unjustly barred from fame:

> *Why write I still all one, ever the same,*
> *And keep invention in a noted weed,*
> *That every word doth almost tell my name,*
> *Showing their birth, and where they did proceed?*

"*All one,*" he said to himself, looking down at the bright paper in front of him, the black letters incised in his graceful Italic script.

"Henry's motto – 'un par tout, tout par un.' But *all one* with whom? The queen, of course. Her motto is *semper eadem - always the same* - not *ever the same*? Ah, but I insert myself – *E. Ver* – between mother and son, showing that we are all one - *Why write I still all one, <u>ever</u> the same.*"

He put down his pen to enjoy his cleverness. Then he frowned. "But to what end? *My name be buried where my body lies!*"

His despair mirrored the gray skies outside. Day after day followed each other, each the same as the other. 'Tomorrow and tomorrow and tomorrow,' he thought to himself.

Finley finally brought word Elizabeth was sinking closer to death. She sat in a chair, refusing to eat anything. Sir Robert told her she 'must' go to bed, at which she erupted: "Must! Is 'must' a word to be addressed to princes? Little man, little man! Thy father, if he had been alive, durst not have used that word." After which, she fell to coughing and her servants were able to carry her to her bed.

Hearing this, Oxford shifted to Derby House to be in London. Finley came with him. "I am to London, my lady," he said to Elspeth. "As a member of the Privy Council, I must be there for what comes." Derby put them in the room by the river where they waited.

———◆◆◆◆———

The end came on March 24 at 3 in the morning. Sir Robert Carey, younger brother of George Carey, Baron Hunsdon, took the ring Elizabeth had promised James as a sign she had passed away and leapt onto his horse. Three days later, he was at Hollyrood Palace on bended knee in front of James VI of Scotland, soon to become James I of England. Carey handed James the ring. In return, James made him a Gentleman of the Bedchamber, and the process of transferring the crown to James began.

Oxford received the news of her death the morning she died. He went to his writing desk and penned the sonnet he had been holding in his mind, not writing it down for fear it would dash his hopes that Southampton would be freed from the Tower:

> *Not mine own fears, nor the prophetic soul*
> *Of the wide world dreaming on things to come,*
> *Can yet the lease of my true love control,*
> *Supposed as forfeit to a confin'd doom.*
>
> *The mortal moon hath her eclipse endur'd,*
> *And the sad augurs mock their own presage;*
> *Incertainties now crown themselves assur'd,*
> *And peace proclaims olives of endless age.*

> *Now with the drops of this most balmy time,*
> *My love looks fresh, and Death to me subscribes,*
> *Since, spite of him, I'll live in this poor rime,*
> *While he insults o'er dull and speechless tribes:*
>
> *And thou in this shalt find thy monument,*
> *When tyrants' crests and tombs of brass are spent.*

Later, Oxford learned that James had signed a royal warrant instructing the Lieutenant of the Tower to release Southampton. The courier carrying James' warrant arrived in London on April 10. The Tower gates were opened and Southampton, on a horse provided by the Lieutenant, rode out into the sunlight of a new day. He had been in the Tower three winters. He wanted nothing more to do with London. He rode through the City and across the Strand, past Whitehall Palace and Westminster Abbey and then south out of London. His path took him between his mother, Elizabeth, her body being prepared for burial in Whitehall, and his father, the 17th Earl of Oxford, dozing in Derby House as he awaited news of what James would do with his son.

By the time Oxford learned of his son's release, Southampton was far from London. Oxford went to his writing desk and sat down to write a sadder sonnet about having to keep himself from the man he knew was his son:

> *O! how thy worth with manners may I sing,*
> *When thou art all the better part of me?*
> *What can mine own praise to mine own self bring?*
> *And what is't but mine own when I praise thee?*
>
> *Even for this, let us divided live,*
> *And our dear love lose name of single one,*
> *That by this separation I may give*
> *That due to thee which thou deserv'st alone.*
>
> *O absence! what a torment wouldst thou prove,*
> *Were it not thy sour leisure gave sweet leave,*
> *To entertain the time with thoughts of love,*
> *Which time and thoughts so sweetly doth deceive,*
>
> *And that thou teachest how to make one twain,*
> *By praising him here who doth hence remain.*

Elizabeth was laid in state. Her funeral took place on April 28. All London turned out to see her coffin carried to Westminster Abbey on a hearse drawn by four horses hung with black velvet. Lords flanked the hearse carrying flags with Elizabeth's family crests on them. The Gentlemen Pensioners, led by Sir Walter Ralegh, brought up the rear, their halberds pointed at the ground. Oxford did not attend. He remained at Derby House.

The people clogged the streets and hung off windows, roofs, and gutters to catch a glimpse of the queen's coffin as it went by. They groaned and wept. Inside the Abbey, her ministers broke their white staves and threw them into her grave, thus ending her reign.

James had started for London on April 5, promising Scotland he would return. He never did. He was feted at every stop on his journey south. When he finally arrived on the outskirts of London, Elizabeth's ministers rode out to meet him at Hatfield.

Southampton had not waited for James to journey so far, however. He had ridden north to Stamford, Burghley's immense estate where James pardoned him and promised to restore his titles and lands. James began to make his word good on July 9; he made Southampton a Knight of the Garter; on the 21st, he restored Southampton's titles: Henry Wriothesley, formerly Mr. Henry Wriothesley, once again became Henry Wriothesley, 3rd Earl of Southampton. To provide him with an income, James gave him the farm of sweet wines the Earl of Essex had previously enjoyed.

All of this activity, of course, was without Oxford's involvement or knowledge. He remained at Derby House, reluctant to return to Hackney because removing himself from London would signify the end of all he had hoped for. Elizabeth was gone and Southampton would never succeed her. Or know who his father was.

Finley and Derby finally convinced Oxford to return to Hackney where he withdrew into his rooms and settled into a deep depression. Timson brought him eye wash to dab his eyes and a string of words written in fair script on a thin sheet of linen to be eaten by Oxford at breakfast and dinner. "Scottish words to ward off the evil eye and restore your health, as written and approved by his Majesty, King James VI in his Buick *Daemonologie.*"

Oxford looked at them. "Joseph and Mary."

"Aye. Father and mother of our good Lord. Eat a word a day – it'll do ye guid."

"I thought paper was deynty and should not be wasted."

"It's not bein' waysted, not on you."

Oxford had lost the will to resist. He let Timson push the folded-up piece of paper into his mouth. He chewed. The bitter taste of the ink flooded his mouth. He swallowed. He felt lost. Alone.

205

Hamlet

Finley refused to let Oxford languish in despair. "*Sic transit Gloriana*," he said one morning, opening the curtains. He thought his chipper remark would revive Oxford, but it had the opposite effect. Oxford thought it was in bad taste because the mourning period for the queen had not ended; worse, Finley's attempt at humor in Latin had fallen flat.

"Well," Finley said, coming back across the room to where Oxford lay slumped in front of his writing desk. "If my attempt at humor is so bad that it rouses his lordship from his lethargy, I have accomplished something of importance today."

Oxford glowered at him.

Finley deposited an armful of notes and manuscripts in front of Oxford. "I have gone through *Hamlet* and compared it to the sources you say you used. Neither Saxo Grammaticus nor Belleforest has a ghost in their story of *Hamblett*. They have no Laertes, no Fortinbras, no gravedigger, no Ophelia, no *Mousetrap* play, *and no pirates!* Furthermore, Hamblett does not die in Denmark; he goes to Scotland and is killed in battle there!"

"S'why I fashioned a different end."

"But ye always borrow. It's what ye've done in every play."

"Who cares where I get a play?"

"We do."

Oxford looked at him differently. "Who?"

"We scholars. We who seek understanding of a work of art need to know the ground from whence it came. A statue comes from a certain marble. Where did it come from? How does the grain and texture affect what the sculptor did with it? Does John Dowd listen to the workers harvesting a crop whilst he creates a new piece of music celebrating their ties to the land? If we know, we can better understand what he creates. In your case, ..."

Oxford turned away. "Mary, mother of ... Can't I just write plays? Must they be laid out on a table and cut into little pieces as if they were a corpse for students to study? It's not the parts that make up the art, Finley; it's the entirety of the work."

"But knowing the source helps us appreciate the play."

Oxford groaned.

Finley leaned forward. "Who was Ophelia?"

Oxford cocked an eye at him. "Who do you think she was?"

"Nan. But Nan didn't kill herself."

"Lisbeth thinks she did." He watched this register on Finley's face. "Lisbeth has claimed that Nan threw herself into the lake behind Hatfield House. Because of how I treated her."

"Oh."

"Didn't know that, did ye?"

"No." He hesitated. "Did she?"

Oxford shrugged. "I wasn't there when she died. If Burghley thought she had killed herself because of me, he would have let me know. But if she had killed herself for any reason, Burghley would have kept it a secret."

"Otherwise, she couldn't have been buried in sacred ground."

"Where is she? She's in Westminster Abbey, Finley. Alongside her mother. You figure it out."

"Oh, so that's what the gravediggers are talking about. How could Ophelia be buried in sacred ground if she killed herself." He scrambled through the pages on the table.

1st Gravedigger:	*How can that be, unless she drowned herself in her own defence?*
2nd Gravedigger:	*Why, 'tis found so.*
1st Gravedigger:	*It must be 'se offendendo;' it cannot be else. For here lies the point: if I drown myself wittingly, it argues an act: and an act hath three branches: it is, to act, to do, to perform: argal, she drowned herself wittingly.*
2nd Gravedigger:	*Nay, but hear you, goodman delver,--*
1st Gravedigger:	*Give me leave. Here lies the water; good: Here stands the man; good; if the man go to this water, and drown himself, it is, will he, nill he, he goes,--mark you that; but if the water come to him and drown him, he drowns not himself: argal, he that is not guilty of his own death shortens not his own life.*
2nd Gravedigger:	*But is this law?*

1st Gravedigger: *Ay, marry, is't; crowner's quest law.*

Finley turned to Oxford. "My lord, you look like you are accusing Nan of doing away with herself *and* her father for covering it up!"

Oxford shrugged. "I kill him in Act III, don't I? I stab him through an arras, like this!" Oxford made a sudden stabbing motion. "He lies there for the audience to wonder about while I harass and annoy my mother and talk to the ghost of my father!" He was enjoying the scene. He looked down at the floor as if Polonius lay there. "*Heaven hath pleased it so, / To punish me with this and this with me.*"

This confirmed to Finley that Oxford was Hamlet. And Polonius was Burghley. And Ophelia, Nan. And so on. But was this madness recent, or had it been festering all these years *Hamlet* had been taking shape in Oxford's mind? "But didn't you think it was Claudius behind the arras."

"Did I?" Oxford looked quizzically at Finley.

"Oh, my lord," Finley said. He decided to stop asking questions. He switched to why Oxford had changed the ending of *Hamblett*. "Hamblett dies in Scotland, my lord. Your Hamlet dies in Denmark."

"Yes."

"Wherefore?"

"*Beowulf.*"

"*Beowulf?* The Norse saga?"

"Old English. I had it from my tutor, Lawrence Nowell, who gave it to me when I was thirteen. He thought I could make a play out of it. I couldn't. I wasn't good yet at adding missing parts. I respected the source too much. When I found *Hamblett*, I took most of *Hamlet* from it but never liked Hamblett going off to Scotland and dying. I needed a better ending. I got it from *Beowulf.*"

Finley was taking this down. He was trying to fit *Beowulf* into *Hamlet*. "Do they end the same?"

"No. I couldn't borrow the dragon Beowulf fought. T'would have upended the play. I took the part where Beowulf fights a duel with poison and a sword: *Its blade was of iron, blotted with poison, hardened with gore.*" He smiled. "And Beowulf wears a helmet surmounted by a boar. How could I resist adding him to Hamlet when I read that?" He turned to Finley. "And, as Hamlet lies dying, he implores his friend to make sure he is remembered."

"Horatio."

"In my play."

Finley had more questions, but Oxford had lost interest. "Put *Hamlet* in proper order, my friend. Convey it to Burbage. I promised it to him once. He will make a fine Hamlet." He rearranged himself in the chair. "And, once done, return to me. There is one more play I must write."

Finley was surprised. "My lord?"

"Lear," Oxford muttered.

"Oh. He who had three daughters."

"And two sons."

"Two sons?"

"Gloucester will have two sons: one got twixt the sheets; the other somewhere else."

"Ah," Finley said. "As you have two sons: one got twixt the sheets; the other somewhere else." A smile began to spread across his face. "Oh, ye'll be both. Like ye were Proteus and Valentine in *Two Gentlemen*, Romeo and Mercutio in *Romeo* …"

"Benedict and Beatrice."

Finley looked at him. "No."

"Yes."

"Henry V and Falstaff," Finley suggested.

Oxford furrowed his brow. "No,"

"Touchstone and Jacques."

Oxford shrugged. They were both having a good time, but Oxford was fading. "Lear," he said. "Lear."

Finley helped him into bed.

"Finley," Oxford said. He was staring at the ceiling as Finley pulled up the blankets. "I am experiencing something most peculiar."

"What is that, my lord."

"I am finding myself at times without words."

Finley didn't know what to make of this. "My lord?"

"My mind has always been a kingdom to me. Words flowed through me like water down the Rhine. Sometimes now there are no words. Great empty spaces with nothing in them."

He turned to look at Finley. "There's something restful about it."

Oxford returned to Derby House as the premiere of *Hamlet* approached. He initially thought he would attend its performance but begged off at the end. Left alone, he gazed out the window and floated away on the soft breeze ruffling the curtains. His right hand rose and fell as he heard the puppets speak his lines. Like every dream dreamed while alone, there were no mistakes. Entrances and exits came and went seamlessly. The players' voices projected to the upper boxes; no one slurred or misspoke what he had written.

Until, that is, the play came to Hamlet returning to Elsinore and coming upon the cemetery. The gravediggers were opening a new grave for Ophelia. Oxford smiled as he heard the gravediggers debate with Hamlet whether Ophelia could be buried in sacred ground if she had taken her own life. He admired how he had folded Nan into Ophelia and reworked the question of how she could be buried in Westminster Abbey if, as Lisbeth claimed, she had died by throwing herself into the lake behind Hatfield House.

But a wispy figure suddenly appeared outside the window, drifting by in the warm air. Oxford sat bolt upright. *Thomas Brincknell!* The figure smiled as it continued past the window. It was on its way downriver to see *Hamlet!*

As the undercook disappeared, Oxford realized the gravedigger's scene was not about Nan. It was about Thomas Brincknell, the poor undercook Oxford had killed when he was seventeen. Where had the undercook's body been taken? A pauper's grave? Unsanctified ground? A coroner's jury had decided he had committed suicide. Falstaff had told them the undercook had run onto the end of Oxford's sword. This was a lie that saved Oxford's life, but had it denied the poor man a life after death?

But surely, Oxford thought, God would see through Falstaff's lie and know the poor man was innocent. Wouldn't he?

Then another thought struck him. What if the undercook was waiting for Oxford to die like the way the Earl of Surrey had waited for Lord Burghley? Oxford quickly glanced around the room. It was empty. The wraith he had seen float by the window was no more.

The room went cold as the sun sank in the west. Wrapped in despair, wondering whether his mind was going now that he conversed with dead earls and undercooks, Oxford sat lifelessly in front of the window, looking out and seeing nothing.

And so it was that those happy few who had seen the premier of *Hamlet* returned full of excitement and didn't notice how subdued his lordship was.

"All London was there, my lord," Robin said as soon as they trooped into his room.

"Burbage will never act another part," Derby announced. "He was larger than life this afternoon. He was magnificent."

"And Shackspear?" Oxford asked.

"Hailed by all," Falstaff said. "He will now be unsufferable."

"And Sir Robert. Was he there?"

"He was," Falstaff said. "He came early and hid himself in one of the upper boxes. I thought he would leave after Burbage stabbed Polonius but he stayed to the end. I had Tupp stick close to him. What'd he say after the play, Tupp?"

"T'wasn't English, I weel say that. He came down the stairs uttering words I have only heard from the weetches in Macbeth!"

They all laughed. Tupp was enjoying the praise. He hitched his tiny pants with his thumbs and started doing a highland gig. Everyone was amazed. He stopped. "What! The new king, he will be from Scotland, no? I learn English, no? Now I learn the highland gig."

"We get it, half-pence," Falstaff said. "To the Boar's Head, then."

"I'd rather stay here," Oxford said, turning away from them.

Derby realized Oxford's leg wouldn't carry him that far. "To the Open Purse, then," Derby said. "In Covent Garden. A celebration."

Oxford still didn't go with them. He didn't feel like celebrating. He listened to them go down the stairs, boisterously laughing and pushing each other. He thought he could hear the air leaving the room with them. Silence replaced it. He felt like parts of him were leaving as well. How many before there was nothing left, he wondered?

206

The Coronation

Oxford began to make preparations to assist James' at his coronation, scheduled for July 25. As Lord Great Chamberlain, Oxford would have the privilege of providing water to James on the morning of his coronation. Oxford had never attended a coronation. Elizabeth had been crowned when Oxford was eight. He was still at Hedingham then and could not recall whether his father, Earl John, had attended the queen as Lord Great Chamberlain. Probably not, given that his father had supported Mary.

Timson was dispatched to Silver Street to have a new ewer made with a boar's head stopper. The old one could not be found. Derby agreed to loan Oxford a basin. Nigel busied himself with converting the forty yards of crimson velvet allotted to Oxford into a suit of clothes that would dazzle His Majesty.

Oxford, of course, had little awareness of all this. He had taken to sitting in front of the window looking out on the Thames. It was July. The wind blew from the southeast, bringing warm, soft air with it. The earth dozed, as he did. He was finding it easier to sleep during the day than at night. His leg hurt him.

He had little interest in the ceremony itself. This was surprising, given that James' coronation would be a first for him and he was the head of a five-hundred-year-old family as well as the last medieval knight living in England. Despite the fact that he would play an important role the morning of James' coronation, it wasn't enough to overcome his reluctance to go. He finally agreed because his son, the future 18th Earl of Oxford, would be watching. Henry had convinced his mother to leave her garden for a few days and take him to the coronation. After all, he told her, as Earl of Oxford and Lord Great Chamberlain, he would have the duty of providing water to James' successor.

Oxford would have preferred not to venture out at all. People were flooding into London, of course. Workers were building arches for James to march through. Ben Jonson had gotten approval to build one; Shackspear had tried as well but didn't have the contacts Jonson had. Besides, there was a sense that James' staff knew Shackspear was not the playwright he claimed to be. Shackspear felt like a man pursuing a woman who always said 'later' until it becomes apparent she really means 'no.' This put him all athwart the beams. He did get the 4 ½ yards of red cloth allotted to him for the coronation, which he immediately thought about selling. He could get a pretty penny for it in Banbury, particularly when a prospective buyer was told the cloth had been issued for the King's coronation. Wedged between making money but missing the coronation and having a suit made *at his expense*, he chose to stay.

James was more generous with Oxford as he prepared for his coronation. He restored Oxford's titles to Waltham Forest and Havering the week before the coronation. Word was sent that Oxford's £1,000 annual pension would be renewed shortly.

———————————

July 25th dawned brisk and blustery. Oxford's leg hurt. That meant it would probably rain. Derby suggested they go to Whitehall in his carriage. He and Lisbeth climbed in. Nigel had put the ewer and basin in a small chest made of osier reeds, which he handed to Timson, who took his seat next to Oxford.

Whitehall was only a few blocks away. Had Oxford not been lame, they could have walked it in a few minutes.

To everyone's surprise, Oxford brought up Nan. "Ye blamed me for your mother's death," he said, looking at Lisbeth across from him. "I figure ye did so because your loss was so great at the time, you being young."

"I was twelve."

"As I was, when Earl John died."

They seemed oblivious to Derby and Timson seated next to them. Lisbeth reached over and took his hand.

"In my grief, I thought only of myself, my lord, and was angry at you because you would live, while sweet, gentle Nan, would not."

Neither spoke for a moment.

"Her death left me living in an opulent house with my sisters. We had servants and the constant care of Lady Mildred and Lord Burghley. They could seem harsh at times but their love and steadfastness was something I was too young to appreciate at the time, but it was genuine."

She looked out the window and then back at him.

"You, my lord, must have suffered much more. You lost your father *and* your mother. You went to a strange house with no family or friends. Yes, the same house I lived in much later, but Lady Mildred and Lord Burghley were *my* grandparents. I cannot imagine what it must have been like for you."

Oxford was touched.

Lisbeth was not done. "My lord, I despise the young woman who told you mother threw herself into the lake behind Hatfield House. That wasn't true. I cannot believe I uttered such lies. I need to erase my false statement."

"Then why did you vex me with it?" Oxford asked.

"Because I hated you at the time. And you were so easy to gull," she added. She rolled her eyes and laughed. "You could be a come-from-the-country bumpkin ready to believe that goblins run down the walls of St. Paul's at night or that sea lizards wait along the Thames to pull you in!"

They all laughed. Even Timson, who, up till then, had been wishing he were somewhere else.

Oxford laughed with them. "I suppose I have always been too willing to accept a story others would reject out of hand." He thought of Yorke. "A flaw, perhaps, in those who love plays."

The carriage came to a halt. "We are here," Derby said, opening the door and climbing down.

Timson followed. "Forgive me," they heard Lisbeth say. She reached out to touch her father's hand again. "A gift to you on James' coronation day."

"On any day," Oxford said. Hand in hand, they disembarked.

⚬✦✦✦⚬

Oxford gave water to the king as he ate breakfast in the ornate bed he had slept in. "Great Oxenford," he said, taking the proffered towel to wipe his lips. "Our thanks for returning the *Buick* to Scotland. We have brought it with us. Like Alexander, who kept the *Iliad* under his pillow, we will keep the *Buick* under ours."

"Majesty," Oxford said, bowing slightly.

"And *Macbeth*. Ye well understand the world we come from. Many thanks for that."

Oxford bowed again.

The morning ablutions over, the king dressed in new clothes. He rode in a carriage the short distance to the Abbey where the coronation took place. A banquet followed in the Great Hall. The lords and bishops queued up to take their places. Oxford and Sir Robert Cecil, made Baron Essendon the week before, crossed paths.

"Congratulations, my lord," Oxford said.

Cecil leaned into him. "*Hamlet*," he hissed. "You treated my sister and father vilely during their lives. That was bad enough, but to paint Nan as Ophelia in *Hamlet* and stab my father through an arras will not go unrevenged. Your name will *never* be associated with your plays, my lord. You will die unknown. Your dream of being the English Sophocles will die with you." He stalked off.

Oxford had expected Sir Robert to be upset about how his father and sister had been treated. 'Frozen like insects in amber,' Oxford calmly thought as he shuffled off toward the Great Hall, 'for future playgoers to see afresh each time *Hamlet* is performed. Such is *my* revenge.'

The passageway he now entered was flanked by the King's Men, Shackspear among them. Resplendent in their crimson garments, they stood at attention as everyone passed. Oxford veered into Shackspear.

"The queen is dead, Willum. Our agreement is at an end."

Shackspear was momentarily taken aback. "Who says, my lord?"

"I do. You've had your fun. I want the world to know I wrote *Hamlet* and all the rest."

"Wot? And I am to give up being famous? Return to being a nameless actor? *Hah!* 'Our Roscius!' Jonson calls out when I walk into the Mermaid." He pushed his index finger against Oxford's shoulder. "I will never die, my lord, as long as there is a theater somewhere and people can read. You, on the other hand," he stepped back, eyeing Oxford, "don't look very well."

"Argh!" Oxford cried out. He looked like he was about to strike Shackspear, but the other lords and ladies in the passageway pushed him on into the Great Hall.

1604

~ 207 ~
Ripeness

Oxford returned to Hackney after the coronation. Timson and Finley helped him up the stairs and into his room at the back of King's Place. He was exhausted. He let Timson help him into bed. Surrounded by his books and furnishings, he turned over and fell into a deep sleep.

He slept forty hours. When he awoke, Timson brought him a broth made from lamb bones. "Rich marrow to bring ye back," he said, fussing over him.

Oxford grunted. He ate some of the soup.

"Angus and Ross thankee for letting them attend King James' coronation," Timson said. "They well-enjoyed it."

"Did they see the king?"

"They did. In his carriage, waving to the pooblic as he went by on his way to the Abbey."

Oxford smiled. 'And wait, my bonnie lads,' he thought to himself, 'till ye see *Macbeth*.' He sat up. But did James have the only copy?'

"Did we keep a copy of *Macbeth*?"

"Well, ye wrote James that ye were sending him the only copy, but Lady Susan would have none of that. She had a fair copy made before I took it to Scotland."

"Lady Susan?"

"Yer daughter?" Timson wasn't sure Oxford understood.

"I know who Lady Susan is, Timson. Why was *she* making a copy?"

"She's got them all," Timson said, mystified by his master's questions. "Robin kept copies while he was your page. When he, well, she, was no longer in yer service, she took what she had to Lady Susan."

"And since then?"

"Lady Elspeth makes sure a clean copy is sent to Lady Susan each time a play is finished *before* a copy is sent to Shackspear."

"Did Shackspear get *Macbeth*?" Oxford asked, worried.

"No, my lord. Only James and Lady Susan. She and Dr. Finley are working on assembling and collating your plays."

"What! I never gave permission for that!"

"Dr. Finley said ye didn't want to bother with saving them while ye were writing them, but they need to be preserved."

Oxford turned away. 'Which means,' he said to himself, glaring at the wall across from him, 'I am no longer needed.' He was about to charge off into imagining his death and funeral, the cortege, the mourners – would there be any? – when Finley came into the room.

"*Leir*, my lord," Finley announced. "You mentioned it before we went to London. Did ye mean *The Chronicle of King Leir*? T'was an old play Henslowe put on in 1594 at the Rose. The Queen's Men played it. No one could remember who wrote it."

Oxford shrugged and made a face, like why ask him?

"Ah," Finley said. "Another play by Anonymous."

"A *joovenile* effort," Oxford said.

"Ye have the script for this *Chronicle of King Leir*?"

Oxford pointed to a box on the dresser. Finley retrieved it. He removed the papers inside. "There are forty versions of Leir, my lord. They all describe how he gave away his kingdom." He turned to Oxford. "Like someone I know."

Oxford assumed a woman's voice. Rosalind's, in fact: "*I fear you have sold your own lands to see other men's; then, to have seen much and to have nothing, is to have rich eyes and poor hands.*"

"Poor, indeed," Finley said. "I have a copy of *Leir* in Cambridge. Henslowe let me copy it. Is this the same?" He began to read:

Leir.	*Speak now, Cordella, make my joyes at full,*
	And drop downe Nectar from thy hony lips.
Cor.	*I cannot paynt my duty forth in words,*
	I hope my deeds shall make report for me:
Leir.	*Why how now, Minion, are you growne so proud?*
Cord.	*Deare father, do not so mistake my words,*
	Nor my playne meaning be misconstrued;
Leir.	*Peace, bastard Impe, no issue of King Leir,*
	Call not me father, if thou love thy life,
	My Kingdome will I equally devide
	'Twixt thy two sisters to their royall dowre.

"'Tis the same," Finley said, answering his own question.

"But not with what I will write," Oxford said. He drew himself up. He was suddenly alive. He swung his legs out and stood up.

Finley backed away.

"Mark this," Oxford said, glaring at him. "The play will be called *The Tragedie of King Lear* – spelled L-E-A-R, not L-E-I-R."

"But it is spelled *Leir* in all the sources, my lord," Finley protested.

"Not in the play I will write!"

Finley's jaw dropped open. Oxford saw it. "Yes, yes, 'Lear' is an anagram for 'earl.' What else could I call it?" He looked at Finley and then toward the window. "I should have done it the first time. My brand, it would have been." This momentarily distracted him, but then he returned to Finley.

"Note well." This Finley took as a command to sit down at the writing desk to capture Oxford's words.

"Lear commands the room," Oxford announced in a strong voice Finley had not heard for quite some time. "He announces he wishes to resign his kingdom and, '*Unburthen'd crawl toward death.*' He asks his three daughters: *Which of you shall we say doth love us most?*"

Finley took up a quill and began writing.

"Goneril and Regan flatter him. When he comes to Cordelia, he says: *What can you say to draw / A third more opulent than your sisters? Speak.* To which Cordelia answers: *Nothing, my lord.*

Lear.	*Nothing?*
Cord.	*Nothing.*
Lear.	*Nothing?*
Cord.	*Nothing.*
Lear.	*Nothing will come of nothing: speak again.*
Cord.	*Unhappy that I am, I cannot heave* *My heart into my mouth: I love your majesty* *According to my bond; nor more nor less.*
Lear.	*How, how, Cordelia! mend your speech a little,* *Lest it may mar your fortunes.*
Cord.	*Good my lord,* *You have begot me, bred me, loved me: I* *Return those duties back as are right fit,* *Obey you, love you, and most honour you.* *Haply, when I shall wed,* *That lord whose hand must take my plight shall carry*

> *Half my love with him, half my care and duty:*
> *I shall never marry like my sisters,*
> *To love my father all.*

Lear.   *But goes thy heart with this?*

Cord.   *Aye, good my lord,*

Lear.   *Let it be so; thy truth, then, be thy dower:*
> *Here I disclaim all my paternal care,*
> *Propinquity and property of blood,*
> *And as a stranger to my heart and me*
> *Hold thee, from this, forever.*

"Different?" Oxford asked Finley. "Better?"

"Stark," Finley said. "A hot knife, cleaving your daughter from you. What is this play about?"

"*Hamlet* is a play about a young man trying to figure out the world. *Macbeth* is about a man in middle years grasping for power. *Lear will be* a play about an old man facing his end." He looked away for a moment. "I will add another dimension: Gloucester and his two sons."

"'Tis not in the original, my lord."

"Gloucester will be another me in the play. He will give me entry into the plot from another angle. He will have two sons; one legitimate, and one not. Gloucester will acknowledge them both at the beginning of the play:

> *I have, sir, a son by order of law, some year elder than this,*
> *who yet is no dearer in my account: though this knave came*
> *something saucily into the world before he was sent for, yet was*
> *his mother fair; there was good sport at his making, and the*
> *whoreson must be acknowledged.*

"Ah," Finley said. "A jest to warm the audience. Shall end well?"

"No. Lear, Cordelia, Goneril, Regan, Gloucester and Edmund will all die."

Finley was surprised to hear this. "In the sources, Cordelia lives. She succeeds Leir and dies peacefully."

"Not in what I will write. Lear will be turned out; Gloucester will be blinded; people will die; and fathers will not know their children."

Finley looked at Oxford. "Nothing," he said.

"Nothing."

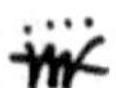

The Rest is Silence

Lady Mary, Dowager Countess of Southampton, descended the stairs from where she had watched Shackspear's latest play, *King Lear*. Her appearance at the bottom showed that the years were beginning to be unkind to her. Described by Oxford once as having the shape of a wide-bottomed merchant ship, she had since turned into a grain barge that had neither front nor rear nor sides. Formidable she remained, however, and not only because she was the mother of the 3rd Earl of Southampton.

"Give grace to God for inventing clothing to save us from having to look at each other as we really are," she announced. Richard Burbage had stripped himself naked by the end of the play to show how far Lear had descended into madness. This was too much for Lady Mary. "A two-penny box is not far enough away from the stage for this kind of performance! What would happen if the audience could sit at the edge of the stage!" She gasped. "Didn't Genesis teach us to wear clothes?"

The rest of the audience ignored her. They thought Burbage's nakedness a brilliant way of showing Lear's madness. Burbage would forever be remembered for his art, not his nakedness. The play left them voiceless, except for the few patrons muttering 'nothing, nothing, nothing,' as they went out the door.

They paid no attention to a huddled figure seated in a chair whose slight frame was hidden beneath blankets folded around him. A tall, thin man stood behind the chair.

Robin, as John Webster, came up. She nodded to the tall man. "Dr. Finley," she said, looking up at him. She bent to one knee and slipped her hand into the blankets.

Falstaff came up, Tupp behind him. The last remaining theatergoers flowed around them like salmon avoiding rocks as they headed for the sea.

"He's dead," Robin said.

Timson immediately bent down and reached in, then pulled his hand out and nodded.

Lady Mary, followed by Lady Lettice, stopped next to them. They looked at each other. Robin stood up. They needed no words to know Oxford had died.

"My Lord of Oxenford," Lady Mary said sadly, looking at Oxford's body hunched over in the chair.

Lady Lettice was angry. "What they've done to this man is a foul crime," she declared. "The greatest writer of all time, denied his rightful fame, the right to claim: 'I wrote *Romeo and Juliet*.'"

"And *Hamlet*," Finley said.

"*Macbeth*," someone newly arrived said.

"*Henry IV*," Falstaff quickly added.

"*Twelfth Night*," Robin muttered.

Lady Mary huffed herself up until she looked like a rooster about to proclaim it was morning. "What they done is as bad as taking a child away from its mother and giving it to someone else."

They all murmured agreement.

"He will be known," Robin said:

> *Absent thee from felicity awhile, Horatio,*
> *And in this harsh world draw thy breath in pain,*
> *To tell my story.*

"Little chance of that happening," Lady Mary said. "Those who know he wrote the plays will die, leaving only the printed plays behind. The title pages will say Shacksmear wrote them. Who will correct that?"

"All the more reason, Lady Mary, to study the plays and find evidence Lord Oxford wrote them," Finley said.

"Footprints," Robin added. "Falstaff stabbing Hotspur in the thigh. If ye know Oxford stabbed the undercook in the thigh, the scene takes on a different light."

"Oxford robbing Lord Burghley's receivers on Gad's Hill," Falstaff said, nodding with pride, "if ye know he robbed Lord Burghley's receivers there when he was twenty-four, ye understand *Henry IV Part One* better."

"*Two Gentlemen of Verona*," Lady Lettice added in her gravelly voice. "Proteus and Valentine, one ever-changing, the other never-changing, both his lordship in *Vere-One-A*."

"Not to mention Lear having three daughters," Finley said, "and Gloucester having two sons, one legitimate and one not, just like his lordship."

"And who else could have written *Timon*, who gave his money away and ended up in a cave?"

"Or wrote a play in which Antonio borrows £3,000 from Shylock when Oxford owed a man named Michael Lok the same amount?"

"And did he get the name *Baptista Minola*, Katharina's father in *The Taming of the Shrew*, from the money lenders he frequented in Italy - *Baptista Nigrone* and *Pasquino Spinola*?"

Shackspear and Jonson slipped by along the wall. Their eyes ne'er looked at those huddled around Oxford's frail body. "Thieves fleeing in the night," Lettice said loud enough for them to hear. Their heads never turned as they disappeared out a side door.

"He's holding a blue bowl in his lap," Robin said. She held it up. "What's that mean?"

Finley didn't know.

"Where does he go now?" Robin asked. "Westminster?" She meant it as a joke. No one laughed.

"Doesn't matter," Falstaff said. "He told us in *Hamlet* what would happen:

> *Imperious Caesar, dead and turn'd to clay,*
> *Might stop a hole to keep the wind away:*
> *O, that that earth, which kept the world in awe,*
> *Should patch a wall to expel the winter flaw!*

Falstaff put his hand on Finley's shoulder. "Ye'll find a safe place for him to put down his head?"

Finley nodded. He put his hands on the chair and turned it around. It had a wheel at the bottom of each leg. As he pushed Oxford out into the gray day, he said:

> *A glooming sadness this day with it brings,*
> *The sun, for sorrow, will not show his head:*
> *Go hence, to have more talk of these sad things;*
> *For never was a story told of more dispraise*
> *Than this, the story of the Earl of Oxord and his plays.*

A furtive figure waited outside the Globe. Shackspear and Jonson tumbled into the street. They were laughing at Richard Burbage stripping himself naked to play Lear. "They'll ne'er forget *that* scene," Shackspear said.

The figure gestured with his left hand for Shackspear to come over; with his right, he waved Jonson away.

Shackspear came over. "Sir Robert."

"The Earl of Oxford is dead. He can never claim he wrote the plays that have your name on them. The door to this part of his life *and yours* has been shut. Do not do anything to open it again."

Shackspear, giddy, put his thumb and forefinger together and brushed them over his lips.

"Do not disappoint me, Willum, or . . ."

Fini

———◆◈◆———

To find out how Shackspear disappointed Sir Robert and what happened in 1616, read the Prologue to Part One. For what happened to Oxford and the facts underlying *The Death of Shakespeare*, read *The Reader's Companion to the Death of Shakespeare* and visit *www.doshakespeare.com*

Lineage Tables

The Earls of Oxford

John de Vere, 16th Earl of Oxford (d. August 3, 1562)

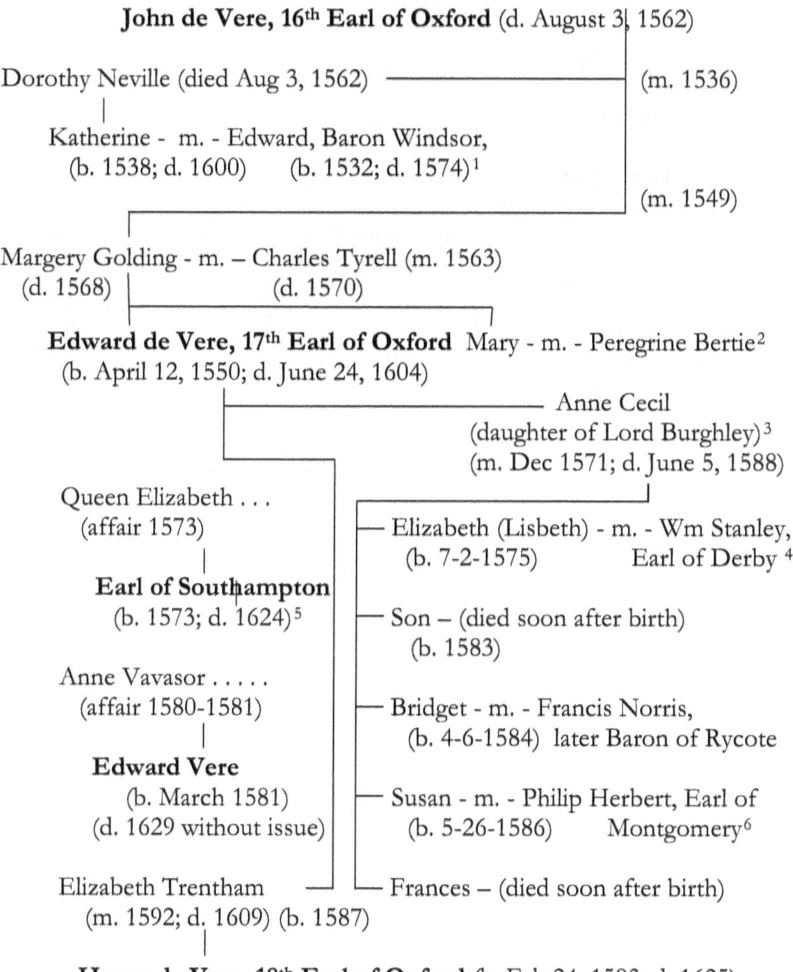

Henry de Vere, 18th Earl of Oxford (b. Feb 24, 1593; d. 1625)

---

[1] Edward, Baron Windsor, died January 24, 1574, in Venice. Oxford's half-sister, Katherine, wife of Edward, Baron Windsor, sued Oxford in 1563 to have their father's marriage to Oxford's mother declared void, which would have 'unearled' Oxford. He was 14 years of age at the time and subject only to the Court of Wards. Katherine's suite was dismissed. She apparently did not refile in the Court of Wards, probably because its head was Sir William Cecil, soon to become Baron Burghley, and Oxford's father-in-law.

[2] *See,* Peregrine Bertie

[3] *See,* The Family of William Cecil, Baron Burghley

[4] *See,* The Earls of Derby

[5] *See,* The Earls of Southampton

[6] *See,* The Earls of Pembroke

William Cecil, Baron Burghley

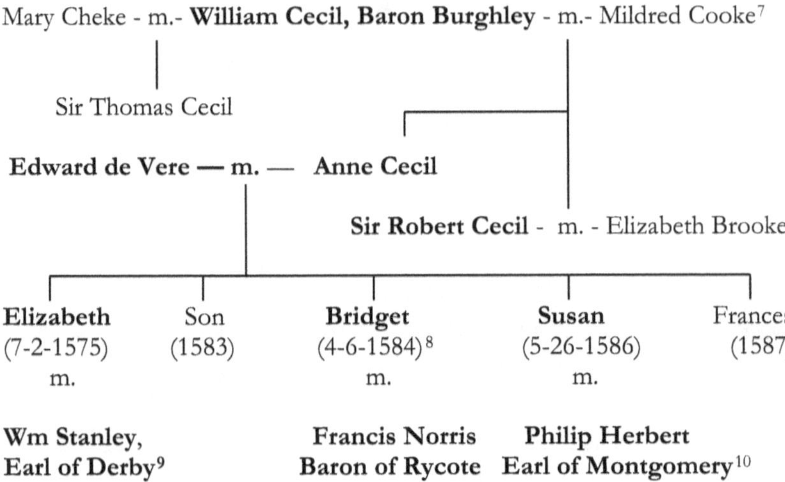

---

[7] Mildred Cooke's sister Anne was the mother of Francis Bacon, later Sir Francis Bacon. Thus, Sir Francis was nephew to Baron Burghley and cousin to Robert Cecil. Sir Francis played a significant role in the trial of Essex and Southampton in 1601. Bacon's interrogation of the two men brought out answers that forced Cecil to come out from where he was hiding to confront Essex as to who had heard him (Cecil) claim that only the Infanta of Spain had the right to succeed Elizabeth on the throne of England.

[8] Burghley tried to get Bridget to marry William Herbert, 3rd Earl of Pembroke, in the summer of 1597 but she rejected him.

[9] *See,* The Earls of Derby

[10] *See,* The Earls of Pembroke

The Earls of Southampton

Thomas Wriothesley - m.—— Jane Cheney
(created 1st Earl in 1547; died 1550)

Henry Wriothesley – 2nd Earl - m. - Mary Brown[11]
(born 1545;[12] died 1581[13]) (daughter of Viscount Montague)

Henry Wriothesley – 3rd Earl— m. — Elizabeth Vernon (1598)[14]
(born Oct 6, 1573)[15]

---

[11] Mary Browne was thirteen when she married the 2nd Earl of Southampton. She supposedly gave birth to his son in 1573. They separated in 1580 because of her alleged adulterous relationship with another man. In an attempt at reconciliation, the Countess sent her young son, the future 3rd Earl of Southampton, to her husband with a letter but the 2nd Earl rejected her offer to reconcile and kept their son away from her. The 2nd Earl died in 1581 but Mary was unable to get her son back because he went to Baron Burghley as a royal ward. In 1594, Mary Brown married Sir Thomas Heneage, who was Treasurer of the Royal Chamber. He died 15 months later in October, 1595, owing an accounting of what he had spent as Treasurer on entertainments for the Queen. The Queen demanded an accounting and the Countess submitted records that mention Wm Shakespeare as being one of the players paid by Heneage in 1594, which is the earliest known reference to William Shakespeare as a member of the Lord Chamberlain's Men. However, the play they supposedly performed before the Queen on the date specified was a play performed by the Admiral's Men; the Lord Chamberlain's Men were performing elsewhere. Since the accounting was made some time after the actual performance, there is a suspicion that the Countess, trying to avoid a massive judgment against her for money her dead husband had spent, was being creative in adding Shakespeare. Ogburn: pp. 65-66, citing Stopes. In January, 1599, almost immediately after her son's marriage to Elizabeth Vernon, she married again, to Sir Wm Harvey, with whom she had been living. Because the 2nd Earl was no longer living, Southampton had to approve the match as the senior male member of the Wriothesley family and apparently balked at her mother's choice.

[12] 5 years of age at his father's death; the Master of Royal Wards sold his wardship to Sir Wm Herbert, who sold it back to Henry's mother, Jane.

[13] The 3rd Earl of Southampton was 2 days short of 8 years old at his father's death. He became a ward of Baron Burghley and lived at Burghley House. Oxford, also a ward of Burghley, had left Burghley House ten years earlier when he came of age in 1571. Thus, the Earl of Oxford and Southampton never lived at Cecil House at the same time.

[14] Baron Burghley (*See* William Cecil, Baron Burghley), as Southampton's guardian, tried to get Southampton to marry his granddaughter, Elizabeth de Vere (Burghley Family; Oxford Family) in 1590, but Southampton refused and reportedly paid a £5,000 fine to Burghley.

[15] There is no documentation for this date except for a letter from his supposed father announcing the news of the birth of a son. There is no record of a baptism. The 2nd Earl was in the Tower in 1571 for his involvement in the Ridolfi Plot; released May 1, 1573 to Sir Wm Moore; July 1573 to his father-in-law, Viscount Montague. The 2nd Earl of Southampton's son Henry was born less than 9 months after his father's release from the Tower. The Queen may have allowed conjugal visits, but the evidence tends to indicate he was only allowed to see his wife in July.

The Earls of Derby

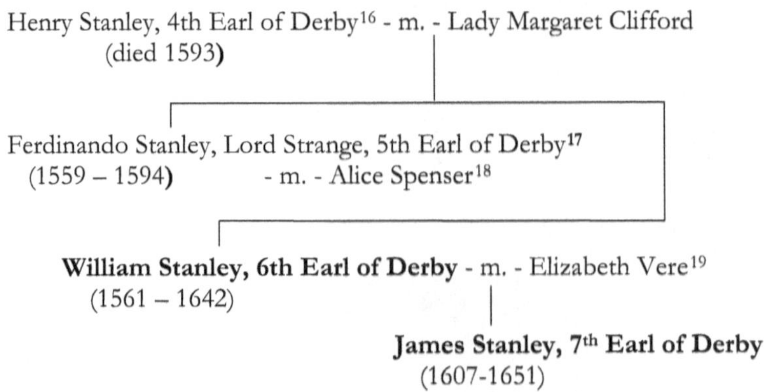

---

[16]   Established Lord Strange's Men, which continued in existence under his two sons, and which performed many of Shakespeare's plays.

[17]   Ferdinando Stanley's mother, Lady Margaret Clifford, was next in line to the throne by virtue of her descent from Mary Tudor. Ferdinando would have become heir to Elizabeth had he survived his mother *and* Queen Elizabeth. However, he predeceased both when he died on April 16, 1594. The succession would have gone to his daughters, who survived Lady Margaret, and not his brother, William, as Oxford's eldest daughter, Elizabeth, is portrayed as believing in *The Death of Shakespeare*. Ferdinando was believed to have been poisoned by a massive dose of arsenic. He had turned in a stepbrother who had tried to enlist him in a plot by the Catholics in exile to put him on the throne as a Catholic king. His act of loyalty, however, made him suspect to both Protestants and Catholics. The relatives ran to the Earl of Essex who took them into his service, which made Ferdinando fearful for his life. Ferdinando raided the main relative's house on April 2. He was dead two weeks later. He may have been poisoned by Burghley (to get him out of the way – Rowland York thought so – see Nelson p. 345), by the Catholic plotters to bring forward his brother, William, who may have been considered a better candidate, or by the relatives of the man he turned in. Burghley moved rapidly to marry Elizabeth Vere to Ferdinando's brother, William, but the wedding had to be delayed. See following footnote. Some of Lord Strange's Men formed the Lord Chamberlain's Men under Baron Hunsdon, which may have been intended to bring the players under control of the Queen. Edward Alleyn joined the Admiral's Men.

[18]   When Henry Stanley died in 1593, his son Ferdinando Stanley succeeded him as 5th Earl of Derby. When Ferdinando died less than a year later, his younger brother, William, should have immediately succeeded Ferdinando as the 6th Earl of Derby. However, Alice Spenser, Ferdinando's widow, claimed she was pregnant. William was engaged to marry Elizabeth Vere. William and Elizabeth had to wait to find out whether Alice gave birth to a son, who would have become the 6th Earl of Derby and 'unearled' William. However, in December 1594, Alice gave birth to a daughter and William became the 6th Earl of Derby. He and Elizabeth Vere married in January, 1594. Some scholars believe *Midsummer Night's Dream* was written for their wedding.

[19]   The eldest daughter of Edward de Vere, the 17th Earl of Oxford. Only the earls used the 'de' after their first names. Thus, Edward Vere, Oxford's illegitimate son, and the fighting Veres, Sir Francis and Sir Horatio, but Henry de Vere, who succeeded his father as the 18th Earl of Oxford.

<u>Peregrine Bertie</u>
(Lord Willoughby de Eresby – 1555-1601)

Richard Bertie (horse master) – m. 1553 - Katherine Willoughby[20]
(died 1580) (Duchess of Suffolk
& Baroness Willoughby de Eresby)
(Widow of the Duke of Suffolk)

Susan Bertie[21] — m. 1570 — Reginald Grey of Wrest,
(b. 1554) later restored as the 5th Earl of Kent (died 1573)

— m. 1581 — Sir John Wingfield

Peregrine Bertie - m.- **Mary (Vere) Oxford** (died 1624)
Lord Willoughby de Eresby (m. 1577/8)
(b. 1555; d. June 25, 1601))

Robert Bertie

---

[20] In 1577, Lady Katherine wrote to Baron Burghley that she would place Oxford's daughter Elizabeth (2 years old at the time) in front of Oxford the next time he came to see her to see if Oxford took to the child in the hope that this would reunite him with the mother, Anne, Burghley's daughter. Nelson: p. 76. Compare *The Winter's Tale*, Act II, Scenes 2 and 3, in which Leontes' baby daughter, which he thinks is not his, is placed in front of him in the belief that he will recognize her as his own. The attempt fails in the play. Whether Lady Katherine put Oxford's daughter in front of him is unknown. If so, it didn't work because Oxford continued to stay away from his wife for quite some time. Lady Katherine is well-known for many things, including talking Henry VIII into letting women read the Bible.

[21] Susan Bertie became Countess of Suffolk upon her mother's death in 1580. Aemilia Bassano was born January 27, 1569 in Bishopsgate, London, into a family of Italian (possibly Jewish) court musicians. At age seven (1576), she went to live with the Willoughby family at Grimsthorpe Castle in Lincolnshire under the tutelage of Susan Bertie. Aemilia arrived four years before Susan's mother, Lady Katherine, died, and may have known something about the letter Lady Katherine wrote in 1577 that is referenced in footnote 20. Upon her mother's death in 1587, Aemilia became Baron Hunsdon's mistress, by whom she had a son, Henry, in 1592. Hunsdon was 45 years older than she was. See, the Lineage Chart for Baron Hunsdon. Bassano thereafter married her cousin, Alfonso Lanier, who died in 1613. A daughter named Odillya lived only ten months. In 1611, Bassano published *Salve Deus Rex Judaeorum*, the first book of poetry published by an English woman. Bassano memorialized Susan in her book as the "daughter of the Duchess of Suffolk." Her son by Hunsdon lived to 1633.

The Earls of Pembroke

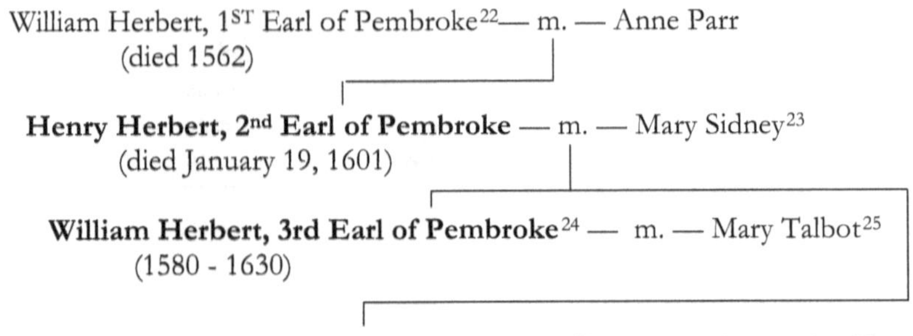

[22]   Established Pembroke's Men, , which continued in existence under his two sons, and which performed many of Shakespeare's plays.

[23]   *See,* The Sidney Family. Mary Sidney, Countess of Pembroke, was Robert Dudley's niece and Sir Philip Sidney's sister. Mary Sidney was Henry's third wife. His first marriage to Catherine Gray was probably annulled when Queen Mary came to the throne. His second wife was Catherine Talbot, who died in 1576. When Henry died in May, 1601, she did not remarry, but remained at Wilton House and became a noted literary figure in Elizabethan and Jacobean England.

[24]   William founded Pembroke College, Oxford, and continued his patronage of Pembroke's Men. He became Lord Chamberlain in 1615. He refused to give up the position until he could secure his brother, Philip, as his successor in 1626. William, therefore, was Lord Chamberlain in 1623 when the First Folio was printed. A relative, Henry Herbert, became Master of the Revels in June of that year. Ben Jonson, one of William's patrons, was supposed to get the office but did not. See, *The Incomparable Pair and "The Works of William Shakespeare"* by Gwynneth Bowen at http://www.sourcetext.com/sourcebook/library/bowen/12pair.htm. William and Philip are described in the dedication to the First Folio as "the incomparable pair of brethren." (Notice that the two brothers were the sons of Sir Philip Sidney's sister, Mary.)

[25]   The dwarfish and deformed daughter of the Earl of Shrewsbury, by whom William had no children. He had an affair with Mary Fitton in 1600 when she was twenty years of age and impregnated her. When he refused to marry her, he was sent to the Fleet Prison. When Mary gave birth to a boy who died, he was released. He wrote a poem about the affair. See Chapter 24 - Lord Willoughby's. He had two children by Lady Mary Wroth, daughter of his uncle, Robert Sidney, after the death of Lady Mary's husband, Richard Wroth.

[26]   Philip had a quarrel with Henry Wriothesley, 3rd Earl of Southampton, in 1610 over tennis. Compare the Earl of Oxford's famous quarrel with Sir Philip Sidney, also over tennis, in 1579.

[27]   The Earl of Pembroke began paying Jonson a stipend of 100 marks per annum in 1616, increased temporarily to £200 a year in 1621. *This Star of England,* p. 1208. Philip became the 4th Earl of Pembroke upon his older brother's death in 1630.

[28]   *See,* Oxford Family. Susan was the Earl of Oxford's third daughter. There is a drawing by Inigo Jones of Susan Vere dancing in one of Jonson's masques. *This Star of England,* p. 1208.

The Lords Hunsdon

Sir William Carey[29] - m. - Mary Boleyn[30]

Henry Carey, 1st Lord Hunsdon[31] - m. - Anne Morgan
(1545)

Mary Hyde - m. - **George Carey, 2nd Lord Hunsdon**[32]

.... **Aemelia Bassano**[33] - m. - Henry Lanier[34]

Henry (b. 1593)

---

[29] Gentleman of the Privy Chamber to Henry VIII. Died suddenly from the sweating sickness June 23, 1528. Henry Carey, his son, was two and became a ward of his aunt, Anne Boleyn. When Anne was beheaded in 1536, Henry was ten. His mother, Mary, died in 1543, and he was returned to his family.

[30] Sister to Anne Boleyn, who was mistress to Henry VIII before Anne. Many believed that Henry Carey's father was Henry VIII, not Sir William.

[31] Born 1526; died July 23, 1596. Appointed Lord Chamberlain in July 1585. Patron of the Lord Hunsdon's Men, and, from 1594, patron of the Lord Chamberlain's Men.

[32] Born 1547; died September 9, 1603. Became 2nd Baron Hunsdon when his father, Henry, died in 1596. However, George Carey did not become Lord Chamberlain on the death of his father. The Queen instead appointed William Brooke, 10th Baron Cobham, to be Lord Chamberlain. Cobham lived in the Blackfriars district and, despite being the patron of the Lord Chamberlain's Men, opposed the attempt in 1597 by James Burbage to have a theater built there for adult companies. This caused Burbage financial difficulty because the lease had run out on the Theatre. Burbage had bought the playing space in the Blackfriars for the Lord Chamberlain's Men to perform plays. Cobham also apparently objected to the name Sir John Oldcastle, one of his ancestors, for the character that became Falstaff. When Cobham died in March, 1597, the Queen appointed George Carey Lord Chamberlain, which post he held until his death in 1603. Cobham's daughter, Elizabeth Brooke, married Sir Robert Cecil on August 31, 1589.

[33] Mistress to Henry Carey; raised in the Willoughby family from age 7. *See*, Peregrine Bertie, footnote 2.

[34] Born in 1593. Assumed to be the son of Baron Hunsdon, by whom Aemilia Bassano became pregnant in 1592. Aemilia married Alfonso Lanier on October 18, 1592. Lanier died in 1613; Aemilia lived to 1645. In 1611, she published the first book of poetry by an English woman, *Salve Deus Rex Judaeorum.*

The Sidney Family

John **Dudley**, Duke of Northumberland

Sir Henry Sidney (1529-1586) - m. - Mary **Dudley** (1561-1621)

Sir Philip Sidney[35] (1554 – 1586)
  (died without issue)

Mary Sidney - m. - **Henry Herbert, 2nd Earl of Pembroke** (died 1601)

William Herbert (1580-1630) - m. - Mary Talbot
3rd Earl of Pembroke

Philip Herbert (1584-1649) - m. - **Susan Vere**
1st Earl of Montgomery
(became 4th Earl of Pembroke after William's death in 1630)

Robert Dudley, 1st Earl of Leicester -m. - Lettice Knollys
(her 2nd marriage)[36]

---

[35] Philip Sidney was knighted in 1583 when he was designated by Prince John Casimir of Poland to represent him by proxy at a ceremony inducting Casimir into the Order of the Garter. Since a representative could not be of a rank lower than a knight, Queen Elizabeth knighted Sidney so he could fulfill the honor. (This parallels William Cecil being made Baron Burghley so that his daughter's marriage to the Earl of Oxford would not be morganatic.) Sidney was wounded at the Battle of Zutphen and died October 17, 1586. His body was brought back to London in a ship with black sails. Pamphlets, poems, and sermons turned him into a national hero. He was not interred until February 16, 1588, eight days after the execution of Mary, Queen of Scots. It is unknown whether this delay was caused by lack of funds to bury him or a conscious decision on the part of Burghley, Walsingham, and the Queen to use Sidney's burial to distract a populace that might have reacted unfavorably to Mary's execution. Thousands of nobles and commoners followed Sidney's hearse to his grave and nothing was heard about Mary's death. *Hidden Allusions*, fn 19a, pp. 247-248.

[36] Lettice Knollys was a grandniece of Ann Boleyn. At age 17, she married Walter Devereux, 1st Earl of Essex, by whom she had Penelope Rich and Walter Devereux, 2nd Earl of Essex, as well as other children. Her first husband died in 1576. She then married Robert Dudley, 1st Earl of Leicester, in 1578. Elizabeth was outraged when she found out about the marriage and banished Lettice Knollys from court for life. It was rumored that she had been carrying on an affair with Leicester while her first husband was still alive. Some even claimed Leicester poisoned her first husband, who died of dysentery in Ireland. She had no children by Leicester. After Dudley died in 1588, she married Sir Christopher Blount, a much younger man, a year later. He was beheaded in 1601, along with her son by her first marriage, the 2nd Earl of Essex, for their participation in the Essex revolt. She lived to 1634, dying at the age of 91 on Christmas Day sitting in her rocking chair.

<u>Margaret Douglas</u>

(Countess of Lennox - 1515 - 1578)

Henry VII (Henry Tudor) — m. — Elizabeth of York

Margaret Tudor[37] (1489 –1541) - m. - **James IV of Scotland** (d. 1513)

m. — Archibald Douglas,
6th Earl of Angus

James V of Scotland (d. 1542) — m. — **Mary of Guise**

Margaret Douglas (1578) — m. — Matthew Stewart,
4th Earl of Lennox

Mary, Queen of Scots (d. 1587) — m. — Henry Stuart, Lord Darnley

Charles Stuart, 1st Earl of Lennox — m. — Elizabeth Cavendish

Lady Arabella Stewart[38]

James VI of Scotland (1542), **James I of England** (1603)

---

[37] Margaret Tudor had other siblings not identified in this table, including Henry VIII.
[38] Lady Arabella was considered a legitimate successor to Elizabeth.

acrostic: a poem in which the first letter of each line spells a name.

alewife: woman who keeps an alehouse; an oily fish.

an: if.

angel: a gold coin worth 10 shillings; called so after the Archangel Michael on one side.

apparitor: process server.

arras: a tapestry, wall hanging, or curtain.

arsenic: poison, referred to as 'inheritance powder.'

Bedlam: Bethlehem Hospital, where the insane were dumped.

bed trick: where a man sleeps with his wife woman but thinks she's someone else.

bergamot: pear-shaped orange the rind of which yields an oil used in the making of perfumes.

besmutched: to besmirch.

bewray: betray; disclose.

bill of exchange: a written document evidencing an obligation to repay a loan.

calliver: a smooth-bore forerunner of the rifle.

cheat: whole meal bread, coarser than manchet bread.

chirurgeon: surgeon; doctor.

Court of Wards (and Liveries): established by Henry VIII to regulate feudal dues, wards, and questions of livery.

eyas: a sparrow hawk.

eyrar: a brood of swans.

felo de se: to commit a felony on oneself, such as suicide.

foul papers: the original drafts of a manuscript of playscript.

froward: forward; brazen.

furniture: baggage.

Gad's Hill: an area on the road from London to Canterbury.

glister: to glisten, to glitter.

gremolata: chopped herb condiment classically made of lemon zest, garlic and parsley.

haberdine: salt cod.

haggard: a mature hawk caught in the wild and trained to hunt.

I Modi: erotic drawings by Giulio Romano.

Ipocras wine: a spiced wine. When strained through a woolen cloth, the cloth resembled Hippocrates' sleeve.

invention: creation, but also a fictitious statement or story; a fabrication.

groat; an English silver coin worth four pence

kickshaw: appetizer, hors d'oeuvres, from quelquechose.

limbo: between Heaven and Hell; where babies went who died before they were baptized.

livery: clothing worn by servants that identified them as servants of a particular nobleman.

manchet: fine white bread.

marriage *in futuro*: a promise to marry in the future, which is not a marriage, although suit can be brought on the contract.

marriage *per verba de praesenti*: a marriage validated by words, even if performed in secret, if followed by consummation.

matrimonium clandestinum: a marriage that rests merely on the agreement of the parties, or a marriage entered into a secret way, as one solemnized by an unauthorized person, or without required formalities.

medlar: apple-like fruit that tasted best as it began to rot.

mon choux: my cabbage; my dear.

moniment: archaic spelling of monument; but also a record without a monument. 'Thou art a moniment without a tomb.'

morganatic; a marriage in which, because one of the parties is not of sufficient birth, the children cannot inherit the parent's title.

motley: jester, a fool; multi-colored cloth.

ne: neither; nor.

Neapolitan Malady: syphilis.

nidicock: a ninny; a fool.

Orpharian: a flat-backed stringed instrument, member of the cittern family.

petits cadeaux: little gifts.

pomander: a mixture of aromatic substances contained in a pierced metal sphere.

quincunx: an arrangement with four points and a fifth point in the middle

Roscius: a Roman slave who became a famous actor.

samphire: samphire, rock samphire, or sea fennel grew on rocky cliffs near the sea and was used as a condiment when pickled and in salads when fresh.

Seneca: a first century Roman philosopher ('readiness is all') and tragedian.

sprezzatura: a certain nonchalance, so as to conceal all art and make whatever one does or says appear to be without effort and almost without any thought about it.

Tycho Brahe: Danish astronomer who argued that the sun and moon orbited the earth.

virginal: keyboard instrument.

ward: a minor under the jurisdiction of a court; a minor whose father, a vassal-in-chief to the king, has died.

weed: clothes.

whiffler: a servant who precedes a noble to make way and announce his presence.

whittawer: a person who converts animal skins into white leather.

wittol: a man who knows he has been cuckolded by his wife and tolerates it.

<u>**Afterword**</u>

Oxford died on June 24, 1604 in Hackney. He is thought to have been buried in Hackney Church since his wife's will in 1612 leaves money to bury her "as near unto the body of my late dear and noble lord and husband as may be: only I will that there be in the said church erected for us a tomb fitting our degree." Hackney Church was pulled down in 1790 and his grave has not been found.

William Shakespeare died on April 23, 1616 in Stratford-upon-Avon. He was buried there in Holy Trinity Church. No one mentioned his passing.

Shakespeare's Sonnets were published in 1609, the year Oxford's widow moved from King's Place in Hackney. An effort in 1619 to publish some of the plays attributed to Shakespeare was blocked. Thirty-six plays attributed to William Shakespeare were published in *The First Folio* in 1623. No one knows who had possession of the scripts in the intervening years. Two more plays have been accepted by scholars as Shakespeare's (Oxford's), making thirty-eight plays in all.

The First Folio was dedicated to two brothers, the Earl of Pembroke and the Earl of Montgomery. The former was engaged to Oxford's older daughter at one time but married William Stanley, the 6th Earl of Derby. The Earl of Montgomery married Oxford's third daughter, Susan. The two brothers are referred to as the two 'incomparable pair of brethren' in *The First Folio*.

The Authorship Question arose in the 18th century when questions arose as to how Shakespeare could have written the plays attributed to him given his apparently humble beginnings. Since then, more than eighty different people have been proposed as the author of the plays, including Edward de Vere, 17th Earl of Oxford; Sir Francis Bacon; Christopher Marlowe; and William Stanley, 6th Earl of Derby.

A separate question is whether the 3rd Earl of Southampton was the son of Oxford and Queen Elizabeth. This is known as the Prince Tudor Theory. *Venus & Adonis* and *The Rape of Lucrece* were dedicated to Southampton but no connection between Shakespeare and Southampton has been found. The first seventeen sonnets urge a young man (presumably Southampton) to marry and have children. C. S. Lewis wondered: "What man in the whole world, except a father or a potential father-in-law, cares whether any other man gets married?" No one has so far claimed Shakespeare was Southampton's father, but could Oxford have been his father? Read *The Phoenix and Turtle* and ask who beauty, truth, and rarity are in this poem? Abstractions, or people? Could they be Elizabeth, Oxford, and Southampton?

<u>**Questions for a Stratfordian**</u>

If you encounter someone who believes the man from Stratford wrote the plays traditional scholarship attributes to William Shakespeare, you might consider asking the following questions:

- Why are 37 of the 38 plays about royalty and nobility (*Merry Wives of Windsor* being the only exception)?

- Why was Shakespeare not punished for plays and poems that clearly satirized the queen (*Venus & Adonis*) and Lord Burghley (*Hamlet*)?

- Why was Shakespeare not punished for staging *Richard II* (his company; his play) the night before the Essex Rebellion?

- Why has no one found a diary that mentions Shakespeare?

- Why has no one found a letter written by Shakespeare, or to Shakespeare, or *about* Shakespeare?

- Why did Shakespeare's will make no mention of books?

- Why did Shakespeare write, in Sonnet 86:

    Why write I still all one, ever the same,
    And keep invention in a noted weed,
    That every word doth almost tell my name,
    Showing their birth, and where they did proceed?

- Why did Shakespeare not write an elegy when the queen died in 1603?

- Why did no one mention Shakespeare when he died in 1616?

- Why was Shakespeare not buried in Westminster Abbey?

- Why does Shakespeare write: *My name be buried where my body is.* (Sonnet 72.) Shakespeare's body is in Holy Trinity Church in Stratford-upon-Avon, isn't it?

Perhaps he didn't write the plays?

Readers interested in further information about

The Death of Shakespeare

can visit

www.doshakespeare.com or *amazon.com*

to find out how to purchase

The kindle version of *The Death of Shakespeare—Part One*

and

The paperback and kindle versions of

The Death of Shakespeare—Part Two

and

The paperback and kindle versions of

The Reader's Companion to the Death of Shakespeare

which contains notes and comments keyed to each chapter